CW00422236

LEWIS CARROLL
AND
THE HOUSE OF MACMILLAN

CAMBRIDGE STUDIES IN PUBLISHING AND PRINTING HISTORY

Roughly contemporaneous portraits of Alexander Macmillan (left, from a photograph by O. G. Rejlander, reproduced by courtesy of the Macmillan Press Ltd), and of Charles Dodgson, taken around 1870.

LEWIS CARROLL
AND
THE HOUSE OF MACMILLAN

EDITED BY

MORTON N. COHEN

AND

ANITA GANDOLFO

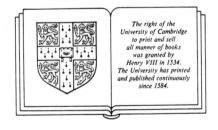

The right of the
University of Cambridge
to print and sell
all manner of books
was granted by
Henry VIII in 1534.
The University has printed
and published continuously
since 1584.

CAMBRIDGE UNIVERSITY PRESS

CAMBRIDGE

LONDON   NEW YORK   NEW ROCHELLE

MELBOURNE   SYDNEY

Published by the Press Syndicate of the University of Cambridge
The Pitt Building, Trumpington Street, Cambridge CB2 1RP
32 East 57th Street, New York, NY 10022, USA
10 Stamford Road, Oakleigh, Melbourne 3166, Australia

Letters of C.L. Dodgson © The Trustees of the Estate of C.L. Dodgson, 1987
Letters from the House of Macmillan © Macmillan Limited, 1987
Selection, Introduction and Notes © Morton N. Cohen and Anita Gandolfo, 1987

First published 1987

Printed in Great Britain at
the University Press, Cambridge

British Library cataloguing in publication data
Carroll, Lewis
Lewis Carroll and the House of Macmillan.
— (Cambridge studies in publishing and
printing history.)
1. Carroll, Lewis — Biography 2. Authors,
English — 19th century — Biography
Rn: Charles Lutwidge Dodgson I. Title
II. Cohen, Morton N. III. Gandolfo, Anita.
828'.809 PR4612

Library of Congress cataloguing in publication data
Carroll, Lewis, 1832–1898.
Lewis Carroll and the House of Macmillan.
(Cambridge studies in publishing and printing
history)
Includes index.
1. Carroll, Lewis, 1832–1898—Correspondence.
2. Authors, English—19th century—Correspondence.
3. Macmillan & Co. 4. Authors and publishers—England.
5. Publishers and publishing—England—History—
19th century—Sources. I. Cohen, Morton Norton,
1921–   . II. Gandolfo, Anita. III. Macmillan &
Co. IV. Title. V. Series.
PR4612.A45   1986   828'.809 [B]   86–8248

ISBN 0 521 25602 X

SE

To
Roger Lancelyn Green
who led the way

CONTENTS

ix

INTRODUCTION

And when quarrels arose – as one frequently finds
Quarrels will, spite of every endeavour –
The song of the Jubjub recurred to their minds,
And cemented their friendship for ever!

The Hunting of the Snark

I

In 1865, an unknown author calling himself Lewis Carroll compelled a leading publishing house, Macmillan & Company, to suppress the first edition of a children's book entitled *Alice's Adventures in Wonderland*. In 1886, the same author, better established, instructed the same publisher to discard the first edition of *The Game of Logic*, also meant for children. In 1889, Carroll condemned the entire first run of ten thousand copies of *The Nursery "Alice"*; and in 1893, he ordered Macmillan to scuttle an entire printing of the *Alice* sequel, *Through the Looking-Glass*.

No publisher today could or would countenance such behavior even from his most treasured author, and ordinarily no Victorian publisher would have done either. That the Reverend Charles Lutwidge Dodgson, a shy mathematics don, could issue such commands from his Oxford aerie and have them carried out to the letter in the bustling offices of the London publisher says much about the character of both Dodgson and the firm of Macmillan, their relationship, and the state of publishing at the height of the Victorian age.

The association between Dodgson and the House of Macmillan began some two years before *Alice* was published, and in spite of some tempests that came close to splitting author and publisher asunder, their ties endured to the very end of Dodgson's life, thirty-five years later.

Those years and the course of the Dodgson–Macmillan collaboration are documented in Dodgson's surviving diaries[1] and in two caches of letters: the original Dodgson letters to Macmillan, now part of the Lewis Carroll archive at the Rosenbach Museum & Library in Philadelphia; and letter books containing copies of the publisher's outgoing letters to Dodgson which Messrs. Macmillan

---

[1] Nine of thirteen manuscript volumes survive and are now, with an accompanying index, in the British Library. They cover Dodgson's life from January 2 to September 25, 1855; January 1, 1856, to April 17, 1858; and May 9, 1862, to Dodgson's death in January 1898. Roger Lancelyn Green's two-volume edition of the *Diaries* contains almost three-fourths of the text. Works cited frequently in the notes that follow are abbreviated; their full particulars appear in the list of short titles on p. 31.

deposited in the British Library in 1964–5. Although four volumes of Dodgson's manuscript diaries are lost to us and the correspondence in the Rosenbach and the British Library archives contains cavernous gaps, the surviving material provides a clear and salient record of the remarkable relationship between the gifted don and his far-from-ordinary publisher.

The purpose of this volume, restricted though it is by publishing costs to a selection of the extant material, is to record the annals of collaboration between author and publisher. It is an engaging tale that throws light not only upon the mind and character of one of the world's most famous writers, but also on the policies and practices of a distinguished publishing house, even as it opens a window onto a period of writing and book production that deserves illuminating. The second half of the Victorian age was a baffling time for both authors and publishers, and we hope that this record will add useful facts and flavors to an important, if eccentric, chapter of author–publisher relations and chart a voyage on the seas of Victorian literature and book publishing as curious as the one conducted in search of the Snark.

The saga opens in Oxford on October 19, 1863, at the first recorded meeting between Dodgson and the head of the publishing firm, Alexander Macmillan. Dodgson mentions it in his *Diaries*: "Went to Combe's in the evening to meet the publisher Macmillan and get . . . [Combe] to print me some of Blake's *Songs of Innocence*, etc., on large paper."[1] Thomas Combe (1797–1872), who brought Dodgson and Macmillan together, was an eminent Oxford figure, director of the Clarendon Press and Printer to Oxford University, a strikingly handsome man and a patron of the arts. Dodgson was well acquainted with him and his wife, was a frequent guest in their home, and had already photographed Combe.[2] Having verses, pamphlets, cards, letters, even menus printed for private use to send to more than one recipient was customary among people of means in Victorian England, and Dodgson indulged himself in this practice all his life. As for getting Combe to print Blake's *Songs of Innocence*, these verses had a special place in Dodgson's affections, for he held with Blake a cherished view of childhood and child innocence. He wished to share with friends his admiration for the verses by giving or sending them printed copies.

II

The early life of Alexander Macmillan (1818–96), whom Dodgson was to meet that evening at Combe's, was closely bound to the life of his brother Daniel (1813–57). They were the younger sons of a Scottish farmer and his loving, literate wife. The father died in 1823, when Daniel was ten and Alexander five. That left the boys' upbringing in the hands of their mother, who encouraged their intellectual and literary leanings. Before long, Daniel was apprenticed for

[1] P. 206.   [2] For Dodgson's photograph of Combe, see *Letters*, facing p. 508.

seven years to a bookseller, one Maxwell Dick, in their home town of Irvine, Ayrshire. From Dick, Daniel learned selling, buying and binding – and more: "to groom and ride horses, to stain and varnish wood, and many things not specified in his indenture."[1] All the time, however, Daniel was reading voraciously, and he filled the gaps in his formal learning with a close acquaintance with the classics and the works of the authors of his time.

After his seven years' hard with Dick, Daniel went as a bookseller's assistant to Stirling, and thence, "full of ambition and hoping for a partnership,"[2] to another bookdealer in Glasgow. But, perhaps from overwork, he grew desperately ill with the dread lung disease so prevalent in Victorian times and had to return to Irvine to be nursed by his mother. He recovered slowly, but when he was well enough, he left Irvine and once more set out to make his fortune, this time in London, a "foreign land."[3] After much unsuccessful searching, he eventually found a place with the publishers Simpkin & Marshall. But the endless hours required ("from Saturday they worked through to six on Sunday morning")[4] were intolerable, and when a Mr. Johnson, a Cambridge bookseller, offered him a post at £30 a year, even though the wages were only half of what he was already earning and despite his reluctance to leave London, he took it.

Daniel spent three years in Cambridge, an important time for him, when he learned about every book on the shelves and grew acquainted with the interesting clientele. They, in turn, were impressed by him: "Learned men came to . . . [the] shop . . . because the wise young Scot was good – and perhaps amusing – company when they were in quest of books," Morgan records.[5] Then he got an offer of another London post, with Seeley's bookshop in Fleet Street, at £60 a year, and he took that. He remained with Seeley's for six years and prospered despite recurring bouts of illness that forced him to return to Scotland to convalesce.

Alexander Macmillan's childhood and early manhood were also burdened by the family's poverty. He attended Irvine High School, but, unable to go on to university, he followed his older brother's example and read hungrily on his own. For two or three years, he taught tough colliery lads in village schools, though, as an usher he had "all the early and most drudgical part of the work. The last year – 1838–9," Alexander noted, "– I had 130 children under my care of the poorest, [in] a school in a mining district, many of them Irish."[6] He soon learned that schoolmastering did not suit him, and he made "spasmodic efforts to enter two widely different professions, the medical and the nautical."[7] For a time, he became an assistant in a chemist's shop in Glasgow and began to know a good deal about medicines and drugs. Then, in what he later called "a somewhat foolish attempt at being a sailor,"[8] he impetuously signed on to the

[1] Morgan, p. 8.   [2] Ibid., p. 11.   [3] Ibid., p. 13.   [4] Ibid., p. 16.   [5] P. 18.
[6] Macmillan, p. xvii.   [7] Ibid., p. xviii.   [8] Ibid., p. xv.

crew of a ship bound for America. That journey cured him of any romantic notions that he had about the sea, and he returned to Glasgow penniless. He turned back to the work he knew, teaching, and took another job as usher at 5s. a week.

In October 1839, as Alexander was approaching his twenty-first birthday, he was summoned to London by brother Daniel, who had procured for him, sight unseen, a post as a clerk at Seeley's at the remarkably good starting salary of £60 a year. The two men shared living quarters and got on well. But their native ambition led them to hope of owning their own bookshop one day. In February 1843, they took a shop in Aldersgate Street, Daniel staying on at Seeley's to insure some income while they established themselves in the new venture. Soon enough, however, they realized that, while holding their own, they could not attract to Aldersgate Street customers comparable in quantity or quality to those of West End bookshops, and they cast about for means of improving their position. Nonetheless, one great event occurred in Aldersgate Street: in November 1843, Daniel and Alexander published the first book to bear the Macmillan family imprint.[1]

Four months after starting the Aldersgate enterprise, the brothers Macmillan heard that the business of an established bookseller in Cambridge was on the market, and with the help of Archdeacon Julius Charles Hare (1795–1855), Fellow of Trinity College and classical lecturer at Cambridge, they bought Newby's at 17 Trinity Street. In 1844 they issued their first catalogue from this address.

At first, the brothers were plagued by debts and creditors. But the new shop's sales began to go well, and they pushed their enterprise forward. Indeed, from the very moment of launch, Daniel dreamed of expanding the publishing side of the business.

I wonder that Cambridge University never sends out good editions of English theologians [he wrote to Hare on June 21, 1844], while Oxford sends out so many, and such handsome books, and so many of them by Cambridge men. If Cambridge were to republish the writings of the best of her sons what a noble array of books we should have. It would be an easy matter to do it. . . . With a subscription of £2 2s. a year, it would be easy to get nearly all the professional men in England and Scotland who had ever been Cambridge men. Jeremy Taylor, or Fuller, or Barrow, would be good books to begin with. . . . Donne, Henry Moore, John Smith, Cudworth, and others might follow. I don't know whether Milton and Howe would have any chance, but a good edition of Milton's complete works is wanted.[2]

With these lofty thoughts about the future, the brothers headed full-sail into the risky seas of publishing. Soon they bought up the business of Messrs Bowes at 1

---

[1] It was *The Philosophy of Training*, "with the suggestions of the necessity of normal schools for teachers to the wealthier classes, and strictures on the prevailing mode of teaching languages," a 92–page treatise by A. R. Craig of Barford Street Institution, Islington, and late Classical Master in Glasgow Normal Seminary (Private Department). See *Bibliographical Catalogue of Macmillan and Co.'s Publications from 1843 to 1889* (1891), p. 1.   [2] Hughes, pp. 163–5.

Trinity Street, where they lived in ample quarters above the shop and took in undergraduates as lodgers to help pay for the upkeep of the house. As early as February 2, 1847, Daniel, writing to his patron, Hare, could assure him: "Things go very smoothly and very prosperously with us, and my brother is a very great comfort and help to me."[1]

The brothers were, in their way, extremely gifted, and, true to their upbringing, possessed the virtues of honesty, thrift, shrewdness and modesty. Still it is remarkable how, coming as they did from a background of poverty and hardship, they pulled themselves up in the world by their boot straps. It was not easy, but it was enormously stimulating and gratifying. Daniel, by now intimately acquainted with the philosophical and the theological controversies of his time, spoke and wrote elegantly about them and could hold his own with the best minds he encountered in Cambridge. Alexander had already edited a volume of Shelley's poetry, which he published anonymously in 1840.[2]

They were clearly more than ordinary booksellers, and the Cambridge community became aware of it. William Wordsworth visited the shop, Thackeray lunched with them, and Charles Kingsley showed them the manuscript of *Alton Locke*. Gradually, Macmillan's took on the aura of pleasant amiability; all were welcome and many came, not merely as customers, but as members of the university community, people with intellectual interests, taste, and convictions, eager to read, to converse, and to dispute. Masters, dons, churchmen, writers, students – all were encouraged to loiter, to browse, to "have a pipe and a chat." An "upper room . . . became a common-room where young men and old men assembled to discuss books or God or social reform"; the bookshop became "a little college in itself."[3] Strong associations were fashioned, deep friendships forged.

That the university elect of Cambridge came to gather under the Macmillans' roof was a tribute to their self-taught learning, their wise judgment in both literary and business affairs, and, perhaps most of all, to a disarming inborn charm that was in no way diminished by their Scots Doric speech.

The poet-journalist Sebastian Evans (1830–1909) later recalled the Macmillan brothers' "genius for faithful friendship."[4] However, the most remarkable element in the Macmillan amalgam was probably high principles. They were far from being mere businessmen; they were men with a mission in life, and perhaps that mission is best set out in a letter that Daniel, still a bookseller's assistant, wrote in 1843, to a friend and fellow bookman in Glasgow:

Bless your heart . . ., you never surely thought you were merely working for bread! Don't you know that you are cultivating good taste amongst the natives of Glasgow helping to unfold a love of the beautiful among those who are slaves to the useful, or what they call the useful? I look on you as a great teacher or prophet, doing work just of the kind that God has appointed you to do. . . . We destroy, and are helping to destroy, all kinds of confusion, and are aiding our great Taskmaster to reduce the world into order, and

---

[1] Ibid., p. 170. [2] Graves, p. 22. [3] Morgan, p. 30. [4] Graves, p. 100.

beauty, and harmony. Bread we must have, and gain it by the sweat of our brow, or of our brain, and that is noble, because God-appointed. Yet that is not all. As truly as God is, we are His ministers, and help to minister to the wellbeing of the spirits of men. At the same time it is our duty to manage our affairs wisely, keep our minds easy, and not trade beyond our means.[1]

With financial security came hopes of marriage and family life. In September 1850, Daniel married Frances Orridge, daughter of a Cambridge chemist and magistrate; in August 1851, Alexander wed Caroline Brimley, daughter of a local merchant who later was Mayor of Cambridge. Her brother was George Brimley, librarian of Trinity College and friend of the Macmillans. In time, Daniel fathered four children and Alexander five.[2]

As highly as the brothers valued the book trade, they grew convinced that their true vocations lay in publishing and were delighted when "men who came into the shop to buy books stayed in the publishing house to write them."[3] Their early successes were encouraging. F. D. Maurice (1805–72), whom they knew through Hare, became one of their authors. In 1852 they published his *Prophets and Kings*; it "sold so rapidly . . . that Daniel believed for a little while that even Maurice might be popular."[4] They also brought out Charles Kingsley's *Phaeton* and Isaac Todhunter's *Differential Calculus*; both proved "solid" investments. In 1855, they published Kingsley's *Westward Ho!*, in 1857 Thomas Hughes' *Tom Brown's School Days* – and each won a large reading public. These two along with Kingsley's later works set the firm on a secure course and helped establish its artistic and financial reliability and independence.

But while the brothers prospered, they still had to contend with ill health. Alexander suffered from sciatica, Daniel from recurring bouts of lung-sickness that forced him to retreat to the south for sea air and to take numerous "cures." Eventually Daniel realized that his illness would never abate fully and, sooner rather than later, would prove fatal. On September 19, 1855, he wrote from Torquay:

At one time I hoped that the long rests I have been able to take, and the wise advice of the best physicians, and the constant care of the most self-denying and loving of wives, and the most rigid attention to all the means prescribed . . . would have restored me to health by God's blessing. But now I have no such hope. . . . every year finds me weaker, and . . . the disease of the lungs increases. So, instead of ever hoping for health, all I can hope for is to maintain a constant stand-up fight with death.[5]

Daniel succumbed less than two years later, on May 27, 1857, but he died knowing that he had established a publishing firm that would survive him and that his brother-partner would look after it and his widow and children. Frank A. Mumby draws an apt comparison between the lives of Daniel Macmillan and Robert Louis Stevenson:

[1] Hughes, pp. 115–16.
[2] Alexander Macmillan's wife died on July 21, 1871, and in the autumn of 1872 he married Emma Pignatel, by whom he had another daughter and son.
[3] Morgan, pp. 33–4.   [4] Ibid., p. 39.   [5] Hughes, pp. 277–8.

Each of them became a master of his craft in the face of physical distress which would have broken the hearts of most men; each knew that he was at death's door, or not very far from it, through the greater part of his life; each passed through that inevitable doorway at the same untimely age – forty-four. And yet each found life good and sweet, and did his best to make it so for others.[1]

Daniel's wife and four children immediately moved into Alexander's home, and the two families became virtually one from then onwards.

Daniel and Alexander had often spoken of opening a branch of the business in London, and it may even have been the notion of establishing a fitting memorial to Daniel that spurred Alexander to pursue this goal vigorously after Daniel's death. He made the dream a reality in 1858 when he opened a branch of the firm at 23 Henrietta Street, Covent Garden. The London office was managed by two of the experienced employees from Cambridge, and Alexander kept in close touch by spending Thursday nights in London. On those evenings he held what came to be known as "Tobacco Parliaments," where the door was open to "any one who liked to come and take part in a modest meal, followed by free and easy discussion of literary and other matters."[2] A round oak table that Alexander had made for his Parliaments bears the autograph signatures of some of the great men that gathered round it, including William Allingham, Thomas Hughes, T. H. Huxley, Francis Palgrave, Coventry Patmore, Herbert Spencer, and Alfred Tennyson.

Another innovation came a year later when Alexander founded *Macmillan's Magazine*, the first shilling monthly ever published. The initial number appeared in November 1859, two months before the *Cornhill* was born. The contents of the *Magazine* were often discussed and decided upon at the Thursday evening Parliaments. Later Alexander also founded the *Practitioner* and *Nature*, and in 1869, he opened a branch in New York. Meanwhile he pushed ahead with the Golden Treasury series, the Cambridge Shakespeare, a series called Vacation Tourists, and a number of other major ventures that took root, flowered, and further enhanced the Macmillan list. By 1863, Macmillan realized that London, rather than Cambridge, was the fitter place for the firm's headquarters. He found a spacious house in Upper Tooting for his large double family and, once settled there, inaugurated "feasts of Talk, Tobacco and Tipple."[3]

When, in that same year, Alexander Macmillan first met Charles Dodgson at Combe's, the story of Alice's Adventures in Wonderland had already sprung from the mind of the quiet, modest, gifted young don. The famous river journey that he had taken with the three daughters of his college Dean and Robinson Duckworth, the friend who sang so well, had occurred more than a year earlier, on July 4, 1862. He had promised the Dean's second daughter, Alice Liddell, then aged ten, to write out the story he had invented on that river journey, and,

---

[1] *The Romance of Book Selling: A History from the Earliest Times to the Twentieth Century* (1967), p. 390.
[2] Macmillan, p. xxx.   [3] Graves, p. 224.

ever true to his word, had gone laboriously about the task, setting the text down in a green leather notebook. Dodgson noted in his *Diaries* (p. 554) the progress he made with the story:

Headings written out (on my way to London)	July 5, 1862
M.S. copy begun	Nov. 13 (Th) ditto
text finished before	Feb. 10, 1863.

Sometime during 1863 Dodgson's friends convinced him that he should publish his fantasy. Alexander Macmillan was a publisher on the *qui vive*, Dodgson an unknown author with an unpublished manuscript on his hands. We do not know if Combe brought publisher and author together with something more than social affability in mind, whether Dodgson, having heard that Macmillan was to visit Combe, asked Combe for the introduction, whether Macmillan, having heard about the unpublished manuscript, asked Combe for an introduction to its author, or whether the Alice manuscript was accidentally mentioned during the evening at Combe's. Whatever the case, we know that the meeting was successful, and soon author and publisher were talking business.

III

Dodgson was some fourteen years younger than Alexander Macmillan. He was born on January 27, 1832, at Daresbury in Cheshire, where his father was Perpetual Curate. In 1843, Dodgson *père* was made Rector of Croft, Yorkshire, and the rectory there became the family home for the next quarter-century. Third of eleven children and the eldest son, Charles enjoyed a happy and lively, if serious and disciplined, upbringing. Unlike the self-educated Macmillan, he received a solid grounding in mathematics and Latin as well as religion from his father even before he entered Richmond School at the age of twelve. From Richmond he went to Rugby, and from Rugby to Christ Church, Oxford, where he lived and worked until his death, 47 years later, in 1898. From 1855 he was Senior Student (the equivalent of Fellow elsewhere); in 1861 he was ordained deacon. But he chose not to take a priesthood or curacy: he was a shy man encumbered by deafness in his right ear and a stammer, handicaps not conducive to parish work.

He had eclectic interests. He was drawn to gadgets and even invented a few himself: all matters mechanical, technological, scientific, and medical fascinated him. He was a better-than-amateur artist and took a continuing interest in art movements of the day. He was an early art photographer before whose lens sat an array of celebrities including Tennyson, the Rossettis, Ruskin, John Everett Millais, and Ellen Terry. He spoke out courageously for the theater as a wholesome source of entertainment and education in an age when the Church usually opposed it. He spent considerable time in London attending theatrical performances, visiting galleries, friends, relatives; he went regularly to

Guildford, where his brothers and sisters lived after their father's death in 1868; and he spent summers on writing holidays at the seaside, usually at Eastbourne.

All his life Dodgson was deeply and genuinely religious, but unlike Alexander Macmillan, he stood apart from the theological storms of the time. He never married, though he wished to and would probably have been happier had he done so. He lived an orderly, careful life, ate little, and, like Macmillan, chose hard work as his road to salvation. He was a compulsive record-keeper: his letter register showed that in the last thirty-five years of his life he sent and received 98,721 letters.

During his entire mature life, Dodgson sought close friendships with a coterie of female children. In spite of some gossip and suspicions about his motives, these were innocent relationships, grounded in an aesthetic that he inherited from the Romantics. The object of his worship was his child friends' beauty and purity. He loved the child's unspoiled, untutored naturalness and what he saw as her proximity to God. He knew instinctively how to speak a child's language, how to capture his young friends' interest, how to engage them in conversation, how to move them, and, best of all, how to make them happy and evoke peals of laughter from them. For his part, he lost his awkwardness – and his stammer – in their presence. These fairy creatures sparked his creative energies, and for them he composed his masterpieces: *Alice's Adventures in Wonderland* (1865), *Through the Looking-Glass and What Alice Found There* (1872), *The Hunting of the Snark* (1876), *Sylvie and Bruno* (1889), and *Sylvie and Bruno Concluded* (1893).

Dodgson fancied himself in a small way a poet: two volumes of verse, in addition to the *Snark*, appeared in his lifetime and one posthumously: *Phantasmagoria and Other Poems* (1869), *Rhyme? and Reason?* (1883); and *Three Sunsets and Other Poems* (1898).

Many of Dodgson's publications, however, were the work of a professional mathematician. They include *A Syllabus of Plane Algebraical Geometry*, published in 1860, three years before he met Macmillan; *Euclid and His Modern Rivals* (1879); *Curiosa Mathematica* (1888, 1893); and *Symbolic Logic, Part I* (1896). He also published a number of works for the amusement and education of young people, including *Word-Links* (1878), *Doublets* (1879), *Mischmasch* (1882), *A Tangled Tale* (1885), *The Game of Logic* (1886), and *Syzygies and Lanrick* (1893).

Dodgson's reputation as an original mathematical thinker has risen in recent years,[1] but his fame rests upon his two great children's classics, the *Alice* books, where his genius for nonsense, parody, satire, irony, paradox – and most of all, that particular brand of Carrollian whimsy – flowered. These books transcend nationality, space, time, and somehow enthrall readers of all ages to this day.

Dodgson died of pneumonia on January 14, 1898, in his family's home at Guildford and was buried in Guildford.

---

[1] The reappraisal resulted from the publication of *Symbolic Logic, Part II*, the book that Dodgson virtually completed before his death in 1898 but that remained unpublished until 1977. See W. W. Bartley III, ed., *Lewis Carroll's Symbolic Logic, Part I and Part II* (1977).

IV

It may seem surprising that Macmillan would have had the temerity to take on an unknown author like Lewis Carroll, but he had supreme confidence in his own judgment, and that faith was one of his greatest assets. His son assures us that, during these early years and for many later ones, Macmillan "himself read practically every manuscript . . . submitted to him."[1] He chose the books that the firm would publish, sought out unsolicited works that he believed should bear the Macmillan imprint, and he pursued writers, known and unknown, whom he wanted to grace his list. He "seemed to have an instinctive perception of what constituted excellence . . . irrespective of his own sympathies," wrote Edith Sichel.[2] If he believed in a work, he contracted for it, and he was far more often right than wrong to do so.[3]

Indeed, Alexander Macmillan's singular independence, his personal resourcefulness, his keen judgment, his willingness to rely solely upon it, and his unbounded mental and physical energies clearly marked the man and lived happily alongside his humility, strong religious faith, and uncompromising generosity.

Actually, the risk that Macmillan was running probably did not seem great to him. Five months before Dodgson and Macmillan first met, Macmillan had brought out Kingsley's *The Water Babies*. Its success may well have encouraged him to consider further forays into children's literature, even as it may have encouraged Dodgson to discuss his manuscript with Kingsley's publisher.

Unfortunately, the record of the beginning of the Dodgson–Macmillan relationship consists entirely of the brief entries in Dodgson's *Diaries*. The first known surviving letter (or, to be more exact, the earliest *copy*, as virtually all of Macmillan's letters to Dodgson that appear here are copies that Macmillan himself routinely made in the Macmillan letter books) is from Alexander Macmillan to Dodgson, dated September 19, 1864, more than a year after the initial meeting between the two men. It went from London to Dodgson's family home, Croft Rectory, Darlington, Yorkshire, where Dodgson was to be found at the end of the summer vacation, and it shows that much had already passed between author and publisher and that *Alice's Adventures in Wonderland* was well along towards being produced.

The letter is typically in Alexander's own hand and full of the sort of suggestions that he was accustomed to make to his authors: "I don't like any of the title pages," Macmillan began. "I will try to get a new specimen and send it

---

[1] Macmillan, p. xxxii.   [2] *The Life and Letters of Alfred Ainger* (1906), p. 63.
[3] He was not infallible, however, and, like other publishers, turned down manuscripts he must later have wished he had taken on. He rejected Thomas Hardy's first novel, turned away Shaw and Barrie, refused to meet Mrs. Humphry Ward's terms for *Robert Elsmere*, and turned down *A Shropshire Lad* (see Graves, pp. 288–92, 396; Morgan, pp. 119, 127–34; and Henry Maas, ed., *The Letters of A. E. Housman* (1971), p. 35).

to you." He suggested specific improvements in the title page and went on to other details. "The headings of the page should give the title of your book – which is very good. *'Fairy Tales'* cannot claim the merit of great novelty!.... The end of October – or early November would be about the best time [to publish]. I don't like ornamental type in title pages. Mr. Tenniel's drawings in the book need no such meretricious help." It is a straightforward letter teaching Dodgson, one imagines, a thing or two about book design.

Within the month, on October 12, Dodgson wrote in his *Diaries*: "Called on Macmillan, and had a talk about the book, but settled little."[1] A week later, on the 19th, Macmillan wrote again to Dodgson, now back at Oxford. "I think all the experiments in the title which you propose will be most effectively made in the sheet by Mr. Combe.... I should certainly incline to put the dedication in *one* size smaller type. . . ."

Dodgson's earliest known surviving letter to Macmillan is dated November 11, 1864, and begins the body of this volume.

V

If 1863 and 1864 were eventful years for Dodgson, emerging as he was as Lewis Carroll, a professional writer for children, it was also a significant time for Macmillan. Expansion was the order of the day: the firm moved to larger quarters at 16 Bedford Street, Covent Garden; Macmillan transferred the firm's headquarters from Cambridge to London; the family was successfully installed at Upper Tooting; and at least one other important event occurred: in spite of his Cambridge bearings, Macmillan was appointed Publisher to the University of Oxford. He took the appointment seriously and dutifully attended the weekly Delegates' meetings at Oxford. His close association with Combe would have been useful, for Combe could proffer insights into the Oxford scene.

In 1864 Macmillan initiated the Globe Shakespeare, from which would grow the Globe Library, a series that included volumes of the works of Burns, Cowper, Defoe, Dryden, Goldsmith, Malory, Pope, Scott, and translations of Horace and Virgil. Chaucer and Milton would follow later. Also in 1864, Macmillan published James Bryce's *The Holy Roman Empire* and George Trevelyan's *Cawnpore and Competition Wallah*. The firm was on solid ground in Covent Garden and the future looked bright.

The progress that Daniel and Alexander Macmillan had made is all the more remarkable when one considers the times in which they grew up and sought to establish themselves. When they came upon the bookselling scene, books were expensive and readers few. In 1825, that early sage of publishers, Archibald Constable, had to explain to Walter Scott that "hundreds of thousands of British subjects who paid luxury taxes never bought a book. Take the single item of hair

[1] P. 222.

powder," he added; "even though it had gone out of style, the number of people who still used it, and paid the tax on it, 'are an army, compared to the purchasers of even the best and most popular of books.'"[1]

Although Constable's efforts to bring affordable books into every home failed, other entrepreneurs struggled to accomplish the same idealistic ends. Henry Brougham and his Society for the Diffusion of Useful Knowledge strove from 1826 on to make high-minded, literate works available cheaply, but, more often than not, he and his Society either undershot or overshot the mark, producing works that were either superficial or too intellectual.[2] These early attempts to appeal to a wide public nonetheless stirred many minds and went hand in glove with the driving forces for educational advances. True, even before the reforms found their pace, before the explosion of enlightenment occurred, the laboring poor included some "whose existence will probably be doubted by many," who, stung by curiosity or impelled by a natural impulse to know more, cultivated hobbies, developed intellectual interests, and bought and read books. Mrs. Gaskell depicts such a one in *Mary Barton* (1847), where Margaret's grandfather spends every penny he can muster on his entomological pursuits.[3] The entire fabric of society was being transformed, and thinking and feeling were rising to new heights of awareness, adventure, even excitement. The more accessible written word accelerated the march of mind for the common man, a movement that would ultimately enhance the dignity of every free-born being, that would guarantee that all people were trained to read and write, that offered everyone a body of essential knowledge – that wrote into law provisions for basic education and made possible a private, personal relationship with books and their contents.

Beginning in the 1830s, an increasing number of innovative publishers were trying to appeal to this sleeping Gulliver of an audience, trying to shake him to wakefulness; to stimulate in him a hunger for facts and knowledge; to stir in him an interest in his heritage, in his world and in stories and poetry. As early as 1829, John Murray was on the scene with his Family Library; then followed Lardner's Cabinet Library, Oliver and Boyd's Edinburgh Cabinet Library, Colburn and Bentley's National Library and Standard Novels, William Pickering's Aldine series. These reprints usually sold for 5*s.* or 6*s.* each. The three-decker volumes, standard fare of the time, cost a prohibitive 31*s.*6*d.*[4] The steadily growing middle class found it progressively easier to purchase 5*s.* reprints through the 1830s and 1840s as their incomes gradually increased. And with increased leisure came a growing desire to develop the intellect. Soon a large portion of the population sought knowledge, wanted to be conversant with the sciences and the arts. Books played a central role in their lives.

[1] J. G. Lockhart, *Memoirs of the Life of Sir Walter Scott*, VII, 126–30, as cited in Altick, p. 208. In the paragraphs that follow, we have drawn liberally from Altick's invaluable work.
[2] Altick, pp. 270–1; and E. L. Woodward, *The Age of Reform*, (1954), p. 474.
[3] See ch. IV of the novel; and Altick, ch. 11.   [4] See Altick, pp. 272–4.

This march of mind was closely tied, of course, to the many innovations that followed hard upon the industrial revolution, during the hot pace of change. The Reform Bill of 1832, the shrinking work week, the movement from country to town and from agrarian to industrial life, the technical advances in machinery, the greater availability of newspapers and magazines, and, in a small way, the effect of the Library Act of 1850 which encouraged free libraries in Britain – all these and more had their effect upon the ability of a working reader to buy books.

Perhaps the greatest change in the book trade occurred because of the technical advances that led to mass production. A cyclical effect emerged: more readers required more books, larger book production forced book prices down, cheaper books encouraged still a larger reading public, and so on. The new wave of reading and learning transformed not only Victorian minds, but Victorian homes as well – just as, in the twentieth century, television has transformed minds and homes – and a huge popular press and a thriving book trade evolved. Robert Chambers' *Cyclopaedia of English Literature*, which appeared in 1843–4, sold over 100,000 copies within a few years of publication.[1]

The 1850s were, as Richard Altick sums them up, "the great turning-point in the history of the English book trade's relations with the mass public." The average price of a book declined by 40 percent between 1828 and 1853; Mudie expanded his circulating library, book clubs flourished, and cheap reprints multiplied; W. H. Smith set up railway stalls that dispensed reading material to the masses; John Cassell made a great success with inexpensive periodicals like *Teetotal Times*, *Working Man's Friend* (in its second year, its circulation reached 50,000), *Cassell's Popular Educator* (Thomas Hardy learned German with the aid of it), *The Illustrated Bible*, and *The Illustrated History of England*. By 1862 Cassell was selling between 25 and 30 million copies of his penny papers annually.[2]

If the 1850s saw the initial explosion of the reading public, the succeeding decades saw the predictable growth of book purchases. By 1879 *Middlemarch* (published in 1871–2) had sold 30,000 copies. In the first half of the century, England's population doubled from 8.9 to 17.9 million; by 1901 it had virtually quadrupled to 32.5 million.[3] Between 1830 and 1890, according to Walter Besant, the reading public expanded from 50,000 in Britain to 120,000,000 in the English-speaking world.[4]

VI

The growing book market provided ample room for the House of Macmillan, both as an innovator in bringing new authors and new titles to the fore and as a

---

[1] See John Gross, *The Rise and Fall of the Man of Letters* (1969), p. 193.
[2] Ibid., pp. 294, 303; see also Royal A. Gettmann, "Colburn–Bentley and the March of Intellect," *Studies in Bibliography*, Fredson Bowers, ed. 9 (1957), 197–213.   [3] See Altick, p. 81.
[4] *The Pen and the Book*, as cited in Sutherland, p. 64.

publisher of quality reprints. Quality had always been an essential ingredient in Daniel and Alexander Macmillan's formula: they sought always to provide the best possible products. Their Evangelical alliance, their endorsement of F. D. Maurice, Charles Kingsley, and Muscular Christianity were intrinsic elements in the dream that Daniel had articulated even as a bookseller's assistant. And in its way, it was the formula for success. Righteous, religious, uncompromising, traditional – these were reliable qualities in people and in business, and these were the emblems of authority that Macmillan's offered and the public sought. The formula succeeded.[1]

Even before Macmillan and Dodgson met, the House of Macmillan had achieved a tone that demanded respect from authors and fellow publishers. "Pray introduce me to Macmillan when you arrive," J. R. Green wrote to W. Boyd Dawkins, on January 15, 1862. ". . . Among the Stanley and Kingsley set Macmillan is the 'pet publisher' of the day."[2]

The status that the House of Macmillan provided was all the more reason for Dodgson to consider himself fortunate to have Alexander Macmillan take on his unknown *Alice*. But in contracting with Dodgson, the publisher was taking less of a chance than the author. Dodgson was to bear all the publishing costs, the cost of illustrating the book, and even of advertising it; Macmillan was simply to sell it – on commission. These terms may seem surprising, but the beginnings of the firm in Cambridge chronicle numerous variations on the theme of commission publishing, and Alexander Macmillan had already had considerable experience along the lines laid out in his agreement with Dodgson.

Publishing on commission was only one of at least six acceptable bases for agreement between publisher and author in Victorian times. Half-profits and joint-accounts were common. In agreements based on half-profits, publishing costs were usually borne by the publisher at the outset but charged against the book's receipts before the author earned anything; and if the sales of the book failed to defray the expenses, the author became liable for half the expenses. If the book's sales covered the expenses, then author and publisher shared additional receipts equally.

Under joint-accounts and joint-profits, either the publisher paid all costs or costs were shared between publisher and author, and the profits divided. Bentley and John Murray often used the joint-account formula. After Dickens was established, he could command seventy-five percent of the net earnings of a new work, fifty percent on reprints under joint-profits agreements.

An author could, of course, sell the copyright of a manuscript outright, as Trollope tended to do, for a given sum of money; he could lease his manuscript

---

[1] Prudery could be another element in the conventional attitude. Alexander Macmillan was at least not immune from it. To a friend who proposed to reissue some eighteenth-century novels, he wrote: "You begin with Richardson, Fielding, Smollett, Sterne. But what are you to do with their dirt? Modern taste won't stand it. I don't particularly think they ought to stand it." Graves, pp. 126, 249, 388–9.   [2] Leslie Stephen, ed., *Letters of J. R. Green* (1911), p. 95.

for a fixed length of time; or he could contract for royalties from the publisher, as most authors do today. Edward Moxon often leased half the copyright of an author's work; he paid nothing in advance, but charged all publishing and advertising costs against receipts. Any balance of receipts that remained after recovering the costs he divided with the author equally. Leasing had certain advantages for authors that outright sale of copyright and royalty arrangements lacked. Dickens, Tennyson, and George Eliot leased their work for limited times and so retained control over the quality of the text and the size of the printings. Leasing kept publishers on their toes, eager to persuade famous authors to renew.

The commission agreements that governed the Dodgson–Macmillan enterprises were common enough through the latter half of the nineteenth century: in 1890, a spokesman for the Society of Authors reported that "at least three-quarters of modern fiction was published on commission." Under this plan, what we think of as the conventional roles of publisher and author often did not exist. The author, as in Dodgson's case, could be responsible for the full cost of producing and promoting the book. The publisher marketed it and, in return, received a fixed ten percent of the receipts. The author stood to gain or lose the bulk of the profit or loss. He took most of the risk and in fact performed the roles and made the decisions that today belong to the publisher. The author determined the size of the book, the quality of the paper, the size and style of the type. He selected the binding; engaged the printer, the engraver, the illustrator; and he paid them. He decided how many books would constitute the first printing. He determined the extent of the advertising, and he set the price for the book.[1]

VII

It is a tribute to both Dodgson and Macmillan that their association did not founder on the rough seas they encountered in launching *Alice's Adventures in Wonderland*. In the face of Dodgson's constant concern for detail during production and his ultimate request that Macmillan scrap the entire first edition, the publisher could easily have thrown up the whole enterprise as not

---

[1] For information on Victorian publishing agreements, we have drawn on the following works: Royal A. Gettmann, *A Victorian Publisher: A Study of the Bentley Papers* (1960), esp. pp. 87–9, 103–15; Frank Arthur Mumby, *Publishing and Bookselling: A History from the Earliest Times to the Present Day* (1930), esp. chs. xiii and xiv; Frank A. Mumby, *The Romance of Book Selling: A History from the Earliest Times to the Twentieth Century* (1967), chs. 11 and 12; Simon Nowell-Smith, *International Copyright Law and the Publisher in the Reign of Queen Victoria* (1968), esp. pp. 50–1; Robert L. Patten, "Slips, Sacred Commodities, and Broadway Bladder," *Review* [Blacksburg, Va.], pp. [1]–24; Joanne Shattock, "Sources for the Study of Victorian Writers and Their Publishers," *Browning Institute Studies*, William S. Peterson, ed., 7 (1979), 93–113; John Sutherland, "The Fiction Earning Patterns of Thackeray, Dickens, George Eliot and Trollope," ibid., pp. 71–92; and Sutherland, esp. pp. 88–94.

worth the candle. But Macmillan remained, at all times, advisory, calm, businesslike, unreproving – and uncomplaining.

Dodgson's dealings with his illustrator were quite different. John Tenniel proved difficult on many counts, while Dodgson, often characterized as fussy and meddling in his relations with his publisher and his artists, was far more patient and indulgent with Tenniel than Tenniel was with him.

Dodgson's admiration for Tenniel's work and the knowledge that the artist's popularity would do his book no harm led him to seek out Tenniel when, with publication assured, he began his search for a professional illustrator. He made his first approach through his acquaintance Tom Taylor (1817–80), dramatist and contributor to (and later editor of) *Punch*: "Do you know Mr. Tenniel enough to say whether he could undertake such a thing as drawing a dozen wood-cuts to illustrate a child's book," Dodgson wrote on December 20, 1863, "and if so, could you put me into communication with him?"[1] A month later, on January 25, 1864, Dodgson, a letter of introduction in hand from Taylor to Tenniel, called on the artist in London: "he was very friendly," Dodgson wrote, "and seemed to think favourably of undertaking the pictures."[2] By June 21 Dodgson was discussing production details with Macmillan. In London that day, he called on the publisher, "who strongly advised my altering the size of the page of the book, and adopting that of *The Water Babies*." From Macmillan's office, Dodgson went to call again on "Tenniell" – he actually misspells the name in his *Diaries* – "who agreed to the change of the page."[3]

Despite the promising start, the passage ahead was strewn with rocks. Contrary to the myth that Dodgson created all the difficulties in the collaboration with Tenniel, Tenniel actually got his every wish. It was he, in fact, not Dodgson, who insisted on having the first edition scrapped and redoing it because he judged the printing to be poor. Although Dodgson acceded in this demand and ordered a second printing at great additional expense to himself, a good many keen observers then and since have been hard put to distinguish between the quality of the illustrations in the two editions.

Given the history of their troubles over *Alice*, one might well wonder how Dodgson ever brought himself to ask Tenniel to illustrate *Looking-Glass*. Clearly, his admiration for Tenniel's work won out over his reservations. But Tenniel, when approached, at first refused on the grounds that he was fully committed for two years ahead. Dodgson sought elsewhere, but found no one good enough who was free. He returned to Tenniel, offered to pay for five months of the artist's services, and in April 1864, Tenniel condescended to do the work "at such spare times as he can find."[4]

This arrangement put Dodgson in the weakest possible position, completely at the mercy of Tenniel's iron whim. In fact, Dodgson's *Diaries* are peppered with disappointment after disappointment over the illustrator's inability to

[1] *Letters*, p. 62.   [2] *Diaries*, p. 210   [3] P. 217.   [4] *Diaries*, p. 270.

meet deadlines, and the upshot was that Tenniel repeatedly delayed publication: "*Looking-Glass* . . . lingers on though the text is ready," Dodgson writes on April 4, 1871, and adds: "I have only received twenty-seven pictures."[1] Ever conciliatory, he did what he could to urge Tenniel on, but wait he had to and wait he did. He made no major decisions about the printing or sale of the book without Tenniel's approval, and when they disagreed, Dodgson usually gave way. He even deleted a large fragment from *Looking-Glass* when Tenniel decided that drawing a wasp in a wig was "beyond the appliances of art."[2] Throughout his collaboration with Tenniel, Dodgson remained ever patient, recording nowhere a harsh word against him.

VIII

By contrast with Dodgson's associations with Tenniel, the tone of the correspondence with Alexander Macmillan is more demanding, some might say *commanding*; at times, one could certainly characterize the relationship with his publisher as "difficult." But Dodgson's dealings with Macmillan are, in essence, less those of a fellow seaman than those of the captain of a ship with his crew: he knows the difference, and he exercises his responsibilities accordingly. Dodgson's letters to Macmillan are frequent, detailed, and businesslike, but they are never rude or huffy. For his part, Macmillan in his letters is correct, straightforward, impersonal, often avuncular and reassuring.

The earliest letter from Dodgson that can be read as a complaint occurs on August 30, 1866,[3] where he regrets that Macmillan went ahead with a new printing without waiting for corrections. But this mild protest does not disturb the harmony between them.

Through the years that follow, Dodgson dispatched a steady barrage of letters to Macmillan. Many contained complaints or objections, but the vast majority concerned details of the manufacture of his books. Commentators have tended to damn Dodgson for the sheer number and frequency of these letters and for his concern with the minutiae of book publishing. "There was never an author more elaborately careful . . . for the details of production," writes Charles Morgan, "or one that can have more sorely tried the patience of his publisher."[4] Dodgson was "almost fanatically anxious to secure artistic perfection," Derek Hudson says, and concludes that "the patience of Macmillan's in the face of a continuous stream of detailed enquiry and sometimes pedantic admonition is something to admire."[5] Warren Weaver finds Dodgson "exceedingly fussy

---

[1] Ibid., p. 297.
[2] Collingwood, pp. 146–9. The deleted wasp fragment came to light in 1974 and has been published on its own and with commentaries. See, for instance, Martin Gardner, ed., *The Wasp in a Wig* (1977); Morton Cohen, "Alice: The Lost Chapter Revealed," *Telegraph Sunday Magazine*, September 4, 1977, pp. 12–21; and "A Suppressed Adventure of 'Alice' Surfaces after 107 Years," *Smithsonian*, 8 (December 1977), 50–[7].   [3] P. 44, below.   [4] P. 79.   [5] P. 153.

about details";[1] Jean Gattégno sees him as "a demanding, indeed an exhausting, author" driven by "'the mania' for quality";[2] and Anne Clark judges him "a difficult and hypercritical taskmaster."[3]

These critics are too harsh. They have not considered well enough that Dodgson lived in an age that embraced a work ethic that is virtually foreign to our own; that he lived in a time when change and perfection were worshipped for themselves, when every self-respecting person agreed instinctively with Browning's Andrea del Sarto: "Ah, but a man's reach should exceed his grasp, Or what's a heaven for?" Dodgson's concerns and behavior were not so much the outward signs of a pernickety personality as the result of his devotion to the Evangelical ethic and his high aesthetic standards. Certainly Macmillan sensed as much and in fact shared Dodgson's fervor and appreciated his goals. He took Dodgson's letters in his stride. He too was bound to Evangelical ideals and never considered himself at fault for insisting upon high quality products for his firm's imprint. Nor did Macmillan complain to Dodgson about the constant stream of letters or about their contents. Their personalities and beliefs were so nearly similar that they were in fact closely attuned in essentials and struck instinctive chords of understanding and sympathy.

Alexander Macmillan was thoroughly experienced in book manufacture, but he must also have known, early on, that in Dodgson he had something more than just another egocentric author. He paid attention to Dodgson's ideas and adopted most of them. Only occasionally did he suggest a course different from the one Dodgson charted, and then, usually, with good reason, based on his wider experience. Especially in the early years of the relationship, Macmillan helped educate the author in the technical processes of book production – and Dodgson proved so apt a pupil that he soon dealt with technicalities like a trained professional.

To acknowledge the shared concerns for excellence is not to make light of Dodgson's demands on his illustrators, printers, engravers, or publisher – and certainly on himself. His personality led him to behave as he did, but his personal circumstances, especially in the early years of the association, also influenced him. He was not wealthy, and when he decided to pay the costs of manufacturing his books, he was risking much more than prudence dictated. On his first ride on the book-manufacturing merry-go-round, he was badly hurt: it cost him a large amount of money that he could not really afford to lose. The only sensible course was to try to insure that engravers, printers, binders, and publishers did the work that he was paying them to do. He simply had to stay alert and to supervise every stage of his books' production. He must at some point have resolved to do just that, and the correspondence with Macmillan shows how he fulfilled that resolve.

[1] P. 23.
[2] *Lewis Carroll: Fragments of a Looking-Glass*, trans. Rosemary Sheed (1976), pp. 134, 140.
[3] P. 135.

What it amounts to, in modern terms, is that Dodgson took upon his shoulders the responsibility of performing the jobs done today by copy editors, production editors, artist-designers, and numerous clerks, technicians, and computers in publishers' offices – a formidable undertaking. Given the arrangements with Macmillan, given the breed of man Dodgson was and the conventions of the time, given the disastrous experience he had over Tenniel's rejecting the first *Alice*, Dodgson's later behavior reflects less personal eccentricity than an effort to achieve a standard of excellence and economy in producing his books that he not only desired, but also had a right to expect.

Some readers may suspect that the formality that both Dodgson and Macmillan assumed in their letters hides some unrevealed animosity. But that is surely not the case. If the letters that pass between them seem, in some respects, curious to our eyes, we must think ourselves back in time to realize that Dodgson and Macmillan were staunch examples of Victorian propriety. Dodgson in his entire life never addressed an adult outside his family by a given name. No friend, no colleague ever was called John or Fred or Harry. In their letters to one another, Dodgson and Macmillan simply complied with the standards of their time, usually addressing each other as "Dear Sir" and only occasionally by the less formal (British) salutation "My dear Sir." Dodgson did not, in fact, get around to writing "Dear Mr. Macmillan" until some time after the approved second edition of *Alice* had become a reality. The subscriptions tell the same tale: "Yours truly," "Truly yours," and occasionally "Very truly yours," followed by "A. Macmillan" or "C. L. Dodgson."

Gradually a full-scale author–publisher relationship took root, not only with Lewis Carroll, author of children's books, but with the combined personality of Lewis Carroll and C. L. Dodgson. In the years that followed, Macmillan published a good many books, over both of the author's names: *An Elementary Treatise on Determinants* (1867), *Phantasmagoria and Other Poems* (1869), *The Hunting of the Snark* (1876), *Euclid and His Modern Rivals* (1879), *Doublets: A Word-Puzzle* (1879), *Euclid, Books I, II* (1882), *Lawn Tennis Tournaments* (1883), *Rhyme? and Reason?* (1883), *A Tangled Tale* (1885), *The Game of Logic* (1886), *Alice's Adventures Under Ground*, the manuscript facsimile (1886), *Curiosa Mathematica, Part I* (1888), *The Nursery "Alice"* (1889), *Sylvie and Bruno* (1889), *Curiosa Mathematica, Part II* (1893), *Sylvie and Bruno Concluded* (1893), *Symbolic Logic, Part I* (1896), *Three Sunsets and Other Poems* posthumously (1898), and various supplements, revisions, translations, later and cheap editions, pamphlets, circular letters, and advertisements to be tucked or bound into his books.

Dodgson's interest in book manufacturing and book distributing never flagged; in fact, as the years passed, he kept up with the new technology and showed a confident command of publishing terms. He continued to be ever vigilant, taking little for granted, anticipating problems, recording his thoughts and expectations clearly and in detail, and giving explicit instructions. Gradually the returns on *Alice* wiped out the arrears he suffered in the first reprinting, and he began to make a considerable profit. But money was not his primary concern, though he was ever cautious in financial matters, and he was by nature precise, accountable, and never wasteful. His primary object, however, was to give the public a book of quality at a reasonable price.

Certainly much of this correspondence proceeded along strictly business lines. But every so often, one letter or another unexpectedly captures something deeply revealing about Dodgson and Macmillan as men. The letter from Dodgson dated December 17, 1871,[1] is a case in point. It is a reply to a letter from Macmillan telling Dodgson that the entire first printing of nine thousand *Looking-Glass*es has been sold in the fortnight since it appeared, that he is printing another six thousand immediately, that he expects that these will sell out rapidly, and that he is consequently ordering still more to be printed.

What author would not welcome such news? Would any ordinary mortal scribbling at his desk or pecking away at his typewriter or word processor feel anything but elation? And how would he respond to his publisher? "More power to you!" probably. Not so Dodgson. His reply begins with some minor details: he acknowledges receipt of ten more copies of the book, asks for copies of the press notices, and deals with another minor item before getting down to Macmillan's good news and the proposal to print more copies. No elation, only caution. He fears haste because haste diminishes the chance of getting work done to a high standard, and he does not wish to vex Mr. Tenniel with any diminution in the quality of the pictures. Macmillan's suggestion that they immediately print another six thousand copies Dodgson terms "alarming," he insists that no short cuts be taken in drying the sheets and that, regardless of profit, they have no further artistic fiascos. Macmillan, instinctively sympathetic, capitulates: "I fully appreciate your desire for excellence," he wrote the following day, "and really do not feel inclined to press our own interests against your high aim."[2]

On the other hand, Dodgson was ever ready to listen carefully to Macmillan, and he often took his advice. In fact he frequently solicited it. What is more, he never took Macmillan for granted. He might be firm and he was often importunate, but he was not obdurate and certainly never disrespectful. Nor did he expect Macmillan to perform miracles. Dodgson appealed to Macmillan on the technical problem of reverse printing for *Looking-Glass*[3] and was gratified when Macmillan could accommodate the idea. He cast a good many other notions at Macmillan and was pleased when Macmillan worked on them with care. When Macmillan, treading on sacred ground, suggested that *Phantasmagoria* be bound in blue covers and not in red, even though he knew that Dodgson was devoted to red, Dodgson saw the wisdom of Macmillan's point and the book ended up with a blue binding.[4]

[1] See pp. 96–9, below.   [2] See pp. 97, 99, below.   [3] See pp. 59, 76, below.
[4] See pp. 35–6, 72, below.

10-31-20-245908

25th August

HOTEL

KAP

Den Texstraat 5B
1017 XW Amsterdam
tel. 020 - 245908

6245908

Familiehotel KAP is zeer rustig en gunstig gelegen in het centrum van Amsterdam.
De verschillende musea, winkels en het uitgaansleven van Amsterdam zijn lopend binnen 5 - 10 minuten bereikbaar.
De RAI is met tramlijn 4 op 10 minuten afstand, vanaf de RAI is de luchthaven Schiphol met de trein zeer snel te bereiken (± 10 minuten).
Ons hotel serveert een uitgebreid Hollands ontbijt.
Wij beschikken tevens over familiekamers.

Family hotel KAP is quietly and favourably situated in the heart of Amsterdam.
Most of Amsterdam's museums, theatres, clubs and shops are within 5 to 10 minutes' walking distance.
RAI Congres and Exhibition Centre is reached in

10 minutes by tram 4 and from there a train goes to Schiphol Airport (approx. 10 minutes).
In our Hotel you can enjoy a sumptuous Dutch breakfast.
Family rooms are available.

Familienhotel KAP mit sehr ruhiger und günstiger Lage im Zentrum von Amsterdam.
Die verschiedenen Museen, Läden und der Amüsementsbetrieb von Amsterdam sind innerhalb von 5 bis 10 Gehminuten zu erreichen.
Das RAI ist mit der Straßenbahnlinie 4 innerhalb von 10 Minuten zu erreichen; vom RAI ist der Flughafen Schiphol per Bahn sehr schnell erreichbar (ca. 10 Minuten.
Unser Hotel serviert ein ausführliches,

Macmillan gave more than technical advice. When Dodgson was beset by doubts over his own judgment, the publisher came to the rescue. A case in point concerned the title of the sequel to *Alice*, about which Dodgson had some qualms. When he shared them with Macmillan, the publisher replied: "The title you chose at first is admirable. Don't let friend or foe disturb you in that. The printer has not arranged it as he might. You shall see it in a modified form. *Behind the Looking-Glass & What Alice saw there* is quite perfect. . . . Don't alter your wording." Dodgson did change the title, of course, but only slightly, and with Macmillan's approbation: "Your new title is admirable," he wrote. "You shall see a proof at once. . . . '*Through*' is just the word – you'll never beat it. . . . Tenniel should make you a wonderful frontispiece from the title."[1]

If Dodgson could, at times, verge on the accusatory, Macmillan could, for his part, be sharp in return, particularly if he detected a faint imputation that, out of some personal motive, he was not heeding Dodgson's instructions. In a letter dated March 19, 1869, on the subject of the German *Alice*, Macmillan wrote: "We have no possible motive for saving you money against your will, and assuredly did not intentionally use one paper knowing you wanted another. I know you wanted a good paper, as like the English as possible. This we took pains to procure. When a reprint is required you shall have English paper. But I have been comparing the two, and there is very little difference to my eye."

Here is another Macmillan reproof: "The 'Behind the Looking-Glass' has only been announced in our Magazine," he wrote on November 9, 1869, in response to what must have been a suggestion that the publisher had rashly publicized the sequel. "It is well to show that you are alive, and not speechless."

Good at public relations strategy himself, Dodgson liked to include a list of his publications in copies of his books, but he was apparently displeased by one such catalogue that Macmillan issued. Macmillan replied to Dodgson's objection on January 5, 1870: "We have only slightly exceeded your wishes. And is it *so* ugly? it is only semi-detached, not printed with the book, and future copies will be bound without it – if you really are aggrieved by it."

In spite of what might seem testy exchanges, the business stance, the Victorian formality gave way in time to a genial, friendly tone, and the humanity of the two men shines through. A good example is Dodgson's letter of February 15, 1869,[2] where he argued for a cheap edition of *Alice*, and Macmillan's where he reacted to Dodgson's suggestion to insert a printed message in all future copies of *Alice* asking his child readers to send him a photograph in care of Macmillan's office.[3] Another of Macmillan's flourishes occurred when Dodgson asked him, towards Christmas 1871, whether it would be wise to put off publishing *Looking-Glass* until after Christmas. Macmillan the wise businessman knew beter: his reply appears below.[4]

Dodgson's partial deafness, his stammer, and his determination to keep his

---

[1] See p. 85, below.   [2] See pp. 77–8, below.   [3] See pp. 84–5, below.   [4] P. 98.

two identities separate combined to keep him from appearing at a good many social gatherings that other Victorian luminaries eagerly attended. He was, for instance, regularly invited to Macmillan's Tobacco Parliaments, and just as regularly declined. This reticence did not, however, prevent a stronger social bond from developing between Dodgson and Macmillan. Before long Dodgson visited the publisher at home and came to know his family. When Dodgson needed a title for what he calls his "book of puzzles," he wrote out some eight possibilities and sent them to Macmillan: "Would your family-circle kindly resolve themselves into a committee of taste, and give me their opinions, collectively if unanimous – otherwise, individually,"[1] Dodgson was evidently quite familiar with the Macmillan family by this time. For his part, he entertained Macmillan from time to time in his rooms at Christ Church. At least once Dodgson dined with Macmillan and his son George at the Garrick Club and accompanied them to the theater. Dodgson's letters to Macmillan from the mid-1870s on allude repeatedly and at times affectionately to members of the Macmillan family.

Macmillan performed a good many services for Dodgson that authors would not today expect of a publisher, and that even most Victorian authors rarely expected. Naturally, the publisher took care of all the ordinary publishing chores, like providing Dodgson with press notices, mailing copies of his books hither and yon, and considering third-party manuscripts which Dodgson referred to him. But, following Dodgson's instructions, Macmillan also had a clerk answer a good many letters addressed to Lewis Carroll, thereby helping Dodgson to maintain the cloak of his cherished anonymity. Macmillan also sent messengers on various errands for Dodgson, not least of all to reclaim a watch from a repairman, and he indulged him in having copies of his books bound in special vellum and in different colors for favorite friends.

The firm searched out addresses from directories for Dodgson; they arranged to have all the speeches from the *Alice* books copied out so that Dodgson could register them as dramas; they found him stationers to sell his *"Wonderland" Postage Stamp-Case*; and they even purchased theater tickets for him. This last courtesy in particular elicits snorts from the critics: how did Dodgson dare to deal so perfunctorily with the great House of Macmillan? But before Dodgson made such a request, he had developed a good, strong, personal relationship with Macmillan. One can even surmise that Macmillan, aware that Dodgson was based in Oxford, might suggest that Dodgson not hesitate to ask and, perhaps, even urged him to avail himself of the company's easy access to London shops and theaters. Dodgson was ever sensitive to the nuances of relationships and always kept to the straight and narrow path dictated by propriety. He would not presume to ask such favors had he not been assured that he might. Nor would Messrs. Macmillan perform them as a duty had they not seen fit to do so:

[1] See p. 108, below.

on at least two occasions Dodgson wrote asking whether his publisher could find employment in his offices for relations of his, once a brother,[1] the other time a nephew. In both instances, the answer was a clear, if polite, no.

Dodgson took a keen interest in Macmillan's list, read a good many books that the firm published, and repeatedly suggested additions, all of which Macmillan & Co. considered seriously. Evidently he performed other, lesser services for the busy publishing house. Morgan reports that Dodgson "knew better than anyone else how to tie up parcels. He supplied a diagram, which long hung in the post-room at Bedford Street, showing how string on all parcels should be, and how the string on all his parcels must be, knotted."[2]

Dodgson's *Alice* books alone must have made an exceptionally good return for Macmillan & Co., and many of his later books exceeded even their expectations in sales. But, more important, because the firm prided itself on its distinguished and dignified authors, Charles Dodgson, and Lewis Carroll even more so, fitted nicely into Macmillan's image of itself.

It became clear in Dodgson's later letters that despite his university income and the considerable profit on the *Alice* books, he did not have much cash to spare, and he calculated his needs and expectations carefully. He was not a bon vivant; he was not extravagant. He lived simply and his tastes were modest. Where did all the money go? The answer is that, in a very quiet way, Dodgson was extraordinarily generous and selfless. Towards the end of his life, he was not only partly supporting his sisters in Guildford but also sending money regularly to more distant relatives and helping to pay bills and to educate a small army of needy friends and acquaintances. Given these commitments, he simply had to protect his resources, to ensure that he made the best of them.

IX

Never one to accept traditional notions without subjecting them to the strictest tests of logic, Dodgson undertook to challenge the practice then prevailing among English booksellers of taking discounts from publishers and allowing discounts to purchasers who paid cash. He was iconoclastic, too, in daring to suggest that booksellers were, on the whole, making too much profit. Such radical notions could easily have disturbed, even destroyed, relations between any author and his publisher. But the Dodgson–Macmillan ties survived even this jolt.

Book pricing and price control were thorny subjects in Britain for most of the nineteenth century. The practice of discounting books (a polite description for publishers competing to offer booksellers the best terms and booksellers underselling one another) went back to the eighteenth century. In the early part of the nineteenth century, selling books for something below their advertised

---

[1] See pp. 87–8, below.   [2] Pp. 110–11.

price was customary. To halt this practice, major publishers banded together in
1829, agreed on a set of rules among themselves, and undertook, by cutting off
supplies of books, to starve out retail bookdealers who sold at less than agreed
prices. For almost a quarter of a century this agreement held fast and control was
maintained over book prices.

But as time wore on, that control became enmeshed in the larger debate over
free trade versus protection, and in 1852 the bookseller John Chapman rallied a
band of articulate authors to the cause of free trade in books. Together they
exerted the pressure needed to bring the recently organized Booksellers'
Association to submit the dispute to arbitration. William Longman and John
Murray argued the case for protection, but, as Richard Altick puts it, "they
were no match for the eloquence of leader-writers in the liberal press and
Gladstone in Parliament."[1] In April 1852, book-price protection came to an
end, and free buying and selling of books became the order of the day: from then
on, booksellers could expect to reap a discount of 2s. or 3s. in the pound from
publishers, and book buyers could obtain a discount from booksellers when
paying cash.

Alexander Macmillan believed strongly in price control. He put his position
eloquently in a letter that he wrote to Gladstone on April 10, 1868:

> I have never been convinced that the decision . . . some twenty years ago, which broke up
> our old trade custom, was a wise decision. Its result has been this – Whereas in former
> years there used to be many booksellers who kept good stocks of solid standard books, one
> or more in every important town in England, and these booksellers lived by selling books,
> the case is now that in country towns few live by bookselling: the trade has become so
> profitless that it is generally the appendage to a toyshop, or a Berlin wool warehouse and a
> few trashy novels, selling for a shilling, with flaring covers suiting the flashy contents, and
> the bookseller who studies what books are good and worth recommending to his
> customer has ceased to exist. Intelligence and sympathy with literature has gone out of
> the trade as a rule almost wholly. I believe the general intelligence of the country has
> suffered by it. My conviction, based on an experience of some thirty years, is that an
> intelligent bookseller in every town of any importance in the kingdom would be almost as
> valuable as an intelligent schoolmaster or parson. How can you get that if you don't pay
> him for his work or thought? I have no doubt that Political Economy and Free Trade
> "buy cheap, sell dear" have some meaning in the world, but they are not God, and may, I
> fear, have become – something else.[2]

Although Altick suggests that Macmillan and other publishers of the day
"probably exaggerated the ruinous effect of underselling upon regular
bookshops" and that, in fact, "the discount system encouraged the reading
habit both by reducing actual prices and by increasing the availability of
books,"[3] the discount system certainly diminished profits for both publishers
and booksellers. It also drove publishers to find cheaper ways to produce books,
and inferior production brought to the shops books of less elegant and less
durable material.

[1] Pp. 304–5.   [2] Graves, pp. 286–7.   [3] P. 305.

However strong Macmillan's views were on discounting, he had an open mind on this as on most subjects, and he was a keen observer of trade practices and a sharp analyst of the current scene. By 1875, when Dodgson proposed to fix the price of his books and to limit or disallow discounts on them, Macmillan was cautious about the suggestion. When Dodgson first sought to alter the terms to booksellers who took his books, thereby diminishing their profit, Macmillan was wary: "When you can come to town I will be very glad to go into the questions you raise," he writes. "I think it would not do in any way to alter terms. . . . In reality the bookseller greatly helps you and his profits are not anything like what you say. . . . Please come and talk it over."[1]

In time they talked, and they exchanged a good many letters on the subject. Dodgson persisted – and ultimately prevailed. Macmillan notified booksellers that Lewis Carroll's books would, in future, no longer bring a 3*d.* discount in the shilling, but 2*d.* instead, and that the publisher would no longer be able to supply "odd books," that is, twenty-one books for every twenty ordered. The news spread quickly through bookselling circles, reaction was swift and heated.[2] Macmillan found himself in a singularly uncomfortable, even embarrassing, position, but he could neither refute logic nor deny Dodgson the right to set the price and condition of sales of his books. He submitted. Dodgson's books thenceforth went from publisher to bookseller on Dodgson's terms, terms that flew in the face of the discounts applied to almost all other books.

The letters between Dodgson and the House of Macmillan now reveal Dodgson guiding the forces that brought about the controls that once again eliminated cutthroat discounting and underselling and set regulations that publishers, booksellers, and authors were once again bound to uphold.

It was no accident that (Sir) Frederick Orridge Macmillan (1851–1936), eldest son of Daniel (and father of the future Prime Minister, Harold Macmillan), emerged as the leading figure in the drama of book discounting. He had gone straight from Uppingham to work for the firm, learned the business through and through, and became a partner in 1876. On March 6, 1890, a letter of his appeared in the *Bookseller* entitled "A Remedy for Underselling" in which he proposed a net system[3] to "abolish discounts to the public altogether."[4] Macmillan's moreover begin to distribute "net books": between July and December 1890 they launched sixteen titles on a net basis, and by 1894 the firm circulated more than a hundred net books a year.[5] Macmillan also refused to supply books to booksellers who would not cooperate. Although Frederick

---

[1] See pp. 112–13, below.   [2] See pp. 365–9, below; Appendix A.
[3] The word *net* meant that the publisher set the *retail* price of the book from which booksellers could not deviate. Limiting or eliminating discounts to booksellers, forcing them to sell at a smaller profit, naturally encouraged compliance with the net system. If a bookseller violated the agreement and sold at a discount, publishers could boycott him. See *Net Book Agreement, passim*; and Barnes, esp. p. 142.   [4] P. 244; reprinted in *Net Book Agreement*, pp. 5–8.
[5] *Net Book Agreement*, p. 17.

Macmillan's original proposal in the *Bookseller* met with stiff opposition, other publishers jumped onto the net book bandwagon as early as 1890 and the movement ultimately led to the Net Book Agreement of 1899, fixing simple rules for book trading and strict controls on discounting. *The Times* and its book club waged war on the Agreement, but they were vanquished: the Agreement survived all assaults, and in 1962 the Restrictive Practices Court, in the first test of the Agreement's legality, upheld it.[1]

Frederick Macmillan was already a partner of the firm by the 1880s, when Dodgson was corresponding with Alexander Macmillan on the very subject of controlling book prices. Looking back upon this time much later, he wrote, "[Dodgson's] attempts to regulate the prices at which his books were sold to the Trade, although they were somewhat troublesome to carry out, were in the end successful, and were to a great extent the foundation on which a few years afterwards we built up the Net Book System which for the last forty years has been the salvation of the Retail Booksellers."[2]

It was Dodgson, then, who unknowingly shaped the terms of the Net Book Agreement and shares with Frederick a place in the history of the book trade and the struggle to control discounting and underselling. True, in 1871, John Ruskin broke with publishers and set up his own firm to produce quality books at a reasonable price. But Ruskin, in selling both to the trade and to the public at the same price and posting books directly to the purchaser, broke with the system entirely.[3] Dodgson worked within the conventional channel of author-to-publisher-to-bookseller-to-reader. He sought to reform the system and succeeded. He deserves an honored place among those who fought for a "just peace" in the nineteenth-century battle of the books.

x

The drama of the Dodgson–Macmillan relationship continued to play through the latter quarter of the nineteenth century: it was not Victorian melodrama, French farce, nor pantomime. As the scenes unfold, they reveal a deepening attachment between the head of the house and this one particular author. These two had weathered a good many storms together, and a natural warm aura enveloped them. Macmillan continued to be gentle and considerate in his letters to Dodgson, and on a number of occasions Dodgson expressed his gratitude to the older man. On April 28, 1871, for instance, he wrote of his "undiminished" confidence in the firm.[4]

Alexander Macmillan gradually gave up his responsibilities to younger

[1] See Barnes, pp. 143–67.
[2] Manuscript letter to Falconer Madan, Christmas Day 1931 (Bodleian).
[3] For the history of Ruskin's efforts to produce quality books economically, see E. T. Cook, "Ruskin and His Books," *Strand Magazine*, 24 (December 1902), esp. pp. 715–7; and *The Life of John Ruskin*, 2 vols., 2nd ed. (1912), II, 330–2.   [4] P. 94, below.

Macmillans, and towards the end of the run, especially through the nineties, Dodgson dealt almost exclusively with Frederick Macmillan. The letters that passed between them were businesslike and polite, but references to the Macmillan family disappear now, and Dodgson seems content, as does Frederick, to restrict himself to practical matters. "Dodgson was . . . a rather pernickety man to deal with," Frederick recalled later, "but I always got on with him well because I recognised that in all his dealings his intention was to do what was honest and fair to all parties."[1]

A diminution in the firm's efficiency apparently occurred, perhaps inevitably as it climbed to the top of the publishing ladder, and Dodgson had more frequent occasions to lament its shortcomings. On December 12, 1889, he went up to London to inscribe copies of *Sylvie and Bruno* to be sent to friends. "I wanted the parcels packed and sent off as soon as possible," he writes,[2] "and the 'hands' provided for the job were (as I found after a long wait) those of a single boy! The *management* seems to be falling off, now that Mr. [Alexander] Macmillan . . . is no longer on the spot," he opined. On the following day he found "further proof of incompetent managing at Macmillan's. I had written on the 8th, to beg they would send me 12 copies of *Sylvie and Bruno* to Oxford as soon as possible. Copies were ready, on Thursday morning. This is Friday evening, and none have come. . . . I fear the Firm is going down, and I may have to find another publisher."[3]

Four years later, on November 21, 1893, he wrote to Frederick Macmillan: "When I also recall the omissions, in advertising, which I pointed out in my letter of October 1, I cannot help feeling that the Firm has suffered much by losing the personal supervision of Mr. Alexander Macmillan . . . and, much as I should regret the having to sever a connection that has now lasted nearly 30 years, I shall feel myself absolutely compelled to do so, unless I can have some assurance that better care shall be taken, in future, to ensure that my books shall be of the *best* artistic quality attainable for the money."[4] Dodgson also found fault with the ever-increasing delays that his requests encountered, and he was deeply troubled by the decline in the quality of the reprints of his books, particularly the *Alice*s. "A great wave of inaction seems to have come over your employees," he wrote on May 27, 1897. "Is it the approaching Jubilee that has so demoralised them!"[5]

In spite of all the difficulties and disappointments, however, Dodgson never broke with the House of Macmillan. The last known letter from Dodgson to the firm bears the date December 15, 1897, less than three weeks before his death; and the last known letter from the firm to Dodgson is dated January 3, 1898, eleven days before the end. In important matters, the association worked until the final curtain. As late as March 20, 1896, Dodgson wrote to Frederick Macmillan: "Thanks for your letter, and specially for what you say about not accepting any share of the profits, should any such accrue, of a French Edition of

---

[1] To Falconer Madan, Christmas Day 1931 (Bodleian).   [2] *Diaries*, p. 476.
[3] Diaries.   [4] See pp. 292–3, below.   [5] See p. 352, below.

Symbolic Logic. It is by no means the first time that I have had to notice, with gratitude, the handsome way in which my Publishers deal with me."[1] But Dodgson's greatest tribute to the House of Macmillan comes in a quotation from his pamphlet *The Profits of Authorship* that his nephew and official biographer has preserved for us:

The publisher contributes about as much as the bookseller in time and bodily labour, but in mental toil and trouble a great deal more. I speak, with some personal knowledge of the matter, having myself, for some twenty years, inflicted on that most patient and painstaking firm, Messrs. Macmillan and Co., about as much wear and worry as ever publishers have lived through. The day when they undertake a book for me is a *dies nefastus* for them. From that day till the book is out – an interval of some two or three years on an average – there is no pause in "the pelting of the pitiless storm" of directions and questions on every conceivable detail. To say that every question gets a courteous and thoughtful reply – that they are still outside a lunatic asylum – and that they still regard me with some degree of charity – is to speak volumes in praise of their good temper and of their health, bodily and mental. . . .[2]

Dodgson clearly knew that, through the years, he had made extraordinary demands upon Macmillan's, but they surely realized, in turn, that he was an extraordinary person and author. They may have regarded him as a rather eccentric Oxford don whom they had to humor and approach with kid gloves, but never, through the thirty-five years, did they patronize him or deal with his suggestions or requirements condescendingly. The underlying mutual respect forged early in the association between Charles Dodgson and Alexander Macmillan endured to the end. Dodgson's books sold steadily, and some of them, certainly the *Alices*, broke sales records. The relationship was, after all, profitable for Macmillan & Co. as well as for Dodgson.

Dodgson's incessant and uncompromising demands upon the firm reflect the nature of the man, the man who, as critics suggest, may have been obsessed by a desire to achieve perfection. But the requirements he set, his flood of instructions, his importunities, were equally the consequence of the terms that author and publisher had forged in the 1860s. Had Dodgson bargained for a royalty agreement, had Macmillan retained all decisions touching upon the manufacture of the books – then all would have been different. Under a royalty agreement, Dodgson might have complained, but he could not have demanded. As it was, because Dodgson paid the bills and undertook the risks, he called the tune.

Dodgson behaved as much like a publisher as an author, and Messrs. Macmillan in turn acted more like contractors or distributors. Dodgson can hardly be blamed for wanting to get value for money, and to him value for money meant a high standard of technical and aesthetic production. He lived, after all, in an age when books were often extraordinarily beautiful, when John Ruskin's and William Morris's handsomely crafted and illustrated volumes led

---

[1] See p. 334, below.   [2] Collingwood, pp. 227–8.

many authors and publishers to aspire to unbelievably grand products.

In the end, perhaps we should ask whether Dodgson's insistence on quality was as misplaced as some think. Pick up a copy of a well-produced *Alice* or *Looking-Glass*, even a *Snark* or a *Sylvie and Bruno*. The red binding, the gold lettering, the gilt edges, the sharp illustrations, the clear print – all make the books still a joy to behold and read. No wonder they bring ever-rising prices at auction. Are we justified, then, in accusing Dodgson of being crabbed when, by giving so much of himself to his publishing enterprises, he ensured that both his contemporaries and future generations would have the pleasure of reading his works and also the satisfaction of seeing objects of beauty, holding them, and owning them?

XI

The text of this volume consists of 351 letters from Dodgson to the House of Macmillan, transcribed from the original manuscripts in the Rosenbach archive, which in turn consists of 479 original Dodgson letters to the publisher. Letters that appear in the body of this volume appear in their entirety. All ellipses in the text of a letter are Dodgson's. In footnotes, however, where passages are quoted from omitted letters, we use ellipses freely. All omitted letters, including those from which quotations appear in footnotes, are listed in Appendix B. Relevant parts of letters that Macmillan sent to Dodgson are quoted in the footnotes. These have been excerpted from the 1137 copies of letters sent to Dodgson in the Macmillan letter books housed in the British Library.

Wherever possible, we have tried to indicate in our notes who wields the pen in the House of Macmillan. In the early days, Alexander Macmillan wrote virtually all the letters himself (and entered a copy of each in his own hand in the firm's letter books). Towards the end Frederick Macmillan takes on the responsibility of dealing with Dodgson's letters, although George Macmillan and G. L. Craik also write. But for a time the impersonal Macmillan & Co. dominates, and it is not clear who does the writing.

In transcribing the letters, we have followed the principles set down in the Preface of *Letters*.

We are indebted to the Executors of the C. L. Dodgson Estate for permission to publish these letters as well as to Macmillan & Co. for their willingness to permit us to quote from their letter books. The Trustees and the Director of the Rosenbach Museum & Library have been most generous in making available to us their huge Dodgson–Macmillan archive, in supplying photocopies of originals and transcriptions of the letters, and in helping in every way to bring this volume into being. Special thanks are due to Gordon N. Ray, who has, from the outset, taken a keen interest in this edition. For help with some particularly knotty problems, we want to thank Nina Burgis, August A. Imholtz, Jr., and

Stan Marx. Professor Gandolfo wishes to express gratitude to West Virginia University for the support she received from the Department of English, the College, and the University, and especially for a Senate Research Grant. We also wish to thank four friends, professional editors in their own right, who have combed the text and given invaluable help: Selwyn H. Goodacre, Peter L. Heath, Cecil Y. Lang, and Richard N. Swift.

M.N.C.
A.G.

SHORT TITLES

Altick   Richard D. Altick, *The English Common Reader: A Social History of the Mass Reading Public 1800–1900* (1963)

Barnes   James J. Barnes, *Free Trade in Books: A Study of the London Book Trade Since 1800* (1964)

Clark   Anne Clark, *Lewis Carroll: A Biography* (1979)

Collingwood Stuart Dodgson Collingwood, *The Life and Letters of Lewis Carroll* (1898)

Diaries   Roger Lancelyn Green, ed., *The Diaries of Lewis Carroll*, 2 vols. (1953)

Diaries   Hitherto unpublished entries from Dodgson's manuscript Diaries housed in the British Library

Graves   Charles L. Graves, *Life and Letters of Alexander Macmillan* (1910)

Handbook   Sidney Herbert Williams and Falconer Madan, *The Lewis Carroll Handbook*, rev. by Roger Lancelyn Green, further rev. by Denis Crutch (1979)

Hudson   Derek Hudson, *Lewis Carroll: An Illustrated Biography* (1976)

Hughes   Thomas Hughes, *Memoir of Daniel Macmillan* (1883)

Jabberwocky The Journal of the Lewis Carroll Society

Letters   Morton N. Cohen, ed., with the assistance of Roger Lancelyn Green, *The Letters of Lewis Carroll*, 2 vols. (1979)

Macmillan George A. Macmillan, *Brief Memoir of Alexander Macmillan* (1908)

Morgan   Charles Morgan, *The House of Macmillan* (1943)

Net Book
  Agreement Frederick Macmillan, *The Net Book Agreement 1899 and the Book War 1906–1908* (1924)

Picture Book Stuart Dodgson Collingwood, ed., *The Lewis Carroll Picture Book* (1899)

Sutherland J. A. Sutherland, *Victorian Novelists and Publishers* (1976)

Tanis and
  Dooley   James Tanis and John Dooley, eds., *Lewis Carroll's The Hunting of the Snark* (1981)

Weaver   Warren Weaver, *Alice in Many Tongues: The Translations of Alice in Wonderland* (1964)

THE LETTERS

Dear Sir,

I have been considering the question of the *colour* of *Alice's Adventures*, and have come to the conclusion that *bright red* will be the best – not the best, perhaps, artistically, but the most attractive to childish eyes. Can this colour be managed with the same smooth, bright cloth that you have in green?[1]

Truly yours,

C. L. Dodgson

---

[1] By the time Dodgson writes this letter, the earliest to Macmillan that we have found, plans to publish *Alice's Adventures in Wonderland* are well advanced. The history of the tale's extemporaneous origin on July 4, 1862, is recorded by Dodgson himself (*Diaries*, pp. 181–2; in the dedicatory verse to the story; "'Alice' on the Stage," *Theatre*, April 1887, pp. 179–84; and in a letter to E. Gertrude Thomson dated July 16, 1885, in *Letters*, p. 591); by Alice Liddell Hargreaves ("Alice's Recollections of Carrollian Days," *Cornhill Magazine*, 73 (July 1932), 1–12; and "The Lewis Carroll that Alice Recalls," *New York Times Magazine*, 71 (May 1, 1932), v, 7); and by Robinson Duckworth in *Picture Book*, pp. 358–60. Dodgson's Diaries chronicle the subsequent events that led him to develop the tale and to consider publishing it. They also record meetings with Alexander Macmillan and John Tenniel that bring us to the point where Dodgson is considering the binding for the book. Macmillan had published Charles Kingsley's *The Water Babies* in May of the previous year in a green binding, and that is probably what the publisher has suggested that Dodgson adopt for *Alice*.

Christ Church, Oxford
November 20, 1864

Dear Sir,

I fear my little book *Alice's Adventures in Wonderland* cannot appear this year. Mr. Tenniel writes that he is hopeless of completing the pictures by Xmas.[1] The cause I do not know, but he writes in great trouble, having just lost his mother, and I have begged him to put the thing aside for the present. Under these circumstances what time should you advise our aiming at for bringing out the book? Would Easter be a good time, or would it be better to get it out before then?[2]

I liked the specimen of red cloth you sent. I have not yet seen the *Children's Garland*, but will look at it.[3] Believe me

Yours truly,

C. L. Dodgson

---

[1] Dodgson first called on Tenniel on January 25, 1864, and recorded (*Diaries*, p. 210) that "he was very friendly, and seemed to think favourably of undertaking the pictures, but must see the book

before deciding." Ten weeks later, on April 5, Dodgson noted (p. 212) that he had "heard from
Tenniel that he consents to draw the pictures for *Alice's Adventures Under Ground.*" On May 2,
Dodgson "sent Tenniel the first piece of slip set up for *Alice's Adventures* – from the beginning of
Chapter III" (p. 215). On May 30, Dodgson, in London, called on the artist and "had a talk" (p.
216); also on June 20, but Tenniel "had not begun the pictures yet" (ibid.); and on the following
day, after a meeting with Macmillan, he again called on Tenniel, who "agreed to the change of
page" that Macmillan had advised earlier in the day (p. 217). On July 17, Dodgson went once
more to Tenniel, but the artist was out and he had to be content with his mother and sister
(Diaries).
² Macmillan replies to this letter on the following day with a note of a single line: "Easter would be a
very good time – say early in April."
³ When Dodgson chose bright red for the cover of *Alice,* Macmillan suggested that he look at a copy
of *The Children's Garland,* as it was covered in "a red cloth such as I fancy you want." *The Children's
Garland from the Best Poets,* selected and arranged by Coventry Patmore, was published in 1863 as
part of Macmillan's Golden Treasury series.

Christ Church, Oxford
December 16, 1864
Dear Mr. Macmillan
I sent you off yesterday the whole of my little book in slip. It is the only
complete copy I have, and I will call for it next week – on Tuesday, most likely.[1] I
hope you may not think it unfitted to come under your auspices. Believe me
Yours truly,

C. L. Dodgson

[1] Dodgson goes up to London on Tuesday, December 20, but does not call on Macmillan until the
following day: "had a talk about the book," he writes (p. 225); "he likes my idea of publishing on
the 1st of April, and says he would like to begin binding about the middle of March."

Christ Church, Oxford
May 24, 1865
Dear Sir,
Thanks for the specimen volume. I like the look of it exceedingly. 3 alterations
I should like made.
(1) The title is incomplete: it should be

ALICE'S
ADVENTURES IN
WONDERLAND

(2) I should like gold lines round the cat side as well as the other. I want the 2
sides to look equally ornamental.
(3) This I am rather doubtful about – but I don't quite like the look of gilt-

edges at one end. As I want it to be a *table*-book, I fancy it would look better with the edges evenly cut smooth, and no gilding.

We hope to begin working off on Monday. My present idea is, to send you 50 copies to be bound first, for me to give away to friends, and the rest of the 2000 you can bind at your leisure and publish at whatever time of the year you think best[1] – but for my own young friends I want copies as soon as possible: they are all growing out of childhood so alarmingly fast.

One of the 50 I should like bound in white vellum: the rest in red like the specimen.[2] Believe me

Truly yours,

C. L. Dodgson

---

[1] The Clarendon Press printed the 2000 copies of the first edition, and the book was bound by Burn of 37–8 Kirby Street, London E.C. Dodgson records the "first copies sent to Macmillan, June 27." All edges are plain, although, according to the bibliographer S. H. Williams, "they are sometimes found gilt" (*Diaries*, p. 554; *Handbook*, p. 30).

[2] The white vellum copy was intended for Alice Liddell, and Dodgson notes (*Diaries*, p. 554) that he "ordered copy to be sent from London so as to be received by Alice on July 4 (Tuesday), 1865," the third anniversary of the famous river expedition to Godstow.

Croft Rectory, Darlington
July 31, 1865

Dear Sir,

Thanks for your letter with its alarming estimate – £100 more than it cost to print the book in Oxford.[1] I rather doubt the wisdom of incurring such a large additional expense, but would like answers to the following questions:

(1) What would be the cost of printing *1000*, instead of 2000?[2]

(2) Would Mr. Clay print from the electro-types (as I should certainly prefer)?[3]

(3) In case we have the first edition so printed, what should you advise me to do with regard to the 2000 printed at Oxford? The choice seems to lie between these courses:

(a) reserve them till next year, to "sell in the provinces" (as has been suggested to me), or to send abroad, but keeping the price to 7*s*. 6*d*.

(b) sell them at a reduced price (say 5*s*.) as being avowedly an inferior edition, stating in the advertisements what the two editions differ in.

(c) get Mr. Clay, or some experienced man, to look them over, and select all such sheets as happen to be well printed – use these along with the London-printed copies, and sell the rest as waste paper.

(d) sell the whole as waste paper.

In case (a) I should of course pay Mr. Combe's bill in full. In the other cases we should of course have to come to some other agreement.

Of these 4 courses, (a) seems to me scarcely honest, and my own opinion inclines to (d). However I should like to know what you think about it.[4] Believe me

Very truly yours,

C. L. Dodgson

[1] Evidently satisfied with the look and feel of his first book for children, Dodgson on July 15 "went to Macmillan's and wrote in 20 or more copies of *Alice* to go as presents to various friends" (*Diaries*, p. 233). Five days later, however, on July 20, he "called on Macmillan, and showed him Tenniel's letter about the fairy tale – he is entirely dissatisfied with the printing and the pictures, and I suppose we shall have to do it all again" (p. 234). Four days after that, on July 24, Macmillan replied, estimating that it would cost £240 10s. to reprint the book. "I protested so strongly against the disgraceful printing," Tenniel later wrote to George Dalziel, "that . . . [Dodgson] *cancelled the edition*" (MS: Huntington Library).

[2] "You would save nearly £100 by printing only 1000 copies," Macmillan writes on August 1. In the end, however, Dodgson had 2000 printed.

[3] "Clay prints from electros," Macmillan adds (same letter). "A more painstaking, conscientious printer never lived" than Richard Clay (1790–1878), according to the *Bookseller* (January 4, 1878, p. 7). Clay would print the second edition of *Alice* and then *Looking-Glass*.

[4] From July 12 on, Dodgson was in London photographing friends. From the 13th to the 17th, he photographed the Terry family and on the 18th moved his camera and other equipment to the home of the Pre-Raphaelite painter John Everett Millais (1829–96) to photograph him and his family. It was Millais who recommended "keeping back the 2000 printed [*Alices*] at Oxford for a future edition" (*Diaries*, p. 234). On August 2, Dodgson "finally decided on the re-print of *Alice*, and that the first 2000 shall be sold as waste paper." He goes on to calculate the costs in detail in his *Diaries* (pp. 234–5):

"Drawing pictures	138
Cutting	142
Printing (by Clay)	240
Binding and advertising (say)	80
	600

i.e. 6s. a copy on the 2000. If I make £50 by sale," he calculates, "this will be a loss of £100, and the loss of the first 2000 will probably be £100, leaving me £200 out of pocket. But if a second 2000 could be sold it would cost £300, and bring in £500, thus squaring accounts and any further sale would be a gain, but that I can hardly hope for." At first, Macmillan agreed to sell the condemned printing as waste paper but later suggested that perhaps it might be sold for "a little above that" to America. On April 9, 1865, Dodgson "called on Mr. Tenniel, who gave his consent to the American sale," and on the following day "called on Mr. Macmillan, and empowered him to sell the Oxford impression of *Alice* in America" (*Diaries*, pp. 241–2). D. Appleton & Co., New York, bought the unbound sheets and published the first U.S. edition in 1866. For more on the complex printing history of Alice and the distinctions between early editions and issues, see *Handbook*, pp. 29–35; Harry Morgan Ayres, *Carroll's Alice* (1936); W. H. Bond, "The Publication of *Alice's Adventures in Wonderland*," *Harvard Library Bulletin*, 10 (1956), 306–24; Warren Weaver, "The First Edition of *Alice's Adventures in Wonderland*: A Census," *Papers of the Bibliographical Society of America*, 65 (1971), 1–40; Selwyn H. Goodacre, "The Textual Alterations to *Alice's Adventures in Wonderland* 1865–1866," *Jabberwocky*, 3 (Winter 1973), 17–20; Selwyn H. Goodacre, "The 1865 *Alice*: A New Appraisal and a Revised Census," *Soaring with the Dodo*, Edward Guiliano and James R. Kincaid, eds. (1982), pp. 77–96; Flodden Heron, "The 1866 Appleton *Alice*," *Colophon*, II (1936), 422–7; Gerard R. Wolfe, *The House of Appleton* (1981), pp. 136–7, 143–4.

Croft Rectory, Darlington
August 30, 1865

Dear Sir,

As several friends are anxious for copies of *Alice's Adventures*, I should like you to bind and send me 25 copies as soon as it is safe to do so. Please let me know how soon this is likely to be. If you have seen any of the new impression, I should be glad to know if the difference is *very* marked between it and the old, with regard to the pictures.[1] Believe me

Truly yours,

C. L. Dodgson

[1] Macmillan's reply is missing.

[Christ Church, Oxford]
November 2, 1865

Dear Sir,

I see you have begun advertising *Alice's Adventures* so write to suggest your substituting "forty-two" for "numerous" – the latter word suggests, to *me*, 20 or thereabouts. I should be glad to have some copies of it when you can get them bound.[1] Believe me

Truly yours,

C. L. Dodgson

[1] Macmillan adopts Dodgson's suggestion: the title pages of both the 1865 and 1866 *Alices* bear the legend "With forty-two illustrations by John Tenniel." Exactly one week after Dodgson writes this letter, he "received from Macmillan a copy of the new impression of *Alice* – very *far* superior to the old, and in fact a perfect piece of artistic printing" (*Diaries*, p. 236).

Christ Church, Oxford
November 12, 1865

Dear Mr. Macmillan,

I duly received 24 copies of *Alice* yesterday. Please send me another 50 with all speed. I am going to recall all the copies I can of the old impression, and substitute new.[1] I think you are right about the gilt edges, and, now that we have begun with them, I should like *all* copies to have them. I am much pleased by the Eversley verdict on the book.[2]

You have not yet answered my 2 questions:

(1) when will the book be really out?[3]

(2) what newspapers, etc., do you propose to send copies to? to which I now add:

(3) is it being kept in type? as, if so, I shall have a few "errata" to send in case more copies are to be struck off.

Sincerely yours,

C. L. Dodgson

[1] "I write to beg that, if you have received the copy I sent you of *Alice's Adventures in Wonderland*, you will suspend your judgment on it till I can send you a better copy," Dodgson wrote, probably to Tom Taylor, on August 3, 1865 (*Letters*, p. 77). Dodgson's nephew records that "all purchasers [sic] were . . . asked to return their copies" and that "the author gave away [the copies he retrieved] to various homes and hospitals" (Collingwood, p. 104). Neither Dodgson nor Tenniel would have believed that a single copy of that "inferior" first edition would bring thousands of pounds when it came up for sale in later times. So choice a book has it become that collectors would trade whole segments of their libraries for a copy of the "first" *Alice*, bibliographers dream of uncovering an unrecorded copy, and literary chroniclers are at a loss to explain how, even in the heyday of Victorian expansion, such extravagant decisions could be made over a children's book as were made over this one.

[2] Having used Charles Kingsley's *The Water Babies* as a production model, Macmillan must have sent a copy of *Alice* to the author of the earlier fantasy, curate of Eversley in Hampshire since 1842. Charles Kingsley's novelist brother Henry also approved of *Alice*. "What a charming book you have published for Dodgson," he wrote to Alexander Macmillan, and in a letter to Dodgson: "Many thanks for your charming little book. My real opinion of it may be gathered from this fact, that I received it in bed in the morning, and in spite of threats and persuasions, in bed I stayed until I had read every word of it. I could pay you no higher compliment in half a dozen pages, than confessing that I could not stop reading your book till I had finished it. The fancy of the whole thing is delicious; it is like gathering cowslips in springtime.. . . Your versification is a gift I envy you very much" (S. M. Ellis, *Henry Kingsley* (1931), p. 138; MS: Harvard).

[3] Macmillan's reply is missing. The precise publication date (if there was one) is unknown, but the British Museum received their copy on November 14 (see *Handbook*, pp. 34–5).

Christ Church, Oxford
November 19, 1865

Dear Mr. Macmillan,

The 50 copies, and the one bound in vellum, have all arrived safe. One of them is deficient of 16 pages (161 to 176). Who ought to be the loser by a mistake of that kind?

In case any papers or magazines should notice the book, I should wish to have copies to keep of the numbers containing the notices. Can you find any one to undertake to look out for them and collect them, or shall I try to get it done at the Bodleian, which I suppose is one of the few places where *all* newspapers and magazines are to be seen.[1]

I shall be very much interested to hear whether you think the sale has made a good start or not.[2] Believe me

Truly yours,

C. L. Dodgson

¹ Macmillan undertakes to supply Dodgson with press notices. For Dodgson's list of them, see the photograph from his Diaries in *Letters*, p. 82. The notices are reprinted in full in the four issues of *Jabberwocky* for 1980.
² Eleven days after he writes this letter, Dodgson "called on Macmillan, who tells me 500 *Alices* are already sold" (*Diaries*, p. 237).

Christ Church, Oxford
November 28, 1865
Dear Mr. Macmillan,
 I have got back the copy, bound in vellum, of the 1st impression of *Alice*. Can the vellum back be transferred to a new copy?¹ In haste,
Truly yours,
C. L. Dodgson

¹ See p. 37, above. Macmillan's reply is missing.

Croft Rectory, Darlington
[after the end of the year, The Residence, Ripon]
December 27, 1865
Dear Sir,
 I forget whether I told you that I have sent Mr. and Mrs. Tennyson a 2nd copy of *Alice*, leaving the other copy to be considered as your present to the boys.¹
 Will you please send me a copy of the *Publisher's Circular*, as I hear they have noticed the book.² You will of course have seen *The Times* notice, and will, I suppose, prefer it to the *Guardian* notice as a pendant to your advertisements.³
 I should be glad to know how the sale progresses.
 Wishing you a happy New Year, I am
Yours truly,
C. L. Dodgson

¹ Dodgson knew and admired Tennyson's poetry from boyhood. In 1856 he published "The Three Voices," a parody of "The Two Voices," in the *Train* (2 (November 1856), 278–84). On August 18, 1857, Mrs. Tennyson's sister, Mrs. C. R. Weld, visited Croft Rectory with her daughter Agnes Grace, and Dodgson took several photographs of the girl. He then evidently sent copies of the photographs to Tennyson by way of Mrs. Weld, and on September 2, he heard from Mrs. Weld that "Tennyson has received the pictures, and pronounces the portrait 'indeed a gem'" (*Diaries*, p. 119). In just over a fortnight after he heard from Mrs. Weld, Dodgson went off with his camera to the Lake District, where the Tennysons were staying at Coniston. On the 18th, he called on the Tennysons, found only Mrs. Tennyson at home, and left his card, adding to his name: "artist of 'Agnes Grace' and 'Little Red Riding-hood.'" On subsequent visits to the house, he met Tennyson and the two sons ("the boys" he alludes to in his letter), dined with them, and, before leaving, took a number of sittings of the poet and his family. In May 1859 Dodgson, on the Isle of

Wight for a holiday, called on the Tennysons and dined with them again. In 1862, Tennyson's publisher, Edward Moxon & Co., brought out *An Index to "In Memoriam,"* suggested and edited by Dodgson but largely compiled by one or more of his sisters. Tennyson approved of the anonymous publication. In the autumn of that year, Dodgson "by permission" dedicated the third volume of *College Rhymes,* an Oxford and Cambridge literary journal that he edited from July 1862 to March 1863, to the poet. In March 1870 Dodgson had the misfortune of offending the Tennysons by requesting that he be permitted to share with friends an unpublished poem of Tennyson's that had come into his hands, and the relationship cooled. (For more on Dodgson and the Tennysons, see *Diaries, passim; Letters,* esp. pp. 34–9, 53–7, 150–3.) For his part, Alexander Macmillan was a great admirer of Tennyson's poetry and staunchly defended *Maud* against the assault of the critics. As early as 1849, the firm published six vocal quartets set to Tennyson poems; Tennyson contributed verse to *Macmillan's Magazine*; and Macmillan began to reprint Tennyson's work in various editions in 1884. That same year, the firm published the poet's play *Becket* and went on to bring out other new works subsequently. Tennyson attended the Tobacco Parliaments in Henrietta Street. "One night in the spring of 1860," Morgan records (p. 53), "he stayed on pertinaciously until the [other] good fellows began to vanish . . . and then . . . had a nice chat on other subjects. By midnight all the guests had taken their leave except an Edinburgh advocate . . . and Tennyson's moment had come. . . . He repeated a long poem in an impossible metre. . . . Its roll is wonderful. The Laureate stayed until half-past one in the morning." In June 1864, Macmillan writes in another letter: "I had Huxley the Professor and Tennyson the Poet dining with me, and better talk is not often to be had" (Graves, p. 224). The same must have been true when Macmillan stayed with the Tennysons on the Isle of Wight (Morgan, p. 57).

[2] The notice appeared on December 8, Macmillan subsequently sent a copy, and Dodgson must have been pleased with it: "Among the two hundred books for children which have been sent to us this year," it reads, "the most original and charming is *Alice's Adventures in Wonderland.*. . . It is a piece of delicious nonsense."

[3] The notice in *The Times* appeared the day before Dodgson writes. It praises Tenniel's work and calls *Alice* "an excellent piece of nonsense." The *Guardian* of December 13 judges *Alice* "absolute nonsense; but nonsense so graceful and so full of humour that one can hardly help reading it through." Macmillan used an excerpt from the *Guardian* notice in their Christmas advertising.

Christ Church, Oxford
March 8, 1866

Dear Sir,

Thanks for the copy of the *London Review.*[1] I had hoped for a larger sale of the book, but perhaps unreasonably. Is it likely to sell at all at Easter? You do not seem to be advertising it with that view.[2]

In the matter of "copies given away" I think you will find that your entry is just 50 too much.

You sent me –	25
and afterwards –	50
to some friends whose	
addresses I gave (say)	10
to newspapers, etc. (say)	30
	115

Will you let me know if I am right?[3]

Yours truly,

C. L. Dodgson

¹ The *London Review* notice appeared on December 23, 1865: "*Alice's Adventures in Wonderland* is a delightful book for children," it reads, "– or, for the matter of that, for grown-up people, provided they have wisdom or sympathy enough to enjoy a piece of downright hearty drollery and fanciful humour. . . . The style . . . is admirable for its appearance of wondering belief, as if the mind of the child were somehow transfused into the narrative – and the book, small as it is, is crammed full of curious invention. Exquisite also are the illustrations . . . a most charming contrast, in their grace, delicacy, finish, and airy fancy, to the ugly phantasmagoria in which so many of the artists of the present day indulge."

² Macmillan addresses himself to the question of advertising in his letter of April 30: "If we go on advertising always, we shall spend an awful amount of money," and he points out that "each copy of your book that is sold is an advertisement." He assures Dodgson that "the book won't drop out of sight."

³ Macmillan's reply about "copies given away" is missing, but Dodgson's manuscript letter bears a note, probably in Macmillan's hand, that reads: "48 of the old edition," which accounts for the discrepancy of "50 too much" in Dodgson's letter.

Croft Rectory, Darlington
August 15, 1866

Dear Sir,

If Mr. Combe was right in thinking that you make a balance of accounts at the end of June, I hope I shall not be troubling you much by asking for some information as to how ours stands – what has come in by sale of *Alice* – and how much you deduct therefrom for publisher's profit – and what the bill for printing, binding, and advertising comes to – and what you allow me for the copies gone to America. At present I know nothing beyond the fact that I am £350 out of pocket, for pictures and for the Oxford printing, which, taken by itself, is not cheering.¹ Believe me

Truly yours,

C. L. Dodgson

¹ Dodgson had dined at the Combes' on July 9 (Diaries), and he and Combe must have discussed the *Alice* finances. Macmillan's reply is missing.

Croft Rectory, Darlington
August 24, 1866

My dear Sir,

Thanks for your letter and information,¹ with which I am very well satisfied. Your magnificent idea of printing *3000* more alarms me a little: *I* should have thought *1000* a large enough venture, considering the sale hitherto² – but if your mention of "a less expensive paper" implies (as I presume it must do) that you propose to lower the price of the book, I am inclined to defer to your judgement in the matter. My idea at first was that 7s. 6d. was too dear.

If however you think we had better keep to 7s. 6d., *then* the paper must be the same as we used before. I can *not* consent to the one being reduced without the other, so that people might say "here is an inferior article sold at the old price."

Let me know when you are ready to print again, that I may send you a list of corrections which I am preparing.

If we decide on the 3000, it would be well, I think, to print on the title-pages "fifth thousand," "sixth thousand," etc.

I should be glad to know what you think of my idea of putting it into French, or German, or both, and trying for a Continental sale. I believe I could get either version well done in Oxford. It would have to be got up, and sold, at a much cheaper rate, if one may judge of their light literature by the specimens that reach England.[3]

It will probably be some time before I again indulge in paper and print. I have, however, a floating idea of writing a sort of sequel to *Alice*, and if it ever comes to anything, I intend to consult you at the very outset, so as to have the thing properly managed from the beginning.[4]

Sincerely yours,

C. L. Dodgson

---

[1] Macmillan's letter containing "information" is missing.

[2] In his reply (August 29) to the present letter, Macmillan points out that "there is a considerable saving per copy in printing 3000 over 1000," and he reminds Dodgson that the new printing would help them prepare for "a fresh Christmas sale this year." Macmillan having allayed Dodgson's fears, Dodgson records in his *Diaries* (p. 246) on September 3: "Macmillan is now printing 3000 more *Alices*; by the end of 1867 I hope to be about clear, if not actually in pocket by it."

[3] In the same letter, Macmillan supports Dodgson's idea of foreign translations and promises to "see after a publisher" if Dodgson decides to go ahead with the notion.

[4] This is the first mention of what will become *Through the Looking-Glass and What Alice Found There*. Macmillan replies (same letter): "I shall be curious to hear about the sequel."

Croft Rectory, Darlington
August 30, 1866

Dear Sir,

You certainly are going to work with promptitude! It is a pity you did not wait for the list of corrections, which I enclose herewith. The question of reduction of price had better wait till we see the book in its finished form, since, if it is to all intents and purposes equal to the last, there will be no necessity to change the price, unless to give it a better chance of sale.[1]

I should like a specimen sheet to be sent to Mr. Tenniel as soon as possible, as I shall certainly not consent to its publication unless he approves of the effect.

When I go back to Oxford I will consult my French and German friends as to translation. Believe me

Yours sincerely,

C. L. Dodgson

If you get any tidings as to how it is selling in America, pray let me know.[2]

[1] "Please send us your corrections at once," Macmillan wrote on the day before Dodgson sends this letter. "We are going to press – indeed the paper is ordered and some little part worked off." In the same letter: "If you like we can reduce to 6s., but really no one will notice the difference in the paper but a skilled person." [2] We find no reply to this query.

5 East Terrace, Whitby[1]
September 28, 1866

Dear Sir,

I have heard from Mr. Tenniel (as I daresay you have also) that he quite approves of the printing of the cuts in the new impression. I shall be glad to know what the printing, etc., of the 3000 is likely to cost, and whether you advise the lowering of the price: it can hardly be done till the first set are all gone, unless they are lowered as well. I have a great idea that there would be a very much larger sale at 6s. than at 7s. 6d. and if it led to our selling more than ⅘ the number we should otherwise sell, it would evidently be worth while to make the change.[2] Believe me

Truly yours,

C. L. Dodgson

Please send me one copy of *Alice* by book post, as I want to give one to a friend here.[3]

[1] In 1854 Dodgson spent the summer vacation at Whitby reading mathematics, and, with some of his family, went to Whitby almost every summer thereafter until his father died and they moved from Yorkshire. At Whitby he lodged with a Mrs. Hunton at this address. On this occasion, he was there from September 13 to October 3 (*Diaries*, pp. 246–7).

[2] "I do think with Tenniel's pictures that *Alice* at 7s. 6d. is a cheap enough book," Macmillan replies on October 4, "and I don't think the reduction to 6s. will make any really material difference in the sale. I will endeavour to make a fresh stir altogether with it, and when we do make any reduction it should be *more* than from 7s 6d. to 6s. and in this case you will have to be content with a cheaper style of working. At present I advise keeping the price as it is."

[3] "I am sorry I cannot send you a copy of *Alice*," Macmillan writes (same letter). "It is quite out of print. Being anxious to do it carefully we have not hurried the printer, but we hope to have copies soon, when we will send you some to Christ Church, unless you instruct us to the contrary." The copy Dodgson requested was probably intended for Edith Jebb. The Jebb family were also in Whitby at the time, and Dodgson was photographing them and going on outings with them. For more on Dodgson and the Jebbs, see *Letters*, esp. p. 122.

Christ Church, Oxford
October 22, 1866

Dear Sir,

I have just received 4 copies of *Alice*. I *hope* to hear that they are 4 survivors of the last impression, that have somehow escaped your notice. Please let me know whether this is the case. *If not*, it is entirely unaccountable to me that *no* corrections should have been made, according to my list, and that the title-page should *not* contain "fifth thousand," as I particularly directed.

But I can hardly believe that your printer would be so negligent, and so await your explanation of the mystery.[1]

Truly yours,

C. L. Dodgson

---

[1] "The 4 copies were of the first edition," Macmillan replies the same day. "A few copies were returned by the trade." For more on the variants of the 1866 *Alice*, see Selwyn Goodacre, "The 1866 Second Edition of *Alice's Adventures in Wonderland*," *Jabberwocky*, Winter 1972, pp. 8–9.

Christ Church, Oxford
October 24, 1866

My dear Sir,

I am very glad to hear that the 4 copies of *Alice* were *not* of the new impression. As a friend is going to town, I shall return you 3 of them – and please send me 3 of the new when they are ready.

Friends here seem to think that the book is *untranslatable* into either French or German: the puns and songs being the chief obstacle. If any of your foreign friends ever express a more favourable opinion, I should be glad to know of it. Believe me

Truly yours,

C. L. Dodgson

Christ Church, Oxford
November 28, 1866

Dear Sir,

As I see you are beginning to advertise the new *Alice*, I write to suggest the introduction of extracts from other reviews than the 2 you have chosen. There are so many to quote from, that it seems a pity to keep to the same always.[1]

I have not yet received any copies of the new impression.

Very truly yours,

C. L. Dodgson

---

[1] The advertisement for *Alice* that appeared in the *Athenaeum* (November 24, 1866) quotes from reviews in *The Times* and the *London Review*. On the day after Dodgson writes this letter, Macmillan replies that he intends to alter the advertisements, that the old quotations were kept by "mischance," that he has "spoken strongly" about the matter, and that it will be "carefully attended to." The advertisement that appeared in the *Athenaeum* on December 15 merely indicates that *Alice* is now in its "5th 1000." No reviews are quoted.

Christ Church, Oxford
November 29, 1866

Dear Sir,

I saw one of the new *Alices* at a shop today. Unless my eyes quite deceived me, the margins are narrower than in the old ones, giving to the book a *decidedly* poorer general appearance. If I am right in this, *pray* have it remedied as far as possible in the other copies not yet cut. If they are printed on smaller paper, I fear it is past remedy this time.[1]

If we get beyond the 7000, we must really return to the old style. So long as it is really handsome, its *paying* or not is a matter of minor importance. Believe me

Truly yours,

C. L. Dodgson

---

[1] "The first edition of *Alice* was printed on paper of an unusual size," Macmillan replies on the following day, on paper not normally kept in stock by stationers. "To tell the truth I was not aware that it was so much larger than the ordinary double crown paper (which was the size I urged you, if you remember, to adopt, and which you yourself agreed to) till this new edition on usual paper came in bound. I have already told our binder to be very careful to cut as little off the edges as possible."

The Residence, Ripon[1]
January 5, 1867

Dear Sir,

I entirely defer to your judgment in the matter of the adverse criticisms. I did not know it was so old a joke.[2]

In the course of these 2 days I have received 2 papers from New York. One, the *Nation*, containing a long and very complimentary review of *Alice:*[3] the other, *Merryman's Monthly* for December, in which they have actually re-printed half the book, and copied about a dozen of the pictures! ending with "Conclusion next month." However, it is so badly printed, both text and pictures, that I don't think it can supersede the purchase of a single copy of the book.[4]

Will you please send a copy of *The Fountain of Youth* addressed to Miss L. S. MacDonald,

12 Earl's Terrace,
Kensington.[5]

I shall be glad to hear when the sale of the 6th thousand of *Alice* commences.[6] Believe me

Very truly yours,

C. L. Dodgson

---

[1] From 1852 Dodgson's father was Chaplain to the Bishop of Ripon and Canon of Ripon. On his vacations, the younger Dodgson sometimes joined his family at The Residence, a second home provided to enable Canon Dodgson to carry out his duties at Ripon Cathedral.

[2] Dodgson had apparently suggested quoting from some negative notices in advertisements for *Alice* as a way of stimulating interest in the book. "I am afraid the joke of quoting adverse criticism along with others is too old to make much stir," Macmillan wrote three days before Dodgson writes this letter. "I will do it if you like. But I don't advise it."

[3] The *Nation* of December 13, 1866, ran a long notice of *Alice* that calls the book "wonderfully clever" and "one of the best children's books we ever met with – a delightful addition to a delightful branch of literature." Lewis Carroll too earns high praise: "The author can make puns that children laugh at and heartily enjoy. . . . If the author does not write novels he ought to do so, for, besides the merits of which we have already spoken, he is quite a master of dialogue; and that is to have one of the rarest of the minor gifts."

[4] On April 4, 1867, Dodgson writes in his Diaries that he "promised to send Mrs. Liddell *Merryman's Monthly* . . . to look at." *Alice* appeared in that magazine's issues of December 1866 (pp. 3–15) and January 1867 (pp. 33–44), making it the first American printing of the story. It appears in double columns with 19 illustrations by Tenniel. The text is virtually as in the 1866 edition, but omits the last four paragraphs (beginning "But her sister sat still . . ."). *Merryman's Monthly* was published by Jesse Haney (1829–1901), founder of a number of papers and magazines, including *Haney's Journal*, which reprinted *Alice* in the issues of March through October 1869. Copies of the two issues of *Merryman's Monthly* are in the Arthur A. Houghton, Jr., Collection at the Pierpont Morgan Library. We are indebted to Stan Marx, founder of the Lewis Carroll Society of North America, for help with this note.

[5] The gift went to Lilia Scott MacDonald (1852–91), eldest child of the George MacDonalds. Frederik Paludin-Müller's *The Fountain of Youth*, translated from the Danish by Humphrey William Freeland, was published by Macmillan in late 1866 with an 1867 publication date. For Dodgson's letter to Miss MacDonald about this gift, see *Letters*, pp. 95–6.

[6] Two days after Dodgson writes, Macmillan reports that they had actually commenced selling the sixth thousand of *Alice* "some ten days ago."

Christ Church, Oxford
February 6, 1867

Dear Sir,

Thanks for the cheque. I was surprised to see it, as I had supposed that you had long ago transferred it to the other side, to help to pay the bill for printing the last 3000. If it is not troublesome to you to furnish the information I should be glad to have some idea how your account is likely to stand, when the 3000 are gone, if that should happen.

In that event, I suppose you would advise printing more, and if so, I should like the pictures to be worked a little more artistically than they were in some of the 5th thousand (where some of the lines are almost lost.) Also I should wish the size of the page to be *half-way* between that of the 4th and 5th thousands. My chief reason for this is, that I am hoping before long to complete another book about *Alice*, and if this is also printed of the "half-way" size, it would bind up with any of the 3 sizes. You would not, I presume, object to publish the book, if it should ever reach completion?[1] Believe me,

Truly yours,

C. L. Dodgson

¹ "I have . . . still a considerable number of copies of this last edition," Macmillan writes to Dodgson on the following day. "The sale of these, deducting expenses, left a balance of over £100 in your favour. When the present 3000 is all sold" and "long continual advertising is not needed, you will have £200 more – that is about £300 in all. We have sold over 1300 of the new edition so it is doing well." Macmillan goes on to assure Dodgson that he will give him fair warning before further reprinting. "I shall be very glad to hear when your new *Alice* is ready," he adds.

[?Christ Church, Oxford]
February 11, 1867

Dear Mr. Macmillan,

I have got a little book, near completion, which I want you to publish for me – *not* one, I am afraid, that can be brought out as "by the author of *Alice's Adventures*." Its title is "The Elements of Determinants,¹ and of Their Application to Simultaneous Equations and to Algebraical Geometry – for the use of beginners."² I am having it printed at the University Press, and fully expect that it will be ready to bring out in another month or so – in good time for next term. It is octavo and, as far as I can guess, will be about 100 pages – but the selling price we can settle hereafter: no price would repay me, I fancy, as I have made so many alterations. The reason I mention it now is, that you may be able to begin advertising it whenever you think fit.

I feel quite undecided as to how many copies to print, at present. That the book is much wanted there can be no doubt: that *my* book will meet the want, may well be doubted – but I am encouraged by the favourable opinion of Mr. Spottiswoode, who is I believe *the* authority on the new subject of Determinants and who has seen most of the book.³ If you are willing to undertake the publication, I will write further. Perhaps you may be able to suggest what sort of number it would be wise to print – also how you would propose to bind it. Should you recommend green cloth and gold lettering, as I see you do for smaller mathematical books?⁴

Yours truly,

C. L. Dodgson

¹ A determinant is "an algebraic expression associated with a square array of number. . . . Determinants . . . simplify the solution of simultaneous linear equations" (A. Adrian Albert, "Determinants," *Encyclopaedia Britannica* (1967), VII, 313).

² "I have been at work for some days on an elementary pamphlet on Determinants, which I think of printing," Dodgson wrote on October 28, 1865 (*Diaries*, p. 236). On January 16, 1866, towards the end of his Christmas vacation, he recorded (p. 238) that "during the [past] fortnight I have been mostly employed on my MS on Determinants." On February 27, he "discovered a process for evaluating arithmetical Determinants, by a sort of condensation, and proved it up to 4² terms" (p. 240). On March 25, he "heard from Mr. Spottiswoode . . . saying that he knows of no short way [of completing Determinants arithmetically], and that he will be very glad to hear from me" (ibid.). On March 29 Dodgson "sent to Mr. Spottiswoode an account of my method for

computing Determinants arithmetically by 'condensation,' and for applying the process to solving simultaneous Equations." Dodgson finished writing his paper on May 12 (Diaries), and on the 29th "received and corrected a proof. . . which was read before the Royal Society on the 17th, and is to be published." It appeared as issue No. 84 in the *Proceedings of the Royal Society*, 1866, as a separate pamphlet. Even after Dodgson wrote this letter to Macmillan, he continued to modify his text: on March 15, he recorded (p. 253): "Went through a grand piece of 'lost labour' in my book on Determinants. About 11 at night I came to a difficulty which seemed to require the re-wording of most of the propositions in the chapter on Equations. I went right through the chapter, and did not get it done till about¼ past 4 in the morning, and the next day I found quite another way out of the difficulty, which made all the alterations unnecessary! This little book . . . has given me more trouble than anything I have ever written: it is such entirely new ground to explore." Dodgson's work with Determinants, according to Collingwood (p. 111), is "largely original" and "has found warm admirers." It also contributes some new words to the English language, for example *adjugate* as an adjective and *determinantal* (see *Handbook*, pp. 39–40, 43).

³ William Spottiswoode (1825–1883), mathematician and physicist, published (1851) the first elementary treatise on determinants and is credited with the rapid development of that subject. He was President of the Royal Society from 1878 until his death and is buried in Westminster Abbey.

⁴ In his reply of the following day, Macmillan does not touch upon the color of the binding, but see Dodgson to Macmillan, p. 58, below. Macmillan suggests a printing of 750 copies and offers to bind a specimen copy for Dodgson's approval.

                                                     Christ Church, Oxford
                                                     March 19, 1867
Dear Mr. Macmillan,

I am strongly advised to try a translation of *Alice* into *French*, on the ground that French children are not nearly so well off for *well* illustrated books as English or German. The great difficulty is, to find a man fit to try it, or at any rate to give an opinion as to whether it is feasible. A friend suggests that I should ask you to enquire of some of the great Paris booksellers – and mentions "Firman Didot"[1] as one who is very likely to know of a writer who would suit. One would wish of course to find some one who had written something of the sort, so as to have some sort of sympathy with the style: if possible some one who wrote verses. The verses would be the great difficulty, as I fear, if the originals are not known in France, the parodies would be unintelligible: in that case they had better perhaps be omitted.

Do you think you could find out anything about it for me? Believe me
                          Yours truly,
                                                     C. L. Dodgson

¹ Dodgson is referring to Firmin-Didot, eminent Parisian printers.

Christ Church, Oxford
March 21, 1867

Dear Mr. Macmillan,

When I wrote to you the other day about getting *Alice* put into French, I did not mention German, because my friend Mr. Bertram,[1] the teacher of German here, was then engaged in examining the book, in order to give an opinion on whether it would go well into German or not.

He has come to the conclusion that it *will* – even the puns: some of them he has himself rendered into German, and his versions could of course be furnished to any one undertaking the task.

Will you try, through some German bookseller, or by any other way you know of, to find a German writer who could and would do it?[2]

Truly yours,

C. L. Dodgson

[1] Robert Bertram, Taylorian Teacher of German at Oxford, 1863–73.
[2] "I am afraid I cannot help you in the matter of translation either into French or German," Macmillan writes in reply (March 22), "and shrink from the idea of entering into any negotiation on the subject.... I have however sent a copy to Baron [Christian Bernhard] Tauchnitz [1816–95, the well known publisher] to see whether he thinks anything can be done, and I would suggest that you should apply to Mr. Gustave Masson with regard to the French translation. I suppose you know him? He is a French Master at Harrow and is doing some work in the Clarendon Press Series."

Christ Church, Oxford
April 17, 1867

Dear Mr. Macmillan,

I have got hold of a capital *French* translator (I believe), for *Alice*. The *prose* he seems to be doing admirably – the verse I cannot judge of well. If you know anyone capable of criticising French verses, I will send you specimens. He is son of M. Jules Bué, our teacher in French here. In fact father and son are both working at it.[1]

You may as well be making ready for printing it in French, as I shall very soon be able to send you the first half.

I should like the paper to be rather larger than the last impression, but not so large as the 7s 6d. one. And could you have the pictures a *little* better worked (or the paper a little better, I don't [know] which is in fault) than in the last impression? Some of them have come out very roughly and imperfectly done, hardly doing justice to Tenniel.

I should think the Great Exhibition is rather a good opportunity for beginning a sale in Paris. Have you heard anything from Baron Tauchnitz?[2] I don't think I have told you of an application I have had from a German lady, who wants to translate *Alice*; I have asked her to do pages 36 and 183 as specimens.[3]

Can you tell me what sort of sum one ought to give for a French, or German translation?[4]

Very truly yours,

C. L. Dodgson

[1] Dodgson first met Jules Thomas Théodore Bué (b. 1817), Taylorian Teacher of French at Oxford University since 1847, on November 4, 1857 (Diaries). Dodgson gave Bué a copy of *Alice* and probably asked him how to find a suitable translator. Bué recommended his son Henri (1843–1929), then Assistant Master at St. Andrew's College, Bradfield, Berkshire, beginning a life-long career as French teacher and translator. Born and raised in England and educated in France, he was proficient in both English and French. However, he lacked credentials as a translator, the reason why Dodgson hesitated and sought a competent evaluation of his skill. For more on the Bués and the French *Alice*, see Morton N. Cohen, "Introduction" to the Dover reprint of Bué's translation, *Les Aventures d'Alice au Pays des Merveilles* (1972); Claude Romney, "The First French Translator of *Alice*," *Jabberwocky*, 10 (Autumn 1981), 89–94.

[2] On the following day, Macmillan writes: "I have heard nothing from Tauchnitz."

[3] "Heard from Aunt Caroline of a Miss Zimmermann, a teacher of German, who would like to translate *Alice*," Dodgson wrote in his *Diaries* (p. 257) on April 13, 1867; "suggested that she should name terms and translate as specimens pp. 36 and 183." "Aunt Caroline," born Hume (1809–75), was the wife of Dodgson's paternal uncle Hassard Hume Dodgson. Antonie Zimmermann's trial translations passed muster, and her *Alice's Abenteuer im Wunderland* appeared in 1869.

[4] ". . . not more than £12 or £13," Macmillan replies on the next day.

[Christ Church, Oxford]
April 19, 1867

Dear Mr. Macmillan,

I am rather puzzled about the mode of publishing translations of English books, and must beg for more information. I had certainly fancied that *you*, as my publisher here, would have been able to negotiate with foreign booksellers, and send out copies. Is it the case however, as you seem to imply, that a new *publisher* altogether must be found, and that the matter will simply rest between him, myself and the printer, without involving you? If this be so, will you kindly inform me, that I may set enquiries on foot among my friends.[1] I do not anticipate difficulty nor do I understand why a foreign publisher should consider the question of *success*, unless I asked him to take some risk on himself. As all the risk will be mine, and he would simply make so much profit on the copies sold, he could not be much concerned to decide whether it would sell well or not.

I am, however, writing rather in the dark as to the whole matter. The cost of translation seems so small that I shall let both translators go on for the present (at least if I get favourable opinions on the *quality* of the work). It would not matter much if neither translation made a "hit." Would Clay be able to print French, or German, or both. And please let me know whether you would undertake the business, or if I ought to apply direct to him.[2]

Very truly yours,

C. L. Dodgson

[1] On the previous day, Macmillan acknowledged Dodgson's announcement that he had found a French translator by emphasizing that it was "not a translator but a *publisher* in France" that was wanted. Macmillan's reply to this letter is missing, but perhaps he wrote none. Five days later, Dodgson "called on Macmillan to talk about the French and German translations of *Alice*" (*Diaries*, p. 258), and they must then have settled a number of questions about the forthcoming translations. Dodgson may even have convinced Macmillan not to seek foreign publishers but to bring the books out himself, as in fact he did: the first German, French – and Italian as well.

[2] Clay would print, but under Macmillan's direction.

Christ Church, Oxford

June 10, 1867

Dear Mr. Macmillan,

I am sending you by tonight's post the French version of *Alice*. There are so many things in it (verses, puns, etc.) on which I should like to collect opinions and suggestions from friends, that I think the best thing will be to have the *whole* set up in slip, and to send me 20 copies. These I will distribute among friends, and after considering and embodying suggestions, I will return it to you to be arranged in pages with the pictures.

Very truly yours,

C. L. Dodgson

Christ Church, Oxford

June 13, 1867

Dear Mr. Macmillan,

To prevent the possibility of mistake as to the French version of *Alice*, I may as well say that I should like *no* change to be made in type anywhere – let the 2 versions match as exactly as possible.

The mouse's tail had better be set up in an upright column to begin with; it is not worth while to take the trouble of zigzagging it, till the words are definitely decided on.[1]

I hope you will order the paper so as to make the book a little broader in the margin than the last edition, though it need not be so broad as the first. In *quality* I should like it more like the first edition. The delicacy with which the pictures are worked off on that paper is far beyond the last impression.

Very truly yours,

C. L. Dodgson

P.S. A friend who has seen the impressions rubbed from the woodblocks (on French paper I think it is) is very anxious for a copy of "Alice playing croquet" done in that way. Could you get one done?

Would it be worth while to have a second set of electro-types done for the German printer?[2]

---

[1] For the variants of the Mouse's Tail, see Denis Crutch, "A Tail-piece," *Under the Quizzing Glass* (1972), pp. 57–8; Selwyn H. Goodacre, "The Mouse's Tail," *Jabberwocky*, 11 (Summer 1972), 9–12.

[2] "As Mr. Macmillan is from home for a few days," George Lillie Craik (1837–1905) writes on the 15th, assuring Dodgson on every point of his letter: that he will send a proof of "Alice playing Croquet" at the beginning of the week; that he will arrange for a second set of electrotypes for the German printer (it would cost about £5); that he will order the larger paper for the next English printing and for the French edition; and that Clay will see to the French edition "if possible page for page like the English one." On June 19, Craik writes that he has "arranged a paper more nearly like that of the first edition." Craik, another Scot, was the nephew of the more famous George Lillie Craik (1798–1866), literary historian, professor of English literature and history at Belfast, author of many standard works including *The History of English Language and Literature* (1861). The younger Craik was educated at Glasgow University, and trained as an accountant before joining the House of Macmillan, where, from 1865 until his death, he was a partner. He supervised most of the financial affairs of the firm and became Alexander Macmillan's right-hand man. "It was a fortunate choice," Morgan writes (p. 69), "for Craik, though he had an artificial leg and other physical disabilities, was precisely what Alexander needed as an administrator – a man full of energy and character." In Alexander Macmillan's words, Craik was "good and wise and careful and kind. I cannot tell you," he wrote to a friend in 1873, "how I have come to love that man. He is a daily comfort and guide to me . . ." (Graves, p. 316). In 1865, Craik married Dinah Maria Mulock (1826–87), author of *John Halifax, Gentleman* (1857) and other books for children.

Christ Church, Oxford
June 18, 1867

Dear Sir,[1]

I fear from your saying you have "asked Clay to *print* a copy of 'Alice playing croquet,'" that you misunderstood my note. What Dalziel[2] did, I believe, was to rub impressions, from the wood blocks, on soft French paper, the result being much more delicate than any prints from the electro-types.

By the way, *who* has the wood-blocks? I can hardly doubt that they are being carefully kept, but, considering the sum I had to pay for them, I should be glad to be certain that they are safe from all possibility of damage.[3]

How many more copies of the English *Alice* do you propose to print this time?[4] I daresay I shall have some "errata" to send you when the time comes. Believe me

Truly yours,

C. L. Dodgson

¹ This and the next three letters are addressed to Craik.
² The Dalziel Brothers – George (1815–1902), Edward (1817–1905), John (1822–69) and Thomas (1832–1906) – were the most famous draughtsmen and wood engravers of their time. As engravers to du Maurier, Tenniel, Millais, Lear, Rossetti, and many more, they cut the blocks for the Victorian children's classics. For more about them, see *The Brothers Dalziel: A Record of Fifty Years' Work* (1901).
³ In his reply (the following day), Craik assures Dodgson that Clay has the blocks "in his fireproof room – so they are in perfect safety." Dodgson's later letters to Messrs. Macmillan underscore his continuing concern about the safety of the wood engravings. Macmillan came to share that concern and saw to their safekeeping. In 1985, the firm's secretary, checking the company's holdings in their vault in the Covent Garden branch of the National Westminster Bank, uncovered two locked black boxes containing all 92 of the blocks, in excellent condition (see "Alice's Original Engravings Found in Vault," *The Times*, October 18, 1985, back page).
⁴ Craik (same letter) suggests a printing of 2500 or 3000 copies.

Christ Church, Oxford
June 24, 1867

Dear Sir,

I have compared the 3 proofs of "Alice playing croquet" with the original one I had from Dalziel – they are completely inferior to it, and in fact are not at all better than those in the printed copies. I should certainly suppose that they have been printed in the ordinary way – I doubt whether Clay *can* execute what I want. Dalziel called the process "rubbing off by hand." I don't know what that means exactly, but the result contains delicacy of detail to which there is no approach in the printed book, nor in the 3 proofs you have sent me.

When the 20 copies in French are struck off, please send me *4* only, and the others to the addresses I will send you.

Truly yours,

C. L. Dodgson

Moscow
August 18, 1867

Dear Sir,

The address will explain my delay in answering your letters.¹ I hope it will not have caused much inconvenience.

You may print 2000, or 3000, of the English *Alice*, as Mr. Macmillan thinks best. I would rather not have 2500 done as in that case the "tenth thousand" might not be all alike. I hope you will have the margins rather broader, and the pictures more perfectly printed. There were some copies of the "7th thousand" that I hardly liked to give away, the pictures looking as if they had been printed from worn-out blocks.

It is quite impossible to print off the French *Alice* at present. In fact, there is not much use in e[ven][2] making it up in pages, as it will probably undergo some alteration. I should be glad if you would send proofs of the French, in slip, as follows:

3 copies to

Miss M. B. Smedley,[3]
Croft Terrace,
Tenby, S. Wales

1 copy to Mr. Capes, Fellow of Queen's College, Oxford.[4] You had better get his initials from the calendar. Address it "to be forwarded," and enclose with it the note herewith sent.

3 copies to myself, addressed

Christ Church, Oxford

where I hope to be in 3 or 4 weeks time. Believe me

Truly yours,

C. L. Dodgson

Letters sent to Christ Church will be forwarded.

---

[1] From July 13 to September 14, 1867, Dodgson travelled on the Continent with his friend Henry Parry Liddon (1829–90), Student of Christ Church, Canon and Chancellor of St Paul's Cathedral, distinguished preacher and theologian. Dodgson's diary of the journey was privately printed as *Tour in 1867* (1928) and reprinted in John Francis McDermott, ed., *The Russian Journal and Other Selections from the Works of Lewis Carroll* (1935). Liddon's diary of the journey has also been published: Morton N. Cohen, ed., *The Russian Journal – II* (1979).

[2] This letter is badly creased and torn. Only the first *e* of this word survives (the remainder is torn away).

[3] Menella Bute Smedley (1820–77), Dodgson's cousin and a poet in her own right, the author of *Lays and Ballads from English History* (1856) and *The Story of Queen Isabella and Other Verses* (1863). Of delicate health, she lived in the seacoast town of Tenby. With her sister, Mrs. T. B. Hart, she published *Poems Written for a Child* (1868) and *Child-World* (1869). She also wrote fiction and popular articles. She was instrumental in helping Dodgson launch his literary career (see *Diaries*, pp. 55–8; 86–7; *Letters*, esp. p. 11; Clark, esp. pp. 86–7).

[4] On the day before Dodgson writes this letter, Liddon sent another off to William Wolfe Capes (1834–1914), Fellow of Queen's College since 1856, Oxford University Reader in Ancient History (1870–7), author of numerous works on ancient and medieval history, asking him to read the proofs of the French *Alice* (for more on Capes, see *Letters*, p. 499; Liddon's letter is in the Gordon N. Ray Collection, New York).

Christ Church, Oxford
October 9, 1867

My dear Sir,

I have not yet even seen any of the German of *Alice*. When you can send me ½ a dozen proofs of it (or so much of it as the printer can manage at once). I want to submit it to various friends for suggestions, corrections, etc., and the verses especially will very likely have to be rewritten altogether. So that there is plenty of time to consider how many copies we should have printed, a point on which I should like to have Mr. Macmillan's opinion.[1] It would be very much more convenient for me, in communicating with my friends, if I could have it all in type at once. Could not your printer hire in some more type? There must surely be printers in London who could do the whole book 3 times over, if necessary. There is also the risk, in printing it off piecemeal, that the different portions of the book may not quite match.

The question of extracts from letters can await Mr. Macmillan's judgement. You could head such a list, if you liked, "The following extracts are vouched for by the author as taken verbatim from the genuine letters of children."[2]

Very truly yours,

C. L. Dodgson

[1] Craik had written the previous day asking Dodgson how many copies of the German *Alice* he intended to print.

[2] Dodgson must have proposed to Craik, in a letter that has not surfaced, that the firm advertise *Alice* with excerpts from letters written by child fans. "I am startled by your proposition . . . ," Craik wrote on the previous day. "It struck me at first as a capital idea, but I scarcely think so well of it after consideration. . . . We would be charged with concocting letters to say what suited the occasion. . . . At all counts I would like to get Mr. Macmillan's opinion before attempting what I am doubtful about." Macmillan's reaction is not recorded, but advertisements for *Alice* did not in fact carry excerpts from children's letters.

Christ Church, Oxford
December 8, 1867

Dear Mr. Macmillan,

I see the *Saturday Review* is bringing out a series of articles, not yet concluded, on "Xmas Books." So far as I know, they have never yet taken any notice of *Alice*: what think you of sending them a copy, experimentally?[1]

No *Determinants* have yet arrived here.[2] The price you have put on the book will do very well, I fancy. Of course I am leaving it to you to send any copies to reviews you may think fit. I mentioned the *Pall Mall*, because I know the editor, and had written to him about it.[3] Believe me

Truly yours,

C. L. Dodgson

P.S. Are there any symptoms of *Alice* selling well this Xmas? When you have sold 9000, I hope you will relent as to the form of announcement: "tenth thousand" would make a very effective advertisement.

Thanks, by the way, for the extract from *Kind Words*. Do you know who the editor is?[4]

[1] "The *Saturday* did notice *Alice* and we have often used their puff," Macmillan writes back the following day. "I enclose it. I am sending them another copy on the chance that they may again take notice of it."

[2] On November 15, Dodgson wrote Macmillan: "My book on *Determinants* is complete at last. Mr. Combe tells me he is sending you word what the printing cost, but I write to beg that you will *not* go by that in pricing the book, but simply charge the usual price of books of that kind. I had so many alterations made that it cost as much as many a larger book, and I shall be quite content to sell at a loss." Two days before Dodgson writes the present letter, Macmillan wrote assuring him that the copies of *Determinants* were dispatched to Combe and should have been received on Saturday, the 7th.

[3] Frederick Greenwood (1830–1909), co-founder and editor of the *Pall Mall Gazette* (1865), had already published Dodgson's letters on "The Science of Betting" (November 19, 20, 1866) and "The Organization of Charity" (January 24, 1867).

[4] On February 28, 1867, *Kind Words: A Weekly Magazine for Boys & Girls* published (p. 71) an extract from "The Mock Turtle's Story," by "permission of the author," and added: "A very droll and amusing book, illustrated by several most admirable engravings." Benjamin Clarke (1836–93), editor of the *Sunday School Chronicle*, author of *The Life of Jesus for Young People* (1868) and other books, was then the Editor of *Kind Words*.

Christ Church, Oxford
December 10, 1867

Dear Mr. Macmillan,

The quotation you send me is part of a notice which appeared in the *Spectator*, December 22, 1866. I have referred to the *Saturday* of that date, and there is nothing resembling it. It is lucky I mentioned the thing, and I hope the *Saturday* reviewer may not have seen any advertisement with the erroneous reference.

The *Determinants* have come and look very well indeed in their brown binding.[1]

Truly yours,

C. L. Dodgson

[1] "My book on *Determinants* came out early in this month," Dodgson writes in his *Diaries* (p. 264) on December 12. The full title is *An Elementary Treatise on Determinants with Their Application to Simultaneous Linear Equations and Algebraical Geometry*.

Christ Church, Oxford
January 24, 1868

Dear Mr. Macmillan,

You would be doing me a favour if you could (without any great trouble) furnish me with the details of our account as it stood at the close of each issue of *Alice*. I want to know what each issue cleared, taken by itself, e.g. take the 3rd and 4th thousands: what did they cost for paper, printing, binding, and advertising? and then what did they bring in (to me) by their sale? Then the same thing for the 5th, 6th and 7th – and then again for the last issue of 2500, so soon as they are all gone.[1]

How many are you printing for the new issue?[2]

Also, what are you doing about German type? I will gladly pay (if necessary) for the hire of more type, so as to be able to submit the book to the criticisms of my friends as a whole, rather than have it printed off piece-meal.[3]

One more question. Have you any means, or can you find any, for printing a page or two, in the next volume of *Alice*, in *reverse*? I mean like this:

$$.\text{rrobrroI} \quad \text{brs} \quad \text{brotxO}$$

If no better way can be found, I suppose there would be no great difficulty in printing it on paper, then transferring it, before the ink dries, to wood, and then cutting and electrotyping as a picture.[4]

Mr. Craik told me I must not look forwards to *Alice* continuing to sell as well as it has hitherto done, but that it would soon settle down into a comparatively small annual sale: is that your prediction also?[5] Believe me

Very truly yours,

C. L. Dodgson

P.S. I have got the *Pall Mall* notice of the *Determinants*. Has it been noticed anywhere else? and is it showing any inclination to sell?[6]

---

[1] "I enclose the statement you want," Macmillan replies three days later. "I hope it gives all the detail you want. It shows a very satisfactory result I should fancy." The statement is missing.

[2] Macmillan does not answer this question.

[3] Macmillan estimates that it would take "*all* the London printers for three ordinary weeks" to set the German *Alice* in full. "May I not send it to Germany?" to be set, he asks. "Clay won't object."

[4] Macmillan foresees no difficulty in having a woodblock cut for the reverse printing, but he thinks it will cost "a good deal."

[5] ". . . it is hardly possible to hope that it will sell long at the present rate," Macmillan writes. "Perhaps we may hit on some new feature to give it a fresh spurt next year."

[6] "We have sold 33 copies of the *Determinants*," Macmillan reports, "and perhaps 7 more may have been sold by our agents. You have given *56* it seems." The notice in the *Pall Mall Gazette* assured its readers that "Mr. Dodgson's original monograph on determinants deserves the attention of mathematicians. . . . At any rate, it serves to show the ability of Mr. Dodgson . . . and it creates a hope that we may have from him the benefit of further investigation in the algebraical wonderland of his choice" (January 11, 1868, p. 156). Dodgson was surely appalled at the oblique reference to *Alice*.

Christ Church, Oxford
January 28, 1868

My dear Sir,

I am much obliged to you for the account, which is very satisfactory. From your sum total of £640 I have to deduct £100 for Oxford printing and £280 for pictures, leaving a clear profit of £250. I enclose a correction which I hope will be in time for some of the edition now printing, as the sentence is nonsense as it stands at present: the error has only crept into the last edition.

By all means print in Germany, if you can *secure* its being done on good paper. I have a horror of the flimsy paper of foreign books. I should be glad to have half a dozen proofs of the whole book.

Now I have a new idea to broach to you. I want to bring out a small volume of verses, most of them reprints from Magazines, but the first and longest quite new. And I should like to give Mr. Combe the printing: will you publish it? My idea is to do all for it that type and paper will do, and to use broad leads. I think none but the best poetry will stand close printing and cheap paper – and that the colour of the binding should match *Alice*. And lastly, I should like to print a *very* small number, say 250. I could hope no better for it than that it should get out of print and require a 2nd edition. If you will publish it at Easter, I will begin printing at once, that I may have as long as possible for correcting and polishing.

Yours very truly,

C. L. Dodgson

P H A N T A S M A G O R I A
and other poems
Lewis Carroll.

Christ Church, Oxford
January 30 [1868]

My dear Sir,

I hope I may conclude from your note that you *will* publish *Phantasmagoria* – on the same terms as *Alice*. Please let me know soon all you can suggest as to type etc.[1] I fancy *Goblin Market* would be a good model in every way.[2] You shall have proofs of the poems. Believe me

Very truly yours,

C. L. Dodgson

---

[1] Macmillan's note is missing, but it is clear from his letter of January 31 that he has undertaken to publish *Phantasmagoria*. He asks Dodgson to look at Matthew Arnold's *New Poems* (Macmillan published it the previous year) as a possible model for his own book of verse. The terms, Macmillan suggest, can be settled "when I see something of the work. . . ."

[2] Macmillan also published Christina Rossetti's *Goblin Market and Other Poems* (1862). Dodgson read the book and admired it (*Diaries*, p. 176). In 1863 he met Miss Rossetti at the home of her brother Dante Gabriel. Dodgson later photographed her and other members of the family and gave her a copy of *Alice*. The acquaintance continued for a good many years. For more on Dodgson and the Rossettis, see *Letters*, esp. p. 61.

Christ Church, Oxford
February 7, 1867

Dear Mr. Macmillan,

I have another money question to ask. Am I right in supposing that you pay money, due to your "publishees," *6 months late*, so that what was due to me in June (£276 I think) I ought to have had about Xmas (which by the way I have not had) – and that the additional £250 or so, due at Xmas, may be looked for next June: is this so? I don't want to appear in the light of a dun, I am in no particular hurry, except that all delay, after the customary time, whatever that may be, is so much loss of interest.[1]

What do you think of the opposite idea for the back of my book? If you like it, could you get it nicely designed, etc., for printing in gold?[2] Believe me

Very truly yours,

C. L. Dodgson

---

[1] Macmillan replies on February 14, enclosing a cheque for the balance due Dodgson. He explains that the firm prepare authors' statements only once a year, in June, as "it is not easy to make them up oftener." What is due the author is paid the following January, Macmillan adds. "You see we sometimes even let it run into February!" He assures Dodgson that the firm do not take it amiss if their authors remind them of their obligations.

[2] Macmillan expresses no opinion of the design Dodgson proposes (same letter) but promises that when *Phantasmagoria* is ready for binding they will try the suggestion.

Christ Church, Oxford
February 16, 1868

Dear Mr. Macmillan,

Thanks for the money, for which I enclose a receipt – I hope a legally valid one. I should be very glad to see you, if you chanced to be in Christ Church about 2 any day, and we could discuss *Phantasmagoria*.[1] We are putting it in type, as I want to have it by me for a while for final touches. Easter I fancy would be a good time to bring it out. If you know of any artist good at fantastic patterns, we might try a cover of the same kind as that of *The Prince's Progress*.[2] There should be something ghostly about it, as that is the subject of the principal poem.

By all means have *Alice* printed in Germany. I thought I had said this before. I received yesterday from you a proof of the first sheet in German, with various MS corrections in the margin. What is it for? Ought it not to go to the printer?[3]

Very truly yours,

C. L. Dodgson

[1] In his letter of February 14, Macmillan mentioned that he was coming to Oxford and added, "Perhaps I may see you." After hearing from Dodgson, Macmillan arranged to meet him on the following Wednesday, but because Dodgson failed to make any entries in his Diaries for February and March 1868, we cannot in fact know whether or not they actually met.

[2] Macmillan published Christina Rossetti's *The Prince's Progress and Other Poems* in 1866. Both *Goblin Market* and *The Prince's Progress* were designed by Dante Gabriel Rossetti. Unlike the "fantastic" pattern that Dodgson seeks, the covers of the two volumes by Miss Rossetti bear a simple pattern of double lines paralleling the borders of the books. Each line ends in a curlicue, and a series of dots arranged symmetrically add emphasis.

[3] Dodgson is right, and on the day after he writes, Macmillan replies asking him to return the proof of the German translation, adding that he will send it on to the German printer.

Christ Church, Oxford

March 8, 1868

Dear Mr. Macmillan,

I have written to Mr. du Maurier about a frontispiece (and sent him a copy of the poem) but on the whole I think I had rather have no "head-pieces" or "tail-pieces."[1] The second part of the volume will consist of pieces of a graver kind, and perhaps we might have a frontispiece for that also – but that can wait till you have seen the principal poem (from which I suppose the picture ought to be taken).

Don't send me my "11th thousand" *Alice* till you have sold the 2nd half of the 10th thousand, so that its coming may be a signal that that is accomplished. I shall be glad to be able to say that we have sold our "myriad."

I forget if I suggested that the German *Alice* should be set up in slip: as there will be probably alterations and omissions, it would be only causing extra trouble to put it into pages now. Believe me

Truly yours,

C. L. Dodgson

[1] "I think *Phantasmagoria* is very likely to be a success," Macmillan wrote three days earlier, and suggested that Dodgson "ask du Maurier if he will do a dozen head and tail pictures with frontispiece." Dodgson admired the work of *Punch* artist George du Maurier (1834–96) and had sent him an inscribed *Alice*. On October 31, 1867, he sent du Maurier a copy of the French *Alice* before it was published "that he might criticise the songs" (*Diaries*, p. 263), and on January 17, 1868, he called on the artist "to . . . thank him for undertaking to look over the French *Alice*" (p. 265). But when Dodgson calls on him again, on April 7, 1868, to discuss illustrations for *Phantasmagoria*, he learns that "Mr. du Maurier is to take a fortnight's perfect rest for his eye, so that my picture is put off for the present" (p. 267).

Christ Church, Oxford
May 20, 1868

Dear Mr. Craik,

I have heard from Sir N. Paton, or rather from the friend to whom he wrote, that he can't undertake the pictures: so I am adrift at present.[1] Believe me

Truly yours,

C. L. Dodgson[2]

---

[1] Dodgson first approached Tenniel (April 8, 1868) to illustrate *Looking-Glass*, but Tenniel told him that there was "no chance of his being able to do pictures . . . till the year after next, if then." Recording this exchange in his *Diaries* (p. 267), Dodgson added: "I must now try Noël Paton." That same day, he "spent a very pleasant evening" at the MacDonalds' in Hammersmith and left a message for George MacDonald, who apparently was away, "begging him to apply to Sir Noël for me about the pictures for 'Looking-glass House.'" On May 19, Dodgson noted (p. 269): "Heard from Mrs. MacDonald, enclosing Sir Noël Paton's letter to Mr. MacDonald. He is too ill to undertake the pictures . . . and urges that Tenniel is *the* man. I wrote to Tenniel again, suggesting that I should pay his publishers for his time for the next five months. Unless he will undertake it, I am quite at a loss." Dodgson could not yet have received Craik's letter of May 19, also reporting that "Sir Noël Paton is very ill," adding that he "has been ordered to the Continent. I fear there is not the chance of his doing anything for some time," Craik concluded. Joseph Noël Paton (1821–1901), conventional painter of scenes from fairy tales, mythology, history, and religious narratives, achieved early popularity and was knighted in 1867 (see *Diaries*, p. 304; *Letters*, pp. 165–6).

[2] In what must have been a fit of absence of mind, Dodgson actually signs this letter "G. L. Craik."

Christ Church, Oxford
June 2, 1868

Dear Mr. Macmillan,

With regard to my unfortunate *Alice II* both Tenniel and Noël Paton appear to be hopeless. Have you seen the pictures in *Fun* signed "Bab"? The artist's name, I am told is Gilbert: his power in grotesque is extraordinary – but I have seen no symptoms of his being able to draw anything pretty and graceful. I should be very glad if you could ascertain (without directly communicating with *him*, so as to commit me in any way) whether he *has* such a power.[1] If so, I think he would do. Some of his pictures are full of fun. But I can't find any one that knows him. Believe me

Truly yours,

C. L. Dodgson

---

[1] "Bab" was of course the pseudonym of (Sir) William Schwenck Gilbert (1836–1911) who was, besides being the librettist of Gilbert and Sullivan fame, a talented cartoonist and illustrator. Three days later, Macmillan writes to Dodgson identifying "Bab" and suggesting that Dodgson look at "a copy of Gilbert's Fairy Tales . . . and so judge of his powers."

Christ Church, Oxford
June 4, 1868

Dear Mr. Macmillan,

Thanks, first, for the *Educational Times'* notice of my *Determinants*: it is a more healthy one to read than if it were all praise – at the same time I cannot avoid a dim suspicion that the writer is not a mathematician and that he has not read much of the book. Nearly all he says is taken from the preface: then he talks of "Proposition-Theorems," an illogical phrase never used by me or any one else, but which he charges me with parading![1]

As to the American question, I have written to ask Mr. Tenniel's opinion, and will write again when I hear from him.[2] Meanwhile, my own inclination is to refuse the electro-types, but at the same time to offer (to Messrs. Appleton first, and then, if they decline, to your present applicant) to print a cheap edition here and send it out. Thus we could secure its being produced in a style not quite unworthy of Mr. Tenniel's reputation, and if Messrs. Appleton had on sale an edition with the pictures fairly printed, and tolerably cheap, I doubt if any other publisher would find it pay to compete with it by mere *copies* of the pictures. What do you think of this plan? and how cheap could we afford to sell it to them?[3]

---

[1] The *Educational Times* notice (June 1, 1868, p. 62), surveys a group of studies on determinants, describes Dodgson's, and concludes about it: "Altogether, the work forms a valuable addition to the Treatises we possess on modern Algebra. With regard to the style of the Treatise we have a remark to make. In his desire to avoid what he calls the 'semi-colloquial, semi-logical form often adopted by Mathematical writers,' Mr. Dodgson runs into the opposite extreme, and makes such a parade of precision with 'Definitions,' 'Enunciations,' 'Q.E.D's', etc. that the work becomes rather a tedious one to read. We should be glad to see much of this ostentation of formality excluded from subsequent editions of the work, if any such should be called for."

[2] On the previous day Macmillan advised Dodgson to sell a set of the electros of the *Alice* cuts to America: "Of course they will work them badly – but on the other hand they will reproduce them in some form too hideous to contemplate if you don't." In his reply to Dodgson's letter, Macmillan on the following day agrees to look into the cost of a cheap edition for America but adds that he doubts that Appleton "will be content with anything but plates."

[3] Dodgson forgets to add a close and signature to this letter.

Christ Church, Oxford
June 7, 1868

Dear Mr. Macmillan,

I have just been told by an Oxford friend, one of our scientific teachers, as a positive fact, that scientific books intended for circulation in America, are sometimes printed in England and sent out, simply because we can print them here cheaper than they can.

If this be true, it seems clear that our proper course is – to offer Messrs. Appleton the refusal of an English edition of *Alice*, and then, if they refuse, to look out some other American publisher, and bring it out there ourselves. If I am rightly informed, we *can* produce it, in America, at such a price, as will make it quite impossible for any one there to compete with the sale by copying the pictures and so reproducing them.

That is my present opinion, but I wait to hear from you again about it.

As to "Bab," I have looked at the "Fairy-tales" which he has illustrated, and my hopes are crushed – it is painfully evident that he can draw *only* grotesques.[1] So, unless you can find me an artist, the MS must remain as – MS.

How is the German edition getting on? They seem to be but leisurely printers.

Very truly yours,

C. L. Dodgson

---

[1] The drawings for which Gilbert is perhaps best known, those in *Bab Ballads*, did not appear in book form until the end of 1868. But the *Ballads* did appear earlier in *Fun*, and Dodgson may have seen them there. Earlier, however, in 1866, Gilbert illustrated a children's book, *The Magic Mirror*, and this is more probably the book that Macmillan steered Dodgson to. Dodgson's ultimate judgment of Gilbert's drawings was shared by at least one reviewer of *The Magic Mirror* (*Nation*, December 13, 1866, p. 467), who judged the pictures "clever and spirited enough" with "considerable power of fun" but added that "some . . . are rather like the work of an amateur, and those which are not comic are not very interesting." *Bab Ballads*, on the other hand, has been called "one of the brightest stars in the galaxy of illustrated books" by Philip James, who goes on to link Gilbert's "wit and punch" in these illustrations to Tenniel's for *Alice* ("Note on Gilbert as an Illustrator," *Selected Bab Ballads* (1955), p. v).

Christ Church, Oxford
June 17, 1868

Dear Mr. Macmillan,

I have just received a proof (2 proofs, I should say) of *Alice* in German, with the MS (which by the way, should have been sent, with a proof, to Miss Zimmermann – not to me – but I will forward it). *I* have only one objection to make to it – but it is a radical one: each page is a line too short, and ½ an inch too narrow. This, of course, throws most of the pictures out of proportion, and spoils the general effect.

There is a second proof enclosed, of the proper size, but this only goes to the 16th page. I think I had better wait till the whole has been set in that size, before forwarding it for correction to Miss Zimmermann.

The book in the smaller size looks very mean. I had rather not bring it out at all in German, than do so in a way that will not do justice to the pictures.

By the way, will they be able to print the pictures properly in Germany? The proofs sent are very hideous.[1] Believe me

Truly yours,

C. L. Dodgson

---

[1] Craik replies two days later and reports that he has written to the German printer to remind him that the instructions were to keep the German and English *Alice*s "as nearly as possible facsimiles." He adds: "I have no doubt it will be all right."

Croft Rectory, Darlington
July 1, 1868

Dear Mr. Macmillan,

If I am right in thinking that June is your month for making up accounts, I should be obliged if you can let me know (roughly if you cannot do it exactly) what sum I may expect to receive from you next January – and whether you are likely to want to print any more *Alice*s this year.

I am yet awaiting information about the proposed American issue.[1] Believe me

Truly yours,

C. L. Dodgson

---

[1] In replying the next day, Macmillan promises to have the account ready "in about a fortnight"; in fact Dodgson receives the statement on August 18. In his *Diaries* entry for August 24 (p. 273), Dodgson calculates "the pecuniary result of *Alice*." Allowing for the loss of the first 2000 copies and the cost of the pictures, he estimates a profit of £55 per 1000 copies. In the same letter, Macmillan also reports that he has written to Appleton offering them 1000 copies of *Alice* at a price which would give Dodgson about 5*d*. a copy but that he has not yet received a reply.

Croft Rectory, Darlington
July 3, 1868

Dear Mr. Macmillan,

Thanks for your offer about the Cambridge man, but I am happy to say I have arranged with Mr. Tenniel to do the pictures – getting on with them as he can, at odd times. We might *possibly* have it ready for Xmas next year.[1]

I forgot to say, with regard to the German *Alice*, that they need not trouble themselves to get into each page the *same* matter as is in the corresponding page in the English. Let them run it on as they like, so long as they place the pictures as near as possible to the text to which they refer. Believe me

Truly yours,

C. L. Dodgson

---

[1] In his effort to help Dodgson find an appropriate illustrator for *Looking-Glass*, Macmillan wrote to Dodgson (previous day) suggesting "a Cambridge man of a really considerable genius." But on June 18, Dodgson "wrote to Tenniel, finally accepting his kind offer to do the pictures (at such spare times as he can find) for the second volume of *Alice*. He thinks it *possible* (but not likely) that we might get it out by Christmas 1869" (*Diaries*, p. 270).

Croft Rectory, Darlington
August 27, 1868

Dear Mr. Craik,

The French *Alice* must wait – and even when printed, I don't want the type broken up at all. If it is usual to make an annual charge for keeping type standing, I will of course pay it.[1] The poems will be ready to come out at Xmas but not before, I think. It will be too soon to begin advertising now, I suppose: when you *do* begin, here is the title:

"*Phantasmagoria and Other Poems* by Lewis Carroll."

I would rather have no allusion to *Alice* in the advertisement.

I forgot to thank you for telling me of *The Times* notice.[2] If you have a spare copy of it by you, I should be glad to have it, but don't trouble yourself to buy it for me, as I can get an old *Times* at Oxford. Believe me

Truly yours,

C. L. Dodgson

---

[1] On the previous day, Craik reminded Dodgson that the French *Alice* was still in type (and had been for nearly a year); he asked whether Dodgson could "do anything to expedite matters" as Messrs. Clay would like the use of their type. The French *Alice* would not appear, however, until August 1869.

[2] On December 26, 1865, *The Times* reviewed *Alice* in a jamboree notice that covered nineteen books. The newspaper ran a second review, this one long and favorable, on August 13, 1868: "*Alice's Adventures in Wonderland* . . . is a very charming production," it reads. "It is the picture of a child's simple and unreasoning imagination illustrated in a dream, and is extremely well and pleasantly written." The notice prints a long excerpt, the Dormouse's story, and concludes: "Certainly we enjoy the walk with Alice through Wonderland, though now and then, perhaps, something disturbing almost causes us to wake from our dream. That it is a little bit too clever every here and there seems to us to be the fault of a very pretty and highly original book, sure to delight the little world of wondering minds, and which may well please those who have, unfortunately, passed the years of wondering."

White Hart, Guildford[1]
September 14, 1868

Dear Mr. Macmillan,

I remember we had a good deal of trouble about the title-page of *Alice*, when done at Oxford, and never got a satisfactory-looking one after all – whereas *your* first attempt was a success. I wish you could send me an idea of a title-page for the poems – *Phantasmagoria and Other Poems* by Lewis Carroll – the size of a page will be $4\frac{1}{2} \times 3$.[2]

Very truly yours,

C. L. Dodgson

---

[1] Dodgson is in Guildford house-hunting. His father died on June 21, and his brothers and sisters had now to leave Croft Rectory. In November, the family moves into The Chestnuts, Guildford, the house Dodgson calls home for the rest of his life and where he dies.

[2] "Since *Alice* was done the Oxford people have greatly improved in the matter of title pages," writes Macmillan on the following day. "As they are printing the book, I think it would be better to let them try and send me a proof."

White Hart, Guildford
September 22, 1868

Dear Mr. Macmillan,

Don't put "with frontispiece by G. du Maurier" in any advertisement of *Phantasmagoria*, as he has just written to say he can't do it[1] – and I am at a loss whom to apply to. Do you know of any one who would do?

What do you think of the enclosed idea for the back of the book?

Thanks for *The Water Babies*. How well Noël Paton would draw a ghost-picture for me, if only he were well enough![2]

Very truly yours,

C. L. Dodgson

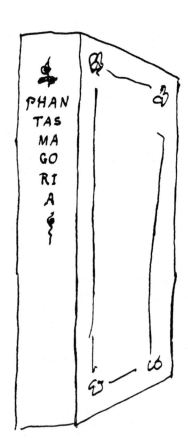

---

[1] Dodgson does not give up easily on du Maurier, however. As late as 1873, he tries yet again to get the artist to "draw for an illustrated edition of *Phantasmagoria*," but that effort also fails (*Diaries*, p. 320).

[2] Noël Paton had illustrated Charles Kingsley's *The Water Babies*.

Christ Church, Oxford
October 17, 1868

Dear Mr. Macmillan,

Thanks for your information about Mr. Proctor: I have written to him.[1]

As to the specimen volume, I like the name at the back: it is picturesque and fantastic - but that is about the only thing I like in the present specimen.

(1) The round ornament at the back is too solid: it should be something more feathery, to match the title above.

(2) The ornament at the side is too small, and it should be something wilder and more fantastic: why not a fiery star?

(3) There should be gold lines, (two at least) *round* each side: and I think some little ornament at the corners: if it were only a twist in the lines, as I have here drawn it, it would be better than a plain right angle.

(4) The two sides should be equally ornamented: I cannot endure a book that has only one side fit to be seen – but the ornaments need not be exactly the same.

(5) The cloth should be a much brighter red, and *not* (as this is) a mixture of red and black: it has the effect of black threads being mixed among the red.

(6) The boards should project a little more beyond the edge of the book.

At present the whole effect is too plain, as if it were a cheap edition. My theory is, that poetry, being a luxurious form of literature, should have all possible luxurious accessories.

The 50 copies which I want bound for private circulation will afford the binder a good opportunity for trying various forms and styles of decoration, and then we can select the best for publication.

I don't like the idea of repeating the name on the side, or of putting a picture of any kind – though it is a clever little drawing.

I see there is no gloss on the paper, even after binding, as there is in *Alice*. Is this an essential difference in the paper? Or is there any way of giving the Oxford paper the same gloss? We are making some rather thicker paper, but of the same texture, I fancy.

Very truly yours,

C. L. Dodgson

[1] On the previous day, Macmillan replied to Dodgson's plea for help in finding a suitable artist to do the frontispiece for *Phantasmagoria*: "The enclosed information about Mr. Proctor may be relied on," he wrote. John Proctor, who sometimes used the pseudonym "Puck," was a distinguished Victorian cartoonist who worked for several magazines from 1866 to 1898. He was perhaps best known as a political cartoonist but had already illustrated *Dame Dingle's Fairy Tales* (1867). Although Dodgson had managed to get Tenniel to agree to illustrate *Looking-Glass*, he probably realized that if he found another artist whose work pleased him and who was free, Tenniel would gladly relinquish the job. Within two weeks of writing this letter (on November 1), Dodgson concludes: "The second volume of *Alice* will after all be illustrated by Tenniel, who has reluctantly consented, as his hands are full: I have tried Noël Paton and Proctor in vain" (*Diaries*, p. 275).

Christ Church, Oxford
October 22, 1868

Dear Mr. Macmillan,

We are printing the poems on paper decidedly thicker, and better toned, and a little larger, so as to give a rather handsomer margin. Please take care the binder doesn't reduce it more than necessary, and that the boards project *well* beyond the margins of the leaves.

I have sent the German *Alice* to Miss Zimmermann, asking her to forward it to you, and to say if she wishes to see another proof. I think there will be no more to alter than the name of the Lizard, which I wanted changed from "Bill" to some German name. It occurs 20 or 30 times in the book, but I think the printer might be trusted to attend to the corrections, without another proof being sent.[1] If Miss Zimmermann is satisfied, will you order the printing off? I think 500 will be a safe number: but if you decidedly advise 1000, I don't object. I trust to you to secure that the pictures are done justice to, and that the paper is *really* good; they seem to me always to print foreign books on blotting paper – perhaps you had better send out paper.

At all events I had rather they were *bound* in England. All foreign books I have ever seen come to pieces directly.

Very truly yours,

C. L. Dodgson

Of course tell them *not* to break up the type.

¹ In the German, the Lizard, Bill, becomes "Wabbel."

Christ Church, Oxford
October 22, 1868

Dear Mr. Macmillan,

On further examining the German *Alice*, I find some mistakes of arrangement which it is essential to correct.

(1) The margin at the top of the page is much too narrow. If you will open out a sheet without cutting it, you will see there is only 1 inch between the titles of 2 pages which lie top to top. There should be *more* than $1\frac{1}{2}$ inch, so as to leave a $\frac{3}{4}$ inch margin after cutting.

(2) The same may be said of the *inner* margin: only here the interval should be $1\frac{1}{2}$ inch *exact*. (It is only 1 inch now.)

(3) The 6 leaves which end with the "Contents" ought of course to be so arranged as to fold one within another,

thus and *not* thus

(4) Will not the *single* leaf, with which they end the book, be very awkward for bindings? Had it not better be double, so that the book will end with one leaf quite blank?

(5) I notice one misprint. In page 57, line 3, there ought to be a (") after (Dir!)

(6) Page 75 end of line 6, insert (") .

Very truly yours,

C. L. Dodgson

P.S. What do you think of covering each side of the *Poems* with a shower of meteors?

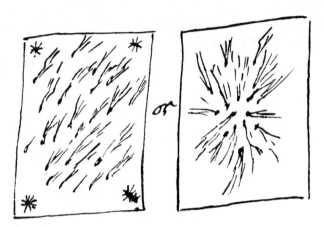

best all radiating to centre.[1]

In the picture of Alice, where she fills the room (page 42, in the German) I observe that the electro-type still has that projection which produces a black spot on the side of the nose. Cannot this be removed with a file? The same fault exists in the electro-type used by Clay.

In page 167, beginning of last line, there is a $\odot$ omitted. I fear there must be many more such omissions. They had better look over the book again, with a view to the punctuation, before printing off.

---

[1] "By today's post we send you two covers on which are depicted more or less successfully your hints of illustration," Macmillan writes to Dodgson on November 12. "We did it on the red first. But these skyey objects seem so homeless without the blue, that we have ventured to see if we cannot induce you to adopt the native colour. Privately I hope you will. It is so pretty." Although Dodgson seems not to record his decision, he is indeed induced: *Phantasmagoria* appeared in blue.

Christ Church, Oxford
December 3 [1868]

Dear Mr. Macmillan,

Would you kindly forward the enclosed to Mr. Proctor for me, as I haven't got his present address. The new *Alice* arrived safe.[1] If you are now going to keep it permanently in type, I wish you would send me a proof, in sheets, on common paper, that I may correct it for the next issue. The punctuation is capable of a good deal of improvement.

I haven't yet heard of any paper arriving for the poems. We must call it a New Year's book: it is too late for Xmas I fear.[2]

By the way, why *won't* Clay attend to the suggestion about the picture of *Alice* at page 45 – in the copy you send me there is still that unsightly mark on the nose, caused by a projection on the electrotype, which ought to be removed.[3] Believe me

Very truly yours,

C. L. Dodgson

P.S. Many thanks for the telegram.[4]

---

[1] Presumably the sixth edition (starting with the 12th thousand), "the first electrotype edition, published October 1868, and . . . the basis of all impressions until the work was reset as the ninth edition" (*Handbook*, p. 35).

[2] In his reply two days later, Macmillan writes that Combe already has the paper for printing, and there is hope that *Phantasmagoria* "may yet be out for Christmas." But the book does not in fact appear until January.

[3] "I hope we will get Clay to attend to the picture on p. 45," Macmillan writes (same letter).

[4] The telegram is missing, but it probably related to Macmillan's letter of November 23 promising to telegraph if he got any early word of results in the Lancashire election. On November 25, Dodgson "wrote a letter to the *Standard*, commenting on a wonderful sentence in *The Times* leader on Gladstone's defeat in Lancashire yesterday. 'The failure of the Liberal policy in one populous district only gives greater weight to the general decision of the country.' I also sent them an anagram which I thought out lying awake the other night.

WILLIAM EWART GLADSTONE
'Wilt tear down *all* images?'"

Dodgson added ruefully: "Neither was published." For more on Dodgson's politics, anagrams, and for possible political models for *Looking-Glass*, see *Diaries*, pp. 275–7.

Christ Church, Oxford
December 9, 1868

Dear Mr. Macmillan,

I shall probably have a lot of MS ready, before the end of this month, to be set up in slip for the new volume of *Alice* – but there is no use in sending it till Clay can begin setting it up: and probably his hands are full just now. Would you let me know whether he could begin it in 10 days' time or so, and whether I am to send it to you or direct to him. I want if possible to get some slip into Mr. Tenniel's hands by the end of the year, now that he has kindly consented to work at it in such odd times as he can find for the purpose.

With regard to the poems – I want to have *some* distinctive mark on the back of those "for private circulation," that one may know them from the others.[1] I leave the selection of it to you: that monogram of yours to be put on the public, *not* the private copies, would do very well, I should think.

I am going to have 100 of them done, instead of 50. But I keep to the number 500 for the copies omitting the Oxford poem. However we shall of course keep it in type a while, so that if (which I can't say I the least expect) there *should* be a demand for more, we could meet it. Believe me

Truly yours,

C. L. Dodgson

¹ Dodgson is planning to issue *Phantasmagoria* in two different editions. Those "for private circulation" are to include a verse parody on Oxford academic politics that he composed and had printed anonymously as a pamphlet in November 1866, entitled "The Election to the Hebdomadal Council." On the following day, Dodgson writes to Macmillan: "Friends are beginning to apply for copies of the poems containing the Oxford squib. Don't you think we had best alter the words 'for private circulation' to 'for circulation among members of Oxford University,' adding, of course, publisher's name and 'all rights reserved,' and sell it for 5*s*. and 5*s*. 6*d*. in the same advertisement? If we do this, I think I shall have *200* printed *with* the squib, and *400 without*." Macmillan replies on the 10th resisting Dodgson's plan for two separate editions, arguing that "*two publications* would cause confusion." While agreeing that the local, topical parody is of less interest to the general public, Macmillan believes it would not detract from the book as a whole. "Your first poem will carry the volume," he assured Dodgson. For more on the verse pamphlet, see *Handbook*, pp. 38–9.

Christ Church, Oxford
December 12, 1868

Dear Mr. Macmillan,

I don't think it will do to include the Oxford poem in all the copies – it is too local and ephemeral: and at the same time I can't undertake to give away, or even to sell, as many copies as Oxford readers may want – not to mention that some Oxford friends might be disappointed if they bought the published volume, and did not hear of the other till afterwards. The best plan seems to me to be this: add to the advertisement

"A few copies have been prepared including a poem on the subject of the Hebdomadal Council at Oxford, which would not be interesting, or even intelligible, to the general public: these may be had, on application to the publishers, at 5*s*. 6*d*. a copy."

I think it very possible that more copies may be thus applied for than we are printing: but it will be very easy to alter the paging back again, and strike off more copies including it.¹

I think it would be well for you to print some fly-leaves (as you did for *Alice*) containing the title page of the published copy, with the additional sentence given opposite, and put one into every copy sold.

Would it not be well to put them also into all copies of *Alice*? and, vice-versa, the fly-leaves of *Alice* might be put into *Phantasmagoria*.

When I say "put into the books," I don't mean them to be fastened in. I have a dislike to books bound up with advertisements.

I have a great heap of the *Alice* fly-leaves, which I will send back, if you can make any use of them.²

Yours very truly,

C. L. Dodgson

P.S. If you don't think your monogram will look well on the "public" copies, what do you say to a simple ⬭ on the back of the Oxford copies, so as to know them from the others?

¹ Macmillan's reply two days later was decisive. "There is no end to the perplexities your proposed scheme will cause," he writes. "Print 500 of the Oxford poem separately and sell it for a shilling." Three days after writing this letter, Dodgson "called at the Press to say that I have given up the idea of bringing out the poems in two different forms. The Oxford poem is to be in all the 600 copies" (*Diaries*, pp. 277–8). The volume appears within the month, and on January 7 of the new year, Dodgson "called on Macmillan and sent off 28 copies of *Phantasmagoria*, which is now ready: 300 or 400 copies have been already ordered by the trade," he notes in his *Diaries* (p. 279), "and I agreed to Macmillan's proposal to print 1000 more (making 1600 altogether)." The volume is in two parts, the first containing thirteen amusing poems; the second thirteen serious ones. The verse is not illustrated. The book takes its title from the first poem, a tale about the trials and tribulations of ghosts. A number of the poems had already appeared in magazines. See *Handbook*, pp. 47–52.
² "Received from Macmillan two hundred of the fly-leaf advertisements of *Alice*, which he has printed by my suggestion," Dodgson wrote in his *Diaries* (p. 243) on May 29, 1866, but "no copy seems to have survived" (*Handbook*, pp. 36–7). A later slip "advertising *Alice* . . . is sometimes found in copies of the first edition (any issue) [of *Phantasmagoria*] tipped in on the front end paper. . . . A similar slip, advertising *Phantasmagoria*, is found in copies of *Alice* dated 1869" (ibid., p. 53).

Christ Church, Oxford
January 21, 1869

Dear Mr. Macmillan,

I was sorry to see *Phantasmagoria* advertised at 6*s.* I fancied we had settled it was to be 5*s.*, which appears to me a much more reasonable price. However I fear it is too late to alter it now, as I suppose a good many copies are out of your hands by this time.¹ But I write to secure the German *Alice* not being charged. more than I should like – as I suppose you have not yet got it ready for sale. Pray do not put it at more than 6*s.* in England, or 2 thalers in Germany: perhaps even that will be too dear.

While writing this, I receive a note from your clerk saying that "J. Parry," and "J. Liddon" have left the houses to which their copies of *Phantasmagoria* were sent. Perhaps the *Court Guide* will give their new addresses: if not, would you send a messenger to ascertain Mr. Parry's address at the Gallery of Illustration, and Mr. Liddon's at "10 Whitehall Place," which is his office, and where he may perhaps be found.² Believe me

Truly yours,

C. L. Dodgson

¹ On the following day, Macmillan replies that "I thought you agreed to 6*s.* when you stuck the Oxford poem in." He assures Dodgson, however, that the price was "very cheap" and would not "stand in the way of sale."
² Dodgson first met John Orlando Parry (1810–79), actor, entertainer, composer, on August 25, 1863, at Whitby. "I had some talk" with him "about the song 'Miss Jones,' which I had sent him" (Diaries). Earlier (June 9 of that year), Dodgson "received back from Mr. J. Parry, my song 'Miss Jones' – he calls it 'clever,' but says 'he does not want a song of the kind at present, and therefore returns it with thanks'" (*Diaries*, p. 197). For more about "Miss Jones," see *Letters*, p. 102. John Liddon (1835?–93) was Henry Parry Liddon's younger brother. Dodgson and the younger

Liddon must have been acquainted in the mid-1850s, when Liddon was an undergraduate at Christ Church. He took a Fourth in Mathematics, went on to become a barrister (Lincoln's Inn) in 1861, and then Clerk in the Ecclesiastical Commission at 10 Whitehall Place. On October 4, 1877, Dodgson notes (Diaries) that he called on Liddon and met his wife and five daughters.

Christ Church, Oxford
January 24, 1869

Dear Mr. Macmillan,

Pray advertise *Phantasmagoria* in any way you like: my only objection was to having *Alice* mentioned on the title-page.[1]

I think I told you that I want to have 2 pages of "reverse" printing in the new volume – such as you must hold up to the looking-glass to read.[2] To cut the whole on wood, like a picture, would be a very expensive process. Various ways of doing it have been suggested – first, my own plan – to print with ordinary type, and with ink that will resist the action of acid, on copper: then pour on acid, and eat down the surface, as in etching – secondly, suggested by a friend, the "bi-chromate and gelatine process": you print on gelatine with something that has the effect of hardening it, and then dissolve away the gelatine in the intervals.

This is so very like the "Anastatic" process on chalk, that it occurs to me it would be best to try that plan first – would you apply to them on the subject? If the work is not too fine for them, I fancy *we* should supply them with the 2 pages, set up in ordinary type: they would print it on their own chalk tablets, from which they would ultimately supply electro-types which we might use in the book just like pictures. If they will undertake the thing, I should like to see a sentence, or even a word or two, done first – and the resulting electro-type printed off with, that we may judge of the effect. The type should be that used for the songs in *Alice*.

I hope you are carrying out the plan of putting a loose fly-sheet advertisement of *Phantasmagoria* into each copy of *Alice* you send out. The converse process is not so necessary.[3]

Yours very truly,

C. L. Dodgson

No doubt you are right about the price of *Phantasmagoria*. I am told that 2 thalers would be a very high price for a book in Germany: could we afford to sell it (*Alice*) for less out there?

---

[1] "I wish you would let me *advertise* it as *by the author of Alice*. Won't you?" Macmillan pleaded two days earlier.

[2] Plans for "Jabberwocky," later modified.

[3] *Alice* certainly needed no such publicity. When Dodgson visited Macmillan on January 8, he recorded that "*Alice* has had a great sale this Christmas, more than 3000 having been sold since June!" (*Diaries*, p. 279).

Christ Church, Oxford
January 31, 1869

Dear Mr. Macmillan,

I have pretty nearly settled in my own mind that it will be too troublesome for the reader to have 2 pages of "reverse" type to make out, and that we had better limit it to one or 2 stanzas (with perhaps a picture over them to fill the page) and print the rest of the ballad in the usual way.[1] If you think with me in this, perhaps you could ascertain whether it would not be best (and nearly as cheap as any other way), to have it printed on a wood-block, and cut and electrotyped like a picture.

Very truly yours,

C. L. Dodgson

[1] "Jabberwocky" appeared with only one stanza of reverse type.

Christ Church, Oxford
February 15, 1869

Dear Mr. Macmillan,

In view of the coming Easter season, I want you to consider once more the idea I once suggested to you – of bringing out a "cheap edition" of *Alice*. My reasons for wishing for it are *not* commercial, strictly speaking – as a commercial speculation, it may very likely not be profitable, or may even be a loss – but *that* I do not much care about. My feeling is that the present price puts the book entirely out of the reach of many thousands of children of the middle classes, who might, I think, enjoy it (below that I don't think it would be appreciated). Now the only point I really care for in the whole matter (and *it* is a source of very real pleasure to me) is that the book should be enjoyed by children – and the more in number, the better. So I should be much obliged if you would make a rough calculation whether you could (by printing on cheaper paper (but keeping to *toned* unless white is decidedly cheaper), by putting more into a page, limiting the pictures to 10 or 12 of the best, and printing these separately (which I suppose would be cheaper than working them with the text: and in this case we might print *them* at any rate, on toned paper), having the edges sprinkled red instead of gilt, and the cover plain red, with no gilding on it except the title) sell the book for (say) half-a-crown, and yet make a profit if there were a good demand for it.[1] I am not Quixotic enough to wish to sell at a loss, but I don't mind its damaging the sale of the other a little, provided we thus put the book within the reach of a new sphere of readers. If the scheme be at all a feasible one, I should much like to try it as an Easter book – and if you wished, something might be said in advertising it to secure people from thinking that it is done because the dearer edition won't sell.

Have not the German *Alice*s come yet? I think I asked you to send me 10 as soon as you could: and I should suggest your sending for more than 50, and advertising it.[2] I rather think it will sell in England.

Very truly yours,

C. L. Dodgson

[1] "We would gain nothing towards a cheaper book by making any change in the plates, etc., as you suggest," Macmillan writes the following day. "Having the book electrotyped we have nothing to pay for but paper and press work and binding. All these might be done at a cheaper rate. The press work would not be *quite* so good of course, and the binding must be in a marked way cheaper. What do you think of a cloth back and paper sides?" With these and other economies, Macmillan believes that "a sale of 5000 copies would leave you about £60 or £70 profit, selling [the book] at 2s. 6d. I will have a copy done up in the style I suggest and you shall see it within a week or so. . . . I propose a light green paper and red cloth back for the 2s. 6d. *Alice* – but you shall see."

[2] In the same letter, Macmillan writes that "the first 50 German *Alice*s are in the binder's hands and 200 more are ordered from the Continent." On April 6, Dodgson writes in his *Diaries* (p. 280): "The German *Alice* came out in February. . . ." For more on this translation, see *Handbook*, pp. 53–5; F. Lösel, "The First German Translation of *Alice in Wonderland*," *Hermathena*, xcix (Autumn 1964), 66–79.

Christ Church, Oxford

February 17, 1869

Dear Mr. Macmillan,

You alarm me by the words "having the book electro-typed, we have nothing to pay for, etc., etc." I hope this does not mean that you have electrotyped the pages, text and all – if it does, there will be a good deal to cancel, I fear, as I cannot endure having the book perpetuated with its present misprints.[1]

Surely my plan, of condensing the matter, by smaller type and thinner leads, would have saved a good deal by reducing the paper to about one-half or so? *You* propose, it seems, to reduce it in *quality*, not in *quantity*. I am half inclined to think the other way would produce a better-looking book – inferior paper takes off so *very* much from the look of a book. But there is a great deal to be said for the plan of getting *all* the pictures in no doubt.

If by my plan, of making it a book of (say) 100 pages, with a dozen pictures, worked off separately, we could manage to sell at 2s., I believe that would be a much better price for the poorer readers than 2s. 6d. If you printed the *text* on cheap paper, and the pictures on good toned paper, I think a dozen, so done, would be more worth having than all 42 on cheap paper. I should like to know what you think of all this – and don't make too much point of having a *profit* on the cheap edition: so long as it just pays its way, I don't care for more.[2]

Please send me an English *Alice*, in sheets, for correction. You promised it on common paper, but I daresay it would cost as much to get one copy worked off for the purpose as to sacrifice one of the existing copies. Only it would be a pity to sacrifice a *bound* copy.[3]

I shall be quite content with paper sides and white edges for the cheap *Alice*.

Yours very truly,

C. L. Dodgson

P.S. As to *America*, isn't it possible for us to arrange with some American citizen to publish *Alice* for us there, so as to secure a copyright?[4] giving him, of course, a share of the profits. I think I have heard of it being done.

---

[1] In his reply of the same day, Macmillan assures Dodgson that even with electrotyping "misprints can be easily corrected in the plates – and this without the danger of fresh ones being made."
[2] "*Wait* till you see my cheap edition," Macmillan urges in the same letter.
[3] Macmillan promises that Dodgson will have a set of sheets from waste paper to correct and adds: "Or if you like, send me a list of errata. That will do as well."
[4] International copyright was not established until 1891.

Christ Church, Oxford
February 20, 1869

Dear Mr. Macmillan,

I have just received the "cheap" *Alice*s, and will begin with a point I want particularly to call your attention to – that the flaw is not yet removed from the block representing Alice in the rabbit's house (where she fills the room) – it is a projection (needing removal both from the wood block and the electrotype) causing a very unsightly mark on the side of the nose. As it has long been an eyesore to me, and I have petitioned you about it several times already, I shall be really obliged if you will remember to get it done, the next time you communicate with Clay. It ought to be done also on the block at Leipsig.

As to the book, I hardly know yet what to say. I like it in many respects, but I should like to consult various friends before I say anything definite. My present impression is that it is too nearly like the 6*s.* edition. People may think it unreasonable to pay 3*s.* 6*d.* or 4*s.* more, merely to get better paper and binding. And I am still very much in favour of the idea of making it quite another book – with only a dozen pictures (only done *well*, on tinted paper), and the text set up again, smaller type, and closer, so as to make the book about 120 pages. Would you please make an estimate of the expense of bringing it out in that way: I cannot help thinking it will be cheaper than the way you propose. I should like the purchasers of the 6*s.* copies to be able to feel that they really did get a good deal more for the money than the purchasers of the cheap edition.[1]

Very truly yours,

C. L. Dodgson

Thanks for the last review of the *Poems* – it is very wholesome reading after the laudations of *Alice*![2]

¹ Macmillan replies on March 4: "I will try to get you an estimate for a book in your proposed new
form in a few days. I am sorry I don't agree with you about doing a new book at all. I think the
same book worked in a cheaper style would do as well for all purposes. But you shall see."

² Our search through the major periodical press turned up no notices of *Phantasmagoria* that
appeared before Dodgson writes this letter. The ones that appear in March and April are almost
all laudatory: "This little book of poems, 'Grave and Gay,' . . . possesses considerable attractions
for all who care to read stories in rhyme," wrote the *Pall Mall Gazette* (March 16, 1869, p. 12). "The
versification is, as a rule, harmonious and graceful. The stories, with the exception of the first, from
which the book takes its name, are very briefly told. The thought is, throughout, transparent. . . .
Of 'Phantasmagoria' itself we cannot speak in terms of very high praise. It reminds one in many
places of 'Alice's Adventures,' but we venture to think that the author tells stories of this kind more
successfully in prose than in verse. To many, however, there is no doubt that the easy, humorous
style in which the piece is written will afford considerable pleasure. . . . The appearance of this
little book – which, without being pretentious, is an *article de luxe* – reflects the highest credit on the
publishers." On March 29, the *Literary Churchman* (p. 141) ran a short notice: "Those who have not
made acquaintance with these poems already have a pleasure to come. The comical is *so* comical,
the grave so really beautiful. . . ." The *Guardian* notice appeared on April 21 (p. 450): "In
Phantasmagoria . . . there are abundant proofs of ability. The book is amusingly varied in its
character. Its covers are decorated with representations of two nebulae which are distinguished
members of the Celestial Phantasmagoria; the poem which gives its name to the volume is full of
real and playful wit, from which the writer passes, without the appearance of painful effort, to
verse of graver mood."

Christ Church, Oxford

May 4, 1869

Dear Mr. Macmillan,

We have at last got the French *Alice* correct, and the whole (except the title-
page sheet) may now go to Press. I write this to you, rather than to Clay, as I
suppose you will have to tell him the number to be done, etc. I should be inclined
myself to say 2000, but you will know best.

The title-page I don't quite like the look of yet, and send you 3 kinds¹ to look at
and decide on. In No. 1, I thought it looked too crowded above, and that the
"AU" in the title was too small, so tried an improvement in No. 2. In No. 3 you
see they have altered the spacing, but not made the "AU" any larger. However,
I now leave the decision to you: the oftener I look at it, the less able I feel to
decide whether it looks right or not.

Of course you will have the paper the same as the English.

There is a favourable notice of *Alice* in the *Contemporary*. I am getting myself a
copy.² As also of the *Nation* of April 8, which contained a notice of it. The
reviewer said he doubted if children would care for it,³ and in the *Nation* for April
15 appears a letter (signed with initials only) detailing how much the writer's
children, and others, like it.⁴ I wish you could, without involving me in a
personal correspondence with the Editor, get me the name and address of the
writer of the letter.⁵

I never see any advertisements of the German *Alice* – do you ever advertise it? I see you don't even include it, or *Phantasmagoria*, in the list of your books in your own *Magazine* – perhaps you consider the latter as hopeless – but the former would, in my opinion, get a respectable sale in England, if it were only made known.

Please give my kind regards to Mr. Craik, and tell him I am now beginning to photograph, so if he thinks he *can* prevail on Sir N. Paton to let me photograph the drawings he told me of, now is the time to send them.[6] Believe me

Very truly yours,

C. L. Dodgson

---

[1] Missing.

[2] *Alice* is one of eleven books discussed in "Children and Children's Books" by A. H. Page in the *Contemporary Review* for May 1869 (pp. 24–25): ". . . though . . . [Lewis Carroll] certainly does not possess anything like Mr. [George] MacDonald's commanding phantasy," Page writes, "[he] has yet a peculiar power in slipping away unseen from the every-day world into a world of strange wonders. But his *spécialité* is that he carries the breath of the real world with him wherever he goes, so that a whiff of it ever and anon passes over what is strangest. Under his disguises of kings and queens, rabbits and eagles, fish-footmen, and the rest, the child must constantly feel himself thrown back, as with a sudden rebound, upon the characters and the scenes of every day. The real and the grotesque, suddenly paired, rub cheeks together, and scuttle off to perform the same serio-farcical play in various ways and with other company." The notice ends with a comment on Dodgson's technique: "Mr. Carroll is just a little forced and artificial now and then, and verges too closely upon the direct and earnest social caricatures. . . . This is a matter which he should be on his guard against, as it has at several points marred this beautiful child's book."

[3] The notice in the *Nation* (April 8, 1869, p. 276) appears in a column of "Literary Notes" and is not much more than an announcement that *Alice* has been translated into German. However, in describing "Mr. Lewis Carroll's most admirable book for children," the writer adds: ". . . only the children care little or nothing for it, and it is to grown people that it is so charming. . . ."

[4] The indignant letter (p. 295) that the *Nation*'s comment provoked came from an American:

Sir:

I beg leave to say that Lewis Carroll's *Alice's Adventures in Wonderland* is liked by many children who, according to *The Nation* of April 8, "care little or nothing for it." The copy which was brought into our family by means of a notice in your paper, more than two years ago, is a standing refutation of your statement, for its covers are almost worn off, and it has been lent to at least twenty children. It was listened to eagerly, besides, in a school where the pupils were allowed, once a week, to read from books of their own choosing; and one little boy, who read it with great delight, and tried in vain to get a copy in Boston, has just been made happy by one from London. Almost every hour I hear the children quote it, or see a grin like that with which the Cheshire cat vanishes, or a milder and more kitten-like one, on the lips of a child too young to read.

C.M.H.
West Roxbury, Mass.
April 9, 1869

Then follows an editor's note: "We probably generalized from too limited an experience."

[5] C.M.H. of West Roxbury, Mass., remains unidentified.

[6] We have no way of knowing how Dodgson's notion of photographing Noël Paton's drawings began, and we find no letters from Craik on the subject. Craik was a personal friend of the artist, and he may have offered to approach Noël Paton on Dodgson's behalf when Dodgson visited the Macmillan offices the previous January 7 and 8 (*Diaries*, p. 279).

Christ Church, Oxford
May 8, 1869

Dear Mr. Craik,

Thanks for your note. I write a line to say – *don't* ask Sir Noël Paton for leave
to photo his drawings. Don't even ask for the children's photos, my former
request – unless you have already done so. Requests refused are so much ground
lost – and perhaps I may meet him some day, and get leave to photo the children
themselves.[1]

I take the opportunity of saying what has occurred to me about selling *Alice* in
America. I suppose we may give up the idea that Messrs. Appleton will give any
order on their own account. But I fancy there would be no difficulty in arranging
with him, or some other bookseller, to sell copies on *our* account – taking no risk
on himself, having a percentage of the profits, and returning the unsold copies. If
any arrangement of this kind could be made, I had rather the copies sent out
should be just the same as we are selling here (or else distinctly inferior and
cheaper: no confusion between the two kinds should be possible – or we shall be
having the cheap ones sent over and sold here as the good ones) – the "same" is
the best idea, in my opinion.

Tell me what you and your partner think of all this.[2]

Very truly yours,

C. L. Dodgson

[1] Craik's note is missing and we cannot tell what obstacles he saw to Dodgson's requests being
satisfied. Dodgson finally meets the Noël Patons on September 15, 1871, when he is in Scotland. "I
had written to Sir Noël Paton," he writes in his *Diaries* (pp. 304–5), "mentioning an intention of
coming to Arran, and had given him time to answer in case he liked to offer a bed. Not hearing, I
thought I had better try a call, and went to Glasgow last night, sleeping at the Queen's. This
morning I got up at 6:30 and reached Lamlash about 11, left my bag at the little inn, and walked
up to Glenkill House. My reception was as kind as it could be. . . . They had arranged a sail for the
afternoon. . . . [and it] gave me a further opportunity of taming the children, who are rather shy
at first, but the most unique 'children of nature' I ever saw, and perfectly charming. I was good
friends with all, when I left at night, chiefly however with the eldest girl, Mona. . . . The whole visit
was delightful. . . . Slept at Lamlash Inn." Eight days later, Dodgson, in Edinburgh, went "armed
with note from Sir Noël Paton, authorising me to have the key to his studio to look over his
portfolios. . . . In the afternoon I spent another two hours or so with . . . [his] drawings, and
enjoyed such a treat as I do not remember *ever* having had in any one day. The drawings are
perfectly exquisite, and almost come up to *my* highest ideals of beauty." Dodgson gives another
account of his visit with the Noël Patons in a long letter to his sister Mary (*Letters*, pp. 165–6): "The
eldest girl, Mona, about 11, would make a grand subject for a picture." He eventually did
photograph her, and in later years, she reminisced about Dodgson in a letter to *The Times* (March
27, 1928, p. 12): "I have . . . two photographs which he took of me in his rooms at Oxford, and of
which I do not approve, as I thought they made me uglier than I was. . . ."
[2] Two days later, Macmillan replies that sending out books to America "on sale" would be "no end
of labour and vexation" and that, furthermore, there were plans for the firm to sell directly in
America, "before long." Macmillan adds that Americans often prefer the English edition, even
though more expensive, and that when the firm began selling directly to America, it would be the
"genuine article" and not an inferior edition. Macmillan would open his New York office in the

autumn of this year, and the imprint "London and New York" appeared for the first time then. The American branch did not become a separate entity (Macmillan and Company of New York) until 1896, after Alexander Macmillan's death (see Morgan, pp. 83, 163–5).

The Chestnuts, Guildford
September 1, 1869

Dear Mr. Macmillan,

I called on Mr. Evans with your card – but the call has produced no result as yet. I think I told you the object of it. I heard accidentally that a Mr. J. Crawford Wilson had had a contribution to the *Gentleman's Magazine* accepted, in which he signed himself "Author of Alice in Wonderland."[1] A proof slip was sent by Messrs. Bradbury and Evans to the "care of Mrs. Gatty," which led to my hearing of it.[2] I wrote to the Editor, enquiring about this Mr. Wilson, and should have thought he would at least have written to disclaim all knowledge of so dishonourable a transaction, and to express his regret that his *Magazine* should have been made the vehicle for it. I wrote to him July 10, and again (enclosing the note to Mr. Evans to forward) August 1, but not a word have I had in reply. On the 16th of August I wrote to Mr. Evans to ask if the letter had reached the Editor,[3] and to that also I have had no answer.

Will you kindly make out from Mr. Evans whether the note reached the Editor, and whether he means to say anything about it, or is content to have a construction put upon his silence which can hardly be a favorable one. I have done all I can to try and get an explanation in a private letter, and I see nothing to be done now but to publish all three letters, adding no comment except the fact that he has refused to answer them.

Please let me hear as soon as you can what you can make out about it, and believe me

Very truly yours,

C. L. Dodgson

---

[1] John Crawford Wilson (1825–90?) was the author of *Elsie; Flights to Fairyland, etc.* (1864), and the resemblance to the title of *Alice* may have led to some confusion in the editor's mind. We do not have Macmillan's reply, but the matter must have been resolved to Dodgson's satisfaction because he never publishes the three letters. Frederick Mullett "Pater" Evans (1804–70) was a partner in the firm of Bradbury and Evans, publishers of the *Gentleman's Magazine*.

[2] Mrs. Alfred Gatty, born Margaret Scott (1809–73), was founder and editor of *Aunt Judy's Magazine* (1866–85). The Gattys lived in Oxford, and Dodgson was well acquainted with them. In August 1867 Dodgson's "Castle Croquet: A Game for Four Players" appeared in *Aunt Judy's Magazine*, and in December of that year, his fairy tale "Bruno's Revenge" appeared. Earlier (June 1866), Mrs. Gatty published a lavish notice of *Alice* in her magazine. For more on Dodgson and the Gattys and for his contributions to the magazine, see *Handbook*, pp. 43–4; *Letters*, esp. pp. 148–9.

[3] Joseph Hatton (1841–1907), author and journalist, edited the *Gentleman's Magazine* from 1868 to 1874.

Christ Church, Oxford
April 15, 1870

Dear Mr. Macmillan,

My title-page hasn't had fair play yet – as the printer doesn't follow out my directions.[1] I want the large capitals to have *more below the line than above*: nearly twice as much. In the corrected copy I send the A and F have slipped a little lower than I meant: the others are about right.

Secondly, the "AND" ought to be half-way between the two lines, and not (as they have printed it) nearer to the upper line.

Thirdly, the 3 lines of title ought to be closer together and not so close to the top of the page.

Fourthly, the comma and full-stop ought to be set lower.

All the above faults I have endeavoured to remedy in the corrected copy I enclose.

I send an uncorrected one with it that you may see the difference.

As to the picture-title you suggested, I forgot to tell you a circumstance which puts an end to the idea at once. Mr. Tenniel has drawn a picture of the looking-glass, with Alice getting through it, to come in at page 11. It will not do to have two different pictures of the same thing.

I am sorry you have given any more thought to the "copyright" subject. My curiosity is quite satisfied, and (as I said before) I have not the least idea of really selling it.[2]

I will ask my Italian friend (Signor T. Pietrocòla Rossetti) if he can give any advice about a publisher.[3]

His own translation of his cousin's *Goblin Market* is printed (and I suppose published) at Firenze. But can't *you* manage that part of the business? Is there no great publisher at Rome you could apply to?

Very truly yours,

C. L. Dodgson

P.S. I have finally abandoned the idea that alarmed you so much, of petitioning for photographs.[4]

I want to have the presentation-copy of the *Looking-Glass* (I mean the one for Miss A. Liddell) bound with an oval piece of looking-glass let into the cover. Will you consult your binder as to whether the thing is practicable? It should not be larger, I think, in proportion to the book, than I have here drawn it.

¹ Two days earlier, Macmillan sent copies of two styles of the title page for *Looking-Glass* for Dodgson to consider. Dodgson must have written numerous letters about the book as it took shape during these early months of 1870, but most are missing. Macmillan's to Dodgson survive as copies in the letter books. The publisher takes a keen interest in deciding the title of the sequel to *Alice*. "The title you chose at first is admirable," he writes on March 21. "The printer has not arranged it as he might. You shall see it in a modified form. *Behind the Looking-Glass & what Alice saw there* is quite perfect." Three days later, he returns to the subject: ". . . as to the main title I decidedly prefer the first form of words: 'Behind the Looking-Glass.' 'Looking-Glass World' is too specific. You answer that there is a *world*. In the first title there is a charming vagueness which I think wholly harmonizes with your peculiar humour. . . . But of course you know your own ideas best. I will content myself with saying that I shall regret it if you do change the title." Dodgson must have written the day earlier or that same day suggesting another change to the title, and Macmillan replied at 4:30 in the afternoon: "Your new title is admirable. You shall see a proof at once. '*Through*' is just the word – you'll never beat it."

² Dodgson must have asked Macmillan to estimate the value of the *Alice* copyright, and on April 12, he replied somewhat astonished: "*Alice*! What is she worth? Who knows! If you want to sell I will give you £1000. I don't think I would like to give more. There are limits to most things. Others might give a little more. But there or thereabout is right." Macmillan returned to the subject two days later: "I have thought a good deal about the value of *Alice*'s copyright. I fancy it would bring about £1000 – maybe £1200."

³ Teodorico Pietrocòla-Rossetti (1828?-83) was a first cousin of the famous Rossettis. He translated Christina Rossetti's *Goblin Market* and would, in time, translate *Alice* into Italian. Dodgson must have met him at the Rossettis'. ". . . a man of more native unselfish kindliness, of stricter morals, or of nicer conscientiousness never breathed," William Michael Rossetti wrote of him, and reported that after living a time in England "without getting into any successful groove of employment," he returned to Italy (*Dante Gabriel Rossetti as Designer and Writer* (1889), p. 12; *Dante Gabriel Rossetti: His Family Letters*, 2 vols. (1895), I, 34–5).

⁴ Dodgson apparently suggested inserting a message in all copies of *Alice* asking each child reader to send him a photograph in care of Macmillan and Company. In his reply to this proposal (March 3), Macmillan wrote: "Did you ever take a Shower Bath? Or do you remember your first? To appeal to all your young admirers for their photograph! If your Shower Bath were filled a-top with bricks instead of water it would be about the fate you court! But if you will do it, there is no help for it, and as in duty bound we will help you to the self-immolation. Cartes! I should think so, indeed – cart loads of them. Think of the postmen. Open an office for relief at the North Pole and another at the Equator. Ask President Grant, the Emperor of China, the Governor General of India, the whatever do you call him of Melbourne, if they won't help you. But it's no use remonstrating with you. But I am resigned. I return from Scotland next Monday a week. I shall be braced for encountering this awful idea."

Christ Church, Oxford
April 21, 1870

Dear Mr. Macmillan,

　　I have received a bundle of 30 title-pages, which I fear are of no use – first, because they repeat the arrangement we rejected long ago, of having the preposition in one line, and THE LOOKING-GLASS in the next line, and next because they omit the second half of the title altogether. The enclosed piece of patchwork represents tolerably what I suggested when I called the other day.¹

　　If you think there is any chance of its being a success, you might have it tried. Twenty copies of any one kind are quite enough for me.

I don't quite like Mrs. Hart not being informed that you have told me the authorship. Some day she or Miss Smedley will be telling me the fact, and then they will see that I have known it before.² Couldn't you tell her or let me do it?

Very truly yours,

C. L. Dodgson

¹ In mid-April Dodgson spent a few days with his family at Guildford and, although no record of a visit to his publisher appears in his Diaries, he probably went up to town and met with Macmillan.

² Elizabeth Anna Hart (1822–90?), Dodgson's cousin, was the wife of Thomas Barnard Hart (1804–80?), an officer in the Indian Army. With her older sister, Menella Bute Smedley, she wrote *Child-World*, a book of verse that contains an early reference to *Alice*; she is also the author of *The Runaway: A Story for the Young* (1872), which Dodgson later recommends to a friend (*Letters*, p. 181). *Poems Written for a Child* was published in 1868, and the title page reads "By Two Friends." Macmillan must have revealed to Dodgson when they met that the authors were Miss Smedley and Mrs. Hart. For more on Mrs. Hart, see Roger Lancelyn Green, *Tellers of Tales*, 4th ed. (1965), pp. 47–8, 93–5, 283.

Christ Church, Oxford

May 1, 1870

Dear Mr. Macmillan,

I am told that Messrs. Clarke & Co., of 13 Fleet Street, are printing in a penny weekly paper, called *Happy Hours*, what they call "extracts" from *Alice in Wonderland*, but what my friend tells me really *are* the book itself. Will you look into the matter. Such a publication is scarcely likely to affect the sale, I suppose: still it won't do to let the law of copyright be infringed.¹

Very Truly yours,

C. L. Dodgson

P.S. When we have the first sheet of the new Volume ready to print, what do you think of electro-typing it, and *at once* printing off 8000 impressions (good) and 5000 (cheap). This would save time very much, if you think it safe to print the sheets at different times.² We might thus perhaps print off Sheet 1 this month, though the last sheet might not be ready to print till August.

¹ *Happy Hours*, a weekly paper for children, published by James Clarke and Co., 13 Fleet Street, printed four long extracts from *Alice* in March and April 1870, as follows:

March 19 "Down the Well" (pp. 188–90);
March 26 "What Happened There" (pp. 206–7);
April 2   "A Mad Tea Party" (pp. 219–21);
April 9   "The Mock-Turtle's Story" (pp. 236–9).

The first installment was preceded by the following: "Perhaps no fairy story in modern times has attained more world-wide celebrity than this relation of Alice's remarkable adventures in the kingdom of the marvellous. No cheap edition has yet appeared of it, and, as its price makes its circulation rather exclusive, a slight sketch of the story, and a few quotations from its fascinating pages, may not be unwelcome to our little readers." In Macmillan's reply the following day, he agrees that this was an "undoubted theft, and a very good one"; he reports that he has written to Clarke and Co. for an explanation. On May 5 Macmillan writes again on the subject, apparently enclosing Clarke and Co.'s reply (missing). Macmillan comments on Clarke and Co.'s defense: "This seems to me a very lame explanation. The 'rather inexperienced editor' went on through four weeks deliberately stealing your book and added the increased insult – that it was because you had no cheap edition. If you like I will instruct my solicitor to demand a sum of money, the suppression of all those numbers, or be content with an apology. I am disposed to demand the suppression of the numbers. If the inexperienced editor becomes experienced in that sort of thing one hardly sees the end of it. Those obscure papers may go on reprinting whatever they like. Tell me what you think."

2 Macmillan replies that no time would be saved by Dodgson's plan and it would cause unnecessary expense.

Christ Church, Oxford

August 8, 1870

Dear Mr. Macmillan,

I am getting more and more down-hearted about my brother:[1] his present life of "nothing to do" is so very bad for him, that I would gladly see him in *work* of any kind, however little pay he got for it. Now it is "borne in upon me" (as Henry Kingsley would say)[2] that *your* house *might* furnish an opening for him that would be just the thing: it is a line of business that would suit him well, and a prospect of some day (supposing he turned out a good man of business) coming in for a partnership would be a very good "look-out" for him in the future. Couldn't you try him (if only temporarily) as a sort of clerk? Put him at a desk in your room, or Mr. Craik's (for I don't think he would like to go behind the counter), and give him accounts to keep, or letters to write, and you would be doing him a real service. Of course the pay would only be nominal till he had got into the way of the thing and had shown himself worth his salt.

He has plenty of brain power, particularly mathematical, and I think you would find him (after a time) really good as an accountant.

I hear that he went to see Mr. Amory,[3] but have heard nothing more. I hope Mr. Amory saw grounds for hope – but whatever chance hereafter presented itself elsewhere, would be all the better for a few years of preparatory work. Please think it over, and believe me

Very truly yours,

C. L. Dodgson

P.S. I am not telling him of this letter – and I think, if you *were* able to offer him any work, it would be pleasanter for him if you would make the offer direct from yourself, without allusion to me.[4]

---

1 Edwin Heron (1846–1918), Dodgson's youngest brother.
2 Dodgson and Henry Kingsley met at Freshwater on the Isle of Wight in August 1864 and remained on good terms thereafter. Dodgson is probably alluding to a favorite turn of phrase of Kingsley's (see *Diaries*, p. 221; *Letters*, pp. 81–3).

[3] Unidentified.

[4] Dodgson evidently approached Macmillan on Edwin's behalf earlier as well. "Nothing occurs to me at the moment that would suit your brother," Macmillan wrote on January 5, 1870, "but if he were in London sometime and could come and talk to me I might perhaps think of something. . . . It will be a pleasure to me if I can be of use." Although Macmillan's reply to this new approach is missing, a note across the top of Dodgson's letter in Macmillan's hand reads: "I have answered this direct. Of course we could not take him." On the following October 10, Dodgson announces "Edwin's commencement of a business-life, in the office of Mr. Ball, Accountant" (see *Diaries*, pp. 271, 273, 290). The young man was not, however, to remain in a business office long. In the autumn of 1871, he entered Chichester Theological College, and then, after holding a number of curacies, he went as a missionary, first, in 1879, to Zanzibar, and then, in 1881, to Tristan da Cunha. He remained there, except for brief visits to London in 1883 and 1885, until poor health and a deep desire to plead for the resettlement of the islanders brought him back to London in 1889. The story of the youngest of the Dodgsons has yet to be told adequately. He was, according to one account of his life at Tristan da Cunha, "beloved by the whole island as one of the saintliest of men": he re-established the defunct church there and served not only as spiritual leader and schoolmaster, but also as potato-patch digger, arbitrator, "postmaster, librarian, meteorologist, [and] social entertainer." In 1981, to celebrate the centenary of his arrival, Tristan da Cunha issued a series of stamps. For more about him, see *Letters*, esp. pp. 534–5; H. Martyn Rogers, "Life on the World's Loneliest Island . . . ," *Landmark*, 5 (1923), 587; Allan B. Crawford, *I Went to Tristan* (1941), pp. 63–4.

Christ Church, Oxford

February 3, 1871

Dear Mr. Macmillan,

In connection with the fact that French and German *Alice*s are occasionally used as lesson-books, and with the fact that my French translator complained of the difficulty of his task, owing to *Alice* being so very "idiomatic," an idea has occurred to me – to print (small and cheap, and without pictures) "Selections" from the book, with the French in a parallel column, for the use of those who wish to learn French for *conversational* purposes, for which it is a great help to know the equivalents for the English idioms that *will* keep occurring to the mind. And the same thing might be done with the German. Of course I should select only those portions that would go *well* into the other language, omitting all poetry and puns. My idea would be to have it a shilling book, as well got-up as can be fairly done for the money, and attractive-looking (perhaps in the same red cover as *Alice*). Not small type, or in any way looking like a common lesson-book. And with gilt edges.

That is my idea. Please think it over, and give me your opinion.[1] If you approve, send me an English and a French *Alice*, in sheets, and M. Bué and I will select a portion to be set up as an experiment.

Yours very truly,

C. L. Dodgson

[1] Macmillan's reply is missing, but the plan was not carried out in Dodgson's lifetime. Over half a century later, however, it was adopted by the Japanese and other foreign-language publishers (see Weaver, p. 46).

Christ Church, Oxford
February 27, 1871

Dear Mr. Macmillan,

I have an alteration to suggest in the arrangement you propose for the American edition of *Through the Looking-Glass*, which I think will be more satisfactory to both of us than your paying me a fixed sum of £10 per thousand.

I find that the actual result, with regard to the profits of *Alice*, has been very nearly the same thing, to both of us, as if we had arranged for you to take 25 per cent on the clear profits, instead of 10 per cent on the gross receipts. Now I don't want *that* arrangement altered; if we substituted the other plan, I should not feel free to insist on fine paper, etc., because I should feel that all extra expenditure was so much off *your* profits as well as off mine.

With regard to the American book, I suppose you will sell at a very small margin of profit, so that 10 per cent on the gross receipts would swallow up all the clear profit, and so make me always a loser. Therefore I don't propose to treat the American book as the English, but simply that you should have 25 per cent on the *clear* profits.

If the clear profits come to about £13 per thousand, the two plans would come to about the same thing – but if they come to much more, or much less, my plan will, I think, be a fairer division of profits than the fixed sum of £10 which you suggest.[1]

Very truly yours,

C. L. Dodgson

---

[1] Macmillan's reaction to Dodgson's proposal has not surfaced.

Christ Church, Oxford
March 8, 1871

Dear Mr. Macmillan,

I have considered the question again, and I really think that, with the matter so complicated and difficult to calculate as you say it is, we had better settle nothing just now. When a few thousands have been sold, we shall see more clearly what the clear profits (if any) are, and can then settle whether £10 is a fair sum to pay me per thousand. I rather expect it will turn out to be too much – but, however it turns out, we are not likely to quarrel for want of a previous settlement.

The book you send me (thanks for it) seems quite good enough in every way for a model for the American edition. I don't half like the idea you suggest, that the American and English editions will be so much alike that only very critical eyes can see the difference. Surely it says very little for English art that an "edition de luxe," where the intention is to produce a book as finely and perfectly finished as possible, should be indistinguishable from an avowedly "cheap" edition? And if this is so, does it not involve the danger of the cheap books returning into the English market? Of course we could not prevent their sale in England. If there is any risk of *this* result, I would rather not attempt an American edition at all. Believe me

Very truly yours,

C. L. Dodgson

Christ Church, Oxford

March 31, 1871

Dear Mr. Macmillan,

Unless it should happen that I have already given the order, will you please send a French and German *Alice*, to "Miss Timiriaseff – care of Rev. H. S. Thompson, English Church, St. Petersburg." She is the lady who, I believe, is going to translate *Alice* into Russian for me.[1]

No use for the printers to begin yet – while we are yet in the very midst of the pictures. The weeks and the months go by, but Mr. Tenniel makes no sign. I fear we shall not get the book out before Xmas if then.[2] Believe me

Very truly yours,

C. L. Dodgson

---

[1] The first Russian *Alice* is a rarity. Warren Weaver spent years searching for a copy. "At Sotheby's on March 3, 1958," he reports in 1964, "there was sold to Maggs . . . a Russian *Alice* dated 1879, having Tenniel illustrations. . . . I have tried for over a quarter of a century to obtain copies of the early Russian editions . . . , prowling the old book shops around the Baltic, in the Russian community in Paris, and elsewhere. I ran an advertisement in a Russian newspaper printed in New York," but all was in vain (Weaver, p. 61). August A. Imholtz, Jr. took up the search more recently and has acquired a microfilm of the copy in the Leningrad State Library. Irony of ironies is that the Berol Collection at New York University contains a copy of the rare edition, perhaps the one sold at Sotheby's in 1958 and probably the only one in the West. It indicates clearly that the book was published in Moscow in 1879, but the translator's name does not appear. We cannot account for the lack of additional information about the translation or the translator in Dodgson's letters and Diaries, nor can we account for the seven-year gap between Dodgson's reference here to the translator and the publication date. (Special thanks to Frank Walker, Fales Librarian at New York University, for help with this knotty problem.)

[2] Although Dodgson had completed the text for *Looking-Glass*, publication was repeatedly delayed because Tenniel did not supply the pictures. On December 22, 1870, Dodgson wrote to Macmillan: "I am going to make a great effort to get the *Looking-Glass* out by Easter. Mr. Tenniel holds out hopes of the pictures being done." On January 15, 1871, Dodgson "sent the slips off to Tenniel: it all now depends upon him, whether we get the book out by Easter or not," he wrote in his *Diaries* (p. 295). "No more pictures have come from Tenniel," Dodgson noted on March 11 (ibid.); "my hopes are now postponed to midsummer." On May 4, Dodgson "heard from Tenniel

the other day, the welcome news that he hopes to have all the pictures done by the end of July at latest" (p. 298). But Dodgson had soon to abandon all hope of getting the book out before Christmas.

Christ Church, Oxford
April 5, 1871

Dear Mr. Craik,

(I address you instead of Mr. Macmillan, because I see the letter comes from you). I own to being surprised at finding that the "American" item was genuine after all: don't imagine me to be writing in a tone of resentment, but I certainly wish the matter had been referred to me before anything was done about it. That I think (considering that I take the whole expense and risk of the book) would have been the best course.

However, the thing is done, and I don't want to quarrel about it, even though the "publisher's 10 per cent" in this case comes partly out of my pocket. But with regard to the future, I must distinctly demur to any such sale – or to any copies being sold *anywhere* at a less price than the regular 4*s*. 2*d*.

Please tell me if you think that I am insisting on more than, as author, I have a fair right to do.

Very probably you will tell me that, unless we let the Americans have them at a lower rate, they will not take them at all. But this would not alter my view of the matter. I am by no means anxious that they *should* take them. And even looking at the thing from a commercial point of view, it seems unwise, when we are intending to send them the new volume on *cheap* paper, to be supplying them with this volume on the *best* paper, and yet at the price of a cheap book.[1]

Hoping to hear from you that you undertake that no more copies shall be sold, whether in America or elsewhere, at less than the 4*s*. 2*d*. you have hitherto sold at, and also that I have not written in too violently aggrieved a tone, I remain

Very truly yours,

C. L. Dodgson

Please let me know how many *Alice*s have been sold *this year*.[2] You give the number since last July, which is not the information I want.

---

[1] Evidently Dodgson somehow learned that Macmillan was allowing *Alice* to be sold in the U.S.A. for a lower price than in England, but we do not have the earlier exchange on the subject. Macmillan himself replied, twice it seems, in the following few days. In a letter with an unclear date, he writes: "You must come and talk the matter over. I confess I have been acting as I thought in accordance with your wishes. . . . Can you come . . . one day next week and go into the subject? Perhaps you can arrange to spend a night at my house as you have more than once half promised to do." Dodgson must have replied that he could not take the time for a journey to London, and on

April 11, Macmillan writes again: ". . . surely you gave me more than once, continually indeed, power to operate in America in such a way as to meet the chances of piracy." He points out that "we made some reasonable profit for you" because "we were at liberty to send out copies at the lowest rate compatible with this end." Again he urges Dodgson to come and talk about the matter, and he adds, "If we sell at 4*s*. 2*d*., we can do *no* American business I fear."

² Macmillan answers the question in a postscript to his April 11 letter: "We have sold since 1 January about 1100 against about 1200 at the same time last year."

Christ Church, Oxford
April 13, 1871

Dear Mr. Macmillan,

I must begin by begging your pardon for having complained without cause. No doubt (though I had forgotten it) I had said enough to warrant the American sale – that has taken place. Still, with regard to the *future*, I would rather have an altogether different arrangement – that is to say:

(1) As to quality of book. I hold to my objection against our selling one and the same book at two different prices. If you think it well to print some on a cheaper paper, and with cheaper binding, I do not object to *their* being sold in America at whatever lower rate you choose to fix. But, whatever I may have said before, I cannot any longer consent to having the *genuine* edition sold cheap.

(2) As to division of profit. As I said with regard to the *Looking-Glass*, the regular arrangement does very well so long as the profits are large as compared with the outlay: in which case you get (say) ¼ of the *clear* profits. I have never looked into the matter or cared much about it, but I am quite confident to acquiesce in *that* result as fair enough for both of us. But when the profits are so small that 10 per cent on the gross receipts is the greater part of (or even more than the whole amount of) the clear profits, it becomes unreasonable. I therefore propose, as to *this* American sale, identically what I proposed as to the American sale of the *Looking-Glass* (still far in the future, I fear!) namely, that you should have ¼ of the *clear* profits, *if any*. If you agree to this, no more need be said, and you can print some cheap ones at once (*taking strict care that none of them are sold in England*): if not, I think I should prefer there being *no* American sale at all. Thanks for information about *Alice*.

Very truly yours,
C. L. Dodgson

Christ Church, Oxford
April 19, 1871

Dear Mr. Macmillan,

I fear we can't have much *talking* at present – unless you come to Oxford. I don't see my way to coming to town till about the middle of June. But if my proposal is not a fair one, by all means make another. I took as *my* basis of calculation the facts about the English *Alice* – which are, taking the gross receipts at 100

expenses	60
publisher	10
author	30
	100

If that *is* a fair arrangement (I assumed it to be so), it doesn't matter, so long as the expenses are 60 per cent on the receipts, whether you take 10 per cent on the *whole* or $\frac{1}{4}$ of the clear profits. But when, as in the cheap editions, the expenses come much nearer to the receipts, the first arrangement seems to me to become less and less reasonable, until the expenses are 90 per cent when we have –

expenses	90
publisher	10
author	0
	100

which I may conclude like a proposition of Euclid, with the words "which is absurd"!

I shall be very glad to know your views as to this way of putting it – and I am by no means sure that it isn't the better and clearer way to have it all in black (I should say "blue")[1] and white.[2]

Very truly yours,

C. L. Dodgson

[1] "Roughly speaking, Carroll used black ink (often faded to brownish) until and including October 10, 1870: then purple ink until about the end of 1890: and then black again until his death," Warren Weaver writes ("Ink (and Pen) Used by Lewis Carroll," *Jabberwocky*, 4 (Winter 1975), 3–4). The first appearance of Dodgson's "blue" (usually characterized as purple, but also as lavender and mauve) in the Rosenbach Dodgson–Macmillan archive is in Dodgson's letter to Macmillan dated December 22, 1870.

[2] "Of course we will act on your instructions," Macmillan replies five days later. "There is no doubt that it is and will be better to print cheaper editions in America, and before the *Looking-Glass* comes we will have an opportunity of discussing the question fully."

Christ Church, Oxford

April 26, 1871

Dear Mr. Macmillan,

The question of selling copies cheap in America is a wider one than I fancied, and had better be all settled at once.

(1) *Alice in French* cost me in printing, etc., 2*s*. 8*d*. a copy. I see you have sold 22 in America at 2*s*. 3*d*. The transaction bringing you 4*s*. 10*d*. as commission, and involving a loss to me of 9*s*. 2*d*.

(2) *Phantasmagoria* – cost me 2*s*. 6*d*. a copy. American sale, 57 at 1*s*. 10*d*. Your profits being 10*s*. 5*d*., my loss £1.18.0.

(3) *Determinants* cost me 6*s*. a copy. American sale, 7 at 2*s*. 6*d*. Your profit being 1*s*. 8*d*., and my loss £1.4.6.

Thus on the 3 transactions your entire profit was 16*s*. 11*d*. while my loss was £3.11.8.

Your profits being so *very* small on the whole transaction, and my loss being so considerable in comparison, I feel no scruple in putting an end to *that* mode of sale altogether, and saying "sell *none* of my books, in America or elsewhere (unless printed cheap for the purpose) at a lower rate than in England." And as to copies printed cheap, it is clear to me that we *must* have some other arrangement than the usual 10 per cent on the gross receipts. I don't want to take up literature in a money-making spirit, or be very anxious about making large profits, but selling at a loss is another thing altogether, and an amusement I cannot well afford.[1]

Yours very truly,

C. L. Dodgson

[1] Macmillan replies the following day pointing out that Dodgson has "overlooked two considerations affecting the questions of profit and loss to us and to you." (1) "A book is not necessarily worth what it cost"; and (2) Macmillan, as publisher, cannot calculate profit *"till we sell.* The beautifullest egg in the world may be in my hand and a broad built mother hen anxious to hatch it," he adds. "I need not apply the moral. But we are not likely to be called in . . . to act again in this matter before I see you. . . . You have put this in our hands, and therefore I did not consult you in each transaction. But of course I gladly give you explanations when anything seems to you difficult or needing explanation. As I said before, a very few moments' talk would settle matters much more clearly."

Christ Church, Oxford

April 28, 1871

Dear Mr. Macmillan,

Thanks for your letter. *One* good would certainly have followed a viva voce talk, that I should not have given you (as I fear I may now have done) an impression that I was in some sort finding fault with what has been done. I didn't mean *that* in the least. I began dealing with your house with full confidence in it in every way – and that confidence is undiminished. All my reasoning was to justify the course I wished pursued for the *future*. I *had* fully considered the argument you mention (that the books, at least the *Determinants*, wouldn't otherwise sell *at all*) and it doesn't alter my decision. My conclusion *may* be only sentimental, though I believe it may be defended on purely commercial grounds as well.

The argument you mention (that you get no profit till a sale has actually occurred) I admit as perfectly true, whether for you or for me, but I confess I *don't* see what it proves.

I suppose we may now consider the question of American sale, for *Phantasmagoria, Determinants,* and *Alice,* as closed – unless you propose to print cheap editions.

As to the projected cheap *Looking-Glass* I wait to hear what arrangement you propose for profits. In great haste

Very truly yours,
C. L. Dodgson

Christ Church, Oxford
May 19, 1871

Dear Mr. Macmillan,

The other day I gave a little dinner-party of 8, and tried an invention of mine, which was so highly approved of, that I think it worth writing to you about.

It is simply to draw up a plan of the table, with the names of the guests, in the order in which they are to sit, and brackets to show who is to take in whom; and that one should be given to each guest (though I only wrote mine once for all).

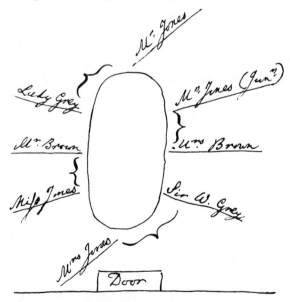

The above will give you a rough idea of what I mean. In the centre (or on the other side) there would be room to write the bill of fare.

Now for the advantages of this plan.

(1) It saves the host the worry of going round and telling every gentleman what lady to take in.

(2) It prevents confusion when they reach the dining-room. (The system of putting names round on the plates simply increases the confusion. Though it would work well *with* this plan.)

(3) It enables everybody at table to know who the other guests are – often a *very* desirable thing.

(4) By keeping the cards, one gets materials for making up other dinner-parties, by observing what people harmonise well together.

I think it would be a good thing to publish such cards, with ornamental borders, and with lines ruled for names, for parties of 8, 10, 12, 14, 16. I fancy they would become popular and sell well.

It isn't a thing I care to make any profit by, and if *you* like to bring the thing out, you are very welcome to it. If not, who would be best to write to? Jenner and Knewstub?[1]

Is it a thing capable of being "entered at Stationer's Hall" and so made copyright? If so, please *enter* it at once (whether you publish it or not) lest some unauthorized person should appropriate the whole idea.[2]

Very truly yours,

C. L. Dodgson

---

[1] Retail stationers, 66 Jermyn Street, London.

[2] "Your ingenious dinner card idea seems worth considering," Macmillan writes four days later. ". . . We could do nothing with it of course. But if you don't mind I will suggest it to some stationer who deals in cards." In the same letter: "You could not copyright it, I think, but I will show it to no one. . . ." Six months later, on November 24, Macmillan replies to what must have been an inquiry from Dodgson about the status of the dinner card idea. He reports that he had submitted the card to a stationer "who deals largely in such things," but had been told that "he cannot think of it now. They are all full of work [just before Christmas]. Meanwhile he gave us the enclosed [missing] which in some degree anticipates your idea." The card was apparently never published. Dodgson records "his little dinner-party of 8" in his Diaries for May 15. The diagram there bears the names of his guests (including three of Dodgson's sisters, his brother Wilfred, Friedrich Max Müller, the orientalist-philologist, and his wife, and Dr. Franz Kielhorn, the Sanscrit authority); the one he sends to Macmillan in this letter bears fictitious names of course.

Christ Church, Oxford

December 17, 1871[1]

My dear Mr. Macmillan,

I have a very important matter to write to you about: so let me dismiss minor matters first.

The 10 copies have come safe, and will last me for a long time to come.[2]

A copy of the *Athenaeum* was sent me by Mr. Ralston, who wrote the review:[3] but the *Globe*, *Examiner*, and *Illustrated*, I should be glad to have – as well as any other periodicals which may contain reviews: you need not ask the question in each case: send *all*.[4]

Twenty-one of the copies sent me have been taken off my hands by my friends, and as I charged them the full price, I shall feel happier about this part of the transaction if you will debit me in your account next month (as I have already credited you in my private account) with 12*s*. 7*d*. – as your percentage on the receipts.

Now for the real subject of this letter.

I have been thinking a good deal about the pictures, and the best way to secure their being really artistically done: I have no doubt that what you told me of, the pressing between sheets of blank paper in order to dry for binding, is the real cause of all the "inequality," which has so vexed Mr. Tenniel in the copies already done: indeed I can see for myself that several of the pictures have in this way quite lost all *brilliance* of effect.

I have now made up my mind that, whatever be the *commercial* consequences, we must have no more artistic "fiascos" – and I am stimulated to write *at once* about it by your alarming words of this morning, "We are going on with another 6000 *as fast as possible*." My decision is, we must have *no more hurry*: and *no more sheets must be pressed under blank paper*. It is my *particular desire* that all the sheets shall in future be "stacked" and let to dry naturally. The result of this may possibly be that the 6000 will not be ready for sale till the end of January or even later. Very well: then fix that date in your advertisement: say that "owing to the delay necessary to give the pictures their full artistic effect, no more copies can be delivered until the end of January."[5]

You will think me a lunatic for thus wishing to send away money from the doors; and will tell me perhaps that I shall thus lose thousands of would-be purchasers, who will not wait so long, but will go and buy other Christmas-books. I wish I could put into words how entirely such arguments go for nothing with me. As to how many copies we sell I care absolutely nothing: the only thing I *do* care for is, that all the copies that *are* sold shall be artistically first-rate.

I am afraid you will be able to urge that I am thus diminishing *your* profits, as well as my own: but I must beg you to bear this for a little while: you will not lose in the long run, I think.

I have already had a bitter lesson in this matter, with *Alice's Adventures*. With all my efforts to keep it up to a high artistic mark, I was baffled at last by that sudden demand (which ought never to have been met!) which led to the working off 3000 in a great hurry. The consequence was, a blow to the artistic reputation of the book which I doubt if it will *ever* quite recover: a general impression got abroad that "the plates were failing, and that the only chance to get a *good* copy was to find one of the earlier thousands." How gladly I would sacrifice *double* the profit which that unfortunate 3000 brought in, if I could only annihilate them off the face of the earth![6]

If any of the sheets of the new 6000 have been already "pressed," and if the pictures seem to have been at all seriously affected by it, these sheets must be destroyed and printed again. Of course *I* pay every penny of the loss entailed by this: it is no fault of Messrs. Clay.

I have written at this length in order to set my reasons fully before you, and to show you how strongly I feel in the matter – and how entirely careless I am how it affects the profit. Indeed, I consider the point as an *essential* one in our relations as publisher and author, and must beg you (with a view to a perfect understanding in the future) to give me your assurance in writing that *"no* copies, either of *Wonderland* or of the *Looking-Glass,* shall in future be dried by pressure under blank paper, but that they shall be stacked and let to dry naturally."

To save time, as the mischief may be going on from hour to hour, I am writing by the same post to Messrs. Clay, directing that no more sheets shall be pressed under blank paper.

Very truly yours,

C. L. Dodgson

---

¹ Although we have no letters from Dodgson to Macmillan for the previous seven months, letters from Macmillan to Dodgson show that Dodgson continued to write to his publisher, chiefly about reprinting *Alice* for Christmas and getting *Looking-Glass* published. At one stage, Dodgson must have considered delaying the publication of *Looking-Glass,* concerned as he always was that haste in printing would result in an inferior book. Macmillan's reply is dated November 6, 1871: "What do I think? That your proposal is worse than the cruellest ogre ever conceived in darkest and most malignant moods. What do I think? Why, half the children will be laid up with pure vexation and anguish of spirit. Plum pudding of the delicatest, toys the most elaborate will have no charms. Darkness will come over all hearths, gloom will hover over the brightest boards. Don't think of it for a moment. The book must come out for Christmas or I don't know what will be the consequence. . . . Don't for any sake keep it back."

² "Heard from Macmillan that they already have orders for 7500 *Looking-Glasses* (they printed 9000), and are at once going to print 6000 more!" Dodgson recorded in his *Diaries* (p. 306) on November 30. Six days later, he "received the first complete copy of the *Looking-Glass*" (ibid.), and two days after that, on December 8, he "received from Macmillan 3 *Looking-Glasses* in morocco, and 100 in cloth. I first sent off 3 to the Deanery (the one for Alice being in morocco), and then sent to friends in Christ Church and to Parker's [Oxford booksellers and stationers] to be packed for book-post, 95 in cloth and 2 in morocco (for Florence Terry and Tennyson), making a total of 99 given away in one day . . ." (pp. 306–7). While selling briskly before Christmas 1871, *Through the Looking-Glass and What Alice Found There,* with fifty illustrations by John Tenniel, bears 1872 on its title page. Dodgson must have asked Macmillan for another ten copies in an earlier letter. On the 16th, Macmillan replied: "The ten shall go to you today, but please don't ask for any more now. We shall want every copy we have, and a good many more before Christmas." For more on the evolution and publishing history of *Looking-Glass,* see *Handbook,* pp. 61–8.

³ William Ralston (1828–89), a Cambridge graduate, was a librarian at the British Museum and a self-taught Russian scholar who specialized in folk and fairy tales. He published an edition of *Kriloff and His Fables* (1868) and *Songs of the Russian People* (1872). Dodgson first met him at the home of George MacDonald and in November 1871 recorded going to hear Ralston tell stories from the Russian to children. In his *Diaries* (pp. 305–6), he notes that "two of them, 'The Demon and the Blacksmith' and 'The Princess Anastasia' will do, with some modification, for telling to little friends." In his unsigned review of *Looking-Glass* (*Athenaeum,* December 16, 1871, pp. 787–8), Ralston wrote: "It is with no mere book that we have to deal here . . . but with the potentiality of happiness for countless thousands of children of all ages. . . ."

4 *Looking-Glass* was well received. The three notices that Dodgson mentions here typify the critical response to Alice's further adventures. The *Globe* (December 15, 1871, p. 3) promised that admirers of Alice would find "the same natural, sensible, simple child that she was when they were first introduced to her" and praised her creator's inventiveness: "It has been said that to write good nonsense is as difficult as to write good sense, but it must be more difficult, as there are very few who deal in the commodity so successfully as Mr. Carroll." The *Examiner* (December 16, 1871, p. 1250) found the sequel "hardly as good" as the original but "quite good enough to delight every sensible reader of any age." The notice praised the "wit and humour that all children can appreciate, and grown folks ought as thoroughly to enjoy." The *Illustrated London News* (December 16, 1871, p. 599) heaped lavish praise upon both book and author: "Who has been with Alice in Wonderland, under the clever guidance of Mr. Lewis Carroll, and has not felt the delight of sympathising with an infant's fresh pleasure in the novelties, the oddities, the impossibilities of fancy innocently wild? . . . Mr. Carroll is a master of this kind of agreeable nonsense, which he manages more effectively as he possesses the trained intellect of a scholar, with the serious poetic imagination and some insight into metaphysical questions, such as are apt to beset the debatable ground between nonsense and philosophic truth. His new story . . . is quite as rich in humorous whims of fancy, quite as laughable in its queer incidents, as lovable for its pleasant spirit and graceful manner as the wondrous tale of Alice's former adventures underground."

5 The day before Dodgson writes this letter, Macmillan wrote him: "We are going on with another 6000 as fast as possible, but I greatly fear we cannot possibly have them before Christmas." In reply to the present letter, Macmillan writes the following day, saying that he has "looked into the question" that Dodgson raised, had an artist inspect the book, who assured him "the cuts [were] *beautifully printed*. On the whole," Macmillan adds, "I do think they are." Macmillan consulted the printer, who "thinks he can fulfil your requirements and let us have copies so as to be on sale by January 23." Macmillan seeks to assuage Dodgson's fears: "I fully appreciate your desire for excellence, and really do not feel inclined to press our own interests against your high aim." But Tenniel must have had his own objections and transmitted them to Dodgson who, in turn, must have relayed them to Macmillan. Three days later, on the 21st, Macmillan writes: "I think Mr. Tenniel hardly realizes all the conditions needful for producing a book like *Through the Looking-Glass.*"

6 We cannot tell precisely which printing Dodgson refers to here, but two letters from the House of Macmillan may be relevant: on September 5, 1871, Craik wrote: "The imperfect printing in the 27th 1000 was no doubt owing to some wearing or breakage in the finer lines in the electro-blocks"; and on November 10, 1871, Macmillan wrote: "I wish you would ask your friend about the *29th thousandth* copy. If it is really so I should be glad to see it."

Christ Church, Oxford
November 26, 1872[1]

Dear Mr. Macmillan,

Will you kindly, with all reasonable expedition on receipt of this, engage a couple of copying-clerks, and have *all* the speeches in *Alice* and the *Looking-Glass* written out, with the names of the speakers, and such directions as "Enter the White Rabbit," "Exit the Red Queen," in the ordinary dramatic form, *and get them registered as two dramas*, with the same names as the books. I am told that is the only way to retain a right to forbid their being represented by any one who may choose to dramatise them. I trust to you to get it all done in such a way as will satisfy the requirements of the law. Please put in *all* the speeches.[2] In haste.

Very truly yours,
C. L. Dodgson

¹ Our files contain only two letters from Dodgson to Macmillan for the calendar year 1872, but letters from Macmillan catalogue a regular exchange of correspondence throughout, principally concerned with sales and additional printings of *Looking-Glass* and with bringing out the Italian *Alice*, translated by T. Pietrocòla-Rossetti. Dodgson received his first copy of it on March 20, 1872 (see *Handbook*, pp. 68–9).

² On October 18, 1872, Dodgson wrote to the novelist and critic Percy Fitzgerald (1834–1925), having read his *The Principles of Comedy and Dramatic Effect* (1870), to ask whether the *Alice* books would make suitable stage vehicles (see *Letters*, p. 180). Fitzgerald believed that the books would suit the stage, and Dodgson registered them as dramas "with a view to keeping control over *this* process" (*Diaries*, p. 315). On the same day that Dodgson writes this letter, Macmillan replies: "Your letter has just come to hand and I will carry out your wishes at once. [I understand that] . . . Wilkie Collins protects himself in this way, and effectually. But when I have had the copying of the conversation done I will send it down to you. You ought then I fancy to add 'stage directions' and the like and then come up to town and you and I can go down together to Stationers' Hall and make you quite secure." In a last paragraph, Macmillan adds: "It will be worth while considering whether you might not *next year* publish them both as dramas." On December 2 Macmillan writes again, telling Dodgson that the "copying of your dialogue is a longer job than we thought, but it is being done and will be ready in the course of this week. I understand that in order to secure the copyright to yourself, *you* should take it to Stationers' Hall and sign the book. Can you come up for that purpose?" On December 26, Dodgson writes in his *Diaries* (p. 315): "I went up once to London during Term – to register as dramas *Alice* and the *Looking-Glass*." He learns five years later, however, that he has not secured adequate protection of the copyright (see p. 142, below).

Private

Christ Church, Oxford
November 28, 1872

Dear Mr. Macmillan,

I want you to execute a little commission for me, in the printing department, *and to keep a secret*. The enclosed MS is a burlesque on the proceedings of a very advanced school of reformers who met in London the other day, to consider the subject of the "re-distribution" of our revenues at Oxford and Cambridge, for the benefit of scientific men, who are not to teach, but only to "investigate." To me (and to others) this seems to savour a little too strongly of a very unscientific affection for the "loaves and fishes."¹ So that there is a grain of serious meaning in the burlesque: still I hope I have made the whole thing extravagant enough to show it is not to be literally interpreted, and so to save it from being personally offensive to any one.

If I get it printed here, people will guess the authorship, and I want to remain "incog." So what I want you to do is, to get it printed at Cambridge (no doubt they have many such squibs on the subjects of the day, just as we have here), and have it on sale at your establishment there. As the matter concerns Cambridge as much as Oxford, it will look quite natural to have it printed there, and it will throw people off the scent as to the authorship.

I suppose you could, in the ordinary routine of trade, and without exciting suspicion, send copies down to be on sale at the Oxford booksellers? To get the thing known of, I should like a single copy to be sent to each Combination-Room at Cambridge, and when copies are sent to Oxford, you might send directions that the same should be done here, only please take care to have "Cambridge" printed on it, so that it may be known to come from there.

I think it will about fill 4 pages of a quarto-sheet. Please have it done in nice readable type, on good paper, and let me have 50 copies.[2]

Let me know when you have managed the "dramatic" business.

How many *Looking-Glass*es are sold? Is there any prospect of much demand this Christmas?[3]

Very truly yours,

C. L. Dodgson

[1] Matthew 14:15–21, 15:32–8; Mark 6:34–44, 8:1–9; Luke 9:12–17; and John 6:5–13.

[2] Macmillan replies the following day that he has sent the manuscript on to his nephew at Cambridge, asking him to put it in the hands of a Cambridge printer and, of course, "to carry out all your instructions." On December 2 Macmillan writes again about the pamphlet, assuring Dodgson that he sent on to Cambridge "your corrections and your list of names for presentation." There is no mention of this burlesque in Dodgson's Diaries, but no diary entries appear between October 24 and December 26, 1872. The publication has never been identified, but it must, in fact, have been printed. A brief note from Macmillan on December 4 reads: "The enclosed, including a note from my nephew will I hope explain itself and be satisfactory. Your correction came too late" (see *Handbook*, pp. 71–2).

[3] Macmillan replies (December 2) that over 3000 copies were sold during the past five months, and there was a good stock on hand for Christmas.

Christ Church, Oxford

February 26, 1873

Dear Mr. Craik,

My sister, Mrs. Collingwood,[1] tells me she has received the little engraving of the "Sleeping Beauty." I cannot clearly remember whether it is *your* present to *me*, and *mine* to her, or whether you gave it to *her*.

In either case, the *frame* was my affair. What do I owe you for it?[2]

With kindest regards to Mrs. Craik, and love to Dorothy[3] (did you give her that little book?) I am

Sincerely yours,

C. L. Dodgson

P.S. Could not you and Mr. Macmillan make a computation as to how many *Alice*s and *Looking-Glass*es will probably sell between this and July, and print that number only, so as to be pretty nearly run out in June? The many thousands, that were "on hand" at the last June balance, were a cause of great and unnecessary loss to me.

[1] Dodgson's sister Mary Charlotte (1835–1911), fifth of the eleven children, married (1869) Charles Edward Stuart Collingwood (1831–98), Rector of Southwick, Sunderland.

² Craik replies the same day that he had given the engraving to Dodgson, "and so we got two blessings out of it." He adds that the cost of the frame would be added to Dodgson's account with Macmillan.

³ Dodgson was well acquainted with the fiction of Dinah Maria Mulock (1826–87) long before he met her and before she became Mrs. G. L. Craik. "I have been lately reading *The Head of the Family*," he wrote in his *Diaries* (p. 42) on March 3, 1855, when he was twenty-three. He called it "a really beautiful story," and after a lengthy critique, concluded that "the character of Ninian is best of all – it is good for anyone to read, even in fiction, a history of such earnest truth and heroism as his." On May 1 of the same year, he wrote (p. 49): "Today I finished reading *The Ogilvies*," which he did not think so good as *The Head of the Family*, but "on the whole it is a very clever and *healthy* story, well worth reading." On December 31, 1857, he records that he "finished reading *John Halifax*, which has pages of beautiful writing in it, as all of Miss Mulock's books have, and shows great power in drawing character" (p. 136). On April 6, 1865, having spent an evening with the MacDonalds, Dodgson records (p. 228) that Mrs. MacDonald "told me that Miss Mulock is going to marry a Mr. Craik," and on the following July 7, when he called at Macmillan's, he "met Mrs. Craik (Miss Mulock that was) whose husband has entered into partnership with Macmillan" (p. 232). Dodgson overlapped with the Craiks at the Noël Patons' in Scotland on September 15, 1871 (p. 304), and Dodgson spent two nights with the Craiks at their home in Beckenham from January 10 to 12 earlier in the year in which he writes here. On the Sunday, Dodgson recorded (p. 328): "Mrs. Craik took me to see a pretty sight, Dorothy asleep – and gave me a little book of verse she has written about her." In January 1869 the Craiks adopted a nine-month-old infant abandoned in a basket in their village and christened her Dorothy Mulock Craik. The Craiks call on Dodgson at Oxford on November 3, 1873 (p. 323), and on April 23, 1874, "Mrs. Craik . . . paid me a visit with her little Dorothy and Mona Paton, and I took photos of all" (Diaries). Again on March 17, 1879, "Mrs. Craik brought her little Dorothy in the morning, of whom I did a photo" (p. 378). In 1887 Dorothy Craik married Alexander John McDonnell Pilkington (b. 1863), a distant cousin of Mrs. Craik. "Yes," Craik replies (in the same letter as above) to Dodgson's query: "Dorothy got and was delighted with the [unidentified] little book. Thanks for it."

2 Wellington Square, Hastings
April 11, 1873

Dear Mr. Craik,[1]

I daresay you are quite right in advising against complying with Tauchnitz's application, but at present I am rather in the dark about the matter. Would you kindly answer me the following questions?

Is it not the case that, whether I give leave or not, he is equally free to *print* the book? If so, I don't see why he asks leave, unless out of civility.

Assuming that, even without leave, he can print and sell the book *abroad*, I then want to know whether the leave affects its introduction into *England*. If I gave leave to publish, could it then be lawfully imported and sold in *England*? Of course it would never do to allow this, as it would diminish our own sale.[2]

If, however, you tell me that under no circumstances could the foreign edition be sold in England, I should then like to know whether you think its sale abroad (supposing it printed with genuine electros) would affect us at all.

I have an idea that the Tauchnitz books cannot lawfully be brought into England, even as private property, and if so, it seems that we should be so little affected by the sale that we might reasonably afford to give leave, and even to sell electros.[3] I wish I could talk to you about it. A few words viva voce would be better than whole strings of hypothetical questions. But I don't know when I am likely to be in town again.

Very truly yours,

C. L. Dodgson

[1] Alexander Macmillan was away on a holiday in Italy. On March 13 Macmillan wrote to say that Dodgson would "find our dear friend Craik up to any emergency I am sure, during my absence."
[2] Craik replies the following day that it would be illegal to import a foreign edition, and although travelers might bring in a few copies, the English sale would not be hurt.
[3] Tauchnitz had applied for permission to publish *Alice*, and Craik had written (the day before Dodgson writes here) suggesting that Dodgson would probably not care to take up the application because "Tauchnitz prints in a very common way and I doubt if you would like to see this." He also assured Dodgson, however, that "unless you gave your consent you never would see it because Tauchnitz is a man of high honour and even though he had the right would not print without your consent." Craik's urging seems to have prevailed, and Tauchnitz never published *Alice* or anything else by Carroll.

Christ Church, Oxford
October 17, 1874[1]

Dear Mr. Craik,

Thanks for your letter and explanations of the accounts.[2] I was not so much dwelling on the wisdom or unwisdom of printing 6000 at once, as on the fact that we had agreed otherwise (but possibly this was *since* the printing), and agreements, whether wise or unwise, should only be altered by mutual consent. So long as this principle is observed, I will cheerfully bear the loss caused by a mistaken arrangement. So once more, please let it be clearly understood for the future that *I do not consent to printing more than 3000 in a set.*

You say that printing 6000 at once is "cheaper" – but in this case it has turned out to be (when all are sold) much dearer. By printing 6000 at once, I lose the interest on nearly £300 during one year – call that £20. Now printing 6000 at once I find costs £321. 1s. 10d. Printing 3000 was charged in 1872 as £169. 0s.9d. and the next 3000 was £159. 0s.6d. – so that printing 6000 *at twice* would have only cost £328. 1s.3d. – the extra cost being £7 – so that by printing 6000 you have *saved* me £7 and *lost* me £20 – total loss £13.

I find you are mistaken in saying you have *not* charged me for printing the 1000 American. It stands in the account you sent me.

"American Edition –
Paper and Printing
1000 copies . . . . £48. 5s. 3d.

But I do not want the loss to fall on *you*: so let it stand as it is. You will need no more copies for 6 years, I expect.

Yours ever very truly,

C. L. Dodgson

P.S. I never got the specimen page of *Phantasmagoria*. You know we agreed that it is to be uniform in *size* (but not necessarily in *type*) with *Alice* – and that the pictures are to be printed separately.[3]

---

¹ We lack letters from Dodgson to Macmillan for the previous six months, but, as before, the Macmillan letters indicate that the correspondence continued throughout.

² On September 3, Craik explained that Dodgson's profits were considerably reduced because Macmillan had printed 6000 each of *Alice* and *Looking-Glass* before Christmas 1872 in anticipation of a much larger sale than materialized. "The sale of both books is considerably smaller this year, but it is a very large sale after so many years, and the books are expensive for children's books," Craik added.

³ Dodgson refers to a projected illustrated version of *Phantasmagoria* that ultimately became *Rhyme? and Reason?*.

Christ Church, Oxford
December 24, 1874
(leaving for "The Chestnuts, Guildford")

Dear Mr. Macmillan,

I wonder if it is a secret who "Elsie Strivelyne" is, or whether you have accidentally overlooked my question.[1] So Sambourne hasn't *yet* begun on *Phantasmagoria* – he talked of doing so a month ago; however I suppose there's no reason to hurry him.[2] Do you think it worth while to try to get it out at Easter? Or wouldn't it be even better to bring it out in the summer?

I am rather frightened to think how old Olive must be getting.[3] Children do grow up so alarmingly quick. However I hope to find a day when I can go over and give them a long call, and renew our acquaintance – as I shall probably spend 2 or 3 nights in town for Pantomimic and Dramatic purposes.[4] Believe me

Very truly yours,

C. L. Dodgson

Why, in your illustrated Catalogue, do you put *Alice* into the 42nd thousand, and the *Looking-Glass* into the 33rd? I fancied they had got some way beyond those figures.

---

¹ In 1874 Macmillan published a children's book entitled *The Princess of Silverland and Other Tales* by Elsie Strivelyne, illustrated by Noël Paton. Although no reply from Macmillan to Dodgson's query about the author has surfaced, the Macmillan letter books reveal her to be a Mrs. MacCallum of Dumblane in Scotland. We can find nothing more about Mrs. MacCallum, nor can we find any other books published by Elsie Strivelyne.

² Edwin Linley Sambourne (1844–1910), *Punch* cartoonist, was the artist Dodgson had enlisted to illustrate the new *Phantasmagoria*. "Sambourne seems to me a very good man indeed for your *Phantasmagoria*," Macmillan wrote on May 21, 1874, "and I would willingly join you in the venture of an edition illustrated by him. . . ." On the day before Dodgson writes this letter, Macmillan wrote that he had recently seen Sambourne, who "has been in Italy for some weeks, but now means to begin on your book."

[3] Olive (1858?–1926) was evidently Dodgson's favorite of the Macmillan children. When he visited the Macmillans in Upper Tooting on January 7, 1873, he met the Macmillan offspring, among them Olive, aged 14 (*Diaries*, p. 317). She married (1886) Norman MacLehose (1859–1931), the third son of Macmillan's closest friend, James MacLehose. Like his father, Olive's husband was publisher and bookseller to the University of Glasgow. Olive wrote *Records of a Scotswoman, Katharine Stuart Macqueen, A Memoir and Account of Her Work* (1920).

[4] An inveterate theatergoer, Dodgson went to the Pantomime on January 6, 7, 9, and 13 of the new year; and indeed he visited the Macmillans at home on the 12th (*Diaries*, pp. 336–7).

Christ Church, Oxford
March 9, 1875

Dear Mr. Macmillan,

I have good news for you – for *us*, I ought rather to say – namely that Mr. Tenniel consents to draw a frontispiece for the book of puzzles, etc. (*Alice's Puzzlebook* is the name I incline to at present.)[1] I think it would be a good thing to get all the MS, that is ready, set up in slip, that I may correct and arrange it at leisure: and of course the first thing is to settle the type. There was something said, the last talk I had with Mr. Craik, about setting up a page of *Phantasmagoria* – in "old-faced" type – but I never received it. I fancy that style would do very well for the puzzle-book too. The page had better be the *size* of *Alice*, but a decidedly smaller type, and thinner leads: instead of 22 lines to the page, we might try 26 or 27.

I enclose the *Castle-Croquet* rules to try the experiment on. Would you get a page of it set up in whatever style you think will look best?[2]

The book will have a few diagrams, but no pictures – and as many of the articles will be very short, and will need something to divide them, and sometimes to end pages, don't you think it would have a pretty effect to use little colophons (or whatever you call them)? Or do you think they would vulgarise the book?

Very truly yours,
C. L. Dodgson

[1] A friendship grew up in the early 1870s between Dodgson on the one hand and Lord Salisbury and his family on the other after Dodgson photographed Salisbury and two of his sons at Oxford. Dodgson sometimes met the Cecils in London and became a regular guest at the lavish New Year's parties at Hatfield House, where his story-telling and puzzle-making became a ritual. "I have been writing verse-riddles for ... [the Cecil children] lately – a new style of composition for me," Dodgson wrote in his *Diaries* (p. 289) on July 28, 1870. He assembled some of the puzzles for publication and recorded (p. 291) on November 30, 1870: "Received a copy of the December number of *Aunt Judy's Magazine*, which contains seven 'Puzzles from Wonderland' of mine. They were originally written for the Cecil children." Five years later, Dodgson took up the idea of Wonderland puzzles again: "Wrote to Tenniel," he notes in his *Diaries* (p. 337) "on the subject of an idea which I entered in my memorandum book [missing], January 8th, of printing a little book

of original puzzles, etc., which I think of calling 'Alice's Puzzle-Book.' I want him to draw a frontispiece for it. (He consented March 8.)" Although Dodgson kept the idea alive to the end of his life and went so far as to advertise it in 1893 as "Original Games and Puzzles," the book never appeared. For more on Dodgson's puzzles and on Dodgson and the Cecils, see *Handbook*, pp. 56–7, 87; *Letters*, esp. pp. 211–12.

² "Wrote out the rules of a new croquet game, for five players, which I have invented and think of calling *Croquet Castles*," Dodgson wrote in his *Diaries* (p. 196) on May 4, 1863. He later revised the game for four players; in fact he refined and reprinted the rules a number of times. Collingwood records (*Picture Book*, p. 271) that Dodgson "elaborated the rules by means of playing a series of games with the Misses Liddell." For more on Dodgson and *Croquet Castles*, see *Handbook*, pp. 23–4, 37–8.

Christ Church, Oxford
March 18, 1875

Dear Mr. Macmillan,

One or two questions about *Phantasmagoria* press for immediate settlement.

First as to *size* of book. I enclose what Mr. Sambourne says – please tell me what you think: I'm rather afraid of its looking like a child's picture-book if we make it too square. Do you think we could compromise the matter by making it the height of *Alice* and a *little* broader.[1]

Secondly as to number of pictures. Here is Mr. Sambourne's suggested list

Phantasmagoria	–	30
Sea Dirge	–	4
Carpet Knight	–	1
*Hiawatha	–	7
*Lang Coortin'	–	7
Melancholetta	–	3
Poeta Fit	–	2
*Beatrice	–	2
Stanzas for Music	–	1
Faces in the fire	–	3
		60

The * means what *he* particularly wants to do.

I expect you will demur to the last three: I can't make up my mind as yet as to "half serious, half comic," or "all comic."[2]

You don't tell me what you yourself think of the specimen-pages of the "Lang Coortin'" and the "Croquet-Rules."

I am inclined to think the verses are in *rather* too large a type for the page. The "Rules" I like better.[3] Haste.

Very truly yours,

C. L. Dodgson

¹ In his reply of the same day, Macmillan disagrees with both Sambourne and Dodgson on the book's size. He writes about experience with "queer shaped" books and insists that "booksellers' shelves and counters don't suit them and besides I am sure private people prefer an author's work to be uniform." On March 20 Macmillan writes again: "I saw Mr. Sambourne yesterday and talked the size over with him. He is by no means wedded to the square and yielded at once to practical reasons for keeping our present size." But before he receives Macmillan's second letter, Dodgson too yields to the publisher's "practical reasons."

² Macmillan replies (March 18) that he cannot judge the idea of the pictures in any detail but very much doubts "the propriety of the mixture of the serious with the comic."

³ "The specimen pages I sent you I thought both good. I really don't think the type of the *Phantasmagoria* volume too large," Macmillan replies (same letter).

Christ Church, Oxford
March 19, 1875
(address to "The Chestnuts, Guildford" till April 8)

Dear Mr. Macmillan,

Your reasoning is clear and convincing. We will keep to the size of *Alice*, and have comic poems *only*. The "type" question I will consider again.

Now I want your advice as to the title of the book of puzzles. It concerns *you* almost as much as me, for I fancy that a taking title is a great help to the sale of a book. Here are some titles to choose among.

× ALICE'S PUZZLE-BOOK

ALICE'S BOOK OF PUZZLES

ALICE'S BOOK OF
ODDS AND ENDS.

THE WONDERLAND
PUZZLE-BOOK.

PUZZLES FROM WONDERLAND

THE LOOKING-GLASS BOOK.

× JABBERWOCKY
AND OTHER MYSTERIES,
BEING THE BOOK THAT
ALICE FOUND IN HER TRIP
THROUGH THE LOOKING-GLASS

If we took the latter title or any modification of it, we should have to begin
with "Jabberwocky" itself; to which I should in that case append the article
from your *Magazine* (if you approved), and three Latin Versions.[1]

Would your family-circle kindly resolve themselves into a committee of taste,
and give me their opinions, collectively if unanimous – otherwise, individually.[2]

You never told me what you thought of "colophons" (that sort
of thing) to divide the shorter articles from each other.[3]

Truly yours,

C. L. Dodgson

Here is another idea for the last title –

JABBERWOCKY

AND OTHER MYSTERIES;

BEING

THE BOOK THAT ALICE FOUND

IN HER TRIP

THROUGH THE LOOKING-GLASS.

1 "The Jabberwock Traced to Its True Source," which appeared in *Macmillan's Magazine* in February 1872, is a delightful spoof created by Robert Scott (1811–87), Master of Balliol College, Oxford (1854–70) and Dean of Rochester (1870–87), co-author with Dean Liddell of *A Greek–English Lexicon* (1843). In the skit, Scott, writing under the name "Thomas Chatterton" claims to reveal the German origins of "Jabberwocky" and supplies the "original German poem" as well. A Latin translation of "Jabberwocky" was made in March 1872 by Augustus Arthur Vansittart (1842–82), Fellow of Trinity College, Cambridge, and printed as a pamphlet by Oxford University Press in 1881. Dodgson's uncle Hassard Hume Dodgson (1803–84), Master of the Common Pleas, also translated the poem into Latin (see *Picture Book*, pp. 364–5). Although "Jabberwocky" was later translated into both Latin and Greek, only these two Latin versions are known to have existed when Dodgson writes this letter. Either he has some other Latin translation in mind which has never entered the mainstream of Carroll parodies and translations or he has conflated the two with Scott's "German" original. For more on the Scott spoof, see *Handbook*, p. 307; *Letters*, pp. 172–3; for more on translations of "Jabberwocky," see Weaver, pp. 71–2.
2 Alexander Macmillan provides his own opinion in his reply the following day, but he does not say whether or not the "family-circle" agreed – or, for that matter, was even consulted: "The first and last titles you suggest are the only ones I care for. All the others are only modifications, with essentially no difference, from the first." He inclines towards the first but suggests that Dodgson himself must decide: "We might have both title pages set and you could judge better in that form."
3 "The question of the colophons I hardly can judge of," Macmillan replies (March 20). "I don't care about them myself – some people do. If I were to decide I would say that . . . in such a book as yours they seem out of place."

Christ Church, Oxford
November 6, 1875

Dear Mr. Macmillan,

I send you the rest of the poem, with the Dedication and Contents and Map.[1] The Preface is not yet written, but I shall want a leaf for it, which I think had better be continuous with the "false" title, and be folded round the frontispiece and title. And I should think the dedication and contents had better be part of the first sheet, which will save sewing them in separately: but of this you will be the best judge.

My arrangement would be as follows

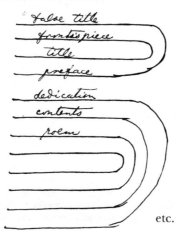

etc.

This would make 21 leaves of text, counting from the dedication-leaf. You might add one more to make an even number, and utilise it for advertising *Alice* on the last page of all, putting "*(over)*" at the foot of the preceding page. (You will observe that the directions for turning over become more and more peremptory as the reader proceeds – "please turn over – turn over – over.")

Please send me *3* proofs of everything – instead of 2, as they generally send.

If you think "brilliant" type for the dedicatory verses will make the heading look top-heavy, try a larger type: but I want it very small.

I want to write another little Christmas letter,[2] to be slightly gummed into each copy sold this year. Is there time to have it done with a coloured heading? a sprig of holly, say? Mr. Holiday would design one.[3]

Mr. Holiday is sending you a suggestion for *blue* cloth covers: I fancy he is right.

Yours very truly,

C. L. Dodgson

---

[1] This is the first mention of *The Hunting of the Snark*, by almost all accounts the greatest nonsense poem in the English language. On July 18, 1874, while Dodgson was walking on a hillside near Guildford, he was struck suddenly by an inspired line of nonsense: "For the Snark *was* a Boojum, you see" (*Diaries*, pp. 334–5). He saw it clearly as the last line of a poem, and over the next year and a half fabricated a network of narrative verse to lead up to it. Along the way, he considered the possibility of publishing the poem. On October 24, 1875, he noted (pp. 344–5): "A sudden idea occurred, about which I wrote to Holiday and Macmillan, of publishing the *Snark* poem this Christmas. . . ." But on October 28, Macmillan wrote to say that the engraver could not possibly cut the blocks for the illustrations in under three months "and even would hesitate to promise that." Macmillan proposed (same letter) that Dodgson publish the poem in the Christmas number of *Macmillan's Magazine* to "serve your purpose in keeping yourself fresh before the public." Two days later, Macmillan repeated the offer: "The publication of your poem in the Christmas number would not in the least interfere with the publication of an illustrated edition at Easter. I think it would rather help than hinder it. . . . It would serve too I think to fulfill the purpose your idea of a Christmas publication aimed at." Dodgson must have declined the invitation, and on October 31 – while his illustrator for the poem, Henry Holiday, was staying with him at Christ Church – he wrote (pp. 345–6): "It occurs to me that as *one* block (the 'landing') is done, it might be worth while to publish at Christmas, using it as the frontispiece: this would have the advantage of keeping the other five pictures, to come out *new*, if the poem is ever introduced into a story." On the following day, Macmillan writes, urging Dodgson not to try to do anything about a "*pictorial* cover" and to be content with a frontispiece. "If it is to be done at all we should decide on our course *now*," Macmillan continues, "as there will be not the least time to consult or devise new ideas. I think a shilling book of this kind might have a considerable sale." Dodgson probably insisted on pictorial covers, and the Macmillan letters that follow concern themselves with details for them. But on November 12, Macmillan writes that he thinks the picture covers, as planned, excessive: "As it is it is a cake which is too thickly coated with sugar." That observation put an end to all plans for Christmas publication: on the 13th Dodgson writes (p. 347): "Heard from Macmillan, objecting to picture covers on both sides as too much 'sugar for the cake.' This confirmed a doubt I have felt for some days as to the advisability of publishing at all with one picture only." Easter publication became the goal. For a comprehensive study of the *Snark*, see the celebratory volume, Tanis and Dooley; see also *Handbook*, pp. 89–92.

[2] In 1867 Dodgson composed a verse of five quatrains entitled *Christmas Greetings from a Fairy to a Child*. He published it in *Phantasmagoria* two years later but it did not appear separately until 1884

(for more on this poem, see *Handbook*, pp. 126–7; Selwyn Goodacre, "Bibliographic Notes on *Christmas Greetings*," *Jabberwocky*, 11 (Summer 1972), 21–3). Dodgson's intention to write "another little Christmas letter" would in time become *An Easter Greeting to Every Child Who Loves "Alice"* (see p. 128, below).

3 The illustrator of the *Snark*, Henry Holiday (1839–1927), was a long-time friend of Dodgson. When the Holidays appear in the *Diaries* for the first time, on July 6, 1870 (p. 289), the artist and the don are already well acquainted. Dodgson records the idea of Holiday illustrating a book for him on January 16, 1874: "Told Holiday of an idea his drawing suggested to me, that he might illustrate a child's book for me. If *only* he can draw grotesques, it would be all I should desire – the grace and beauty of the pictures would quite rival Tenniel, I think" (*Diaries*, p. 326). Obviously, Dodgson had no specific book in mind just then, but by November 23, when he first mentions the *Snark* in his *Diaries* (p. 334), Holiday is already at work on the illustrations. That same entry reveals that "Ruskin came, by my request, for a talk about pictures Holiday is doing for the 'Boojum' – one (the scene on board) has been cut on wood. He much disheartened me by holding out no hopes that Holiday would be able to illustrate a book satisfactorily." Dodgson may have been disheartened, but his own faith in Holiday persisted. The copy of the *Snark* that he inscribed to the artist reads: "Presented to Henry Holiday, most patient of Artists, by Charles L. Dodgson, most exacting, but not most ungrateful of Authors." It is one of the few instances when Dodgson put his real name in a book by Lewis Carroll. For more on the Dodgson–Holiday friendship, see Henry Holiday, *Reminiscences of My Life* (1914), esp. pp. 165, 244–6; "The Snark's Significance," *Academy*, January 29, 1898, pp. 128–9. For more on Dodgson and Ruskin, see *Letters*, p. 326.

Christ Church, Oxford
December 21, 1875

Dear Mr. Macmillan,

In the early part of January I hope to get the *Snark* set up in its final form, with the additional matter, etc., so as to have ample leisure for verbal corrections before you electrotype. So I should be glad to have the question of pictures settled *now*. The more I think of your proposal to work them off separately, on paper of the same colour as the book, the less I like it.[1] My own expectation would be to find text at the back. There are only two courses which seem to me endurable – one, to have the pictures quite distinct from the text, on a different coloured paper – the other to have them printed along with the book, with text at the back of each picture, as we did with *Alice*.

The latter plan, unless you seriously object, is what I prefer on the whole.[2] If you can tell me you approve of this, I can begin at once arranging the first sheet. We shall have nearly 60 pages, altogether, I expect.

Thanks for catalogue of Xmas Books.

Very truly yours,
C. L. Dodgson

1 Macmillan made this suggestion in a letter dated November 23.
2 In his reply the following day, Macmillan reports that the plates could be printed with or without text at the back but that he is inclined to the latter as the plates will then "gain in clearness by the absence of type on the back." He adds: "At the same time I have no sort of objection to your plan if you prefer it, except that the pictures will certainly *look* better, and the book will be so many pages thicker, a very desirable thing, where the cost is so great in proportion to the appearance."

The Chestnuts, Guildford
December 28, 1875

Dear Mr. Macmillan,

I am going to write you a letter which you will think unusually commercial – for me. I have been analysing the *Alice* accounts and have come to some startling conclusions as to the undue amount of booksellers' profits (not *publisher's* profits, with which I am entirely satisfied) which I wish to lay before you, with the practical result which I wish to deduce.

The average result, on a sale of 40,000, is as follows –

Ordinary Sale		*Per copy*	*Per 1000*
Expense of production	–	2s.5½d.	£122.18.4
Publisher's profit	–	5d.	20.16.8
bookseller's profit	–	1s.5d.	70.16.8
discount to public	–	7d.	29. 3.4
author's profit	–	1s.5½d.	56. 5.0
		6s.0d.	300. 0.0

"Trade Dinner" Sale		*Per copy*	*Per 1000*
Expense of production	–	2s.5½d.	£122.18.4
publisher's profit	–	4d.	16.13.4
bookseller's profit	–	2s.0d.	100. 0.0
discount to public	–	7d.	29. 3.4
author's profit	–	7½d.	31. 5.0
		6s.0d.	300. 0.0

Now first as to "trade dinner." I don't think you can ever have realised that this complimentary privilege, apparently given by one publisher to another, comes almost wholly out of the author's pocket. Every 1000 you allow a bookseller to buy at the reduced price, is putting £29 into his pocket, of which you subscribe £4, and I £25. Now *you* probably are his friend, and wish to benefit him. *I* am a stranger to him, and owe him nothing, and am altogether disinclined to give him so large a present.

So I hope you won't take it ill, or think me as reflecting on *your* position in the matter, when I say that no more books of mine must be sold in this way. I have more to say, but must post this today, as I don't know when your "trade dinner" occurs, and fear it may be about this time.

Yours very truly,

C. L. Dodgson

P.S. My next point is that I want to raise the price charged to booksellers, from 4s. 2d. to (say) 5s. 2d. But I will write more fully about this. Tell me how much you think such a change would reduce the sale, by making *booksellers* less anxious to order it (it would make no difference to the *public*). Instead of selling 1000, what should we then sell? 800? 700?[1]

---

[1] Dodgson here begins a long campaign against what he considers booksellers' excessive profits. He was not wrong in principle. During the second half of the nineteenth century, booksellers got the lion's share of what the public paid for a book, and profits were closely tied to the practice of underselling competitors. Booksellers demanded large discounts from publishers, and large firms were often able to undersell their smaller competitors. Bookselling was consequently a precarious business. Dodgson's perceptions are, of course, limited by his own position as author and his lack of familiarity with the realities of bookselling. Macmillan replies the following day and tries to broaden his understanding: "When you can come to town I will be glad to go into the questions you raise. I think it would not do in any way to alter terms. The result to you is not inconsiderable. In reality the bookseller greatly helps you and his profits are not anything like what you say. He keeps stock, takes risks of various kinds and helps you more than you guess. Please come and talk it over."

The Chestnuts, Guildford
December 29, 1875

Dear Mr. Macmillan,

I now go on to my *second* point – the inordinate profit made by booksellers, on ordinary sales, even without the exceptional privileges of a "trade dinner," as compared with your profits, and with mine. On every 1000 copies sold

your profit is	£20.16.8
mine is	£56. 5.0
the bookseller's	£70.16.8

This seems to me altogether unfair: his profit should be the *least* of the three, not the *greatest*. Authors (I don't mean myself specially, but authors in general) give time and brain-work to an indefinite (sometimes enormous) amount: all this is worth money, and their profits should be, it seems to me, the largest of all. Publishers give a large amount of time and attention, in advertising, etc., and deserve a handsome profit. But the bookseller gives neither time nor attention: he simply opens a shop, and invests money in books – in many cases he has not even the trouble of choosing what to buy: the public order the books they want through him. All *he* deserves is sufficient profit to enable him to allow to his ready-money customers the usual 10 percent discount, and clear a good interest on his money besides: and in calculating this interest it ought to be remembered that he often "turns over" the same money several times in a year. If the publisher allowed him (say) 15 percent discount, and he allowed his customers 10, he would then be clearing 5 percent 3 or 4 times a year, i.e. he would *clear* 15 or 20 percent annually on his capital. Surely this is enough?

But you are allowing him (in the case of *Alice*) 33 percent discount, so that he clears *23* percent several times a year!

Now if, instead of charging him 4*s*. 2*d*., which, with the "21 as 20" rule, is practically 4*s*., you were to charge him 5*s*. 2*d*., which would practically be 5*s*. 1*d*., just consider what the effect would be –

Proposed Tariff (A)

		Per copy	Per 1000
Printing, etc.	–	2*s*.5½*d*.	£122.18.4
publisher	–	6	25. 0.0
bookseller	–	4	16.13.4
discount to public	–	7	29. 3.4
author	–	2*s*.1½*d*.	106. 5.0
		6*s*.0*d*.	300. 0.0

But if you think this scheme (by which the bookseller clears 6–⅔ percent) is too violent a reduction, let us see the effect of a milder scheme. Charge 4*s*. 8*d*. (practically 4*s*. 6½*d*.)

Proposed Tariff (B)

		Per copy	Per 1000
Printing, etc.	–	2*s*.5½*d*.	£122.18.4
publisher	–	5½*d*.	22.18.4
bookseller	–	10½*d*.	43.15.0
discount to public	–	7*d*.	29. 3.4
author	–	1*s*.7½*d*.	81. 5.0
		6*s*.0*d*.	300. 0.0

This makes the bookseller clear nearly double as much as you do, and seems to me quite exorbitant: still I should be content to have it tried for a year, and should be curious to see how much it reduced the sale. As it would increase my profit in the ratio "$\frac{1}{7\frac{1}{2}}$ to $\frac{1}{1\frac{1}{2}}$," i.e. "39 to 27" or "13 to 9," I could well afford to have the scale reduced in the same proportion. And if for every 1300 we now sell, we could sell, on the new tariff, anything over 900, I should be a gainer by the change.

There is another evil I forgot to mention, arising from the enormous discount allowed by publishers to booksellers: it is that it enables mere adventurers, who embark no capital on books, to underbid the regular booksellers, by allowing the public 25 percent discount, and even more.[1] Now if a bookseller can afford to give 25 percent discount, when he receives 33, he can on the same principle, afford to give 10 when he receives 18 – and much more can he afford it when he receives (as he would do on "proposed tariff (B)") 25 percent discount.

I reserve my *third* point (the question what discount to allow to the booksellers on the *Snark*) till I hear what you think about the first two. I will only say here that I do not think there would be the same risk, in trying a new tariff for the

Snark, which we should run if it were my first book. In that case, if the booksellers objected to so small a discount, and declined to order the book, it would probably destroy the sale altogether: in this case I am vain enough to think that even if the booksellers withdrew their patronage, the public would still insist on having it: and if they could not get it at their bookseller's, they would order it direct from you, and so *you* would get all the retail profit as well as the wholesale. In fact, if *that* were the result of the experiment, I should be inclined to propose advertising that you would send the book "post paid" to any address in the United Kingdom.

Whatever I do in the matter, I wish to act in concert with you, and in harmony with your opinion. The changes I propose are all in your favour as well as mine: the only loser by them being the hitherto overpaid booksellers.[2]

Yours very truly,
C. L. Dodgson

P.S. If I were to publish a letter (as I have some notion of doing) on the subject of "Booksellers' profits and authors' profits," would you have any objection to my giving the history of *Alice* as an illustration?

---

[1] Dodgson here points to the basis of the problem. At this time, no means existed for controlling or defining booksellers' terms to clients, and, as Dodgson notes, a bookseller might set up in a town and, by cutting prices sharply for a short time, drive the other booksellers out of business. In order to survive, booksellers began to deal in other goods as well. The problem was a concern of Alexander Macmillan, and as early as 1864 he considered proposals for altering current practice. Nothing came of these plans, however, until 1890, when his nephew Frederick Macmillan began a program of reform that ultimately led to the Net Book Agreement of 1899. For more on the Net Book Agreement, see pp. 25–6, above; Morgan, pp. 193–207; *Net Book Agreement*.

[2] In his reply on the following day, Macmillan again suggests that he and Dodgson discuss the whole question, but he also tries to show that Dodgson has not taken all the facts into account: "In your calculation of the profits to the publisher and the bookseller you overlook the fact of the expenses of their respective business: rent, clerks, etc. In a wholesale business this does not come to less than 5 or 6 percent on the returns. This would reduce our profit to about one-half what you say. In the retail booksellers' case those expenses are a good deal more – from 7 to 10 percent, and besides that he has risks of injured stock – and either bad debts or he may have to wait for his money. I have experience of retail business very carefully conducted and I know how much all those things lessen profit. I wish you would come and talk this matter over."

Christ Church, Oxford
December 30, 1875

Dear Mr. Macmillan,

A very happy New Year (and many of them) to you and yours! Thank you for your note received this morning: I am quite prepared to find that I have overstated the case against booksellers, and shall be very glad to have data on which to modify my statement. A conversation with you is always pleasant, but *writing* has several advantages – the chief perhaps being that you have something tangible to refer to afterwards, instead of mere memory. So that as to *this* matter I shall be grateful if you can find leisure some day soon to write me, as briefly as you like, a more just statement than I have succeeded in drawing up.

My rash proposal to raise the terms on *Alice* is very likely an impracticable one – but the *Snark* is new ground, and we can experiment more freely. What do you say to pricing it at 3s., and charging the booksellers 2s. 6d. (i.e. with the usual allowance of "21 as 20" about 2s. 4d.).[1]

Very truly yours,

C. L. Dodgson

[1] "About the terms of the trade I am sure it would be hazardous in every way to alter them," Macmillan writes on January 5. "Your natural desire to formulate by figures the respective share of profits all the parties concerned get, is in effect impossible. You remember the old story of Robin Hood and some one else who tried to split the willow wand with him. The rival hits it on the side. Robin says, 'Well shot, but you did not allow *for the wind.*' This not allowing for the wind is the fault of all abstract calculators. . . ." Macmillan then puts the hypothetical case of John Smith, Bookseller of Middlemarch, who orders six copies of *Alice* for Christmas sale. He sells four and "is left at the end of his season with two unsold copies. They get shabby from his very anxiety to sell them. Little Miss Nelly Puss, aged 6¾, asks Mrs. Shrewd Puss, her loving but careful mother, if she might not have it. Mrs. Shrewd Puss says 'Yes, my dear, but that copy is *handled.*' . . . Mrs. Shrewd Puss is sure that Mr. John Smith will order a *fresh* copy. John Smith's two copies may be on hand for many months, till he is obliged to offer them for 6d. or 1s. under the ordinary price so that at next Christmas he may have quite *fresh copies.* Then he orders *one or two.* But he is told that instead of 4s. 2d., he must pay 5s. 2d. My dear friend, need I go on with the parable?"

The Chestnuts, Guildford

January 3, 1876

Dear Mr. Macmillan,

Thanks for your letter. The additional data are valuable, though I am not quite clear how far, in such a summary, it is necessary to trace the money. Whether we say that 1s. 5d. of the 6s. 0d. goes to the bookseller, or that 1s. 5d. goes, partly to the bookseller, and partly to his landlord, and partly to his non-paying customers, the result is much the same so far as the author is concerned. I don't clearly understand what you mean by the bookseller's expenses being 10 percent on his returns. In this case, where the bookseller pays 4s. for the book, and sells for 6s. (or, giving discount, for 5s. 5d.), is the 10 percent calculated on the 5s. 5d. he *receives*, or on the 1s. 5d. he *clears*? i.e. do his expenses amount to 6½d., or to 1$\frac{7}{10}$d.?

In any case it seems to me that a system by which, out of the 3s. 6d. which the public pays (in addition to paying for the cost of production), only 1s. 1½d. finds its way into the author's pocket, is capable of improvement.

There is a question about the *Snark*, which I want settled *at once.* I am quite willing to have the pictures worked along with the poem, but without text at the back, if you [are] sure that will look well. But it seems to me that that will oblige us to have all the pictures (except of course the frontispiece) on right-hand pages: now, two of them refer to concluding verses of cantos. Will this look well? ⅔ of a page blank, and *then* a picture?

By the other arrangement (of having text at the back) it would look like this:

the picture is now imbedded in the poem, and looks much more natural, I fancy.[1]
Please consider this point, and believe me

Very truly yours,

C. L. Dodgson

---

[1] "There is no reason why the cuts to the *Snark* should be on the right hand page more than on the left," Macmillan replies two days later. Dodgson apparently persists in his wish to have the pictures and text back to back, and the *Snark* ultimately appears that way.

The Chestnuts, Guildford
January 17, 1876
(I go to Oxford on the 19th)

Dear Mr. Craik,

Many thanks for the cheque, for which I enclosed a signed receipt.

Please take a memorandum to advertise the *Snark* "to be published on the 1st of April." Surely that is the fittest day for it to appear?[1]

When Mr. Holiday has designed the simpler covers which I have asked him to do, I suppose they had better begin printing covers at once, as 10,000 must take a long time to prepare. The *colour* had better be red, I think, to match *Alice*. And don't you think, with such a thin book, it will look best to print the title lengthways, as here drawn?

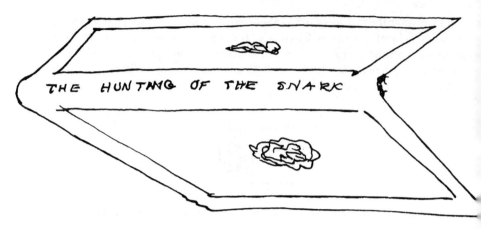

The "richly emblazoned" copies I should like done in that dark blue cloth which Mr. Holiday recommended.

I will look at Walter Crane's books when I have an opportunity.[2]

Very truly yours,

C. L. Dodgson

[1] Once the hope of publishing the *Snark* at Christmas 1875 was abandoned, both Dodgson and Macmillan consistently referred to it as an "Easter book."

[2] Walter Crane (1845–1915) was a favorite of Craik, who probably recommended the artist to Dodgson, always in search of good illustrators. Beginning in 1874, Macmillan published a series of story books by Mrs. Molesworth, all illustrated by Walter Crane, who gave Craik credit for bringing him the work.

Christ Church, Oxford
February 3, 1876

Dear Mr. Macmillan,

I will repeat my questions.

(1) You said in your letter (dated November 12) "Might not the advertisements 4 pages, or 2 leaves, go in simply as advertisements? the p.t.o does not approve itself to my feelings or judgement." Does this mean that you object to the way the advertisements are put into the *Looking-Glass*? (asked in my letter dated November 22).[1]

(2) (asked November 22) What do you propose to do about America?[2]

(3) (asked January 15) What do you think of the plan of having *two* prices? a simple cover at (say) 3s., and a richly decorated one at 1s. extra?[3]

(4) (suggested January 17) I should like it advertised "will be published on the 1st of April." Do you approve?[4]

(5) (suggested January 17) I think title had better be printed *lengthways* on back. Do you approve? And should it be plain type, or shall I ask Mr. Holiday to draw fantastic letters for it?[5]

(6) (asked January 28) Do you approve of using *new* extracts from Reviews in the advertisements? We have gone on so long with the same set. I could send you some to choose from.[6]

(7) (asked February 1) Can the covers you have sent me be used for binding copies for me to give away?[7]

(8) (asked in another letter, the same day). Could covers be done on red cloth like *Alice*, but substituting white, grey, or cream-colour, for gold? What price would they be?[8]

Now as to the covers. I think, for *gold*, the best colour is red – the same red as *Alice*. It is far more taking than the blue Mr. Holiday advised. *That* would have done beautifully for a volume of poems meant for aesthetic adults. *This* book is meant for children. I don't at all like the mixture of black and gold – and I don't like any of the other covers – except the plain black and grey, which is a nice contrast, and would look well if the black and grey could be interchanged within the border: but that of course cannot be. As it is, with a nigger bellman, a black sail, and scalloped

clouds (caused by converting into *clouds* what should be sky *between* clouds) it won't do at all.

My present ideas tend towards – cream-colour on red (the white being *sunk* will protect it from soiling) at 3*s*. – gold on red at 4*s*. What say you?

Clay will be able to go to press long before the end of February. The text is all in type already.

Very truly yours,

C. L. Dodgson

---

[1] We do not have Dodgson's letter of November 22, 1875. Macmillan answers Dodgson's various points in his letter of the following day. "What I objected to in the p.t.o. on the *text* page has been removed; as it stands now it is all right."

[2] Macmillan reports that he wrote to his nephew, Frederick Macmillan, the firm's agent in America; he "wishes to . . . print the book there paying you 10 percent on the selling price. Do you object to this? Or will you allow copies to be sent out on the same sort of terms as we have sent the other books?" Again, the Dodgson letter to which he refers, dated November 22, is not in our files.

[3] "The objections to two prices and two bindings are very strong," Macmillan writes. "We were quite aware of the faults you point out on the grey and black cover. The block was cut for *gold* and we will require a new block if you decide on this style. Our binder, whom I have just seen, says he can obviate all the defects you mention and is very sure that it would come out beautifully. I wish you would settle on this and throw all the other styles on one side."

[4] Macmillan replies with a question: "Do you want us to advertise April 1 *now*? You have not got your blocks yet. Won't it do if we begin to advertise say in the March Magazines?"

[5] "By all means let Mr. Holiday cut the letters for the back . . . ," Macmillan writes.

[6] Again, "By all means send us new extracts. Would you mind sending them to me and I will instruct our advertising clerk?" We do not have Dodgson's letter of January 28.

[7] "We can use the covers we sent as specimens when the book is ready," Macmillan writes. Both letters that Dodgson wrote on February 1 are absent.

[8] "Our binder has been at work to get a white or cream-coloured pigment to print on cloth but has not succeeded yet and has no hope of being able to achieve it for six or eight months if at all. At present it is impossible."

Christ Church, Oxford

February 5, 1876

Dear Mr. Macmillan,

Many thanks: my questions are all answered now. I proceed to answer *yours*.

I strongly object to any electros going out to America, or *anywhere* out of Messrs. Clay's hands. By all means print some here and send out on the same terms as for *Alice*.

I like very much the idea of black and grey done the reverse way (so far as *inside* the border: of course we retain grey as the colour *outside*). Please have one block cut so at once and let me see the effect. For my own 200 copies I shall want gold on red. I don't want them sent round to the booksellers, but surely there would be no harm done by advertising that copies may be had, bound to match *Alice* and with the design in gold, at 1*s*. extra? As it is, you have 2 prices for *Alice*, you know, in cloth and in morocco. I like the *red* cloth for gold better than either of the blues.[1]

I am sorry that a cream-coloured pigment is so fearfully difficult to obtain. I should have thought you might have advertised for a ton of it and got it in a week. However the black and grey will look nearly as well and will last better.

If you approve of advertising for April 1, and don't think the public will regard it as a hoax, you will be the best judge as to when to begin. *I* should have thought about the middle of February: but if you think that too soon, do as you think best.

I have no doubt at all that the picture-blocks will be ready by the 20th. 7 of the 9 are cut already (though needing some finishing touches) and the other 2 I believe are in hand.

I will ask Mr. Holiday to draw title for back.

Very truly yours,

C. L. Dodgson

I will send extracts from Reviews. In cutting the new cover-block they may as well avoid the mistake they have made in the present one, of putting a star in front of the rigging!

---

[1] Although the general issue of the *Snark* was buff-colored cloth, Dodgson had four other combinations printed for his private use (see p. 127, below).

Christ Church, Oxford
February 6, 1876
Dear Mr. Macmillan,

I enclose extracts from Reviews, for you to select from as you think best. Could you not select *two* sets, and use one for advertisements in papers, etc., the other for the list of my books at the end of *Alice*?

Please let me know whether it will be necessary to electrotype the picture-blocks separately and then, after putting them in their places, to electro the book as a whole. Will it not be enough to put the wood-blocks themselves in among the type, and then electro the book? And would this method involve *any* risk of the wood-blocks (which will contain some very delicate cutting) getting injured?[1]

Now for a suggestion which has just occurred to me. When you have got the lengthways title cut for the back of the book, I want you to print it (or the same words in ordinary type, which would do just as well) on the paper wrapper. The letters had better slope a good deal, so as to be easily read as the book stands upright. The advantage will be that it can stand in bookstalls without being taken out of paper, and so can be kept in cleaner and more saleable condition.[2]

I should like the same thing done for *Alice* and the *Looking-Glass* for the future – and even those on hand, which are already wrapped in plain paper, might be transferred into printed covers: of course *I* would pay for the trouble of transferring – which may perhaps be a day's work for one of your men.[3]

Very truly yours,

C. L. Dodgson

---

[1] Macmillan replies on February 19 that each plate was electro'd separately, and each page of the book was also electro'd by itself "and put into sheet form separately." He assures Dodgson that care was taken of both the blocks and the electros, so there was no fear of injury from the process itself.

[2] Dodgson's suggestion "may claim a share in the ancestry of the book ... 'jacket'" (Morgan, p. 110), and the wrapping is well known not only for its vertical spine title but also for advertising three other Carroll books. See G. Thomas Tanselle, "Book-Jackets, Blurbs, and Bibliographers," *Library*, 26 (June 1971), 110–11.

[3] "We are printing the wrappers for *Alice* and *Looking-Glass* and will get them on the books as soon as possible. It is not the question of a man's work, but it involves the whole of the arrangements in our warehouse being disturbed," Macmillan writes (February 19).

Christ Church, Oxford
February 11, 1876
Dear Mr. Macmillan,

Here are 2 designs by Mr. Holiday for a back-title. For my own part, I like the one with smaller letters best – but you and the binder will be the best judges.

Is there any other pigment besides black that could be used? If so, I should like to see specimens. Mr. Holiday wants to give his opinion on the colour for the cheaper cover. I am telling him he had better communicate with you.[1] For the *dearer* covers I hold to *Alice* red, and gold.

Very truly yours,

C. L. Dodgson

P.S. I am sending Messrs. Clay MS for a Preface, which will occupy about 2 pages – and telling them I think it should be in smaller type than the poem, and closer leaded (from 25 to 30 lines in a page). If you think this wouldn't look well, please let them know what you advise. I think a book looks very bad when the Preface is more handsomely printed than the text: the contrast should always be the other way.[2]

---

[1] In his letter of February 19, Macmillan replies that the only other possible pigment would be red, "which would not do." He points out that if Dodgson wants to publish by the first of April, they had best stay with the black on grey combination and adds: "You have no idea of the work required to get any of these experiments made."

[2] "I quite agree with you about the way the preface should be printed," Macmillan writes (same letter).

Christ Church, Oxford
March 1, 1876

Dear Mr. Macmillan,

With reference to the letter, forwarded by George,[1] from the Polytechnic, I heard the other day from Mr. Boyd (an Oxford man, who has set to music the songs in *Alice*, etc.)[2] asking my leave to use the pictures in "a lecture for children" on my books at the Polytechnic – and asking what terms I should ask for vesting "the right of representation" in him. I told him he *might* use the pictures, but that I could not vest such a right in any one person, as I had already given leave for them to be published as magic-lantern slides, which of course involved the right to *exhibit* the slides. (By the way, you never told me how that matter ended: you undertook to arrange the thing with the slide-maker, and I think were to ask for some remuneration. The application was made, in January 1875, by Mr. W. L. Breare, Sun Lane, Burley-in-Wharfedale, Leeds.)[3] I am writing to Mr. Boyd to ask what sort of entertainment is proposed, as, if it is dramatic, or involves the the recitation of the book, I can not give leave without knowing more about it. I will write again when I hear from him. It certainly does not look like a case in which payment should be expected from *my* side![4]

No more book-covers are come – nor any proofs of the pictures. Have they not electrotyped them yet?[5]

Very truly yours,

C. L. Dodgson

¹ George Augustin Macmillan (1855–1936), second son of Alexander, came into the firm in 1874 and became a partner in 1879. His special interests were music, the classics and natural history. For more on his association with the firm, see Morgan, esp. pp. 166–8.

² *The Songs from Alice's Adventures in Wonderland* was published in 1870. William Boyd (1845–1928), composer, friend of Charles Gounod, tutor to Charles Kingsley's son Lorenzo, and, towards the end of his life, Vicar of All Saints, Norfolk Square, published music regularly. "His knowledge of music made the services [at All Saints] a delight," wrote *The Times* (February 17, 1928, p. 19), "and many notable people attended the church." For more on Boyd and Dodgson, see *Handbook*, pp. 57–9; *Letters*, pp. 168–9.

³ See p. 126, below.

⁴ We do not have the letter that George Macmillan forwarded to Dodgson, but on February 29, George Macmillan wrote: "I enclose a letter which we think must be meant for a joke! The idea is too delicious, that you should pay them something for doing what they have no earthly right to do without your permission. If the copyright were ours we should be inclined to ask them to pay something like £500 for the right to present *Alice* on the stage. It would be a just reward for their insolence. Please return the letter with your answer." In a letter dated March 2, Alexander Macmillan writes: "I think you had better take the Polytechnic people into your own hands. Don't you think so? Their impudence is droll." Dodgson must have given permission because on April 18, 1876, he "Went to the Polytechnic . . . to see Mr. G. Buckland's Entertainment *Alice's Adventures*" (*Diaries*, pp. 352–3). "It lasted about one and a quarter hours. A good deal of it was done by dissolving views, extracts from the story being read, or sung to Mr. Boyd's music; but the latter part had a real scene and five performers (Alice, Queen, Knave, Hatter, Rabbit) who acted in dumb show, the speeches being read by Mr. Buckland. The 'Alice' was a rather pretty child of about 10 (Martha Woolridge) who acted simply and gracefully. An interpolated song for the Cat, about a footman and housemaid, was so out of place, that I wrote afterwards to ask Mr. Buckland to omit it." Dodgson goes a second time to see the performance, on June 10: "The new version is very much the same," he records, "except that for the 'footman' song is substituted one about 'a naughty little boy,' part of which I think I must protest against as too horrible to be comic."

⁵ In his letter of March 2, Macmillan writes: ". . . the engraver pleads for the book being worked from *Wood*. If we do 10,000 from those delicate cuttings you will get little more use of the blocks."

Christ Church, Oxford
March 3, 1876

Dear Mr. Macmillan,

On no consideration whatever are the wood-blocks to be used for printing from. That is *one* fixed principle I wish to be borne in mind: and another is:

The date of publishing is not to interfere *in the least* with the goodness of the printing, binding, etc.

If necessary, postpone the publishing: but take *full* time to produce a first-rate article. I had rather wait another year, if necessary, then have it fall short of the best we can do.

The dark picture will do very well, I think. That it should not look intelligible is one of its merits!¹

The 9 proofs (which arrived safe this morning) complete the thing. There are no more to come.

I should like to *see* a specimen of the "reversed" grey and black cover before it is settled on.

Please advertise for April 1 as long as there is a hope of our getting it out by that date.[2] In haste.

Very truly yours,

C. L. Dodgson

[1] In his letter of March 2, Macmillan also called Dodgson's attention to the fact that one of the blocks was not printing clearly and "seems . . . impossible to render in ink." Macmillan is referring to the illustration for the eighth fit, "The Vanishing," which appears in the first edition of the *Snark* facing p. 83. It is a dark picture but delicately engraved and beautifully printed with the ghostly quality that Dodgson wanted for the end of the poem:

> They hunted till darkness came on, but they found
> Not a button, or feather, or mark,
> By which they could tell that they stood on the ground
> Where the Baker had met with the Snark.
> In the midst of the word he was trying to say,
>   In the midst of his laughter and glee,
> He had softly and suddenly vanished away –
>   For the Snark *was* a Boojum, you see.

For variants of "The Vanishing," see Tanis and Dooley.

[2] On March 15, Macmillan writes: "You are advertised in all Saturday weeklies this week."

Christ Church, Oxford

March 12, 1876

Dear Mr. Macmillan,

I think you must have misunderstood something in my letters. I didn't mean to ask for *any* more "proofs" (except only of the title-sheet, which has now come, and which I hope to return, marked "Press," today), but meant to say "print off as fast as you like." All I want is, for my own satisfaction, that as they work off each sheet, they should post *one* copy to me. Surely that won't be much extra trouble?

What you say about "enquiries what we can or cannot do under certain contingencies" puzzles me. I want you to go straight on, without pausing to think of "contingencies," only being careful that nothing suffers from hurry, the exact day of publishing being of much less importance than the doing all thoroughly well.[1]

I hope it is needless to say that all "sideways" pictures (all of which are to be on *left*-hand pages) ought to face *inwards* like this.

But I mention it, as I saw a book the other day, in which a "sideways" picture faced *outwards*.[2]

Very truly yours,

C. L. Dodgson

P.P.S.[3] On second thoughts, I send *you* the corrected proof of the title-sheet. It will save time if *you* will kindly undertake to see that it is properly done, instead of sending *me* any more proofs.

As to the Dedication, I am nearly in despair: they seem unable to correct one part of it without getting another part wrong. I sent back one proof with some stops to be corrected, and the next proof that came introduced the novelty of omitting three whole words! When you get the corrected proof, please read it with a magnifying-glass, and see that no fresh mistakes are introduced.[4]

In the matter of "spacing" in printing, Messrs. Clay are *not* very satisfactory. They are far too fond of having a very open line followed by a *very* crowded one – sometimes so crowded that the words are almost continuous. I suppose the setting up is done in the first instance by boys, or persons not experienced in "justifying" – but it is tiresome to an author to have to revise with such minute attention.

[1] "We really must go straight on now with no pauses to enquire what we can and what we cannot do under certain contingencies," Macmillan wrote the previous day, "which take no end of time and work to discover." He added: "I *think* we can get out by April 1 now the binding is settled."
[2] Another confusion apparently arose over the illustrations. On March 15, Macmillan writes: "I took for granted that you had, with Mr. Holiday, marked the pages in your proofs opposite to which each picture was to go, and put *titles* to the pictures so that they might be identified. I suppose that in the former books you worked with Tenniel who is familiar with these things. But the printers whom I told to print a list of illustrations on the last leaf of the title sheet write to say they don't know what the titles are, and don't seem to be quite sure whether their placing is right." Macmillan returns the rough proofs and adds: "I am afraid that you have not quite realised that all instructions for printers should be written on *proofs* and not in letters," and he goes on to say that if Dodgson had any doubts that the printer would understand his instructions, he should not only mark the proof but write to Macmillan who would see that the instructions were carried out.
[3] In another fit of absence of mind, Dodgson writes a P.P.S. where there is no P.S. Or did he consider this entire letter a postscript to his previous one?
[4] The dedication had to be put right for more than aesthetic reasons: it was a double acrostic verse to one of Dodgson's all-time favorite child friends, Gertrude Chataway. See *Letters*, pp. 230–6.

Christ Church, Oxford
March 17, 1876

Dear Mr. Macmillan,

A friend has made the suggestion – a very wise one, it seems to me – that if we put an advertisement inside the "grey-and-black" *Snark*, that it is to be had in red-and-gold for 1*s.* extra, it will simply make it impossible for any one to give the book as a present. No one would like it to be on record, in the book itself, that it was a cheaper kind than he could have bought. This difficulty might be avoided by having the advertisement on a loose fly-leaf – but I fancy the best plan will be to advertise the red-and-gold copies in the newspapers only, and *not* in the "grey-and-black" copies. Could not the advertisement end something like this. "Copies with the outside designs in gold may be had as follows: – cloth 4*s.* 6*d.*; morocco –/–; vellum –/–."

We are running it *very* fine for April 1, and I am beginning to be nervous about the pictures not being "made up" properly, or the sheets being hastily dried, or something done badly in order not to miss that date. *Please* remember that even as late as April 9 (say) will do perfectly well.[1]

Have you any technical name for that greenish blue which Mr. Holiday chose for the covers? I shall want you to bind me some copies in it, and it would be convenient to have a name for it when I want to order it.

Very truly yours,

C. L. Dodgson

P.S. As to Routledge – I don't think our views quite harmonise.[2] *You* take the publisher's view, doubtless, that it might injure the sale of the book. But really *I* don't feel much fear of that. And as to anything of mine being included among (respectable) collections of Nursery Rhymes, it is a classical position I have not hitherto aspired to. I should rather like, than otherwise, to be represented in a *good* collection of such things. But if you do not like to enquire from Messrs. Routledge about it, I do not mind writing myself. Those poems are already included in *Comic Poets of the Nineteenth Century.*[3]

Please answer my question of March 1 about the magic-lantern slides.[4]

---

[1] They made the April 1 publication date (see p. 129, below).

[2] George Routledge (1812–88), originally a bookseller like Macmillan, began publishing in 1843. Unlike Macmillan, however, he built his reputation as a publisher of cheap literature. His "Railway Library," a series of 1*s.* books, eventually ran to 1060 volumes. We do not know what precisely Routledge suggested to Dodgson, but surely it involved reprinting some of Dodgson's verse. The first mention of the offer occurs as a postscript to Macmillan's letter of March 15, in which he emphatically advised: "*Absolutely refuse* Routledge's proposal. *It is monstrous.*" Although Dodgson seems inclined to consider the approach, Macmillan again advises against doing so on March 20: "I am quite willing to write to Routledge if you give me leave to tell him that we must decline to give him leave. I have no doubt it is the right thing to do." No further reference to the Routledge proposal enters the letters: Macmillan's advice probably prevailed.

[3] *The Comic Poets of the Nineteenth Century,* ed. by William Davenport Adams (1851–1904), was published by Routledge in 1876 and contains six poems by Lewis Carroll. In arguing against the undocumented Routledge proposal, Macmillan writes (March 20): "The fact that you gave leave to Mr. Davenport Adams to put your poems into his volume . . . is the strongest possible reason why you should not do the same sort of thing again. The man is a mere *pushing* person with no power of discrimination. The book was offered to us. I had it up and looked carefully over it. It was obvious that the man had as much sense of what was *classical* in what he calls comic poetry as I have in what is classical in the 'theory of Determinants.'"

[4] Macmillan replies (March 20) that Craik corresponded with the man who had applied to produce magic-lantern slides of *Alice* and asked him "what he would give in the way of terms, but so far as I can learn he never answered."

Christ Church, Oxford
March 21, 1876

Dear Mr. Macmillan,

I am afraid you don't have my letters before you while answering them – otherwise you would have perceived a question you do not answer, and an answer to a question which you repeat.[1]

My question was, what is the technical name of the blue which Mr. Holiday chose for the *Snark*? I may be wishing to order copies in it, at times. There is also a green, very like it, and by candle-light hardly to be distinguished from it, of which you have sent a specimen: how am I to name *that* when I want it?[2]

I am sending you the 2 covers, to be returned to me as they are, after noting the colours. I shall speak of them as "dark blue" and "dark green," unless you can give me more definite names.

I also send 4 miscellaneous covers to be used for binding 4 copies for me. I want you to bind for me:

100 in red and gold (of course gold on *both* sides)
20 in dark blue and gold
20 in dark green and gold
2 in white vellum and gold.

An artistic friend suggests that these 2 ought to have "red gold" edges. Do you know the phrase?[3]

As to the Appletons, I wrote to say we had arranged for American sale. I don't want any thing more done about it, as I *don't* wish to sell them electrotypes. If they choose to pirate it, that isn't *my* fault: but it isn't likely, is it? if you send out plenty, to be sold cheap (but *not* at a loss, please) before they could get theirs ready.[4]

Are you not going to advertise in the Daily Papers? Don't be too economical. I am almost afraid it will be out before the country booksellers will have heard of it.[5] Haste.

Very truly yours,

C. L. Dodgson

---

[1] Macmillan replies the following day: "Your fear is certainly needless. I always have your letter or letters before me when I answer them. The questions you put are always full of interest, sometimes of perplexity, like Lord Dundreary's question 'If you had a brother, would he like cheese?'" (Lord Dundreary is a lazy, brainless fop of a peer in Tom Taylor's 1858 play *Our American Cousin*.)

[2] Macmillan answers (same letter) that there is no technical name for the two colors but that after consulting the binder his suggestion would be to "call one Morris & Fallmen *blue* and the other Morris & Fallmen *green*."

[3] "I quite understand what red gold edges mean for the vellum copies," Macmillan writes (same letter).

[4] On March 16, Macmillan wrote to suggest that Dodgson allow the firm to handle negotiations with Appleton about American rights to the *Snark*. In his letter of March 20, Macmillan inquires about the status of the negotiations with Appleton: "Have you written to Appleton or shall I communicate with them? My only fear is that they, or some other house, may reproduce the *Snark*

pictures by some of the easy and bad processes, and make a book even more inferior than printing from electros will give, if the book takes the American fancy. If you like to write to the London agent of Appletons, saying you leave it with me I will see him, and, if I found reasonable terms, I would let him have them." Macmillan clearly favors selling the electros, but Dodgson is unalterably opposed.

[5] "Our travellers have shown and we have sent notices to nearly every important bookseller in the country," Macmillan writes (March 22), but he does not answer Dodgson's query about advertising in the daily papers.

Christ Church, Oxford
March 26, 1876

Dear Mr. Macmillan,

If there is ample time for me to see another proof of this letter, I may as well do so: if not, I entrust it to you to see that these corrections are all properly made, and the paper cut so as to make equal margins round the border-line. If you look through it against the light, you will see that the first page does not fit upon the second as it ought: I suppose this will be duly adjusted when they print off.

Please order enough copies to put one into every copy of the new book, and of both the *Alice*s, which you are likely to sell before the end of April (no need to leave off putting them in the moment Easter-day is past) and to have a few hundred over.[1]

How soon will there be 50 red, 20 blue, 20 green, and 2 vellum ready for me to write in? If you *could* get the 2 vellum ones done first, and send them to me here, I should be glad – as I should like to send off those 2 *as soon as possible*. If you *do* send them, you might put a couple of each other colour along with them. But if the vellum cannot be done sooner than the rest, I may as well come to town and write in them: I can come any day, if you will let me know when you can undertake to have them ready for me – the sooner the better.[2]

I looked in vain, perhaps too hurriedly, for our advertisement in yesterday's *Saturday, Spectator*, and *Athenaeum*. If there, it is very artfully concealed.[3]

Very truly yours,
C. L. Dodgson

---

[1] The letter to which Dodgson refers is *An Easter Greeting to Every Child Who Loves "Alice"*. On February 5, 1876, when Dodgson was still referring to the *Snark* as his "Easter book," he wrote in his *Diaries* (p. 349): "In the afternoon I wrote a large piece of MS of 'An Easter Letter' which I am again thinking of printing to insert in copies of my Easter Book. I am afraid the religious allusions will be thought 'out of season' by many, but I do not like to lose the opportunity of saying a few serious words to (perhaps) 20,000 children." The four-page pamphlet is meant to cheer his child readers: he urges them not to fear the end of life, for purer and greater pleasures await them in the brighter sunrise after death. *An Easter Greeting* appeared in a number of Dodgson's books and was later pirated (see *Handbook*, pp. 92–5; *Letters*, pp. 247–51.)

[2] On the day after Dodgson writes this letter, Macmillan replies asking whether Dodgson would be coming on "Wednesday." On the same day, Dodgson writes Macmillan: "You don't say whether it is Wednesday *morning* or *afternoon* that you mean. Unless you telegraph to the contrary

tomorrow, I shall interpret it 'morning' and shall most likely be with you by soon after 11, returning here the same day. If the books cannot be warranted to be ready so soon, I had better come on Thursday morning instead." In his *Diaries* entry for Wednesday, March 29, Dodgson writes: "Went up to town for the day, and spent from eleven till nearly five at Macmillan's writing in about 80 presentation copies of the *Snark*" (p. 351). For more on the publication of the *Snark*, see *Diaries*, pp. 351–2; *Handbook*, pp. 89–92; and Tanis and Dooley, *passim*.

3 Macmillan replies (March 26): "You were prominently advertised on the back of last *Saturday* and *Academy*. You will equally appear in next *Spectator* and *Athenaeum*. We have sent the enclosed postcard [missing] to over 6000 booksellers all over the country. I think it is known the *Snark* is coming."

Christ Church, Oxford

May 12, 1876

Dear Mr. Craik,

In the first place, have you *entirely* dropped the subject of a cheap *Alice*? I heard from Mr. Macmillan on April 8, that he would get an estimate for a 2*s*. edition, and that is the last I have heard about it.[1]

In the second place, I want you, and him, seriously to advise on another matter, which I have mentioned before, the idea of re-publishing the comic portion of *Phantasmagoria*. The following are the points I want you to consider.

(1) The *Snark* has now been out long enough, I think, for you to form an idea (with the help of the opinions of friends, and reviews, the *Standard* especially!) whether Mr. Holiday would be likely to succeed as an illustrator of *Phantasmagoria*.[2]

(2) If you think he *would*, then comes a most important commercial question – how much it would be prudent to lay out on pictures. I am not particular about making much by it, and should be fairly content if it were to pay its expenses in (say) 2 years, and after that bring in some profit. To start the subject, I suggest an ideal case: could we reasonably expect to sell 5000, at a price which would bring *me* £50 per 1000?[3] In that case I might afford about £200 for pictures (£100 to artist, and £100 for engraving), which would give perhaps a dozen pictures (more, if many were small) – no very large allowance, as compared with the *Looking-Glass* and its 50 pictures. All these figures are mere guess: but I should like to have *some* definite notions before making any overtures to Mr. Holiday.

(3) I suppose we had better keep to the *Alice* size?

(4) I presume the blocks used for the cover of *Phantasmagoria* are still in good order, and would do for the new edition?[4]

Yours very truly,

C. L. Dodgson

Don't leave off putting "Easter letters" into *Snark*s and *Alice*s – at any rate till end of May.

On the 25th April I ordered 1000, to be sent to Mr. C. A. Owen: did they go, and when?[5]

[1] On April 7 Macmillan wrote promising to get an estimate for a 2s. *Alice* "in a week or ten days," and a letter from George Macmillan on April 18 also took up the subject: "With regard to the cheap *Alice*, my father is strongly of opinion that the only difference should be in the paper, type, and binding, and that the illustrations should stand as they are." Craik replies to the present letter on May 16 and gives the estimate. Alexander Macmillan is suffering a bout of sciatica about this time, which may account for the delay.

[2] Craik replies (same letter) that the question of an artist is complex and would be best resolved in personal discussion. Dodgson's reference to the *Standard* suggests that it reviewed Holiday's drawings negatively, but he is probably confusing the *Standard* with the *Saturday Review*. The brief notice in the *Standard* (April 24, 1876, p. 3) does not mention Holiday but condemns the *Snark*: "Mr. Carroll, having made one success in the domain of 'delicious romance,' has essayed another and failed. There is neither wit nor humour in this little versified whimsicality; its 'nonsensicalities' fail either to surprise or to amuse." The *Saturday Review* (April 15, 1876, p. 502) applauded the *Snark* but added that "the illustrations display that strange want of any sense of fun which distinguishes most comic draughtsmen in these days."

[3] Craik agrees (same letter) that by "rough calculation" Dodgson might expect £50 per 1000 on such a book.

[4] Craik answers affirmatively to questions 3 and 4 in the same letter.

[5] Craik writes (same letter): "We sent the thousand letters to Mr. Owen as you asked . . .," but he does not say when the firm sent them. Dodgson might have had these letters sent to the Polytechnic where he had seen *Alice* performed (see pp. 122–3, above), to be distributed to the students. More than a year later, Dodgson must have received an application from the Polytechnic to permit them to perform *Alice* again. He records in his *Diaries* (p. 363) on June 18, 1877: "Wrote to Mr. Owen, one of the directors of the Polytechnic, in answer to his letter, received yesterday, proposing to reproduce *Alice*: I declined to give leave, and explained (1) that I objected to interpolations, and meant any future dramatic version to be the book itself; (2) that I meant to charge a 'royalty,' if it were ever to be done again." Three days after that, Dodgson writes (Diaries): "Heard from Mr. G. Buckland, who had assumed that I had given my consent. . . . I sent him a copy of the letter I had written to Mr. Owen."

Christ Church, Oxford
May 18, 1876

Dear Mr. Craik,

Please be prepared to sell *Easter Greetings* separate, if asked for: I have been asked if I will not allow them to be sold, and of course I have no objection. You will know best what to charge: only remember that I want neither to gain nor lose by it: so you will have to add together (1) cost price of printing (2) a margin to cover expense of postage, etc. (3) (if you wish to take your 10 percent commission) $\frac{1}{9}$ of the sum of (1) and (2). Do not charge any more than is needed for these purposes.

Thanks for your answers to my questions: but my question about Mr. Holiday was not so much a matter of *taste* as a *commercial* one, whether you think his pictures "take" with the buying public. The new specimen-page you send me is identical with the one I sent to Mr. Macmillan on April 6 – i.e. it is 29 lines to the page.[1] The page of *Alice* is 22 lines: in my letter of April 6, I asked Mr. Macmillan to have one set up, intermediate to these, *viz.* 25 lines to the page. This I should like to be done. The type of the 29-line page looks to me too small for children to read comfortably. I don't think the 2s. price essential: 2s. 6d. would perhaps be cheap enough. We must not produce a really inferior article.

Please send me another 200 Easter letters.

Thanks for *Inverness Courier.*[2]

Yours very truly,

C. L. Dodgson

---

[1] This sentence and the rest of the paragraph refer to the proposed 2s. *Alice.* On June 26, Craik writes: "I send you a specimen of the *Alice* page in the shape you asked. . . . if you approve of it, I will tell you how an edition at half a crown will repay. . . ."

[2] The review of the *Snark* in the *Inverness Courier* (May 11, 1876, p. 3) considers the possibility that the book is political allegory. It concludes: "Various ingenious interpretations might be put upon this, but we prefer to look upon the poem as nonsense pure and simple, and as such it will be eagerly welcomed by the children." The poem is "disappointing, though there are passages which, taken alone, may vie with some of the happiest rhymes in *Alice.*" Of the illustrations, the *Courier* writes: "We miss the delicate grace of Tenniel . . . ; by the side of those in *Alice*, these in the *Snark* look poor and coarse. . . ."

Christ Church, Oxford
October 30, 1876[1]

Dear Mr. Craik,

Many thanks for your letter, and for the very satisfactory money-accounts for the year.[2] I think we had better defer *publishing* a cheap *Alice.* What I wanted one *printed* for, chiefly, was to have copies to give away to Hospitals, etc. Perhaps after all these can be done as cheaply without setting up new type. Would you make an estimate of how cheap it could be done? I should want 500 *Alices* and 500 *Looking-Glasses*, on cheap (but not thin) paper – no gilt edges nor gilt ornaments outside – but a strong cover, which would not easily come to pieces, and if possible a *gay* one: I might even say *gaudy.* What can you suggest, which would please the eyes of little children and yet would be cheap? Some of those cheap picture-books have very pretty outsides.

The edges of the leaves had better not be left white: they would get dirty so soon. Would marbling be much cheaper than gilding?[3]

Very truly yours,

C. L. Dodgson

---

[1] We have found no letters from Dodgson to Macmillan between May 18 and October 30, 1876, although six replies come from the firm to Dodgson during that period.

[2] The account is missing, but Craik reported in his letter of October 27 that "the sale [of *Alice*] is still very good. . . ."

[3] Dodgson had long been a benefactor of sick children. Printings of *Alice* or *Looking-Glass* which did not meet his rigorous standards were occasionally "presented by the author for the use of sick children." In 1876, he decided to have cheap copies of both books printed expressly for children's hospitals. He recorded on July 6, 1876, that he "took to the University Press the MS of a new

circular to send round to Hospitals, etc., offering *Alice* and *Looking-Glass* for the use of sick children" (*Diaries*, p. 354). In Craik's reply (November 2) he agrees that binding the books more cheaply is preferable to an entirely new edition and suggests that "marbling the edges" might allow them to produce the books at 1*s*. 11*d*. or 2*s*. a copy. On the following June 25, Dodgson writes to Macmillan: "I am again sending round circulars to the Hospitals, to get the information which I could not get satisfactorily last time, with a view to giving *Alices*, etc. I am sending them printed envelopes addressed to you. You will know them by their being numbered 1, 2, etc. Please do not forward them to me as they arrive, but keep them for me, and when all have come in, you can send them in a parcel." On July 18, Dodgson writes from Eastbourne asking Macmillan if he would "kindly forward to me here whatever circulars have now come in. . . ." For more on Dodgson's books for children's hospitals, see *Handbook*, pp. 70, 95, 169–70; *Letters*, p. 150.

Christ Church, Oxford
November 22, 1876

Dear Mr. Craik,

I have several important matters to write about.

(1) I have been going through the accounts and find several items to be corrected:

The American *Alice* has a balance of £3.10*s*. against me, which ought to go into the "General Statement."

The American *Looking-Glass* has a balance, on the whole year, of £3. 11*s*. 7*d*. against me; and *not* (as stated) a balance of £18.11.11 for me, followed by £27.7.5 against me (i.e. £8.15.6 against me).

The "$\frac{3}{4}$ to author,$\frac{1}{4}$ to publisher" arrangement can only come into effect when there is a gain *on the year's account*. That was the arrangement I made with Mr. Macmillan: it is an obvious mistake to reckon a bit of the year, by itself, as gain, and take $\frac{1}{4}$ of that, unless you *also* take a $\frac{1}{4}$ of the loss on the remaining bit. But clearly the proper thing is to take the year as a whole.

The "General Statement," when thus corrected, shows only £606.10.2 (instead of £632.3.8) as due to me in January 1877.[1]

I enclose the papers: please let me have them again.

(2) Please make a memorandum *not* to advertise the French, German, and Italian *Alices* any longer. The sale does not pay for the advertising. You will say perhaps that, without advertising, there will be no sale at all. My answer is "I greatly prefer no sale at all to selling at an annual loss. In money matters, zero is preferable to a negative quantity!"

(3) Please make another memorandum, to sell no more *Determinants*, in America or anywhere else, at less than 7*s*. 6*d*. *More* than that I don't insist on: the few left may go at that, but it is too absurd to be selling a book, that cost more than 8*s*. a copy to produce, at 2*s*. 6*d*.! Please send me 10 of the copies you have left. The other 17 will probably last you till 1900.

(4) I am rather curious to know if you have had *any* applications for the Easter letters by themselves – and if so, what did you sell them at? (I said "sell at cost-

price.") A lady-friend was very anxious I should authorise their sale, but I suspect it was a mere fancy of hers that there would be any demand for them.[2]

Very truly yours,

C. L. Dodgson

[1] Although Dodgson published in England entirely at his own risk, with Macmillan earning a commission on sales, the American sales were accounted for on a royalty basis. In Craik's reply (November 24), he explains: "The half profit arrangement is one of the commonest arrangements we have, and we ought by this time to know how to make out the accounts. The principle is that we take all the risk and account for each edition separately – giving you a share in the profit of each edition. On this principle there is no oversight in the way these accounts are stated. Of course we can have no objection to account in the way you proposed," Craik continues, "for it is obviously for our advantage but you may never receive anything." He goes on to explain that by figuring on the year as a whole (as Dodgson believed right) rather than by edition (as Macmillan did) any new printing near the end of the year would erase profits for that year. Craik concludes: "After this explanation I will wait to hear before altering the accounts."

[2] Craik writes (same letter) that "we have sent 120 of the *Easter Letters* to Cambridge, charging them 6*d*. a dozen." Dodgson has the *Easter Greeting* reprinted for sale to the public in 1880, 1881, 1883 and 1887 (see *Handbook*, pp. 91–5).

Christ Church, Oxford
November 25, 1876

Dear Mr. Craik,

I know the "all the risk and half the profit" plan quite well: but that isn't exactly the arrangement on which we have been going. If you refer to the accounts, you will see that you are allowing me $\frac{3}{4}$ the profit: and I had not understood that you, under these circumstances, undertook *risk* at all. I mean that I had been under the impression that, supposing no more profits were to come in, the "balance against," which you are carrying on into the next year, would remain as a valid debt from me to you. I now understand you that, in such a case as that, *you* would bear the loss. However, the case is hardly worth providing for, it is so very unlikely to arise.

I withdraw my proposal as to making up accounts at the end of the year. Please let me have the papers again, and I will alter them back: I don't mind their being untidy – that is *my* fault.

In the long run, it would come to much the same thing, whenever you made up the accounts. Your gloomy picture of the possibility that I might "never get any profits," if you always printed an edition just before the end of a year, could only be realised if every edition were much larger than the last. For if they were the same size, and if the proceeds of an edition were (as of course they must be) greater than the cost of producing an edition, it would not matter whether they were set against the cost of the edition *itself* (as in your plan), or against the cost of the *next* edition (as in the "annual account" plan): in either case there would be a clear profit to be divided.[1]

Please keep a look-out among illustrated books, and let me know if you see any artist at all worthy of succeeding to Tenniel's place.[2] I should *much* like to write one more child's book before all writing-power leaves me. Believe me

Very truly yours,

C. L. Dodgson

[1] Craik replies with a single sentence on the following day: "Let us then keep the accounts as I rendered them at first."

[2] In the same letter, Craik writes: "You should look at *Baby's Opera* by Walter Crane. I think for humour he is superior to Tenniel. I remember you did not admire some things I showed you of his but this new book is unusually good." We do not know whether Dodgson looks at *Baby's Opera* or not, but in a letter to Macmillan dated November 26, 1877, he writes: "The *Cuckoo-Clock* has converted me into an admirer of Mr. Walter Crane's drawings, and I am writing to ask if he is open to a commission to do a few drawings for me." Macmillan published Mrs. Molesworth's *The Cuckoo-Clock* (by "Ennis Graham," her pseudonym at the time), with illustrations by Walter Crane, that year. Indeed, Dodgson and Crane correspond, and Crane agrees to Dodgson's exacting terms. Nothing, however, comes of the proposed collaboration. Crane gives us an account of what happened: "Lewis Carroll . . . wrote to me . . . saying he had been looking out for a new illustrator for a forthcoming work of his, as . . . Tenniel would do 'no more.' This Mr. Dodgson evidently greatly deplored, and naturally felt that it would be most difficult to find a substitute. His letters gave one the impression of a most particular person, and it is quite possible that he may have led Tenniel anything but a quiet life during the time he was engaged upon his inimitable illustrations. . . . I believe I agreed to meet his views if possible, but my hands were so full of all sorts of other work that I fear the year went by without my being able to take the matter up" (Walter Crane, *An Artist's Reminiscences* (1907), pp. 184–6; see also *Letters*, p. 322).

Christ Church, Oxford
February 4, 1877

Dear Mr. Macmillan,

Can it be true, what a friend reports to me, that the *Looking-Glass* is out of print? And if so, how can it possibly have happened? Surely there must have been some strange carelessness, on the part of whoever is responsible for the re-printing, in letting the stock run too low before putting a fresh 3000 in hand? And I suppose that to be "out of print" just now, in the Xmas Season, means to lose the opportunity of a good many possible sales.[1]

How has the *Snark* sold during the Xmas Season? *That*, I should think, would be a much better test of its success or failure than any amount of sale at its first coming out. I am entirely puzzled as to whether to consider it a success or failure. I hear in some quarters of children being fond of it – but certainly the Reviews condemned it in no measured terms.[2]

Have you taken your young people (or your young "person" – for I suppose Olive still considers herself young) to see that most charming performance, the "Children's Pantomime" at the Adelphi?[3]

Yours ever truly,

C. L. Dodgson

¹ Macmillan replies the following day that Dodgson's anonymous friend is wrong: there are more than 1300 *Looking-Glasses* on hand, and, Macmillan adds: "I cannot find that we have ever been out of it for a day."
² Macmillan reports (same letter) that some 15,000 copies of the *Snark* have been sold since its publication in April 1876. "This does not look very like a failure," he concludes, but adds that it was not so great a success as Dodgson's other books. "It is no doubt very *Queer!* But never mind the critics," he urges. For critical reservations on the *Snark*, see pp. 130, 131, above. On January 13, 1877, Dodgson wrote thanking Craik for "*Punch*, with the allusion (I can hardly say 'review'!) of the *Snark*." The "allusion" appeared among "Some Christmas Books" (January 6, 1877, p. 297): ". . . next on the table is *The Hunting of the Snark* by Lewis Carroll, who, as he never appears in print except at this festive season, ought to be known as the Christmas Carroll. The *Snark* is very distinctly related to the Jabberwock, but it is *not* the Jabberwock," the notice concludes.
³ Dodgson saw *Goody Two-Shoes*, the Children's Pantomime at the Adelphi, on January 13 and thought it "a really charming performance" (*Diaries*, pp. 359–60). He must have recommended it earlier to Macmillan, who, in a letter the following day, writes: "Under a misapprehension I took some 'young persons' to . . . *Cinderella* . . . played most amusingly by children. I thought at the time that this was what you recommended. It is very good. I don't know whether I shall accomplish the Adelphi." Dodgson apparently did not see *Cinderella* that season.

Christ Church, Oxford
March 2, 1877

Dear Mr. Macmillan,

I hope I'm not making a troublesome request in asking you to get me 4 tickets for the Adelphi Pantomime for Saturday afternoon (the 10th).

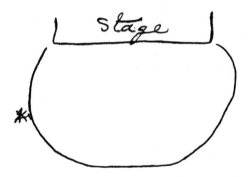

I want them dress-circle, front seats, about the place I have put a *. Two of them are for children under 12 (I mention in case children may be "half-price").¹

Very truly yours,

C. L. Dodgson

We cannot arrive much before the thing begins – so, unless such seats are *numbered and reserved*, it would be better to get stalls (near middle of 2nd or 3rd row) but I'm afraid little children wouldn't see so well from the stalls.

¹ Macmillan reports three days later that he has procured the tickets, and on the appointed Saturday, Dodgson "went to town. . . . Picked up Evelyn and Olive Brooke on the way to the Adelphi, to see the Children's Pantomime for the second time . . ." (*Diaries*, p. 361). The young ladies were the daughters of Stopford Augustus Brooke (1832–1916), Honorary Chaplain to the Queen, author of numerous theological works and books on English literature.

Christ Church, Oxford
March 26, 1877

Dear Mr. Macmillan,

Many thanks for the Exeter Hall tickets.¹ If you sent a boy from the shop to get them, and the Adelphi tickets, would you give him a shilling, and charge it to me? But if it was your son to whom I am indebted, I decline to offer *him* a shilling! I want to ask a question of you, relating to that circulation I made about how the money is apportioned that is paid (by the public) for *Alice*. If you tell me the answer involves one of the secrets of the trade, I say no more: but hope you will at least not think it a piece of unjustifiable curiosity, as it is my own book I am asking about.

Somebody or other told me that publishers charge so much for "printing and binding," but do not pay that sum to the printers, but that part of it remains in their hands as commission. Of course I have not a word to object to such an arrangement, if it is customary. But my question is, if the sums put down for printing, binding, and advertising are in excess of the sums actually paid, what percentage is the excess? And similarly, if the sum put down as received by sale is short of the true sum, what percentage is the defect? With this information I should see *exactly* what proportion of the 6*s*. charged for a copy, goes to the printer, what to the publisher, and so on – which it would be very satisfactory to me to know.²

Very truly yours,

C. L. Dodgson

¹ Two days later Dodgson travels from Guildford to London with four sisters and a brother-in-law to hear *The Messiah* at Exeter Hall (*Diaries*, p. 361).
² Craik answers the questions on the following day: "With commission books such as yours, we add 10 percent to the printing charges," but the printer charges the firm 10 percent less than the general public, "so . . . the cost of printing is as it would have been if you had gone direct to the printer." He goes on: "The advertising charges are a small percentage above the cost price, but the insertion of your books in . . . [*Macmillan's*] *Magazine* is half price and the advertising in all our Catalogues is at a very trifling – almost nominal cost. So I should say there is virtually no commission on the advertisements. The books are accounted for at the trade price – that is at the price we sell to the booksellers. We have a 10 percent [commission] which appears in the account on sales. The above are I understand the customary charges for commission books."

The Chestnuts, Guildford
March 30, 1877

Dear Mr. Craik,

Many thanks for your full explanations about commissions and percentages, which I consider eminently satisfactory.

I think it is not premature to tell you (but don't let it go beyond yourselves, at present, as it *may* come to nothing) that I have some hope of getting *Phantasmagoria* illustrated after all, by Mr. Sambourne.[1]

All we have settled so far, is that he is to draw 4 or 5 pictures for the "Lang Coortin'." So I want you to set up a specimen page of it, the *Alice* size of page. As to type, I think I should prefer 5 stanzas to the page: 4 would look too much spread out, I fancy. The *Snark* I see has only 3 stanzas to the page, but then the lines are so long and so often turn the corner that it makes a better show than any short metre would do. We might try two specimens – one with 4 stanzas to the page, and the other (same type but closer leading) with 5. If I go no further in the business, I shall probably ask you to print the "Lang Coortin'" and pictures by itself, not for publication, but merely to give to friends.[2]

Very truly yours,

C. L. Dodgson

[1] Earlier negotiations with Sambourne (see pp. 104–7 above) came to naught. On this day, however, Dodgson "Heard from Sambourne, asking if I have arranged for having *Phantasmagoria* illustrated, as he again thinks he can undertake it. I wrote at once to re-open negotiations" (*Diaries*, p. 361).

[2] Although on April 6 Craik offers to print "Lang Coortin'" separately, nothing comes of the proposal. Dodgson continues to negotiate with Sambourne for years to come.

Christ Church, Oxford
May 1, 1877

Dear Mr. Macmillan,

I shall take it as a favour to myself (though I ask it on behalf of a lady-friend, Mrs. Hatch by name) if you will kindly inspect (or give to one of your "readers" to inspect) the MS of a novel, on which she has tried her "prentice han'."[1] And having done, would you kindly write me word what you think of it, and, if you think it good enough for publishing, whether you would be willing to undertake it, and on what terms – in fact, as the lawyers say, would you "advise generally on the whole matter." I have read none of it myself: even if I had time, I don't see that it would be any use, as you would no doubt prefer judging for yourself. The MS is coming to you by carrier.[2]

Very truly yours,

C. L. Dodgson

¹ Mrs. Edwin Hatch, born Bessie Cartwright Thomas (1839–91), was the wife of Edwin Hatch (1835–89), Vice-Principal of St. Mary Hall, Oxford (1867), and University Reader (1883). Dodgson was a friend of the Hatch family for more than twenty-five years and frequently entertained and photographed the children. For more on Dodgson and the Hatches, see *Handbook*, *passim*; *Diaries*, *passim*; *Letters*, esp. p. 185; Evelyn M. Hatch, ed. *A Selection of the Letters of Lewis Carroll . . . to His Child-Friends* (1933), esp. pp. 92–3.

² On the following day, Macmillan writes to say that he would be happy to consider the manuscript. On June 4, George Macmillan writes to Dodgson rejecting the manuscript and leaving it to him to decide how much of the reader's report to transmit to Mrs. Hatch. In part the report read: "All that can be said is that there is a centre of interest in the action of the story; that the characters are people with pleasant manners; and that the grammar and style are of a cultivated person." The novel was apparently never published.

Christ Church, Oxford
November 4, 1877

Dear Mr. Macmillan,

I see I never told you which I preferred of the two title-pages (with inscriptions for Hospitals). I like the *smaller* inscription best. We had better prepare 200 copies of each book, as I shall want about 150 of each at once, and the rest can be put aside for future donations. Please send me a specimen of binding as soon as you can, and tell me how you think the edges had better be done – "sprinkled with red" is *my* notion.

The Euclid book is a harder matter than I expected, to finish to my satisfaction. However I have got some MS into the printer's hands, and hope to have the whole in type (in slip) by the end of this month: that will give me the Xmas vacation for final alterations and arrangement in pages, and we may get it printed by the end of January. My fellow-lecturer here thinks February would be a good time to publish it, as it would catch all the schoolmasters, fresh from their Xmas tours, and well *before* their Easter tours begin. What say you?

Very truly yours,

C. L. Dodgson

P.S. I expect the book will be between 150 and 200 pages.¹

¹ "Have been at work, every day and all day, at my protest *Euclid and His Modern Rivals*," Dodgson wrote in his *Diaries* (p. 358) on the last day of 1876. He continued to work on the book during his summer vacation of 1877: on September 29, he recorded: "Am writing *Euclid* pamphlet 6 or 8 hours a day now" (p. 366). On October 23, back at Oxford, he was "writing the *Euclid* book day and night" (Diaries). We cannot tell which of his fellow lecturers Dodgson refers to here.

Christ Church, Oxford
December 11, 1877

Dear Mr. Macmillan,

The "Elliston Family" (who advertised *Alice in Fairyland* in Brighton) are at the "Theatre Royal, Gloucester" (engaged for the Pantomime). Unless you see any objection, would you, as publisher of *Alice*, write to Mrs. Elliston, not threatening any proceedings, but mentioning that the dramatic copyright of the book is secured, and asking where you can get a copy of the libretto. If she declines to furnish the information, I think it would be an awkward circumstance for her, if I ever took legal proceedings. Perhaps it would be well to enclose a stamped envelope for reply.

You can write from yourself only, or "by the author's request," as you think best.

Very truly yours,

C. L. Dodgson

P.S. As to the Hospitals?

Christ Church, Oxford
December 15, 1877

Dear Mr. Macmillan,

The "Hospital" copies of *Alice* and the *Looking-Glass* have just come. The binding, and the sprinkled edges, will do capitally. Please note the following particulars:

(1) The inscription, "Presented for the use of Sick Children" must be on the *title-page* as well as the cover. It is well to have it on the cover too, but it might easily not be seen there, and would of course vanish if the book were rebound. But it is absolutely essential to have it on the title-page also, as a security against the books ever getting into the market. If, as I fear is the case, the new impression has been worked off without inserting it on the title-pages, it must be added by hand. It would not be difficult I suppose, to set up the phrase in a small frame with a handle, and stamp it on every title-page. You sent me 2 title-pages for choice. I enclose the one I prefer.

(2) I under-estimated the numbers needed. Please prepare *300* copies of each book.

(3) In binding, cut out the advertisement-page.

(4) None of these copies are on any account to be sold to any body: but *all* kept for me, somewhere where they have no chance of getting mixed with the books on sale.

(5) I should be very glad if you and the binder could devise a rather stronger way of keeping the sheets together at the back. *Bound* books seem to have an inner back of a much more solid nature than these. But they ought to be quite as strong as bound books, to bear the wear and tear of childish hands. If the thing cannot be managed in cloth backs, then try half-binding, with leather backs and cloth sides. The extra cost doesn't matter in the least: the essential point is that the books shall be able to stand an exceptional amount of knocking about without coming to pieces.

So much for the "Hospital" books.

I enclose our last attempt at a title-page for my *Euclid* book: which I hope you will approve of. To me it seems to be just the thing. Do you see that the *World* and *Figaro* have announced that I am doing "a burlesque Euclid"?[1] (I am just about the last person in the land who would think of so dishonouring the great mathematician!) I have not thought it worth while to contradict it.

As to the dramatic copyright question. Your saying that the registering was done "3 years ago" lost me an hour, I should think, in hunting journal and letter-register for the years 1874 and 1875. At last I find that it was at the end of 1872:[2] I took the two MS books to Stationers' Hall (you did not go with me), and the following is a copy of the document I received.

"Copyright Registry,
Stationers' Hall.
No. 3251
2 British Entry 10*s*.
12 December 1872"

there is a signature I can't make out.

If you have any doubt whether the registration has or has not secured me the dramatic copyright, or as to my exact rights of preventing others from dramatising the books, I can easily get a legal opinion on that point. One thing seems clear – that it cannot require "publication and sale" of the drama, as you suggest. Many dramas are never printed for sale at all, but are acted from MS: and yet are undoubtedly copyright.

Who is responsible, I wonder, for the astounding statement that appears in the advertisement at the end of *St. Nicholas Magazine* for December (published by Scribner, New York)? In a list of books sold by "Macmillan & Co. 22 Bond Street, New York" I see "Now ready, the hundredth thousand *Alice's Adventures in Wonderland*, etc., etc., *Through the Looking-Glass*, fiftieth thousand." Surely your namesakes are not selling the *American* reprint of *Alice*? And the *Looking-Glass* was never reprinted there at all, that I know of. I am sorry to see such a name as "Macmillan" at the end of a statement which seems to me to be absolutely false.[3]

With best wishes for the season to you and Mrs. Macmillan, "Miss" Margaret[4] and "Miss" Olive, I am

Very truly yours,

C. L. Dodgson

[1] Dodgson seems to conflate burlesques here. Indeed the *World* announced that he was writing such a work (November 7, 1877, p. 12): "The well-known author of *Alice in Wonderland*, etc., has, I hear, a new work in the press, which treats of Euclid in a serio-comic way. Those who read with wonder and despair that marvellous piece of nonsense the *Hunting of the Snark* will look forward with nervous expectancy to the new production of 'Mr. Lewis Carroll.'" But what appeared in *London Figaro* had nothing to do with Dodgson's work on Euclid but was a notice of a burlesque of *Alice* (November 14, 1877, p. 12): "*Our Trip to Blunderland*, published by Blackwood and Sons, is a children's book written after *Alice's Adventures in Wonderland*. There are illustrations by Charles Doyle. The author, 'Jean Jambon,' is Col. J. H. A. MacDonald, the Solicitor General for Scotland. . . . 'Jean Jambon' is the French equivalent of 'John H.A.M.'" Years later, Dodgson, compiling a list of books of the *Alice* type, includes this *Blunderland* (*Diaries*, p. 486).

² See p. 100, above.
³ We do not have Macmillan's reply.
⁴ Alexander Macmillan's eldest daughter, Margaret, was one year older than Olive, or about twenty at this time. She married (1889) Louis Dyer (1851–1908), classical scholar from Chicago, a friend of her brother Malcolm (they had been at Oxford together).

Christ Church, Oxford
December 18, 1877

Dear Mr. Macmillan,

Thanks for your letter.

Please send me (I go to "The Chestnuts, Guildford" on the 22nd) one of the "Hospital" books with the "extra strong" binding, before you go on with them. I doubt if *any* cloth binding will do, and rather expect that I shall want leather backs.

Euclid, etc., won't be ready, I fear, till about Easter. I am not nearly satisfied with it yet: the subject is very complicated, and requires much thought. You had better not put out any notices about it *yet*. Also I think we may as well let the *World*, etc., alone. When we come to advertise, I think it will be well to add, to the title, a few words of explanation, and then people will see that it is *not* a funny book.

I will get a legal opinion on the copyright question.

Thank you. I should like very much to come and see your Mary.¹ But do not suppose *she* is the chief attraction of your house.¹ My views about children are changing, and I *now* put the nicest age at about 17!

Yours very truly,

C. L. Dodgson

¹ Mary (three or four years old at this time) was the elder of two children that Alexander Macmillan had by his second wife, born Emma Pignatel (they married in the autumn of 1872). Mary in turn married (1896) James MacLehose, 2nd, the brother of her sister Olive's husband, Norman MacLehose. James MacLehose was also a member of the Glasgow firm of booksellers and publishers established by his father. Mary later married John Victor (b. 1877). For more about Olive, "the chief attraction," see p. 105, above.

Christ Church, Oxford
December 20, 1877

Dear Mr. Macmillan,

It is unfortunate that you have misunderstood me, but I daresay it was my fault, in not expressing myself more clearly. Nothing was further from my thoughts than that the binding should go on without our having settled exactly what it was to be, which of course cannot be done until I have seen a specimen which appears to be the right thing.

Whether the copies are sent round at Christmas, or Easter, or any other time, is a matter of quite minor importance. The only thing I really care about is that the copies, when given, shall be worth giving. And as it is a matter of pure outlay, out of my own pocket, I am not inclined to throw my money away by giving copies that are not really durable.

I am going to "The Chestnuts, Guildford," on Saturday the 22nd so would you kindly send me a copy there, and at the same time let me know how many of them are already bound?

If the binding does not seem strong enough for much handling, it might still be possible to utilise those that are already bound (if not too many) by giving them to some hospitals where there are very few children. But I shall be quite willing to pay for their being bound over again, if necessary, as this present binding has been gone on with owing to a mistake.

If your binders are very busy just now with other work, I have no objection to wait awhile.

Very truly yours,

C. L. Dodgson

Christ Church, Oxford
December 27, 1877

Dear Mr. Macmillan,

I have just got the legal opinion on dramatic copyright which I told you (in my letter of December 18) that I would ask for. It is entirely against me, and is to the effect that *any* one may dramatise a book, and that if the author does so, and registers the drama, it only secures the *drama* from being copied, not the book. So we cannot interfere with the Elliston family. What did you say in your letter to them? I should still like to see their drama, if a copy is to be had.[1]

Please give my best thanks to George for his kind trouble on my behalf.[2]

I have just noticed your advertisement of the two *Alice*s in the Christmas number of the *Monthly Packet*, in which there is no mention as to which "thousand" it is in. Will you please see that it is not omitted in other advertisements?[3] When a book has had a good sale, I think that very fact is a valuable advertisement, and ought to be kept before the eyes of the public. Believe me

Very truly yours,

C. L. Dodgson

---

[1] In his reply four days later, Macmillan encloses a copy of the firm's letter (missing) to the Elliston family and reports that he had yet to receive a reply. Macmillan writes to Dodgson again on January 7: "I enclose the answer from the Elliston family [also missing]. Shall I ask them to send the MS or will you write yourself?" Although no further reference to the Ellistons and their *Alice* libretto appears in the letters we have, Dodgson meets them within the year. On January 4, 1878, in Brighton to visit friends, he goes to the pantomime *Jack and the Beanstalk*, "which was extremely

good as a whole. There was a pretty scene of children," he adds, "the leading child being Clara Elliston, a graceful and pretty child . . ." (*Diaries*, p. 368). On August 3 of that year, again at Brighton, Dodgson "called on the Ellistons, and had about 5 minutes (it being near train time) to make personal acquaintance with Clara, who seemed a nice, bright child, neither too forward nor too shy" (Diaries). An advertisement appeared in the *Eastbourne Chronicle* of September 21, 1878, announcing "A Grand Afternoon Performance" on September 27 and 28, "each day at Five for the convenience of the juveniles of the gentry: THE ELLISTON FAMILY OF BURLESQUE ENTERTAINERS will have the honour to appear in their New, Original and Select Drawing-Room Entertainment entitled '*Alice in Fairyland.*'" On September 28, Dodgson, at Eastbourne, records: "The Elliston family gave a performance of *Alice in Fairy-Land* in Diplock's Assembly Rooms. . . . it was a very third-rate performance. . . . none of them could articulate so as to be audible: and the singing was painfully out of tune" (Diaries). Dodgson calls on the Ellistons again in Brighton in early January 1879 (*Diaries*, p. 376) and goes on calling on them and admiring Clara's acting and singing through the next few years.

2 What service George Macmillan performed for Dodgson at this point is not made clear in the letters we have.

3 In his reply of December 31, Macmillan promises to "try to keep the numbering of the *Alice*s before the people."

Christ Church, Oxford

March 4, 1878

Dear Mr. Macmillan,

Could you suggest the proper course to take in the following case?

A German Teacher, with wife and children, has settled in England, being told there was a good opening for him: but all he has got is a mastership in a middle-class school, at £20 a year, and 3 pupils at 2*s*. 6*d*. a lesson. Consequently, he is in great difficulties, but he is not asking for charity, as he prefers *earning* an income, if possible. He has, in MS, 70 books translated from the German, which he wishes to sell to some publisher (he thinks they are worth about £1 a piece). Would it be of any use to send you a few of them to look at? Or could you suggest any other publisher, to whom it would be worth while to apply? I understand he is a well-educated and most respectable man, and one really deserving that some trouble should be taken to help him – which I should be very glad to do, if only I knew how to set about it.[1]

Yours very truly,

C. L. Dodgson

1 "Your German friend's case seems to me wholly hopeless in a publishing sense," Macmillan replies the following day. "The mere fact that he has done seventy books is startling. If he will send me a list of three or four of those he thinks most important I will tell him whether I feel it of any use to look at them." On March 19 Dodgson writes again on the subject: "I enclose a list [missing] of the works of the German teacher, about whom I wrote to you on March 4. The number '70' was evidently a mistake. If you can't do anything with them yourself, could you name any publisher to whom it might be worth his while to apply?" On the 20th, Macmillan reports that he cannot publish any of the translator's work: "I cannot conceive any rational English publisher undertaking any of them." We are not able to identify the translator whose cause Dodgson was trying to advance.

Christ Church, Oxford

April 11, 1878

Dear Mr. Craik,

I am grieved to hear what a disastrous effect my suggestions of other coloured inks, etc., have had! They were meant merely *as* suggestions – not as orders. Pray consider them wholly and unreservedly withdrawn: and give the reins to your fancy.[1]

The type of Arnold's poems looks charming.[2] I should like to have a page of *Phantasmagoria* itself set up in it: and would you send me 2 or 3 impressions. I shall want to send one to my artist.[3]

What do you think of the idea of printing no more *Hunting of the Snark* by itself, but embodying it (of course in the new type) with *Phantasmagoria?* It would make a more respectable volume than the comic part of the old book will be by itself.[4] How long is the present stock of *Snark*s likely to last?

Very truly yours,

C. L. Dodgson

I leave on 13th for "The Chestnuts, Guildford."

P.S. Messrs. Kegan Paul and Co. decline the *Index to "In Memoriam"* – deterred, I fancy, by the fact that, though nearly 1000 were sold between 1861 and 1871, none have sold since.[5] That, I think arises from the public having lost sight of it. What I want you to do is this: you will receive from Messrs. Ward & Lock about 100 copies in sheets and 50 in cloth. I want you to send me 20 of those in cloth (not till after Easter Tuesday, as I shall be away), and to keep the rest to sell for me. When next you print lists of my books to go at the end of *Alice*, please add the *Index*. That will help to make it known. And I think a little advertising might be tried, but not enough to swallow up the receipts, as there are only a few pounds' worth to sell. However, if there seems to be a fair demand, I would reprint it. Suppose you spend a couple of pounds on advertising, and then we can see if there is any chance of a sale for it.[6]

---

[1] The inks may be for variant bindings, of course, but Dodgson and Craik had probably, at some point, discussed printing the text of the *Alice* books in a variety of colored inks (see Dodgson's next letter). At any rate, Craik wrote on the previous day: "As to the coloured inks we once spoke of, I have done nothing more. I feel confident I could make a good result if I were left to myself – but the suggestions you made were so contrary to what I think that I lost heart," and he added: "If you will leave it to me I will do my best for you – but if not I can only communicate your suggestions to the printers."

[2] On April 8, Craik sent Dodgson a sample page for the proposed new volume of verse and described it as made up using the type of Arnold's poems. Macmillan & Co. had been publishing Matthew Arnold's poetry since 1867; most recently they had brought out the two-volume *Collected Poems* of 1877.

[3] On April 2, Dodgson wrote in his *Diaries* (p. 370): "Yesterday I sent back to Sambourne, with approval, his first drawing on 'The Lang Coortin'.' I have now three artists drawing for me: the others being Walter Crane (for 'Bruno's Revenge') and Frost (for 'The Three Voices')." Nothing

however, comes of Dodgson's negotiations with Sambourne and Crane, and the illustrations for *Rhyme? and Reason?* are provided by Arthur Burdett Frost (1851–1928), the American illustrator best known for his drawings for *Uncle Remus*. On the previous January 7, Dodgson wrote to Frost as "a stranger," complimenting him on some drawings in *Judy*, "which seemed to me to have more comic power in them than anything I have met with for a long time," and asking "whether you would be willing to draw me a few pictures for one or two short poems . . ." (*Letters*, p. 298). On April 24, Dodgson calls on Frost in London, on May 2 Frost visits Dodgson at Christ Church, and the collaboration succeeds (*Diaries*, pp. 370–1). For more on Dodgson and Frost, see *Letters*, pp. 304–5, 308–9.

On April 16 Craik replies advising Dodgson to keep the *Snark* separate for the time being because it is selling and he is sure that the new *Phantasmagoria*, as they continue to call the new volume of verse, will also sell without the help of the *Snark*.

When Ward, Lock & Co. absorbed the firm of Edward Moxon & Co., Dodgson turned to his own publisher, and on March 28, 1878, wrote asking Macmillan whether he would take on the remaining stock and market the books. Craik replied on the following day suggesting that Dodgson be in touch with Kegan Paul, Tennyson's current publisher, as the more appropriate outlet.

Craik advises (April 16) against advertising the *Index* and suggests instead that Dodgson sell off the books as remainders. They "might be got rid of quietly to some of the country booksellers," he writes.

The Chestnuts, Guildford
(till Tuesday – afterwards at "Christ Church, Oxford")
April 20, 1878

Dear Mr. Craik,

Thanks for the specimen of "Phantasmagoria" in the new type. Would you send me 2 or 3 copies of it? (I have an impression that I asked this before.)

The pages of *Alice* in red and black look very like what you sent to Oxford: I will take them with me next week and compare them. Do you think red type comfortable for the eyes? (That is only a *negative* suggestion, and so I hope will not dishearten you! One *positive* suggestion occurs to me – which I make in fear – it is, have you ever considered the effect of *gold* type?)

Your advice about "the policy of isolation"[1] (as Mr. Gladstone would call it) for the *Snark* is sound, I have no doubt, and I accept it.[2] But I entirely demur to selling off the *Index* as a "remainder." *My* hope is, not only to sell these, but to reprint. The book itself is surely still selling, and I don't see why we should not sell another 1000. At any rate I should like it added to the list of my books at the end of *Alice*. I find by Moxon's list that the selling price was "2s. in cloth, and 5s. 6d. for binding with *In Memoriam*." As to further advertising, would you tell me what it would cost to put it into your lists for a few months – or better, how you think £2 could be most usefully spent in advertising it.[3]

Would you send me to Oxford any hospital letters that may have come in.

Yours very truly,
C. L. Dodgson

[1] Two days before Dodgson writes, Gladstone, in a speech in London, contrasted Britain's actions in the Crimean War, when it represented "the union of Europe against a public wrong," with the unilateral demands that Disraeli's government had recently made on Russia in what Gladstone saw as "a rage, a passion for isolation" that bid fair to plunge the nation into an unnecessary war. For the text of Gladstone's speech, see *The Times*, April 19, 1878, p. 6.

[2] But on the following February 4, Dodgson reverses himself when he writes to Macmillan: "Please don't print any more *Snark*s. I think I shall put it, pictures and all, into the new volume. So the present form of it had better get out of print." Then on February 14, another reversal: "I see by my letter-register (what I had totally forgotten) that I had made the same proposal, some months ago, about including the *Snark* in the volume of *Phantasmagoria*, and that Mr. Craik had then advised strongly against it: so I withdrew the suggestion."

[3] Craik waits until Macmillan returns from holiday in Italy before replying on May 1: "We are of course anxious to do anything you wish and I am sorry to seem to hesitate about it. . . . There are, however, reasons that are difficult to explain that would make it inconvenient for us to publish . . . [the *Index*]. The natural publishers are Kegan Paul & Co., and if they don't see their way to it – I would advise as I did before, that you should sell the copies off. We will help you in any way we can. If our travellers could privately dispose of them at a reduced price, this would settle the matter – but we are averse from appearing as the publishers. The stock lies here and it is for you to say what is to be done. Pray use us in any way you like except as publishers." Dodgson acquiesces in a letter dated May 7. On May 8, Macmillan reports that he is sending 20 copies of the *Index* to Dodgson for his private use. Kegan Paul evidently reverse themselves, for on the 28th, Craik writes: "We have sent the remaining copies . . . of the *Index* . . . to Kegan Paul & Co. I am glad you have arranged with them, for in the hands of Tennyson's publishers I feel sure more can be done with the *Index*."

Christ Church, Oxford
June 30, 1878

Dear Mr. Macmillan,

What do you think of adding to your Art Hand-books (*House Decoration*, etc.) one on "the Art of Reading and Speaking"? A friend of mine, who has made a study of that subject, would much like to try and write such a book for you: he has rather a knack of smooth and lively writing.[1]

By the way, your *Brief Biographical Dictionary* is provokingly incomplete, in not giving the *day* as well as the year, of birth: this is often quite as interesting a fact as the day of death, and is also necessary for computing the *age* at any given period.

Suppose one wished to know which of the two great rivals, Bonaparte or Wellington, was born first, your dictionary gives one no help.[2]

Yours very truly,

C. L. Dodgson

Please bind me 12 *Alice* and 12 *Looking-Glass* in "leatheret and gold" but don't send them off yet.

[1] From 1876 to 1883, Macmillan published an "Art at Home" series, a dozen volumes in all, including *A Plea for Art in the House* (1876) and *Amateur Theatricals* (1879). The volume Dodgson refers to appeared in 1876; it is R. and A. Garrett, *Suggestions for House Decoration in Painting, Woodwork, and Furniture*. We cannot identify Dodgson's "friend." Macmillan replies (July 1) that

they have already taken two books on "articulation" for the "Art at Home"series and that that is as much as they ought to give to any one form. "Thanks to you and your friend all the same."
2 *A Brief Biographical Dictionary*, edited by Charles Hole, was published in 1865 and reissued with considerable alterations and additions the following year. Macmillan replies (same letter): "If the birth [day] had been added . . . it would have very much increased the size. We had to make a choice as to what to give and omit. The amount and general accuracy of the information given in the space seem to me wonderful." But Dodgson will not be silenced on the subject. On the following day, he writes: "If you ever bring out another edition of the *Biographical Dictionary*, you could, I think add the births without increasing the width of the page, by printing thus: 15,6,1815–2,7,1878."

7 Lushington Road, Eastbourne[1]
August 30, 1878

Dear Mr. Macmillan,

I have made an annoying discovery in the 42nd thousand of *Through the Looking-Glass*. Both the Kings are omitted from the chess-diagram. They are in their proper places in a copy I referred to of the 10th thousand: but in *which* thousand the misprint first appeared I have not the means to discover.

The first thing to be done (and please have it done without delay) is to print a slip of paper, and insert it in all copies still in hand.

I enclose MS of slip.

The next thing to be done is to ascertain in *which* thousand it began. If many thousands are now in the hands of the public with the wrong diagram, I *think* we ought to advertise the erratum: but I will wait to hear from you before settling this point.[2]

I hope you are not forgetting that when the existing grey-and-black covers of the *Snark* are exhausted, I wish to have no more of them printed, but red ones instead, with circular medallions, about which I wrote some time ago.[3]

Yours very truly,

C. L. Dodgson

1 In 1877 Dodgson began spending summer holidays at Eastbourne. On July 31 of that year he moved into lodgings at this address, the home of Mr. and Mrs. Benjamin Dyer, where he had "a nice little first-floor sitting-room with a balcony, and bedroom adjoining" (*Diaries*, p. 364).
2 In a long letter dated September 10, Macmillan reports that he cannot be sure where the error occurred, but he is "inclined to believe that it was in the 22nd thousand. Up to the 21st the title sheet was not stereotyped. . . . But when we were going to press with the 22nd thousand it was thought better to stereo the title sheet as the rest was done. It seems to me probable that when the form was passing from the compositor's hands to the electrotyper's those two squares may have dropped out and were replaced by blanks. . . . What is certain is that no copy between the 28th and the 44th had a King in the chessboard! . . . it may be earlier. It is a consolation . . . no one of these . . . 16 thousand copies gave its readers less delight for the omission – so that practically it has been of little consequence, though it is a kind of mistake that ought not to have happened, and I am glad that you discovered and pointed it out. I am inclined to think that if any reader found out that the Kings were not there he must have given them credit for being 'behind the Looking-Glass.' Now as to how to mend matters? We are just to reprint, and of course will restore their majesties to their

place – but to arrange about the past? I would either let it alone or write a half chaffy note to the *Athenaeum* or *Pall Mall.*" We have found neither an erratum slip nor any advertisement about the error. According to the *Handbook*, the Kings were first omitted in the 25th thousand, 1872, and replaced, with a new and enlarged board, in the 45th thousand, 1878 (p. 101).

3 "The *Snark* will appear in her red costume as soon as the few greys remaining are sold," Macmillan assures Dodgson (in the same letter).

7 Lushington Road, Eastbourne.
September 26, 1878

Dear Mr. Macmillan,

Many thanks for the very satisfactory annual budget. I hope you won't think me a great bore in the matter of wanting theatre-tickets, but really you are the only friend I have who is handily situated for procuring them. Could you kindly get me a couple of stalls at the Olympic for Saturday, October 5 (near the middle of the 2nd, 3rd and 4th row).[1] And, by the way, if the procuring of tickets (which you have several times so kindly done for me), involves the sending of a shop-boy or any one who would accept a gratuity for his trouble, would you add to the favour by remunerating him, on my behalf, with a half-crown, or whatever sum you think would be handsome in return for his various journeys.

That misprint in the chess-diagram I found out while trying to prove to two little friends here that it ends in a *real* check-mate – in which, as I tried it on a recent copy, I need hardly say I signally failed.[2]

Yours very truly,
C. L. Dodgson

1 On the following day Frederick Macmillan replies, sends the tickets, and explains that "in my uncle's absence I opened your letter."

2 Alexander Macmillan asked (September 10) how Dodgson had noticed the error. We cannot tell for certain which pair of young friends helped Dodgson discover it. Perhaps they were Margie and Helen Dymes, or Agnes and Evelyn Hull, or other pairs of friends whom Dodgson saw during his working holiday at Eastbourne.

Christ Church, Oxford
October 19, 1878

Dear Mr. Macmillan,

Please thank your son for his letter about Mr. J. Mount. The permission may be repeated, of course.[1]

We shall be ready to set up my book about Euclid in pages very soon now: it is nearly all in slip. How many lines should go to a page, and what-sized paper should we use? As the text is the same width as Birks' *Physical Fatalism*, I suppose the book had better be that size.[2] In that case it must be either 31 or 30 lines to the page. I incline to 30, to get a little more margin. We shall have running titles at top of page.

Another matter to settle will be binding, etc. If you have no objection, I should like red cloth (my favourite colour), and the name in quite plain gold letters at the back: and the edges cut and mottled red. I *don't* want the reader to have to cut the leaves, and then to have the rough and unequal edges in his way when he wants to refer from one page to another.

I hope we shall get it out by December. Is it too soon to announce it now? If not, I want to ask the Editor of the *Pall Mall* to announce it, as he kindly did my last.[3]

Yours very truly,
C. L. Dodgson

[1] George Macmillan wrote the day before about a Mr. Julian Mount who the previous June had asked on behalf of a music publisher for permission to set music to the words of "The Walrus and the Carpenter." The permission had been granted, but now Mount was writing from a different publisher for the same permission. "Julian Mount" was the pseudonym of William Marshall Hutchinson (b. 1854) who published sixty-four songs between 1878 and 1884, many of them based on words of well-known poets like Byron, Burns, Poe, and Shakespeare.

[2] In 1876 Macmillan published *Modern Physical Fatalism and the Doctrine of Evolution* by Thomas Rawson Birks (1810–83), Professor of Moral Philosophy, Cambridge (1872). The book is octavo, as Dodgson's *Euclid* would ultimately be; the Birks book has 311 pages, *Euclid* 299.

[3] Macmillan replies two days later that it is not too soon to announce the book but advises sending the announcement to the *Athenaeum* at the same time as to the *Pall Mall*, "else they will not put it in." He adds: "Please send *us* the paragraph." On October 23, Dodgson writes to Macmillan: "I have adopted your suggestion, and sent the description of the book to the Editor of the *Athenaeum*, which I think will be a more suitable paper than the *Pall Mall*. I thought it best not to send it to *both*. I can't send you the 'paragraph' for I haven't ventured to suggest one. I have given him the facts, to select from and express as he likes. I daresay he will only give a few words of description." The "Literary Gossip" column of the *Athenaeum* carried the notice on the 26th: "Mr. C. L. Dodgson, Senior Student and Mathematician Lecturer at Christ Church, has nearly finished a volume, which will be out by the end of November, and will be called *Euclid and His Modern Rivals*. The book will contain reviews of several modern geometries.

Christ Church, Oxford
October 31, 1878

Dear Mr. Macmillan,

If there is an edition of Wilson's *Geometry* since 1869, with any material alterations, please send me a copy: if not, the 1869 edition will suit my purpose.[1]

You ask how many copies I think of printing of *Euclid and His Modern Rivals*. I should say "250, and keep the type standing for a few months." I don't expect any sale, to speak of: and feel sure the total result will be a loss: so you must regulate the selling-price, not by what it will have cost to produce, but simply by the average price of such books.

Yours very truly,
C. L. Dodgson

[1] *Elementary Geometry* was the work of James Maurice Wilson (1836–1931), classical scholar and author of theological works. His book on geometry was first published by Macmillan in 1868, and new editions appeared in 1869, 1873, and 1878. Dodgson does not seem to know about the later edition, but it matters not because Macmillan replies (the following day) that a new edition is "almost ready" and should appear "within a fortnight." Macmillan has no copy of the earlier editions, and he asks Dodgson if he should send him a copy of the new edition when it is ready.

Christ Church, Oxford
November 3, 1878

Dear Mr. Macmillan,

The book will contain, as nearly as I can calculate, 14 sheets like the enclosed – i.e. 224 pages. I want to have an extra sheet blank at the end, paged consecutively with the book, of paper that will bear writing on: so you may reckon on 240 pages. I see you talk of "sending" paper here for it: no doubt you know best, and I leave all such details to you, but it sounds to me a little like "sending coals to Newcastle," as the Press manufactures paper.

Please send me the new edition of Wilson *in sheets*, as soon as they are passed for the press. I have 2 bound copies already, and so do not care to have another, and it will save time not to wait for the binding.

Puss in Boots is a pretty picture: but I can't write for Annuals. I am getting quite callous to such requests now, I have so many sent me. It's only the *name* they want: ask the next Editor who mentions the thing to you which he would pay most for – an article written by me, but unsigned – or an article written by the first man he finds in the street, but signed "Lewis Carroll"! I have no doubt the *name* is worth some money by this time (a result largely due to my good fortune in choosing a publisher!) but I don't care to make money by writing in periodicals.[1]

Yours very truly,

C. L. Dodgson

[1] The picture in question is a reproduction of a painting by (Sir) John Everett Millais, whom Dodgson had known since 1864. Millais painted *Puss in Boots* in 1877, and it was exhibited the same year. Two days earlier, Macmillan wrote: "The manager of the *Graphic* brought me this morning a very pretty proof of a coloured reproduction of one of Millais' pictures. They want you to write a few lines to accompany it, and I told him to apply to you direct as time presses with them. If you find you can do it I think it would be well you should: apart from pleasing Millais it will help as an advertisement of your book." However, after receiving Dodgson's reply, Macmillan writes (November 5): "Your answer to the *Graphic* is very much what I expected – and what in your circumstances I would have given."

Christ Church, Oxford
[November 10?, 1878][1]

Dear Mr. Macmillan,

Thanks for the copy of Mr. Wilson's new book. It is almost entirely different from his former book, and will require to be reviewed separately in my treatise – thus perhaps causing a further delay: still I hope we may be out by Christmas. The verses which you sent me in 1872 began like this:

> "First they pull up the fish:
> It can't swim away: for a fish that is funny.
> Next 'tis bought, and I wish
> That a penny were always the adequate money."

The reason I asked the question is that, when you sent me them, I sent you back an *amended* version, as they were rather halting in metre: and I see (in a parody of *Alice* which has appeared in *Fun*) these very verses – not the original ones, but the amended version. So I conjecture that you shewed my amended version to the writer (whoever it was), and that he has adopted the new readings. Was it so?[2]

Yours very truly,

C. L. Dodgson

[1] The letter is undated, but Macmillan's letter of November 1 promising a copy of Wilson's book within a fortnight helps place the date.

[2] Dodgson's 1872 letters on the *Fun* parody are missing. On May 4, 1872, Macmillan wrote to Dodgson: "The *Fun* parody did not strike me as being very funny, but it is of course not unpleasant to have such 'marked attention' paid you even by such people when it is kindly." In response to the present undated letter, Macmillan writes on November 11: "1872! That is six years ago. I have no recollection of the verses you refer to. Where did they appear? Have you got them?" And on November 18: "I have no record, and no recollection of your *Fun* correspondent. The only person connected with *Fun* that we are aware of having known was . . . Tom Hood the younger. He was a good fellow and if he brought the verses I might have given him your version. As he has been dead some years I fear the riddle is harder than any one even Alice proposed." The parody, "Alice in Numberland," appeared in *Fun* as part of a series called "Specimens of Celebrated Authors" ("Alice" on October 30, 1878); the verse that Dodgson quotes in the letter appears as:

> First pull up the fish.
> It can't swim away: for a fish this is funny!
> Next 'tis bought; and I wish
> That a penny was always its adequate money.

For more on the parody, see *Handbook*, pp. 100–1.

Christ Church, Oxford
January 30, 1879

Dear Mr. Macmillan,

I hope we shall be able to bring out *Euclid and His Modern Rivals* during February. Will you see about binding? I suppose we had better have an experimental "dummy" copy bound. I enclose a sheet (which need not be returned) and if you allow for 16 such sheets, you will be almost exactly right.

I have given up the idea of having any blank leaves at the end. My notion for binding is a rough red cloth (like the cheap *Alices*), and the title in gold on the back – no other ornament – edges to be cut smooth and left white.

A lady told me the other day she had met with cheap *Alices* (those printed for sick children, she believed) *on Sale*. Surely they were all sent to me?[1]

Yours very truly,

C. L. Dodgson

P.S. Could you get me, through your American connections, a book on the Beaver, by Mr. Lewis H. Morgan, of New York – illustrated with photographs of Beaver dams and lodges.[2]

[1] Because Alexander Macmillan is unwell, Frederick Macmillan replies the following day that Dodgson's friend "must have been mistaken" about the cheap *Alices* or that "some of the hospitals must have sold the copies given them."

[2] Lewis Henry Morgan (1818–81), social evolutionist, was one of the founders of modern anthropology. The book Dodgson wants is *American Beaver and His Work* (1868), where Morgan records his observations of the beaver's habits and sharply criticizes "metaphysicians" who, "lest the high position of man be shaken or impaired," hesitate to acknowledge that animals manifest human characteristics. Macmillan eventually sends Dodgson a copy of the book, but not until December, explaining (December 8) that their agent in New York "made some mistake."

Christ Church, Oxford

February 27, 1879

Dear Mr. Macmillan,

I have one more remark to make on a subject which I presume (not having heard from you about it) that you are still considering, the price to be put on *Euclid and His Modern Rivals*. It will be safe, I think, to put on it the full price such a book ever bears: no one is likely to buy the book casually, but every purchaser will buy it because he really wants to have it, and will not be in the frame of mind to give up buying it because it is a shilling dearer than he expected. There is a good deal of "table-work" in it, which is costly printing, so you may safely take the maximum price for a book of that size.[1]

Yours very truly,

C. L. Dodgson

[1] On February 14, Dodgson wrote: "I am this day sending to the Press the first batch of sheets, marked 'Press.' They will print 250 and keep the type standing. You have never told me what price you propose to put on the book. It should be a price which would be fairly remunerative for *future* issues. These 250 will necessarily be sold at a loss: there has been so much alteration." In his reply (February 28), Macmillan concurs with Dodgson's view that there is no point in setting a cheap

price on *Euclid and His Modern Rivals*. "But the price is one of the last things we settle," he adds: "as we like to see what a book looks like, outside and in and also what it has cost." He believes it should be either 6*s.* or 7*s.* 6*d.* In the end, the first edition went for 7*s.* 6*d.*, the second for 6*s.*

Christ Church, Oxford
April 7, 1879

Dear Mr. Macmillan,

Thanks for list of periodicals.[1] If any of them should review my book, and you should be sending me (as on former occasions) the bits cut out, would you kindly tell whoever cuts them out to allow a good margin (which I can afterwards trim off), and not to shave them so close as was done with some of the reviews of *Alice*. I remember sending a remonstrance about them, to which your clerk replied that he "could not allow a margin without cutting into the surrounding matter" – which was no doubt true, but was hardly a sufficient reason![2]

Have you sold any copies yet, and do you think there is any chance of your wanting more than the 250 copies?[3]

Yours very truly,

C. L. Dodgson

[1] On April 2, Macmillan sent Dodgson a list of periodicals (missing) to which review copies of the book had been mailed. Earlier, on March 27, Dodgson "went to Parker's, and wrote names in thirty-four copies of *Euclid* . . . , to be sent off at once (*Diaries*, p. 378). *Euclid and His Modern Rivals* "by Charles L. Dodgson, M.A., Senior Student and Mathematical Lecturer of Christ Church, Oxford," is "one of the outstanding examples of serious argument cast in an amusing style, designed to prove that for elementary geometry a revised Euclid is better than any proposed modern substitute. The form is dramatic: Minos and Rhadamanthus, with occasional help from Euclid himself and 'Niemand,' sit in judgement on twelve (or in some sense nearly twenty) Euclid-wreckers and their manuals, and much fun results, with comic and conclusive discomfitures of all kinds. . . . This is the most elaborate mathematical work produced by Dodgson, and at the same time a piece of literature" (*Handbook*, pp. 101–2).

[2] On the following day, Macmillan replies: "It will be safer to send you the actual papers in which reviews of your *Euclid* appear. I have ordered this done."

[3] Macmillan replies (same letter) that 54 copies of *Euclid* had actually been sold with 47 more in the hands of agents; probably half of the latter were also sold. But "as the book was only published on April 1, it is impossible to predict about the sale." Macmillan suggests that it is "very probable" that more will be wanted, and he promises to "keep our eye on the sales and give you due warning."

Christ Church, Oxford
May 9, 1879

Dear Mr. Macmillan,

Are you keeping an efficient look-out for reviews of *Euclid and His Modern Rivals*? I ask the question, because I happen to know of *two* reviews already which you have not sent me. One was in *Vanity Fair* for April 12. This I possess, so you need not send it me. The other was in the *English Mechanic*, about a week ago I think: and this I have not got, and should be glad to have.[1]

Many thanks for your kind intimation of the days of your "receptions" in Bedford Street: but (how many "buts" there are in life!) I fear that in such an assembly it would be almost impossible to preserve an incognito. I cannot of course help there being many people who know the connection between my real name and my "alias," but the fewer there are who are able to connect my *face* with the name "Lewis Carroll" the happier for me. So I hope you will kindly excuse my non-appearance.

Very truly yours,

C. L. Dodgson

[1] *Vanity Fair* found *Euclid and His Modern Rivals* "absolutely refreshing" and explained that "this is a book marvellous for the labour contained in it, and still more marvellous for the brightness and humour with which the ponderous stuff of geometry is handled" (p. 208). The notice in the *English Mechanic* is longer. It points to the trend among modern mathematicians to disparage Euclid as deficient. Dodgson puts the opposite case well, it says: "the ideas intended to be conveyed are clearly and definitely expressed, and Euclid quite holds his own." The notice concludes: "On the whole . . . we regard our author as having triumphantly proved that, so far, no work has been produced which is comparable with Euclid's immortal *Elements*, as an introduction to geometry for *beginners*" (May 2, 1879, pp. 174–5).

Christ Church, Oxford

May 16, 1879

Dear Mr. Macmillan,

The news that the first 250 of *Euclid and His Modern Rivals* are sold, is as welcome as it is unexpected.[1] I shall take the opportunity of reprinting to make considerable alterations, profiting by the criticisms and suggestions that have reached me, but you shall have another 250 as soon as possible. The covers of course can be prepared at once. As it will be, in some respects, a different book, I should like to have "SECOND EDITION" printed on the cover. I fancy it would look best in italic capitals, towards the lower end of the blank space: but you will be the best judge on this point, and I leave it to your taste.

The enclosed papers may be interesting to your family circle.[2] The "Glossary" here alluded to I am printing here, and intend to ask *you* to publish it for me, on the usual terms. I will shortly send it you in sheets, and a title-page for your kind criticisms. We never can manage the title-page at the University Press, and always need your skill to produce an artistic one.

Very truly yours,

C. L. Dodgson

Thanks for *English Mechanic* and *Saturday Review*.[3]

¹ On the previous day, Macmillan wrote that all 250 copies of *Euclid* were sold and suggested printing another 250.

² The "papers," a word game that Dodgson invented at Christmas 1877 and originally called *Word-Links*, will become *Doublets*. "The rules are simple enough," Dodgson wrote. "Two words are proposed of the same length; and the Puzzle consists in linking these together by interposing other words, each of which shall differ from the next word *in one letter only*. . . . As an example, the word 'head' may be changed into 'tail' by interposing the words 'heal, teal, tell, tall.' I call the two given words 'a Doublet,' the interposed words 'links,' and the entire series 'a chain'. . . ." *Vanity Fair* printed Dodgson's rules and three trial Doublets in late March and early April 1879 and then on April 19 inaugurated a Doublets competition. The first separate edition of *Doublets* (1879) contained a glossary of some 1400 legitimate words. For more on *Doublets*, see *Handbook*, pp. 99–100, 102–5, 107–8.

³ The *Saturday Review* ran a long notice of *Euclid*. It quotes Dodgson's rationale for the form of his book: "It is presented in a dramatic form, partly because it seemed a better way of exhibiting in alternation the arguments on the two sides of the question; partly that I might feel myself at liberty to treat it in a rather lighter style than would have suited an essay, and thus to make it a little more acceptable to unscientific readers." Then the reviewer objects: "Mr. Dodgson has brought great knowledge and acuteness to his task, but we must regret the form in which he has cast his book – not on the score of his 'abandoning the dignity of a scientific writer' by putting his argument into dialogues between the ghost of Euclid, an examiner, and an imaginary German Professor – but, because to our mind the effect is to make the argument much harder reading than it would be otherwise." The reviewer, evidently one of the "modern rivals," insists that "it must not be made an article of faith that nothing better than Euclid is possible" (May 10, 1879, pp. 592–3).

Christ Church, Oxford
May 30, 1879

Dear Mr. Macmillan,

I think it is too small a book for a cloth cover,¹ so, if you are clear that 2*s*. will be too much to charge with a paper cover, then I suppose we must make it 1*s*. 6*d*. – unless an intermediate price be possible. What do you think of 1*s*. 9*d*.? Or of 1*s*. 8*d*.? I think

PRICE FIVE GROATS

would look rather original. But 1*s*. 6*d*. (out of which I suppose you would credit *me* with 1*s*. Is that so?) would barely cover the cost of production.

Very truly yours,

C. L. Dodgson

They tell me at Parker's they have 13 unsold copies of *Euclid and His Modern Rivals*, which I daresay they would be glad to let you have again. Perhaps these, with the 11 I sent you, will really satisfy the remaining demand. I am in no hurry to enter on the trouble and cost of a second edition, unless there is a *real* demand for one.

¹ "If you make . . . [*Doublets*] 2*s*. I think you should put it into limp cloth," Macmillan wrote two days earlier. In fact if appeared in cloth boards.

Christ Church, Oxford
June 6, 1879

Dear Mr. George Macmillan,

I am very much obliged by the trouble you have kindly taken in getting me the tickets. I did mean Saturday, but my chronology had got a little mixed.[1]

The University Press tell me your house have written for a copy of *Doublets*, so I send a proof, in its present state. There will be 8 more pages when it is complete. I sent your father a copy before, but he (unnecessarily) returned it: I don't want this back.

I propose to have a coloured paper cover, as your father advised: and would be glad if he would say whether it would do to price it 1*s*. 9*d*., or 1*s*. 6*d*., or my new idea of "PRICE FIVE GROATS."[2]

Yours very truly,

C. L. Dodgson

---

[1] Dodgson's original request is missing. The next record of a theatrical outing on a Saturday occurs on June 28, when Dodgson takes the eldest MacDonald daughter, Lily, to the Lyceum to see Ellen Terry in W. G. Will's play *Charles I* (*Diaries*, p. 381).

[2] Alexander Macmillan replies on June 7: "Anything more than a shilling would certainly look absurdly dear for a little thing like this. But of course you can make it eighteen pence if you like."

Christ Church, Oxford
June 10, 1879

Dear Mr. Macmillan,

The only chance of avoiding selling at a loss (which I think would be slightly absurd, besides that I can't afford it) seems to me to be to add the "limp cloth cover" which you once advised, and make it a 2*s*. pamphlet. If I had known how dear such small type would be, I would have printed it larger: but the mischief is done.

I should like a bright red cover, with the name in gold, in ornamental letters. Could you have a specimen done?

They want *you* to send them paper. I think I should like *toned*, of fine quality, so that it will take ink, as readers will have to add new words in MS. Please send them enough paper for 500.

Yours very truly,

C. L. Dodgson

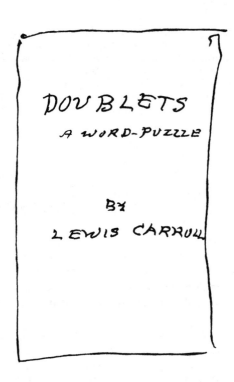

There will be 40 pages – i.e. 20 leaves. Shall it be in 2 sheets, or all folded in one, so that one sewing will do for all?

The Chestnuts, Guildford
June 22, 1879

Dear Mr. Macmillan,

I am at a standstill for want of knowing whether you want the pamphlet (40 pages) sent to you all folded as one sheet (so as to have one sewing only) or as two sheets, or how. Please decide the point and tell me as soon as you can.[1]

As yet I do not know whether you approve of the red cloth cover, etc., and the 2s. price – but these details can wait. The great object now is to get 250 copies *printed*: and, as I told the Editor of *Vanity Fair* it would be ready by the end of the month, the time is short.[2]

I want you to let *Vanity Fair* have copies on the same terms as booksellers.

Yours very truly,

C. L. Dodgson

158

June 26, 1879

[1] "We have instructed the printer to put your little tractate into three sections. It could not have been well put into cloth covers otherwise," Macmillan writes the following day.

[2] Dodgson was acquainted with the editor of *Vanity Fair*, Thomas Gibson Bowles (1842–1922). He called on Bowles the preceding January and had "a very pleasant two hours with him and Mrs. Bowles." In March Bowles came to Christ Church, dined with Dodgson in Hall and sat for Dodgson's camera (*Diaries*, pp. 377–8). *Doublets* was a regular feature in *Vanity Fair* from March 29, 1879, to April 9, 1881. For more on Dodgson and the Bowleses, see *Letters*, pp. 556–7, 840–1.

"care of Mrs. Bayne[1]
30 Gordon Place,
Campden Grove, Kensington"
June 26, 1879

Dear Mr. Macmillan,

Thanks. I like the design, except that the lines look to me too close together: however that is a matter of which you and your binder will be the best judges. I should like to have a dummy-copy done in red and gold (really bright red): it isn't worth while trying black and gold: for I think it essential that it should look *gay*.[2]

As to supplying the Editor of *Vanity Fair* on the bookseller terms, if (as I gather from your letter) it is unusual, and you feel any objection to it, please don't do it. Perhaps it will be the simplest plan after all to consider such copies as supplied to *me*, and to address them "Lewis Carroll, Esq., care of Editor of *Vanity Fair*, 13 Tavistock Street."[3]

I will tell you how many to send when they are ready. I only want 250 bound *to begin with*: but I think another 250 may be wanted, so that I may not be very much out of pocket after all.

I shall be at my present address till Monday. After that address to Guildford again.

Yours very truly,

C. L. Dodgson

[1] Mrs. Thomas Bayne (d. 1888) was the mother of Dodgson's oldest friend, Thomas Vere Bayne (1829–1908), whom he had known from childhood. Bayne and Dodgson were contemporary undergraduates and dons at Christ Church. Dodgson frequently visited Mrs. Bayne in London and escorted her to art galleries and to the theater. On June 24 he recorded (*Diaries*, p. 380): "Guildford to London, where Mrs. Bayne kindly gives me a bed." For more on Dodgson and the Baynes, see *Letters*, esp. p. 92.

[2] On June 24 Macmillan sent Dodgson a sketch for the cover design of *Doublets* and suggested making up two dummy copies, one in red and gold, the other in red and black, for Dodgson to choose from.

[3] Dodgson had arranged for *Vanity Fair* to offer *Doublets* for sale directly to its readers. On July 5, the following notice appears in the paper: "By the 15th of July there will be ready for delivery *Doublets* by Lewis Carroll, containing a history of the game, the revised rules, and a glossary of admissible

words, bound in a portable form. The price of *Doublets* is two shillings. It is published by Macmillan and Co., but it can be obtained at *Vanity Fair* Office. Intending purchasers are requested to send their orders at once to ensure early delivery." In reply to Dodgson's request of June 22 that *Vanity Fair* have copies of *Doublets* "on the same terms as booksellers," Macmillan writes (June 26): "The publisher of *Vanity Fair* is naturally treated as a bookseller – any newspaper publisher is so treated. Let him order as many copies of that or any other book we publish and he will have them at trade price. I wrote hurriedly and may have failed to convey what I meant that this is a matter of course."

address "Chestnuts, Guildford"

July 3, 1879

Dear Mr. Macmillan,

The red cover looks very nice: but it is much to be wished that binders would simply follow their instructions! I had said "fill it with *blank* paper, of the kind we are going to use," and I was going to utilize the book for MS entries of *Doublets* and their solutions. Instead of doing as he was told, your binder has actually filled it with leaves from some religious book! which of course I instantly cut out: the contrast between the contents and the title outside was too outrageous.

I return the cover, and if you can utilise it for me by putting in the blank paper I asked for, please do so. But it isn't worth while wasting a new cover on another dummy.[1]

So there is no further demand for *Euclid and His Modern Rivals*? In that case I have saved myself a good deal of expense by *not* printing the second edition. By the way, do you advertise it at all, and if so, where? As a general rule, I think I ought to leave to *your* judgement the entire subject of advertising, but I venture to break the rule for once, as I have so often lately seen lists of your books, in which it might naturally occur, without any mention of it. Also friends tell me they have never heard of it. Surely it ought to be advertised pretty regularly in such papers as the *Athenaeum*, *Spectator*, etc., and should be included in your lists of educational and scientific books? If the public don't hear of it they are not very likely to ask for it.[2]

Yours very truly,

C. L. Dodgson

---

[1] "You shall have the blank paper red book," Macmillan writes the same day.

[2] In the same letter, Macmillan writes: "I enclose a list of advertisements sent out of *Euclid*. They and catalogue expenses will cost you about £12. May we spend more?" A week later, Macmillan writes again on the subject: "We have sent you the 4 copies of your Euclid book. This leaves us with only 6 copies. Is it worth while advertising for that number if you don't mean to reprint, which I could not advise. . . ." Both a *Supplement* to *Euclid* and a second edition would appear in 1885 (see *Handbook*, pp. 132–3).

Christ Church, Oxford
July 12, 1879
Dear Mr. Macmillan,
The enclosed advertisement of a "scarce" book may amuse you. I hope there
will be a rush of buyers to secure such a rarity![1]
I agree with you about not advertising *Euclid*, etc., any more.
You will shortly receive 250 copies of *Doublets*. Best cover *all*, I think: and send
me 50, and 100 to the *Vanity Fair* Office, 13 Tavistock Street, and keep 100 to sell.
You will be the best judge about advertising it.
Yours very truly,
C. L. Dodgson

[1] The enclosure is missing; the "scarce" book was probably one of Dodgson's that was still in print.

Christ Church, Oxford
November 25, 1880[1]
Dear Mr. George Macmillan,
Please give Miss Graham (of "Warwick House, Salisbury Square") the leave
she asks for, to reproduce the "Mad Tea Party" on a tablecloth.
I have just had a talk with Mr. Acland Troyte, a former pupil of mine who
wants your father to publish a little book for him.[2] He seems to be suffering from
a nervous fear, not uncommon to authors, that publishers are an inscrutable
race, who make money vanish as if by magic, and never render up any profits to
their victims. What *other* publishers may do, I know not, but I gave him full
assurance that he was in good hands. Also I advised, as a large sale seems by no
means likely, that, if your father is willing to publish on the usual terms of the
publisher taking "all the risk and half the profit," he should accept the offer.
Thanks for mention of gilt-edged "Globe" books.[3] If you have Shakespeare
and Pope, I should like them. I have no list of the "Globe"s at hand. Perhaps you
would kindly send me one, marking those which are to be had with gilt edges.[4]
Yours very truly,
C. L. Dodgson

[1] Our files contain no letters from Dodgson to Macmillan between October 30, 1879, and
November 25, 1880, and this is the only Dodgson letter we have for the 1880 calendar year.
[2] John Edward Acland Troyte (1849–1932) had been a Christ Church undergraduate (B.A. 1872,
M.A. 1875). George Macmillan thanks Dodgson on November 29 for his "good word with Acland
Troyte to whom in fact we have made the offer you indicate." In 1881 Macmillan publishes
Troyte's reflections on his military experience, *Through the Ranks to a Commission.* Troyte later wrote
a memoir of his father, *A Layman's Life in the Days of the Tractarian Movement* (1904) and a *Guide to
Dorset County Museum* (1918) of which he was curator.
[3] Macmillan's Globe Editions began in 1864, the result of Alexander Macmillan's idea of publishing
a scholarly text of Shakespeare's plays at a low price. The name Globe was also Macmillan's

notion, and he held to it against his editors' opposition. The volumes were an immediate success, and by 1870 the Globe series included works by Malory, Scott, Burns, Defoe, Goldsmith, Pope, and Spenser. Macmillan's own words best describe the venture: "Under the title Globe Editions, the Publishers are issuing a uniform Series of Standard English Authors, carefully edited, clearly and elegantly printed on toned paper, strongly bound, and at a small cost. The names of the Editors whom they have been fortunate enough to secure constitute an indisputable guarantee as to the character of the Series. The greatest care has been taken to ensure accuracy of text; adequate notes, elucidating historical, literary, and philological points, have been supplied; and, to the older Authors, glossaries are appended. The series is especially adapted to Students of our national Literature; while the small price places good editions of certain books, hitherto popularly inaccessible, within the reach of all." Globe volumes retailed at 3s. 6d.

⁴ In a letter to Macmillan that is missing, Dodgson must have asked about the gilt-edged Globe books, and in a reply the day before the present letter, George Macmillan wrote: "I am afraid I omitted to answer the question in your last letter about the gilt-edge copies of the Globe books. We gave up issuing them because the demand was so small, but we have a few odd copies left I believe if you will let me know what you want." However, on November 29, George Macmillan writes again, to say that he had been mistaken and the last gilt-edged Globes had been sent to America. He offers instead "a cheap bound edition . . . which might be useful though I cannot say it is very ornamental, save the Shakespeare which is at least inoffensive and of which I send a specimen on approval." Dodgson must have put another question, to which Macmillan replies on December 4: "It is true that we now print the Globe Shakespeare on white paper instead of toned. These copies of the 1865 edition have the advantage that they are among the first that were printed from the plates so that the typography is clearer. But we could easily bind the present edition for you in the same style." Dodgson's reply to this offer is also missing.

Christ Church, Oxford
January 25, 1881

Dear Mr. Macmillan,

With reference to the illustrated edition of *Phantasmagoria* (which of course I shall want *you* to publish for me), Messrs. Dalziel write to propose that the dozen (or so) blocks they have already cut shall be electrotyped. No doubt this must be done: shall I tell *them* to get it done, or simply to send the blocks to *you* (or to Clay?) to be electrotyped and then safely stored away? Please tell me what I had better say.¹

Mr. Frost has been delayed by illness, but he is now at work on the other pictures, and I quite hope we shall get it out next year. We had better use the designs for the old cover: I hope you have the dies.

Very truly yours,

C. L. Dodgson

I went to *The Cup* the other night, and thought it charming.²

¹ In his reply the next day, Macmillan writes: "It will certainly be better that Messrs. Clay who have to print the book should be responsible for the electrotyping. Please tell me when you know that the blocks are going to them and I will instruct them."
² Dodgson went to a performance of Tennyson's two-act tragedy at the Lyceum on Monday,

January 17 (Macmillan had obtained the tickets for him), and so delighted was he with the play and with Ellen Terry's performance that he commemorated the occasion in verse and recorded his reaction in a long entry in his *Diaries* (p. 393). He goes to see *The Cup* again on April 18 and finds it "even more enjoyable a second time, than when I first saw it" (p. 395). For more on *The Cup* and Dodgson's verse entitled "The Lyceum," see *Letters*, pp. 403–5, 411, 417–18.

7 Lushington Road, Eastbourne
August 17, 1881

Dear Mr. Macmillan,

Thanks for sending the "Pearl" Byron, which I will keep. I showed it to the bookseller here, along with his agent's letter denying the existence of the book. He seemed surprised, and I suppose will make enquiries as to his agent's state of mind! He *appears* to be crazy.[1]

I *don't* think you would be doing anything unreasonable towards Mr. Murray, if you were to bring out a "Globe" Byron, *without* Don Juan. It would be bought by a great number of people, who would never buy the "Pearl" edition, nor even allow *Don Juan* to enter their houses. And, omitting so large a piece of the book, you could enlarge the type to the size of your Shakespeare, if not even larger. All "copyrights" *must* have expired by this time.[2]

Mr. Tenniel is going to make some changes in the figure of "Alice," so I have telegraphed to you to stop the work on two of the pictures, in which she occurs, and I may as well add the others – i.e. please tell them only to do the frontispiece and the picture at p. 63, till they receive further orders.[3]

Please tell them to take great care of that coloured frontispiece: I want to have it fastened into the book again, as a unique specimen of colouring done by the artist himself.

Also please send Mr. Tenniel an *Alice* in sheets, that he may mark his alterations and cut the pictures out one by one. It seems a pity to spoil a bound copy for this purpose.

Yours very truly,

C. L. Dodgson

[1] We have no letters from Dodgson to Macmillan between January 25 and August 17, 1881, but the Macmillan letter books produce the customary flood of replies to the missing Dodgson letters. Dodgson obviously took a keen interest in the Macmillan Globe editions. On February 7, 1881, George Macmillan wrote: "The 'Globe' Editions you want bound are put in hand and shall be sent to you as soon as possible. We have several times thought of a 'Globe' *Arabian Nights* but never quite seen our way to its production. It may come some day perhaps." On May 18, Alexander Macmillan wrote that the firm had already considered the Latin poets for the Globe editions, but that it could not be done "in the Globe form under two or three volumes, to be at all reasonable. . . . Wordsworth is still a good deal in copyright," he wrote (same letter). "We have had negotiations on the subject, but there are difficulties which we could not see our way to overcome." About Byron, "my friend Mr. Murray has an edition which is in Globe size and sells at 3*s*. 6*d*. The type is too small, but we don't care to rival a brother publisher needlessly." On July 29, Craik

wrote that "Murray's 'Pearl' edition of Byron's is to be had at any bookseller's," but Dodgson could not find a copy and Alexander Macmillan sent him one on August 16.
2 John Murray (1808–92), head of the publishing firm that bears his name, had himself prepared the edition of Byron's complete works. Murray's father, also John Murray (1778–1843), had been acquainted with Byron and acquired many of his poems in manuscript. Murray's Pearl Byron carried a notice challenging any other publisher to produce a better edition: "Although various editions are circulated purporting to be 'Byron's Works,' none are complete except those bearing the imprint of the publisher of this Edition, who retains the copyright of pieces which no one else has the right to reprint. In addition to this, he has taken the pains to collate carefully text by the original MSS. in Lord Byron's writing, which are in his possession, and has thus been able to discover and expunge numerous errors from which no other edition is free. He ventures, therefore, to invite comparison between this and any recent Edition, on the score of accuracy, completeness, and price." Alexander Macmillan replies on August 23: "Have you seen Matthew Arnold's selections from Byron [published by Macmillan in the Golden Treasury series]? If not go to that intelligent bookseller you have at Eastbourne and invest 4s. 6d. or whatever less he charges and you will have a Byron without his nudities and rudities. But the play without Hamlet would be a joke to a Globe Byron without *Don Juan*. *Don Juan* contains far and away his best poetry. Look at Arnold's selections, and read his preface." Dodgson's reply is missing, but Macmillan writes again on the subject on November 3, explaining that he sometimes published "selections" because the firm recognize "the fact that for many people selections are best." He sends Dodgson editions of Byron, Wordsworth, and Shelley, and adds: "Your other suggestions I fear we cannot act on. Keats we have often thought of for a Golden Treasury book, but I have reason to know that any existing edition can and will be improved on, though circumstances stand in the way. We have an edition of Coleridge in four volumes – which is the best – and may consider a Globe form later on. It has often been talked of among us."
3 Tenniel is working on *The Nursery "Alice"*, which Dodgson conceived earlier that year, "with pictures printed in colours, to be larger and thinner than the original with a selection of the text and of the pictures, and to sell for about 2s. I fancy such a book would have a sale of its own," Dodgson wrote (*Diaries*, p. 394) on February 15, "and would not at all interfere with the sale of the complete 6s. edition." On April 13 of this year, Macmillan wrote about Dodgson's proposal: "Please give me a list of the pieces you propose to include, and of the pictures you wish to reproduce. You should consult Mr. Tenniel on this and also on the colourist." On April 21, Macmillan wrote a long letter pointing out the complex nature of colour printing and added: "A recent French process has been brought before us and we are going to do Mrs. Molesworth's next book in this way. We hope soon to see some proofs of these, and estimates. . . ." Dodgson evidently exchanged many letters on the subject with both Macmillan and Tenniel until the book became a reality. For more on *The Nursery "Alice"* and its tangled publication history, see *Handbook*, pp. 160–3 and the entire issue of *Jabberwocky* for Autumn 1975.

Christ Church, Oxford
May 13, 1883[1]

Dear Mr. Macmillan,

Thanks for the 2 reviews you have sent me – from the *Glasgow Herald* and the *Educational Times* – of my *Euclid I, II*, 2nd edition.[2]

I have several questions to ask.

(1) Would it be best to have the volume of Poems[3] folded in sets of 16, or of 8, pages in a sheet? I see *Alice* is done in 8's, but the *Looking-Glass* in 16's. The latter I suppose costs less for binding, as there would be only half as much sewing to do. Is there any advantage in the 8's?[4] (The book must *not* be electrotyped as a

whole, as I shall want to correct the text from time to time: it must be printed from movable type, for the text, and electrotypes for the pictures.)

(2) I want the cover to have – like *Alice* – a head in a circular medallion on each side. What were the 2 you had cut in brass for the later copies of the *Snark*?[5] We may use *one* of them: the other should come out of *Phantasmagoria*.

(3) I want the book printed on a cheaper paper than *Alice*. Mr. Craik said (in his letter dated June 12, 1882) that this is "one of Dickinson's expensive papers," and that you could provide a cheaper paper and would be "prepared for the bulk of people not observing the difference." How much cheaper do you mean? As I said in my letter dated June 9, 1882, considering that the Chiswick Press, and Messrs. Hazell, Watson & Viney, both undertake to produce a book in a style "fully equal to *Alice*," though charging less than half the price for paper, I think it might be worth trying what *you* can do at $\frac{2}{3}$ the price. Would you get a few pages of *Alice* (including a picture or two) worked off properly on some paper of that price (or a little dearer if you think that too low a figure) that I may compare it with *Alice* on the dear paper?[6]

(4) I want the book to be announced as "in the Press" by my friend the editor of the *St. James's Gazette*. About how long before it appears should the announcement be made?[7]

(5) What would be the difference in cost between gilt edges, as in *Alice*, and coloured edges (a uniform tint, *not* marbled)?[8]

(6) I shall wish the 2nd thousand to have "second thousand" on the title-page: then "third thousand," and so on. Is this done with *Alice*? I mean, is the change made for *each* thousand, or do you print 3000 at a time with the same title-page?[9]

(7) Which thousand are you in now, for *Alice* and for *Looking-Glass*?[10]

I will send you, shortly, a scheme I am concocting for publishing this new volume. Its chief novelty is in the reduction of the bookseller's profits, which seem to me exorbitant: but you and I will be better off.

Very truly yours,

C. L. Dodgson

---

[1] Again an enormous gap appears in the file of Dodgson letters to Macmillan while Macmillan letters to Dodgson continue at the usual pace.

[2] Dodgson printed his *Euclid Books I, II* for private circulation in 1875. It was not a defense of Euclid, like *Euclid and His Modern Rivals*, but a rectification of the original form of Euclid's *Elements*, Books I and II, for modern use. Macmillan published a revised version of this 1875 work in 1882; it sold for 2s. "This book is admirably suited to Oxford men who require to know the first two books of Euclid, and desire nothing more," wrote the *Glasgow Herald* (April 24, 1883, p. 6). "It is charmingly neat, 'free from all accidental verbiage and repetition,' and yet Euclid. Mr. Dodgson's slight alterations of the text . . . are fully stated and explained in the introduction. As a frontispiece we find a chart of the propositions of Book I arranged in logical sequence." The *Educational Times* (May 1, 1883, p. 147) begins by describing the book: "The present differs from the first edition of Mr. Dodgson's little work in the substitution of words for ten algebraical symbols there used, an alteration which will commend itself to many. . . . Mr. Dodgson . . . has

brought his considerable experience to bear upon the modelling of this exposition of Euclid's method."

[3] *Rhyme? and Reason?* to be.

[4] In his May 21 reply, Frederick Macmillan writes that the difference in the sheets was of no advantage to the binder, and as the same size paper had been used for both *Alice* and *Looking-Glass*, the paper had obviously been cut by the printers "to suit their own convenience."

[5] The Bellman and the Beaver.

[6] Frederick Macmillan replies (May 21): "We propose to use a cheaper paper than has hitherto been used for *Alice* and *Looking-Glass*. We understand that you wished that done and have ordered some for a reprint of *Alice* which is just going to press. We will send for a sheet as soon as one is printed off that you may see how it works."

[7] Frederick Greenwood, who had been the Editor of the *Pall Mall Gazette*, broke with the paper's owner in 1889 and founded the rival *St. James's Gazette*. Dodgson's allegiance went with his friend from the *Pall Mall* to the *St. James's*. "The book had better not be announced . . . till, at earliest, a fortnight before it is ready for publication," Frederick Macmillan replies (same letter).

[8] F. Macmillan reports (same letter): "The cost of binding with gilt edges (like *Alice*) would be 98s. per 100 copies, with coloured edges 88s. and with plain cut edges 80s.

[9] Macmillan replies (same letter): "We alter the number on the title page with each thousand copies of *Alice*, and will do so with the new book."

[10] "We are now in the 70th 1000 of *Alice* and the 52nd 1000 of *Looking-Glass*," Macmillan replies (same letter).

Christ Church, Oxford

May 20, 1883

Dear Mr. Macmillan,[1]

Would you kindly get me a couple of good "stalls" for the afternoon performance at Drury Lane on the 29th, to be given for the Actors' Benevolent Fund. They are a guinea each, I see. I should like to have them in the 3rd, 2nd, front, or 4th row – and fairly central.[2]

I have an idea for the binding of the poems, which I should like to see tried. It is a bright, rather light, green for the cover (as near the fresh green of hedges in Spring as we can get) and that the edges of the leaves shall be marbled creamy-white and pink (which would give the sort of effect apple-blossoms have, when seen against a background of green foliage). Would you kindly have a piece of paper marbled in this style, and send it me, along with some different shades of green cloth: and I will show them to artistic friends.[3]

Hoping to receive before long your answer to my letter of the 13th, I am

Very truly yours,

C. L. Dodgson

[1] In replying to this letter on the following day, the sixty-four-year-old head of the firm, writes: "My nephew Fred has been going into the various points of your letter of the 13th and will write you either this afternoon or tomorrow," thereby charting a new course for the Dodgson–Macmillan relationship. Alexander Macmillan's health was not good (on April 14, 1882, he asks Dodgson to "pardon my writing through an amanuensis: my fingers are rheumatically stiff."), and from 1880 onwards the Macmillan letters reflect the increased participation of the younger family members

in the business. Alexander's second son, George, had been working in the firm since 1874, and Alexander's nephew Frederick (Daniel's eldest son) had returned to the London office in 1876, after five years in the New York branch of Macmillan and Co. More and more, Alexander delegated responsibilities to these younger men. Gradually, he withdrew from the business, and when his eldest son, Malcolm, died mysteriously in 1889, the mantle fell entirely upon Frederick and George, who, by that time, were able partners. The firm suffered no shock from the transfer of management. Dodgson did not welcome the change, he so valued his long association with the founder of the firm, and although his letters are, more and more, answered by Frederick, George, or even by the impersonal "Macmillan and Co.," he continues to address his own letters to Alexander Macmillan. He grows convinced that after Alexander Macmillan surrendered the mantle to his successors, the firm is never the same: on December 12, 1889, he writes: "The *management* seems to be falling off, now that Mr. Macmillan (who is very old) is no longer on the spot" (Diaries). For more on the transition in management of the firm, see Morgan, esp. pp. 135–40.
2 Alexander Macmillan sends the tickets on the following day. On the 29th Dodgson "met Lucy Walters and took her to the Drury Lane performance for the Actors' Benevolent Fund," which includes "a bit of *Iolanthe*," the trial scene from *The Merchant of Venice*, scenes from *The Rivals*, and a number of other offerings (*Diaries*, p. 417). For more on Dodgson and Lucy Walters, see *Letters*, p. 699.
3 Macmillan replies (May 21) that he thought either "*creamy pink* or primrose edges" might do but emphasized "*single colour*," adding that "*mottle* of any kind I very much doubt." Dodgson must have insisted on mottling, and in his next letter (May 26), Macmillan writes: "We are sending you by rail today two specimens of binding with primrose and apple blossom – *single* colour. . . . Mottling seems to be extremely hazardous. The light green and creamy pink edges look to my eye very charming. I hope also ، yours."

Christ Church, Oxford

June 4, 1883

Dear Mr. Macmillan,

I am now ready to put before you my ideas as to publishing this new volume, and will be glad to know what you think of them.

First, as to the name:

RHYME?

AND REASON?

is, I think, original: and may prove attractive. Do you know if it has been used already?[1]

Next, as to the terms of publishing. This book will be about 210 pages, and will contain more than 70 pictures! I think the *publishing* price may fairly be 7*s*. 6*d*., or even 8*s*. But that does not concern *me* so much as what you are to fix as the price for the *trade*, for that is all for which you will account to me. This price I wish to be 6*s*. (At present I am speaking only of *credit* prices – to be paid within a year: I will speak of ready-money prices afterwards.) I wish you to announce that this abatement includes *all* the usual abatements, such as selling 25 and 24, etc., and that no further abatement will be made.

The transaction between you and me I want to be of this kind. *Debit* me with the expenses of paper, printing, and binding, merely (advertising I will speak of soon). In this matter I want you to make your usual profits, and charge your usual commission on what you actually pay. Then *credit* me with 6s. for every copy sold. Then as to your commission as publisher: this, on 6s., would be only 7½d., which I propose to raise to 1s., making this cover the advertising. For here I wish to try a novel experiment, by leaving it to *you* to advertise as much or as little as you please. I do not think there is any commercial flaw in such an arrangement, as it is clearly the interest of the publisher to advertise, so long as it increases the sale, and does not cost more than 1s. a copy: if for instance you thought that another £20 spent in advertising would cause an extra 1000 copies to be sold, I fancy you would find it worth your while to do it, and thus to get another £30 of profit.

Deducting this 1s. from the 6s., it leaves 5s. to credit me with. So that our account would be a very simple one: "Paper, printing, and binding . . . copies, £. . . . Sale of. . . . copies, at 5s., £. . . ."

You would, I suppose, allow the bookseller discount if he paid within 3 months, and more if he paid ready money: and the same to your *retail* customers: but all that would be a matter for your own convenience, with which *I* should be unconcerned. For you pay me, in January, the receipts of a year ending the previous June – which is practically much the same as if, instead of being spread over a year, they were concentrated on its central point, and all came in during one January and were paid to me one year afterwards, so that no discount is due from *me*.

I shall be glad to hear what you think of all this.[2]

Yours very truly,

C. L. Dodgson

---

[1] The reply from "Macmillan & Co." on the following day agrees that "the title you have chosen for your new volume seems to us appropriate and attractive," and adds: "We should have thought that it might just as well be called *Phantasmagoria and Other Poems* like the first edition, but you no doubt considered and rejected this idea." *Rhyme? and Reason?* is, of course, the title settled on, and Dodgson does not learn until December 1883 that there is another book in print that uses the same title without the two question marks (see *Letters*, p. 518).

[2] "We are quite ready to adopt the plan you suggest for its publication," Macmillan & Co. write (same letter). "We honestly confess that we do not think it will be popular with the booksellers and it is possible that their dislike to any change in their ordinary terms may be prejudicial to the sale of the book. As far as we ourselves are concerned we shall be quite satisfied with the profit you propose to allow us and will undertake that the advertising shall be adequate. . . . Would it not suit you equally well," the letter continues, "if the retail price was made 8s. 6d.?"

Christ Church, Oxford
June 5, 1883

Dear Mr. Macmillan,

Thanks for the copy of the *Snark* just received. You can omit it from the printed list, as you propose, as there are only special copies left.[1] Now that I see

the 2 medallions, I think the "Bellman" the best to use for the new volume.
Could you have the new head enclosed in the same-sized circle? Also (if it is not
too late to suggest it) could you have the 2 *Alice*s, that are to be done in bright
green cloth – one with marbled (pink and cream coloured) edges, and the other
(as Sir F. Leighton suggests)[2] a rather lighter shade of the same green as the
binding – lettered outside in the usual way? The two you have sent me are
rendered useless for giving away by having no lettering outside – not even the
name of the book: and I fear the omission cannot be remedied now.

Have you made the addition I suggested, to the advertisement of *Euclid I, II?*[3]

Yours very truly,

C. L. Dodgson

---

[1] George Macmillan wrote on the previous day that the *Snark* was "quite exhausted" except for
thirty copies especially bound for Dodgson's own use, and added: "I think therefore it would be
right to omit it from this list unless you specially wish it to stand."

[2] Sir Frederick Leighton (1830–96), P.R.A., later Lord Leighton, the well-known artist, was
probably one of the "artistic friends" whom Dodgson consulted about the binding of his new book
(see p. 165, above). Dodgson first called on Leighton in July 1879, although he had already
corresponded with the artist, and reported being "much taken with" the man. He called on him
again in 1881 (*Diaries*, pp. 381, 394; *Letters*, pp. 346, 347).

[3] We cannot tell what "addition" Dodgson refers to here.

Christ Church, Oxford
June 6, 1883

Dear Mr. Macmillan,

Having your *general* consent to a change in the method of publication, I will
now send you the exact details, which I have carefully thought out.

First, before I forget it, I hope it is clearly understood that the reprint of *Alice*
you are now doing is *not* to be on a cheaper paper. I have at present a decided
objection to cheapening (without notice) the paper of an *existing* book. With a
new book it is different. I have not yet received the *sheet* of *Alice*, worked on the
cheaper paper, which I asked for.

As to the title of the new book, I rejected *Phantasmagoria and Other Poems* as
misleading, since the new volume differs from the former one, in omitting the
serious poems, and in adding the *Snark*.

As to the terms of publishing. To adopt your suggestion of making the retail
price 8*s*. 6*d*., in order that the trade-reduction might be the usual thing, would
undo the whole object of the system I propose. My reason for taking a new line is
that I consider the difference, between the retail-price and the trade-price, to be
too great, and the booksellers' profit to be too great. If, in reducing it, I incur
their hostility, so be it: the system needs reform, in my opinion, and reformers
must often face hostility.

Here is my scheme:

I want you forthwith to advertise to the following effect (the exact wording I leave to you to settle):

"After the 30th of June, 1883, Mr. Lewis Carroll's two books, *Alice's Adventures in Wonderland*, and *Through the Looking-Glass* will be printed on a rather cheaper paper, and will be sold on the following terms. To the public, the prices will be 5*s*. 6*d*. and 6*s*. respectively: to the trade, a reduction of about 20 percent will be made, i.e. the prices will be 4*s*. 4*d*. and 4*s*. 9*d*. respectively – no other allowances (such as 25 as 24) being made. The above prices are for payment within the year: for payment within 3 months, 5 percent discount will be allowed, and for ready money 10 percent. A volume of poems, now in the press, which will contain most of *Phantasmagoria and Other Poems*, with the addition of *The Hunting of the Snark*, with more than 70 illustrations, will be sold to the public for 7*s*. 0*d*., and to the trade for 5*s*. 6*d*.; discount being allowed as in the case of the other two books."

Your own 10 percent commission on these 3 prices would be 5½*d*., 5$\frac{7}{10}$*d*., and 6⅗*d*., which I propose to raise to 8*d*., 9*d*., and 1*s*. respectively, so that you will credit me with 3*s*. 8*d*., 4*s*., and 4*s*. 6*d*. respectively, for every copy sold – *you* undertaking the advertising.

I may as well add that I should be quite willing, if you wished it, to allow *you* the same discount, for payment within 3 months, which I wish *you* to allow to the public and the trade. This would entail the making up our account at the end of each quarter, and settling by the middle of the following quarter. "Ready money" payment we need not consider: I am sure it could never be managed.

One thing more. When books are reprinted (as you are now doing with *Alice*) close to the end of a financial year, I think that either the *number* should be reduced, so that not more than (say) 1000 copies are "in hand" on June 30 – or, if that would not be a convenient plan, the printing should not be *all* charged in the year then expiring, but some of it should be carried over into the next year, so that the expenditure and the receipts for the same books may, to a large extent, be included in the same account.

You do not say whether anything can be done with the two *Alices* you have sent me with blank covers. If they could be lettered, they would do well to give away.

Very truly yours,

C. L. Dodgson

Christ Church, Oxford

June 7, 1883

Dear Mr. Macmillan,

(For simplicity's sake, I address *all* my letters to *you*, whether the one last received has come from yourself, Mr. Craik, your son, or your nephew. I trust I do not seem discourteous to any of them in this.) The specimen sheets of *Alice* on

2 kinds of paper have come. Please tell me *how much cheaper* the proposed paper is.[1] To me the difference in appearance seems so trifling that I am inclined to think it would be quite unnecessary to announce to the public that a cheaper paper was to be used, and might even mislead them, and create an impression that the new copies were going to be distinctly inferior in quality to the earlier ones.

Please tell me what difference, per 1000 copies, it will make to me to use the cheaper paper.[2]

Very truly yours,

C. L. Dodgson

---

[1] Macmillan & Co. report on the same day that the proposed paper was 3*d.* per pound cheaper.
[2] The same letter indicates that the difference per 1000 copies would be £9.11*s.*3*d.*

Christ Church, Oxford
June 11, 1883

Dear Mr. Macmillan,

You will not, of course, put out any advertisement till we have agreed as to all the details. Now that I see the proposed paper, I think we need not even cheapen *Alice*, as I propose, but can sell it on the same terms as the *Looking-Glass*.[1]

Also, instead of the "discount" terms I proposed, I think it would be fairer to offer "5 percent discount for payment within 6 months: and 10 percent for ready money." This seems more reasonable than dividing the year, unequally, into 3 and 9 months.

Thanks for card about *Spectator* notice of *Euclid I, II*. You need not send me a copy, as I have one here.[2]

Very truly yours,

C. L. Dodgson

---

[1] In a letter of the same date, Macmillan and Co. reply: "We regret to find that by a mistake Messrs. Clay have printed off nearly the whole of the new edition of *Alice* on the cheaper paper of which we sent you a specimen. We are sorry it should have happened because it was against your wishes, but as a matter of fact we do not think anyone will be able to tell the difference and (as we explained in our last) it will put about £20 into your pocket."
[2] The notice in the *Spectator* (June 9, 1883, p. 749) is a single paragraph: "Mr. Dodgson does not think with those who would supersede Euclid altogether, but he regards the 'Elements' as being capable of improvement. The changes are not great, but they are of some importance, and all tends towards simplicity. There is a very neat alternative proof of ii, 8, reducing the length by about nine parts out of ten. In this edition, words have been introduced, in the place of algebraical symbols."

Christ Church, Oxford
June 15, 1883

Dear Mr. Macmillan,

Thanks for the "Memorandum of Agreement."[1] I don't see any alteration in it to be needed, and I think you may as well advertise the new arrangement at once. We will try it for a while (I should like to try it for a year, or half-a-year at least) and then we shall see whether any further change is desired by either of us. It is but a mild onslaught I have made, so far, on the booksellers' profits: and will hardly be likely to incur their hostility. However, if it *does*, my inclination would be to say "one may as well be hung for a sheep as for a lamb!" and cut down their profits a little more.

When are the other 2 *Alice*s coming.[2]

You can advertise the *name Rhyme? and Reason?*

Very truly yours,

C. L. Dodgson

[1] Macmillan sent the agreement on the 13th, "covering all the points mentioned in your letters of the last few days." The letter added: "You say that you would be willing to allow us the discount that we are to give and in order that this may be accomplished we propose that we shall be allowed to avail ourselves of the 10 percent for cash by paying you in advance for the 250 copies of the books as we order them from the binder."

[2] On the 16th, Macmillan reports that the binder was at work on the other two copies of *Alice*.

Christ Church, Oxford
June 24, 1883

Dear Mr. Macmillan,

Thanks for sending the two duplicate copies of the "Agreement," which is a most satisfactory embodiment of my views. I have signed both copies, and return one to you.

The first clause leaves it uncertain *who* has the control of the details of printing, so that, as a mere matter of *law*, it would be in your power to order an unlimited number of copies, and to change the paper, binding, etc. However, it is of course understood that the author has the control, and that no details will be carried out without his actual or implied consent. In fact, of course no change would be made of any kind, without consulting me, with the one exception of the *numbers* ordered, as to which we have hitherto gone on the system of your ordering at your own discretion. I don't want that system altered, and I wish to withdraw what I once proposed, about dividing the cost of an edition between one year and the next, when more than 1500 copies are on hand on June 30. I think that would be needlessly complicated: and I shall be quite content with a general understanding that care shall be taken to avoid having any large numbers on hand on June 30. The nearer we are to being run out on that date, the better for me. No doubt it is also true that the larger the stock of unsold copies at that date, the better for *you*: but I don't think the accidental advantage of being paid for the printing a year before you have to account for selling comes legitimately under the head of "publisher's profits."

I think the advertisement ought to be out *before* July 1, and that the new book should be named also, so that the booksellers may have fair notice. Hence, though I fear we can't get it out till well on in July, I have sent Mr. Greenwood details of it, that he may announce it in the *St. James's Gazette*, telling him that we shall begin advertising it in a few days. He will probably announce it at once.[1]

Very truly yours,

C. L. Dodgson

---

[1] No announcement appeared, however, in the *St. James's Gazette* in June or July, nor do Macmillan include *Rhyme? and Reason?* in their advertisement in the paper on July 23.

Christ Church, Oxford

August 1, 1883

Dear Mr. Macmillan,

I had forgotten that you ceased to keep the *Index* on sale in 1878, and I suppose you had forgotten it too, as I see it is still in the list of my books. Please withdraw it at once.[1]

As to the *Easter Greeting*, I must ask your advice. Friends have again and again begged me to let it be sold separately, and I wrote years ago to ask you to do this, and supposed (as you raised no objection) that it was being done.[2] Can you recommend a bookseller, with whom you could arrange that he should be named as the person from whom copies could be had, and that you should send him (say) 1000, for which he should pay nothing, but merely account to you for *sold* copies? I don't want any profit on them, so you could arrange to charge him just enough to cover the cost of printing. The difficulty you raise as to selling for me so cheap a book suggests a question. What is the lowest-priced book you *are* willing to undertake? The little pamphlet on *Lawn Tennis Tournaments* which I asked, in my letter of July 29, whether you would publish (you do not notice the question) will be 8 pp., and cannot I think be charged more than 6*d*. Is that too cheap for you?[3] In that case, I suppose I must employ some publisher who is also a bookseller. Can you suggest one? I should be glad of an answer as soon as you can conveniently give it, as I should want him to advertise it without delay. It must not be mixed up with the "Lewis Carroll" books, as I am putting my real name to it (my usual course with *mathematical* books).

Yours very truly,

C. L. Dodgson

¹ Dodgson is mistaken. Macmillan never agreed to sell his *Index to "In Memoriam"* (see pp. 144–6, above), and Dodgson's memory has betrayed him also about the reason that the *Index* is in his list of works (see p. 177, below).

² "We do not quite understand what you wish done about the *Easter Greeting,*" Macmillan & Co. wrote on July 31. "We have hitherto been in the habit of inserting it in copies of *Alice* and *Looking-Glass,* and we shall be glad to continue to do so if you like. The tract has never been sold and we fear that if you want to sell it we are hardly the people to manage it for you, as we have not the proper machinery for dealing with such a thing. We are publishers and not booksellers so that the public would not come to us direct nor do we wish for them. . . ."

³ On August 2 Macmillan agrees to "undertake the sale of your pamphlet on *Lawn Tennis Tournaments* – the retail price being sixpence." The pamphlet developed from a letter which Dodgson published in the *St. James's Gazette* of August 1, 1883 (the same date as the present letter), entitled "The Fallacies of Lawn Tennis Tournaments." Dodgson argues that in a tournament where all competitors beaten in the first round (and subsequent rounds) retire, the best player usually wins the first prize, but the odds are against subsequent players being placed second, third, and fourth according to their skill. For more, see *Handbook,* pp. 111, 120; *Letters,* pp. 682–3.

Christ Church, Oxford
August 6, 1883

Dear Mr. Macmillan,

Will you kindly post enclosed.

As to the *Lawn Tennis* book, I will send you copies at once, and shall be quite content to have the retail-price 6*d.,* trade-price 5*d.,* and that you should allow me 4*d.* Only in this case *I* will pay for the advertising, as that item will cost probably a good deal more than the book will ever clear. I want you to advertise it at once, daily, and rather widely – at least in the *St. James's, Field, Land and Water, Sporting and Dramatic News,* and wherever else you think desirable. The title is *Lawn Tennis Tournaments, the true method of assigning prizes, with a proof of the fallacy of the present method, by Charles L. Dodgson, M. A. Student and late Mathematical Lecturer of Christ Church, Oxford.* I am printing on the back of it "By the same Author: *Euclid I, II.* Second Edition, 1883. Crown 8 vo. 2s. Macmillan & Co." and adding an extract from the preface. I hope 2*s.* is right? If you want further copies of *Lawn Tennis* (I am sending you 200) please order of, "The Messrs. Baxter, 69 St. Aldate's, Oxford."¹

Many thanks for what you say about *An Easter Greeting,* but I fear it would not meet the wishes of my friends, who would certainly want to buy *single* copies. If you can't suggest a bookseller, I think of going to Harrison, of Pall Mall, corner of St. James's St., as my sisters deal with him. Please tell me what you are charging me for its production, per 1000.²

The primrose-edged *Alice,* asked for in my letter of July 27, has not yet arrived.

Yours very truly,
C. L. Dodgson

¹ On July 30, Dodgson wrote in his *Diaries* (p. 419): "Am now printing at Baxters' my pamphlet on *Lawn Tennis Tournaments.*"

[2] On August 2, Macmillan & Co. wrote: ". . . although we cannot undertake to sell single copies, it has occurred to us . . . that we might do them up in packets of 25 or more copies and offer them for sale at sixpence. If you approve we are willing to do this." On the 7th, Macmillan wrote to assure Dodgson that Harrison of Pall Mall would be "very good people" to sell the pamphlet. They also reported that the net cost per 1000 was £1.12*s*.0*d*.

Christ Church, Oxford
August 8, 1883

Dear Mr. Macmillan,

I had forgotten I had given you the Eastbourne address. Please address *here* till further notice.

By all means sell the *Lawn Tennis* pamphlet as you propose.[1]

Will you kindly apply to Mr. Harrison, and arrange with him for selling the *Easter Greeting* (as it is a "Lewis Carroll" publication, I cannot do anything *myself* about it). Please tell him they are to be sold at 1*d*. apiece, or 12 for 9*d*., or 100 for 5*s*. and that you will charge him per 100 the usual trade terms: and further, that you will send him 1000 to begin with, and that he need not pay for any till he has sold them. Please let me know as soon as you can if you succeed in arranging this.[2] If the above terms leave you a reasonable profit above the £1.12*s*. cost per 1000, would you kindly take the whole thing on yourself, and leave me out. I revoke that last sentence,[3] as I see it would lead to your losing, if there were no sale.

Thanks for the *Bookseller*. I was much interested to see what "A Firm of London Booksellers" think about it.[4] It shows clearly that the public are interested in knowing what the trade-price is, and what discounts you allow: and of course I shall announce it in my "list of books." I *hope* you will also do it in advertising the books, but as that is now wholly in your own hands, I can do no more than express a hope.

I am going to publish an explanation of my new terms of sale, and to give a history of the sale of *Alice*, and of the booksellers' profits, and *my* profits. Would you mind my completing the thing, by naming cost-price of book and *your* profits? I cannot see what harm it could do to name them, but of course, if you object, I must leave out those 2 items.[5] The booksellers' letter (which I mean to quote *entire*) will furnish admirable matter for criticism – specially that wonderful sentence "it will be necessary to explain to every customer that no discount can be allowed because the author refuses to allow the seller to give it to the purchaser" (!)

I hope you will get your 200 *Lawn Tennis* pamphlets by the end of this week.

Very truly yours,

C. L. Dodgson

[1] On August 7, Messrs. Macmillan wrote: "We think that the *Lawn Tennis* pamphlet had better be sold on the usual trade terms . . . , and we will charge our commission of 10 percent on the proceeds.

We would rather confine the experimental terms to the 'Lewis Carroll' books for the present."
2 On August 14, Macmillan & Co. report that "Messrs. Harrison of Pall Mall have undertaken to sell the *Easter Greeting* on the terms mentioned in your letter of the 8th inst." Thenceforth, the following announcement regularly appears in Macmillan's list of "Works by Lewis Carroll": "Mr. Lewis Carroll, having been requested to allow *An Easter Greeting* (a leaflet, addressed to children, and frequently given with his books) to be sold separately, has arranged with Messrs. Harrison, of 59, Pall Mall, who will supply a single copy for 1*d*., or 12 for 9*d*. or 100 for 5*s*."
3 Dodgson actually writes *sense* for *sentence*.
4 On the day he writes this letter, Dodgson records in his *Diaries* (p. 419): "Got from Macmillan [the August issue of] the *Bookseller* containing a letter from 'A Firm of London Booksellers' about my new 'trade-price,' and proposing that the booksellers shall agree not to buy any of my books(!) I mean at once to write a letter, or pamphlet, or both, to tell the public what booksellers' profits really are, and that I am trying to reduce their present monstrous proportions."
5 See p. 176, below.

7 Lushington Road, Eastbourne
August 15, 1883

Dear Mr. Macmillan,

I will give you a sketch of the paper I am preparing, and then I hope you will see your way to allowing me to name *your* profits as well as my own. My "case" is that the order, as to profits, *ought* to be "Author, Publisher, Bookseller" and that it is monstrous that the Bookseller should come first: in my new plan he is lowered to the *second* place: but I am very doubtful if the reform goes far enough. Here are the contents of my paper:

Letter from *Bookseller*, with remarks.

Account of share borne by the 3 parties in producing a book:

(1) *Bookseller* – gives no time, thought, or trouble – merely sinks a little capital.

(2) *Publisher* gives time, thought, trouble, and results of experience. (Here I propose to say something of the amount of trouble I give *you* in bringing out a book.)

(3) *Author* gives brain-work chiefly – but of a kind not always procurable from *any* quarter, but scarce, and so worth much.

Account of *Alice*, as hitherto sold. Retail price 6*s*.: actual cost of production 2*s*.: leaving 4*s*. profit, which has been divided thus:

Author	1*s*. 2*d*.
Publisher	8½*d*.
Bookseller	2*s*. 2½*d*.

Result of this monstrous arrangement, in booksellers underbidding each other, and allowing absurd amounts of discount, etc. Purchaser for ready money ought to be content with 10 percent.

Ruskin's plan gives Bookseller *nothing*, and would in this case leave 4*s.* for Author and Publisher to share.[1]
Mine divides it thus:

Author	2*s.* 2*d.*
Publisher	10*d.*
Bookseller	1*s.* 0*d.*

This, however is a "credit" transaction; and here the Bookseller makes 20 percent on his outlay, at the end of year. But by ready-money dealing, he would buy for 4*s.* 6*d.*, and sell for 5*s.* 5*d.*, thus making rather over 20 percent *at once*: so that he can turn his money many times in the year.

I very much *hope* you will allow me to name the above details: of course, if you object, I must lump together the cost and your profits as one item: but it will make an awkward statement, and general readers will be probably quite as much at a loss as I am to guess what reason there can be for keeping *your* share of the profit a secret, while mine and the Bookseller's are exactly stated.[2]

With many thanks for your letter and the various things you have done or are doing, I am

Very truly yours,

C. L. Dodgson

---

[1] For some time, John Ruskin had been battling the problem of unacknowledged profits and percentages in bookselling. In 1871, he began to distribute and sell his own books, with George Allen engaged as business manager. He explained his departure from conventional practice in the advertisement to *Sesame and Lilies* (1871): "It has long been in my mind to make some small resistance to the existing system of irregular discount in the bookselling trade . . . not in hostility to booksellers, but, as I think they will find eventually, with a just regard to their interest, as well as to that of authors. Every volume of this series of my collected works will be sold to the trade only; who can then fix such further profit on it, as they deem fitting, for retail. . . . Every volume will be clearly printed and thoroughly well bound; on such conditions the price to the public, allowing full profit to the retailer, may sometimes reach, but ought never to exceed, half a guinea, nor do I wish it to be less. . . . The price of this first volume to the trade is seven shillings." Even this specific statement of the price to booksellers did not stem the tide of booksellers' efforts to undersell one another; consequently in the following year Ruskin issued even more stringent restrictions. He fixed the price of his books at 9*s.* 6*d.* for the plain volumes, and 19*s.* for the illustrated, with no abatement, and they could only be obtained from Smith and Elder or George Allen. Eventually Ruskin's books could only be obtained *directly* from George Allen and only for cash. Far from destroying Ruskin's sales, the practice proved immensely profitable and established George Allen as a major publisher (W. G. Collingwood, *The Life and Work of John Ruskin* (rev. ed. 1900), pp. 284, 294; Derrick Leon, *Ruskin: The Great Victorian* (1949), pp. 515–16).

[2] On the previous day, Macmillan & Co. wrote: "We shall be obliged if in anything that you publish with regard to the sale of your books you will refrain from going into particulars as to our profits. It seems to us that it will answer all purposes if you say that we have been paid by a commission." Craik replies to Dodgson's present letter on the following day: "We do not think there is any objection to the publication of such a statement as you propose as far as we are concerned. I have not attempted any verification of your figures, but you have doubtless made careful estimates." He also expresses concern over the possibility that Dodgson might prove "a loser" in trying to reform bookselling because the trade would certainly be antagonistic to "the complicated and exceptional terms" on which Dodgson's books were to be had.

7 Lushington Road, Eastbourne
August 17, 1883

Dear Mr. Macmillan,

First, let me revoke what I said about *your* having forgotten that the *Index* had left your hands, and still gone on advertising it. The lapse of memory is all mine. I now find that I got Mr. Kegan Paul to send *me* all the copies, and that I asked you to keep it in the list of works, meaning to send you a copy, if one were ever asked for. However, nobody seems to want them.

Secondly, I am very much obliged by your permission to publish the details I named to you, as to profits on *Alice*. I have no doubt the *booksellers* are now very hostile to me, and perhaps will refuse to keep my books. *If* they do, *our* next move (I hope you will agree with me) is obvious, and constitutes a real "checkmate." It is to announce that any one, finding a difficulty in getting the books, has only to send you a money-order (5s. 5d. for *Alice*, or 6s. 4d. for *Rhyme? and Reason?*) and the book will be sent carriage-free – thus costing the purchaser exactly the same as if he got it of his local bookseller. And it will be well worth your while to pay the carriage, since every such sale will represent one that would otherwise have been a "trade" sale – so that you will get 5s. 2d., instead of 4s. 6d., for *Alice* (I think Parcel Post would be 3d.), and 6s. 1d., instead of 5s. 3d., for *Rhyme? and Reason?*. However, we had better keep this move in reserve, till we have clear evidence that the booksellers are really lessening the sale.

Thirdly, I look in vain in the *Standard* and *St. James's* for advertisements of *Lawn Tennis*. Please advertise it daily for the next 2 or 3 weeks. *One* advertisement, now, is worth a dozen a month hence.[1]

Very truly yours,

C. L. Dodgson

Advertisements appear in the *St. James's Gazette* on both August 28 and 29 (p. 16). Dodgson was creating his own publicity as well, with letters on "The Fallacies of Lawn Tennis Tournaments" in the *St. James's Gazette* of August 1, 4 and 21, which, in turn, provoked other letters from readers.

7 Lushington Road, Eastbourne
August 21, 1883

Dear Mr. Macmillan,

To complete my case, about booksellers' profits, etc., I need one or two more details, which I shall be much obliged by your furnishing me with.

(1) The average interval between the payments falling due, and being paid, in the case of the paper-maker.

(2) ditto for the printer.

(3) ditto for the binder.

(4) ditto for the booksellers, in paying you.

(5) As to the 5 percent discount allowed to booksellers, is that allowed in *all* cases, or only when they pay ready money?

I cannot make a perfectly accurate estimate till I know if these transactions are ready-money or credit.[1]

Yours very truly,

C. L. Dodgson

[1] "Mr. Craik is away for a few weeks' holiday," Macmillan & Co. write on the following day, "and as all matters connected with the accounts are in his hands, we regret that we are not in a position to answer your questions."

7 Lushington Road, Eastbourne

August 22, 1883

Dear Mr. Macmillan,

I hear that an article has appeared, either in the *Athenæum* or the *Academy*, on our new system of selling books. I should be glad if you could find it and send me a copy.[1] It was only yesterday I discovered that the number of the *Bookseller*, which you sent me, contains, besides the letter from "A Firm of London Booksellers," an editorial article which takes the opposite side. Did you see it?[2]

On further thinking over the letter I wrote you August 17, I have come to the conclusion that it would be a good thing, in case you are willing to adopt the suggestion, that I should at least *mention*, in my letter on the subject, that we are prepared with that move, if it should prove necessary. I should put it something like this – "I do not anticipate that booksellers generally will act in the spirit of this letter, and raise any difficulty in supplying the public with these books: if, however, we find that this is done, Messrs. Macmillan authorise me to announce that they will be prepared to supply the books carriage free: so that country purchasers, who like to send them the retail price, less 10 percent discount, will be able to get them on exactly the same terms as they would from their local bookseller."[3]

I don't think I mentioned to you that I want to republish the letter as a 6*d.* pamphlet, and of course hope that *you* will sell it for me.

Very truly yours,

C. L. Dodgson

[1] On the following day, Macmillan & Co. reply that the only notice was a paragraph in the *Athenaeum*, a copy of which they send him. It appeared in the "Literary Gossip" column on August 11 (p. 180): "Mr. Lewis Carroll, following in the steps of Mr. Ruskin, in his new book *Rhyme? and Reason?* reduces the usual trade allowance to booksellers to twopence in the shilling, so that the discount booksellers who take off threepence in the shilling cannot in this case do so without incurring loss. This departure from trade custom will doubtless prejudice booksellers against the book, and probably interfere with its sale. The retail bookseller's profit by competition is reduced

to a minimum, and indications constantly occur of the depressed condition of the retail trade."
2 The *Bookseller* editorial supported Dodgson's effort, and the September issue of the journal continues the controversy with two more letters and an editorial. On the day before he writes this letter, Dodgson recorded in his *Diaries* (p. 419): "During yesterday and today I have written nearly all of the letter I mean to send to the *St. James's* on 'Authors and Booksellers.'" The letter does not appear, but in the following year Dodgson prints a pamphlet entitled *The Profits of Authorship*. No copy of it has surfaced, but Collingwood (pp. 227–8) quotes a paragraph from it. Morgan suggests (pp. 113–14) that it may never have been published, but it certainly was printed. Craik writes to Dodgson on January 7, 1884: "Thank you for letting us see the proof of your pamphlet *The Profits of Authorship*. We have certainly nothing to complain of but on the contrary to acknowledge the kind way you refer to us. We do not attempt to discuss your theory or your figures. If we publish for you I think we should deem it right that you should state that all you say is on your own responsibility and that you have no reason to say that we concur with you. It is only truth to say that we have tried to dissuade you from the mode of publishing you now pursue." For the text of the *Bookseller* letter signed "A Firm of London Booksellers" and the *Bookseller*'s August 1883 editorial, see Appendix A below, p. 365; see also *Handbook*, pp. 130–1.
3 Macmillan and Co. reply (August 23): "We should strongly advise you not to publish such a sentence as that suggested in your letter of yesterday. It will be better, we think, to take it for granted that the booksellers will not object to the new plan. To make an offer to supply books direct would seem like a bid for their enmity. Besides, we do not for a moment suppose that any booksellers will refuse to supply your books. They may decline to speculate in them, or to buy them to stock on the chance of reselling, but will be certain to get them to order."

7 Lushington Road, Eastbourne
August 24, 1883

Mr. Dodgson supposes, from the delay in answering his questions, that Mr. Macmillan is out of town as well as Mr. Craik, as he could certainly have answered the questions at once.

It is certainly an inconvenient arrangement that there should be no one on the spot capable of answering such questions. They are, however, questions that need no reference to books and either Mr. Macmillan or Mr. Craik is quite sure to be able to answer them at once, as the arrangements with the printer, bookseller, etc., as to interval of time for payment, must of course be fixed and permanent.

He will thank them, if it is not already done, to forward the letter 44147, at once, to whichever of the two partners is most readily accessible.[1]

Messrs. Macmillan & Co.

1 Dodgson in referring to his letter of August 21 uses the number he assigned it in his Register. He began to keep his Register of Letters Received and Sent, with a *précis* of each alongside its date and entry number, on January 1, 1861, less than a month before his twenty-ninth birthday, and maintained it diligently for the remaining thirty-seven years of his life. The Register has not survived, but Collingwood records that the Register consisted of twenty-four volumes and the last number recorded there was 98,721 (S. D. Collingwood, "Lewis Carroll: An Interview with His Biographer," *Westminster Budget*, xii (December 9, 1898), 23. Macmillan & Co. reply the following day: "In reply to questions 1–3 in your letter of August 21, we beg to say that from printer, paper

maker, and binder we get 12 months' credit without discount. . . . With regard to questions 4 and 5, we should say that in any argument founded on it you had better assume that the bookseller gets 5 percent discount from the trade price for cash only. Roughly speaking these are the terms, but as a matter of fact booksellers buy at much better rates. Our regular terms are 6 months account with 2½ percent discount at settlement, but our traveller calls upon every customer in the country twice a year, and on those occasions takes orders to account at 5 percent discount. Naturally booksellers make up their stock and buy as much as they can at the larger discount. Then the exporting houses who send to India and the Colonies get extra discounts varying from 7½ to 10 percent on everything they buy, while some of the larger wholesale (Row) houses pay monthly and get discounts averaging 10 percent on all they buy."

7 Lushington Road, Eastbourne
August 28, 1883

Dear Sirs,

I will now put before you the statistics, on which I based the agreement we have made as to future sales, and a summary of which I propose to publish – and I shall be glad if you will, at your earliest convenience, examine them and correct them if necessary, as any serious error might require the agreement to be altered, and in that case the sooner the new terms are announced, the better.

As to cost of printing, etc., I took the following furnished by you, of 2000 *Wonderland* September 1880.

	Actual cost	Publisher's commission
Paper –	£57. 7s. 6d.	£5. 14s. 9d.
Printing –	£44. 14s. 0d.	£4. 9s. 9d.
Binding –	£88. 0s. 0d.	£10. 0s. 0d.
Advertising –	£10. 13s. 6d.	£1. 1s. 6d.
Total –	£200. 15s. 0d.	£21. 6s. 0d.

This gives actual cost of production, etc., 2s. a copy.

Publisher's commission on this is almost exactly 2½d. a copy.

I then took trade-price as 4s. 2d., and deducted 1/25th for the "25 sold as 24": this gave 4s. as sale-price, and publishers' commission on this is nearly 5d. The publishers' whole profit is (exactly) 2.556 + 4.8 = 7.356, which I called 7½d.

Publishers of course make an additional profit, by selling copies to the Trade in smaller lots than 24, viz. 4s. on every 24 thus sold, i.e. 2d. a copy. Not knowing how many copies you thus sell, I do not know what to allow for this. In my letter of August 15, I put it at 1d., assuming that *half* the copies sold went in small lots. I should be glad if you would make out, taking the sale of 2000 or more as your basis, what your average profit is under this heading.[1]

The Booksellers' profit I took as 2s. (difference between 6s. and 4s.) + the 2½ (i.e. 5 percent) discount you allow them on the 4s. This item must now be corrected, as you tell me the 5 percent ought to be considered as a discount for ready money: and, as all the other items are taken as payable within 12 months, we must do the same in this case. Is it fair to say that, *if* the Bookseller did not pay for 12 months, you would expect 4s. a copy? Or, if not, what would it be?

My profit I took as the residue when all these items were deducted from 6s.

If you make no correction in the above items, the summary I propose to publish is

Division of Profit hitherto:

Bookseller	2s.	0d.
Author	1s.	3½d.
Publisher		8½d.
	4s.	0d.

Division in future:

Bookseller	1s.	0d.
Author	2s.	2d.
Publisher		10d.
	4s.	0d.

Your profits, under the new system, I reckon thus: I make the new cost-price 11d. instead of 1s. 9d. by knocking off the 1d. for advertising, and your commission on that is 2d. Then I add 9d., the difference between 5s. and the 4s. 3d. you are to credit me with. That gives 11d. I then deduct 1d., because *you* undertake advertising.

I take no account of the change in the value of the paper which we are making, as it does not affect the *Booksellers'* profits – the point at issue in what I am about to publish. The reduction in value of paper (about 2d. a copy) will of course make a difference to *you*: your commission on printing, etc., being thereby reduced ⅕ of a penny per copy: or 16s 10d. per 1000 copies. If you wish it, we can allow for this in a supplementary agreement.

But let us first get the statistics made *quite* accurate.

Faithfully yours,

C. L. Dodgson

---

[1] On the following day, Macmillan & Co. reply to this question of odd books: "We charge, as you know, 25 books as 24 and 13 as 12½, but this does not mean that a bookseller must buy 13 copies of the *same* book in order to get the allowance. If he breaks up an order for 13 books selling at the same price we always 'sort' them, as the trade expression goes, and he is charged for 12½ volumes though

7 of them may be a book of comic poetry and the other 6 a book of sermons. You will see therefore that we do not make much extra profit by selling books in small numbers, and also that it would be next to impossible to trace the copies that had been sold by themselves and those which had been sorted up in 25s. or 13s."

7 Lushington Road, Eastbourne
August 30, 1883

Dear Sirs,

Thanks for letter of August 29. The statistics now stand thus:

> Division of Profits hitherto:
> Bookseller – 　　2s 0d.
> Author – 　　　　1s. 5d.
> Publisher – 　　　7d.

(instead of taking your 10 percent on printing, etc., and on trade-price as *separate* items, which introduces an extra halfpenny, I take it on their sum total – 10 percent on "2s. + 4s." is only 7.2 pence).

In my last letter, page 4, the first 2 lines should be "I make the new cost-price 1s. 11d. instead of 2s.

You may cease now to advertise *Lawn Tennis* unless the demand has been so great that you advise going on.

Please tell me, as soon as you conveniently can, if the above statistics are correct.

Faithfully yours,
C. L. Dodgson

7 Lushington Road, Eastbourne
August 31, 1883

Dear Sirs,

It had not occurred to me that the sentence you quote was liable to such an interpretation.[1] All I meant by it was to tell the public the terms on which *you* are prepared to sell the books: the price at which the *booksellers* sell is a matter for *them* to settle: as you most truly say, *I* have no power to control it. I have altered the words, so as to make the meaning perfectly clear. It now stands "Messrs. Macmillan are prepared to sell the above-named books to the Trade at an abatement of 2d. in the shilling (no odd copies), and to allow discount, both to the public and to the Trade, of etc., etc." I trust this will remove your objections, and that you will include it – or words to the same effect – in your own advertisements.[2] I have just discovered a mistake in the statistics I sent you. I had not observed that the 5 percent discount (which I had deducted from the profits I had at first assigned to the Bookseller) had to be added to *your* profits, not to mine, since you charge it to me. In fact, the actual proportions (calculated on a sale of 2000, of which you gave me the items), are:

Cost of production	2s.	0d.
Bookseller's profit	2s.	0d.
Author's profit	1s.	2d.
Publisher's profit		10d.
	6s.	0d.

so that (curiously enough, as it was not arranged for) *your* share of the profits is exactly the same under the two systems of sale.

Faithfully yours,

C. L. Dodgson

---

[1] On the previous day, Macmillan & Co. wrote: "We see from the proof of the last sheet of *Rhyme? and Reason?* that you have inserted a paragraph with regard to the terms on which your books are sold. We thought that you had agreed to omit this: we hope at all events you will do so now. Such a public explanation would serve only to alienate booksellers because it implies that author and publisher are dictating terms to them." Furthermore, Macmillan & Co. had already explained Dodgson's new terms to all their customers, and "what they are now is well known throughout the trade. The publisher and author can control the price at which their books are sold to the trade, but they cannot fix the rates at which the retail booksellers shall sell to the public. You can make it difficult for booksellers to 'undersell' by giving them only a moderate margin of profit, but if a bookseller chooses to make a present of the whole of his profit to the public you have no power to prevent him."

[2] In reply to the present letter, the firm write the following day: that they are prepared to accept the amended announcement of price "with one slight alteration." Rather than the phrase "to allow discount, both to the public and to the Trade," Macmillan suggest the phrase "to allow discount for cash both to the public and the Trade." They stress that "we cannot say anything that would give people the impression that they could buy books from us on credit – for we do not open retail accounts and have no intention of doing so." On September 14, Macmillan & Co. add: "Since we last wrote to you Mr. Alexander Macmillan has returned from abroad and we have discussed the question of inserting the paragraph about the terms in the advertisement at the end of your book. Mr. Macmillan is strongly of opinion that the paragraph in question should not appear at all on the ground that in the first place it looks like a bid for retail custom on our part, and this we decidedly object to, as we have no wish to be retail booksellers, and secondly that the terms on which booksellers buy are of no interest to the public."

7 Lushington Road, Eastbourne
September 17, 1883

Dear Mr. Macmillan,

I am sorry to find that you wish to revoke the letter of September 1. Of course I accept your revocation, though it throws a bewildering uncertainty over all previous letters signed "Macmillan & Co.," any one of which *may* have been written in your absence. At any rate I hope you were present when our "Agreement" was signed.

You do not, I think, quite understand my position in regard to these new terms of sale. I am trying, in one small instance (viz. the sale of 3 little books) to set an example to other writers of insisting on the reduction of the exorbitant profits of the booksellers – which of course carries with it the reduction of the exorbitant discount purchasers now exact from *them*. It is of course a dangerous experiment, so far as my own money-interests are concerned: but I hope to get the sympathy, not only of the authors, in whose interests I am acting, but also of the general public. To do this, I must convince the purchaser of two things (1) that he cannot reasonably expect to purchase *Alice's Adventures*, ready money, for *less* than 5s. 5d. – (2) that he cannot reasonably be expected to give *more*.

To prove (1), I must not only show him that, as an abstract question, 10 percent is a reasonable rate of discount; but I must also fully inform him as to the increased price the bookseller has to pay, making it impossible for him to have the old rate of discount. This makes it essential to publish, as widely as possible, the terms on which you sell to the trade.

To prove (2), I must furnish him with the address of *at least one* bookseller who is prepared to sell the book for 5s. 5d. Otherwise he is quite at the mercy of his local bookseller.

You remarked, most truly, in your letter dated August 30, that we "cannot fix the rates at which the retail booksellers shall re-sell to the public," alluding merely to the *ready-money price*: but it would have been equally true of the *credit-price*. In fact the announcement "price 6s." has no meaning at all, unless it means that *somebody* is prepared to sell the book – if not for 6s. with a year's credit, at any rate for 6s., less *10 percent* discount, for ready money. And *this* I had always understood you *were* prepared to do. The fact, which comes quite unexpectedly to me, that you really object to be announced as ready to sell the book to the public for ready money, would, if I were now *beginning* to publish, make it obvious that I must find another publisher, one who will also sell retail. But, after so long and so pleasant a connection, I am most reluctant to transfer the "Lewis Carroll" books to another publisher, and I think I see another way out of the apparent "dead-lock." Do you think you can find a bookseller in London who will undertake to deal on the new terms, and who is willing to have his name published as ready to allow 10 percent discount for ready money? If so, the announcement in the List of Works might run thus:

"Messrs. Macmillan and Co. will supply the above-named books to the Trade at an abatement of 2d. in the shilling, allowing 5 percent discount for payment within 6 months and 10 percent for ready money. Messrs. x x x x x x x x x will supply them to the public, allowing 10 percent discount for ready money."

If you cannot find such a bookseller, and would rather cancel the "Agreement" than be held to the clause in it regarding retail sale, I will not press the point, but will find another publisher. But it would be a matter of sincere regret to me.[1]

Very truly yours,

C. L. Dodgson

¹ "We will do as you wish," Alexander Macmillan replies two days later. "I was always doubtful of your enterprise though I greatly sympathise with your aim in trying to stop the foolish disparity of nominal and actual price. A *trade* concert many years ago tried to stop it. Lords Macaulay and Campbell . . . made Murray and Longman bend to their will, as we do to yours now. . . . But are you right?"

Christ Church, Oxford
December 9, 1883

Dear Mr. Craik,

"Peccavi!" It *was* my doing, I admit, that so few *Rhyme? and Reason?* were printed: and your firm advised a larger number. I am sorry if any one is put to inconvenience.¹

What I am now writing about is to beg earnestly that *no* risk may be run of the execution being deteriorated by hurrying the work. Whether we have more copies ready by Christmas, or Easter, or any other time, is a matter to me of no importance at all, compared with the having printing, binding, etc. all of *first-class* quality. Please secure *that*, at any rate, whatever else we miss.

One sign of haste I fear I saw in the copies I received the other day. Many of them had either been folded crooked, or the text [on] one side of the paper not truly placed with regard to the other side. There are many pages of text that lean visibly to one side. That evil will I hope be remedied in the next issue.

While these 2000 are being printed, would you see about getting some paper with a deeper tone, on the chance of yet more copies being called for?

As to these 2000, and any further issue you may think advisable, I say as I said in my telegram – "print at discretion."²

Yours very truly,

C. L. Dodgson

Messrs. Dalziel write that they have a book published for them by Routledge, also called *Rhyme and Reason*.³ It is a pity: but I fear it's too late to alter the name. We must hope that the two question-marks in *my* title will keep the two books distinct.

¹ Three days earlier, Craik wrote: "As I telegraphed we have already subscribed 1300 – actually 1330 copies and we have only 888 copies to supply the demand. It is a great pity we printed so few – but I understand it was your doing and contrary to our advice. We shall do our utmost to get copies of the reprint before Christmas but I very much fear it will not be possible." On December 6, Dodgson recorded in his *Diaries* (p. 422): "Arrival of 12 copies of *Rhyme? and Reason?*" The volume consists of eleven poems reprinted from *Phantasmagoria and Other Poems*, *The Hunting of the Snark* in its entirety, and five poems not printed in previous volumes. Henry Holiday's illustrations for the *Snark* are reprinted, and sixty-five illustrations by A. B. Frost appear for the first time. (For more about *Rhyme? and Reason?*, see *Handbook*, pp. 122–3; Selwyn H. Goodacre, ". . . An Annotated Hand-List," *Jabberwocky*, Autumn 1977, pp. 107–11.) On the last page, beneath the list of "Works by Lewis Carroll," two notices appear:

"N.B. In selling the above-mentioned books to the Trade, Messrs. Macmillan and Co. will abate 2*d.* in the shilling (no odd copies), and allow 5 per cent. discount for payment within six months, and 10 per cent. for cash. In selling them to the Public (for cash only) they will allow 10 per cent. discount.

"Mr. Lewis Carroll, having been requested to allow "An Easter Greeting" (a leaflet, addressed to children, and frequently given with his books) to be sold separately, has arranged with Messrs. Harrison, of 59, Pall Mall, who will supply a single copy for 1*d*., or 12 for 9*d*., or 100 for 5*s*."

2   Craik wrote (December 6): "It is unfortunate that the paper makers have just enough paper in stock to print 2000 copies. . . ." The new issue of the volume does not, however, become available before Christmas. "We expect to publish the new issue of *Rhyme? and Reason?* before the 20th," George Macmillan writes on January 3. "You expressed a wish that it should be carefully printed," he continues. "We have therefore avoided giving Messrs. Clay any excuse for hurrying over it. I hope the result may justify the delay."

3   H. W. Dulken, *Rhyme and Reason* (1869).

Christ Church, Oxford
October 12, 1884

Dear Mr. Macmillan,

I want you to publish a little pamphlet for me, which I am printing at Oxford, on Parliamentary Representation. Here are the details. I am using a handsome type, and a page about 7 × 5 outside measurement. I expect it will be 30 pages, or more. I don't think it will need a cover. I propose to have merely the name outside, and the title-page on the next leaf. I should think 1*s*. would be a good price for it. I shall put my own name to it.[1]

You shall have an early proof, of course: but I hope these details will be enough to enable you to say whether you will publish it. I should want you to do it on the *old Alice* terms; i.e. making your usual allowance to booksellers, charging me with advertising, etc., etc.

It will need pretty brisk advertising for a short time. When the Franchise business is settled, of course, the sale will come to an end.[2]

I hope to be able to send you 2000 copies by the 24th, or thereabouts: and I want a copy sent to every Member of Parliament (not to the Houses of Lords and Commons, but to their private addresses). This will need nearly 1200 copies, and it will be well to set to work at once, getting a lot of half-penny wrappers addressed ready for this.

Please let me know at once whether you will do it: as, if you say "no," I must forthwith arrange with some one else.[3]

Yours very truly,

C. L. Dodgson

P.S. What do you think of advertising "Price 1*s*. – *Free by post*"? It would only deduct 1/2*d*. from the profit on every copy you sold by retail: and it would be much more tempting to purchasers – 1*s*.1/2*d*. is a tiresome sum to remit.

Thanks for bound volumes.

¹ The pamphlet that Dodgson proposes in this letter is *The Principles of Parliamentary Representation*. It consists of fifty-six pages and appears in a private edition before the end of 1884. Electoral reform was in the air at this time, and Dodgson was taking an active part in the ensuing debate. Four of his letters on proportional representation appeared earlier in the year in the *St. James's Gazette*, and on July 5, an article by him appeared in the same paper. He presumably had extra copies of the article printed, and on July 8 sent one to Lord Salisbury. On the following day, Lord Salisbury replied, acknowledging the need for reform, but he implied that it was virtually impossible to get a patient hearing for anything "absolutely new . . . however Conservative its object. . . ." One day later, Dodgson, in a letter to Lord Salisbury, pleaded: ". . .*please* don't call my scheme for Proportionate Representation a 'Conservative' one! . . . Most sincerely, *all* I aim at is to secure that, *whatever* be the proportions of opinions among the Electors, the *same* shall exist among the Members. Such a scheme may at one time favour one party, at one time another: just as it happens. But really it has *no* political bias of its own." Dodgson's theory of parliamentary representation assumes a two-party political system in which each side knows the number of its own supporters and controls their votes. He views an election as a two-person zero-sum game in which the votes one party wins the other party loses and whose outcome depends both on the number of supporters each side has and on the strategy each side adopts. Assuming each side adopts "optimal" strategies, he calculates the percentage of voters represented on the average in any given electoral system. Comparing these percentages, he can judge which system is the most representative. He concludes that the largest percentage of voters is represented where each constituency has four or five seats and where each elector has a single vote. For more on Dodgson and electoral reform, see *Handbook*, pp. 111, 129–32; and *Letters*, pp. 544–5, 554–5.

² The Franchise Bill of 1884, introduced by Gladstone, was designed to extend to rural householders the rights enjoyed since 1867 by borough voters. It provided for near-universal male suffrage and envisioned adding two million voters to the rolls, nearly four times the number added in 1832 and twice the number in 1867. The Bill passed the Commons easily on June 26, but in July the Conservatives in the Lords attempted to amend it by requiring the Government to join to it a complete plan for redistributing Parliamentary seats. The controversy continued, and a second reading of the Franchise Bill was scheduled for November 18. The Bill was passed on December 6, 1884.

³ Alexander Macmillan replies on the following day: "It is with great reluctance that I say no to any request of yours but we never publish a pamphlet without regret. The labour involved is out of all proportion to any result that is satisfactory to us, and we are in the middle of our busiest season. The sale of pamphlets has practically ceased since Reviews and letters to the papers came to be adequate means of communication between the public and its teachers." All the same Dodgson has the pamphlet printed by Messrs. Baxter of Oxford and sold by Harrison and Sons of Pall Mall. On November 5, he records in his *Diaries* (p. 430): "At last received 50 finished copies of the pamphlet. So I hope that during today and tomorrow, copies will go to all M.P.'s."

Christ Church, Oxford
October 17, 1884

Dear Mr. George Macmillan,

I have given in my corrected copy of *Euclid I, II* at the Press, and they will begin printing off on Tuesday, if they hear by then how many the 3rd edition is to consist of.¹ And they hope to be able to send you copies by the end of the month.

With regard to Mr. Pryke, I find there are still 50 copies waiting at the Press: so I have written to ask him to let me know how many he wants, and they shall be sent direct from here.²

How had we better settle about the payment? It seems to me that, as the books don't go through *your* hands, the simplest plan would be for Mr. Pryke to pay *me* (2*s*., less 10 percent for ready money, I presume is what I ought to ask), and then for you to charge me in your account with 10 percent commission on the receipts (e.g. if he takes the 50, I charge him £4. 10*s*., and you charge me 9*s*.). But I don't care how it's done.[3]

Don't you think, after so encouraging a letter, it might be well to advertise it rather more than last year? I see you spent £4. 15*s*. 0*d*. in the year. Would £10 be very extravagant?[4] If only other schoolmasters would take the same view as Mr. Pryke, we should have a great sale.

Very truly yours,

C. L. Dodgson

[1] George Macmillan replies three days later: "We hardly think it would be worthwhile to print less than 1000 copies of the new edition of *Euclid*, and we are communicating with the Press to this effect."

[2] William Emmanuel Pryke (1843–1920), Headmaster of the Royal Grammar School, Lancaster (1872–93), went on to be Canon Residentiary of Exeter (1908–20). Pryke had written to Macmillan for copies of *Euclid I, II*, but none was to be had because the book had gone out of print. George Macmillan had, in turn, asked Dodgson how to respond to Mr. Pryke.

[3] George Macmillan replies (October 29) that it would be "decidedly better" for all copies to be sent "in the ordinary way," and adds: "As you are aware, we believe in the wisdom of sticking to the ordinary channels of trade."

[4] In the same letter, Macmillan advises against increasing the expenditure for advertising, pointing out that for "our own school books" a budget of £4. 15*s*. 0*d*. for the year would be considered "fully adequate." He also reminds Dodgson, however, that the choice was his and the firm would do as he instructed. Dodgson's reply to this is missing, and although on November 13 George Macmillan mentions that the firm were advertising *Euclid I, II*, he does not indicate that they were doing more than they had previously intended.

Christ Church, Oxford
March 22, 1885

Dear Mr. Macmillan,

I have a project to submit to you, for a fresh venture in publication, which I hope will meet with your approval. For myself it will probably prove a considerable loss, as I expect the cost of production will be enormous: but it will at any rate put an honest penny into *your* pocket! My idea is to publish, in facsimile, the original MS book of *Alice's Adventures*, which was done in printing-hand, with pen-and-ink drawings of my own.[1] The book contains 90 pages, 7½ inches high, by 4½ wide.

Now, supposing you to approve the idea, the first question to settle is how to produce the facsimile: and on that point I hope for valuable advice from you. I have seen such things done by lithography, but I do not *at all* like any results that I have ever seen: they look rough, and gritty, and quite wanting in delicacy of finish. My own idea is (unless you have some better plan to suggest) to get Messrs. Dalziel to photograph it, page by page, upon wood-blocks, and cut them like ordinary pictures: and then Messrs. Clay would electrotype the blocks, and we could print copies *ad libitum*.

The book would be thin, and squarish – about the size of *Lucy's Wonderful Globe*[2] (which size I think we agreed on for *The Nursery "Alice"*, did we not?), and would look charming, I think, in white "leatherette" with gilt edges: but these are details we need not discuss at present.

As there would be nothing new for *me* to do (except to write a short introduction), we might easily get it out by next Xmas, might we not?

But I had better wait to hear what *you* have to say about all this, before troubling you with any more questions.[3]

Very truly yours,

C. L. Dodgson

[1] On March 1 Dodgson wrote to the original Alice, then Mrs. Hargreaves, to ask permission to publish the facsimile and to borrow it from her for the purpose (see *Letters*, pp. 560–1).

[2] *Little Lucy's Wonderful Globe* by C. M. Yonge, published by Macmillan in 1871 (second edition 1872, third 1881).

[3] On the following day, Alexander Macmillan replies: "Such a reproduction as you speak of of your original MS would be really interesting. I quite agree with you that lithography generally is woolly and gritty. But the wood seems to me by no means certain of anything beyond serious expense. If you send me up the MS I will go carefully into it. There are several new processes that are worth considering."

Christ Church, Oxford

July 3, 1885

Dear Mr. Macmillan,

I hope to find that you are willing to publish another little book for me, on the same terms as the two *Alice* volumes. It will be a reprint of a mathematical tale that I contributed to *The Monthly Packet*, in chapters, seven of which I enclose: they were reprinted in this form for giving away. The book will be perhaps 120 of these pages, and I have got half-a-dozen illustrations done by Mr. Frost, two of which I am sending to be cut by Messrs. Swain,[1] whom my artist-friend prefers to Messrs. Dalziel.

Would you have a page or two of this set up to look at? And do you approve of my idea of having the *Alice* page, and type, but closer "leading"? Such a roomy page seems to me only suitable for *children's* books. I should like the book (being fiction) to range with *Alice*.

The whole thing is ready for the printer, and the 6 pictures won't take long. We could easily bring it out as a Christmas book.[2]

Very truly yours,

C. L. Dodgson

¹ Joseph Swain (1820–1909), one of the most eminent engravers of the time, engraved Tenniel's and other artists' drawings for *Punch* and did work also for *Cornhill, Once a Week, Good Words,* and *Argosy.* He had already engraved the *Snark* for Dodgson in 1876.
² "Romantic Problems: A Tangled Tale" was the early title of *A Tangled Tale,* the book that Dodgson proposes here. All ten "knots" of this series were first published in Charlotte Yonge's *Monthly Packet* between April 1880 and March 1885. Dodgson's "Preface" to the volume tells us that "The writer's intention was to embody in each Knot (like the medicine so dextrously, but ineffectually, concealed in the jam of our early childhood) one or more mathematical questions – in Arithmetic, Algebra, or Geometry, as the case might be – for the amusement, and possible edification of the fair readers of . . . [the *Monthly Packet*]."

Christ Church, Oxford
July 8, 1885
Dear Mr. Frederick Macmillan,

It seems quite clear that the only chance of getting a *good* facsimile of the book (and no other is worth doing) is that the process-man should do it *all,* including negatives, if it can be managed without the book going into any hands but mine.¹

I want to make it clear to *you* that this point is *essential.* I know, by sad experience, the result of putting valuable papers into workmen's hands, whatever guarantees are given of careful treatment. I had a beautiful set of proofs, rubbed off on that thin paper from the blocks of *Rhyme? and Reason?,* and these Messrs. Clay borrowed to guide themselves in printing the book, promising that all possible care should be taken, and that they should be returned uninjured. The result is that there is hardly *one* of them, that is not creased, bruised, and soiled: the set is entirely spoiled and (as you know) cannot now be replaced. I know exactly the state I should get this MS book back in, if I let it go (under whatever guarantees) into workmen's hands. It would not be *much* injured, perhaps – a few creases, and a few thumb-marks – just enough to spoil the look of it as a whole. This book has been lent me, as a great favour, by the lady to whom it belongs, and I am responsible to her for its being returned *absolutely* intact.²

Now the best plan seems to me to be for Messrs. Waterlow to send over a competent man to do them *here.*³ He can have the use of my studio, and dark room for developing. If there are any secrets in the developing, I should know nothing of them, as I should not see the process: the only essential is that, wherever the book is to be placed to be photographed, *I* must place it: no other hands must touch it. If there are secrets in *this* part of the process, which I should thus learn, Messrs. Waterlow may be sure I should hold myself bound in honour to tell nobody of them, and to make no use of the knowledge.⁴ If they *can* send a man, I should like to settle *first* about terms, that there may be no misunderstanding. My idea would be that, besides the regular charge for doing the MS, I should pay the man's return-ticket (2nd class) and the cost of conveying the camera, etc., etc., and a fixed sum per day *towards* his board and lodging (it would be unnecessary to pay the *whole*, as he cannot live, even in London, for nothing). He would find the "Roebuck," Corn Market (family and commercial hotel), the best to stay at, as it is very near Christ Church. I would give us as many hours, each day, as he chose to work. If this plan is agreed on, he had better come by the earliest train on Monday, and stay till the 92 negatives are done.

It is not worthwhile discussing any other plan, till I know what is thought of this.

I am glad you will publish *A Tangled Tale*.[5]

Mr. Tenniel has finished colouring the 20 enlarged pictures for *The Nursery "Alice"*, and I hope you will soon hear from Mr. Evans about it.[6] I will shortly send you some selected portions of text, to set up for it. Believe me

Very truly yours,

C. L. Dodgson

[1] Frederick Macmillan wrote to Dodgson on May 8 to suggest a photographic process for the facsimile *Alice*. But several attempts to have a sample page made up for Dodgson's approval failed because of faulty negatives, and Macmillan suggested that the "process people" should do all the work to ensure good quality.

[2] Mrs. Hargreaves (see *Letters*, p. 588).

[3] The firm responsible for the photographic processing was Messrs. Waterlow and Sons, Finsbury Square.

[4] Four days later Frederick Macmillan replies stressing the extraordinary secrecy of the process. He explains: "The fact is that all these mechanical engraving processes are more or less secrets and the superiority of one process over another is due to some little thing in the manipulation which the man using it has discovered. They make a rule therefore of refusing to exhibit their methods."

[5] Frederick Macmillan wrote on July 7: "We shall be happy to publish the book about which you wrote on Friday last."

[6] Edmund Evans (1826–1905), famous color printer, who printed color books by Richard Doyle, Walter Crane, Caldecott, and Kate Greenaway, and who would print *The Nursery "Alice"* in 1889.

Christ Church, Oxford
July 16, 1885

Dear Mr. George Macmillan,

As I see you are now returned, I address this to you: but I have no definite idea to *which* of all your numerous corps I ought to send communications on books: however I suppose it all comes to the same in the end.

The photographer you have sent me is a great success, and is making splendid negatives of the MS book.[1] I find he is willing to undertake the zincograph process as well: so I have arranged with him to do it all for me, and will tell him to send the zinc-plates to Messrs. Clay. I will let you know when this is done, and I would like you to instruct them (as they are *your* employees, not mine) to electrotype them, so as to keep the zincs uninjured, in case more electrotypes should be wanted in future.

How many copies of the book would you advise to have printed? My own idea is 10,000: but you will be much the best judge of this question.[2]

It might be well to order a supply of the tinted paper, to match *Alice.*

I enclose a suggestion of a title-page. If you have a better to suggest, please send it me: if not, Messrs. Clay had better set this up, that we may see what it looks like.

Yours very truly,

C. L. Dodgson

[1] The photographer that Macmillan recommended was a Mr. Noad of Hawthorne Cottage, Eastham, Essex.
[2] The size of the printing would not be decided for some time: see p. 212, below.

7 Lushington Road, Eastbourne
August 19, 1885

Dear Mr. Macmillan,

My brother, lately returned from Tristan da Cunha, thinks *you* a likely man to be able to advise him in the following difficulty.

He has been informed that a letter, written by a Captain of a ship, on the subject of Tristan, appeared in some Scotch paper about the first fortnight of last June. He has failed so far to find the paper: and all he seems to have made out is that it is *not* in the *Glasgow Herald.* It is important to trace the letter, and he was thinking of "advertising" (but *where* he does not seem to know). But, before doing so, he wants me to apply to *you* for advice. Would you kindly suggest what should be done, if anything occurs to you?[1]

I take the opportunity to ask what you think of the following idea as to the second edition of *Euclid and His Modern Rivals.* To have a number of copies struck off, by themselves, of the 2 sheets containing the title, preface, and contents: and to send these to all the Schools, etc., to which you sent *Euclid I, II,* and to which (I suppose) you send your Monthly List. The contents, in full, would be much more likely to find out a possible purchaser than any advertisement.

If you approve this, please let me know how many copies to work off (on *thin* paper, I suppose?).[2] Of the book itself I propose to print only 250.

Yours very truly,

C. L. Dodgson

I have ordered 5000 copies to be sent you of the fly-leaf containing list of Mathematical works.

[1] Dodgson's youngest brother Edwin, the missionary to the island of Tristan da Cunha, was in London to seek assistance for the desperately poor islanders (see *Letters,* pp. 609–10). Frederick Macmillan, "in my uncle's absence," replies to Dodgson's inquiry on August 24, reporting that a

search has been made through six Scottish newspapers but without result and suggesting that "if it is important that the letter should be found . . . the best plan will be to insert an advertisement in one of the Scotch papers – the *Scotsman* would probably be the best – offering a small reward – say 10s. – for the information." We do not know whether the Dodgson brothers took Macmillan's advice or whether they found the item they were searching for.

2 In the same letter, Macmillan agrees with the suggestion: "If you will have 3000 copies of the 2 sheets of *Euclid and His Modern Rivals* struck off on thin paper in the way you propose we shall be happy to send it out with our monthly list and with our Catalogues to Schools. It will certainly be more effective than a mere advertisement."

7 Lushington Road, Eastbourne
September 25, 1885

Dear Mr. Macmillan,

We shall begin printing off the new edition of *Euclid and His Modern Rivals* directly. I suppose you approve of 250 as the number?

I think it would give it a much better chance of sale if the price were reduced: 7s. 6d. is alarming, and I don't want the price to do much more than cover the *current* cost of production, without counting the corrections, which are an outlay once for all. Now they tell me the current cost of producing 250 is about £16. Suppose they were sold (in the usual way – not on the *Alice* system) at 5s., would not that yield me a very handsome profit on £16? I reckon, roughly, that, if you sold them all, you would have to remit to me not far from £30. Is that so, allowing for advertising, etc.?[1]

You shall have your 3000 copies of title and contents as soon as price is fixed.[2] Will they know at the Press what you mean by "thin paper," or will you send them a specimen?[3] Believe me

Very truly yours,

C. L. Dodgson

1 Macmillan & Co.'s reply on the following day includes calculations for printing 250 copies; they show a profit to the author after expenses of only £13. 15s. 7d. On November 18 Dodgson writes in his Diaries: "Received 2 copies of 2nd edition of my *Euclid and His Modern Rivals*."
2 An advertisement for *Euclid and His Modern Rivals* (see p. 192, above).
3 In their reply, the firm write that they have already given the Press "exact instructions as to the weight of the paper on which the circular is to be printed."

Christ Church, Oxford
November 3, 1885

Dear Mr. Macmillan,

Thanks for the vellum-bound books.

I send a copy of the *Tangled Tale* – a little incomplete, but there will be enough to enable you to say what the price ought to be. The blocks have gone to Messrs.

Clay to be electrotyped: and I hope to pass the whole for "Press" very soon. How many should we print, do you think?

I would like the cover to be red, with gold lines, to match *Alice* – and a medallion on each side – the heads of the 2 Knights on the cover next the title-page, and the Dragon on the other cover. I send prints of the two, with circles cut of paper to show how much should be included. The Dragon will have to [be] reduced a little, so as to match the other. The print I send for the Knights will do very well to cut the medallion by: but the other is rather rough, being a photo-zincograph of the drawing, and it will be better to wait for a print from the electrotype of the wood-block now being sent to Messrs. Clay. The book will be decidedly thinner than *Alice*: so I think the title had better be printed *along* the back, as you did with the *Snark*.

As soon as we have agreed on the price, you can, if you think fit, begin announcing it as "nearly ready."[1]

Very truly yours,

C. L. Dodgson

[1] Two days later Dodgson writes again: ". . . 5*s*. will do well for *Tangled Tale*, I *think*. But I doubt if it is not too dear. Consider that it has only *6* pictures, instead of 40! Don't you think 4*s*. would be enough?" On the 9th, Macmillan & Co. write suggesting a retail price of 4*s*. 6*d*., "a much more usual price than 4*s*." On the 23rd, they write suggesting that 2000 copies would be wise and advising against any number smaller than 1500.

Christ Church, Oxford
November 10, 1885

Dear Mr. Macmillan,

I think 4*s*. 6*d*. will do very well: and, as this is $\frac{3}{4}$ of the *Alice* price, we have a very simple rule for calculating the items of the business, thus:

	Alice		Tangled Tale
Retail price –	6*s*. 0*d*.	–	4*s*. 6*d*.
Trade price –	5*s*. 0*d*.	–	3*s*. 9*d*.
Macmillan & Co.'s price –	4*s*. 4*d*.	–	3*s*. 3*d*.
deduct for advertising	1*d*.	–	1*d*.
	4*s*. 3*d*.	–	3*s*. 2*d*.

(This last item you have, by a miscalculation, made 3*s*. 1*d*.)[1]

However, this 1*d*. (for cost of advertising, when borne by you) does not, I think, fairly meet the case of the *first year* of a book, when you would naturally advertise more freely. So I propose that, for the first year, you should charge me for advertising, according to the advertising done, and allow 3*s*. 3*d*. a copy as royalty. After a year, if the sale goes on, we can make it, if agreeable to you, 3*s*. 2*d*. a copy, *you* undertaking the advertising.

Very truly yours,

C. L. Dodgson

¹ In a letter the firm sent to Dodgson on the previous day.

The Chestnuts, Guildford
December 26, 1885

Dear Mr. Craik,

To begin with, I wish a very happy New Year to Mrs. Craik, and yourself, and Dorothy.

Your letter leaves no room, I fear, for any further doubt as to *whose* shoulders ought to bear the blame of the spoiled copies (if there are any: I still hope my one copy may prove to be the only one) of *A Tangled Tale* – namely, the shoulders of that eminent firm of publishers, Messrs. Macmillan & Co.!¹ It is certainly not the printer, or binder, who no doubt had full instructions from *you*: and most certainly it is not the author, who never even suggested a *date* for bringing out the book, and who has done his very best to impress on the minds of his publishers that he is *absolutely* indifferent as to what time in the year his books appear, or whether they have a great or small sale, but that the *one only* thing he cares for is, that the work shall be done at sufficient leisure to secure the *best possible* artistic results. You will probably demur to this, and ask *when* I have ever expressed all that. In that case, let me remind you that this question has arisen before now (on the occasion of some *Looking-Glass*es being bound too soon after printing), and that I then wrote my views fully and clearly. As you have probably not kept the letter, let me copy part of it to refresh your memory. "Christ Church, December 17, 1871. x x x x x I have now made up my mind that, whatever be the commercial consequences, we must have no more artistic fiascos. x x x My decision is, we must have *no more hurry*: and *no more sheets must be pressed under blank paper*. It is my *particular desire* that all the sheets shall in future be 'stacked' and let to dry naturally. The result of this may possibly be that the 6000 will not be ready for sale till the end of January or even later. Very well: then fix that date in your advertisement. x x x x x You will think me a lunatic for thus wishing to send away money from the doors; and will tell me perhaps that I shall thus lose thousands of would-be purchasers, who will not wait so long, but will go and buy other Christmas books. I wish I could put into words how entirely such arguments go for nothing with me. As to how many copies we sell I care absolutely nothing: the one only thing I *do* care for is, that all the copies that *are* sold shall be artistically first-rate. I have already had a bitter lesson in this matter, with *Alice's Adventures*. With all my efforts to keep it up to a high artistic mark, I was baffled at last by that sudden demand (which ought never to have been met!) which led to the working off 3000 in a great hurry. The consequence was a blow to the artistic reputation of the book which I doubt if it will *ever* quite recover: a general impression got abroad that 'the plates were failing, and that the only chance to get a *good* copy was to find one of the earlier thousands.' How gladly I would sacrifice *double* the profit which that unfortunate 3000 brought in, if I could only annihilate them off the face of the earth! If any of the sheets of the new 6000 have been already 'pressed,' and if the pictures seem to have been at all seriously affected by it, these sheets must be destroyed and printed again. x x x x x I have written at this length in order to set my reasons fully before you, and to show you how strongly I feel in the matter – and how entirely careless I am how it affects the profits. Indeed, I consider the point as an *essential* one in our relations as publisher and author, and must beg you (with a view to a perfect understanding in the future) to give me your assurance in writing that '*no* copies, either of *Wonderland* or of the *Looking-Glass*, shall in future be dried by pressure under blank paper, but that they shall be stacked and let to dry naturally.' "[2]

At the same time I wrote to Messrs. Clay as follows: "Mr. Dodgson writes to tell Messrs. Clay that, whatever be the demand for more copies of *Through the Looking-Glass*, the printing is *not to be in the least hurried*. Also *no more sheets are to be dried for binding by pressing under blank paper*: they must be 'stacked,' and let to dry in the natural way. x x x If the deliberate printing and drying should result in the 6000 copies not being ready for delivery till the end of January, or even later, Mr. Dodgson will be quite content."

I doubt if you could easily suggest stronger or clearer language for an author to use, in order to exonerate himself from *all* responsibility in case any books of his should suffer in future from hasty printing or binding.

There will, I trust, be no loss to bear in this matter: but, if there is, what I have here copied makes it abundantly clear who ought to bear it.

Will you kindly send me, here, 6 *Euclid and His Modern Rivals*.

Thanks for the condemnatory critique (from a Perthshire paper) of my *Euclid I, II*.[3] Such critiques are very wholesome reading!

                                                        Very truly yours,

                                                                        C. L. Dodgson

---

[1] Dodgson received his first copy of *A Tangled Tale* on December 22, and he must have written off to Macmillan immediately to complain about the printing and possibly intimating that some or all of the copies might have to be cancelled. Craik replied on December 23, suggesting that perhaps Dodgson's advance copy might be the only poor one, and added: "I do not think any one is to blame but yourself" for holding back the proofs and thereby not allowing enough time for the printing, let alone the drying, before Christmas. In the copy that Dodgson received, he wrote "spoiled by being bound while damp, see pages 34 and 47." Selwyn H. Goodacre notes that "examination of these pages indeed reveals distinct off-setting of the illustrations onto the facing page of text. In fact, off-setting is clearly seen with all the illustrations, and in places with the text as

well." We cannot tell how Dodgson was reconciled to permit the edition to go out to the booksellers, but he was. Perhaps Craik's letter of the 28th helped to assuage Dodgson's concern: "I thoroughly appreciate your care that your books shall not suffer from hasty preparation," he writes, and continues: "In the present case I do not think there is any cause for alarm or blame. I have a copy in my hand now which is quite perfect and I hope what you have seen is a mere exception. . . . You wrote on November 21: 'Both books (*A Tangled Tale* and *Alice Under Ground*) should be worked off and bound, as soon as may be' . . . and indeed there is another letter of yours enquiring the date of publication. . . . I believe you will never hear a word of censure. . . .'" Goodacre notes that ultimately "Dodgson's complaint must have been heeded, as the later 'thousands' are very clean." (See *Catalogue of the Furniture, Personal Effects, and the Interesting and Valuable Library of Books . . . of the Late Rev. C. L. Dodgson . . . Sold at Auction* (1898), Lot 707; and Selwyn H. Goodacre, "Bibliographical Notes on 'A Tangled Tale,'" *Jabberwocky*, Winter 1975, p. 8.) For more on *A Tangled Tale*, see *Handbook*, pp. 108–9, 136–8.

2   See pp. 96–9, above.

3   The notice appeared on December 21 in the *Perthshire Advertiser* (n.p.): "With so many excellent text-books of 'Euclid,'" it reads, "we do not see any necessity or justifiable reason for the publication of this. Mr. Dodgson assigns its merit to the fact that the text of his edition is (as he has ascertained by counting the words) less than five-sevenths of that contained in the ordinary editions. He is correct in saying, however, that on comparison with all other systems of geometry, no treatise has yet appeared worthy to supersede that of Euclid. Postulates, axioms, and definitions are mixed up together. Some explanatory notes are appended. The text and diagrams are very clear. . . . He errs in not giving any exercises to which the pupil can apply his ingenuity, and by which he may test his progress."

The Chestnuts, Guildford
January 12, 1886

Dear Mr. Macmillan,

Thanks for the critiques, in the *Warrington Guardian* and the *Perthshire Advertiser* on *Tangled Tale*.[1]

I am sorry to say that Mr. J. H. Noad is not going on satisfactorily, and I think you ought to know about it, as it was on your recommendation I went to him. He has been employing Mr. John Swain, of 58 Farringdon Street, to do the zinc-blocks from his photographs, and in November Mr. Swain wrote to tell me that Mr. Noad had taken away one lot (30 blocks) though still owing £5.15.0 for them, and that they had in their hands a 2nd lot (40 blocks) for which he had yet to pay. I thought it very likely he was in money-difficulties, so sent him £15 "on account" and begged him at once to send Messrs. Clay the rest of the blocks. I heard from him on November 19, acknowledging the £15, and promising to send the rest of the blocks at once. Since that he has made no sign, though I wrote November 21, and December 7, 11, and 27. On December 26 I heard from Mr. Swain that he had been obliged to begin a County Court suit to recover his dues from Mr. Noad, but had stopped the suit on his promising to pay on a fixed day, which however he had not done. The total amount due, on the 70 finished blocks, was £24.8.6. On hearing this, I paid Mr. Swain his dues and asked him to send the 40 blocks to Messrs. Clay; and wrote to tell Mr. Noad I had done so (and should debit him with the amount in our account).

The book consists of 92 pages; so there are still 22 photographs to go to Mr. Swain, before the zinc-blocks can all go to Messrs. Clay. And meanwhile there is no getting anything, not even a letter, from Mr. Noad! He may have left the country for anything I know. Can you ascertain anything about him?[2] The original MS has been returned, I am happy to say; but Mr. Noad has *another* MS book of mine in his hands, which I wanted done in facsimile, and that I should be very unwilling to lose.[3] Believe me

Very truly yours,

C. L. Dodgson

[1] The *Warrington Guardian* (January 6, 1886, p. 3) gave only a few lines to the book: "This story, which originally appeared as a serial in the *Monthly Packet*, is now produced in tasteful binding, and illustrated by Arthur B. Frost. Totally unlike Mr. Carroll's popular *Alice in Wonderland*, as this volume is, it will probably be popular amongst that class of readers who delight in solving problems of any kind. . . ." The *Perthshire Advertiser* (January 8, 1886, n.p.) gave it more attention, but not the kind an author seeks: "Mr. Carroll has deserved so well of humanity as the author of *Alice's Adventures in Wonderland*, that one is really very unwilling to appear to notice any of his works in an unfavourable way. Yet a perusal of *A Tangled Tale* makes one wish that he had kept to Wonderland, and left these problems to men who were unable to write better books." The reviewer describes the book and continues: "There are two questions that claim one's notice in such a work, the quality of the problem with its solution, and the sort of tale it is embedded in. . . ." He finds no fault with the tales, but he questions Carroll's credibility as a mathematician: "We do not know how far Mr. Carroll may have studied mathematics . . . yet we are quite unable to accept some of his views." The writer then proceeds to question specific solutions to the knots and concludes: "We are sorry to speak of these things, but while the idea of the book is good, and while the problems are well suited (as a rule) for quickening the powers of those who engage in their solution, yet we cannot but wish that the time given to them by Mr. Carroll had been employed in giving us rather some further peeps into his own Wonderland."

[2] Macmillan & Co.'s reply on the following day promises to "send someone down to East Ham tomorrow" to try to get the blocks from Noad.

[3] This is *The Rectory Umbrella*, seventh of the eight Dodgson family domestic magazines that Dodgson had contributed to, illustrated, and edited in his youth. He recorded in his *Diaries* on July 18, 1885 (p. 438): "Mr. Noad left, taking with him *The Rectory Umbrella*, which I am thinking of getting him to facsimile for me – but whether for 'private circulation,' or publication, I have not yet made up my mind." Although four of Noad's zincograph proofs of the manuscript survive at Christ Church, *The Rectory Umbrella* was not published until 1932 (see *Handbook*, pp. 4–5, 220).

Christ Church, Oxford
January 29, 1886

Dear Mr. Macmillan,

I am annoyed to find that Messrs. Clay have been for some time cutting down, more and more, the margins of my books. Here are 3 measurings –

Alice   –   14th thousand   – $7\frac{3}{8} \times 4\frac{7}{8}$
  ,,   –   17th   ,,   – $7\frac{1}{8} \times 4\frac{3}{4}$
Tangled Tale   – $7\frac{1}{8} \times 4\frac{5}{8}$

I do not consider that I have been well treated in this being done without any permission from me: and I strongly disapprove of the change.

Will you kindly take care that it be distinctly understood that in future none of my books (the 3 *Alice* books, *Rhyme? and Reason?* and *Tangled Tale*) is to have its pages cut down to less than $7\frac{3}{8} \times 4\frac{7}{48}$.[1]

The *inner* margin of *Tangled Tale* is too narrow – being only $\frac{1}{2}$ inch instead of $\frac{5}{8}$. The book looks quite mean by the side of *Alice*.

Very truly yours,

C. L. Dodgson

[1] On February 23 Macmillan & Co. write: "The binders have gone carefully into the question of the size of your books and they say that they cannot get them up to anything larger than *A Tangled Tale*. What surprises them is to hear that they ever cut the books down . . . they have always intended to keep to a uniform size and were under the impression that they had done so. They would very much like to see the copy of the 14th thousand of *Alice* which measured $7\frac{3}{8} \times 4\frac{7}{48}$." Dodgson obliged and sent the book. On March 1, Macmillan & Co. write again: "The binders now find that they will be able to bring all your books up to the size of the 14th thousand of *Alice* . . . and all copies bound in the future will be uniform with that."

Christ Church, Oxford
March 27, 1886

Dear Mr. Macmillan,

The 2 copies of *The Children's Garland*, bound in morocco, which I ordered in November, never came, and the order was no doubt forgotten: please erase it, as I do not want them now.[1]

Did I mention that Mr. Tenniel has sent me the 20 pictures, coloured by himself, as well as a fresh set of 20 proofs?[2] What is the process of printing, by which the pictures will appear along with the text? Will Mr. Evans print both, or will Messrs. Clay send him the sheets ready printed, with blank spaces left for the pictures? I have no idea when the text will be ready – certainly not for some time to come, I am so overwhelmed with other business.

I hope you got, safely, the 32 *Tangled Tales* I sent you on February 18. I have not yet got the 4 copies of the "3rd thousand" I asked you to send me.

Many thanks for your promise (received March 2) that they shall have broader margins in future: also for my specimen *Alice* back again.

Many thanks also for a long series of notices, condemnatory of *Tangled Tale*.[3] I feel rather tempted to send a few of them to Miss Yonge (at whose request it was written) and say "and this blighted reputation I owe to *your* baneful influence!" Spite of this chorus of blame, it is selling pretty well, don't you think?[4]

Lastly, as to Mr. Noad. Will you let me know what, if anything, you have done in the "detective" way, and whether you have any hope of finding him? I have hitherto taken no step myself, but left the matter wholly in *your* hands. If, however, you tell me you have got to the end of your resources, I will try and set other machinery going. So soon as it is *proved* that there is no hope of recovering the 22 missing negatives, I will at once borrow the book again, and arrange with Mr. Swain to have those pages photographed, etc., over again: but it seems rash to go to all that expense, while we may hear, any day, that Mr. Noad has been found, and that the negatives are all right.[5] Believe me

Very truly yours,

C. L. Dodgson

---

[1] *The Children's Garland from the Best Poets*, selected and arranged by Coventry Patmore, was published by Macmillan in 1863. Dodgson probably intended to give them to child friends at Christmas.

[2] For *The Nursery "Alice"*, still "in progress."

[3] The critical reception of *A Tangled Tale* ranged from lukewarm to antagonistic. The review in the *Pall Mall Gazette* (January 4, 1886, p. 5) describes it, praises the illustrations, and points to the "higgledy piggledy mixture of sense and nonsense that at once compels a reading." It concludes: "Still, we decidedly prefer the simple nonsense of *Alice in Wonderland* (even *Through the Looking-Glass* took its chess a little too seriously). Mathematics will be mathematics, carroll you never so wisely. Children's stories, alas! will soon not be children's stories at all in this improving age."

[4] On February 17, Macmillan wrote to advise Dodgson that their stock was "now reduced to 96 copies" and asked permission to print another 1000 copies.

[5] On January 26 Macmillan wrote to say that Noad had given a false address and was nowhere to be found. They intended to make further efforts to locate the elusive photographer, he adds. On February 19, the firm wrote to say they "regret that we have been unable to catch Mr. Noad. We sent down one of our head clerks to East Ham and he found the house of Noad's mother but they said that Noad himself did not live there. We found out that he had an address in town but it turned out to be only the office of a man for whom he did things on commission. . . . If you are willing to go to the expense of employing a lawyer we suppose that Noad might be taken by means of a detective for we fancy he sleeps at East Ham though his mother denies it." Two days after Dodgson writes this letter, the firm add: ". . . [Mr. Noad] is a very slippery person. If you will authorise us to employ a detective we think we could probably get hold of him without much expense, but before doing so we shall be glad to know exactly what property of yours is in his possession. . . . We understand that there is a manuscript book which you gave him to reproduce and a certain number of negatives of the MS of *Alice* made for you when Mr. Noad was at Oxford. Have you paid him for these?"

Christ Church, Oxford
March 30, 1886

Dear Mr. Macmillan,

I will go to work at the text for *The Nursery "Alice"*: but I fear Mr. Evans will have to wait some time.[1]

Certainly I will authorize you to employ a detective to find Mr. Noad, and will trust to you not to involve me in ruinous outlay.[2]

The property he has of mine, and of Mr. Synge's, is as follows:

(1) Negatives of 22 pp. of *Alice Under Ground* (probably done on 11 glasses only: possibly more) already paid for by me: and ought to have been delivered, long ago, to Mr. John Swain, 58 Farringdon Street, E.C.

(2) A MS volume, called *The Rectory Umbrella* belonging to members of my family.

(3) Six coloured sketches belonging to Mr. W. W. F. Synge, Lislee House, St. John's Road, Eastbourne.[3]

I have another piece of business to consult you about, in reference to Mr. Synge. I have undertaken the publication of a book of poems of his, written for children, and he will send you the MS. When you have had time to consider it, I shall be grateful for answers to these questions:

(1) Are you willing to publish it for me, on same terms as we at first had for *Alice?*

(2) What sized-page, and what type, would you recommend? (It would be well to set up a specimen page. *My* idea would be a *nearly* square page – just a trifle higher than its width: about the height of *Alice* but broader.)

(3) What binding? (I think I have seen books of yours with a pretty dove-coloured grey cloth: that, with sprinkled edges, would do well, I should think.)

(I forgot to say, as to type, that I think the same as *Rhyme? and Reason?* would do very well.)

As soon as I have the whole in slip, I will get it illustrated, and send the wood-blocks to Clay to electrotype.

The *price* to sell at we cannot of course discuss, until you can see it as a whole, pictures and all.

In getting the text set up, I shall wish you to communicate with Mr. Synge (when once we have settled on type, etc.), by sending all proofs for correction to *him*. But in all the *money* part of the business, please communicate with *me* only.

I should like *toned* paper to be used, but not a very costly kind. You are using a rather cheaper kind now for *Alice*, are you not, than what we began with?

About a dozen pictures will be enough, I expect: so I should think 3 or 4 months will do for drawing and cutting. In that case I presume you could bring it out as a Xmas book?

My agency in the matter will be wholly in the background, and I had rather not have my name mentioned in any way, in connection with it.[4]

Very truly yours,

C. L. Dodgson

---

[1] Macmillan & Co. wrote on the previous day that Edmund Evans, the color printer, had agreed to print *The Nursery "Alice"* but would appreciate being able to work on it at once "as he is not overcrowded with work at this time of year and could give special attention to it, while later on his hands are very full."

[2] Macmillan never actually employed a detective in the Noad affair. Their letter of June 1 of this year explains: "We have done nothing in the matter of employing an amateur detective to find Mr. Noad. We think with you that it would be in every way best that such a person should be employed by you direct." Dodgson later sought advice from friends, but abandoned the idea of engaging a detective when he learned that "all detectives are scoundrels" (see *Letters*, pp. 632–3; 647–8).

[3] William Webb Follett Synge (1826–91), diplomat and author, was a neighbor of Dodgson's

family in Guildford. He had previously published, *inter alia, A Tale of the Wandering Jew and Other Verses* (1850) and two novels: *Olivia Raleigh* (1875) and *Tom Singleton, Dragoon and Dramatist* (1879). For more on Dodgson and the Synges, see *Letters*, p. 175.

[4] Macmillan & Co. reply three days later: "We have received the MS of Mr. Synge's poems and write to say that we are willing to publish them because you ask us to do so. Had they come to us independently we should have refused, for it does not seem to me that they are likely to achieve much success: but we may be wrong." Specimen pages were set up almost immediately for Dodgson's approval, and on April 10 he visits Macmillan's in London "to have a talk about Mr. Synge's poems" (*Diaries*, p. 441). The result was *Bumblebee Bogo's Budget*, a book of verse for children.

Christ Church, Oxford

June 7, 1886

Dear Mr. Macmillan,

Many thanks for your kind trouble about the tickets. Please send the two for June 12 *here*. I fear I hardly allow you time enough, I make my plans so hastily, and when Friday noon comes without any tickets, I have to telegraph (as I generally leave here at 9 a.m. on Saturday) for fear of their coming here too late.[1]

Thanks also for various (more or less cutting) cuttings of reviews of the *Tangled Tale*. If ever you have to print any more, let me know in time, to send corrections, etc.

Next, *of course* you are quite welcome to include the pieces you name in Miss Woods' book. "The Walrus," etc., seems to be a general favourite with those who want to extract from the 2 *Alices*.[2]

Lastly, as to *The Nursery "Alice"*, I will try to get the text done soon, but I am very busy on other things.[3] Moreover, I have something to say about the American sales, which will, I expect, modify the views of your American Agent as to his idea of taking 1000 of them, or even of taking any at all.

With the end of this month (i.e. the end of *our* financial year) I wish the exceptional arrangement, as to letting the Americans have my books, to cease, and that *all* shall henceforth be served on the terms named on the fly-leaf at the end of each book. I expect you will be inclined to say, as I think you said when we made the arrangement, that, if I won't let them have my books cheap, they will do without them: but my answer is, "*let* them do without them, by all means." If you will refer to our annual accounts, you will see that the difference it would make to *us* would be absolutely trivial. They are even quite welcome to pirate them, if they like: such reproductions can *never* compete, in the *English* market, with copies printed by Clay. And, as to the coloured edition, I rather hope they *will* try to pirate it: I should be very curious to see the result![4]

Very truly yours,

C. L. Dodgson

¹ On the following day, Macmillan & Co. write: "We have sent you the tickets for June 12 as requested." On the 12th, Dodgson takes Beatrice Earle, one of his young friends, to *The Mikado* (*Diaries*, p. 442).

² Three days earlier, George Macmillan wrote: "Would you have any objection to "The Walrus & the Carpenter" and one or two pieces from *Phantasmagoria* being inserted in a small poetry book for Schools which is being compiled for us by Miss Woods, of the Clifton High School for Girls? Your permission would of course be duly acknowledged." On the 8th, Macmillan & Co. add: "We are much obliged to you for permission to include 'The Walrus,' etc., in Miss Woods' collection of poems."

³ On the 2nd, Macmillan & Co. wrote ". . . to ask whether there is any chance of your being able to go on with the "Children's *Alice*" soon. We ask because our American agent is over here at present and he says that if the book is out early in the autumn he will buy 1000 or more copies, but he will not take it after about the middle of October."

⁴ On the 8th, Macmillan & Co. write: "Your determination not to allow special terms to America will naturally modify our Agent's view as to the number of copies he will want of *The Nursery 'Alice'*. There will be no difficulty in invoicing any copies of your books that we may export in future at the regular English price and we will take your letter as an instruction to that effect, to come into force at the end of the month. . . . You will remember perhaps that our New York Agent has plates of the earlier books and that he has invested a considerable sum of money in buying up the plates of other people who have printed the books. We cannot ask him to sacrifice these, but what he prints will not be the English Edition or appear on your authority. Anyone in America who wants the genuine English Edition will have to pay the same price as in England."

Christ Church, Oxford
June 9, 1886

Dear Mr. Macmillan,

Thanks for your letter. I hope I need not say I am ready to withdraw any proposal which would cause loss to you or your Agents. I find a letter, in which you asked to be allowed to have "a set of plates" made of *Rhyme? and Reason?* for America, undertaking to make them at your own cost and pay me a royalty of 10 percent on the American price for copies sold. I presume we had similar agreements for the 2 *Alices*. (The letter is dated May 21, 1883.) Is it these plates that you allude to in the words "we cannot ask him to sacrifice these"? I do not ask you to "sacrifice" them (i.e., as I suppose you mean, "destroy" them) but simply to sell all copies, printed from them, on the same terms as in England. I will ask you to ascertain the full amount you spent in making the plates and debit it to me. The plates will then be my property: and I should wish that all of them that are in good condition, should be stowed away, ready to replace any of the London set that get worn or damaged; and that all, not in good condition, should be destroyed.

I observe you also say that your agent has (on your account, I presume you mean) "invested money in buying up pirated plates" (implying, I suppose, that you spent this money with a view to being repaid by an American sale). I think you will find this is a mistake. To the best of my recollection, you wrote to the effect "We have an opportunity of buying up the pirated plates: shall we do it?"

And I wrote to the effect "Certainly. Buy them at my expense, and destroy them." At all events, if I did not *then* use the words "at my expense," I do so *now*. Whatever it cost to buy them up ought to be debited to *me*.

But there is one paragraph in your letter to which I demur. You say "what he prints will not be the English edition or appear on your authority." To print and publish *any* copies from these plates, except for me, would (I believe I am correct in saying) be an infringement of the copyright, which I have not parted with, and do not intend to part with. However, to make the matter perfectly clear, I have altered what I wrote on p. 1, and wish to pay for the plates in any case. By doing this, and by also repaying you (if *you* paid it) the cost of buying up the pirated plates, I hope I shall secure you from all risk of loss under the new arrangement.[1]

How did that business end, of using a stronger binding for *Euclid I, II*? Did you rebind the copies in your hands? And does the University Press now use such a binding as you approve?[2]

The Savoy tickets for June 12 have come: many thanks for them.

Very truly yours,

C. L. Dodgson

---

[1] We do not have Macmillan's reply to this letter.

[2] In a letter dated June 30, the firm apologize for having neglected Dodgson's question about the binding for *Euclid I, II* and explain: "We rebound all the copies in our hands in a strong binding which we think is quite satisfactory: they are all sold now, and the book as you know is reprinting. We think the best plan for the new Edition will be for you to allow us to get the binding done for you in the new style. If you approve of this kindly instruct the Clarendon Press people to deliver the book to us in sheets."

7 Lushington Road, Eastbourne
August 22, 1886

Dear Mr. Macmillan,

I have several matters to write about.

(1) Next time you want more copies printed of *Euclid I, II*, or of *A Tangled Tale*, please let me know, that I may send corrections. I may say the same of *all* my books, in fact. I keep copies by me, and mark misprints, etc., as I chance to notice them.

(2) You never made a more judicious present than when you gave me your Golden Treasury Wordsworth.[1] It is a real delight to me: so handy, so well printed, and so well selected – containing pure gems *only*. I should like a copy of *Scotch Song*. And won't you give the world a Golden Treasury Burns?[2] Also a volume of "Lake Poets" would be very acceptable. I would take for it Coleridge, Keats, Hood (serious poems only, or *perhaps* admitting the "Ode to Rae Wilson") and Hartley Coleridge. I don't know if Hood ever actually lived in the

Lake country, but he would suit the others very well. His "Haunted House" ought by no means to be omitted, long as it is.[3]

(3) The machinery I have set in motion to find Mr. Noad has so far succeeded that we have found him, and he has undertaken to complete and hand over the remaining 14 blocks for *Alice's Adventures Under Ground*.[4] I hope you will receive them in a few days: and there will then be no obstacle to finishing the job, and bringing the book out.

(4) As to Mr. Synge's Poems. He has got (written by some friends) music for 8 or 10 of the poems. Could we introduce this without largely increasing the cost of production?[5] If not, I give up the idea, for I *cannot* hope for a large sale for the book, and am beginning to make up my mind that the nett result *must* be – loss!

Very truly yours,

C. L. Dodgson

---

[1] Macmillan's Golden Treasury series was inspired by Palgrave's *Golden Treasury of English Songs and Lyrics*, which Macmillan published in 1861. It led to a long series of anthologies, including Coventry Patmore's *Children's Garland* and Matthew Arnold's selections from Wordsworth (1879) and Byron (1881). From time to time, Macmillan included in an advertisement an unidentified comment that appeared in the *British Quarterly Review*: "Messrs. Macmillan have, in their Golden Treasury Series, especially provided editions of standard works, volumes of selected poetry, and original compositions, which entitles this series to be called classical. Nothing can be better than the literary execution, nothing more elegant than the material workmanship."

[2] Macmillan immediately sends Dodgson the volume, *Scottish Song*, compiled and arranged by Mary Carlyle Aitkin (1874), as well as "a little edition of Burns," which, while not a Golden Treasury, is "equally pretty."

[3] On the 24th, Macmillan & Co. write: "Mr. [Alexander] Macmillan is away from London at present but when he returns we will put before him your suggestion that a volume selected from the writings of the Lake Poets should be added to the Golden Treasury Series."

[4] In his letter to Mrs. Alice Hargreaves (November 11, 1886), Dodgson explains that instead of a detective, he was advised to engage a solicitor, who in turn insisted that he would never get his blocks back unless he took legal action. This he unwillingly did and had the experience of testifying in court (see *Letters*, pp. 647–8). *Alice's Adventures Under Ground* is the full title of the original manuscript book of *Alice's Adventures in Wonderland* (see *Handbook*, pp. 143–6).

[5] In the same letter as above, Macmillan & Co. write: "The addition of the music to Mr. Synge's book would naturally increase the cost and we should greatly doubt whether it would have a corresponding effect on the sale." Dodgson abandons the idea of printing the music in *Bumblebee Bogo's Budget*.

7 Lushington Road, Eastbourne
September 13, 1886

Dear Mr. Macmillan,

Would you kindly send this note by a messenger? Mrs. Carlo has moved to the opposite side of the street, but I do not know the number, so can think of no other way of reaching her than sending it by hand.[1]

Have you any idea as to the cover of *Alice's Adventures Under Ground*? The book will be about the thickness of the *Snark*. I assume that it must be red cloth and gilt

edges, to match the other *Alice*s. But we cannot have medallions: my drawings
are too bad for that. So *my* idea is to have the title printed in gold, in some fanciful
way, on one side, no gold lines, and the back and the other side left without
device.

If you approve the idea, can you find an artist to design a good title?[2]

Very truly yours,

C. L. Dodgson

[1] William and Phoebe Carlo were the parents of Phoebe Ellen Carlo (b. 1874), a successful child actress. Dodgson first saw her perform in 1883, and in 1885 he called on the Carlos "to make acquaintance with little Phoebe. . . ." Later Phoebe went on outings with Dodgson in London and visited him at Oxford (*Diaries*, pp. 434, 435, 438). On the 17th, Macmillan & Co. write: "We regret to say that our messenger was unable to find Mrs. Carlo. She was unknown at No. 30 . . . and inquiries among the neighbouring tradesmen produced no good result. We therefore return your letter." But surely Dodgson succeeds in getting in touch with the Carlos because Phoebe plays the first Alice in the West End when Savile Clarke's "dream play" opens in December of this year. For more on Dodgson and the Carlos, see *Letters*, esp. p. 582.

[2] In a letter of the 20th, Macmillan write: "We shall send you a drawing for the cover of *Alice's Adventures Under Ground* in a few days."

7 Lushington Road, Eastbourne
October 7, 1886

Dear Mr. Craik,

Thanks for yours of October 5.[1]

(1) I do *not* want *The Game of Logic* to have gilt line round front side – merely fancy title on front side, and title (whether fancy or plain) along back. For the former I should like to see a design, in style of *Alice Under Ground*.

(2) As to *price*, I find the cost of production will be about 1*s*. 1*d*. a copy (envelope, etc., included). So, on the principle adopted for my other books, the price of book, etc., should be 3*s*.: and you should pay to me 2*s*. 2*d*., for every copy sold, till 30/6/87, charging *me* with what you spend on advertising: after that, if the sale continues, you might allow me 2*s*. 1*d*., and do the advertising yourselves.

(3) I accept your suggestion of having *one* price only for envelope, etc., sold separately. Each will cost me about 1½*d*.: so I propose to price it at 3*d*., and to be allowed 2*d*. for each sold.

(4) How many shall we print? *I* say 250 books, and 1000 envelopes.[2]

(5) Thanks for offer to send some paper to Messrs. Baxter: but I prefer their dealing direct with the maker. They print many other things for me. We have found the right kind.

(6) I enclose a List of Works, with corrections. I think it would be well, now we have room enough, to name each translation by itself, and each in its proper language. Also the date should be given of first publication, for each.

(7) The summons, taken out against Mr. Noad, will be settled probably on the 9th. If we fail in getting the 14 blocks (or negatives), I will then at once borrow the MS book again, and get the missing 14 pages re-photographed. Thus, in any case, we can get it out by Christmas; and Messrs. Clay had better get paper ready for 500 copies.

Yours very truly,

C. L. Dodgson

P.S. I will send you the colours for the card counters.

¹ On July 24 of this year, Dodgson recorded in his *Diaries* (pp. 442–3): "The idea occurred to me this morning of beginning my 'Logic' publication, not with 'Book I' of the full work 'Logic for Ladies,' but with a small pamphlet and a cardboard diagram, to be called *The Game of Logic*. I have during the day written most of the pamphlet." On October 3, Dodgson took up the subject of *The Game of Logic* with Messrs. Macmillan in a postscript longer than the body of his letter: "P.S. Would you get me an estimate of the cost of binding *The Game of Logic* in red cloth, with fancy title in gold, and edges simply cut and left white. . . . Of course I want it published on same terms as my other books: so we must fix such a price as will allow, to author, enough to cover binding, the other expenses (which I have calculated to be 7*d*.) and the probable cost of advertising. . . . For first year I want you to charge *me* with the advertising, whatever it happens to be. If it lasts more than a year we may then make an arrangement about this, as with the other books. . . . The actual cost of an envelope, card, and 9 counters, will be about 1*d*. Shall we sell at '3*d*. for one, or 12 for 2*s*. 6*d*., or 50 for 7*s*. 6*d*.'?" Craik replied on the 5th giving figures of costs and suggesting alternate sales prices either 3*s*. 6*d*. or 2*s*. 6*d*.
² On the following day, Macmillan & Co. write: "We think it would be a pity to print fewer than 500 copies. It will be annoying to have the book go out of print just before Christmas when the sale may be expected to be brisk."

7 Lushington Road, Eastbourne
October 10, 1886

Dear Mr. Macmillan,

(1) I have another correction for the new Editions of *Alice* and *Looking-Glass* and for the next Edition of *Tangled Tale*. In each case I wish the price to be stated on the title-page, just above the word "London," in small capitals (Italic), to match *Rhyme? and Reason?*¹

(2) I enclose the proof, you sent *me* of "List of Works," with corrections. Please send me *two* fresh proofs, as I always like to have one to keep by me.

(3) I agree with your proposal to print 500 "Logic Game," and will order accordingly, when I pass it for Press.

(4) As to selling it in America, I accept 1*s*. 6*d*. as "royalty," if that is what you think reasonable.²

(5) What do you propose as to selling *Alice Under Ground* in America?

Very truly yours,

C. L. Dodgson

¹ On September 28, Dodgson wrote: "Thanks . . . for the estimate of result of reducing price of *Rhyme? and Reason?* to 6*s*. I wish that reduction to be made at the end of this month. . . ." Dodgson must have asked for the estimate in a missing letter, and on September 20 the firm reported that the next 2000 copies, if sold at 6*s*. rather than the 7*s*. of the earlier copies, would produce a profit for him of £213. "It is for you to decide whether this would be satisfactory," Macmillan added.
² On October 8, Macmillan & Co. asked if Dodgson would accept 1*s*. 6*d*. for each copy sold to the firm's American agent.

7 Lushington Road, Eastbourne
October 11, 1886

Dear Mr. Macmillan,

Messrs. Harrison have most courteously, though with a natural regret, assented to the change as to publication of *The Game of Logic*,[1] and they say they will be happy to give you the name of the firm who had undertaken to supply the card counters – for which Messrs. Harrison were going to charge me 3s. 3d. per 1000. I enclose a piece of the card-board (sent as specimen of *card*, not of *colour*) which they propose to use: it seems to me a trifle too *thin*: but the glossy surface is just what I want. The *colours* I want to be rose-colour and a sort of grey, or light brown. The piece of ribbon and the bit of grey, or brown, paper enclosed are almost exactly the two colours I want: they are a pretty contrast, and, if you put them behind the 2 circular openings in the enclosed piece of paper, you will see that they show well against the white (the card-board diagram will be on white card).

Would you get the name of the firm from Harrison (unless you have some one else you would prefer to employ) and get him to try how nearly he can match these two colours in glazed card-board, slightly thicker than this specimen? The counters must be exactly $\frac{3}{4}$ inch diameter.

We had better have 1000 diagrams printed, I think: which will require 4000 red, and 5000 grey, counters.

Please remember, when "List of Works" is passed for Press, that there will be 1000 wanted to bind up with *The Game of Logic*, and 500 for *Alice Under Ground*, besides what you will want for the 2 *Alices*. However, it will be well, I think, only to print it in small quantities – so as to be able to make the necessary alterations from time to time.

Thanks for copy of annual account, received today.

Very truly yours,

C. L. Dodgson

P.S. I am sending Mr. Macnaghten a *Looking-Glass* for his little girl, as she already has *Alice*: and I am asking him to return the *Alice*, which you sent there the other day, addressed to me at 29 Bedford Street.[2] When you get it, will you forward it to me at Oxford, along with the solitary copy of *Doublets* which you now have in hand.

We do not know what "change" in the publication of *The Game of Logic* Dodgson refers to here. How Dodgson and the Macnaghtens became acquainted is a mystery. On September 23 of this year, Dodgson recorded in his Diaries: "Heard from Mr. Macnaghten that they will be glad to see me, if I call." On September 25, Macmillan & Co. wrote that they had sent a copy of *Alice* "from the author to Miss Ella Macnaghten." On October 3, Dodgson asked Craik: "Will you kindly have a copy of enclosed (which please return) sent to – Mc Naghten, Esq., 6 Stanhope Terrace, Hyde Park. Perhaps you can add Christian name." On the 5th, Craik wrote: "I return your copy of the letter to Alfred Macnaghten. We have copied it and sent it. No reply has been received as yet." In mid-October Dodgson includes Ella Macnaghten among his "child friends this season" (*Diaries*, p. 444), and on November 4, Dodgson in London calls on the Macnaghtens, meets Mrs. Macnaghten, "whom I had not seen before, but Ella received me as an old friend" (Diaries). Alfred Hill Macnaghten (1848–1915) was the grandson of Sir Francis Workman Macnaghten (1763–1843), 1st Bt of Dundarave; Mrs. Macnaghten was Arabella Marie (d. 1931), daughter of William Betts, of Frenze Hall, Norfolk. Their daughter, Ella Margaret, married (1910) Capt John Colloyran Mitchell, 12th Royal Lancers, who was killed in action in 1914.

7 Lushington Road, Eastbourne

October 13, 1886

Dear Mr. Macmillan,

(1) Thanks for note. I suppose the correction had been made in some earlier edition of *Alice*?[1]

(2) Do you send parcels to America, in which you could include for me an *Alice* and a *Looking-Glass* that I want to send as presents to a friend in New York?[2]

(3) I am happy to say we have at last frightened Mr. Noad into surrendering to Mr. John Swain, what we demand. I have directed Mr. Swain to prepare the 14 zinc-blocks, and hope they will be delivered to Messrs. Clay in a week or two. As soon as they have taken the electrotypes of these 14 pages (the other 78 are, I hope, electrotyped long ago), they can arrange the book in sheets, and we ough to have the book out by Christmas.

(4) I enclose the title-sheet with a few corrections.

(5) Please let me have an estimate of the current cost of printing and binding assuming the type, etc., as ready set, and thence calculate what the price ough to be, so that the "allowance to author" may cover the current cost, and leave reasonable margin over.

Very truly yours,

C. L. Dodgson

P.S. I go, on October 16, to "The Chestnuts, Guildford," and on October 18 t Christ Church.

---

[1] On the previous day, Macmillan & Co. wrote: "In writing to Mr. Craik on the 7th inst: you gav us a correction for *Alice*: page *116*, line 6, for *their* read *the*. We cannot find the word *their* at the plac referred to."

[2] No further reference appears to Dodgson's proposed gifts, and we cannot identify the intende recipient.

Christ Church, Oxfor

October 27, 188

Dear Mr. Macmillan,

Mr. Savile Clarke, who is preparing (with my sanction) a stage-version of *Alice* and *Looking-Glass*, wants to have "blocks" of some of the pictures.[1] Pleas have electros done for him of any he likes to order. (The "blocks" themselves, i.

the original wood-blocks, must, of course, *never* be entrusted to *any* body: they are far too precious: but I suppose the electros required would have to be done from them. It does not hurt the wood-blocks, does it, to take electros from them?)

I enclose the 2 title-pages, with the alterations I would like made. I like the look of a title-page much better *without* stops.

Very truly yours,

C. L. Dodgson

---

[1] Henry Savile Clarke (1841–93), a minor playwright, drama critic and newspaper editor, prepared a two-act operetta based on *Alice* and *Looking-Glass* that was first performed on December 23, 1886. Dodgson was closely involved in planning the production and suggested Phoebe Carlo for the role of *Alice*. He recorded that when he received the application from Savile Clarke, he sent his consent "on condition of 'no *suggestion* even of coarseness in libretto or in stage business'" (*Diaries*, p. 443; *Letters*, pp. 636–7). Dodgson's impression of the play when he first attended it on December 30 is recorded in his *Diaries* (p. 445): he has reservations but "as a whole, the play seems a success." The stage version was published in 1886 with some of Tenniel's illustrations – the reason for this request. For more on the play and the play text, see *Handbook*, pp. 146–9; *Diaries*, pp. 443–8; *Letters*, pp. 643–5, 657; Lewis Carroll, "'Alice' on the Stage," *Theatre*, N. S. IX (April 1887), 179–84.

Christ Church, Oxford
November 5, 1886

Dear Mr. Craik,

On my return here I found a letter from your firm, dated November 3, advising that both *Alice* and *Looking-Glass* should be reprinted at once. Apparently the writer was not aware that a letter to the same effect reached me on September 30, since which I have been in communication with you about corrections, etc., for the new issue. The finally corrected title-pages reached me at Guildford, before I saw you: will you kindly pass them for 'Press'?[1]

The above-named letter also mentioned Mr. Savile Clarke's play as a possible cause for an increased sale of both books – thus taking a different view from what *you* expressed viva voce.[2] Greatness has its penalties: and a great firm is liable I suppose to such differences of expression owing to its letters being sometimes written by one person and sometimes by another.

Anyhow, *I* take the view that we had better provide for an *increased* sale: and, as I observe that *Alice* sells about twice as fast as the *Looking-Glass*, I think we might venture on (say) 5000 *Alice*s and 3000 *Looking-Glass*es. Would you take means to secure that the "making ready" shall be done really well? I fancy I have noticed in some recent copies of *Alice*, a falling off in this respect. If once the public get an idea that the *early* thousands are the only ones worth buying, the sale will soon die out.[3]

Believe me

Very truly yours,

C. L. Dodgson

¹ The letter that Dodgson found waiting for him (dated November 3) read: "The present stock of *Alice* is *544* copies and of . . . *Looking-Glass 448.* This would be enough to carry us over Christmas under ordinary circumstances," the writer continued, "but in view of a possible increase in the demand which may result from Mr. Savile Clarke's play we write to suggest that we should go to press at once with new Editions as it would be very annoying to be out of either of the books."

² Although Dodgson does not record in his diaries any visit to the firm at this time, he did call on them on November 4 and discussed details with Mr. Craik (see Dodgson's next letter).

³ On November 8, Craik replies: "If there is any defect in the plates it is due to the frequent workings – three thousand printed at separate times do more harm than 10,000 printed all at once. It is the getting ready and moving the plates that cause injury to them." On the following day, Dodgson writes: "When electros get damaged, new ones should be prepared: this we agreed years ago."

Christ Church, Oxford
November 9, 1886

Dear Mr. Macmillan,

In order to save the repeated "makings-ready" for successive issues of *Alice Under Ground,* I am ready (as I told Mr. Craik when I called on November 4) to take the risk of printing 5000 at once.¹ But we can't print the *title-page* till we have fixed the price. So please, at your earliest convenience let me have an estimate of cost of 5000 copies, for paper, "making ready" and printing, and binding; also the prices you propose to sell at, to the public and to the bookseller; also what you would in that case credit to me for each copy sold; also what royalty you would propose to credit to me for each copy sent to America.

I am hoping to receive from you a specimen copy, bound, of the *Game of Logic*: and some more specimen colours for the counters.²

Very truly yours,

C. L. Dodgson

¹ Originally Dodgson suggested printing 10,000 copies of the book (see p. 192, above, July 16, 1885), but on July 21, 1885, George Macmillan wrote: "I am afraid we take a far less sanguine view than you do of the probable demand for the book. To print 10,000 seems to us quite out of the question. We greatly doubt whether as many as 1000 will be sold. It may be much less. But in any case we could not honestly advise you to print more than 1500, or at the very outside 2000. Even then you might well be left with 1500 unsold copies on your hands. People are by this time so much accustomed to plain type that it is only a collector here and there who will buy a facsimile from MS. That is our serious conviction." Dodgson hastily retreated, and in answer to a missing letter, George Macmillan wrote on August 6: "We think you are quite right to print only 500 at first of the Facsimile. The best time to publish would be the first week in December." On October 27, 1886, Macmillan and Co. reported: "We have now received an estimate for printing *Alice's Adventures Under Ground* and we find that owing to the difficulty of 'making ready' the process blocks of which the book consists the expense of printing 500 copies will be proportionately very much higher than the cost of 1000. . . . We think therefore that it is worth your while to consider whether you had not better have 1000 copies printed off at once. It is not probable that 500 would last more than a very short time, indeed we will ourselves take 250 for America if we can have them at a reasonably low price." On the following day, Dodgson replied: "I agree to your proposal to print 1000 . . . instead of 500. . . ."

² On November 1, Macmillan sent Dodgson colored cardboard samples for his approval, but

apparently he did not like them. On the day before he writes this letter, Craik wrote: "We have tried in several places but without success to get cardboards nearer the colour you selected. Those you have are the nearest and I think you had better have them unless you yourself can find more suitable. Without troubling you to write let us arrange if we don't hear from you by Wednesday that you agree to the colours you have." On the same day as Dodgson writes the present letter, he writes again "in haste": "I do *not* agree to the present colours. I will get card-board made of the colours I want."

Christ Church, Oxford
November 18, 1886

Dear Mr. Macmillan,

(1) Thanks for sheets of *Alice in Wonderland*: but I said "from p. 157 to end of *chapter*" only, not "to end of *book*." I return the superfluous sheets, as they may possibly be of use to you.

(2) Please tell me what gilt edges for *Alice Under Ground* will cost per 1000, and whether you approve of the terms I proposed on November 14.[1]

(3) Ought we not to have a "memorandum of agreement" for it and the *Game of Logic*?[2]

(4) I find they have only worked off *500 Game of Logic*. Shall we go on with more at once, or wait till you have sent copies around by your agents, to see what sort of sale it is likely to have?[3]

(5) Please send me 2 sets of *Game of Logic* in sheets, along with the bound copy which I hope is being done.

Very truly yours,

C. L. Dodgson

[1] On the 14th Dodgson wrote: ". . . would the following arrangement satisfy you? To make the price 4s. To allow me, at first, 2s. 11d. for each copy sold, and charge me for all spent on advertising. After June 30, 1887, to allow me 2s. 10d. and do the advertising yourselves." On the 19th, Macmillan and Co. reply that gilt edges would cost 2½d. per copy extra and that they agree to all the terms Dodgson proposed on November 14.
[2] The firm promise (November 19) to send a formal agreement for both the facsimile *Alice* and *The Game of Logic*.
[3] Macmillan advise that it would be best to see how many copies are ordered by the trade before deciding how many more to print off.

Christ Church, Oxford
November 21, 1886

Dear Mr. Macmillan,

I am not at all easy about the printing of *Alice Under Ground*. Each page is generally good, by itself (except that the pictures are now and then too light or too dark, defects which I have pointed out to Messrs. Clay), but the pages are not *so placed that the tops of two opposite pages shall be on the same level*. In some cases I fancied it was a mere accident in mis-folding the sheet sent to me: but I have tried re-folding in vain: the fault is in the placing the blocks together.

Now, I wish it to be quite clearly understood, both by you and by Messrs. Clay (I am writing to them also) that this defect would be, in my view, a fatal one. I don't at all care to have an exactly uniform top margin all through the book, but, when two pages face each other, it is *essential* that *their* top margins shall be fairly equal.

In some of the sheets sent to me, one top margin is a full$\frac{1}{4}$ inch broader than the one facing it.

I have warned Messrs. Clay that no sheets ought to go to Press till this defect has been remedied, as they would be no use for binding, and I should be forced to return them. And I may as well say to you also (to avoid all misunderstanding) that I could not allow copies, thus disfigured, to be sold: it would spoil the whole thing, as this is essentially an "edition de luxe." And of course it follows from this that I could not recognize the printing of such sheets as an execution of my order for the printing, or as work that I ought to pay for.

I think it would be *most* desirable to get a few copies completed, and *bound*, that we may be sure it is all right, before the 5000 copies of even a single sheet are worked off.[1]

Very truly yours,

C. L. Dodgson

---

[1] On the next day, Macmillan & Co. write: ". . . with reference to the printing of *Alice Under Ground* . . . we have seen Clay on the subject. It was fully understood that they were to send you each sheet as it was 'made ready' and to wait your approval before working it off. It would not be possible to have all the sheets 'made ready' at the same time as each sheet would occupy a machine and the whole of the rest of the work of the printing office would be at a standstill, but if each sheet is submitted to you before being worked we think the result will be satisfactory. There is no doubt that the tops of the opposite pages should be on the same level."

Christ Church, Oxford
November 23, 1886

Dear Mr. Macmillan,

(1) I return copies of the two agreements, signed, about *Alice Under Ground* and *Game of Logic*.

(2) Messrs. Clay have sent me a fresh set of sheets of *Alice Under Ground*. The first sheet is all right, and I have marked it press: the others I have corrected, as there are still places where opposite top-margins are unequal.

(3) Thanks for the two bound copies of *Game of Logic* and the 2 sets in sheets. The red and *black* cover need not be repeated: I don't like the effect. The fancy title in gold comes out very well, but it is not *placed* right: a title that is designed *obliquely* is essentially one to go into a *corner*; to put it symmetrically in the middle

is to sacrifice its quaint look entirely: please move it up into the upper left-hand corner, so as to leave a clear ½ inch above, and a clear ⅜ inch at side.

(4) The outer margins are mostly ¼ inch too wide, and the upper margins about ⅛ too wide (sometimes it is the *lower* margins that are too wide: the book is badly folded, and the margins are by no means uniform). Considering that the inner margins are a bare ½ inch, ¾ inch outer margin would be ample. As a consequence of giving too much margin, the *boards* are too large, and the book does *not* range (as it ought to do) with *A Tangled Tale*.

(5) The "List of Works" at the end is so placed as to have a full½ inch more top-margin than the rest of the book. Consequently it looks as if it were dropping out.

(6) The sheets are not yet quite dry enough for binding. Consequently the thick lines of the diagram, which serves as frontispiece, appear in a reversed state on the title-page.

(7) So soon as the sheets are dry, would you send me one copy bound in crimson morocco with gilt edges, and 120 in red cloth.

(8) I am not clear whether I have mentioned to you that I am engaged on another child's-book, for which Mr. Harry Furniss is drawing pictures, and which (I need hardly say) I wish *you* to publish for me. May I assume that you will be willing to do so?

(9) The less it is talked of the better, as we have *no* chance of having it ready earlier than Xmas of 1887, and I consider 1888 a more likely date.

(10) But I should be glad to get parts of it set up in slip, as I am a little nervous about the risk of the MS being destroyed by fire: and I could never *remember* it all. How soon would it be convenient for Clay to do some of this? I suppose they will be too busy for it until after Christmas.

(11) I *expect* the book will be about as large as the 2 *Alices* together, and I want it to have 50 or 60 pictures – perhaps even more![1]

Very truly yours,
C. L. Dodgson

P.S. Have those 200 title-pages gone to Mr. Synge. The corrected proofs (about which he wrote to you) are *here*: he had sent them to me, not to you as he supposed.

---

[1] Dodgson is working on *Sylvie and Bruno*. On March 1, 1885, he wrote Harry Furniss (1854–1925), "a very clever illustrator in *Punch*," asking if he was available to draw for him. On March 9, Dodgson recorded in his *Diaries* (p. 432): "Heard from Mr. Furniss, naming terms, etc., and wrote accepting them, and proposing to send him a poem to begin on. I named Christmas 1886 as a *possible* date, and Christmas 1887 as a more *probable* date, for completing the story. Mr. Furniss has sent me some drawings to see of children and girls, which I think charming." On the day after Dodgson writes this letter, Macmillan & Co. reply: "We are very pleased to hear of the new book and shall be glad to have what is finished put into type at once if you will let us have the manuscript. We shall of course say nothing about the book outside in the meantime." For more on Dodgson and Furniss, see *Letters, passim*, esp. pp. 574, 1090–1; Clark, pp. 242–6.

Christ Church, Oxford

December 1, 1886

Dear Mr. Macmillan,

Thanks for specimen copy of *Game of Logic*. I fear it will not do yet. Further change is needed.

(1) I said, in my letter of November 23, "please move title into upper left-hand corner, so as to leave a clear $\frac{1}{2}$ inch above, and a clear $\frac{3}{8}$ inch at side." This has only been partially attended to. *Both* margins are $\frac{3}{8}$ inch.

(2) I said "the outer margins are mostly $\frac{1}{4}$ inch too wide, and the upper margins about $\frac{1}{8}$ too wide (sometimes it is the lower margins that are too wide; the book is badly folded, and the margins are by no means uniform). A $\frac{3}{4}$ inch outer margin would be ample. As a consequence of giving too much margin, the *boards* are too large, and the book does *not* merge, as it ought to do, with *A Tangled Tale*."

None of this has been attended to. The margins continue as they were. The book is as badly folded as ever (please look at pages 2, 3, 14, 15, 18, 19, 22, 23, 26, 27, 38, 39, 52, 53, 68, 69, 70, 71, 74, 75, 76, 77, 80, 81, 86, 87, 90, 91). And the boards are exactly what they were, viz. about $\frac{1}{8}$ inch too long, and $\frac{1}{4}$ inch too wide.

I fear that, as a whole, the book does very little credit to your binder. A binder's first, and chiefest, duty is, I imagine, to make pages, which have to face each other, an exact match, i.e. to bring their headlines to a true level.

I think it *most* desirable that the binding should not be proceeded with, generally, until a copy has been properly bound, and approved of.

Very truly yours,

C. L. Dodgson

Christ Church, Oxford

December 5, 1886

Dear Mr. Macmillan,

Thanks for new bound copy of *The Game of Logic*.[1]

(1) The lettering is all right now.

(2) As to the boards, you are quite right. I *had* been measuring too early a copy. By all means keep to the present sized board, viz. $7\frac{1}{2} \times 5$, for *all* my books. As to the broad outer margin, I see that this is necessitated by the printer's having made the inner margin too narrow.

(3) I realise that your binder is *not* to blame for opposite pages matching badly, but that it is the printer's fault.

(4) In other ways the printing is unsatisfactory. First (a matter of my own doing) I chose a paper not quite so good as what you are using for my books. Secondly, I learn from the printer that it is set up with *old* type, which obliged

him to damp the paper so much that the letters print a little too *thick*, and the effect is not nearly so good as the clear elegant type of *A Tangled Tale*. This, and the crooked printing show me that, to get the *best* results, it does not do to trust local printers.

The appearance of the book is not up to the standard I have set myself. I have well considered the matter, and have come to the following decision:

(a) to ask you to get the book printed by Clay, in *new* type, to match the Appendix to *Tangled Tale*. That is, I think, the same sized type as it is now in, so they will probably be able to print it off page for page. I have a few little corrections to make, which I will send you (I have a copy in sheets), but they will not alter the paging.

(b) to give up the idea of bringing the two books out together. No doubt Messrs. Clay are very busy just now, and would prefer delaying the *Logic* till after Xmas. Let us be content with getting out *Alice Under Ground* for Xmas, and let the *Logic* come out next year.

(c) I would rather that these Oxford copies were not sold in England *at all*. But they will do very well for the Americans, who ought not to be very particular as to *quality*, as they insist on having books so very cheap. You need be in no hurry about binding these, as of course they must not begin to be sold in America until the English edition is ready.[2]

(d) I would still like the 50 copies bound, as already ordered, in cloth (but *not* the morocco one), as I don't want to keep my friends waiting till next year for their promised copies.

(e) I am quite content to wait till next year for the reprint: but, *if* Messrs. Clay arc ready to begin at once, I will send you the corrections forthwith.

Very truly yours,

C. L. Dodgson

P.S. This change in arrangements for printing will need a new written "Agreement". The book must *not* be electrotyped.

---

[1] On the previous day, Macmillan & Co. wrote: "We are sending you by this post another copy of *The Game of Logic*. (1) The Lettering is now exactly according to your instructions – viz. $\frac{1}{2}$ inch from the top of the cover and $\frac{3}{8}$ inch from the back. (2) The size of the board is exactly that of *A Tangled Tale* and all your other books. We have measured it with a dozen copies taken from stock to be sure of this. If it does not agree with your copy of *A Tangled Tale* we think you must have one of the copies bound up before a uniform size for your books was adopted. (3) If the margins are not all even it is the fault not of the binder but of the printer. The pages are not printed straight on the paper and no amount of folding will make them so. . . ."

[2] On the day he wrote this letter, Dodgson records in his *Diaries* (p. 445): "The printing of *The Game of Logic* (by Baxter at Oxford) has not been a success: and I wrote today to Macmillan my decision to have it printed again by Clay, for England, and send these 500 to America – just what happened in 1865 with *Alice*, when the first 2000, done at the University Press, turned out so bad that I condemned them to the same fate."

Christ Church, Oxford
December 7, 1886

Dear Mr. Macmillan,

I sent a corrected copy of *Game of Logic* to Messrs. Clay directly I got your telegram.[1] There will be some risk, no doubt, of mistakes, if I do not see proofs, as there is a good deal of MS alteration, though I have taken care to keep the *pages* the same. But I do not mind running that risk, just for the copies that will be needed *at first*, in order to fulfil my fancy of publishing the 2 books absolutely *together*.[2] You have not told me what the Trade have ordered. How many copies do you think will meet demand (say) till middle of January? Then we could work a second impression at leisure.[3]

Very truly yours,

C. L. Dodgson

[1] "We have telegraphed to you to say that Mr. Clay can undertake the reprint of *The Game of Logic* and to ask you to send the corrections you speak of," Macmillan & Co. wrote on the 6th. "Unless you wish to see proofs (which we think will be unnecessary as what is wanted is a page-for-page reprint)," the letter continued, "Clay will be able to deliver perfect copies to the binder on Monday next – 13th inst. and the book can be published before Xmas as originally arranged. We will send you in a day or two a specimen page for the *new book* in the style suggested by you in your letter of December 3 [missing]."

[2] Dodgson must have changed his mind again, about publishing by Christmas, and he writes off to Macmillan on the 8th instructing them accordingly. His letter is not in our files, but on the 9th Macmillan & Co. write in reply: "In consequence of your letter received this morning we have stopped the printing of *The Game of Logic* and told Messrs. Clay to let you see proofs."

[3] On the following day, the 8th, Macmillan & Co. reply: "We have not sent round to the London trade for orders yet, as it did not seem safe to do so until something had been decided about the date of publication, but now that we can promise it before Christmas we will take the orders at once."

Christ Church, Oxford
December 17, 1886

Dear Mr. Macmillan,

I am much pleased with the bound copy of *Alice Under Ground*. How many are being worked off? I see I said, on November 9, that I was ready to take the risk of doing *5000*: so I hope that is the number you are doing.[1]

I shall want 150 myself, in red cloth (50 will do to begin with), and I should be glad to have, as soon as can conveniently be managed, 3 special copies, one in white vellum, one in dark green morocco, and one in purple morocco.

I am having a lot more counters sent to you. They are invoiced as 21200 grey and 14750 red. The former lots were called 1000 of each, and I retained 120 red and 150 grey. So that you ought to have, now, 15630 red and 22050 grey: i.e. enough red for 3900 copies and enough grey for 4400 copies.[2]

I am awaiting your answers on various points.

Very truly yours,

C. L. Dodgson

¹ "Received first bound copy of *Alice's Adventures Under Ground*," Dodgson writes in his *Diaries* (p. 445) on the day that he writes this letter, and adds: "The photographing of the MS book was begun July 15, 1885: so it has taken just 17 months to bring out." This first of numerous facsimile volumes is the earliest version of the *Alice* story. The text is in Dodgson's own careful hand script, and it is illustrated with thirty-seven of Dodgson's own drawings. It is less than half as long as the published version of *Alice*. The original remained the property of Alice (Liddell) Hargreaves, for whom Dodgson had written it out. For more about the original manuscript book, its sale at Sotheby's in 1928, its resale in the United States, its purchase by a group of American Anglophiles who then presented it to the British Museum (1948) in appreciation "of the courage of these islands in protecting liberty during two great wars," and publication details, see *Handbook*, pp. 143–6, *Letters*, pp. 561, 588, 597, 647–9; Luther H. Evans, "The Alice Manuscript," preface to *Alice's Adventures Under Ground* (Ann Arbor: University Microfilms, Inc., 1964); and *Jabberwocky*, Autumn 1978. Five days later, on the 22nd, Dodgson writes in his *Diaries* (ibid.): "Today begins the sale of *Alice's Adventures Under Ground*. Tomorrow is the first performance of *Alice in Wonderland* at the Prince of Wales' Theatre. A tolerably eventful week for me!"

² Macmillan & Co. reply on the same day confirming that they were printing 5000 copies of *Under Ground* and add, perhaps with a touch of Carrollian whimsy: "We presume you do not wish us to count the cardboard counters. We will take the numbers stated to be correct and will be careful not to lose any."

Christ Church, Oxford
December 19, 1886

Dear Mr. Macmillan,

I think we shall find the best way to use the ornamental title to *Bumblebee* will be to put it as "false title," and to put the name, without the foliage, on the cover.

I hope this may be in time to prevent your sending *here* the 50 *Alice Under Ground* I asked for. I shall go in a few days to "The Chestnuts, Guildford"; so, if you will send *20* there (with Envelopes and Counters)¹ it will suffice; and some day soon I will arrange with you to come to town, and inscribe about 120 copies, for you to send for me by Parcel Post (which I should prefer to Book Post, as you can put in pieces of whole paper, so as to thoroughly guard the corners).

As for *The Game of Logic*, the *fewer* we print at a time, the better. I should think 500 at a time would be enough. I shall probably make alterations *every* time we reprint.

Very truly yours,

C. L. Dodgson

¹ The perils of publishing two books simultaneously are evident here. The envelopes and counters belong to *The Game of Logic*, not *Under Ground*. In his letter of December 17, Dodgson asked Macmillan to send him copies of *Under Ground* for his private use, and he writes this letter to ask that a portion of his private copies be sent to him at Guildford "with Envelopes and Counters." On December 5, he had also asked for fifty copies of the spoiled *Game of Logic* to be sent to Oxford. He is absent-mindedly conflating the two books here. No reply from Macmillan appears in our files, and one wonders how they dealt with the request.

Christ Church, Oxford

January 23, 1887

Dear Mr. Macmillan,

A letter, which I received from Messrs. Burn & Co., on the 20th, about *Alice Under Ground*, contains a sentence I do not like *at all*. It is this: "it (the book) was bound in a very great hurry."

This I suppose was done in order to get it out before Christmas.

I believe I have already expressed my wishes on this point, but, as I do not seem to have made them fully understood, I may as well repeat that I *do not care*, in the least, for any book of mine being brought out at any particular season: it matters nothing to me in what week, or month – I may even say year – the book appears: what *does* matter to me, very seriously, is that it should be done with all the leisure necessary to produce the *best* results that we can give the public for their money. You may say "the sale would have been less if it had been delayed." By all means. *Let* it be less: I am quite willing it should be so.

I have laid it down, as a fixed principle, that I will give the public (profit or no profit) the *best* article I can: I consider that any "very great hurry" involves very serious risk of the article *not* being the best I can give: and I shall be really much obliged if you will take measures to prevent any such hurry on future occasions. Believe me

Very truly yours,

C. L. Dodgson

P.S. I think you now have 2000 Logic Cards in Envelopes – 1000 with title of book printed on Card and Envelope: the other 1000 plain. If you will return the plain ones to "Messrs. Baxter, 89 St. Aldate's, Oxford," they shall be printed like the others.

I have now passed the whole book for "Press": so the binding can be put in hand at once, and the advertising begin as soon as you think it expedient.

Please send me 20 copies in red cloth, as soon as ready, and one (which can follow) in purple morocco with gilt edges. I shall be coming to town soon, and will then inscribe about 50 copies, to be sent off by Parcel Post.

Christ Church, Oxford

January 27, 1887

Dear Mr. Macmillan,

With many thanks, I enclose receipt for £585.8.7. When *I* so nobly disavowed, and when *you* (i.e. Mr. Craik) gave me credit for disavowing, all pecuniary motives in connection with *Alice Under Ground*, I think we *both* forgot that none of the profits (see P.S. to Preface) will come to me![1]

I suppose you will be now sending round the *Logic* to the Trade, for orders. I should like to know what sort of orders you get.

Very truly yours,

C. L. Dodgson

¹ In sending Dodgson his annual check on the previous day, Craik wrote: ". . . I admire your indifference to pecuniary result and I think we are now all fully impressed." The postscript to Dodgson's preface to *Under Ground* reads: "*The profits, if any, of this book will be given to Children's Hospitals and Convalescent Homes for Sick Children: and the accounts, down to June 30 in each year, will be published in the St. James's Gazette, on the second Tuesday of the following December.*"

[Christ Church, Oxford]
January 29, 1887

Dear Mr. Macmillan,

Really, the more I look at these copies of *Alice Under Ground*, the more vexed I am at their having been bound in such a hurry. I am just sending off a copy to a friend, and, on examining it, I find that, at pages 20, 21, pages 46, 47, pages 48, 49, and pages 80, 81, the right-hand page (judging by the *inner* top corners, which are the points that ought to match) is a full line higher than the left-hand page. The *artistic* effect of all such copies is, to a great extent, *spoilt*.

I find that, in my letter dated November 21, 1886, I used these words: "I have warned Messrs. Clay that no sheet ought to go to Press till this defect has been remedied, as they would be no use for binding, and I should be forced to return them. And I may as well say to you also (to avoid all misunderstanding) that I could not allow copies, thus disfigured, to be sold: it would spoil the whole thing, as this is essentially an "edition de luxe." And of course it follows from this that I could not recognise the printing of such sheets as an execution of my order for the printing, or as work that I ought to pay for."

After that warning, I believe I should be strictly within my *legal* rights if I insisted on all copies, spoiled like the one above-described, being cancelled, and not counted as part of my order. But, considering the peculiar difficulties in folding this book, and that you (with the best intentions) were making the binders work in a hurry, I shall let it alone.

But please understand (that we may not quarrel about it when the time comes) that if a similar thing happens in future, I will have no mercy at all, but shall come to town and myself examine the whole impression, and cancel all spoilt copies, and decline to reckon them as part of my order.¹

Very truly yours,
C. L. Dodgson

P.S. We have a second 1000 Logic Cards ready to send when wanted.

---

¹ Craik replies on February 1: "I think you exaggerate the defects in *Alice Under Ground*. Burn is the finest binder in England and we believe altogether unmatched by any other. . . . It was casually said that your books were done hurriedly, but Burn did not mean to imply that they were so badly done that they were inferior. I think the hurry scarcely perceptibly affected them. I say this in defence and explanation. I hope there will be no shadow of further difficulty for I repeat what I said before that I cordially sympathise with your enthusiasm for perfection."

Christ Church, Oxford
February 2, 1887
Dear Mr. Craik,

Thanks for your letter, and for your taking in such good part my rather fierce letter.

But surely it is the *printer*, not the *binder*, who is responsible for ill-matched pages? So, at least, I was assured when I complained of the uneven pages in the bound copies of the Oxford impression of *The Game of Logic*. Your binders said the pages were not placed evenly on the paper, and that it was impossible to bring them right, however they were folded. I fancy it is Messrs. Clay who are responsible in this matter, not Messrs. *Burn*.

When will the *Logic* be out? And have the Trade ordered any?[1]

Very truly yours,

C. L. Dodgson

---

[1] Two days later, Craik replies that, in his letter of the 1st, he wrote about "the *binder*" because "I thought you had fastened on some remark of his and had brought him in as guilty. As to the *printers* I daresay they do err and I fancy there is a lack of the *perfect* accuracy you like in the Underground *Alice*. We will do what we can to keep them up to your mark." He adds: "It is proposed to publish *The Game of Logic* on the 21st, but it has not been subscribed yet – so I cannot tell you what the Trade have ordered." On the 21st, Dodgson noted in his *Diaries* (p. 449): "Coming out of *The Game of Logic*." The book embodies Dodgson's effort, with the aid of diagrams, humorous examples, and counters (cards), to instruct young people in deductive logic. The *Handbook* (pp. 142–3) calls it "a failure. . . . A schoolboy might understand the game, but would certainly not be amused by anything except the examples. . . . The usual vein of humour, however, runs through the whole book, with excellent effect, but . . . it is too light to bear the superstructure." For more on *The Game of Logic*, see *Handbook*, pp. 149–50; and Jeffrey Stern, "*The Game of Logic*," *Jabberwocky*, 10 (Winter 1980/1), 3–10. On February 25, Macmillan report: "Up to this date we have sold 332 copies besides 54 which have been sent to Agents. In addition to these, 250 of the Oxford Printed Edition have been sent out to America." On March 4, Dodgson goes to Macmillan's to inscribe 49 copies (*Diaries*, p. 449).

Christ Church, Oxford
March 16, 1887
Dear Mr. Macmillan,

I have gone through *Alice's Adventures* and made a tolerably exact estimate of the text and pictures which I should retain for a cheap edition, supposing it done in the style of the specimen page which Mr. Craik gave me a few weeks ago There would be about 112 pages, containing 24 pictures. The paper would be, of course, of a cheaper kind than what we use in the 6s. edition: at the same time, I would rather not have it *thin*. How would the paper suit, on which your *Selection from Wordsworth* is printed? The boards might be covered with bright red *paper* instead of cloth: no ornamentation on the sides, but the name in gold along the back: edges of leaves cut smooth and left white. Would you send me an estimate for 10,000 copies (printed from electrotypes): and also say what a second 10,000 would cost.[1]

Very truly yours,

C. L. Dodgson

[1] No reply from Macmillan to these queries is in our files.

Christ Church, Oxford

March 21, 1887

Dear Mr. Macmillan,

(1) I don't want to hurry Messrs. Clay needlessly in the matter of *Bumblebee*, etc., but really they are very long over the title-sheet. On February 23, I wrote asking them to set it up as soon as the book was all arranged in pages (so that they could draw up a table of contents). This condition was fulfilled on March 1, just 3 weeks ago. For myself, I would not mind the delay, but Mr. Synge is *very* anxious to see the book completed, and I should be sorry to keep him waiting longer than necessary.

(2) Is the die (or whatever it is called) ready, for doing the whole frontispiece in gold on the cover?

(3) Are the 500 copies of the text being worked off? (I passed it all, for "Press," on March 5.)

(4) You have not sent me the list (asked for on March 13) of the Papers to which you propose to send copies.[1]

(5) I have heard nothing of the fate of the paper (on computing dates) sent to you on March 15 for the Editor of *Nature*. (I am assuming you to be the publishers.) If the Editor does accept it, I would be glad to have it sent me, in slip, for corrections.[2]

(6) I have some corrections for your *Sunday Book of Poetry*, when you reprint it.[3]

(7) I have been thinking over what you said (on March 11) about your preferring, if it were left to you, *not* to advertise the terms on which you sell my books to the Trade: and I should be glad to meet your wishes as far as possible.[4] What I regard as *essential* is that the Public should know the *price* of the book (*that* we secure by putting it on the title-page) and the discount they can get, if they choose to buy direct from *you*. Would you be satisfied if the advertisement were reduced to "In selling the above-named books to the Public (for cash only), Messrs. Macmillan will allow 10 percent discount." But my fear is that this would involve you in difficulties with the Trade, who would expect more allowances than you could afford to give them. However, we might think this over, and perhaps make a new agreement to begin next July.[5]

Very truly yours,

C. L. Dodgson

¹ On the following day, Macmillan & Co. promise to "hurry Clay" with the proof of the title sheet and to send a copy of the cover for *Bumblebee* by post. In their letter of the 22nd, Macmillan enclose the list of newspapers to which they propose sending presentation copies of Synge's book, but the list is missing.

² Macmillan were indeed the publishers of *Nature*. The magazine was conceived in 1868 by (Sir Joseph) Norman Lockyer (1836–1920), astronomer and spectroscopist. Lockyer was Alexander Macmillan's "consulting physician with regard to scientific books and schemes," and when he proposed a journal devoted to science, Macmillan did not hesitate. Lockyer was made editor and retained the post for fifty years, during which he enjoyed absolute editorial independence, even though the journal consistently lost money. *Nature*'s aim was to assert the rights of science to an honored place in national service, linking science with community life. It also sought to report early information of all advances made in any branch of material knowledge and to provide a forum for the discussion of scientific questions (see Morgan, pp. 69, 84–7). This is the first of three contributions that Dodgson would publish in *Nature*. It embodies his discovery of a formula for finding the day of the week for any given day of the month, an idea he recorded in his *Diarie.* (p. 449) on March 8 of this year. Macmillan's reply on the following day reports that Dodgson': letter was forwarded to the editor of *Nature*, that it is "now in type," and a proof would be sen shortly. Dodgson's paper appeared in *Nature* on March 31 (see *Handbook*, p. 150; *Letters*, pp 965–6).

³ Macmillan's *The Sunday Book of Poetry*, selected and arranged by C. F. Alexander, was a popula Golden Treasury anthology that was published in 1865 and reprinted six times by 1887. *A* collection of sacred poetry for children from eight to fourteen, it included selections from Milton Keble, Crashaw, Newman, Wordsworth – but not Lewis Carroll. On the 22nd Macmillan & Co write: "We shall be much obliged if you will let us have the list of corrections for *The Sunday Book c Poetry* as we are just about to print a new Edition," and on the 23rd Dodgson sends them.

⁴ Dodgson raises the delicate subject again in response to a letter from Macmillan & Co. of Marc 11, in which Macmillan reported: "We have today received a letter from some customers of ours Messrs. Brown & Sons, of Hull – who say that they wrote to you with reference to the announcement at the end of *Alice* as to the terms on which your books were supplied, and that yo informed them that we alone were responsible for the notice in question. We think there must be some mistake about this. We have always been under the impression that you insisted on the appearance of the announcement. Had the matter been left for us to decide we should certainl have omitted it, and will do so now if we hear from you that we have the option of doing so."

⁵ On the following day, the firm reply: "We do not think that any change in the form of the announcement as to the price at which your books are to be sold is worth making. The bookselle object to it being stated that the public can buy your books at a discount from the advertised price as they consider that whether they give any discount or what it is to be is a matter to be settle between their customers and themselves. The announcement that we are prepared to give 1 percent for cash practically obliges every bookseller to do the same and this is what they do not like We understand, however, that you regard this as an essential part of your scheme, and this bein so, we do not think that any mere change in the form of the announcement would do any good. Dodgson replies on the 23rd: "The booksellers are quite right in considering 'that whether the give any discount or what it is to be is a matter to be settled between their customers an themselves.' Who wants to interfere with them? . . . And surely they must grant *you* the right settle what discount *you* will give, and to advertise your intentions. . . . When they say that *yo* announcement that you will give 10 percent practically obliges every bookseller to do the sam your best answer perhaps would be that, whether *you* announce it or not, *others* announce eve larger discounts: you might quote one or two (I think Harrison, of Pall Mall, advertises '2*d*. in th shilling off *all* new books') and ask whether *these* advertisements oblige all booksellers to give 2*d*. the shilling!"

Christ Church, Oxford
April 3, 1887

Dear Mr. Macmillan,

(1) It is, I think, a most dangerous rule that you are adopting, in sending me printers' proofs, and saying that, if you "hear nothing to the contrary the next morning," you will consider it is passed for "Press." Suppose you were printing 10,000 copies of some book, and sent me a sheet, with some absolutely fatal mistake, with that message. There would be a *double* risk: first, your letter might fail to reach *me*: secondly, my answer might fail to reach *you*: and in either case there would be 10,000 sheets worked off, which would have to be cancelled. Kindly let it be understood, in future, that *silence*, on my part, means *dis*approval; and that nothing is to go to "Press," *unless I have written to say so*. Considering that, in my case, all the printing is done at my cost and at my risk, I hope you will not think this too dictatorial.[1]

(2) You are evidently anxious to get the book out by Easter. This is a matter I do not care about *in the least*. I had much rather wait a long time than have the thing done badly through haste. I have several times already said this same thing – with regard to binding in a hurry, etc., and I trust you understand me now. Never mind Mr. Synge being in a hurry: *I* am responsible for this book, and I will *not* consent, after the very great trouble I have had with it, to let all be spoiled at the last in order to save a few days.

(3) We have been very near spoiling this book by the title-sheet. Both Dedication and Preface were unsightly. The Dedication needed breaking up into more, and shorter, lines. Also they had omitted a word, to which Mr. Synge attaches great importance. And as to the Preface, it would simply have *killed* the book, and made all the text look mean, in comparison with such large type. I have the strongest objection to a Preface in larger type than the book.

(4) I always like to have 2 proofs sent me of anything – one to return and one to keep. You only sent *one* of this, which I had to send, with corrections, to Messrs. Clay. I have asked them to send me 2, and to send 2 to Mr. Synge, as I have promised him he shall see each sheet before it goes to Press.

(4) I have not yet received the specimen binding, with the design placed centrally, which I asked for in my letter of March 27. I wish to make sure it will look well, before authorising that arrangement.

(5) Was that paper of mine, that I sent through you to the Editor of *Nature*, ever published?[2]

Yours very truly,
C. L. Dodgson

---

[1] On March 30 Dodgson wrote Macmillan: ". . . Mr. Synge, who is in very bad health, is fidgeting himself a good deal about the book, and I am really anxious, for his sake, to get it completed." Here Dodgson is reacting to Macmillan & Co.'s letter of April 1, in which they enclosed a proof of the title page for *Bumblebee* and added: "Unless we hear from you to the contrary tomorrow morning

we shall take it for granted that this sheet is all right." Macmillan & Co. reply (April 4): "We quite agree with you that no sheet of any book of yours should be printed off without your written approval and we had no wish when writing to you . . . to establish a precedent for any different method of procedure. We understood however from your former letter that you and Mr. Synge were anxious to have copies of the book before Easter and this would have been impossible unless we could print off immediately. We shall of course now take care that the printing is gone on with deliberately and without undue haste."

² In the same letter: "Your letter to *Nature* appeared in the last number of that journal. We are sending you a copy by post."

Christ Church, Oxford
April 6, 1887

Dear Mr. Macmillan,

(1) Thanks for *Educational Year Book*,¹ the number of *Nature* containing my letter, and the new cover for *Bumblebee*.

(2) The cover is exactly as I directed: but I find it *looks* as if the design were too much to the right. I think the eye takes, as left-hand margin, the *average* leaves, and takes the projecting flower as an exception. It should be moved ⅛ inch to the left, so as to leave a clear inch between the last E of "Bumblebee" and the edge.²

(3) You have not yet sent me an estimate for a cheap *Alice*, asked for on March 16.³

(4) Nor the 100 *Easter Greetings*, asked for on April 1.⁴

(5) Whenever you want to reprint anything of mine, please let me know, as I generally have some corrections on hand.

Very truly yours,
C. L. Dodgson

¹ On the day before, Macmillan & Co. wrote: "We have sent copies of *The Game of Logic* from the author to the schoolmasters marked by you in the *Educational Year Book* and are returning the book to you by post."

² "We will send you after Easter another cover for *Bumblebee* altered in accordance with your latest directions," Macmillan & Co. write on the 7th. "The binders do not begin work again until today week."

³ In the same letter: "We find that the cost of paper, printing and binding the first Edition of 10,000 copies of an abridged *Alice* making 102 pages like the specimen you have would be £260. Subsequent Editions would cost £239. This Estimate is for binding in paper boards with gilt lettering which we find can be put on the side as well as the back without extra expense." The writer adds: "At the risk of appearing to offer you advice for which we have not been asked we cannot help saying that the wisdom of publishing an abridged Edition of your books seems to us doubtful. If it does not sell it is of course not worth doing, and if it does sell it seems to us it is likely to injure the complete book. If anythng of the kind is to be done would it not be better to bring out a cheap Edition of the complete book without abridgement? Such a book would have an *enormous* sale and would cost very little more to produce than the abridged Edition."

⁴ "The *Easter Greeting* has been reprinting," the firm report in the same letter. "We are trying to get some copies to send you tonight."

Christ Church, Oxford
April 10, 1887

Dear Mr. Macmillan,

Please do not trouble the binders to do another cover, for approval, for *Bumblebee*. It would do very well as it is: but would be a little improved by moving the design as I suggested on April 6.

When I get the revised title-sheet, I fully expect to be able to telegraph to Messrs. Clay that it may go to Press: and then you can begin binding as soon as the sheets are dry.

Please have 25 copies done with *gilt* edges (the ordinary copies are to have *white* edges), and of these send 20 to Mr. Synge and 5 to me.

Mr. Synge wants *one* copy bound in [a] special way. That copy he had better buy for himself: and he will give you his own directions about it.

You can begin advertising the book as soon as you think fit.

Also I suppose we had better have, as usual, a written agreement as to its publication, etc.

Far from thinking your advice uncalled-for, in the matter of the cheap *Alice*, I am very grateful for it, and feel tolerably sure that your view is right.

I would like to have an estimate for 10,000 copies of the complete book, stipulating – as the point of chief importance – that the pictures must be *well* printed.[1] Please take "advertising" as one item of cost (and *not* to be reckoned, as with my other books, as 1*d*. a copy, leaving you to advertise, as you think fit, at your own cost. That arrangement I do not now think the best: and I shall ask you to rescind it, next June, for my other books). And then I should like to know what you advise the *price* to be. One shilling would be a *most* desirable price, if I could possibly produce a respectable book and get clear a margin of profit; but that I fear cannot be: I am inclined to propose 1*s*. 6*d*. for each book alone, and 2*s*. 6*d*. for the two bound together.

I may as well mention here another change I want made in our terms of sale – to begin next June 30. It is that the "Trade" allowance shall be 1½*d*. in the shilling instead of 2*d*. Mr. Ruskin's theory, of allowing *no* abatement to the Trade, I still think unreasonable. But I feel that the purchaser ought *not* to expect more discount than 10 percent for ready money. And this the bookseller can well afford to give him, if he himself can get 2 1¼ percent (which he will do in this case). The practice of booksellers, of underselling each other by offering such excessive discount as 2*d*. or even 3*d*., in the shilling, is an absurdity that I do not think need be at all recognized.[2] Believe me

Very truly yours,

C. L. Dodgson

P.S. Thanks for the 100 copies of the *Easter Greeting*. In future editions of my books, instead of putting it, and the *Xmas Greeting*, in as separate leaflets, I think we will print them at the end of the book, as we have done with *Alice Under Ground.*

¹ On the 20th, Macmillan & Co. send their estimate for a cheap edition of *Alice* unabridged: ". . . we find that 10,000 copies could be produced for £357 and subsequent Editions of the same number for £322. The volume will contain 160 pages printed on paper one-sixth thinner than that used for the 6s. Edition and the binding will be limp cloth lettered on the back and side but not in gold. The printing of the woodcuts is to be equal to that of the present Editions. This book might be sold for 1s. 6d. but we think it would do just as well at 2s. and of course the result to you would be much better in that case. This point of course you will decide for yourself."

² In the same letter: "We hope you will reconsider your proposal to reduce the bookseller's allowance on your books to 1½d. in the shilling. In the first place we are afraid that the booksellers who have now become more or less accustomed to the present rates will be very much enraged at a further reduction of their profits and will refuse to keep your books in stock at all or even to supply them to order. In the second place, which is much more to the point we do not think that 21¼ percent which according to your calculation is what the bookseller would make under the new plan is enough to pay him. A bookseller's turnover is comparatively small and his risk in the way of books which become unsaleable and shopworn is considerable, and we should be surprised if there are many men in the trade whose working expenses do not amount to 10 percent of his gross profit and . . . your proposed arrangement is not enough for him to live or keep his wife and children on."

The Chestnuts, Guildford
(leaving for Oxford today)
April 25, 1887

Dear Mr. Macmillan,

Many thanks for your letter, and explanation of the financial position of the booksellers: if that is as you believe, it does look as if I could not, in fairness to them, make any further reduction in their profit. I will carefully consider all you say on this point, and also what you say of the hostility likely to be roused: this point however does not seem to me so weighty as the other, as you anticipated much the same result from the first reduction, but I do not see any appreciable result as yet.

As to the "agreement" about *Bumblebee,* etc.: it needs considerable alteration, as it seems to me. I have altered it into what looks to me a more satisfactory form, and I add some remarks.

(a) The *copyright* is surely Mr. Synge's. If this is so, legally, any agreement, in which he is not one of the parties, would be null and void. I see no use in alluding to the matter.

(b) I should prefer *all* matters of debit and credit, between us, to be settled at the usual times, i.e. the accounts to be made up to June 30 each year and settled in cash in the following January. It does not seem quite reasonable that I should pay printing, etc., 3 months after date, unless the receipts on the sale are also paid to *me* 3 months after they come in. If however you wish for more prompt payment than the present system involves, I would have no objection to *half-*

yearly settlements, e.g. that the accounts should be made up to June 30, and settled in July: and again made up to December 31, and settled in January.

(c) I do not wish to have *any* copies disposed of at a lower price: but any unsold copies may be handed over to me in *one* year, if you like: we shall be quite well able to judge, at the end of a year, whether there is a reasonable prospect of a further sale.[1]

Please send to me, at Christ Church, Trench's *Medieval Church History* and *The Victorian Half-Century*.[2] Believe me to be

Very truly yours,

C. L. Dodgson

P.S. The "cheap" *Alice* plan looks very promising. I would like to see a sheet of it set up on the paper you propose to use: and to see a specimen of the kind of cover you propose.

---

[1] Craik writes the following day: "I see no objection to any one of the alterations you suggest in the Agreement." He encloses a revised agreement incorporating Dodgson's emendations.

[2] Macmillan published *Medieval Church History* by Archbishop Richard Chenevix Trench in 1877, and a second edition appeared in 1879. The book developed from a series of lectures that Trench gave and was designed to impart "a certain acquaintance with church history" to those "who cannot make of it a special study." *The Victorian Half-Century*, a Jubilee Book compiled by Charlotte Mary Yonge, was published by Macmillan in 1886 with an advertisement that it contains "a portrait of . . . the Queen." It was reprinted twice in 1887.

Christ Church, Oxford

April 27, 1887

Dear Mr. Craik,

I thank you for so readily agreeing to my suggestions, and I enclose a signed "Agreement."

Please tell Mr. James Upton, of Cambridge Street, Birmingham, that, for all matters connected with the Drama of *Alice in Wonderland*, application should be made to "H. Savile Clarke, Esquire, Cleveland Lodge, Westbourne Park," the author of the Drama.[1]

I shall, some day soon, want you to publish for me, a book on Logic, going a good deal further than the *Game*.[2] I want it to range with my other books in *height*, but the pages will have to be square, as it will have diagrams, one of which I enclose. Will you be considering how such a thing had better be reproduced? The *words* ought to be ordinary *type*, I think. If done by hand, however neatly done, they would not be so easily read as if printed.

Very truly yours,

C. L. Dodgson

[1] "Will you say how you would like the enclosed communication from James Upton answered?" Craik wrote in his letter of the previous day.
[2] Dodgson is already at work on what William Warren Bartley III has called "one of the most brilliantly eccentric logic textbooks ever written: a work in three parts, or volumes, titled simply *Symbolic Logic*." Part I would not, in fact, appear until 1896. (See Bartley's edition of *Lewis Carroll's Symbolic Logic*, 1977.) The diagram Dodgson encloses is missing.

Christ Church, Oxford

May 9, 1887

Dear Mr. Macmillan,

Thanks for specimen-diagram. The lines are all rather too thin: the eye does not easily follow a thin line for any distance. And the type is not nearly large enough: it should be as large as there is room for. Also rather *thicker* type would be better, I think. Is there not a kind called "antique" that would be more legible? This sort of thing

Not all x

Also, have they not got ordinary *accented* letters? x^1 is a very poor substitute for x'. Wherever they print *mathematical* books, they keep them in stock. In Price's *Differential Calculus*, x' and y' are used by the thousand.[1]

I enclose the MS for further experiments.

With regard to what you said about printing, etc., being paid for in 3 months, am I not right in thinking that *we* have never yet had any such arrangement?[2] I cannot remember a book-account being settled between us at any other time than the annual settlement in January.

Is the sheet of the cheap *Alice*, that I asked for, in hand?

Very truly yours,

C. L. Dodgson

Will you kindly get me 2 seats (front of dress-circle, near centre) at Toole's Theatre, for Saturday afternoon? either *next* Saturday, or, if all the good front seats are gone, then Saturday week, or even Saturday fortnight.[3]

[1] *A Treatise on the Differential Calculus and Its Application to Geometry* (1848) by Bartholomew Price (1818–98), Dodgson's tutor and friend.
[2] Dodgson refers to *Bumblebee Bogo's Budget*, finally published on April 29. No reply to this letter is in our files.
[3] "To town for the day with Maggie Earle as my companion," Dodgson records in his *Diaries* (p. 450) on May 14. In the afternoon they went to Toole's theater and saw an undistinguished double bill. John Lawrence Toole (1830–1906), comedian and toastmaster whom Dickens and Thackeray praised, was one of Dodgson's favorites. In 1882 Toole leased the Folly Theatre, renamed it Toole's, and with his own company produced comedies and burlesques there.

Christ Church, Oxford
June 14, 1887

Dear Mr. Macmillan,

Many thanks for sending me the 2 Lyceum tickets.[1]

I have considered what you said about changing the terms with the booksellers, and have decided to let things remain as they are, for another year at any rate.

As to the cheap *Alice* –

(1) Let it be "old-faced" type.

(2) Let there be *28* lines in the page, so as to keep the shape of the existing page, viz. $5\frac{1}{8} \times 3\frac{1}{2}$.

(3) I wish to have the dedicatory verses, and the 3 supplementary pages at the end, omitted. They would not be appreciated by the poorer classes, for whom the cheap edition is meant: and I feel clear that the purchasers of the 6*s*. edition ought to have something more than those who get the cheap one.

(4) As a further distinction, I wish the number of pictures to be reduced, by leaving out the less important ones. Those I wish to be retained are 27 in all, as follows:

Frontispiece, pictures at pages 1, 10, 15, 26, 35, 48, 51, 55, 59, 63, 64, 65, 66, 81, 88, 91, 93, 97, 113, 117, 128, 141, 150, 170, 177, 188.

This omission of 15 pictures ought to make a real difference in cost of production. Would you have the saving estimated? It might possibly enable us to sell cheaper than at present proposed.[2]

(5) Would it not save trouble and cost in binding, if the title page, etc., were included in the 1st sheet of 16 pages, or 8 leaves? The "false" title, frontispiece, title-page, and contents, would occupy 4 leaves: so 4 leaves of text might be included in the same sheet.

So much for the cheap *Alice*.

After the end of this month, I wish the "1*d*. per copy for advertising" to be cancelled in all our agreements. I would prefer that you should advertise as you think fit, and charge it along with the binding, etc. And you would then allow me 1*d*. more, per copy of every book, than you now do.

Very truly yours,

C. L. Dodgson

---

[1] Presumably to see Henry Irving and Ellen Terry in a Shakespeare play. Dodgson goes to the Lyceum on the 18th, but he records in his Diaries that he "had telegraphed to Miss E. Terry to get . . . stalls: failing that, she gave us a box. . . ." On the 18th Dodgson sees Miss Terry and Henry Irving in *Much Ado*. The tickets that Macmillan procured might have been for another performance of the same play or for another play in the Irving–Terry repertory.

[2] On the following day, Frederick Macmillan writes, saying ". . . we take the liberty of asking you to reconsider your decision as to the omission of 15 of the less important illustrations. From the point of view of economy it is not worth while doing, for it would make no appreciable difference in the

cost of production, whereas on the other hand we think it might interfere with the sale. In our opinion the true plan to adopt in publishing a cheap edition is to give everything contained in the original edition but printed and bound in a cheaper form. If you leave out anything you produce not a cheap Edition but an abridgement which is quite another thing and which many people will refuse as being incomplete. We are further inclined to think that you contemplate too great a reduction in price. We consider that if you made the books 2s. each (1s. 8d. to the trade) you will be making them cheap enough to command a very large sale and at the same time the difference between the sale price and the cost of production would be enough to give you a fair margin of profit."

7 Lushington Road, Eastbourne
July 6, 1887

Dear Mr. Macmillan,

I have considered your proposal to include *all* the pictures in the cheap *Alice*, and decided to accept it: and I see there is not nearly such a risk of loss as I had calculated on. We had better have the Dedication, and final pages, as well.

But a new idea has occurred to me, and I would like to know, before we go on, what you think of it. I bought your 2s. edition of *Haworth's* yesterday, and like the look of the book very much, and think the type much more readable than the one proposed for the cheap *Alice*. What would you think of bringing it out as one of that Series?[1] You would have to put one line less in the page, and to make the text $\frac{1}{8}$ inch wider: so that, in order to have uniform margins, the page, and therefore the book, would have to be $\frac{1}{4}$ inch wider: but it would be the same height, and would range with the rest of the Series. The cover might be just the same colour and style as that of *Haworth's*, with one of the pictures (viz. "shower of cards") printed outside.

In the page, at present proposed, there would be 280 words: in the one I now suggest, only 245: so that the number of pages in the book would be increased by $\frac{1}{7}$th.

If you see no objection to the plan, would you make an estimate for producing 10,000 copies? Then I shall see what the profit will be per copy.[2]

By the way, in your letter of June 2, you say "supposing that the retail price was 2s. 6d. and that you allowed us 4d., etc., etc." Is not this a mistake?[3] If the retail price were 2s. 6d., the trade-price would be 2s. 1d., on which your "commission" of 10 percent, would be $2\frac{1}{2}d$.

Very truly yours,

C. L. Dodgson

P.S. I shall be glad to have another proof of that Logic Diagram, as I have several more to send you, when once we have got one satisfactorily done.

---

[1] *Haworth's*, a novel by Frances Hodgson Burnett, appeared in 1879 and was reprinted in 1880. In 1887 the edition that Dodgson refers to here was published at 2s. In their reply two days later,

Macmillan & Co. send Dodgson a specimen page of *Alice* set in the same type as the 2*s. Haworth's.*
² In the same letter, Macmillan estimate the cost of the proposed *Alice* in the same style of binding as *Haworth's* at £412 for 10,000 copies, adding that "this would pay you very well if the retail price were fixed at half-a-crown as we have suggested."
³ Dodgson's figures are correct, and Macmillan apologize for their error in their letter of July 8.

7 Lushington Road, Eastbourne
July 12, 1887

Dear Mr. Macmillan,

Before settling type, etc., for the cheap *Alice*, I think we ought to consider well the various possibilities. I find that the original *Alice*, the *Tangled Tale*, and *Haworth's* are all the same type (what is its name?), and only differ in *leading*, having respectively 22, 25, 27 lines to the page: the number of pages in the book being, for the 3 styles, 192, 172, 160.

The smaller "old-faced" type, which you suggested, would be 28 lines to the page, and would give a book of 132 pages.

The number of words in a page would be, for the 4 styles, 180, 205, 220, 280.

My first question is, is there not some *intermediate* type, that would give (say) 250 words to the page (which would make the book contain 144 pages)? (It had better be leaded to 27 lines in a page of $5\frac{1}{8}$ inches long.)

My next question is as to the quality of paper. It seems that we can make almost any reduction we like in the cost of the book by using cheaper paper.

You tell me that, with the small type, the first 10,000 would cost £357 (i.e. $8\frac{1}{2}d$. each), and a subsequent edition £322 (i.e. $7\frac{3}{4}d$. each).

Also that, in *Haworth's* type and binding, 10,000 (you don't say whether first or second: I suppose you mean *first*) would be £412 (i.e. 10*d*. each): so I suppose a subsequent 10,000 would cost about £387 (i.e. $9\frac{1}{4}d$. each).

Roughly speaking, the intermediate size I am thinking of would cost (with the paper you are proposing to use), about $\frac{1}{10}$th less, i.e. £370 (9*d*. each) for first set, and £348 ($8\frac{1}{4}d$. each) afterwards.

Could it be done for about this cost with toned paper?¹ In that case we might sell for 2*s*. 6*d*.

The other course (which I should prefer, if the book would look respectable), would be to use a rather cheaper paper, and sell for 2*s*. I cannot make up my mind which plan would be best, and would be glad of your advice.

I fancy 2*s*. would be a better selling price, and that there would be an advantage in having it at the same price as the rest of the *Haworth's* series (as I presume you will make it one of the series), but you will be the best judge of this.²

I should like the *Looking-Glass* to be issued, cheap, at the same time: and, when we have settled about type and paper, I should like 10,000 of each book to be worked off, to issue next Xmas.

What price would you propose for America? Whatever reduction you think necessary, can we not save it by simply using a cheaper paper? If they *won't* give the English price, I think they have no right to expect an equally good article.

Very truly yours,

C. L. Dodgson

---

[1] In their reply two days later, Macmillan & Co. write that toned paper cost no more than white paper and could easily be used.

[2] Macmillan reply (same letter) that "the price might just as well be 2*s*. 6*d*.," and added that "the adoption of the lower price would only reduce the profits without increasing the sale." They explain that *Alice* cannot be put into their "Two Shilling Novel" series as it is not a novel in the ordinary meaning of the term, but, more important, because Dodgson's books are sold on different terms from novels like *Haworth's*.

7 Lushington Road, Eastbourne
July 15, 1887

Dear Mr. Macmillan,

Thanks for letter and estimates. One or two points in my letter you have not noticed.

(1) I think I should like the type to be *intermediate* to "small pica" and "pica." Is there such a type?[1]

(2) What paper do you propose to use? How much cheaper than what is now used for *Alice*?[2]

I think the limp binding will do very well: and I agree to your proposed price of 2*s*. 6*d*. In that case, what reduction would you propose for America? And can we save that reduction by giving them a cheaper paper?[3]

Another thing I want to see the "intermediate" type for, is that I think it would be suitable for the new book.[4] If there is no such thing, then we had better print uniform with *Tangled Tale*. As soon as we have settled on type for new book, I want to have a lot of it set up in slip. I am hard at work at it, down here. Mr. Furniss has promised to devote the summer to the pictures for it: so I hope we shall make great progress this year, and perhaps be able to publish it next Easter.

Very truly yours,

C. L. Dodgson

P.S. Are you advertising Mr. Synge's book still? Or do you not think it worth while? How is it selling?[5]

---

[1] In a letter on the previous day Macmillan & Co. sent two separate estimates for the cheap *Alice*, one based on the use of small pica type, the other on pica.

[2] Replying to these two queries on July 16, Macmillan write: "There is no type between pica and small pica. Would not the old-faced small pica which you saw as a specimen for the cheap Edition

of *Alice* do for the new book? It is very pretty type." And: "The paper we propose to use for the cheap *Alice* is 1½*d.* per lb. cheaper than that used for the six-shilling edition. It is as cheap as paper good to print woodcuts on can be."

3 Macmillan write (same letter) that they will not send any copies of the cheap *Alice* to America as their agent there "has a set of plates and can print a cheap Edition for himself for less than he can import it."

4 *Sylvie and Bruno.*

5 Macmillan reply (same letter) that £11 was spent on advertising, but at the moment it is being advertised only in *Macmillan's Magazine*. "The sale as we feared has not been very good," they add.

7 Lushington Road, Eastbourne
July 18, 1887

Dear Mr. Macmillan,

Thanks for letter of July 16. You tell me that the paper you propose for the cheap *Alice* costs 1½*d.* per pound less than what is used for the 6*s.* edition. But that conveys no idea to my mind, as I do not know what the paper, used in the 6*s.* edition, costs per pound – nor yet how many pounds are used for 1000 copies.[1]

As to type – I think the cheap *Alice* had better be in small pica, and the new book in pica – both to be "old-faced."

I would like to see specimen pages of these, the small pica, having 27 lines in a page 5⅜ inches long (measuring from lower edge of 1st line to lower edge of last line): and the pica having 24 lines in the page.

Very truly yours,

C. L. Dodgson

1 "The price of the paper we propose to use is 5*d.* a lb, and it will take 55 reams weighing 100 lbs. each to produce 10,000 copies," Macmillan & Co. reply two days later.

7 Lushington Road, Eastbourne
August 6, 1887

Dear Mr. Macmillan,

We have got the right thing at last.[1] I like the look of both the narrowed pages, very much. The small pica will do very well for the cheap *Alice* and *Looking-Glass*, and the pica for the new book.

You can put the cheap books in hand as soon as you like and can electrotype the sheets as fast as I pass them for Press.

As soon as you know how many pages the cheap *Alice* will contain, I would like you to bind up that quantity of blank paper, in a cover such as you propose to use. It will not be waste of labour: I have found similar books, that you have bound for me, very handy as MS books, as the paper will take ordinary ink.

Now that we have settled the type, etc., for the new book (we will call it "Four Seasons" for the present),[2] I should be glad to get a good deal of it set up in slip:

and I enclose a portion (originally published in *Aunt Judy's Magazine*) to begin with.[3]

Of course you will take all needful precautions that none of the new book is seen by "outsiders"?

Did you write, for me, to that doctor, whose letter you forwarded to me on July 8? And what was his name? *I* couldn't read it.[4]

Very truly yours,

C. L. Dodgson

---

[1] Macmillan sent Dodgson specimen pages for the cheap *Alice* on July 26, 28 and August 5.

[2] "Four Seasons" was the early working title of *Sylvie and Bruno*, and Dodgson seems to have debated over the title as he worked away on the text. In July 1888 he refers to the book as *Sylvie and Bruno* (*Diaries*, p. 463), but in an 1889 letter to Macmillan he still refers to "Four Seasons" (see p. 259, below). However, less than a month later, he asks Macmillan about printing *Sylvie and Bruno* (p. 259, below).

[3] The earliest published portion of *Sylvie and Bruno* appeared in *Aunt Judy's Magazine* in December 1867 as "Bruno's Revenge," a short story (see p. 83, above).

[4] On the following day, Macmillan send the name "Tibbits," but no further information on the correspondence appears.

---

7 Lushington Road, Eastbourne

August 29, 1887

Mr. Dodgson wishes to send copies of some of his books to the children who acted in the *Alice* drama. He has a list of addresses, but, as they were obtained some time ago, he wishes to ascertain if they are still correct. He will therefore thank Messrs. Macmillan to send, to each of the following list, a copy of the following letter, and a stamped envelope, for the reply, addressed to Messrs. Macmillan. After a week has elapsed, he wishes to have the replies.

The letter should run thus:

"Messrs. Macmillan request to know, on behalf of Mr. Lewis Carroll, whether the address of this letter is correct, or, if not, what the correct address now is. A stamped envelope is enclosed for the reply."[1]

---

[1] Enclosed in Dodgson's letter is a list of thirty-five names and addresses of the little actors and actresses. Macmillan have duly printed the circular letter that Dodgson asked for, but by omitting the crucial word *letter*, garble Dodgson's first sentence. One recipient returns the circular (it is now part of the Macmillan file) on which she inserts an asterisk after the word *this* and writes at the bottom: "Query: What this?" On September 11, Dodgson writes from Eastbourne to say: "I hope to call in on Friday, to inscribe books for you to send to the children whose addresses you have been getting for me . . . ," and indeed on Friday, the 16th, he records (*Diaries*, p. 455): "To Macmillan's and inscribed 41 books to go to children who had acted in *Alice*."

7 Lushington Road, Eastbourne
October 7, 1887
(address will be, till Tuesday evening, "Chestnuts,
Guildford" – after that "Christ Church, Oxford.")
Dear Mr. Macmillan,
Don't you think we ought to have something on the title-page of the cheap
editions, to mark the distinction? I thought of placing, at the top,
[CHEAP EDITION].[1]
Thanks for information about copies of *Bumblebee* sent to America.[2] As to the
advertisement in the *Publishers' Circular*, I would prefer the picture of 2 children
wading.[3] I think the *pictures* are the best, possibly the only, chance, of a further
sale: for I have a *very* moderate opinion of the merits of the verses. However the
reviews, Mr. Synge tells me, are of another opinion, and "have vied with one
another in laudation"![4] They don't seem to have much affected the sale: but, if
you think it would be worth while to append to any of the advertisements
extracts from these laudatory notices, and will apply to Mr. Synge, I have no
doubt he will supply you with copies of the best of them. I have not read any of
them myself, having come to the conclusion that newspaper-notices of books are
entirely worthless.

By the way, I hope you did not misunderstand what I said (October 3) about
numbers of my books *on hand*. I did not mean to charge *you* with imprudence, but
to say that I thought it would be imprudent in *me* to keep so far ahead of the sale.
Not only is there the outlay caused by paying for printing, a year before profits
come in: but there is the danger of loss by *fire* of (say) £500 worth of property –
for which (as you rightly point out) *you* would have no liability: so the loss would
fall on me. I think we need not print any more *Alice* or *Looking-Glass* till after June
1888.

How many *cheap* books do you propose to print?[5]
Very truly yours,

C. L. Dodgson

---

[1] Two days later, Macmillan & Co. agree that the inexpensive *Alice* books should have some
indication on the title page that they differ from the 6s. editions, but they resist using the word
"cheap" as "not a nice word to see on a book." Instead they suggest that perhaps "people's
edition" would be "pleasanter." These editions consequently become the "People's Edition"
(see *Handbook*, pp. 154–5; Selwyn H. Goodacre, "Lewis Carroll's 1887 Corrections to *Alice*," *Library*,
5th Ser. xxviii (June 1973), 131–46; and Peter Heath, review of the *Alice* illustrated by Barry Moser
(1982), *Analytical & Enumerative Bibliography*, 8 (1984), 204–11).
[2] In a letter of August 23 of this year, Dodgson resisted sending *Bumblebee Bogo's Budget* to America at
a loss, but then Macmillan reported (October 4) that they had arranged to sell the book in
America at 10 percent less than the trade price, and to compensate Dodgson were not charging
their own 10 percent commission on the American sales. They explained: "The result is therefore
exactly the same to you: we having given up our 10 percent commission to our American agent."
[3] Three days before Dodgson writes this letter, Macmillan asked his advice about which picture

from the Synge book they should use for advertising in the Christmas number of the *Publishers'*
Circular.
4   *Bumblebee Bogo's Budget* by A Retired Judge, with eleven illustrations by Alice Havers, was not
widely reviewed. The notice that appeared in the *Athenaeum* (August 16, 1887, p. 180) was
approving but cautious: "The Retired Judge who writes . . . [it] has a fine turn for nonsense. Now
nursery nonsense, when it is traditional, has a charm about it, but we never know whether new
nonsense is going to live." Dodgson's reservations were obviously shared by Macmillan and would
be supported by any reasoned assessment of the book today. Dodgson was probably responsible for
the illustrations. He first saw and admired the work of Alice Mary Havers (1850–90), who was
married to the artist Frederick Morgan (1856–1927), in 1883 and wrote to her about her "lovely
illustrations." On December 30, 1885, he called on her to make her acquaintance, and again on
June 5, 1886, he called on her in London "for a talk about the pictures for Mr. Synge's Poems"
(*Diaries*, pp. 416, 440, 442). She also drew one illustration for *Sylvie and Bruno*. For more about
Dodgson and the artist, see *Letters*, esp. p. 711.
5   Two days after Dodgson writes, Macmillan & Co. remind him that all estimates were for editions
of 10,000 copies as "the books could not be produced so cheaply in small quantities."

The Chestnuts, Guildford
October 10, 1887

Dear Mr. Macmillan,

I have two ideas to submit to you for consideration in connection with the
cheap editions of the two *Alice*s.

One is that it may be worth while to bring out, besides the two books in
separate covers, the two bound together in one cover. For this purpose, I would
omit the *Easter Greeting*, etc., at the end of the *Wonderland* part, and let the last
page of the text be immediately followed by the "false title" of the *Looking-Glass*.
Also I would put *both* pictures on the cover, which would make it a specially
attractive book. And lastly, I would put it at *less* than the 5s. which the two
would cost separately. Perhaps 4s. 6d. would be low enough to tempt purchasers:
but I am much inclined to believe that 4s. would be far more likely to "pay," as
many people, who wished to buy *one* of the two books, would be induced to buy
both when they found it would be only another 1s. 6d.

Another idea is that it would be well to ascertain *at once* from the booksellers
how many they would be likely to order, in order to print more than the 10,000
of each, if that should seem desirable. For this purpose it might be well to bind up
a lot of dummies (containing one sheet of text, and the rest blank paper) and
send one to each of the booksellers with whom you usually deal. It would not,
surely, cost more than a trifle to bind up a number (even if it came to hundreds)
of these. That would be a great saving of time, over the plan of sending round
two or three by your agents: and another advantage of each bookseller having
·   one to *keep* would be that he could show it to his customers, and thus get orders, in
anticipation, from *them*.[1]

Surely, they ought to have the cheap *Looking-Glass* in hand by this time, and
not wait to finish off the other? It will take some time to get it properly arranged.

Very truly yours,
C. L. Dodgson

P.S. I suppose the real question to ask, if we had to choose between 4*s.* and 4*s.* 6*d.* as price for double book, would be "is it likely that taking off 6*d.* from the price would increase the sale in the ratio of 8 to 9? Such a question *you* perhaps can answer: it is quite beyond *me.*

---

¹ Two days later, Macmillan & Co. reject this idea as too expensive and add: ". . . as the books are well known in their present form anything beyond an intimation that they are to be published for half-a-crown each is unnecessary." They suggest instead that as soon as a publication date is firmly fixed, but not before, they send out postcards to "some of our principal customers (say 1000 or 1500 of them)," as "booksellers will not order books to be delivered at some indefinite time." ² Macmillan urge (same letter) that the price of the two books in one volume should be no less than 4*s.* 6*d.* and add that they do not think reducing the price to 4*s.* would help the sale.

Christ Church, Oxford
November 2, 1887

Dear Mr. Macmillan,
　If you have not yet worked off the title-sheet of the new edition of *Rhyme? and Reason?* please let me know, as I would like to insert a preface.¹
Very truly yours,
C. L. Dodgson

Macmillan & Co. reply the next day that the title sheet of the new edition of *Rhyme? and Reason?* is not worked off yet and Dodgson may therefore insert a preface. "Preface to the Fourth Thousand" is dated December 1887 and simply states which poems have appeared earlier in print and where and indicates that the illustrations for the *Snark* appeared in the original 1876 volume of that poem, the others in the first edition of *Rhyme? and Reason?.*

Christ Church, Oxford
November 6, 1887

Dear Mr. Macmillan,
　(1) I don't like the look of the Easter Letter facing the last page of the cheap *Alice.* I would prefer that the blank leaf (which at present comes at the end of all) should come between the text and the Easter Letter. Can it be so arranged now? Even if those sheets have been electrotyped, I suppose the electro-plates can be cut up and re-arranged. I am writing to the same effect to Messrs. Clay, in hopes of preventing the electros from being done wrong.
　(2) This would make the *combined* volume contain a blank leaf between *Alice* and *Looking-Glass,* which would be a good arrangement.
　(3) What do you propose to put at *back* of cover of combined volume? (I think we settled that the two sides should have the two pictures.)
　(4) Would it not be well, as soon as some cheap *Alices* are ready, to send

specimens round to the booksellers, to get orders, that we may have some idea
what the demand will be, without waiting till the other volume is ready?
Yours very truly,
C. L. Dodgson

P.S. I doubt if the combined volume would look well with the two titles running
up the back, side by side. How do you think it would look in some such style as
the sketch enclosed?[1]

---

[1] Missing.

Christ Church, Oxford
December 4, 1887
Dear Mr. Macmillan,
The cover for the double volume of *Alice* will do very well, except that the title
at the back should be all in *black*, instead of being part black and part red. As it is
the word "Wonderland" is lost, the red being nearly invisible at a short distance
Please put title, along back of each of the *single* volumes, all in black also.[1] If they
are already printed, never mind.
The cover for *Bumblebee* will do very well.
Before settling its price, I should be much obliged if you will give me a rough
estimate of
(1) the total cost of production of 1000 copies (remembering that the book will
be only 64 pages).
(2) the sum you propose to spend in advertising.
(3) the sum you would have to pay to me, if you sold the 1000.
Then I shall be able to judge what I am likely to clear per 1000 sold.[2]
Thanks for what you tell me about the booksellers and my terms of sale.[3] I will
write more about this hereafter.
Yours very truly,
C. L. Dodgso

---

[1] "Passed, for electrotyping, the last sheets of the People's Edition of *Alice*," Dodgson wrote in his
Diaries on November 3, and on December 10, he noted (*Diaries*, p. 456) that on December 6 he
received "a complete copy of the People's Edition. . . ." On December 16, he writes (ibid.
"Passed, for 'Press,' the title-page of the double volume of People's Editions of *Alice* and *Looking-
Glass*. That ends *my* part of the work." On the same day he writes to Macmillan: "I have received
this title-page from Messrs. Clay, but think I had better return it to *you*, as I don't understand what
directions to give him. I leave the matter in your hands. . . . I have marked it 'Press,' thinking
not worth while to electrotype it, as probably only a few copies of the double volume will be called
for. . . . If you think it better to electrotype this title-page, do so. . . . Please take care that,
binding the two books together, the Easter Letter and Xmas Verse are *not* put at the end of *Alice*
but only at the end of the *Looking-Glass*." On January 11 Dodgson writes in his Diaries: "Yesterda

I received complete copies of the People's Edition of *Looking-Glass* and of the double volume." For more on these three People's Editions, see *Handbook*, pp. 154–5, 247–8.

2 On October 7 Macmillan wrote to say that a new edition of *Bumblebee* was needed, and on October 11 Dodgson inquired what they thought of trying a cheap edition, to sell at 2*s.* 6*d.* On October 12 Macmillan replied that it would be impossible to produce an edition of 250 at that price. "The way to make the printing cheaper is to work off a number of copies – say 2000 – but there is little good in doing that unless we can sell them. We think very little of the verses and as we told you when we agreed to publish them we should not have undertaken to bring them out except to oblige you. It seems to us that the best plan will be to print another 250 from the standing type and keep the book at the present price. But of course we will do anything that you wish." Dodgson evidently rejected Macmillan's advice in a missing letter, and on October 25, Macmillan wrote: "We find that by closing up the type of *Bumblebee Bogo's Budget* so that the book will make 6 sheets instead of 10½, an Edition of 1000 copies can be produced for £45.15.0. This of course could be sold profitably for 2*s.* 6*d.*" Two days after Dodgson writes the present letter, Macmillan reply enclosing an "Estimate of the result of selling the 1000 copies now being printed of *Bumblebee* – supposing the price to be 2*s.* 6*d.* retail," but the enclosure is not in our files.

3 On November 29, Macmillan & Co. wrote: "We are subscribing the cheap Edition of *Alice's Adventures* and regret to find that owing to the terms on which it is published the booksellers are not very much inclined to help us. For instance one large retail bookseller in the City says that he loses by selling your books simply because his assistants do not remember about the peculiar terms and continually sell the six shilling edition for 4*s.* 6*d.*, that being the regular price for books published at six shillings. This same man says that if the cheap Edition of *Alice* is issued at the regular trade rates so that he may retail it at 1*s.* 11*d.*, he will at once order 2000 copies; but as it is he will only take 50 and will not trouble himself to put the book on his counter or to push its sale in any way. We think it right to tell you this in order that you may see that the sale of your books is in some degree influenced by the terms." Although our files contain no reply from Dodgson to this tale of woe, a letter from Macmillan dated December 12 indicates that Dodgson again suggests publishing a pamphlet with a statement of his views on bookselling and the reasons for the terms he insists upon. Macmillan agree to publish the pamphlet but again advise against it: "We do not think you will make many converts, as it is to the bookseller not merely a question of profit, but of the inconvenience and loss of time involved in selling one author's books on different terms from all the rest." Dodgson apparently abandons the idea of the pamphlet.

Christ Church, Oxford
January 15, 1888

Dear Mr. Macmillan,

I am very much obliged to you for anticipating the usual time for settling our account. The sale of People's Edition seems to *me* eminently satisfactory: is it more, or less, than you had anticipated?[1]

Next time you are writing, I would be glad to know how many of the People's Edition of *Bumblebee* have sold.[2]

Allow me to point out a serious omission in your Book of *Scottish Song*. It provides no means for finding a song of which the *title* only is known. The unfortunate reader, who does not happen to remember the first line (as was *my* case the other day, when wishing to find "Auld Robin Gray"), has no choice but to turn over the book, page by page, till he comes to the song he wants. An alphabetical index to titles of songs would make the book complete.[3]

Very truly yours,
C. L. Dodgson

1 Macmillan's letter and the account are missing, and no reply to this question appears until April.
2 On February 2, Macmillan & Co. report sales of about 500 copies of the cheap edition of _Bumblebee Bogo's Budget._
3 For _Scottish Song_, see pp. 204–5, above. No reply from Macmillan to Dodgson's suggestion is in our files.

Christ Church, Oxford
March 19, 1888

Dear Mr. Macmillan,

I have been making an extraordinary blunder all this time, in that "caution" at the end of the "List of Works," by confusing together two foreign correspondents and ascribing the paper in _Aunt Judy's Magazine_ to the wrong one! There seems to be a fate against that unfortunate story being ascribed to its _real_ author.[1]

Please have the enclosed correction made at once in the standing type of the "List of Works": and, with regard to the unsold copies in which the mistake stands, I would like an "erratum" slip printed, and inserted in each copy. It will cost me something, no doubt, the time and labour needed for putting it into thousands of books: but I feel that I _ought_ to have it done, in justice to the two ladies whose names I have so unfortunately confused together.[2]

Yours very truly,

C. L. Dodgson

1 Dodgson's corrected "Caution to Readers" explains: "On August 1st, 1881, a story appeared in _Aunt Judy's Magazine_, No. 184, entitled 'The Land of Idleness, by Lewis Carroll.' The story was really written by a lady, Miss Cato Schaap, of 40, West Zeedijk, Rotterdam. Acting on her behalf Mr. Carroll forwarded it to the Editor: and this led to the mistake of naming him as its author.' Dodgson, if he is not pulling our leg, has been publishing the wrong name in the "Caution," attributing the story to 'Fräulein Ida Lackowitz, of 14 Lottumstrasse, Berlin." And to add further confusion to the mystery, in later "Caution"'s, he reverts to Fräulein Lackowitz. On May 18, 1894 Dodgson writes Macmillan: "Thanks for calling my attention to the 'Caution to Readers' in the 'List of Works.' It has appeared quite long enough, I think, and may now be withdrawn." An essay on the problem takes us round the mulberry bush reciting all the pertinent questions: did the two foreign ladies even exist? did either of them write the story? is the story in fact by Dodgson himself? are the two foreign names inventions, even anagrams? But, alas, answers are there none (see Selwyn Goodacre and Jeffrey Stern, "The Land of Idleness – An Enquiry," _Jabberwocky_ 1 (Winter 1983/4), 18–20). Now let us consider: Goodacre and Stern – a comedy team? an anagram?
2 On the following day, Macmillan & Co. write: "We will have the type of the 'Caution' put right and will print an Erratum slip to be inserted in all the unsold copies of your books."

Christ Church, Oxford
April 4, 1888

Dear Mr. Macmillan,

I want you to publish a new book for me, to match _Euclid and His Modern Rivals._[1] I want to bring it out in parts, as fast as completed, in paper covers like the "Henrici" *Supplement* to *Euclid*,[2] etc. May I assume that you will be willing to do it, on the same terms as the *Euclid*, etc.?

I would get it printed at the University Press, where the *Euclid*, etc., was done. I observe that you have ceased to advertise the cheap *Alice*. No doubt you are wise in doing so, but I would like to know whether the reason is that the sale is so small that you think advertising would exhaust the profits, or so large that you think advertising no longer necessary.[3]

Very truly yours,

C. L. Dodgson

[1] *Curiosa Mathematica, Part I*, which would be published in August. Macmillan & Co. reply on April 6 that they would be "very pleased" to publish Dodgson's new book on the same terms as his *Euclid*.

[2] Dodgson refers to his *Supplement to Euclid and His Modern Rivals containing A Notice of Henrici's Geometry*, in which he takes to task yet another modern rival of Euclid: Olaus Henrici's *Elementary Geometry* (1879). Macmillan published Dodgson's 55-page booklet in April 1885 (see *Handbook*, pp. 132–3).

[3] In their letter of April 6, Macmillan explain that they have not advertised the cheap *Alice* much since Christmas not because of any problem with sales but simply because it did not seem prudent to spend money on advertising at this time of year. They promise to "take care to keep the books forward when the occasion comes" and add: "We think the sales have been very satisfactory. We have disposed of 6000 *Alice*, 3500 *Looking-Glass*, and 1200 of the double volume."

Christ Church, Oxford
April 25, 1888

Dear Mr. Macmillan,

There certainly ought to be a list of my mathematical works, on a fly-leaf, at the end of each of them. I do not see any in the copies I have by me of *Euclid and His Modern Rivals*, or *Euclid I, II*, but I fancy such a fly-leaf *has* been printed. Have you got one? And if not, shall we print one at the Press here?[1]

It ought to be done in 2 sizes – one for *Euclid and Rivals*, the other for *Euclid I, II*.[2]

Have you any copies, of either, not yet in boards? The fly-leaf might be bound in with *them*: and, as to those already in boards, I would like to have copies of it inserted, loose.

I shall want you to put the new book into boards, with grey cloth, like *Euclid I, II*.

I will send you a title-page as soon as I can, for your opinion as to how it *looks*. An artistic title-page is, I think, a very important feature in a book.

Very truly yours,

C. L. Dodgson

[1] Frederick Macmillan replies the same day: "There ought certainly to be a list in each of your mathematical books though we cannot find that one has ever been printed. If you will kindly instruct the Clarendon Press people to print one off and let us have 215 copies we will insert it in the

books now in stock." On May 30, Dodgson reports in a third-person letter to Macmillan that he "has given order for the 215 copies of the 'List of Mathematical Works' to be sent to Messrs. Macmillan, to be inserted in the copies still on hand."

2 "The same list will do for both books if there is an ample margin round the type as we can cut it down for the smaller volume," Macmillan write (same letter).

Christ Church, Oxford

May 23, 1888

Dear Mr. Macmillan,

I had no such idea in my mind as that *you* should publish my cousin's little story, and wonder what words of mine could have been interpreted to mean "with the view of our accepting another by the same hand." I must have expressed myself very badly. What I *do* mean is, would you look at the little printed book, and then, with your large experience of books and men, say whether you think there is *any* quarter where the MS might have a chance of acceptance: or even if the story would have a *reasonable* chance of paying for the cost of printing – in which case, as I said (or at least *meant* to say!) I should probably publish it at my own cost.[1]

Yours very truly,

C. L. Dodgson

[1] Although Dodgson's original request is missing, this letter and Macmillan's letter of the previous day make clear that Dodgson asked Macmillan to give an opinion of the merits of a story written by a cousin. On May 22, Macmillan wrote: "In answer to your letter we write to say that we think it would not be worth your while to send us the story you speak of with the view of our accepting another of the same hand. For some years past we have practically given up the publication of books for children with the exception of those by yourself, Mrs. Molesworth and one or two others who are old clients and whose reputation is established; and it does not seem to us probable that we should be tempted to make a further venture in the line of juvenile literature by a story which has been found unsuitable by the S.P.C.K. and several other publishers." In reply to Dodgson's present letter, Macmillan & Co. write (the following day): "If you will send the MS of the story you speak of we will read it and let you know whether we can suggest anything as to its disposal. It will be very little more trouble to read the MS than the printed book and it seems to us that it will be more useful for us to read the story for which a publisher is wanted than the one which has already appeared." After reading the manuscript, Macmillan send it to Dodgson's cousin, the author, and on May 30, Dodgson pens a third-person barrage: "Mr. Dodgson writes to say that Messrs. Macmillan made a great mistake in sending the MS to the lady, instead of returning it to him. He had given no such direction, but had merely sent it for Mr. Macmillan's opinion and advice: he will be glad to be informed whether they can suggest any one at all likely to publish such a thing, in order that he may decide what step to take next." Two days later, Macmillan & Co. reply: "We should not have sent it back without first communicating with you if we had realised that this was the manuscript about which you had written to us, but you had not in either of your letters mentioned the name of either the story or its author and there was nothing on the manuscript so far as we saw to connect it with you. We must apologise for the mistake. It is difficult to give any advice" the letter continues, "as to the best course to pursue. In our opinion it would not if published have much chance of repaying the expenses of publication, but of course we may be wrong, and some other publisher more in the way of bringing out books for children might think

differently. We should think that it might be offered either to Messrs. Griffith & Faran of St. Paul's Church Yard, or Messrs. Hatchard of Piccadilly." On April 8, 1889, Dodgson records in his Diaries: "Heard from Messrs. Wells Gardner, Darton, & Co. that they are willing to publish . . . *Evie* in their shilling series." Dodgson's cousin Elizabeth Georgina Wilcox (1848–1934), who married (1891) Charles Francis Egerton Allen (1847–1921), is the author of *Evie; or, The Visit to Orchard Farm*, published by the firm Dodgson mentions in 1889. Dodgson acted as literary advisor to "Georgie," and the last of his own writings to appear in print in his lifetime is an introduction to her story *The Lost Plum-Cake*, which indeed Macmillan publish in 1898.

Christ Church, Oxford
June 16, 1888

Dear Mr. Macmillan,

The new book is to range with *Euclid and His Modern Rivals*. It will have (counting Preface) about 80 pages. I should like a *grey* cover like *Euclid I, II*. I enclose title-page, frontispiece, and idea for cover. If you approve, would you have the diagram cut?

Shall we print 250?

Very truly yours,
C. L. Dodgson

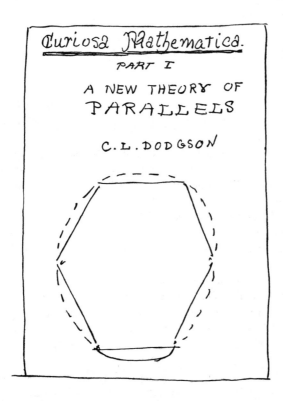

Christ Church, Oxford
July 6, 1888
Dear Mr. Macmillan,

I have now passed the whole of this book for "Press", and have told them to print 250 copies, on toned paper, and to send you 100. If you wish to modify that order, please write to University Press.

As soon as you have got some copies bound, please send one to the Editor of the *St. James's*.[1] He begged me to send him "an early copy." Also please send me a dozen.

I would like to see a list of the periodicals to which you propose to send copies.[2]

Many thanks for the very efficient way in which the tickets were procured for the 3 theatres.[3] They are all excellent seats.

Very truly yours,
C. L. Dodgson

[1] Frederick Greenwood.
[2] On August 3, Macmillan & Co. send Dodgson a list of fifteen papers to which they propose to send *Curiosa Mathematica, Part I*, and they invite Dodgson to add to or subtract from the list.
[3] On June 28 Dodgson telegraphed Macmillan for the theater tickets. On July 2, he saw the matinée performance of *Bootle's Baby*, an adaptation of John Strange Winter's story by Hugh Moss, at the Globe, and was disappointed in Minnie Terry, Ellen Terry's niece, as an actress. Macmillan had sent tickets for that same evening, but Dodgson fails to record the name of the play or what he thought of the performance. On July 3, he saw Alfred C. Calmour's *Amber Heart* at the Lyceum: "a pretty and poetical piece: but I couldn't realise any pathos in it, even with Ellen Terry's exquisite delivery of the lines . . ." (*Diaries*, p. 460).

Christ Church, Oxford
October 14, 1888
Dear Mr. Macmillan,

Will you kindly inform Mr. A. Silver, of 84 Brook Green, that Mr. Lewis Carroll has no objection to his using Tenniel's pictures for the wall-paper which he proposes to design. Please add the suggestion that the *longer* the paper can be made, before the pattern repeats itself, the better: the thing has been already tried once, but the pattern repeated itself in about 2 yards of length, so that, even in a small room, the same picture would recur many times, with a very tedious effect. Twenty yards of length, before the pattern recurs, would be none too long.

Will you send me 6 copies of *New Theory of Parallels*?[1]

I hear, from the University Press, that you want 250 more of *Euclid I, II*. So I have sent them a list of corrections, and have told them that I want my "List of Mathematical Works" to be placed at the end of the new edition.

Yours very truly,
C. L. Dodgson

¹ The sub-title of Dodgson's latest book, *Curiosa Mathematica, Part I*, is "A New Theory of Parallels." The preface is signed July 1888, and Dodgson must have received his first published copy in August. It is, as the *Handbook* describes (p. 158), "a scientific attempt to improve Euclid's 12th Axiom about two lines unequally inclined to a transversal, compared with his 35th Definition (of Parallel Lines) and certain Propositions."

Christ Church, Oxford
December 3, 1888

Dear Mr. Macmillan,

I sent a specimen stamp-case to Messrs. De La Rue, at your suggestion.¹ They are not willing to take it up for themselves, nor to make them at my cost: but are willing to *sell* them, if I can get them made.

Then I sent it to Mr. Neville (who published Macklin's *Folding Chess-Board*, which is something in the same style), to see if he would take it up, or else make it for me. I sent it on November 20, signing "Lewis Carroll," and giving "29 Bedford Street" as address. No answer came. I wrote again, November 27, enclosing a blank postcard for reply. No answer has yet reached me. Will you kindly (unless you have just sent, or are just sending, his reply) send a messenger to the place, to get some kind of reply? Possibly Mr. Neville is away, and my letter of November 20 is yet unopened (it is done with a "type-writer,"² not in MS). Please do not mention my real name, but ask what reply he has to make to Mr. Carroll's application.

The address is

> Mr. H. Neville,
> 7 Queen Victoria Street.

In case this application fails, can you tell me of any working stationer, or some such man, who would make the cases for me, at so much a thousand?³ I want them made of stiff paper, and there would be some sewing needed (which might be done with a sewing-machine). I would ask Mr. Edmund Evans to print coloured covers, to be pasted on them. I am thinking of utilising some of the *Alice* pictures for the purpose.

Yours very truly,

C. L. Dodgson

¹ This is the first reference to *The "Wonderland" Postage Stamp-Case*. Dodgson recorded that he invented it on October 29, 1888, and immediately thought about getting it published (*Diaries*, p. 465). In a letter dated November 13, Macmillan suggested that he apply to Messrs. De la Rue "who are large wholesale stationers and moreover hold the contract for printing postage stamps." The stamp case is not, however, published until 1890, when Dodgson issues it with a small pamphlet, *Eight or Nine Wise Words about Letter-Writing*. A photograph of the stamp case appears in *Diaries*, p. 519; *Eight or Nine Wise Words* appears in *Letters*, pp. 1157–68. For more on the stamp case and the pamphlet, see *Handbook*, pp. 170–3.

² Dodgson acquired his first typewriter on May 4 of this year. For more on Dodgson and the typewriter, see *Diaries*, p. 459; *Letters*, p. 706.

³ On December 16 Macmillan report that Neville had left Victoria Street seven years before and "as his name is not in the Directory, and he left no address behind him, we cannot trace him."

Christ Church, Oxford

December 20, 1888

Dear Mr. Macmillan,

Please get me 3 couples of *front* seats, dress-circle, for matinées of *Alice* at the Globe – for 3 different days, not later than January 15, and as far apart from each other as can conveniently be arranged. The best part of the circle is the left-hand end, as you face the stage: and next to that the other end.

Also a couple of stalls, 2nd or 3rd row near middle, for a matinée of *Little Lord Fauntleroy* at the Opéra Comique – for some other day. Keep the 4 days as far apart as you can.

Don't give my *name*, in any case. If they want some name, to book the tickets, give the name "Mortimer."

Please send the tickets, any day after this week, addressed to me at "the Chestnuts, Guildford." Don't get any for December 31 or January 1. I should prefer their all being for next year.¹

Yours very truly,

C. L. Dodgson

¹ The first revival of Savile Clarke's *Alice* opens at the Globe Theatre on December 26, with Dodgson's child friend Isa Bowman in the title role. Dodgson sees the revival on January 3, 7 and 15, and is pleased with the production (*Diaries*, pp. 467–8; *Letters*, p. 723). He sees *Little Lord Fauntleroy* on the 10th: "not so good a cast as last time" (*Diaries*, p. 468).

Christ Church, Oxford

February 1, 1889

Dear Mr. Macmillan,

Will you kindly write to Mr. C. T. J. Hiatt ("Sandon, Wellington, Salop") that Mr. L. Carroll *did* once take (in 1863) a fairly good photograph of Mr. D. G. Rossetti, but regrets that he has no copy of it that he can lend him.¹ It is possible that Mr. W. M. Rossetti (of 5 Endsleigh Gardens, Euston Square), or Miss Rossetti (of 30 Torrington Square, Bloomsbury), may possess a copy of it, and may be willing to lend it.

Will you also let me know how many copies you have on hand of *The Hunting of the Snark* by itself, and in what bindings. (I fancy we have used *3* kinds, one large designs, in gold, on red cloth; another, the same designs, in black, on white cloth; a third, small medallions, in gold, on red cloth).[2]

Also I want to know how many copies you would advise to print of *The Nursery "Alice."*

Very truly yours,

C. L. Dodgson

[1] Although Dodgson stopped photographing in 1880, his fame as an art photographer was already established. He became acquainted with the Rossetti family in 1863 and photographed them several times at their home (*Diaries*, pp. 201–5). Dante Gabriel Rossetti's obituary in the *Graphic* (April 29, 1882, p. 416) is accompanied by a print "from a photograph by Lewis Carroll." A Dodgson photograph of the poet also appears in William Michael Rossetti's "Portraits of Rossetti," a series of three articles that the *Magazine of Art* published in 1888 and 1889 (see the December 1888 issue, pp. 59–61), where W. M. Rossetti writes: "'Lewis Carroll' is (or at any rate then was) a very skilful amateur photographer, and in 1863 he took an amicable pleasure in levelling his camera time after time upon the painter's form" and then describes each of Dodgson's photographs of his brother. When W. M. Rossetti's memoir of his brother was published in October 1889, it bore a 'Lewis Carroll' photograph of the poet-artist as a frontispiece. For more on Dodgson and the Rossettis, see *Letters*, esp. pp. 61–2. Mr. Hiatt remains unidentified.

[2] On February 16, Macmillan apologize for having neglected to answer Dodgson's question about the *Snark* and enclose a statement (missing) of the stock on hand.

Christ Church, Oxford
February 17, 1889

Dear Mr. George Macmillan,

Thanks for information about *Hunting of Snark*. I have a dozen or more copies on hand, that I can send you if necessary. I wish the book to be replaced on the "List of Works," and enclose MS, to be inserted, next time you print more "Lists." When the copies on hand are sold, I should like a few more to be printed (I think I would like more lines in a page, next time), as those large designs for the cover are too good to be wasted.

I have asked several times, but all in vain as yet, for your estimate for *current* cost (excluding *all* initial outlay), per 1000, of *The Nursery "Alice"* (which will have 64 pages). All I want, from *you*, is an estimate for *paper*, and *binding*: the rest I can ascertain from Mr. Evans. Also I want to settle how many to print, and what price to put on it? Can't you give any opinion on these matters without seeing a complete copy? *That*, I fancy, would be a very inconvenient thing for Mr. Evans to produce, before the *number* is settled: as he would have to get *all* the colour-blocks into work, before even working off a single sheet. I enclose 24 pages, in hopes that will enable you to form a sufficient idea of the book. If you can't *imagine* the pictures coloured, I daresay Mr. Evans can supply you with a few of the coloured prints.

As to the *number* to print, I offer no suggestion. *You* (I mean the *firm*, of course, not you the individual!) will be the best judges on *that* point.

As to *price*, my own idea is 2*s.*, if that would give a fairly good profit on *current* expenses. The *initial* outlay I am content to reckon as *loss*, to begin with: a loss to be gradually recovered, if the sale lasts long enough.[1] Believe me

Very truly yours,

C. L. Dodgson

[1] Macmillan & Co. write on February 19 and explain that they have been delayed in answering Dodgson's questions by their search for paper suitable for color printing, but they expect to be able to give the estimate in a day or two. They send it on the 21st. For a printing of 20,000 copies, the publishers estimate that paper, printing, and binding could be done "for something under 1*s.* 3*d.* a copy." Macmillan suggest a retail price of 3*s.*, reminding Dodgson that the customary price for colored books for children is 5*s.* or 6*s.*

Christ Church, Oxford
February 22, 1889

Dear Mr. George Macmillan,

I have received from you an estimate of the cost of printing 20,000 *Nursery "Alice"*: and, though I did not ask for it, and it is not of much use to me, I am much obliged for it.

What I *have* asked for, and would be really glad to have, so soon as you can manage it, is information on following points:

(1) What would be cost of producing 1000, excluding all *initial* expenses, i.e. for instance, suppose 20,000 had been prepared and sold: what would be cost of printing a single thousand more? (I only want *your* part of the cost. Mr. Evans' share I can ascertain from *him*.)

(2) What would be a good price to put on it? Would 2*s.* be too much? Would 2*s.* 6*d.* be likely to hinder the sale?

(3) How many do you advise to print?

Perhaps you will say that sending estimate for 20,000 is a virtual answer to (3). But do you *really* advise so large a number? How long do you expect it would take to sell them?

(By the way, your estimate of £1223 for 20,000 is quite incomplete, since it takes no account of (a) colouring pictures (b) cutting wood-blocks – these items would add about 3½*d.* a copy, raising it to 1*s.* 6¼*d.* a copy).[1]

Very truly yours,

C. L. Dodgson

[1] "We gave you an estimate for printing 20,000 copies of *The Nursery 'Alice'* because there is a considerable saving in printing a good large Edition and it seems to us that there would be a very good chance of disposing of that number of copies," Macmillan & Co. write four days later. "In

accordance with your request we now send estimates for Reprints of 1000 and 5000 copies" (missing). "We have nothing to add to what we said in our last letter as to the price," the letter continues. "We think it should be 3s. charged at 2s. 6d. to the trade (we presume that you wish the book offered on your usual terms, otherwise of course the retail price will be 3s. 6d.)." Finally: "We quite understand that our Estimate did not include the cost of colouring the pictures or engraving the woodblocks. . . ."

Christ Church, Oxford
February 27, 1889

Dear Mr. Macmillan,

Thanks for letter dated February 26.

It looks as if some former letter of yours had gone astray, as you say "we have nothing to add to what we said in our last letter as to the price," whereas no letter, that has reached me, has named *any* price: the last said "we will write about the price." Again you say "the former estimate was for paper printing and binding only," whereas the only one I have received contains the words "including the cost of composition and electrotyping."[1]

The number 20,000 is larger than I dare risk. I am not very hopeful about the sale, and think that 10,000 may very likely take more than a year, or even more than 2 years, to sell. So let us begin with 10,000. I have told Mr. Evans that that is the number.

I agree with you as to price, and am having 3s. printed, as price, on title-page. I wish the sale to be on our usual terms: i.e. you will credit me with 2s. 3d. for each copy sold.

I am just incurring a yet further cost, by getting Miss E. G. Thomson to design a picture-cover, which I expect will add much to the attractiveness of the book.[2] Believe me

Very truly yours,

C. L. Dodgson

The full title now is *The Nursery "Alice"*, containing coloured enlargements of twenty of the pictures drawn, for *Alice's Adventures in Wonderland*, by John Tenniel; with text adapted to Nursery readers, by Lewis Carroll; the cover designed by E. Gertrude Thomson.

---

[1] Dodgson seems to have forgotten Macmillan's letter of February 21, to which he replied on the following day. No letter from Macmillan with the phrase that Dodgson quotes, "including the cost of composition and electrotyping," is in our files. Macmillan replied to the present letter on the 28th sending a copy of their February 21 letter.

[2] Dodgson met the artist Emily Gertrude Thomson (1850–1928) in 1879, after admiring some Christmas cards she designed (*Diaries*, pp. 380–1). From then on she enters the *Diaries* frequently (see also *Letters*, esp. p. 321).

Christ Church, Oxford
March 24, 1889
Dear Mr. Macmillan,
Will you kindly write to Mr. S. Cheetham, of 8 Acresfield, Bolton, to say that
Mr. L. Carroll is not competent to give "permission to produce a representation
of *Alice in Wonderland*." He should apply to the author of the play (H. Savile
Clarke, Esq., Cleveland Lodge, Westbourne Park, London), without whose
permission a performance of the play, where a charge is made for admission,
would be illegal.

Thanks for further information about Tom Hood. No doubt you are right.
Would you kindly get me a copy of the sentence in the *Nineteenth Century*, on
which my letter was based? It occurred in an article entitled "Literature for the
Little Ones," in the October number, 1887.[1]

As to the number to be printed of the 2nd edition of *A New Theory of Parallels*,
you base your advice on the supposition that I mean to distribute the type. But I
have no such intention. Shall we print 250, and send you 100?[2]

Very truly yours,

C. L. Dodgson

---

[1] "Literature for Little Ones" (pp. 563–80) is a long critique of books available for children. When
the writer deals with Carroll's work, the first thing he does is accuse him of plagiarism: "Between
Tom Hood and Mr. Lewis Carroll – to call Mr. D. C. Lutwidge by his famous *nom de plume* – there is
more than a suspicion of resemblance in some particulars. *Alice's Adventures in Wonderland* narrowly
escapes challenging a comparison with *From Nowhere to the North Pole*. The idea of both is so similar
that Mr. Carroll can hardly have been surprised if some people have believed he was inspired by
Hood. . . . Though *Alice* . . . and . . . *Looking-Glass* are, of course, undeniably clever and possess
many charms exclusively their own, there is nothing extraordinarily original about either, and
certainly the former cannot fairly be called, as it once was, the most remarkable book for children
of recent times. Both . . . would be but half as attractive as they are without Mr. John Tenniel's
illustrations. . . . Mr. Carroll's style is as simple as his ideas are extravagant. This probably
accounts for the fascination which these stories of a child . . . have had over the minds of so many
thousands of children and parents." Dodgson wrote a letter to the Editor, which appeared in the
November number (p. 744): "Sir, – I find it stated, in an article . . . in your October number, that
my little book, *Alice's Adventures in Wonderland* . . . was probably suggested by the late Mr. T.
Hood's *From Nowhere to the North Pole*, first published in 1864. May I mention, first, that I have
never read Mr. Hood's book; secondly, that I composed mine in the summer of 1862, and wrote it
out, in the form lately published in facsimile, during 1863? Thus it will be seen that neither book
could have been suggested by the other. . . . As it is, in my view, and no doubt in that of many
others of your readers, an act of dishonesty to imitate another man's book without due
acknowledgement, I trust to your sense of justice to allow this reply to the charge brought against
me in the above-named article to appear in your forthcoming number." Dodgson must have
grown suspicious of the publication date of the Hood book as reported in the *Nineteenth Century*
article, and he must have asked Macmillan for more information. On March 26 of this year,
Macmillan reply: "We think there is no doubt as to the date of the publication of *From Nowhere to the
North Pole*. We had sent to the British Museum and find that the copy of the first Edition deposited
there is dated 1875. It was probably published before Xmas but dated in advance in accordance
with a common but bad habit followed by many publishers." Macmillan add that a review of the
Hood book that appeared in the *Athenaeum* for December 12, 1874, describes it as "a fantastic story
in the style of *Alice's Adventures*."

[2] In their reply of the 26th, Macmillan & Co. agree to the number Dodgson suggests.

Christ Church, Oxford
April 18, 1889

Dear Mr. Macmillan,

The 2 fresh proofs have come: the corrected copy was *not* enclosed with them: however I think I remember what the corrections were.

Would it not be well, in the copies sent round to booksellers, to put some marginal mark (such as a pointing hand) to call attention to the *forthcoming* book? I leave it to you to do as you think best.[1]

The *cover* for *The Nursery "Alice"* is not ready yet: but the whole *book* is passed for "Press." I have asked Mr. Evans to send you 2 sets of the sheets, as soon as they are dry: and I will be obliged if you will have them full-bound, one in brown morocco, the other in purple morocco, with gilt edges, and the title in gold, and some little ornamentation, which I leave to your taste.

If you get the tickets I have telegraphed about, please post them to me at "The Chestnuts, Guildford," where I shall be for a week.[2]

C. L. Dodgson

[1] Dodgson is reading proof of his "List of Works."
[2] On April 24 Dodgson attends a performance of *Richard III* in London (Diaries).

Christ Church, Oxford
April 28, 1889

Dear Mr. Macmillan,

You chose me excellent places at the Globe, except that they were a little too *central*. Next time I want tickets, I will ask you, if I think of it, to avoid the central 3 seats in the 1st row, and the central 4 in the 2nd. So long as theatres keep up the absurd practice of placing the conductor so that his head and shoulders come above the footlights, the occupants of these seats have their view intercepted by him.

Would it not be a good plan for you to have a telegraphic address? Some one word, to put before "London." As it is, in telegraphing to you, 7 words are needed for the address, leaving only 5 (in a 6*d.* telegram) for the message.

Very truly yours,

C. L. Dodgson

P.S. Would you kindly send copies of the enclosed to all the London Theatres? It will want about 40 copies, I think. Of course you will charge me for the time and trouble, as well as postage.[1]

---

[1] In the 1880s a strong movement had developed to prohibit the employment of young children. Dodgson kept a close watch on proposed legislation governing the employment of children in the theater, wrote letters to the press on the subject, and tried to influence public opinion generally. On July 19, 1887, his letter entitled "Children in Theatres" appeared in the *St. James's Gazette* protesting the idea that children under ten should be forbidden employment on the stage (see *Diaries*, pp. 452–3). In June 1888, in his article "The Stage and the Spirit of Reverence" that appeared in *Theatre* (N.S. xi, 285–94), he again defends the theater as an uplifting social force. In early April 1889, the House of Commons passed a bill prohibiting the employment of children under the age of ten, and in the four months before the bill reached the House of Lords, considerable agitation arose over the issue. On May 18, for instance, *The Times* reports a week of protests and demonstrations at the Home Office by both sides ("Employment of Children at Theatres," p. 13). The main opponents of the bill were theater managers who sought to have child actors excluded from the legislation. In the course of the controversy, John Coleman (1831–1904), actor, dramatist, theatrical entrepreneur, asked Dodgson for a copy of his 1887 letter on the subject that had appeared in the *St. James's Gazette*. "I sent it," Dodgson wrote in his *Diaries* (pp. 472–3) on August 4, "and a new one, which he has printed in today's *Sunday Times*, of which he has sent a copy to every member of the Lords!" Dodgson's "new" letter, entitled "Stage Children," was reprinted in the September number of *Theatre* (N.S. xiv, 113–17). Both letters defend acting as a profession for children, and in the latter Dodgson outlines a set of model regulations: ". . . I do not believe," he writes, "that the law can absolutely prohibit children under ten from acting in theatres without doing a cruel wrong to many a poor struggling family, to whom the child's stage salary is a Godsend, and making many poor children miserable by debarring them from a healthy and innocent occupation which they dearly love." Which of his theatrical publications he is here asking Macmillan to circulate is not clear. When the bill for the Protection of Children is debated in the House of Lords on August 5 of this year, a move to exclude children in theaters from the bill is defeated, but an amendment is accepted prohibiting employment in theaters only of children under the age of seven.

Christ Church, Oxford

May 31, 1889

Dear Mr. Macmillan,

I have two literary projects to submit to your leisurely consideration: there is no hurry for a decision in either case.

They are not books that need to be *written*: selecting and editing is all that is needed.

The first is a selection of passages of the Bible, 10 or 20 verses long, suitable *to learn by heart*, and store up in the memory to repeat to one's-self. Such a book would be invaluable to invalids who lie awake in the night, to old folk when the eyesight is failing, also as food for thought in railway-journeys, solitary walks, etc. It should be a *small* book (say 6 inches high by 4 wide), printed on white paper, in large legible type, and if possible so arranged that the whole of the selected passage should be visible at one opening of the book.[1]

The other is a book for children: a selection of readings from the Bible, each to take about (say) 15 minutes leisurely reading. Each chapter should if possible have a *picture*. These would not need to be drawn afresh: there are hundreds of good ones in existence, not copyright, which would only need copying. The book should be squarish in shape, for the sake of the pictures, and a handy size: perhaps 6 inches high by 5 wide.

I would undertake the editing, in each case, conscious as I am that there are many who would do it better, if they had time and inclination: but it is better I should do it than leave it undone.

I believe the first would sell fairly well. The sale of the second I feel tolerably sure would be *enormous*.

Very truly yours,

C. L. Dodgson

---

[1] Dodgson has in mind "such passages as would do to say over to one's self, in sleepless nights, etc." (*Diaries*, p. 468). "We shall be happy to publish the two volumes of Selections from the Bible which you propose on the usual terms," Macmillan write on June 4. "The Readings for Children would no doubt have the largest sale, and on that point it would probably be best to get it out first."

Christ Church, Oxford

June 5, 1889

Dear Mr. Macmillan,

I am glad you approve of the 2 books of Biblical Selections. But I think the one of passages to be learned by heart will be the best to do first, as it will be so easily done, needing nothing, beyond the actual word of Scripture, except a short preface. The other will take a long time, on account of the pictures.

It would be well to try some specimen pages for each book, that we may settle on size of type, etc.

You may take Samuel I 3 as a specimen of "Child's Bible" (omit last verse): and Matthew V 1–16 as one of the passages to be learned by heart.

With regard to pictures, I do not know "Schnorr" as an artist:[1] but I do not like the peculiar *German* style, nor do I think it desirable to have a series by any *one* artist: a *family-likeness*, among people *not* related, is by all means to be avoided. *I* should like each picture to be by a separate artist.

By all means print 5000 more 2*s.* 6*d. Looking-Glass.*[2]

As to *Nursery "Alice"*'s for America, which will need price to be omitted from title page, I find that the 2 leaves, which contain the title page and the dedication, have a common hinge, so that that couple of leaves is all that needs reprinting. I have told Mr. Evans to do 1000, that we may have some in hand, in case they order more after the first 500.[3]

Very truly yours,

C. L. Dodgson

P.S. Would Joseph Swain be a good man to do the pictures? I do *not* want them reproduced by any "process," but would rather incur the heavier expense of having them photographed on wood, cut as wood-blocks, and electrotyped. We might get him to do one as a specimen, as soon as we have settled on size of page.[4]

---

[1] In their letter of June 4, Macmillan agreed that plenty of good pictures might be copied and added: "We should think that the best for the purpose would be a German series – Schnorr's – which you very likely know." "Schnorr von Carolsfeld" was a household name among illustrators. Four members of the family engaged in book illustration throughout the nineteenth century and were well known in England and France as well as their native Germany. The current Schnorr, Ludwig II (1824–1905), carried on the family tradition of excellence. Schnorr were best known for their Biblical illustration, and their *Die Bibel in Bildern* (1853–6) contains over 200 large wood engravings, some of which were reproduced in John Keble's *Christian Year* (1875), giving the name Schnorr considerable vogue in England.

[2] Macmillan reported (June 4) that their stock of *Looking-Glass* was very low and they would print 5000 copies unless Dodgson advised to the contrary. They added the assurance that, because the books would not be ready until July, the cost would come into the next year's accounts.

[3] In a postscript to a letter Dodgson sent Macmillan on April 29 he wrote "Mr. E. Evans has suggested to me his idea that some *Nursery 'Alice'*s should be printed *without* the 'price 3s.' on the title-page, in order to send to America: but I decided *against* it. If the Americans want to buy any, let them pay the same as our booksellers: it is a good deal *less* than they would have to pay for any other book of the same kind. Nor am I the least inclined to send them copies un-priced, so that they can charge as high as they like. It is *for the protection of the public* that I want the price printed on every title-page." On the following day Macmillan wrote: ". . . we may say that the American booksellers cannot be expected to supply it to their customers at the equivalent of 3s. unless you wish to give them a very much greater discount, as there is an import duty of 25 percent . . . that has to be paid on every book taken into the United States." Dodgson must have had second thoughts in a letter that followed, missing from our files, and on May 2, Macmillan wrote: "We think the best plan will be for us to write to our American agent and find out what number of copies of *The Nursery 'Alice'* he will take. We will do so at once." On June 4, Macmillan wrote to say that their "Agent in New York writes to say that he will take 500 *Nursery 'Alice'* to begin with."

[4] Dodgson is referring to the proposed book of selections from the Bible. Macmillan agree (June 14) that Swain would be good for the engraving and add: "If you can decide upon some particular picture he might engrave it as a specimen."

Christ Church, Oxford

June 23, 1889

Dear Mr. Macmillan,

(1) Will you kindly get me 2 stalls (front or 2nd row) for *Little Lord Fauntleroy* at the Opéra Comique for Wednesday afternoon the 26th: and leave them at Mr. Wells, 431 Strand: and let me know you have done so?[1]

(2) Please *stop* the binding of the 2 *coloured Nursery "Alice"* in morocco: and substitute 2 of those done in *brown* ink only.

(3) The other 4, in brown ink only are to be covered in covers, done in brown ink only, which Mr. Evans will send you.

(4) The 2 copies, with *colour*, and without covers, to be sent to me at Oxford.

(5) The leatherette copies of *Alice Under Ground* have arrived. Thanks.

(6) It is a great disappointment to me to have to postpone, till Xmas, the publication of *The Nursery "Alice"*, but it is absolutely necessary. The pictures are *far* too bright and gaudy, and vulgarise the whole thing. *None must be sold in England*: to do so would be to sacrifice whatever reputation I now have for giving the public the *best* I can. Mr. Evans must begin again, and print 10,000 *with Tenniel's coloured pictures before him*: and I must *see* all the proofs this time: and then we shall have a book really fit to offer to the public.[2]

(7) As to the 10,000 already printed, I want you (as soon as you get the covers, and the 1000 special title-pages and "list of works" prepared for America) to cover 500, and send them out, and see if they will buy the lot. The present arrangement is, you know, that you are to account to me, for all copies sold (whether here or in America) at 2*s*. 3*d*. each: but, if you can sell *the whole 10,000* in America (which would be £1125), I am willing to knock off the £125.

Very truly yours,

C. L. Dodgson

---

[1] Dodgson's sees *Little Lord Fauntleroy* for the third time on the 26th: "Marion Terry is now 'Mrs. Erroll,' and does it very sweetly and pathetically," he writes in his *Diaries* (p. 472).

[2] The publication of *The Nursery "Alice"* is a tale of enormous knots and tangles. Dodgson was obviously appalled when he first saw the printed color illustrations and exiled them to America. But because he had already promised copies of the book to friends, he ordered a few printed in brown ink only, for his private use. Selwyn H. Goodacre provides evidence that five variants appeared with *1889* on the title-page and three with *1890* (see his "*The Nursery 'Alice'*: A Bibliographical Essay," *Jabberwocky*, Autumn 1975, pp. 100–19; the other essays on the book in the same issue of the journal; see also *Handbook*, pp. 160–3).

---

7 Lushington Road, Eastbourne
July 16, 1889

Dear Mr. Macmillan,

Thanks for your letter. As you have already sent my offer to America, and as I fully authorised you so to do, of course I adhere to it, and am willing that you should account to me, for the whole 10,000, during this year, at 2*s*. a copy.[1] But it must be understood that the offer only holds for the *whole* number, and only for *this* year.

Very truly yours,

C. L. Dodgson

[1] On the previous day Macmillan & Co. wrote: "We certainly think that you might charge 4*s.* for *The Nursery 'Alice'*. The price paid for it by the public will even then be rather less than what they have to give for books published on ordinary terms at 6*s.* We wrote to America by last Saturday's mail. If you get an offer for a reasonable number of the inferior edition at 2*s.* we think you might accept it." On August 17: "Our American Agent writes to say that he will take 4000 copies of *The Nursery 'Alice'* if he can have them at 1*s.* 6*d.* a copy. This is less than you asked, but it is still over cost price, and considering that you had determined to destroy these copies rather than sell them in England, it will be £300 to the good. We shall be glad to know what you decide to do." Dodgson must have rejected the offer in a missing letter, and on August 21, Macmillan write: ". . . we have no objection to your offering the 10,000 condemned copies to an American publisher though we do not think it probable that you will find anyone prepared to pay a higher price than we offered – 1*s.* 6*d.* per copy. We should of course *not* expect any commission on a sale with which we had nothing to do."

7 Lushington Road, Eastbourne
September 10, 1889

Dear Mr. Macmillan,

The French *Alice*, for which I wrote on August 30, has not yet arrived.

It won't do to announce the new book (as you propose) *yet*. So many of the pictures yet remain to be drawn, that I am by no means certain we can get it out by Xmas.[1]

I shall be willing that you should (as you propose in your letter received August 23) print an American edition, on the same terms[2] as you did with regard to the 6*s.* editions of the 2 *Alice*s.

I have several questions to ask about the new book (entitled, at present, *Four Seasons*):

(1) In your letter, received August 23, you advise *against* printing 20,000 to begin with, and advise *10,000*.[3] I am quite inclined to yield to your experienced advice, *provided that*, when you gave it, you were in full recollection of the following facts,

(a) that, when we brought out *Through the Looking-Glass*, you advised to print *12,000*;

(b) that this number proved quite inadequate, the whole impression being ordered by the booksellers before any were ready, and the book being, in consequence, "out of print," for a whole month, in the middle of the Xmas season;

(c) that, in spite of this misfortune, we sold 20,000 in the first 6 months. *Were* you in full possession of these facts, when you wrote?[4]

(2) The volume has grown on my hands so much that I doubt if it will be less than 300 pages. Please give a rough estimate of *current* cost of (say) 5000 copies, this size; putting number of pictures at 40.

I have asked Mr. Evans to do *14* (not 44) copies, in brown ink, of *Nursery "Alice"*.

Very truly yours,

C. L. Dodgson

1 Macmillan wrote on August 21: "We shall be glad to know whether we are at liberty to announce the book [*Sylvie and Bruno*] in our list of forthcoming publications and if so under what title."

2 Namely, for Macmillan to print the book at their own cost in America and pay Dodgson a royalty for each copy sold.

3 In their letter of August 21, Macmillan & Co. wrote: "We are inclined to think that 20,000 would be rather a large edition to print of a new book selling at 6s. and would suggest 10,000 to begin with. There would be no economy in the rate of production for the larger number."

4 "In view of our experience with *Through the Looking-Glass* it would perhaps be best to print 20,000 copies of the new book as you at first suggested," Macmillan & Co. reply three days later.

7 Lushington Road, Eastbourne

September 26, 1889

Dear Mr. Macmillan,

I have just received the 14 copies of *Nursery "Alice"* in brown ink, and am sorry to say the covers must be done again. Mr. Evans, in printing the covers, has made the extraordinary mistake of allowing nothing for the *thickness* of the book. The consequence is that the figure of the hare, on the reverse side, is $\frac{5}{8}$ inch to the right of the centre; i.e. there is $1\frac{1}{4}$ inch more margin on the left than there is on the right.

The look of the book is entirely spoiled by this mistake.

I don't know whether it is a case where the binder can be required to bind them again at his own cost: but I must say I think it was *very* stupid of him, when the first copy was obviously wrong, not to stop the work *at once* and announce that the covers were printed wrong.

I suppose I must pay for the 2nd binding: but what I want to know is whether it can be done by pasting fresh covers *over* these, or whether the books must be taken out of these covers and bound afresh. If the former is the case, then I want to know how much width must be allowed, extra, on account of the double thickness of paper. I should guess $\frac{1}{4}$ inch, but the binder ought to know.

I am going to tell Mr. Evans to print 14 fresh covers, and want to know exactly what directions to give.

It has just occurred to me that *perhaps* it might be managed by merely having the "hare" printed again, and pasted on over the reverse side of the cover, leaving the front side untouched. Would this look well, or would the edge show too much, where the new piece of paper came to an end?[1]

I am sending you the 14 copies again.

Very truly yours,

C. L. Dodgson

1 "We are sorry to hear of the mistake in binding the 14 brown copies of *The Nursery 'Alice'*," Macmillan & Co. reply the next day. "We will get fresh covers from Mr. Evans and have them bound over again without expense to you."

7 Lushington Road, Eastbourne
October 6, 1889

Dear Mr. Macmillan,

(1) Would it not be a good plan to print 10,000 copies of *Sylvie and Bruno* to begin with, and then, while these are drying, to work off a second 10,000? Would not that enable the binding to begin much sooner than they would if the whole 20,000 were worked off at once?

(2) Mr. Joseph Swain is anxious about the pictures. They are very delicate work (and of course must not, on *any* consideration, be *hurried*), and he fears he cannot finish them by the end of October, which was the date at which I told him they would be wanted. So I want to allow him, if possible, more time. Will you kindly consider, in consultation (if necessary) with Messrs. Clay and the binder, what is the latest date at which the *last* picture-block ought to be delivered to the printers, and then send word to Mr. Swain?

(3) I shall be glad to have your immediate answer to the question whether we can manage 25 lines to the page, or must be content with 24.

(4) Please tell me the amount, *per copy sold*, of the "Royalty" I get from America, for my 6*s.*, 4*s.* 6*d.*, and 2*s.* 6*d.* books, in return for my supplying electros, from which they can print, if they like, copies as good as the English ones. The sums paid are so trivial, that it occurs to me that it would be more worth my while, instead of sending out any electros of the new book, to take my chance of selling *English* copies (of course with prices omitted). No doubt that involves the risk of somebody out there issuing a *pirated* edition: but that would necessarily be so greatly inferior to the English one that I don't think it would be a formidable rival. However, all this depends a good deal on the amount of the "Royalty."[1]

(5) Please send the 14 brown-ink *Nursery "Alice,"* to me at *Christ Church*, not *here*.

(6) Let me know when you have the 12 copies bound, of the first lot of coloured ones: and I will send you the addresses to which they are to go.

Very truly yours,

C. L. Dodgson

Please post enclosed card.

---

[1] In Macmillan & Co.'s reply on the following day, they answer the questions in the preceding four numbered paragraphs as follows: (1) Not much time would be saved by printing *Sylvie and Bruno* in two installments of 10,000 each because "once a sheet has been made ready on the machine it is best to print off the whole number." (2) Much time could be saved if Swain would send the exact measurements of the woodblocks not yet ready and if Dodgson would advise the printer where those prints go in the text. The sheets could then be prepared and the text electrotyped. (3) Getting 25 lines to the page was not difficult: ". . . we think it will be an improvement on 24." (4) Dodgson receives 10 percent of the American retail price as royalty. They explain: "If we make *Sylvie and Bruno* $1.25 . . . as we probably shall, the royalty will be 12½ cents per copy."

Christt Church, Oxford
October 11, 1889
Dear Mr. Macmillan,

Thanks for your letter, but you don't quite understand my question about
Mr. Swain. What I want is to give him *as much time as possible* for the wood-cuts, so
as to avoid all risk of hurrying the work. What you suggest as "the best plan" –
viz. "to get him to deliver the blocks as soon as he possibly can" – is the very thing
I am anxious to avoid.[1] If you will kindly tell me at what date the binding ought
to *begin*, I think I can get the information I want from Messrs. Clay.[2]

The American business is a very unsatisfactory prospect. If they have
electrotypes sent them, so that they can print at between 1s. and 2s. a copy, and
sell at 5s. a copy, it seems to me that a Royalty of 6d. is very small. As you don't
deal with American booksellers, and as I am in communication with several,
would you object to my ascertaining whether better terms can be had? Or rather
(as merely asking questions would not commit us to anything) would you mind
my dealing with someone other than your agent, if I can get better terms? Of
course I should wish *your* profits to be untouched by the change: and you could
tell me what those are (as I presume you make a profit yourselves in the
American sales); and you should have the same.[3] Believe me

Very truly yours,

C. L. Dodgson

Please send me a dozen of the first lot of *Nursery "Alice"*, as soon as they are
bound. Mr. Evans reports the covers as ready. Also please take care the right
covers are used, as there are 2 kinds – the *darker* paper for the 1st set, and the
lighter for the 2nd set (which are to be printed on *white* paper).

P.P.S. Have you considered the question of *price* for the new book? It will be
nearly *double* the size of *Alice in Wonderland*, and will have 45 pictures by Harry
Furniss. It seems to me worth consideration whether we shall be wise in selling it
at the same price as *Alice*.[4]

---

[1] Eager to publish *Sylvie and Bruno* for Christmas but still intent on preserving the book's quality,
Dodgson asked Macmillan how long it would take Clay after he received the last block from
Swain. Macmillan replied (October 10) that it was impossible to judge and "depends on
circumstances." The only thing they could promise was to see that Clay lost no time, and they
suggested that if Dodgson wanted to get the books out, he should "get Swain to deliver the blocks
as soon as he possibly can."

[2] Macmillan reply (October 14) that if Clay could deliver perfect copies of *Sylvie and Bruno* to the
binder on December 2, the book could be bound and published by Friday, December 13. They
add: "We do not think it should be any later than that to get the advantage of the Christmas sale."

[3] Macmillan & Co. go on to say (October 14): "We are afraid we misled you by our remark that 'we
did not deal with American booksellers.' What we meant to explain was that we have no direct
dealings with them from here and that we could not therefore dictate the price at which they were

to sell your book. What we propose is that the book should be published by Macmillan & Co. of New York which, although carried on as a distinct business from this, belongs to us and is managed for us by an Agent. He has direct accounts with every bookseller of importance in the United States and is, to say the least, in as good a position to sell your book as anyone else in the Union. The discounts given by American publishers to their customers are very large and expenses of carrying on business in America are heavy and the disproportion between the retail price of the book and the royalty we offer is therefore not so large as it appears. If our agent publishes your book at 5*s.* ($1.25), he will not get more than half price for it, and after paying you the royalty will have 2*s.* left for paper, printing, and binding. We are willing, as we said in our former letter, to give you a royalty of 10 percent on the retail price of every copy sold, and we may now say that if you please we will pay you £100 on publication on account of this royalty. We bought up the plates of a pirated Edition of *Alice* and the *Looking-Glass* at a considerable expense some years ago in order that the books might be in our hands, and we should be very sorry to lose the publication of the book that is now in preparation. We can honestly say that we do not think you could do better for yourself by going to any other publisher."
4 The price of *Sylvie and Bruno* was not settled for more than a month.

Christ Church, Oxford
October 15, 1889

Dear Mr. Macmillan,

Thanks for letter. It answers all my questions but one, in which I failed to make my difficulty understood: I will try to express it better.

Your answer about binding enables me to tell Mr. Swain that, if we can deliver the *last* block to Messrs. Clay before the middle of November, we shall do. What frightened him was the idea that he was expected to finish them all *by end of October*.

I accept your view as to pricing at 6*s.*

As to American booksellers, I had never dreamed of "dictating to them the price at which they should sell." I had imagined that, by omitting all statements of price, on title-page, etc., they were left free to ask any price they chose. I will go into the question of the 6*d.* royalty hereafter. I daresay I shall come to the conclusion that it is as much as I can fairly expect. It is 8½ percent. In your next sentence you say you are willing to give a royalty of 10 percent, adding "as we said in our former letter." You have never said it to *me* before: and, if 8½ is really as much as is reasonable, I don't the least want *10*.[1] But I'll go into that matter another day.

Now for the unanswered question, which I will now repeat in other, and I hope clearer, words.

"When I first came to you, some 25 years ago, you told me your own 'commission' was '10 percent on receipts by sale.' That, combined with the fact that we allow 2*d.* in the shilling to booksellers, would seem to leave 4*s.* 6*d.* as sum to be credited to me. I find we have agreed on putting it at 4*s.* 4*d.* I cannot remember *why* we agreed on that deduction of 2*d*. I want you to remind me *what the reason was*."[2]

I hope I've made my question intelligible *this* time. In great haste

Very truly yours,

C. L. Dodgson

Kindly forward, as soon as you can, the 12 bound copies of the 1st set of *Nursery "Alice"*.

---

[1] On the following day, Macmillan & Co. write: ". . . we propose to pay you 10 percent of the American retail price whatever that may be. In view of the size of . . . [*Sylvie and Bruno*] we shall probably see our way to fix it at $1.50 in which case your royalty would be 15 cents = 7½*d*."

[2] In the same letter: "We really do not remember at this distance of time what was your reason for fixing the price we were to pay for *Alice* at 4*s*. 4*d*. Our impression is that after going very carefully into the figures you came to the conclusion that this price would give us a fair remuneration for our trouble. The terms were not suggested by us and agreed to by you but *vice versa*."

Christ Church, Oxford
October 19, 1889

Dear Mr. Macmillan,

I have just received a parcel containing 12 of the 14 "brown-ink" copies of *The Nursery "Alice"* rebound, and 12 of the first set of coloured ones, bound.

The brown-ink ones will do very well, now that the covers have been done the right width.

The 12 coloured ones I have packed up again, and will send them to you by train on Monday. Every one of them cracked to pieces on simply being opened. It seems needless to add that I decline to pay for such exceptionally bad binding: books, so bound, would be dear at 6*d*. apiece!

They are surely not done by the same binders who did the brown-ink ones? For *those* open flat, very nicely, without any cracking at all.

There is another fault in the coloured copies, which has nothing to do with the *binding*. I am writing to Mr. Evans about it. It is that the leaves all *curl up*, when the book is opened, in contrary directions, alternately. I tried the effect, in one copy, of rolling them round a wooden roller, one one way and the next the opposite way, to take the curl out: but it was a tedious process, and very difficult to get them to go flat.

All this is a serious matter for me, who am, as you know, negotiating for the sale, in America, of the 10,000 over-bright copies: and I wanted these dozen to send as samples. I am asking 2*s*. 3*d*. apiece for the books: but it is very doubtful if any one would give even the odd 3*d*. for such books as these. It would be ridiculous to offer them as samples.

As soon as Mr. Evans sends you some *flat* sheets, will you get them properly bound? I should think it would be well to employ some other binder than the one who did these 12: or (if you think these have gone wrong from some temporary cause) I think it would be well to warn the binder that what is required is that the books *shall open flat without cracking in two*, and that, unless they will stand that ordeal, he will not be paid – though the mere *not paying* for the binding is poor compensation for me, who have to bear the loss of the spoiled copies.

Will you also get a dozen of the *2nd* set of coloured ones properly bound (taking care to see, beforehand, that the sheets are *flat*). I want them simply for *giving* away: none are to be sold as yet: as part of the bargain I am offering to American booksellers is that, if any one will give £1000 for the whole impression, I will postpone the issue of the other set for 6 months: and I do not yet know if that offer will be accepted, though one firm mention it as a possibility.

The 2nd set (as I have already mentioned) are to have whiter covers than the first. The books are to be printed on *white* paper, but I do not know if any are ready yet. I should think they ought to be so, as Mr. Evans reported the paper as "ready" on August 16th.

What became of the other 2 of the 14 brown-ink copies which were to be re-bound? I should be glad to have them as well.

Very truly yours,

C. L. Dodgson

P.S. Just as I said, in the case of the 14 brown-ink ones, when first bound, that it was very stupid of the binder not to *stop* binding, when he could see that the covers were all crooked, so I say, in the case of these coloured ones, that it was very stupid of him to go on binding them all, instead of at once reporting that the sheets had too strong a *curl* in them to be fit for binding. I'm afraid your binder goes to work like a *machine* – and not a remarkably good machine either! I suppose he is the same man who bound that copy of *Alice Under Ground* in morocco, and decorated it with medallions belonging to another book.[1]

---

[1] Frederick Macmillan replies three days later: "We are very sorry that you should have been so much inconvenienced about the binding of *The Nursery 'Alice'*. We are putting 12 more copies of the coloured book in hand and hope that the binder (to whom we have spoken seriously) will get them right."

Christ Church, Oxford
October 25, 1889

Dear Mr. Macmillan,

The result of my enquiries about American "royalties" is to satisfy me with your offer of 10 percent on the published American retail-price. You can therefore arrange with Messrs. Clay to take a second set of electrotypes (I have already told him 2 sets will be wanted) and send them out to your American agent.

As to the *curled* leaves of the American *Nursery "Alice"*: I wrote, to complain of it, to Mr. Evans; but he declares they were sent *flat* to 29 Bedford Street. It must therefore have been some one of *your* people who conceived the by no means good idea of *rolling up* the sheets before forwarding them to the binders.[1]

A friend here suggests, as a possible reason for the backs all cracking, that perhaps they were bound *too soon*, before the sheets were properly dry. This of course must *not* be done: however long we have to wait, to have the sheets properly dry for binding, wait we *must*.

As to a word, for you to register as telegraphic address, I will suggest a few that occur to me.

1. *Ems.* This is a pun on the two M's which you use in your monogram. And it has the advantage of unusual brevity.
2. *Fitzmillan* – "Fitz" is of course equivalent to "Mac."
3. *Omillan* – (ditto ditto)
4. *Apmillan* ("Ap" being Welsh for "Mac")
5. *Barmillan* (Hebrew prefix – meaning "son of")
6. *Benmillan* (ditto)

Very truly yours,

C. L. Dodgson

P.S. Of course there is large choice of *non*-real words, made out of certain letters, taken in proper order, of "Macmillan." But gibberish is not easy to remember – e.g.

7. Maclan.
8. Maan.
9. Maian.
10. Min.

(I have taken them *symmetrically* in every case: i.e. equidistant from centre.)[2]

---

[1] "Mr. Evans's accusation against us of having rolled the sheets of *The Nursery 'Alice'* is quite without foundation," Macmillan & Co. write the following day. "However we made him deliver the next lot to the binder himself in order that he should not again be able to lay the blame on our shoulders. We hope that the new copies will be ready for you on Monday."

[2] Macmillan wrote on October 24 that they had attempted many times to find a word acceptable to the post office authorities and also meaningful, but without success. Someone else had already registered *Macmillan–London* and such things as *publishers, book,* and *booksellers* were already appropriated too. They added: "We should be very greatly obliged to you if you could suggest some words that might do. Unfortunately, the Post Office does not publish any list of registered addresses and will not tell us what words have been appropriated until we send them a list when they return it saying that all the words are taken." To Dodgson's list in the present letter, Macmillan reply the following day: "We are much obliged to you for your suggestions for a telegraphic address. We will try the Post Office with them and will let you know." Months later, on March 3, Macmillan add: "The Post Office authorities refuse to accept any word that is not either a real proper name, or to be found in the English Dictionary. As they also decline to let us know what words are taken up, we hardly know what to offer them."

Christ Church, Oxford
October 29, 1889

Dear Mr. Macmillan,

The dozen *Nursery "Alice"*, just received, seem quite satisfactory. It is perhaps needless to say that I *don't* expect books to be so bound as not to be breakable "by main force." I suppose the binder means to imply that I used "main force" on the previous lot. I can only say that I opened them as I would open any other books, and as I opened the "brown ink" copies, which I presume were bound by the same man, and which showed no symptoms of breaking.[1]

I am sorry to tell you that Mr. Joseph Swain says it is quite impossible to finish the pictures for *Sylvie and Bruno* in time for Xmas.

Please give me your opinion on the following points.

(1) I reckon, roughly, that we might get the book worked off by the middle of December, and the sheets dry for binding early in January. My idea is that it would be worth while to advertise it, among other Xmas books, as "in the Press: will probably be ready by the middle of January." I fancy many purchasers of Xmas books would *wait* for it. But it is a point as to which you are *far* the best judge.

(2) The sale will necessarily be *much* less, this year, than it would have been if we could have got it out by Xmas. I fancy the wisest course, now, would be to print 10,000 only, and store up the rest of the paper. To print 20,000, and sell (perhaps) 5000, would bring my account for June 1890 terribly on the wrong side!

On October 17th I asked you to send me 4 sets of sheets of *Parallels*[2] 2nd edition. On October 20, I asked for the other 2 *"brown ink" Nursery "Alice"*. Neither of these requests has been performed.

Yours very truly,

C. L. Dodgson

[1] When sending the second lot of *The Nursery "Alice"* on the previous day, Macmillan wrote: "The binder has taken great pains with them and believes that the backs will stand any amount of *fair* usage. Of course no book printed on such heavy paper as this can be bound so that the back cannot be broken by main force."

[2] Dodgson refers here to the sub-title of *Curiosa Mathematica, Part I*. A second edition appeared earlier this year.

Christ Church, Oxford
October 30, 1889

Dear Mr. Macmillan,

Mr. Furniss is going to arrange to employ other wood-cutters, besides Mr. Swain, so as to have all pictures cut simultaneously.[1] By that means the pictures may perhaps all be ready by (say) the 10th of November, and all the sheets passed for press. Can you make a similar arrangement for *printing*? Messrs. Clay work off 32 pages at once (that will be from 10 to 12 workings altogether), and, doing them consecutively, they said it would take a month. That only means about 3 days for each set of 32 pages. Hence, if you could get 5 other printers, and divide the work among the 6, giving each of them 64 pages to work off, all the sets of 32 pages would be going on at once, and the whole thing would be printed in a *week* instead of a month. That would bring us to (say) the 20th of November, and then there would just be time to get the sheets dry by December 2, the day you named when they ought to be delivered to the binders.

All this would of course involve a lot of extra expense: but I'll stand that: it seems worth while to make a push for it, rather than miss the Xmas sale.

Will you kindly go into the matter *at once*, and see Clay and other printers, and let me know if the thing can be done or not, on the assumption that the sheets can all be passed for Press by the 10th.[2]

Very truly yours,

C. L. Dodgson

Thanks for *Wilfred*.[3]

[1] On the following day, Macmillan & Co. express satisfaction with the plan to use other engravers; they add that they intended to make that very suggestion themselves.

[2] In the same letter, Macmillan object to Dodgson's plan to employ several printers, arguing that "it is doubtful whether first class printers would accept work under such conditions, but even supposing that this could be arranged, we do not think you could rely on getting work of equal quality throughout." They suggest that Clay put several machines on this work and assure Dodgson that the printer was willing to do so.

[3] A. Winthrop, *Wilfred: A Story with a Happy Ending*, New York: A. D. F. Randolph & Co., 1880, 2nd ed. 1889. On October 3, Macmillan acknowledged ordering Mrs. Winthrop's *Wilfred* from New York, presumably at Dodgson's request.

Christ Church, Oxford
November 2, 1889

Dear Mr. Macmillan,

The only chance seems to be to hold a general consultation of all concerned.[1] I will come to town tomorrow, and hope to be with you by about 11, and am writing to Mr. Webb who is Mr. H. Furniss' Secretary, to ask him to meet me there at 11½, and also to Messrs. Clay and Mr. Joseph Swain, to ask each to send some one, fully informed in the matter, at same time. The *chief* difficulty is as to blocks *begun* by Mr. Swain, and which he says he has not now time to finish. I don't at this moment see what can be done about them: but a general consultation may help.[2]

Please be prepared with all information on *your* part. I should think you had better have some one from your *binders* at hand, to answer any questions as to *binding*. I am asking Mr. Webb to get representatives of any engravers he recommends, to meet us in consultation.

Very truly yours,

C. L. Dodgson

I propose to leave here by 9 a.m. train – 1st London post reaches me at 8 a.m.

---

[1] The summit conference took place because on October 30, after Dodgson had written to Macmillan about the extra wood engravers to help complete the plates, he received a telegram from Furniss "announcing the thing to be impossible: so after all the publication must be deferred" (*Diaries*, p. 475). Macmillan refused to accept defeat, however, and wrote on November 1: "We cannot believe that it is impossible to get the pictures for *Sylvie and Bruno* finished, unless it be the case that Mr. Furniss has not completed the drawings. In fact, if you will now put the unengraved drawings in our hands we will undertake to get them all finished within a week." They added: "We think it would be worth your while to do this; it is a serious thing for you to lose the Christmas sale."
[2] Apparently the consultation helped. "The outcome is, that we are to get it out this Christmas: it will be tough work," Dodgson writes in his *Diaries* (p. 475) on the 5th.

Christ Church, Oxford
November 4, 1889

Dear Mr. Macmillan,

Will you kindly write at once to Messrs. Gebbie & Co., 900 Chestnut Street, Philadelphia, telling them that you have given your consent to my "offering to an American publisher" (I quote your letter of August 21, 1889) the 10,000 *Nursery "Alice"*, which I decided not to sell in England.

They have written to ask me "in what relation" they would stand, in case they bought these books from me, to your "New York Branch" – and also (which is merely the same question in other language) "what Messrs. Macmillan's position in the American market would be to those books," in case they purchased them. Would you kindly give them an answer to this question: I don't know enough about it to answer it myself.

They evidently fear being placed "in a contentious position," and I fancy they suspect that *my* offering the books is the result of a quarrel between yourselves and me![1]

Very truly yours,

C. L. Dodgson

---

[1] If Messrs. Macmillan answered this letter, we have not found the reply.

Christ Church, Oxford
November 13, 1889

Dear Mr. Macmillan,

The length of *Sylvie and Bruno* has far exceeded my calculations: I now find that it will be close on 400 pages, if not over that number. That is, it will be almost exactly equal to *Alice* and the *Looking-Glass* (for which we charge 12*s*.) put together, though with only 47 pictures instead of 92. Under these circumstances, I must beg you to carefully re-consider the question of *price*, and see if you do not think we might fairly put on another shilling, or even 1*s*. 6*d*. When one sees, in the advertisements, children's books charged at 6*s*., by quite unheard-of writers, and merely stated to be "illustrated," without even an artist's name, it does occur to me that we might fairly go a little higher. I have no wish to be exorbitant, but merely to be in reasonable relation to other books.

If, on full consideration of the size of the new book, you still think it best to sell it at 6*s*., I am content to adopt your view: but we ought to remember that, while it will be possible, at any time, to *lower* the price, it will be quite impossible to *raise* it.[1]

Very truly yours,

C. L. Dodgson

P.S. If you chance, this time, to bind up a sham copy, as a specimen of the cover, would you use *blank* paper, instead of odd sheets of the book? Then I could make real use of it – whereas the other is a mere dummy, of no use whatever.

Did you arrange a telegraphic address? One other word has occurred to me – "Maximilian."

---

[1] Macmillan write on the 19th that after careful consideration, they believe the price should be 7*s*. 6*d*., and "as that is your idea too, we will consider it as settled at that figure."

Christ Church, Oxford
November 21, 1889

Dear Mr. Macmillan,

I am most happy to be able to announce that Mr. Furniss has telegraphed to me that he is *satisfied* with Mr. Cooper's work. So we shall have all the blocks in Messrs. Clay's hands in a day or two, and they will be able (on their own showing) to begin delivering copies for binding before December 2.[1]

Of course I shall not pass the title-page for Press till I get an answer from you to my letter of yesterday, about price.[2]

As to the terms, between us, on which it is to be published. Although neither of us can remember the *reason* for which we came to the agreement that your "commission" was to be 13⅓ percent, instead of 10, yet I feel sure that it was a satisfactory one; and I do not wish to propose any other terms for the new book. The result would be that, if we sell at 7*s.* 6*d.*, you will credit me with 5*s.* 5*d.* for each copy sold. If that arrangement satisfies *you*, I think it would be superfluous to have another signed "agreement."[3]

Are the medallions done yet?

Very truly yours,

C. L. Dodgson

You can announce the book as soon as you like.

I see you advertise *Bumblebee*, etc., with extracts from Reviews, which suggests to me to say "Don't advertise any of *my* books so." I think you already know that I don't even want to *see* any reviews, should any appear, of *Sylvie and Bruno*. P.S. Do you know of any place in London, where they would supply me with "Cambridge scribbling paper" (a folio ream at a time) which would fairly match the enclosed specimen, in quality and in thickness? The stationer here, who used to supply this kind, says he cannot get any more. And the paper he now sends me is thin, flimsy stuff – not nearly so pleasant to write on. I have none left of the good kind, except what is written on; so am obliged to send a paper with a calculation on it, which I haven't time to copy, and so would like to have it back again.[4]

---

[1] Cooper was the engraver engaged to supplement the work of Swain. The printing was completed by the end of the month; Dodgson records receiving the final sheets from Clay on November 30 (*Diaries*, p. 476).

[2] Dodgson's letter is missing, but Macmillan's of the 21st suggests that Dodgson wondered whether the price of 7*s.* 6*d.* for *Sylvie and Bruno* would diminish the sale. Macmillan reassure him that people might resent a price increase "for no apparent reason – but *Sylvie and Bruno* is such a much larger book that the increase in price must appear reasonable to everyone."

[3] On the 22nd Macmillan & Co. accept Dodgson's terms as "most satisfactory to us" and agree that it will be unnecessary to have any more formal agreement.

[4] On the 23rd Macmillan send Dodgson two specimens of scribbling paper to select from. On the 29th we find them writing: "We are sorry the scribbling paper did not suit you after all," and they offer to try again "on receipt of a sample of the kind of thing you want."

Christ Church, Oxford

November 25, 1889

Dear Mr. Macmillan,

Mr. Furniss' pictures lose so much of their beauty by the necessary reduction, that I have an idea of bringing out (when we have published the 2nd Part of *Sylvie and Bruno*) a picture-book containing some of the largest engraved full-size or nearly so; and, if that is to be done, Mr. Swain may as well be going on, at his leisure, with the selected ones out of Part I.

But the question must be well considered, first, on the score of expense. I do not wish to publish it, if it is *certain* to be a dead loss.

Suppose I select 30 pictures altogether. The book would be about 15 inches wide by 12 high: with ornamental cover (which I would get Mr. Furniss to design), and *white* (not gilt) edges. I should like the pictures to be all on *right*-hand pages, with explanatory text opposite. There would not be much text needed. There would be about 48 pages in the book.

Would you kindly make rough estimates of

(1) the *price* that we could reasonably put on it.

(2) the *number* we might reasonably hope (say in 3 years) to sell.

(3) the cost, per 1000, for paper, printing, and binding: assuming electrotypes, of text and pictures, to be in existence.[1]

Yours very truly,
C. L. Dodgson

P.S. Please send me 4 proofs of "List of Works," as corrected for new book. It had better be same as in *Nursery "Alice"*, except that the "thousands" should be corrected to date, and new book inserted at end of list.

Also please bind 3 (instead of 2) copies of *Sylvie and Bruno* in morocco – one purple, one brown, and one dark green.

---

[1] Macmillan & Co. reply on the next day: "It does not seem to us that there would be a sufficiently large public for such an enlarged reproduction of Mr. Furniss's drawings as that suggested in your letter, to render the undertaking profitable. To engrave 30 wood blocks 10 x 6 inches in size would cost at least £450 apart from the paper, printing and binding. We do not think you could ask a high price for such a book nor expect to sell a large number of copies. We should certainly advise you strongly against the undertaking." Dodgson apparently drops the notion.

Christ Church, Oxford
December 5, 1889

Dear Mr. Macmillan,

I want to publish the enclosed stamp-case. The outer-case is not the right colour yet: the title is not right yet: the name "De la Rue" was only provisional (I find they do not wish to be the publishers): and the price is going to be 1*s.*, instead of 9*d*.

What I should like best would be for *you* to publish it, and advertise it along with my books: but I fear you will think a shilling article too trivial to be worth troubling about. If you *were* willing to publish it, I would be glad to make the same terms with you that I proposed to Messrs. De la Rue, viz. that *I* shall get them made at my own expense, and supply them to you in any numbers (not less than 100) you wished for; and that you should credit me with 6*d*. for every copy sold.

If you don't care to undertake it yourselves, do you think you could find me a stationer or bookseller, in a large way of business, who *would* undertake it?[1]

Very truly yours,

C. L. Dodgson

[1] On the 7th Macmillan decline the stamp case and suggest Messrs. Parkins and Gotto of Oxford Street, prominent stationers.

Christ Church, Oxford
December 8, 1889

Dear Mr. Macmillan,

Thanks for your suggestion of Parkins & Gotto: I will send them a stamp-case.

Thanks also for the welcome information that you will have some *Sylvie and Bruno* ready for me on Thursday. I hope to be with you about 11.[1] Please send me a dozen *here* as soon as you can.

The 3 "morocco" copies will look better, I think, *without* the medallions.

I don't think I need trouble you to send me a list of the Reviews, etc., to which you propose to send copies: the list that you had for *Rhyme? and Reason?* will do very well. Only please *don't* send copies to any of the following.

> *Pall Mall Gazette*
> The *World*
> *Truth*
> The *Whitehall Review*
> The *St. Stephen's Review* (or some such name)

and please *send* copies to

> *National Review*
> *Notes and Queries*
> *Monthly Packet*
> *St. James's Gazette*
> *Church Bells*
> *Academy*

I have had 2 very characteristic replies from American booksellers about *The Nursery "Alice"*. One declines it because the colours are "not bright enough"(!) The other says the price I ask (2s.) is a great deal too much; and that, if any one there found it worth while, he would reprint it, and sell it for a great deal less than that(!) If they *do* bring out a pirated version in America, please get me a copy: it will be a curiosity in brilliant, but cheap, colour-printing.

Have you sent out the electrotypes yet, to your American branch, of *Sylvie and Bruno*? And how soon will they begin publishing?[2]

Very truly yours,

C. L. Dodgson

I am bringing about 150 labels ready written.

¹ On November 30 Dodgson recorded in his *Diaries* (p. 476): "Received from Clay the remaining sheets of *Sylvie and Bruno*: so the whole book is now printed, and Macmillan has advertised that it will be ready on the 13th." On December 12, Dodgson writes (ibid., p. 476): "Went to town for the day, to write in about 150 copies of *Sylvie and Bruno* which will be published tomorrow." Dodgson actually sent out 148, but he was unhappy with his treatment at Macmillan's and adds to his Diaries entry of the 12th: "I wanted the parcels packed and sent off as soon as possible and the 'hands' provided for the job were (as I found after a long wait) those of a single boy! The *management* seems to be falling off, now that Mr. Macmillan (who is very old) is no longer on the spot." Dodgson must have expressed his dissatisfaction at Macmillan's, and the firm's letter of December 13 takes up the problem: "We think you did not realise that six people were engaged with the packing and sending off of your book although you only saw one or two. When the packing began one boy could keep up with you, but in the afternoon *three* were busily employed in packing only, and it happened that yesterday we were particularly busy with sending out review copies of your book and others which we are publishing today. The work went on until it was too late to post any more copies." *Sylvie and Bruno* has a long history of growth. "It was in 1874, I believe, that the idea first occurred to me of making . . . 'Bruno's Revenge' the nucleus of a longer story," Dodgson writes in the "Preface" to *Sylvie and Bruno*. "As the years went on, I jotted down, at odd moments, all sorts of odd ideas, and fragments of dialogue, that occurred to me – who knows how? – with a transitory suddenness that left me no choice but either to record them then and there, or to abandon them to oblivion. . . . And thus it came to pass that I found myself at last in possession of a huge unwieldy mass of litterature – if the reader will kindly excuse the spelling – which only needed stringing together, upon the thread of a consecutive story, to constitute the book I hoped to write." The "Preface" goes on at some length and gives us a good many insights into Dodgson's manner of composition and his own attitudes to and beliefs in what we call inspiration. He thought highly of *Sylvie and Bruno*, of the forty-six illustrations by Harry Furniss and the one by Alice Havers, and he clearly expected it and its sequel to occupy a fair place alongside his two *Alice* books. But these fairy tales have never attracted the critics' approbation, for, unlike Dodgson's earlier works of imagination, they are weighted with moralities and solemn passages, and, perhaps worst of all, succumb to the fashion of the day of couching children's speech in baby talk. The books contain a great deal of excellent material, nevertheless, not least of all the poetry, and deserve more attention. For more on *Sylvie and Bruno*, see *Handbook*, pp. 163–6; *Jabberwocky*, Summer 1975.
² On December 16, Macmillan & Co. write that the American edition would be published in January 1890.

Christ Church, Oxford
January 16, 1890

Dear Mr. Macmillan,

Thanks for your letter.

I have made a calculation about *Nursery "Alice"*, and find that to accept the offer of your American Agent, of £75 per 1000, would be to sell *at a loss*. It is just under cost-price. I think, if you were to communicate that to him, he would see that it is *not* a reasonable offer. You may also tell him that I am willing to sell 1000, as an experiment, for £80 (I mean, of course, that you should credit me with the full £80: I can't even undertake to pay *carriage*, out of so small a sum): and, if he finds they sell easily, I hope he will see the reasonableness of allowing a little more for subsequent thousands.¹

You don't tell me what you think of the *prospects* of the sale of *Sylvie and Bruno*. Isn't a month enough to enable you to form a guess as to the period in which we may hope to sell the 20,000?²

Very truly yours,

C. L. Dodgson

¹ Macmillan & Co. write the following day to accept "on behalf of our American agent your offer of 1000 copies of *The Nursery "Alice"* for £80."
² On the day before Dodgson writes, the firm reported the figures for the first month's sale of *Sylvie and Bruno*: 8614 copies "disposed of," with 8100 actually sold; 299 to agents, "and probably most of them sold"; and the balance given away either by Dodgson or to the press. In reply to Dodgson's question about "prospects," Macmillan reply on January 17 that "it is quite impossible to form any idea from the sale of a new book during the first month what the subsequent rate of sale is likely to be." In 1898, the year of Dodgson's death, *Sylvie and Bruno* was selling its thirteenth thousand; the first edition did not go out of print until 1942.

Christ Church, Oxford
February 28, 1890

Dear Mr. Macmillan,

Thanks for your kind proposal to carry on *Rhyme? and Reason?* account, if against me, from June 1890 to June 1891. You can print the 500.¹ Please state on title-page what *thousand* you are in.

I've thought a good deal about the *Quality* of the recent impressions of the 6s. *Alice* and *Looking-Glass*: and am not at all comfortable about them. They are so distinctly inferior to the earlier ones: and I don't wonder to see, as I did, a day or two ago, in a second-hand catalogue, an 1866 *Alice* advertised at £4.4.0. I *fear* one cause is that Messrs. Clay have lost all interest in the book, after printing so many thousands, and do not trouble themselves further about "bringing up" the pictures, but simply aim at getting the thousands worked off with the minimum of trouble. They don't realise what a heavy disappointment it is to the author, to fail in his intention to give only *best* quality to the public.

Another cause may *possibly* be the having lately used (as we agreed to do) a rather cheaper paper. Do you think this is so? In that case, by all means let us return to the dearer paper, even if it swallows up most of the profits.²

Mr. Evans told me, some time ago, that he would have the new 10,000 *Nursery "Alice"* (on *white* paper) ready by end of February. So please make all necessary arrangements for bringing it out at Easter: and advertise it well.³

I observe that you are no longer advertising *Sylvie and Bruno*. Is it that you think it no use? Or have you spent the £100 I authorised? If the latter is the case, and if you think more advertising desirable, by all means spend more.⁴

Have you got a telegraphic address yet?⁵

Very truly yours,
C. L. Dodgson

¹ It took four letters from Macmillan to obtain Dodgson's permission to reprint *Rhyme? and Reason?*. They first wrote on February 17 to report that the stock was exhausted, and they proposed printing another 500. Dodgson's reply is missing, but Macmillan's letter of February 19 clarifies his objections: "We are afraid you are right about the comparative quality of the picture-printing in the editions of *Rhyme? and Reason?* of 1883 and 1887. We have today had a serious talk with Messrs. Clay and Sons on the subject, and they are willing to guarantee a result equal to that in the first edition if you will allow the book to be reprinted." On February 25 Macmillan wrote again to

say that they were waiting for permission to reprint, again promising Dodgson that Clay would do quality work. Again Dodgson's reply is missing, but Macmillan's next letter (February 27) assured Dodgson: "If you will allow us to reprint it we shall be quite willing, in case there is a balance against the book at June 30 to carry it over to next year's account."

2 Macmillan reply on March 3 but conflate the subject of the first paragraph with the next two paragraphs: they submit samples of paper for reprinting *Rhyme? and Reason?* for Dodgson's approval instead of responding to his question about the paper used for *Alice* and *Looking-Glass*.

3 Macmillan reply (same letter) that the book would be published on March 25 with suitable announcements. This is, of course, the second printing of *The Nursery "Alice"*.

4 In their reply (same letter), Macmillan & Co. write that they have not yet spent £80 advertising *Sylvie and Bruno* and have not stopped advertising but "have lately only been inserting it when we had prominent positions, such as the back page of a paper, at our disposal." They explain further: "We think that in this way the book may be kept forward for some time without exceeding the expenditure (£100) which you authorised."

5 Macmillan did not succeed in getting a cable address until the next year. On January 30, 1891, they write Dodgson: "You will be glad to hear that we have at last succeeded in registering a telegraphic address – and that after tomorrow messages addressed to *Publish-London* will reach us." It is Macmillan's cable address to this day.

Christ Church, Oxford
April 3, 1890

Dear Mr. Craik,

Messrs. Kennett & Co. write that the stamp-case does not suit their line of business: so I must again appeal to your kindness to try and find a stationer who will undertake to keep it on sale, on condition of being supplied with them, in any quantities, at 6*d*. each. Could you send a man round to the principal stationers? (I would pay all expenses.)[1] If so, how many cases shall I send you to show as specimens? Will you kindly avoid letting any of them suppose himself authorised to treat, on my behalf, with *other* tradesmen? Messrs. Kennett & Co. had somehow got this idea into their heads, and had applied to Messrs. De la Rue to know if *they* would sell it for me! I would rather negotiate with strangers through *you*, not through *other* strangers.

How is *Nursery "Alice"* selling?[2]

Yours very truly,

C. L. Dodgson

1 On March 26 Macmillan suggested that Dodgson send his stamp case to Messrs. Kennett & Co. On April 8 Craik replies to this letter saying that it would be useless to apply to the "principal stationers" as "they have been already applied to and they have declined." He adds: "I fear you must accept the verdict that there is no practical use in the invention . . . ," a verdict that Dodgson rejected. We cannot tell exactly when Dodgson expanded the concept to include his essay *Eight or Nine Wise Words about Letter-Writing* or when he applied to Emberlin and Son, 4 Magdalen Street, Oxford, but he inscribes a copy on June 18, and on June 28 he receives an estimate "for the future supplies of *Wise Words*." On July 2 he records in his *Diaries* (p. 478): "Sent Emberlin, in order to begin sale of the '*Wonderland*' *Stamp-Case*, 75 of them, with 150 *Wise Words*, and 950 envelopes." The combination sold for 1*s*. Six years later, on April 20, 1896, Dodgson writes to Macmillan again about the stamp case: "It has occurred to me, with reference to the '*Wonderland*' *Postage*

Stamp-Case, advertised at the end of my 'List of Works,' that I should be very glad if you could see your way to allowing me to add it to the 'List,' and to yourselves selling it for me, on whatever terms you may consider reasonable. The *Eight or Nine Wise Words about Letter-Writing* is a separate book, and I am thinking of adding to it a Chapter on Reading, and one on Talking; but this would still leave it small enough to be put into the envelope along with the *Stamp-Case*." On the following day, Frederick Macmillan rejects the notion once more: "I am afraid we cannot offer to undertake . . . it. It really comes into the category of 'Stationery' or 'Fancy Goods' in which we do not deal, and we are so much pressed for room in our warehouse that we do not feel that we can devote space to what does not properly belong to our business." (See *Handbook*, pp. 170–3.)

² In a letter of April 8, Craik enclosed a report of the sales of *The Nursery "Alice"*, but it is missing.

Christ Church, Oxford

June 24, 1890

Dear Mr. Macmillan,

Now the annual sale of my books has reached so large a figure as to bring in (I hope) quite a respectable addition to your income, it occurs to me that I may fairly ask for slightly better terms for myself. I am obliged to look to £.s.d. a little, as the calls on me, relatively to my income, are enormous.

Deducting 2*d.* in the shilling, as booksellers' allowance, and then 10 percent as your "commission," really amounts to deducting 25 percent. We have been proceeding on the plan of deducting rather more than this. I propose that you shall in future account to me, for all sold copies of "Lewis Carroll" books, at the rate of ¾ of the published price. I mention this now, because we are close to the annual winding-up day; and it would be convenient that the new agreement, if accepted by you, should take effect on and after July 1, 1890.[1]

Very truly yours,

C. L. Dodgson

¹ Macmillan & Co. do not accept Dodgson's proposal: they state their objections in their letter dated June 28. They write that from his proposal "we understand that in future we should account to you for the 'Lewis Carroll' books at ¾ of the published price. That is to say, for every copy sold of the half-crown edition of *Alice* we should pay you 1*s.* 10½*d.* You will remember the terms (fixed by yourself) on which we have to supply the trade: 2*d.* in the 1*s.* off retail price, with 10 percent discount for cash. That is, for a half-crown book, 2*s.* 1*d.* less 10 percent – 1*s.* 10½*d.* As most of the copies of your books are bought for cash in order that the discount may be secured, our profit under your proposed arrangements would be simply the use of the money from the time the book was sold until our accounts were settled with you. We are happy to say we are not sufficiently in need of capital to make such an arrangement worth our while." The letter concludes: "We consider that the terms on which we have been working for some years past are equitable, and we hope that on consideration you will allow them to remain as they are."

Christ Church, Oxford

June 30, 1890

Dear Mr. Macmillan,

We seem to be rather at cross-purposes.

You say "the terms (fixed by yourself) on which we have to supply the trade

discount from the publisher: so he can reply "Very well: then I will get it from London." It is also partly in the *bookseller's* interest, as he can now reply, to any one demanding *more* than 10 percent discount, "you cannot get more, even from the publishers."

Did you suppose that "they," in the last sentence of the notice, stood for "the booksellers"? It stands for "Messrs. Macmillan."[1]

Very truly yours,

C. L. Dodgson

Don't send the Hospital replies just yet.[2]

[1] In their reply the following day, Macmillan & Co. urge Dodgson to abandon his idea of an "explanatory paragraph." They argue that while at one time retail customers were used to being able to obtain a 25 percent discount, this is no longer the case with many books being sold on special terms, so "this reason for the existence of the paragraph no longer holds." Furthermore, they cite Dodgson's letter of June 30 (missing), where he writes: "I am not at all anxious that you should allow *any* discount to the booksellers," to which Macmillan counter: "This being so, we do not see why you should ask us to print a paragraph to say how much discount we will allow. We think it a matter that we should be allowed to explain privately to our customers."

[2] Dodgson gave a great many copies of his books to children's hospitals. He published *Circular to Hospitals* (1872, 1890) and *Letter and Questions to Hospitals* (1876), which he sent to hospital managers offering them copies of his books. He also printed a *List of Institutions* (1890), a catalogue of hospitals to which he sent his circulars. For a return address, he usually used Macmillan & Co. On July 7 the firm wrote: "We have now received between 90 and 100 replies to your circular to the Hospitals. Shall they be forwarded to you?" For more on these circulars, see *Handbook*, pp. 70, 95, 169–70.

7 Lushington Road, Eastbourne
July 11, 1890

Dear Mr. Macmillan,

You say you "do not think that any explanatory paragraph as to the terms on which my books are supplied to the Trade is necessary or even advisable." But the rest of your letter shows that you have misunderstood my *objects*, in making the announcement at present published with the "List of Works," in two important particulars. I am sorry the wording of that announcement has turned out so obscure and misleading, but really it is a *most* difficult thing to write an English sentence which shall be absolutely unmistakable. The 2 points I allude to are these:

(1) You say, as a reason for the non-necessity of the existing announcement, "So many books are published at 'net' prices, that buyers are no longer surprised to find that they cannot get discount." But that is only *half* my object. It is true that I want buyers to understand that they must not expect to get *more* than 10 percent discount: but I *also* want them to know that they *can* get *as much as* that (by writing to the Publishers direct). The fact, that "so many books are

published at net prices," might possibly secure the *first* half of the object I aim at: but it would not touch the *second*.[1]

(2) You quote my remark, that "I am not at all anxious that you should allow *any* discount to the booksellers," and then you say "this being so, we do not see why you should ask us to print a paragraph to say how much discount we will allow." But that is *not* my object in printing the paragraph. I print it, *not* in order that the public should know how *much* discount you will give, but how *little* – not that they should know the *minimum* limit of the discount allowed to the Trade, but its *maximum* limit. I fear you will find that last sentence totally obscure: so I will try and express it another way. It would quite answer my purpose, if the announcement ran thus: "will abate not more than 2*d.* in the shilling (no odd copies), and allow not more than 5 percent discount for payment within six months, and not more than 10 percent for cash." The sentence would look very queer, but it would quite answer my purpose, as it would show the public that they could not reasonably expect the bookseller to give more than 10 percent discount for cash. That part of the announcement is wholly meant in the interest of the *booksellers*: but, if they dislike its appearance in print, and prefer to *tell* any customer, who says "of course you give 3*d.* in the 1*s.* discount for cash?": "we cannot afford it: we are not allowed enough discount, by the publishers, to make it possible" – it is worth considering whether we can omit that clause in future.

I had better state, as clearly as I can, the objects to be secured, and, if you can devise any new form of advertisement, securing these objects, and more acceptable to the booksellers, I shall probably be willing to adopt it.

I will take *Sylvie and Bruno* as an instance.

(1) I wish the public to know that the book *can be had* for 7*s.* 6*d.*, and thus to be protected against any bookseller asking *more* than this. (The object is already secured by printing the price on the title-page. With many books this is not done, and the consequence is that a dishonest bookseller can take advantage of his ignorant customer, by asking more than the published price.)

(2) I wish the public to know that, if they choose to pay ready money, the book *can be had* for 7*s.* 6*d.* less *10 percent discount*, and thus have the remedy in their own hands, if the local bookseller declines to sell on those terms, by getting the book from *you.*

(3) I wish the public to know that the booksellers *cannot reasonably afford* to allow *more* than 10 percent discount for cash.

Very truly yours,

C. L. Dodgson

Please send me 4 *Sylvie and Bruno.*

---

[1] The reference here to "books published at net prices" reflects a development in the book world, spearheaded by Macmillan & Co., which would culminate in the Net Book Agreement in 1899. The problem of bookseller's profits which Dodgson had tried to address with his insistence on special terms for his books was endemic in the publishing business and a concern to all involved.

Booksellers reserved the right to sell at any price they chose, and because the margin of profit for the bookseller was usually small, unscrupulous booksellers managed to drive many competitors out of business by relying on a profitable "side" enterprise. Except for isolated attempts to address the problem (like Ruskin's and Dodgson's), nothing was done to regulate or reform the practice. Finally, in 1890 Frederick Macmillan proposes a remedy in a letter published in the *Bookseller* (March 6, 1890, p. 244). In the letter, Macmillan says that the time is ripe to settle the underselling question because, although it has been a serious issue for many years, it has "recently assumed such proportions that it is rapidly becoming impossible for a bookseller, pure and simple, dealing in current literature to make a living profit from his business." He continues: "Although this is no doubt a matter that primarily concerns retail booksellers, it is of serious importance to authors, publishers, and all concerned in the production of books, and also to book buyers and those interested in the welfare of letters. A well-stocked book shop is a centre of mental culture, and any disorganisation of trade that renders the existence of such centres difficult or impossible is an injury to the community." Macmillan suggests that publishers take the initiative, not, however, "with the expectation of any direct advantage to themselves as publishers" but with "the view of benefiting their customers and assisting in the settlement of a difficult problem." He proposes that all books be published in one of two categories – Net Books, to be sold at the published price without discount, or Subject Books, to be sold subject to discount at each bookseller's discretion. This would be a temporary measure, and the development would be in the direction of publishing all books eventually at "net" prices, so that the price to both bookseller and customer was clearly understood by each party and there would be an end to the perpetual discounting that wreaked economic havoc in the book world. Macmillan reasons that "the ease with which, when in isolated cases books have been published at *net* prices, the bookseller has been able to sell them without discount, leads me to think that a general movement in that direction would be unattended with any real difficulty." Macmillan & Co. initiate the movement by publishing sixteen net books in 1890, and the number then rises yearly, so that in 1897 they publish 137 net books. Other publishers follow suit, and although the percentage of net books is small, the direction of the trend is unmistakable. The watershed is the 1899 Net Book Agreement between the Publishers' Association and the Associated Booksellers. Today the net book is the rule rather than the exception. For a full discussion of the subject and its aftermath, see *Net Book Agreement*; see also pp. 23–6, above.

7 Lushington Road, Eastbourne
July 20, 1890

Dear Mr. Macmillan,

After duly considering your letter of July 7,[1] I have decided to accept the 2 conditions, there laid down, on which you are willing to account to me, for the copies you sell, at $\frac{3}{4}$ of the advertised price.

In future, then, let the "N.B.," at the end of the "List of Works," run thus: "N.B. In selling Mr. Lewis Carroll's books to the Public (for cash only) Messrs. Macmillan & Co. will allow 10 percent discount."

You can, if you like (of course at my cost) have this new "N.B." printed separately, and pasted over the existing "N.B." in all the copies now in stock. If that is done, you will, I suppose, regard the new arrangement as commencing (say) on August 1st.

Thanks for the 4 *Nursery "Alice"*, and for rebinding the faulty copy of *Sylvie and Bruno*.

Very truly yours,
C. L. Dodgson

P.S. It occurs to me to add, to avoid all risk of future misunderstanding, that any such arrangement as letting a bookseller have 13 copies as 12 (if you should think it worth your while to make it) would be a matter between you and *him*, and would not enter into your account with *me*, where they would appear as "13 copies sold."

P.P.S. I have asked Messrs. Parker to send you all the "Hospital" copies of *Alice* and *Looking-Glass*, that are left, in order that you may send them round along with the *Nursery "Alice"*. There are some 20 or 30 answers to the Circular yet to come in: but there is no need to wait, for all to come in, before we begin sending round. I will send you, very soon, a list of about 100 Hospitals and Homes, for whom parcels are to be made up.

[1] See pp. 277-8, above.

7 Lushington Road, Eastbourne
July 22, 1890

Dear Mr. Macmillan,

Your letter of July 21 is very welcome.[1] I was beginning to feel doubts as to the arrangement I had proposed. Had you closed with the proposal, as it stood, I was prepared to abide by it: but your not having done so gives me an opportunity, which I am very glad to have, of reconsidering the whole question. Please consider my proposal as, for the present, withdrawn.

So long as the advertisement continues to be issued in its present form, I think the enclosed P.S. a desirable (I may say "necessary," considering how it has been misinterpreted) addition to it. I shall be glad to know if any amended wording of it occurs to you.

You will observe that I have inverted the order of the clauses in the notice itself, thus avoiding the ambiguity of the word "they" in the second clause of the existing notice.

Very truly yours,
C. L. Dodgson

N.B. In selling Mr. Lewis Carroll's books to the Public (for cash only) Messrs. Macmillan & Co. will allow 10 percent discount. In selling them to the Trade, they will abate 2*d.* in the shilling (no odd copies), and allow 5 percent discount for payment within six months, and 10 percent for cash.

P.S. – Mr. Lewis Carroll has learned with regret that the above announcement has given annoyance to some of the Trade, who have failed to perceive that its second clause is published in *their* interest, in order that their customers may know that they cannot reasonably expect the usual "*3d.* in the shilling" discount for cash. The first clause is published in the interest of the *Public*, in order that they may know, in case their Bookseller should decline (as he has a perfect right to do) to allow them so much as 10 percent discount for cash, that they can get it by applying direct to the Publishers.[2]

(Proposed form of notice,
for "List of Works.")

---

[1] In it Macmillan & Co. wrote: "In reply to your last letter we write that in our opinion the paragraph with reference to the terms on which your books are sold had much better be omitted from the advertisements altogether and nothing put in its place. It seems to us that the author and his publisher should fix the retail price of a book, but that they should leave the question of what deduction if any is to be made for cash payment to be settled between the bookseller and his customer. The competition between booksellers is such that there is not the slightest chance of your books being sold too dear. Booksellers are much more inclined to take off too much discount than too little. So far as we ourselves are concerned," the letter went on, "we have no wish whatever to supply books to the public direct, in fact we avoid doing so as much as possible as we think it undesirable to compete for trade with our own customers, the booksellers. Of course when you or any other client of ours, orders a book we are very pleased to get it for you but we do so to oblige you, not because we wish to sell books at retail. We have neither the machinery for such a business nor the wish to encourage it."

[2] In their reply to this letter on the following day, the firm explain that they object to the printed explanation in principle rather than in form. They remind Dodgson that back in 1883 when he orginally proposed special terms for the sale of his books their "principal objection to the scheme was to the paragraph in the advertisements which is now under discussion." They "gave way" only to oblige him and now know from the results that the printed announcement caused much ill feeling among booksellers. Because of this, they explain, "we have always been anxious to suppress it." When Dodgson wrote to them a few weeks before with his new proposal, "we looked into the matter and found we should be selling your books at a gross profit of something less than 5 percent. We do not think this enough to cover the cost of working expenses and the risk of bad debts . . . but we considered that as your books were not infrequently reprinted we made a fair commission on the manufacture, and we thought it would be a good opportunity to please our customers if we could put your books on the same basis as others published at so-called *net* prices. We therefore offered to accept your terms if you would allow us to withdraw the announcement which 'the trade' has regarded with such hostility. This, then, is our position. We wish to publish your books on terms acceptable to you, and we are willing to do so at a rate of profit which we deem inadequate if we can withdraw the advertisement which is, and always has been, a source of annoyance to the retail booksellers. We will agree to sell your books to the trade at a rebate of *2d.* in the *1s.* with such other allowances as may seem fit to us, and we will agree to account to you for all books sold at ¾ of the advertised price, but we cannot undertake to sell to anybody who is not a bookseller at anything but the published price. . . . We feel sure that the retail booksellers would welcome the withdrawal of the advertisement that has given them so much annoyance and we hope you will believe that we are acting in your interest in asking you to let us withdraw it."

7 Lushington Road, Eastbourne
July 25, 1890
Dear Mr. Macmillan,

I thank you sincerely for your full and candid and most interesting explanation.

I quite see the reasonableness of your wish to withdraw any announcement as to acting yourselves as retail-booksellers. My wish to retain that announcement rested on the fact that it *secured* to a private purchaser the getting 10 percent discount. But from what you tell me, I think he would be secure of getting this, even from his local bookseller. That being so, I see, at this moment, only *one* objection to accepting the terms you offer: and that is, your saying that the resulting profit, to yourself, would be such as you deem to be "inadequate." *No* arrangement, which leaves *you* in that position, can be satisfactory to *me*.

Now, without making any further definite proposal, I should be glad to know whether the terms I am about to name would be deemed "adequate" by you.

First, I will give a few statistics. *Sylvie and Bruno* sells at 7*s.* 6*d.* Three-quarters of that would be 5*s.* 7½*d.* At present you credit me with 5*s.* 5*d.*: i.e. with ¾ of the selling price, less $3\frac{19}{27}$ percent on that ¾. Now

$$5s.7\tfrac{1}{2}d., \text{ less } 1 \text{ percent,} = 5s.6.825d.$$
$$,, \quad\quad ,, \; 2 \quad\quad ,, \quad = 5s.6.15d.$$
$$,, \quad\quad ,, \; 3 \quad\quad ,, \quad = 5s.5.475d.$$
$$,, \quad\quad ,, \; 3\tfrac{19}{27} \quad ,, \quad = 5s.5d.$$

Would a commission of 2 percent, on the amount credited to me, make the terms what you would consider "adequate"?

If that were so, our new agreement would embody the following conditions: (1) that the present announcement, as to terms of sale, be *wholly* expunged, (2) that in future you credit me, for each "Lewis Carroll" book sold by you, with ¾ of the published price, less a commission of 2 percent on the sum so credited. (This 2 percent would be most conveniently calculated, once for all, on the whole sum credited to me on account of sold copies.)

Very truly yours,

C. L. Dodgson

---

[1] ". . . we consider that the terms you suggest are quite fair to us," Macmillan & Co. write three days later, "and . . . we will accordingly as from July 1, 1890, account to you for the Lewis Carroll books at ¾ of the retail price less 2 percent. We are much obliged to you for meeting our views as to the advertisement."

Christ Church, Oxford
December 7, 1890
Dear Mr. Macmillan,

Thanks for sending those 4 copies of the *Snark*.

Here we are within 3 weeks of Xmas, and it is a long time since I have come across any advertisement of either *Sylvie and Bruno* or *The Nursery "Alice"*. I have great confidence in your judgement in this matter: still I *will* venture to say that I think you are overlooking *the* one opportunity for securing a sale of them. If they are not to be advertised *now*, at what times *would* you do it? I can hardly suppose that you believe, either that they are so universally known that further advertising is *superfluous*, or that they are so little likely to please that further advertising is *useless*. If neither of these is the case, I should certainly wish you (unless you have some reason, that has not occurred to me, for advising to the contrary) to spend at least £20, during this month, in advertising these 2 books (which, in *my* belief, would sell better if better known). Under our present (to me most comfortable) arrangement, whereby *I* pay for all the advertising, and whereby, the more it is done, the better for *you* (for I presume you charge me more than you pay – just as with the printing, etc.), I feel no scruple in expressing my wishes.[1]

Very truly yours,

C. L. Dodgson

P.S. If you, on considering the matter, think it would be worth while to spend *more* than the £20 I have named, please to let me know.

[1] In a letter of the same date, Macmillan & Co. assure Dodgson that his books "shall be well advertised between this [date] and Christmas."

Christ Church, Oxford
December 13, 1890

Dear Mr. Macmillan,

Will you kindly send me *separate* accounts for the two impressions (10,000 each) of *Nursery "Alice"*, down to June 30, 1890.

The *first* impression was over-coloured, and condemned *not* to be sold in England: and you got me £95 per 1000, for 4000 of them, from your American Agent.[1] Cannot you get him to take some more of them. I would take £70 per thousand – or £200 for 3000 – or, if he will take the whole 6000, I will take £375 (which is at the very low rate of 1s. 3d. a copy).[2]

These last two offers only hold good till January 31, 1891, the money to be paid to me in July, 1891, less the cost of binding.

Why did you bind 500 copies (you don't say which impression) at 60s. 5d. per 100, instead of 45s. 10d., the price charged for the others?[3]

Very truly yours,

C. L. Dodgson

[1] Although Dodgson clearly writes "£95 per 1000," earlier letters indicate that he settled for £80 per 1000 (see pp. 273–4, above). On February 7, 1890, Macmillan sent Dodgson a check for £287.10.0 "in payment for the 4000 copies of *The Nursery 'Alice'* sent to America."

[2] Two days after Dodgson makes this offer, Macmillan write that they are offering the remainder of the rejected first printing to their American agent. But on April 22, 1891, they report that they have not received another order from America and are trying "our most likely Australian customers." On April 23, they add: "We have today seen the London representatives of the three Australian booksellers most likely to speculate in *The Nursery 'Alice'*. One of these would not take any at all, another offered to take 100 at 1*s*. 6*d*. and a third said he would take 500 at 1*s*. 3*d*. per copy. We fear that these offers will not be satisfactory to you." On the following day, Dodgson writes: "You can let the Australian Agent have the 100 . . . which he offers to take at 1*s*. 6*d*. (I mean . . . *nett* – no *discount* allowed): and you had better warn him that in a few months, probably, the price may be raised to £80 per 1000. The other offer I *decline*." In the same letter, Dodgson goes on: "I should much like to send some to the American Hospitals and Homes, where there are sick children. Could you get me any statistics?" On April 25, Macmillan report that they are "writing to New York" to see if they can find a book that lists the appropriate institutions, and on May 15 they send Dodgson a copy of *Charities of New York*. On May 31, Dodgson thanks them for the book: ". . . it has not proved much use, as it only names *one*, and gives no details: but it has told me all about the Charity Organization Society there, which appears to be in touch with Branches all over the States: so I am going to apply to them to put me in the way of getting the information I want."
[3] In their letter of December 15, Macmillan write that the copies which cost 60*s*. 5*d*. per 100 to bind "were those done in accordance with your instructions in a special style for presentation to the Hospitals."

The Chestnuts, Guildford

January 9, 1891

Dear Mr. Macmillan,

Thanks for parcel, containing 1 *Alice* (red), 1 *Looking-Glass* (red), and 4 *Nursery "Alice"*.

I have just noticed an extraordinary thing. The *Alice* is "83rd thousand" and dated "*1886.*" The *Looking-Glass* is "59th thousand" and dated "*1887.*" Yet these are the exact thousands you quote *now*. And, most certainly, we have not sold *none* in the last 3 or 4 years. Is it possible the printers have gone on altering the "thousands" only, and *not* altering the date? It seems scarcely credible that such an amount of absence-of-thought should exist in any London Printer.

As it stands, the title-page is utterly misleading.

This really must not go on. I cannot allow my readers to be so misled.[1]

Very truly yours,

C. L. Dodgson

[1] No error was involved, as Macmillan explains in a letter of the same date. When Dodgson's books were printed, complying with his wish, Macmillan numbered each thousand separately. The 1886 printing of the 6*s*. *Alice* was of 5000 copies, that is the 79th to 83rd thousands. In 1891 the 83rd thousand of that printing was being sold, but, of course, the date refers to the printing date, not the sales date. The same is true of the *Looking-Glass*: 3000 copies were printed in 1887 (the 57th, 58th, and 59th thousands), and the 59th thousand was being sold in 1891 with the date "1887," the date of printing.

Christ Church, Oxford
July 2, 1891
Dear Mr. Macmillan,

I fear my last letter was not clearly expressed: I will try and make it clear.

(1) I did *not* request you to find warehouse room on your own premises for the sheets of *Nursery "Alice"*.

(2) I *do* decidedly object to paying, for warehouse room, either to, or through, Mr. E. Evans. I think it would be a very bad precedent: and I want to wind up my account with him.[1]

My request to you is not, I hope, a very troublesome one. It is simply that you will select some place where the sheets can be warehoused, which would be convenient for yourselves when wishing to procure more sheets, and give the necessary orders, charging me with the expense incurred. Messrs. Clay occur to me as the best people to employ: but I leave it to your choice.[2]

As to your kind offer to "undertake the insurance of my stock and wood-blocks at rate of 10*s*. per £100," it occurs to me that it would be better to employ an ordinary insurance company. That *you*, whose property is risked along with mine, should act as an insurance company for me, seems an undesirable arrangement. I would not willingly insure with even a regular company, if I knew that, supposing *my* property were burned, the same fire would also destroy *their* available assets. But perhaps I have misunderstood you?[3] Believe me

Very truly yours,

C. L. Dodgson

---

[1] Dodgson's letter preceding this one is missing, but Macmillan's of July 2 indicates that he wanted to transfer the stock of *The Nursery "Alice"* from the color printer Edmund Evans. Macmillan write: "With regard to the stock of *The Nursery 'Alice'* we regret to say that we have so little warehouse room that we cannot make room for it. All our printers keep the bulk of the stock of the books they print for us and we do not see why Mr. Evans should not do the same; particularly if you have no objection to paying him for warehouse room."

[2] Four days later, Macmillan write that they would try to make arrangements with Clay to warehouse the stock. They add: "It is, of course, a very unusual thing to ask one printer to keep stock of a book printed by another, and even though we make them some payment, we shall consider ourselves under considerable obligation to Messrs. Clay for helping us out of this difficulty." Dodgson's reply to this is also missing, and Macmillan's next letter, on July 8, simply adds: "We will arrange about the stock. . . ," but they do not specify the nature of the arrangement. The stock did not, in the end, go to Clay: a letter dated August 6 reports that Macmillan "arranged with our binder to take over the stock of *The Nursery 'Alice'* from Mr. Evans."

[3] Dodgson misunderstood. On July 6, Macmillan clarifies: "We merely meant that we would add the insurance of your books to our own policies which are already very considerable." They go on to say that, naturally, Dodgson is free to arrange for his own insurance if he prefers. Dodgson apparently allows Macmillan to proceed, for on July 8 they report that Clay does not have his woodblocks insured, and if Dodgson will send the publisher an estimate of their value, Macmillan will have them insured as well. On August 6, Macmillan & Co. give Dodgson the details of his fire insurance: "We have taken out an insurance policy on the wood blocks of your books for £1600. With regard to the printed stock, it is scattered about: some at the printers, some at the binders,

and some at our own warehouse, and it varies in amount from time to time. We think the best plan will be for us to charge you with the insurance on the value of the stock on hand at July 1st of each year, and to hold ourselves responsible in case of fire. We have large floating insurances on our own stock, and we will so arrange them as to include any property of yours that may be in our keeping."

Christ Church, Oxford
December 23, 1891

Dear Mr. Macmillan,

I am glad to find myself once more in communication with an *individual* member of the Firm as in past years, when Mr. Macmillan Senior was able to be daily at the office.[1]

I enclose Messrs. Blackie's letter: and have sent them the permission they ask for.[2]

As to the opinion you have kindly procured for me: when you did a similar thing last April, I wrote offering to pay for it, and of course am equally ready to do so now: by all means enter the 2 guineas against me in our account. You will see, by the enclosed letter, that in April you took the course of *declining* remuneration. If you would like to "amend the record" (as the lawyers say), and to charge for that opinion also, I have no objection to your doing so.

What you say about the opinion, viz. "such things are written for our guidance and not to be forwarded to the authors," is puzzling. Am I to pay 2 guineas for this opinion, and still not to be free to make the only possible use of it by communicating it to the writer? That would seem hardly fair.

I am surprised, and a little indignant, at your reader's having taken the liberty of *marking* (though only in pencil) a MS which was merely sent him to *read*. He appears to have mistaken his function, and to have thought he was asked to *correct it for the Press*. Kindly have all the marks *very* carefully erased, and at once: the longer they remain, the harder they will be to get out. I should be indeed sorry for my lady-friend to learn her mistakes in *that* way. If it were necessary to tell her of them, I had rather do it myself.[3]

I wish you, and the whole family, and Firm, a very happy Christmas.

Very truly yours,

C. L. Dodgson

[1] Dodgson apparently objected, in a letter that is missing, to receiving letters signed "Macmillan & Co.," a circumstance he had endured now for about a decade (see pp. 165–6, above). On December 12, Macmillan & Co. wrote: "If it would be more satisfactory to you to address your letters to one individual member of our firm we would suggest your writing to our Frederick Macmillan who usually answers you." From this time on, then, Dodgson's salutation "Dear Mr. Macmillan" is intended for Frederick Macmillan and, henceforth, letters going to Dodgson are usually signed "Frederick Macmillan."

[2] The Blackie letter survives. It is a request to include "The Walrus and the Carpenter" in a School reading book which the competing publisher had in preparation.

³ Earlier in the month, Dodgson arranged with Macmillan to have a manuscript novel sent to them to evaluate and possibly publish. The author is named (in letters in both directions) as "C.G.S.," but we cannot even guess at her identity. Macmillan rejected the manuscript, and we have no evidence that it was published elsewhere.

Christ Church, Oxford
March 13, 1892[1]

Dear Mr. Frederick Macmillan,

In answer to your letter about the application of Mdlle. Piguet for leave to publish a French translation of *Through the Looking-Glass*, I write to say:

(1) Please to explain your sentence "the period, during which the right of translation is reserved, has expired." I should have thought it would not expire till the expiration of the *copy-right*, which lasts, I believe, "for 40 years, or for 10 years after the death of author, whichever period is longest." What is the law as to "reserved right of translation"?

(2) On December 12th, 1888, you sent me a letter, from a "Mons. Jacques du B........." (I could not read the name) of "29 Rue Fortuny, Paris," asking leave to publish a French translation of *Through the Looking-Glass*. In reply, I authorised you to give him leave. I have no record of anything being said about selling him electros of the pictures, or of any further negotiations. And I have no idea if the book ever came about. Before answering Mdlle. Piguet, you had better trace the history of this affair.[2]

(3) If Mons. Jacques has published a translation, with the pictures, I think it would not be fair on him to authorise a rival publication.[3]

I await further information, and am

Very truly yours,

C. L. Dodgson

¹ This is the only Dodgson letter in our files for 1892.
² On March 11 Frederick Macmillan explained that "the right of translation is not the same as the copyright and only lasts 10 years." He went on to say that although they no longer held the right of translation, they had some control over translations because no publisher would print an edition without the illustrations, which were still in copyright and for which permission had to be obtained.
³ Frederick Macmillan wrote on the 16th to say that M. de Berwick had been unable to find a publisher for his translation of *Looking-Glass*, and if Dodgson consequently wished to make an arrangement with Mlle. Piguet, "the best plan will be to tell her that she must in the first place find a publisher willing to purchase electros of the illustrations and bring out the book." No further correspondence on this subject enters our files nor is there any record that Mlle. Piguet's translation was ever published. For a summary of translations of *Looking-Glass*, see Weaver, pp. 67–73.

Christ Church, Oxford
February 1, 1893

Dear Mr. Macmillan,

Many thanks for cheque, for which I enclose receipt.

I want to lay before you, for the approval of the Firm, and for any suggestions that may occur to you, some details as to a treatise on Logic, that I am preparing for publication.[1]

My idea is to divide the work into 3 Parts, viz. "Elementary," "Advanced," and "Higher," and to publish them *separately*, in paper covers (or perhaps stiff covers, like picture-books), and also the 3 Parts in one volume, in cloth.

I think we could sell each part for 3*s.* (the price of *The Game of Logic*), and the volume for 7*s.* 6*d.*

The first Part would cover much of the same area as *The Game of Logic*, which has a board sold with it, with red and grey counters. This board would also serve for use with the new book. And I think it would add immensely to the popularity of the book, if the diagrams in it could have *coloured* discs, to represent the counters. Do you think this could be done at reasonable cost? *Printing in colours* would I fear be impracticable, as the diagrams would have to be embodied, here and there, in the text. My idea is to have them printed as circles only, and the colour added by *hand*. I should not expect a *large* sale, 250 at the outside. And the colouring would be of the very simplest nature – only *two* colours to be used, and only circular disks to colour: a boy of 12 could do it quite well. What sort of cost do you think would be incurred, for colouring 250 copies, with (say) 100 discs in each?

Another point I want your opinion on is this. I have been at the book for 20 years or more, and have a mass of MS on hand: but I doubt if any one, but myself, would understand it enough to get it through the Press. So if, at my decease, it were still in MS, it would all be wasted labour. What I want to do is, to get it all into type, and arranged: then it could be utilised, even if I did not live to complete it. I could do this in the course of the next 3 or 4 months; and then I should want to publish Part I only, and keep Parts II and III standing in type for a year or more, as it would need a great deal of revision, and correction, for which I should submit copies, in slip, to all my friends. Could this be managed? Of course I should be willing to pay interest on the value of the type thus locked-up.[2]

Very truly yours,

C. L. Dodgson

---

[1] Dodgson has been working on *Symbolic Logic*. On January 23 he recorded in his *Diaries* (p. 496): "Working on Logic. I am thinking of getting most of the book into type, and getting friends to criticise it."

[2] Frederick Macmillan replies on the following day: ". . . it seems to us that the best plan will be to have it printed at the Clarendon Press. . . . [They] would also no doubt be prepared to undertake the colouring of the discs, which I think under the circumstances had better be done by hand as

you suggest. . . . We shall of course be glad to publish it for you on the usual terms." Four days later, in reply to an intervening letter from Dodgson that is missing, Macmillan changes his mind: "I did not understand that the Logic was to be a 'Lewis Carroll' book. There will be no difficulty about getting it printed at Messrs. Clay and I will arrange with them."

Christ Church, Oxford
February 7, 1893

Dear Mr. Macmillan,

I am glad to hear there is no difficulty in having my new Logic book printed by Messrs. Clay. Your proposal, that it should be printed at the University Press, was no doubt made in ignorance of the fact that *The Game of Logic* was printed by Messrs. Clay. You are also evidently not aware that it was published under the name of "Lewis Carroll." I will now write to Messrs. Clay about it. It will have to be worked off in a very peculiar way. There will, *quite* certainly, be many alterations needed, so soon as I get copies into the hands of my friends, and ask them for suggestions: so it would be quite a waste of paper to work off more than a few copies at a time: I think 50 copies will be quite enough for each edition. Of course that will be much more costly than working off (say) 250 at a time: and very likely the book will be a loss to me. This, however, I don't at all mind. The loss will only affect *me*: I am glad to feel that *your* profits will be all the same, in whatever way the copies are worked off.

Will you kindly get me 2 front stalls for the "Avenue" Matinée of *A White Lie* on February 18?[1] I don't want any other than *front* row: and I had rather have them *not* central. Central stalls are apt to have their view interfered with by the conductor, who is sometimes perched up much too high. If there is choice of sides, I would rather be to the *right*, as you face the stage – as I am deaf of my right ear.

Very truly yours,

C. L. Dodgson

[1] Macmillan send the tickets for Sydney Grundy's *A White Lie* on February 8, and Dodgson's *Diaries* (p. 497) confirm that he attends the performance on the 18th as planned.

7 Lushington Road, Eastbourne
August 16, 1893

Dear Mr. Macmillan,

I hope you will excuse the rather peremptory tone of yesterday's telegram. One cannot explain fully in a telegram, at $\frac{1}{2}d$. a word: and I particularly wished to make it perfectly clear that not a single additional copy of the first edition was to be sold: as it was evident that the meaning of my former letter had failed to reach you, and that you were intending to go on supplying the 1st edition of *Pillow-Problems* to purchasers. Of course I assume that it had *not* happened that my meaning had been understood, but that it was *not* intended to carry out my wishes. It would be as clear to you, I feel sure, as it is to me that Publishers and Authors could not possibly work together on *those* terms.

Of course any applicants for copies, at present, must be told that the book is out of print.

One point I had forgotten to notice when I wrote – the unsold copies in the hands of agents. Please at once recall these, if any, and supply, instead of them, copies of the new edition, as soon as you get it.

The improvements in the 2nd edition are so important, that any purchaser of the book might reasonably consider he had been very hardly dealt with, if, with the new edition on the point of appearing, he was allowed to buy a copy of the inferior edition.[1]

Very truly yours,

C. L. Dodgson

---

[1] "Pillow-Problems Thought Out During Sleepless Nights" is the sub-title of the second part of *Curiosa Mathematica*. It is a set of seventy-two problems, chiefly in algebra, plane geometry, and trigonometry, and it was published in late spring 1893. On January 21, Dodgson recorded: "During the month I have had at Guildford I got into the printers' hands the rest of the MS of *Pillow-Problems*" (*Diaries*, p. 496), and a letter from George Macmillan of March 3 reported that "the volume of *Pillow-Problems* is now nearly all in type, and we will include it in our list of announcements." Dodgson's letter requesting that the book be withdrawn from sale is missing, but Frederick Macmillan assured him on August 14 that "the first Edition of *Pillow-Problems* shall be withdrawn from sale as soon as we receive the copies of the second Edition which you say are being worked off." The phrase "as soon as we receive the copies of the second Edition" probably suggested to Dodgson that Macmillan was disregarding his early request to withdraw the first edition from sale immediately and inspired both his telegram and his letter. In a reply also dated August 16, Frederick Macmillan reassures Dodgson: "We quite understand that no more copies of the first Edition of *Pillow-Problems* are to be sold under any circumstances, and we will at once recall those that are still in the hands of agents." For more on both editions of *Pillow-Problems*, see *Handbook*, pp. 181–2.

Christ Church, Oxford

November 21, 1893

Dear Mr. Macmillan,

I have a serious matter to write to you about.

Having promised to give a copy of *Through the Looking-Glass* to a lady-friend, and having no copies on hand, I wrote to you for 6. They arrived this morning, and I have been examining them.

The paper is not properly "toned," and is nearly white: *that*, however, is a trifle.

Of the 50 pictures, 26 are over-printed, 8 of them being so much so as to be quite spoiled. The book is worthless, and I cannot offer it to my lady-friend. I am glad to find that it belongs to an impression of only 1000, and that you have 940 on hand. On no consideration whatever must any more of this impression be sold. The 940 copies must be at once destroyed, and the book must be "out of print" for the present.

Evidently there has been gross carelessness, on the part of Messrs. Clay in the "making-up" of these pictures. This fact has so far undermined my confidence in them, that I have stopped the working off of the sheets of *Sylvie and Bruno Concluded*. I dare not run the risk of having to cancel an impression of 10,000 copies of a book of 400 pages. The delay will probably prevent the book coming out this season, and so entail on me the loss of hundreds of pounds: but *any* loss is preferable to having a worthless article sold, in my name, to the public.

But, while I lay great blame on Messrs. Clay, as printers, I can by no means acquit *you*, as publishers. I consider it to be part of the duty of a publisher to examine the books received from the printer, and to refuse to take them, if improperly printed.

When I also recall the omissions, in advertising, which I pointed out in my letter of October 1, I cannot help feeling that the Firm has suffered much by losing the personal supervision of Mr. Alexander Macmillan.[1]

But this latter matter is simply one of pecuniary loss to *me*, and is trivial compared with the offering worthless books to the *public*.

It has always been, with me, the one point of *supreme* importance, that all books, sold for me, shall be the *best* attainable at the price: and, much as I should regret the having to sever a connection that has now lasted nearly 30 years, I shall feel myself absolutely compelled to do so, unless I can have some assurance that better care shall be taken, in future, to ensure that my books shall be of the *best* artistic quality attainable for the money.

I am sending you a marked copy of the book complained of, and shall wait to hear what you have to say about it, and about the prospect of the new book being properly printed, before authorising any of the sheets to be worked off.[2]

Very truly yours,

C. L. Dodgson

---

[1] Dodgson's letter of October 1 is missing, but Frederick Macmillan's detailed reply of October 2 indicated that Dodgson had criticized Macmillan's advertising practices in some detail. Macmillan explained that some books were not being advertised because new printings were still in press, but he concluded apologetically: "We will follow out your instructions as to advertising the other books."

[2] Dodgson's *Diaries* (p. 503) also record his reaction to the defective *Looking-Glasses* (same day). On the following day, Frederick Macmillan replies: "I have been very much concerned at the contents of your letter . . . the more so because I find that your complaints . . . are well founded. I sent for Mr. Clay this morning and I find that the reason for the unsatisfactory appearance of the book is that the plates from which many thousand copies have been printed are worn out, and that the only thing to do is to reset the book and make new electrotype plates from the original woodblocks. If you will agree to have this done Messrs. Clay and we will be happy to share

between us the cost of the cancelled copies." Macmillan also encourages Dodgson to reconsider his decision to halt production of *Sylvie and Bruno Concluded*, promising that each sheet will be sent to him for approval and any faults he finds with the printing will be corrected immediately. Macmillan concludes with a conciliatory note: "I hope you will believe that there is no intention on our part to neglect your books, and that we are most anxious to second you in your desire of offering to the public, books, that in artistic quality, are the best obtainable for the money." For a full discussion of this debacle, see Selwyn H. Goodacre, "Lewis Carroll's Rejection of the 60th Thousand of *Through the Looking-Glass*," *Book Collector*, 24 (Summer 1975), 251–6.

Christ Church, Oxford
November 23, 1893

Dear Mr. Macmillan,

Though this will, no doubt, cross a letter of yours, I think it best, considering how pressed we are for time, to write tonight.

First, I wish to apologise for the curtness of the phrase "breach of contract" in my last telegram.[1] Of course I do not for a moment suppose that there has been any *conscious* "breach of contract" on your part. It was merely a brief way of stating (what perhaps you were not aware of) that there had been a definite contract entered into, between Mr. Alexander Macmillan and myself, on that very point. I wrote about it some years ago, and Mr. Macmillan wrote in reply, undertaking that worn electros should never be used, but that, when any electro showed signs of being worn, a fresh one should be taken from the wood-block. It was not to be a matter referred to *me* for decision: it was to be done, as a matter of course, as soon as needed. So I think it is pretty certain that *I* am not responsible for any loss that may be incurred by selling damaged copies, and having to exchange them for good ones.

Secondly, let it be clearly understood that this "exchanging" must go as far back as the damaged copies go. The batch worked off, previously to the 1000 now on hand, consisted of 3000, and was worked off between June 30, 1886, and June 30, 1887. If it should turn out that these 3000 were worked from worn-out plates, so as to be artistically worthless, we are *bound* to exchange any of them, that may be returned for that purpose, for new copies. It admits of no discussion at all: it *must* be done, I am going to advertise that any holders of copies of the 60th Thousand can have them exchanged for good ones: and the question to be settled is, whether the advertisement is, or is not, to include the 57th, 58th, and 59th Thousands. I have sent for two copies of the book, given away in 1891 and 1892, to be returned to me: and they will probably serve as sufficient samples, as they are almost certain to belong to that batch.

Further discussion may, I think, be deferred till this point is settled.

Very truly yours,
C. L. Dodgson

---

[1] The telegram is missing.

Christ Church, Oxford
November 24, 1893

Dear Mr. Macmillan,

I will first reply to your two letters received this morning.

It would be very convenient if, when referring to what you suppose me to have meant, in my letters or telegrams,[1] you would quote my *actual words*, on which you formed the supposition.

You say:

"I did not intend to imply that many thousand copies of *Through the Looking-Glass* had been printed from worn-out plates."

My reply is, that I never supposed you *had* intended to imply this, or any other, assertion as to how many copies had been so printed. I simply enquired *what the number was.*

In your second letter, you say:

"If your proposal is that we should agree to take back any copies of *any* previous edition with the printing of which the possessor is not satisfied, I do not see how we can agree to it."

I am really curious to know what words of mine led you to use the phrase "with the printing of which the possessor is not satisfied." Kindly quote them. It had not even entered into my *thoughts* to make the *possessor* the judge in his own cause. My meaning was, that, if we (you and I) found, on examination, that any *previous* impression had been worked from worn-out blocks so as to be practically worthless, fresh copies *must* be supplied to any holders who chose to return their copies. And I considered it fair that your Firm should bear the cost of this, as you had undertaken to supervise the quality of the printing.

I am happy to say that this question is not likely to arise. I have got back a copy given in October 1891, and find it belongs to the 58th Thousand. I have examined it all through, and find that the pictures are *quite* satisfactory. One or two are a little too heavy: but most of them are very good indeed. My own suspicion is, now, that Messrs. Clay have been laying on the electrotypes, the blame they ought to have taken on *themselves*: that the electrotypes are *not* worn-out but that the "making-up" for printing had been very carelessly done – probably they did not make new cushions at all, but used the old ones: and these probably had got quite dry and hard, and were practically useless. I wonder if you could ascertain whether this was so? I suppose they may be trusted not to tell a *falsehood*, in answer to a question? So I should like you to ask them whether they "made-up" *new* cushions for the pictures, or used the old ones.

This disaster with the *Looking-Glass* made me anxious about *Alice*, and I have been examining a copy of the 84th Thousand. I find it is distinctly *inferior* to the early copies: and some (about a dozen) of the electrotypes are either beginning to wear out, or else have been badly "made-up." I have not the skill to know which. All the rest are *very* good: and I think it throws great doubt on the truth of the statement that one set of electros are worn out by printing 60,000, when the *other* set are in such good order after printing 84,000. Of course some or all of the *Wonderland* electros *may* have been renewed: but if so, there has been an omission in the bill: certainly "new electros" ought to be charged to *me*. I am perfectly ready to pay for them whenever needed. The *one* essential point is, to *keep the quality of work up to the same standard*. This has been my *chief* wish, in connection with the 2 *Alice* books: and it is a *great* annoyance to me to find that I have *not* kept faith, as I hoped to do, with my readers, and that they have been buying inferior goods of me.

No more *Wonderland* are to be printed, from the present electrotypes, till I give permission.

Deferring, till next year, further discussion of the 2 *Alice* books, I will now tell you my wishes as to *Sylvie and Bruno Concluded*.

You will not be surprised to hear that this *Looking-Glass* business has weakened my confidence both in Messrs. Clay's carefulness, and in *your* vigilance.

I must have some questions answered, and some promises given, before I can venture to order the new book to be worked off.

In answering this letter, will you kindly refer to the *numbers* of the questions.

(1) Your Firm undertook that the quality of the printing of the pictures should not deteriorate. To secure this, it was necessary that they should either warn Messrs. Clay to keep a watch on the pictures and give instant notice if any electro seemed worn, too much to print *well*: or else that they should themselves keep watch. Did they give such orders to Messrs. Clay?

If the answer be "no," then I ask.

(2) Did they intend to keep watch themselves, and to examine all books (or at least sufficient samples of them) received from the printers?

If so, then

(3) Whose fault was it that the 60th Thousand were put on sale without inspection?

If the answer to (1) be "yes," then I ask

(4) Whose fault was it that Messrs. Clay failed to announce to you that the electros were too much worn to print from?

Somebody must be to blame, for this miserable "fiasco"; and the culprit must be traced out, if confidence is to be restored between us.

(5) You will not, I think, regard me as exorbitant in saying that I must have a written undertaking, signed by whoever represents your firm, that you will in future inspect samples of any batch of books received from the printers, and satisfy yourselves that the quality is *good*, before selling any.

(6) I must also have a written undertaking, signed by Messrs. Clay, that they will in future keep a watch on the quality of the pictures, and that, if they find them falling off, and have reason to think that new electros are needed, they will at once give you notice.

On receiving satisfactory answers to these questions, and the 2 written undertakings, I will telegraph to Messrs. Clay permission to work off the sheets already passed for the Press, and will send them the rest of the sheets, with a few corrections, to be corrected and worked off.[2]

I will dispense with seeing sample sheets, after "making-up," which you proposed I should do. It would cause great delay, and I think it needless: for I know, perfectly well, that Messrs. Clay *can* produce quite first-rate work. They have the "rubbings" to guide them: and that ought to be quite enough.

The "dummy" volume of *Sylvie and Bruno Concluded* has reached me, and will do extremely well. I think the Medallions *capital*.

Very truly yours,

C. L. Dodgson

---

[1] During the fracas over the 60th thousand *Looking-Glass*, Dodgson sent Macmillan several telegrams, all missing, Before he wrote this letter, he sent off a short note (same date) to Macmillan: "If the 940 *Looking-Glass* are not yet destroyed, keep them. It has just occurred to me that they might be *given* away, to Hospitals, Institutes, etc. Any, so given, I will pay for the printing of." He adds a postscript: "I am writing fully by Registered Post."

[2] The disagreements were resolved in a meeting between publisher and author which Dodgson recorded in his *Diaries* (p. 504) on November 25: "Mr. Frederick Macmillan, happening to be in Oxford, called, and we talked over the *Looking-Glass* business. I have procured copies of the previous impression, of three thousand, and find them so good that I am nearly sure the failure of the 60th Thousand was due to bad 'making-up,' and *not* worn-out plates. This is confirmed by the fact that, in an *Alice* of the 84th Thousand, the pictures are still mostly good. He is to send me written undertakings, from the Firm and from Clay, to secure me against this happening again, before I authorise working off any of the sheets of the new book. Probably we shall run it *very* fine, now, the getting it out by Christmas. The rejected 60th Thousand not being yet destroyed, I am going to give them away (and shall therefore pay for the printing)."

Christ Church, Oxford
November 28, 1893

Dear Mr. Macmillan,

I thank you for the two written undertakings, signed by yourself and Messrs. Clay, though the variations, from the form which I suggested, have made them both, from a legal point of view, valueless. I enclose fresh forms of both, and will thank you to return them, as soon as you can, signed and dated.

You will no doubt like me to explain my remark about these "variations."

In *your* undertaking, you use the phrase "samples of every Edition of any of your books." This gives *no* promise as to my *illustrated* books, none of which are published in "Editions."

Also you use the phrase "printed by Messrs. Clay." This gives *no* promise as to any *other* printer: and there is nothing to prevent you changing your printer tomorrow.

Also you make the test, of quality of work, to be that it shall be "up to the standard of previous Editions" (see my remark, above, on this word) "which you have approved as satisfactory." These last words make the test practically useless, as it would throw on me, if ever I complained of non-fulfilment of this undertaking, the impossible task of producing some previous copy, and of proving that you *knew* that I "approved of it."

In Messrs. Clay's undertaking they use the phrase "we shall at once call your" (i.e. Mr. Dodgson's) "attention, etc." Of course it ought to have been "Messrs. Macmillan's attention."

Also, after thus describing the undertaking which they say they understand I wish for, they go on to say "we are quite prepared to give this undertaking." Being "prepared to give" is no more the same thing as "*giving*," than being "prepared to pay a bill" is the same thing as "*paying*" it!

However, I feel no doubt that you and Messrs. Clay will sign the two undertakings enclosed:[1] and accordingly I have telegraphed to Messrs. Clay to work off the 12 sheets which I had already passed for "Press," and I am sending them, today, 4 more sheets, to have a few corrections made (which I will trust them to make) and then to be electrotyped and worked off. This will make 256 pages passed for "Press" – i.e. $\frac{4}{7}$ of the whole book.

But I have not yet received the Preface, even in slip: so that it will most probably be 10 days, or more, before the *whole* can be passed for Press.

Now let me remind you of *another* agreement, which I made, not long ago, with your firm – immediately after some books of mine had been spoiled by hasty drying (by pressing between blank sheets of paper, which had taken off so much of the ink as quite to rob them of all *brilliance* of tone). It was, that in future no books of mine, offered for sale, should be dried in that way, but that all such should be dried deliberately, in the ordinary way, so as to secure the greatest possible *brilliance* of tone.[2]

I don't mind this risk being run, with the 200 copies required for *giving* away: but it must *not* be run with any of those for *sale*. If the copies to be *given* away suffer, it is merely that my gifts are not quite so good as I should like them to be: but, if the *sold* copies suffer, it is that I fail in what has been *my chief* object all along, to give the public the *best* I can for their money.

So please understand that I wish *this* condition observed, even if it should oblige us to postpone the issue of the book to next year.[3]

Very truly yours,

C. L. Dodgson

---

[1] On the following day, Frederick Macmillan writes: "I enclose a written undertaking couched in the terms suggested by yourself, and have no doubt that Messrs. Clay will do the same." Although we have no further letters from Dodgson on this subject, Macmillan's of December 1 indicates that there was at least one more revision of the undertakings before Dodgson was satisfied.

[2] In his letter of November 29, Macmillan reports that "the old system of doing this by pressing them between mill boards has for some time been abandoned."

[3] *Sylvie and Bruno Concluded*, with forty-six illustrations by Harry Furniss, missed the Christmas sale period. It was officially published on December 29. Dodgson receives a dozen copies on December 24 and inscribes copies at the Macmillan office on December 27 and 28 (see *Diaries*, p. 505; *Handbook*, pp. 184–6).

Christ Church, Oxford
January 26, 1894

Dear Mr. Frederick Macmillan,

I enclose, with thanks, a signed receipt for £660.16.5.

Mr. Craik tells me you are "getting an estimate of the cost of resetting" the *Looking-Glass*. This is superfluous trouble. We have hitherto done without estimates in printing the *Alice* books: I have entire confidence in your charging me only what is reasonable. Moreover, it is premature trouble. The first question is "do any, or all, of the sheets, *need* re-setting?" My present opinion is that *none* do – that there is no reason why the 61st 1000 should not be as good as the 59th; and no reason why the electros of the *Looking-Glass* should not last as long as those of *Alice*, from which 84,000 have now been worked.[1]

Please answer my question, in letter of 25th, as to cost, per 100, of binding the "Hospital" copies.[2]

With regard to the 940 spoiled *Looking-Glass*es, which I hope to give away, I have a question to ask. It seems to me that, considering that your Firm accept the responsibility of the "fiasco," which has inflicted heavy loss on *me*, causing me to miss the December sale of my new book, and thereby lessening my profits for the current year by (probably) some hundreds of pounds, it would not be reasonable to charge me anything over *cost* price for printing and binding: even *that* is all dead loss to me, as I am *giving away* the books: but it is *not* a case where you can reasonably make a *profit* for yourselves. I *think* I might, not unreasonably, ask you to bear part of this outlay: but this I forbear to do. I merely ask you to charge *me* no more than it costs *you*. My question is, whether you accept this view of the matter?[3]

When *are* those crimson morocco books coming? They are for a very dear friend, for whom I was anxious to get them as soon as possible. The order was given before the sheets were ready; and the sheets were delivered to the binders more than a month ago.[4]

Do not forget that I want 12 copies of the new book bound *with edges uncut*.[5]

Where are the "Hospital" copies of the 2 *Alice* books? (This question I asked some time ago, but you have omitted to answer it.)[6]

Did the 5 books, inscribed on December 27th for Mrs. Macmillan, Mrs. George Macmillan, and Mrs. Maurice Macmillan, reach their destinations?[7]

Very truly yours,

C. L. Dodgson

[1] On January 24 Craik wrote inviting Dodgson to set a date when he could be in London to arrange personally the details for reprinting *Looking-Glass*. On the 25th, Dodgson replied: "At present I am suffering from lumbago, and dare not travel. Could we not arrange the matter by letters? It is a process that *I* (with a very treacherous memory for conversations) would much prefer, as I should then have it all, in black and white, for reference." Craik replied the same day agreeing that all could be settled in an exchange of letters. Three days after Dodgson writes this letter, Frederick Macmillan sends two pulls of "Gentleman dressed in white paper" from *Looking-Glass*, "one of them from the original wood block and the other from the Electrotype as it now is; if you compare

them," Macmillan writes, "you will see that the lines in the latter have become coarse and that the delicacy of the picture as it originally stood has to a great extent disappeared. I do not understand why the Electros of *Looking–Glass* have not worn as well as those of *Alice*," he continues, "but it is a fact that they have not, and as I do not think anything really satisfactory could be done by patching up the plates, I should like to have your permission to instruct Messrs. Clay to make an entirely new set from which a really first rate 61st thousand can be printed. I will get them made as cheaply as is consistent with excellence and we will charge you no commission."

² On January 31, Macmillan reports that the price for binding the Hospital copies of *Alice* and *Looking-Glass* was fifty-five shillings per hundred.

³ The rejected sixtieth thousand *Looking-Glasses* were bound and given away. On the previous December 8, Dodgson wrote Macmillan: "Please prepare a stamp, to be impressed at the top of the title-page of every copy given to Mechanics' Institutes, etc., similar to the one you made for books to be given to Sick Children – only substituting, for 'Sick Children' the words 'Mechanics' Institutes, etc.'" The *Advertisement* recalling the rejected copies appeared in *The Times* on December 2, 1893, and a separately printed version was inserted in copies of *Sylvie and Bruno Concluded* (see *Handbook*, pp. 67–8, 183). Macmillan writes in his letter of January 29: "As regards the unlucky 60th thousand, we will certainly charge them to you at a cost price: we have no wish to make any profit out of them."

⁴ Macmillan writes (January 29): "I am sorry that we have not been able to send you the crimson morocco copies of the new book yet. The binder promised them on Saturday last but has disappointed us. I hope to be able to send them within a day or two."

⁵ "The 12 copies of edges *uncut* will be sent you immediately," Macmillan writes (same letter).

⁶ ". . . I find that they were all sent to Parkers by your instructions," Macmillan writes on January 31, "afterwards returned to us, also by your instructions, and finally all distributed to Hospitals in the year 1890."

⁷ No reply to this question appears in our files. Perhaps the ladies in question were nudged to write to Dodgson directly.

Christ Church, Oxford

January 31, 1894

Dear Mr. Macmillan,

You have given me a fright by sending me a "pull" from one of the original wood-blocks of the *Looking-Glass*. Such a thing should never be done without real necessity; and I particularly request that it may not be done again, as there is not the slightest need for it. Even if there were no early copies of the book accessible, there are of course the "rubbings" from the wood-blocks, to refer to, of which I have a set. But, in fact, any early copy of the book is quite enough for purposes of comparison.

And now as to the other "pull," marked "from the Electro." Before taking it as any evidence whatever as to the state of the electro, it is of course essential to know whether a new "overlay" had been made for it. You surely know as well as I do, that without a proper "overlay" no electro will print well. I feel no doubt, now, that the 60th 1000 were worked off without taking the trouble to "make up" afresh, and that Messrs. Clay used the overlays made 3 years before, which no doubt had become hard and dry and useless.¹

And there is very good evidence before me that they have used these same overlays for these 2 "pulls." I have compared the one, marked "from the original woodblock" with an 1872 copy of the book, and the difference is obvious. The "pull" is altogether of inferior quality. You speak of producing "a really first-rate 61st thousand." I certainly cannot accept *this* quality as "really first-rate." Unless we can come a greater deal nearer, than this, to the beauty of the earlier copies, I will not have the book reprinted at all.

Now, do you think we can fairly expect Messrs. Clay to act with any zeal, in preparing evidence against themselves? Are they at all likely to do their best to get a good result from the electros, on which they seek to lay all the blame, while well aware that a *successful* result would serve to convict them of gross carelessness in working off the 60th thousand? For myself, I do not think we can.

You say "I do not understand why the electros have not worn as well as those of *Alice*." Neither do I.

It might perhaps produce unpleasant feeling, between you and Messrs. Clay, if *you* were to take the step of having the matter tested by some other printer. This consideration is not so important for me: so I will now take the matter into my own hands. Kindly send me the electro of the sheet containing the "Railway" picture.[2]

Many thanks for what you say about not wishing to make any profit for yourselves out of this unlucky 60th 1000.

Very truly yours,
C. L. Dodgson

[1] On the following day, Macmillan writes to say that he had himself "enquired upon this point some time ago and found that all the overlays had been specially made afresh." Moreover, the pulls that he sent for comparison were "flatpulls," done without overlays so that the actual condition of the electro could be judged.

[2] In the same letter, Macmillan encloses the picture Dodgson asks for.

Christ Church, Oxford
February 9, 1894

Dear Mr. Macmillan,

On December 17, 1893, I sent you instructions for a new stamp, to be used for title-pages of books presented to Reading-Rooms, etc. I have not yet seen the result.[1]

I am told that a new Periodical, *Chimes*, is announced, claiming *me* as a contributor to the first number. I know nothing of it. Would you look out for it, and see if it infringes copyright?[2]

With reference to the application of Mrs. E. A. Worsdell (28 King Street, Lancaster) to be allowed to buy copies of spoiled *Looking-Glass*, for a reading book, I think it would be best to make a small charge, and not give them – if you don't mind the trouble of receiving the money from her, and crediting it to me.

In that case, would you kindly write and ask her if she would like to buy copies at 1*s*. apiece: and how many she would require. (She would have to wait till some are bound in the *plain* binding used for Hospitals.)

Please send me 4 *Alice Underground* in *red*.

Very truly yours,

C. L. Dodgson

---

[1] Macmillan replies on the same day: "I enclose an impression of the new stamp which was ordered by your instructions in December last."

[2] In the same letter, Macmillan promises to look into the *Chimes* question, but no further reference to the new periodical enters our files. *Chimes*, a monthly magazine of poetry, fiction, music and drama, ran for only eight numbers, from March to November 1894. Neither Dodgson nor "Lewis Carroll" appears as a contributor.

Christ Church, Oxford
February 10, 1894

Dear Mr. Macmillan,

Thanks for proof of stamp. It will do very well now.

Please have 250 of the spoiled *Looking-Glass* bound in the strong plain binding we use for Hospitals. If you have not a specimen-copy to show to the binders I will send you one from here. It has the title on the back in gold. The rest of the cover is plain red, the medallions being impressed but not gilt. On the upper part of the cover is impressed, in Old English,

Presented for the use of Sick Children.

I should like a similar heading to be impressed on these 250 covers – viz.

Presented for the use of Mechanics'
Institutes, Reading-Rooms, etc.

The edges of the book are cut and sprinkled.

I return Miss Bailey's letter. Will you kindly tell her that there is no such person as "Canon Dodgson"; that the Rev. C. L. Dodgson, of Christ Church, Oxford, has published some mathematical books with you; that you have submitted her letter to him; and that he has given you the enclosed circular, to send in reply to her letter.[1]

Very truly yours,

C. L. Dodgson

In reprinting *Looking-Glass*, how would it do to electro *picture*-pages *only*, and use old electros for the rest of the text?[2]

---

[1] For the purpose of answering unsolicited letters from unknown readers addressed to the Rev. C. L. Dodgson (and its numerous varieties) as the author of the *Alice* books, Dodgson had printed up *The*

Stranger Circular (1890), which reads: "Mr. Dodgson is so frequently addressed by strangers on the quite unauthorized assumption that he claims, or at any rate acknowledges the authorship of books not published under his name, that he has found it necessary to print this, once for all, as an answer to all such applications. He neither claims nor acknowledges any connection with any pseudonym, or with any book that is not published under his own name. Having therefore no claim to retain, or even to read the enclosed, he returns it for the convenience of the writer who has thus misaddressed it." For more on the subject, see *Handbook*, pp. 168–9; Selwyn Goodacre, "The Stranger Circular," *Jabberwocky*, Autumn 1974, pp. 11–12.

2 On February 12, Frederick Macmillan replies: "It would of course be possible to insert new electrotypes of the illustrations in the *Looking-Glass* and to use the existing plates of the text, but it would not make so satisfactory a job as having new plates throughout."

Christ Church, Oxford
February 12, 1894

Dear Mr. Macmillan,

There seems to be a curious fatality about the 2 volumes of *Sylvie and Bruno*, which I ordered to be bound in crimson morocco. First, the thing was, evidently, forgotten altogether – the other morocco volumes reaching me on January 12, and the crimson ones on January 31st. And now I find that they are bound wrongly. The volume lettered *Sylvie and Bruno*, contains the title-sheet and preface of Volume i, and the *text* of Volume ii: while the one, lettered *Sylvie and Bruno Concluded* contains the title and Preface of Volume ii, and the *text* of Volume i.

Please let me have answers to the following questions:

(1) Can the covers be used again?

(2) If the books are taken to pieces, and arranged properly, would it entail much cutting down of the edges?

I ask this because I should like, if possible, to keep the same books: as they were inscribed on January 31, and *new* copies would have to be inscribed with a later date. Nevertheless, if the re-binding of these copies would at all spoil their appearance by narrowing the margins, then we must have new copies.[1]

I think you will agree with me that, whatever has to be done, to rectify the mistake, the binder ought to do *without charge*. It is entirely *his* fault.[2]

Very truly yours,

C. L. Dodgson

1 Frederick Macmillan replies the following day that "under the circumstances, there is nothing to be done but to bind another copy." However, as Dodgson was so concerned about the inscription, Macmillan offers to take from the existing copy "the leaves on which your inscription occurs and bind them up in the new copies."

2 Macmillan agrees and assures Dodgson that "the binder shall, of course, only charge for one set as the blunder is his, and perfectly inexcusable."

Christ Church, Oxford
February 28, 1894

Dear Mr. Macmillan,

I am now engaged on getting the first Part of *Symbolic Logic* through the Press. Messrs. Clay have just set up the Contents, a proof of which I enclose.

I pointed out to them the four different kinds of title that would be needed – Part, Book, Chapter, Section – and that types should be used, so different as to show clearly which was subordinated to which. And I told them I thought *they* would be the best judges of what to use. Now that I see the result, I withdraw that opinion. They don't seem to understand the thing at all: the different titles are scarcely distinguishable. If you turn to the foot of slip 5, where Chapter, Book, Chapter, come together, you have to look closely to see which is the superior heading, and which the inferior.

Messrs. Clay have shown *no* inventive faculty at all. They have tried *all* the titles in upright caps printed solid; and have made no use at all of the other kinds of type, viz. caps spaced out, italic caps, large italic non-caps. By using these, very distinct headings could be obtained.

Your firm have no doubt had large experience in such things. Would you try (taking Mr. Craik into counsel, specially: I have confidence in his taste) to devise some way of doing the headings which will show clearly their subordination to one another?[1]

Very truly yours,

C. L. Dodgson

Thanks for 25 *Game of Logic.*

---

[1] "I enclose a specimen type which Clays have set up for the headings to your *Symbolic Logic*," Frederick Macmillan writes on March 6. "The three divisions of part, book and chapter, seem to be pretty clearly indicated."

Christ Church, Oxford
March 5, 1894

Dear Mr. Macmillan,

Will you kindly get 6 copies of the two volumes of *Sylvie and Bruno* bound, for me to give to Lending Libraries. I want each volume divided into *three*, so as to make 6 volumes altogether, lettered at back, like this:

The covers to be red, but without the medallions and gold lines; and the edges to be sprinkled red.

Vol   I to end of p. 128.
Vol II pp. 129 to 270
VolIII pp. 271 to end,
Vol IV to end of p. 146

Vol V 147 to 286
Vol VI pp. 287 to end.
I have lately made the acquaintance of a lady artist, who has done some
beautiful book-illustrations. She was then "Miss Laura Troubridge," but is now
"Mrs. Adrian Hope."[1] One of her books is quite lovely – *Little Thumb*, by Hans
Andersen, published by Mansell & Co., 271 Oxford Street, at 2*s*. 6*d*. Another is
The Little Mermaiden: *that* does not give so good an idea of her skill, as she has
drawn the pictures twice over, and the published book is *not* the best set. The *best*
set appeared in some Magazine – perhaps the *Strand*. She lent me the original
drawings, which are very beautiful. And she also lent me the (unpublished)
coloured illustrations for *The Queen of Hearts*, and music, written for it (I believe
she has the copyright) by Mr. Alfred S. Gatty.[2] This book I have undertaken to
mention to you, as she seems rather inexperienced in publishing, and is glad of
my help in thus bringing it to your notice. The pictures are *most* charming, and, if
properly reproduced in colour, would make one of the prettiest picture-books
out. You would find it worth publishing, I think. May I ask her to send you the
pictures for inspection?[3]

Very truly yours,

C. L. Dodgson

P.S. I wrote February 9 about a letter you were to write to Mrs. Worsdell. Has
she answered it?[4]

Are the 250 copies of spoiled *Looking-Glass* yet bound in "Hospital" binding,
about which I wrote February 10?[5]

These "Magic Pens" are about the best I ever wrote with.[6]

---

[1] Laura Elizabeth Rachel Troubridge (1858–1929), who married (1888) Adrian Charles Francis
Hope (1858–1904), enters Dodgson's Diaries on August 31, 1893, when he records showing
visitors "drawings Mrs. Hope has lent me," and again in 1896 when she visits him at Oxford
(*Diaries*, p. 525). Her illustrated version of Andersen's *Little Thumb* appeared in 1883, and she
illustrated Andersen's *The Story of the Mermaiden* in 1888.

[2] (Sir) Alfred Scott Gatty (1847–1918), composer and musician, was the son of Margaret Gatty,
founder and editor of *Aunt Judy's Magazine*, and her husband, Alfred Gatty, D.D. (1813–1903),
Dodgson's long-time friends. In 1877 he published *Little Songs for Little Voices* which contains
mostly his own compositions and includes three songs from the *Alice* books.

[3] Frederick Macmillan writes the following day: "I know the work of Miss Laura Troubridge. 'The
Little Mermaiden' appeared in the *English Illustrated Magazine* when it belonged to us. We shall be
very pleased to look at her illustrations for *The Queen of Hearts* if she cares to send them, but I do not
think it very likely that we shall see our way to make her an offer for publication, for experience has
made us rather afraid of coloured picture books." *The Queen of Hearts* illustrated by Laura
Troubridge was not published by Macmillan, nor, it seems, by anyone else.

[4] Macmillan agrees to receive payment directly from Mrs. Worsdell and writes on the following day
that she was purchasing thirty copies at one shilling each.

[5] In the same letter, Macmillan writes that these copies are ready and "can be sent out whenever
you give us instructions."

[6] Dodgson obtained "Magic Pens" from Parkins and Gotto and often recommended them to
friends. A detailed description of Magic Pens, however, eludes us (see *Letters*, p. 1011).

Christ Church, Oxford
May 24, 1894

Dear Mr. Macmillan,

Thanks for your letter about *Sylvie and Bruno Concluded.*[1] I am quite satisfied that its small sale is not at all due to insufficient advertising; and that more advertising would have done no good, either for it or the *Nursery "Alice"*. Don't do any more *extra* advertising: it seems to be only throwing money away. I did not know the reviews had been unfavorable.[2] If the reviewers are right, the book does not deserve to sell: if they are wrong, it will gradually get known by people recommending it to their friends.

As to that letter and bill you have sent me, from the "Authors' Clipping Bureau," I must ask you to investigate as to *whose fault it is* that the name "Rev. C. L. Dodgson" has reached those people. The bill is made out in that name: and in their letter they quote your "favor of April 11, directing us to discontinue sending clippings to Rev. C. L. Dodgson." Of course you yourself know, perfectly well, that my name is *never* to be given to outsiders, in connection with "Lewis Carroll." It must be one of your subordinates who have made the blunder. I am much vexed about it, and beg you will investigate the matter, and reprimand whoever is to blame.[3]

The order, sent through you in July 1890, was to send clippings to "Miss Dodgson, Chestnuts, Guildford" about books by "Lewis Carroll." Will you kindly refer to your copy of the letter, and see if "Rev. C. L. Dodgson" was named in it?

The clippings have always been sent, hitherto, to Guildford: but this morning I received a packet of them, addressed "Rev. C. L. Dodgson" to your care. This I have sent back to Boston, with one of my printed circulars saying that Mr. Dodgson acknowledges no connection with books not published under his name.

This new bill is, of course, *not* to be paid. They know, perfectly well, the terms on which they do business: and you, no doubt, stated the matter clearly in your letter of July 1890.

They require prepayment of 5 dollars: in return for which they undertake to go on sending clippings, till they have sent 100. When that is done, the transaction is at an end.

If they sent *more* than 100, it is entirely their own affair. I never authorised them to do so, and I will not pay for them.[4]

Very truly yours,

C. L. Dodgson

P.S. For your convenience, I will add a history of the communications with these people.

July 12, 1890) I wrote to you "send 5 dollars to Authors' Clipping Bureau, 186 Washington Street, Boston, to prepay 100 cuttings about me, to send to Guildford."

April 7, 1894) I received a letter from them (addressed "Rev. C. L. Dodgson, Chestnuts, Guildford." I forgot to complain about this at the time) saying "We send by this mail 7 clippings relating to your books, and enclose statement of account to date. Miss Dodgson's remittance, through the Messrs. Macmillan, of $5.00 in advance, paid for the first one hundred clippings, so that a second remittance is now due. We shall be pleased to have you send either by postal order or through your publishers, as may be most convenient to you." (I do not find any "account" enclosed in this letter.)

April 9, 1894) I wrote to you "tell 'The Writer' no more cuttings are required."

May 23, 1894) I received from you their letter "Your favor of April 11, directing us to discontinue sending clippings to Rev. C. L. Dodgson, is at hand, and we have given the necessary instructions to our Readers. We enclose bill for the clippings mailed to Rev. Mr. Dodgson to date." Also a bill

> "Clippings 1 to 200 – $10
> 26 July, 1890 – by cash $ 5
>
> Amount due $ 5

---

[1] On May 18, Dodgson wrote Macmillan: "I am disappointed at the small sale of *Sylvie and Bruno Concluded*. Do you think you are advertising it enough? . . . I authorised you at the end of last year, to make a considerable outlay in advertising several of my books – particularly *The Nursery 'Alice'*, which I think you had not advertised for about a year. Do you think the outlay made any difference in the rate of sale of those books? If advertising does them no good, there is no use wasting money on it." On the 21st, Frederick Macmillan replied saying that they had spent about £55 on advertising *Sylvie and Bruno Concluded*, "so that the unsatisfactory sale cannot be the result of insufficient advertising. I am afraid it is chiefly due to the tone of the reviews that have appeared." In the same letter, Macmillan wrote: ". . . I regret to say that the experiment of advertising *The Nursery 'Alice'* does not appear to have been particularly successful. I find that the sales from October 1893 to March 1894 are considerably less than for the corresponding months of the previous year."

[2] The reviews were not universally unfavorable. The *Saturday Review* (January 27, 1894, p. 106) praises the story "as dream-like in humour and fantasy as anything in *Alice's Adventures*" and calls the illustrations by Furniss "the best work in book-illustration that the artist has yet published . . . admirable for invention, spirit, humour, and ingenuity." The *Athenaeum* (January 27, 1894, p. 112), on the other hand, asks "Where is the wit; where are the 'flashes of merriment'? The story – if story 'it can be called which shape has none' – has, however, been constructed on a theory. . . . Is *Sylvie and Bruno* intended as a child's book? If so, will any child ever read the long preface or require the index? . . . There are many good things in this book, of course, but it is much too long."

[3] In his letter of May 28, Frederick Macmillan reports that he has investigated the matter and no one at Macmillan & Co. is to blame: Dodgson's instructions were followed and no use made of his real name. Macmillan adds, however, that "the Americans are very fond of breaking veils of anonymity, and you will find your books always catalogued in American bibliographical publications under your own name." Macmillan concludes that the information about the identity of "Lewis Carroll" probably came from some publication.

[4] Macmillan suggests (same letter) that Dodgson return the account to him and the publisher would write to the clipping bureau explaining that only one hundred cuttings were ordered (and prepaid), and, therefore, the second five dollars would not be paid.

7 Lushington Road, Eastbourne
September 17, 1894
Dear Mr. Macmillan,

Don't you think it would be worth while to spend some money on advertising *Sylvie and Bruno Concluded* in good time for the Christmas sales? It has hardly had a good chance yet, as the *Looking-Glass* business made it so late last winter, and probably diminished the sale by several thousands, and my profits by many hundreds.[1]

I was grieved to see the contrast between the two volumes which you sent me the other day. The "Conclusion," put side by side with the first volume, looked so wanting in brilliancy, so faded, as to be decidedly of inferior quality to the first. I fear your printers' work is not up to its ancient level. And their services have proved a very "white elephant" to me! The loss they have caused to me by their gross carelessness (for which they have never expressed the slightest regret) in giving you no warning about those *Looking-Glass*es, is probably over £500: and the inferior quality of the new book will no doubt affect its sale, and cause a further loss.

Very truly yours,

C. L. Dodgson

[1] Frederick Macmillan replies (September 19) that he does not think it advisable to spend additional money on advertising, but, of course, the firm would do so if Dodgson wished it. On September 28, however, Dodgson goes up to London to consult both Macmillan and Craik, and together they decide to offer both *Sylvie and Bruno* books and *The Nursery "Alice"* at reduced prices for the Christmas sale (*Diaries*, pp. 514–15). The result is not a great success. Macmillan writes in a letter of December 17: "I am afraid that the offer of *Sylvie and Bruno* on special terms has not had any very marked effect on the sales. I find that we have sold at special prices 34 copies of Part I and 23 copies of Part II. In the case of *Nursery 'Alice'* the result is slightly better. We had sold practically no copies at all up to the time of the reduction, and we have since then sold 72. On the whole I should think that it would be best to return to previous terms after the 1st of January."

7 Lushington Road, Eastbourne
September 18, 1894
Dear Mr. Macmillan,

I was just going to give away the enclosed copy of *Nursery "Alice"*, when I discovered that it has been spoiled (in the binding, I suppose): every leaf is puckered. Please to stamp it with the "Hospital" stamp, and put it aside. It must not be *sold* on any account.

Please send me a good copy.

Also please have an examination made of the copies now on sale, and let me know how many more (if any) are spoiled in like manner.

If there are many, so as to make it highly probable that some have been sold, I shall [have] to incur *another* outlay in advertising, in order to get them returned and changed for good copies.

However, I will hope, till I hear to the contrary, that this is a solitary instance.[1]

Very truly yours,

C. L. Dodgson

---

[1] "I am having all the stock carefully examined," Frederick Macmillan writes two days later, "but I have no reason to think that the damaged copy was due to anything but an accident which did not affect any of the other copies." He adds: "I think you ought to know that not a single copy of *Through the Looking-Glass* was returned to me in consequence of your advertisements."

Christ Church, Oxford
November 30, 1894

Dear Mr. Macmillan,

On opening the parcel, containing the 6 copies of the *Sylvie and Bruno* books, bound in 4 volumes each set, I found that the volumes were labelled i, ii, instead of *, **, as ordered in my letter of October 24.[1]

Considering that, in the "General Index," "i" means the first book, and "ii" the "Conclusion," this lettering is most confusing. I tried to get them altered (at least enquired about it, of a binder here) but it cannot be done.

I hope you won't be offended with me for saying that I do *not* like having my instructions ignored without consulting me about it.

A similar case (of quietly setting aside my instructions) occurred last August, when I asked you to write for me to Messrs. Deacon and Co., and sent you, on August 23, the substance of what I wanted written. In October I got from them a copy of the letter they had received from you, and found it necessary to write to them again, telling them my former reply had been improperly transmitted. On that occasion I got my letter copied by a young lady friend.

If you do not like writing letters for me, I will get them copied elsewhere: but, when you *do* undertake it, I think I may fairly expect that they shall be written according to my instructions.[2]

Very truly yours,

C. L. Dodgson

---

[1] Dodgson's letter of October 24 is missing, and Frederick Macmillan's reply (also October 24) simply confirmed that Dodgson had ordered *Sylvie and Bruno* bound according to special instructions. Macmillan replies to the present letter on December 1: "I am very sorry that the binder has not followed exactly your instructions with regard to the *Sylvie and Bruno* books in 4 volumes. If you will kindly send them back I will either have them put right or (if that turns out to be impossible) rebound at our expense."

[2] Frederick Macmillan investigates this complaint and reports to Dodgson on December 1 that the problem lay in his sending "the substance" of what he wants to say which could be (and apparently was) misinterpreted. Macmillan suggests that in the future Dodgson send the precise words he wishes to use and they would be copied exactly. Macmillan adds: "I can assure you that we have no wish to avoid writing letters or doing anything else of the kind to oblige you."

Christ Church, Oxford
December 5, 1894
Dear Mr. Macmillan,

Many thanks for your kind offer to rebind the *Sylvie* books: but the matter is too trivial for that, even if alteration were impossible. But I have thought of a remedy that will meet the case, viz. in the 2 volumes of the "Conclusion," to increase the "ɪ" to "ɪɪɪ," and the "ɪɪ" to "ɪɪɪɪ": then there will be no risk of confusion. I shall have to send the 12 volumes to *you*, to be done, as, oddly enough, the binders here have no "ɪ"s of the right size!

As to the letter to Messrs. Deacon, I quite understand that the omission of part of my letter was a mistake, and not a very unnatural one. In future I will adopt your excellent suggestion, and send you the exact words that I wish to be copied.

As to *Rhyme? and Reason?*, I would like to wait till it is sold out. There are some changes I wish to make in it, next time we print it: but there will be no harm in its being out of print for a while.[1]

Thanks for the trouble you have had in the matter of Mr. Powell's *Musa Jocosa*.[2]

Very truly yours,

C. L. Dodgson

[1] On December 4 Macmillan asked Dodgson for permission to reprint *Rhyme? and Reason?* because the stock was down to forty-two copies.

[2] *Musa Jocosa: Choice Pieces of Comic Poetry*, selected and arranged by George Herbert Powell (1865–1924), was published in 1894 by Bliss, Sands, and Foster of London. Lewis Carroll is represented with "The Walrus and the Carpenter," "Father William," and "Jabberwocky" (pp. 155–68). A. A. Vansittart's Latin version of "Jabberwocky" also appears. On November 22, Frederick Macmillan wrote: "If you will kindly send up your copy of *Musa Jocosa* we will get Mr. Powell to inscribe it."

Christ Church, Oxford
April 5, 1895
Dear Mr. Macmillan,

What you say, as to our understanding regarding reprints, agrees with my own impression. The records I fail to find are of my letters authorising 10,000 *Alice* (people's edition) and 5000 *Looking-Glass* (people's edition) to be printed in the year ending last June. Kindly give me the dates.[1]

I'll see about preparing *Rhyme? and Reason?* for a reprint: but I'm giving *all* my time, and brains, just now, to Part ɪ of *Symbolic Logic*: and I should like to get *that* through the Press first.[2] Most of the MS is now in Messrs. Clay's hands.

The book will, I expect, be about the size of *A New Theory of Parallels*. Do you think it would be possible to sell it for *one* shilling, and *just* to cover the current expense of production? I can't afford to sell it at a *loss*, but I would be content with one halfpenny profit per copy![3] If any of your school-books is got up in the style you would recommend, I should be glad to see a specimen.

Very truly yours,

C. L. Dodgson

[1] Dodgson's letters immediately preceding this one are missing, but from the Macmillan letters it appears that Dodgson wrote to ask what their understanding was concerning reprints of his works. On the previous day, Frederick Macmillan wrote: "In reply . . . I write to say that our understanding is that no one of your books is to be reprinted without consultation with you." In reply to the present letter, Macmillan writes the following day: "I cannot find your letter authorising us to print the last Editions of the People's *Alice* or *Through the Looking-Glass*. They were both printed during the first part of 1894."

[2] On the previous day, Frederick Macmillan wrote to remind Dodgson that on the previous December 4 they had asked permission to reprint *Rhyme? and Reason?* because only 42 copies remained. ". . . the stock is now quite exhausted," Macmillan writes, "and if a new edition is to be printed it had better be put in hand."

[3] On April 6 Frederick Macmillan replies that a shilling "seems a very low price" and adds that it would be preferable to get an estimate from the printer before suggesting a price.

Christ Church, Oxford

April 9, 1895

Dear Mr. Macmillan,

I am inclined to agree with you that we shall not be able to sell the *Logic* at 1*s*. I'm afraid 2*s*. will be the lowest we can put it at. Do you get a large sale for any 2*s*. school-books? You have not sent me a specimen of the sort of style of get-up you would recommend.

As to those reprints of People's Editions (15,000 altogether: 10,000 *Alice* and 5000 *Looking-Glass*) I feel sure now that the matter was *not* referred to me. My *memory* is not reliable: but I have a letter-register, and enter a précis of every letter received and sent: and there is no record of any such correspondence. I will tell you how I came to look into the matter. My last receipts from you were, financially, a most disappointing amount. I had hoped for *hundreds* more: and it was a very serious deficiency, and difficult to meet. And the other day I went through the account, to see *how* the misfortune had come.

The *great* cause of loss was of course my having so entirely miscalculated the chance of sale for *Sylvie and Bruno Concluded*. Instead of *10,000* copies it would have been much wiser to print *2000*. *You*, I presume, shared my false hopes, as you never made any suggestion for a smaller issue. Well, *that* mistake accounted for about £500, expected but not received. For *that* waste of outlay I have only myself to blame.

But, on looking over other accounts, I was surprised to find these 15,000 copies, which I felt pretty sure I had never authorised. If the matter *had* been referred to me, I should almost certainly have said "no" to the *Alice* reprint, and reduced the other from 5000 to 1000: and that would have made a difference of nearly £200 in my receipts.

The average sale of *Alice* (taken on 5 previous years) is 4800. You *began* the year, which ended June 30, 1894, with 5714 in hand – amply sufficient for the year. And in fact you did not sell so many in the year: and, of the 10,000 which you printed, 9559 were still on hand at the end of the year. This needless operation cost me £160, within a few shillings. And the needlessly large number of the *Looking-Glass* (whose average sale is 3000, and you began the year with 2635, so that *1000* would have been quite enough to print) cost me some £30 or £40 more.

I've no doubt you *thought* you had written to me about reprinting, and I don't want to dwell on the matter further. Mistakes will happen, in the best conducted businesses. But I think it well to point out that this mistake of yours has been a very costly one to *me*. When I was already in some financial straits, owing to my own rashness in spending a needless £500 on printing *Sylvie and Bruno Concluded*, it was a little hard on me to have to waste another £200 owing to a mistake of my Publishers.

Of course the money will *ultimately* come in: but, for that current year, the blow was a heavy one.

However, I feel pretty sure that you will be in future more careful to refer to me before committing me to such large losses.

Reprints, especially in such large amounts, should always come near the *beginnings* of our financial years, so that there may be some receipts by sales, to balance the outlay: and should be so arranged as not to *end* our financial year with a large number of unsold copies on hand. (In the case of the unfortunate *Alice*, you *ended* our year with *two* years' supply in hand!)

I have pointed all this out to you, in a previous letter, I feel sure. But it is not for *me* to complain of forgetfulness in others. Those, who live in glass houses, should never throw stones!

Very truly yours,

C. L. Dodgson

The Chestnuts, Guildford
April 15, 1895

Dear Mr. Macmillan,

I will now answer your letter dated April 10.

As to *Symbolic Logic*; you say you can not "give an exact estimate of cost." *That* is of course impossible, at present: and I did not ask for it: what I want to know is, supposing it were about the size of *A New Theory of Parallels*, what style of cover, and what sort of paper, you would suggest, in order to *minimise* the cost of production.[1] I thought you might have some school-book which would serve as a specimen.

As to the reprints of People's Editions: you say "I cannot pretend to say with certainty, at this distance of time, whether or not I consulted you before going to Press." In asking you the question, I had fancied that you great business-houses had a much more perfect system for letters than my letter-register, and that you kept actual *copies* of all the letters you sent. *I* only record a précis of each: but *I* could easily give, for any year since about 1865, the *substance* of our correspondence for the year.

You say you "cannot agree with me" as to your action having "caused loss": and that the only loss is "interest." That was just what I meant to say – that there was no *ultimate* loss: in fact I used the words "of course the money will ultimately come in." So we *do* agree.

You point out, quite rightly, the mistakes in my calculations, caused by not counting copies used for the double book.[2]

Still, allowing for that, I think that, if I had been consulted, I should have limited the reprint to 1000 each, just to clear the year: and then, when July came, I should have been ready to sanction printing 10,000 *Alice* and 5000 *Looking-Glass*, as I quite see the advantage of printing large numbers at a time.[3] Thus there would have been (say) £150 more to receive during 1895.

To a large house like yours, with (no doubt) a large capital, it probably matters next to nothing whether such a trifle as £150 is paid *now* to you, or a year or two hence. It is, as you say, merely a question of losing the interest. But to a man of limited means, who has to regulate the expenditure of each year so as, if possible, to get it out of the *income* of that year, a year's delay is a more important matter. As you have been so kind as to offer to pay some more cash *now*, I will gratefully accept £150, which I shall then be able to reckon as part of my income for 1895, and which will enable me at once to do several things which I had most reluctantly abandoned as being impracticable.[4]

Whenever you have any spare hands to put on to the task, it would be well to begin drawing up a list of the schools and colleges to which we ought to send prospectuses of the *Logic*-book, marking those that ought *also* to have copies of the book itself.

Very truly yours,

C. L. Dodgson

---

[1] Macmillan reply the next day that the best and cheapest binding would be the one already in use for Dodgson's *Curiosa Mathematica*.

[2] In his letter of April 10, Frederick Macmillan calculated that with the sale of the combined volume of *Alice* and *Looking-Glass* included, the average sale was over 6000 copies annually, not the 4800 Dodgson estimated.

[3] While Frederick Macmillan admits and apologizes for neglecting to consult Dodgson about the reprints (same letter), he argues that the large printing was not really a loss because the much smaller printing that Dodgson would have ordered would have cost him significantly more in the long run: ". . . the saving per copy in printing five thousand copies instead of one thousand is something like fifty percent," Macmillan writes.

⁴ Macmillan concluded his letter of April 10 with the offer to send Dodgson a check for £200 at once against the amount that would be due him in January 1896. The check for £150 which Dodgson requests accompanies Macmillan's reply of April 16. On the 17th Dodgson writes: "I am really grateful to you for your kindness in paying me that £150, and I enclose receipt, signed."

The Chestnuts, Guildford
April 19, 1895

Dear Mr. Macmillan,

I think it will be quite easy, before the middle of May, to make an exact estimate of the current cost of production, per 1000, of the *Symbolic Logic*. As to the *cover*, I thought you had told me that a cheaper cover might well be used than we have used for *Curiosa Mathematica*, viz. thinner boards, and the cover cut flush with the book: however, I will look at some school-books, and write again.

Besides the list, which you have kindly undertaken to make, of Professors, etc., to whom copies of the *book* might be sent, we shall need a *much* longer list, of masters and mistresses of schools, to whom copies of the circular *letter* should be sent. It would save you much trouble, to get the *Educational Yearbook* (which you may charge to me) and use it as your list, ticking off the names on the margin, as fast as they are sent off.¹ As soon as we know what sized envelope will be needed, it will be well to prepare some, with a notice printed, above the address, to this effect.

SYMBOLIC LOGIC by LEWIS CARROLL
PART I. ELEMENTARY
A fascinating Mental Recreation for the Young

How do you think that would do?

You suggest that the circular letter had better be in *writing*, reproduced by some "process"; and no doubt that has some advantages over a *printed* circular, which is so often thrown into the waste-paper-basket, wholly unread. But there are arguments on the other side, which I would like you to consider.

It is *much* more easy, in a printed circular, to gather the meaning of a sentence as a *whole*, without the necessity, attaching to a *written* letter, of reading each individual word. My own feeling, as to *written* letters, is that one does not willingly undertake the trouble of reading it a *second* time. Now *this* circular I want to be read *several* times: and I think, to most people, it is *less* trouble to read a printed paper 2 or 3 times through, than to read the same thing in MS *once*. If only we make the heading of the paper, and the notice on the envelope, sufficiently *attractive*, I think very few of the masters and mistresses would fail to read it through.

At present, I am inclined to have it a *printed* circular: but I should like to know what you advise after reading what I have said.²

Don't you think it would be quite safe to send circulars in envelopes *un*-fastened, merely with the flap tucked in? That would reduce postage from 1*d*. to ½*d*. – an important item if we send out many thousands.

Very truly yours,

C. L. Dodgson

Please to send me, at Oxford, 4 copies of each of the 2 Parts of *Curiosa Mathematica*. Also a copy of *The Divine Library* by Kirkpatrick.[3]

---

[1] In his reply three days later, Macmillan reports that the firm keep a superior and more comprehensive manuscript list of schools and propose using it to send out advertisements of *Symbolic Logic*.

[2] Macmillan agrees with Dodgson (same letter) that a printed circular would be better, and it is duly printed (see *Handbook*, pp. 192–3). On November 1, 1894, Dodgson hatched an idea for advertising his books that has since become standard practice. In a letter to Macmillan, he wrote: "Do you think we could induce one of the Daily Papers (I should prefer the *Standard*), for a reasonable sum, to fold a copy of the leaflet [advertising all the 'Lewis Carroll' books] inside each copy of one day's issue of the Paper? It would be a novel form of advertising, and one that I think would attract attention. Of course I would pay for the printing of the necessary leaflets. How many would they be? A quarter of a million?" But Frederick Macmillan replied (November 2): "It would be quite hopeless to propose that the leaflet should be inserted in any of the great daily papers. They would not listen to such a suggestion for a minute." The notion seems then to have been dropped – and re-invented by the high-powered advertising forces much later.

[3] *The Divine Library of the Old Testament* (1891) by Alexander Francis Kirkpatrick (1849–1940), Regius Professor of Hebrew at Cambridge and Canon of Ely (1882–1903).

Christ Church, Oxford
May 4, 1895

Dear Mr. Macmillan,

You need not wait till I have seen the sheets of Messrs. Lippincott's Continuation of *Alice*, before coming to a decision as to whether *you* will be the publishers of it in England. Whether it be extremely good, or extremely bad, or have any intermediate degree of merit, *my* view of it would be exactly the same, viz. *absolute* disapproval. I entirely agree with you in thinking such a publication impudent and offensive.[1] I am getting legal advice as to whether we have any power to prevent its being published in England.

I have been reconsidering the question of printing those 6000 special envelopes, in which to send, to all Schools, my circular letter about *Symbolic Logic*; and have come to the conclusion that it will not be worth while to incur that additional expense, and that it will do very well if it can be sent round with your other circulars and catalogues of Educational Works.

Will you, then, kindly let me know

(1) At what times in the year you send your Catalogues.

(2) To how many Schools you send them.

(3) What you would charge for the trouble of putting a copy of my circular letter into each envelope.

I think you might, quite fairly, charge me with a share of the cost of printing your envelopes, writing the directions, and posting.

The fact, that the circular is to include a specimen-page, settles the question of size and type. The letter will be in the form of a pamphlet, probably of 8 pages, the size of *Curiosa Mathematica*. It can be printed on *thin* paper, if that be necessary to avoid increasing cost of postage.

The book might be *announced*, as "in preparation," in the Catalogue you send round in June: but without naming any *price*, as I cannot fix it so soon.[2]

I *hope* to get it through the Press before Christmas: but the labour of perfecting it is tremendous.

As to the cover, I like the *look* of your *Anglo-Oriental* Reader, better than the Clarendon Shakespeare-plays: but the sides are not *stiff* enough for a book of 200 pages. However, we can go into that matter when the book is nearer to completion.[3]

If you issue a new edition of that *Reader*, I would advise careful *revision*: I have marked no less than 22 places where words are entered under wrong headings, so that the unfortunate Oriental scholar will learn to *mis*pronounce them! Believe me

Very truly yours,

C. L. Dodgson

---

[1] Two days earlier, Frederick Macmillan wrote that a representative of Lippincott & Co. of Philadelphia had called and told Macmillan about the impending publication of "a continuation of *Alice in Wonderland*" and asked whether Macmillan would be willing to publish it in England. Macmillan wrote to Dodgson that the firm would publish the book only if Dodgson were eager for it to appear. Macmillan concluded by offering his opinion that "the idea of a continuation of *Alice* by another hand strikes me as both impudent and offensive." When Macmillan receives the present letter and learns that Dodgson shares his views, he replies (May 6): "I am writing to Messrs. Lippincott's agent to tell him that you and we strongly disapprove of the continuation of *Alice*." The book in question (also bound in red) was not so much a continuation as an imitation. *A New Alice in the Old Wonderland* by Anna M. Richards, Jr. (1895) tells the story of a little girl, Alice Lee, who loves the *Alice* stories, eats too much cake before bedtime and has a dream (almost 300 pages long!) in which she meets most of Dodgson's characters in a variety of similar situations. Mrs. Richards lacks Dodgson's narrative skill and imagination, and it is not surprising that the book did not enjoy a great success.

[2] ". . . we shall be sending catalogues to about twenty thousand schools at the end of November," Frederick Macmillan writes on May 6, "and if you think fit we shall be willing to enclose the *Symbolic* circular in the parcel. We should not charge you anything for folding up the circular or writing the directions, but if the addition of your circular involved an increase in the cost of postage as it might very likely do, we should propose to charge you with that." On the 8th, Dodgson replies: "I am most truly grateful for your great kindness, in undertaking, without charge, the gigantic task of enclosing my circular in your 20,000 envelopes. The extra halfpenny postage, if it should entail it, must of course be charged to *me*. Still, £40 is a serious item, and must be avoided if possible. Will you kindly tell me what your envelope and its contents will weigh (to within a quarter of an ounce)?" To which Macmillan replies on the 9th: "We cannot at this date tell exactly

what circulars we shall wish to send out in November and I think the whole matter had better stand over a bit."

³ On April 22, Macmillan sent Dodgson a copy of one of their Anglo-Oriental readers as a sample for *Symbolic Logic* because it had "the cheapest possible binding."

Christ Church, Oxford
May 20, 1895

Dear Mr. Macmillan,

I have an idea for reprinting the serious poems, from *Phantasmagoria*, etc. (published in 1868), with some pictures that have been drawn for me by Miss Thomson.[1]

I will put down my notions, and shall be glad to hear whether you approve them, or can suggest any alterations.

The page to be 6 inches wide, 8 high. Text $5\frac{1}{2}$ or 6 high. About 4 lines to the inch. Old-faced type, intermediate to Small Pica and Long Primer. The pictures to be in the centres of blank pages, without even lines round them.

I am sending some MS to Clay, to have a couple of pages set up as an experiment.

The pictures are all of fairies. I think it will make a very pretty-looking book.

The cover I think should be *dark*, as they are serious poems: some colour that will not fade (as all purples do). Is not *brown* a good lasting colour?[2]

Very truly yours,
C. L. Dodgson

¹ This is the first mention of *Three Sunsets and Other Poems*, which would appear posthumously in February 1898. Frederick Macmillan replies two days later with some reservations about whether or not "there is likely to be a remunerative sale," as "there is not much sale for serious poetry nowadays." But he adds that should Dodgson decide to publish, "we shall of course be pleased to do our best to assist you."

² In the same letter Macmillan does not think brown "sufficiently attractive" and would be inclined to suggest green, but he adds that it would be best to wait and have Dodgson look at specimens in several colors at the appropriate time. *Three Sunsets* ultimately appeared in green cloth.

Christ Church, Oxford
May 26, 1895

Dear Mr. Macmillan,

I suppose, not having heard to the contrary, that you approve of my description of the *Symbolic Logic*, and are putting it into type for your Catalogue.[1] Could you conveniently manage, when you have got it into type, to work off 100 copies as leaflets, which I could insert in letters sent to friends? It would help to make it known.[2]

As to the "Serious Poems" (not that I am thinking of *that* as a title: my present idea for a title is *Three Sunsets, and Other Poems*), I may as well tell you how the matter stands. Miss E. G. Thomson has drawn me a dozen very charming pictures of fairies. These I had meant to insert in the book of "Games and Puzzles,"[3] which is already partly in type, the page being the same size as the *Game of Logic*. But I find that, when reduced to $3\frac{1}{2}$ wide, most of them suffer so much as *pictures* that it would quite spoil the beauty of the set. They ought to be $4\frac{1}{2}$ wide, most of them, and thus need a page $6\frac{1}{2} \times 8$ (the book must be pretty nearly *square*, as many of the pictures are broader than they are high). They have cost me a good deal of money, which will of course be entirely wasted if I do not publish them at all: and the public would lose the sight of a beautiful set of pictures. Also to publish them, reduced to $3\frac{1}{2}$ wide, would be nearly as bad. The best way I can see out of it is to sacrifice yet a little more money in getting them cut, $4\frac{1}{2}$ wide.

My notion is to regard the whole cost of the pictures, drawing and cutting, as money *spent*: and to price the book merely with regard to the current cost of producing it. It will be a thin book, 50 or 60 pages only; and perhaps we might manage to sell it for 2*s*. 6*d*., or even 2*s*. And if we only print 250, there would be no great loss, whether it sold or not.

Very truly yours,

C. L. Dodgson

P.S. I have consulted a legal friend about the possibility of stopping the publication, in England, of that imitation of *Alice*: and I find that, though we should probably have a strong case, yet the taking legal action might easily lead to my having to appear in Court, and having to acknowledge the identity of my real name and my pseudonym. *That* would be worse for me than any money loss which the sale of the book could entail: so my conclusion is to let them alone.

[1] Three days earlier, Frederick Macmillan wrote that Macmillan & Co. were going to press with a catalogue to be sent to schoolmasters in June, and he asked Dodgson if he would briefly describe the "aims and object" of *Symbolic Logic* for the catalogue, as "the title alone looks a little bare."
[2] On the day after Dodgson writes this letter, Macmillan replies that unfortunately it is necessary to keep the type of the catalogue standing for six months, and it would not, therefore, be possible to work off Dodgson's description separately until that time had elapsed.
[3] The drawings are of fairy children without dress in various poses and combinations. They do not relate to the text they grace (see *Handbook*, pp. 203-4).

Christ Church, Oxford
June 14, 1895
Dear Mr. Macmillan,

Many thanks. I had not understood your meaning. It was not worth while setting up the short description a second time, as I shall circulate the longer one among my friends. Still, as it is done, it would be a pity not to utilise it as a leaflet.[1] It had better be all on one page, I think. What do you think of the enclosed sketch of it?[2]

There is *another* book that I have been long working at, as to which I should be glad to know if you will be willing to publish it, in order that I may get some of it set up in slip, to submit to friends. It will be an attempt to treat some of the religious difficulties of the day from a logical point of view, in order to help those, who feel such difficulties, to get their ideas clear, and to see what are the logical results of the various views held. Venn's Hulsean Lectures, which I have just met with, called *Characteristics of Belief*, is very much on those lines, but deals with only *one* such difficulty.[3]

Very truly yours,
C. L. Dodgson

[1] After having written that they could not reprint Dodgson's catalogue description of *Symbolic Logic* separately, Macmillan apparently had the type reset to print off copies for Dodgson's private use. On the previous day, Frederick Macmillan wrote: ". . . the type is standing and we can print off 100 or 200 copies as you may instruct us."

[2] Missing.

[3] *On Some of the Characteristics of Belief, Scientific and Religious*, the Hulsean Lectures for 1869 by John Venn (1834–1923), was published by Macmillan in 1870. Venn was a lecturer in logic and moral philosophy at Cambridge for many years. In the introduction to the book, he explains his purpose: "The following discourses are intended to illustrate, explain, and work out into some of their consequences, certain characteristics by which the attainment of religious belief is prominently distinguished from the attainment of belief upon most other subjects." Venn adds: "The method of treatment here adopted is logical and not metaphysical." Collingwood later writes (*Picture Book*, p. 344): "Among the books which death prevented Lewis Carroll from completing, the one on which his heart was most set was a collection of essays on religious difficulties, for he felt that, as a clergyman, to associate his name with such a work would be more fitting than that he should be known as a writer of humorous and scientific books. However, it was not to be so; he only lived long enough to finish one of the several papers . . . ," on the subject of eternal punishment. That essay appeared posthumously in *Picture Book* (pp. 345–55) for the first time. Dodgson's letters to an Agnostic and his letters to an Invalid give further insights into what he might have written in the proposed book (see *Letters*, indexes).

7 Lushington Road, Eastbourne
August 5, 1895

Dear Mr. Macmillan,

I am seriously anxious about the accuracy of the "List of Works" at present inserted in my books, and will be much obliged if you will at once look into the matter yourself, as it evidently will not do to trust it to Messrs. Clay without your own supervision.

The other day I sent them a proof of the circular letter about *Symbolic Logic*, arranged in pages, with instructions to make an 8-page pamphlet, 4 pages to be occupied by the letter, and 4 by the "List of Works." I enclose a proof of these last

4 pages, which I beg you to examine, and to compare with the "List" in *Sylvie and Bruno Concluded*. You will see that it is an entirely bygone version of the "List." Several books, that we have announced as "in preparation," are omitted altogether: the paragraph about *Sylvie and Bruno Concluded* could never have been in the "List" itself at all, as it contains the words "by Lewis Carroll" (which of course would be absurd in a "List" headed with my name), and it does not mention the *number* of illustrations: it has evidently been copied from some *newspaper* advertisement, issued before the book was completed. And, worst of all, the "List" contains that vexatious misprint, of "wonderful" for "wonderland," which I corrected at least a year ago.

This startling instance of incompetence, or carelessness, on the part of Messrs. Clay, has made me very uneasy. I fear I must ask you to take the trouble of ascertaining, as to *each* of my books now on sale, whether any copies, that are still unbound (of course the *bound* copies are beyond remedy), whether it is supplied with the latest edition of the "List of Works." All incorrect copies of the "List," not yet bound up, must of course be withdrawn and replaced by correct copies.

Please let me know, as soon as you conveniently can, how the matter stands.[1]

Very truly yours,

C. L. Dodgson

Kindly send me a copy of your little book of *Selections from Wordsworth*.[2]

---

[1] The following day, Frederick Macmillan reports that the "List of Works" Dodgson was sent was not supplied by Macmillan & Co. and was apparently taken from something which existed before Dodgson's last corrections. Macmillan proposes printing an entirely new list that he will send to Dodgson for approval "in a day or two." On September 7, Dodgson writes again: "Messrs. Clay tell me they are waiting, before sending me a revise of the *Logic* circular, till you have finally corrected the 'List of Works.' I thought the proof you sent me on August 16 *was* your final revise? If I have not miscalculated the weights, you will be able to send it to all your 20,000 schools without any increase of postage. If so, I should like that done. How many schools ought to have presentation-copies of the book?" On the 9th, Macmillan replies that Clay was confused: the "List of Works" *was* finally corrected, and Clay was being instructed to send Dodgson a revise of the *Logic* circular. In the same letter, Macmillan reports that they plan to send presentation copies of *Symbolic Logic* to 220 school teachers and would send Dodgson a copy of the presentation list for his approval.

[2] This could be the copy of Wordsworth that Dodgson gave to May Barber, whom he visited this summer and to whom he gave an anthology of Wordsworth's poems with the inscription: "May, with love from Lewis Carroll" (see *Letters*, p. 1113).

7 Lushington Road, Eastbourne
October 9, 1895

Dear Mr. Macmillan,

Thanks for tickets, annual account, and the books just received. I will send you the address to which to forward the 3 tickets you have now in hand.[1]

We ought at once to go into the subject of the paper, and binding, for the first part of *Symbolic Logic*, in order to fix the *price*, which of course should be named in the Circular Letter.

I can now tell you the *size* of the book: it will be just under 184 pages, counting in the "List of Works."

Now my wish, as you know, is to sell it for the *lowest* price we can afford. Please keep that in view, in choosing a paper and a binding. But we must also remember that it will be used (by those who take it up) quite as much as any School-book: so the paper must be good enough, and the binding strong enough, to stand a good deal of thumbing, and opening and shutting.

I should be no judge of the paper, with only a specimen-piece of it to go by: the best way, to come to a clear idea as to what the finished book will be like, would be to bind up a dummy copy. The binding should be such that the book will open tolerably *flat*; for the reader, in working the examples, will need to have it lying open before him.

As to the cost of *printing*. You need not make any allowance for the *initial* cost, which I know will be great. All you need to ask Messrs. Clay is, assuming the type to be all set, what they would charge for printing 250. Of course the cost per copy will be much less if they print 1000 at a time; but I think we must fix the price so as to cover the cost when only 250 are done at a time.

Do you think it would help the sale (I am far more anxious to sell *many* copies than to make money by it) if you offered it to the booksellers, *not* at a "net" price, but with full reduction, and selling them 13 copies as 12?[2]

I enclose the 1st sheet, and also a copy of the Circular letter.

Very truly yours,

C. L. Dodgson

[1] On Saturday, October 12, Dodgson goes for the third time to see Augustus Thomas' *Alabama*, with Marion Terry acting, at the Garrick (see *Letters*, p. 1075).

[2] Macmillan replies on October 16 that he believes *Symbolic Logic* should be priced at 2s. But he also explains that he would prefer not to use "the old system of giving thirteen copies as twelve" because a new system was being adopted with the "net books" of invoicing books to the trade at 9½d. in the shilling. He proposes terms for *Symbolic Logic* of 9d., in the shilling, less 7½ percent, which would leave Macmillan "a profit of one half penny in the shilling with which we shall be content."

Christ Church, Oxford
October 17, 1895

Dear Mr. Macmillan,

I am much obliged to you for your letter. If I understand it aright, it amounts to this. Each copy will cost me (if we print 250 at once) 8¾d. (say 9d.). You propose to sell at 2s., and to credit me with 1s. 4½d. a copy, and say that you will thus make a profit of 1d. a copy, which will content you. *My* profit would be 7½d.: our profit (between us) 8½d.

Now I should be glad if you would answer the following 2 questions, before we fix the price.

(1) Suppose we sold at 1*s*. 6*d*., instead of 2*s*. What would be our total profit? (It is a puzzling question to me: *I* make it 4*d*., instead of 8½*d*.: i.e. 3*d*. for me, and 1*d*. for you.)

(2) Suppose we sold at 1*s*. 6*d*., instead of 2*s*. Would this be likely to make a *real* difference in the sale? Would 1*s*. 6*d*. be a distinctly better selling price? (If so, I would gladly submit to my profit being reduced from 7½*d*. to 3*d*. I am *much* more anxious to sell *many* copies than to make profit.)[1]

Very truly yours,

C. L. Dodgson

---

[1] Macmillan replies on the following day: "I cannot believe that the sale of the book would be any better at 1*s*. 6*d*. than at 2*s*. Schoolmasters adopt books because they fancy they will be useful not because they are cheap, and supposing the price of a school book is reasonable, the sale is not affected by sixpence one way or the other."

Christ Church, Oxford

October 19, 1895

Dear Mr. Macmillan,

I write in haste, as I see your specimen book is your "File Copy": so perhaps you are in a hurry to get it back. Please send me an ordinary copy of it, or any book with a similar cover, as I should like to have a specimen by me for reference and to show to friends till we have settled on binding and paper. Best send a book done on thicker paper. I presume *some* of your school-books do not show the printing through? If, however, *all* do so, then please bind a dummy copy, of the paper you propose to use, with at least *one* sheet of it printed on both sides of the paper: *what* you print matters little: but, if it has to be done by Clay, they may as well print a sheet of the *Logic*. Also please let me know what difference the thicker paper will make in the cost.[1]

As to the profit on the book, if priced at 1*s*. 6*d*. which you put at between 4*d*. and 4¼*d*., dividing it into 3½*d*. for *me*, and between ½*d*., and ¾*d*. for *you* (i.e. less than the penny with which you said you would be content), I should certainly wish the division (if we adopt that price) to be 3*d*. for *me*, and between 1*d*. and 1¼*d*. for you.

As to your advice to price at 2*s*. instead of 1*s*. 6*d*., I should be disposed to accept it without demur, but that it is evidently based on a misunderstanding, on your part, as to the nature of the book. This must be removed, and *then* I shall be glad to know if you still prefer 2*s*. to 1*s*. 6*d*.

You say "Schoolmasters adopt books because they fancy they will be useful, not because they are cheap, and, supposing the price of a school book is reasonable the sale is not affected by sixpence one way or the other." This shows that you have not yet read any of my circular letter, as I have there explained clearly that this book is *not* offered as a "school book." In the present state of logical teaching, it has *no* chance of being "adopted" as "a school book," as it would be of no use in helping its readers to answer papers on the Formal Logic, which is the only kind taught in Schools and Universities. It teaches the real *principles* of Logic, and it enables its readers to arrive at *conclusions* more quickly and easily than Formal Logic, but it does *not* enable any one to answer questions in the form at present demanded. I have no doubt that Symbolic Logic (not necessarily *my* particular method, but *some* such method) will, *some* day, supersede Formal Logic, as it is immensely superior to it: but there are no signs, as yet, of such a revolution.

My book aims at supplying a mental *recreation* – most useful and helpful, but *not* a school book.

Now that you understand this point, it may perhaps modify your view as to price. That a book at 1*s*. 6*d*. should have *no* chance of selling better than one at 2*s*., is certainly a paradox, and *sounds* almost incredible. However, you must have had large experience in selling books at both prices, and I should be willing to adopt your view, if you still hold to it now that you know that my book is *not* a "school book."[2]

Very truly yours,

C. L. Dodgson

---

[1] Two days later, Frederick Macmillan writes that Clay is printing a sheet of *Symbolic Logic* on the paper intended for the book and will send Dodgson a dummy copy within the week.

[2] Macmillan replies (same letter) that he *still* believes *Symbolic Logic* should be 2*s*. He argues that if it is unfitted for class teaching and therefore unlikely to be adopted as a textbook, "its sale is likely to be very limited in any case. We do not believe that this limited sale could be made into an extended one by lowering the price from 2*s*. to 1*s*. 6*d*. However, the matter is of course in your hands and if you wish to make it 1*s*. 6*d*. we can have no objection."

Christ Church, Oxford
October 23, 1895

Dear Mr. Macmillan,

In answer to your question ("May I take it that in future we are to account to you for all your books at the same rate, viz. 9*d*. in the 1*s*., less $7\frac{1}{2}$ percent?") I can only say, today, that my letter (agreeing that the *Symbolic Logic* should be priced at 2*s*. and accounted for to me at 1*s*. $4\frac{1}{2}d$.) did not contemplate the case of *any* others of my books. The terms on which *they* are sold have been the subject of much consideration and correspondence, as you know, and were thoroughly agreed on by both of us. If you wish them altered, which will re-open the whole question, of course I am ready to reconsider the matter: but it would take a good deal of time, and I am extremely busy. I presume there is no *immediate* need for going into the matter?[1]

Very truly yours,

C. L. Dodgson

[1] We have no reply to this letter.

Christ Church, Oxford
October 27, 1895

Dear Mr. Macmillan,

I am well satisfied with the look of the dummy-copy, and I think the paper will do very well now (you have not told me what difference it will make in the cost of production to use this thicker paper instead of that used in the Arithmetic-book).[1] But I think it would be better to interchange the 3rd and 4th lines on the cover, and to have "PART I. ELEMENTARY" in the place, and in the type, of "LEWIS CARROLL," and to put my name *below*, and in the smaller type. Thus the title will all come together, and the more important fact (that it is *elementary*) will be in the larger type. Do you approve of this alteration?

I suppose you will very soon know what the Catalogues will weigh, that you intend to send round in November, and whether the additional Circular Letter will or will not make a difference in the postage. Please let me know how this will be.[2]

Very truly yours,

C. L. Dodgson

How many copies of the book shall we print?[3]

[1] On the following day, Frederick Macmillan writes that no increase in cost is involved, as the thicker paper was allowed for in the estimate.
[2] In the same letter, Macmillan writes: "I am afraid we shall not be able to send out the Circular letter about *Symbolic Logic* free of cost if it remains in its present form. We can do so if you will cut it down to four pages by leaving out the advertisements of your other books. Even then it should be printed on thin paper."
[3] Macmillan suggests (same letter) printing 500.

Christ Church, Oxford
October 31, 1895

Dear Mr. Macmillan,

I am disappointed with your letter. I thought I had put my 2 questions clearly; but you do not answer *either* of them. I will try again.

(1) As to catalogues, and cover, which are to be sent to the 5000 schools. What is the exact weight (*without* any letter of mine)?

(2) As to catalogues, and cover, which are to be sent to the 20,000. Same question.

Please give the weights to within $\frac{1}{10}$th of an ounce. You can weigh with ordinary weights to within $\frac{1}{2}$ an ounce: and you can finish with the enclosed envelopes, each of which is exactly $\frac{1}{10}$.

The leaving out the "List of Works" won't suit me at all. It would be a sacrifice of a most valuable opportunity. Our ordinary advertising seems to be simple waste of money. Take *The Nursery "Alice"* for instance. I get plenty of evidence that most people don't know of its *existence*, even. I believe it would sell *well*, if only we could get its existence *known*.[1]

Very truly yours,

C. L. Dodgson

[1] Frederick Macmillan replies on the same day, explaining that there are two separate batches of catalogues. The first, which will be sent to 20,000 schools, must be light enough to go for a penny; the second, which goes to 5000 higher schools, is heavier and must cost $1\frac{1}{2}d.$ to send. If Dodgson would agree to send *only* to the latter schools, his 8-page letter could be sent without difficulty because of the $\frac{1}{2}d.$ margin. Macmillan also explains that he cannot give the weights within $\frac{1}{10}$ of an ounce because the catalogues are not yet printed and stitched. He does not, however, wish to "run the thing so close as to weight" that the slightest variation in the thickness of any sheet of paper might render the package overweight and put the recipients to expense for extra postage.

Christ Church, Oxford

November 1, 1895

Dear Mr. Macmillan,

Thanks for your letter.

I want the Circular (the 8 pages, and *not* on thin paper) to go to the 20,000. This, it is clear from your letter, will cause the 15,000 packets to cost $1\frac{1}{2}d.$, instead of $1d.$ The Circular weighs exactly $\frac{1}{4}$ ounce; so the packet will weigh between 4 and $4\frac{1}{4}$ ounces.

Fifteen thousand half-pence are £31.5.0.

Now I should like to know how much of this you think it would be fair that I should pay. It is needless to point out that it will enable you to send, to these 15,000 schools, all the extra papers and catalogues that are now sent only to 5000; and a good deal more, if you liked, as you will have an ample margin to deal with.

Of course, if you say "we *don't* want to send *anything* more to the 15,000 and the packets we shall send will be such that, leaving out your Circular, they will be under 4 ounces," it would be fair to charge the whole £31.5.0 to *me*. But I fancy it is more likely that you will be willing to share the expense, and to utilise the occasion by sending, to the whole 20,000, what you now send to only 5000. In that case, *you* will be the best judges as to what would be a fair division of the expense.

I await your answer before coming to any decision.[1]

Very truly yours,
C. L. Dodgson

---

[1] Three days later, Frederick Macmillan writes: ". . . we shall be pleased to send your eight-page circular to all the twenty thousand schools if you will allow us to charge you ten pounds (£10) as a proportion of the expense of doing so." Dodgson's reply is missing, but Macmillan's letter of November 6 indicates that he accepted the proposal.

Christ Church, Oxford
December 22, 1895

Dear Mr. Macmillan,

I want to consult you about the Advertisement, of books to be given away, which is to occupy the last page of the Logic-Letter in the 4000 copies which are to go round in *Crockford's Clerical Directory* (and also in the *Clergy List*, to which I am making a similar application, in case they are willing to circulate them).[1] And I shall be much obliged if you will consider the matter, and let me know your opinion, as soon as you can, as we have no time to lose.

My wish is to offer, to all Incumbents or Curates, copies of *Looking-Glass* (60th Thousand) for use in Village Reading Rooms, or to lend to invalids: also copies of *Nursery "Alice"* (toned) to show to children, or lend to sick children: also of *Sylvie and Bruno* (both volumes, to be bound in *plain* covers, merely with name, and with sprinkled edges) for Village Reading Rooms, or to lend to invalids.

It will be *many* years before we can hope to *sell* the great number of *Sylvie* on hand, and I would gladly give away (say) 1000, that they may give pleasure *somewhere*.

Now I have not time to receive applications *myself*, and send instructions to you to forward books. Would you mind the applications being addressed to *you*, and that you should act on a general instruction to forward *single* copies to any genuine clerical address (it would, of course, be satisfactory to *verify* them, by reference to the *Clerical Directory*, and I would gladly pay for the trouble of doing this), and, where application was made for more than one copy, to exercise your own discretion as to sending them.

If you would do this, it would dispose of *one* difficulty: but there is another – the *cost* of postage, or carriage. If, as I hope, we may find it possible to give away some thousands of books, the cost, whether by Parcel Post [or otherwise], would be between £50 and £100: and *I* cannot afford to spend that sum, though, if each applicant pays for his own parcel, it would not be felt, anywhere. But how can this best be secured? The following ways occur to me, and I shall be glad to know, which, if any, you approve of.

(1) To announce that the books will be sent as Railway parcels, to be paid for on delivery.

(2) To announce that applicants must send stamps (it would be for you to fix the *amount*, per book) to defray cost of Parcel Post. This plan would require the *return* of the stamps, in case applications came in for more than we could supply. Perhaps *this* difficulty might be met by announcing that, in case the books asked for could not be sent, the stamps would (after deducting 1*d.* for postage) be returned.

In *any* case the distribution will involve a great deal of *clerk*-work, for which of course I would pay.[2]

Please address your reply to "The Chestnuts, Guildford," whither I go tomorrow.

Very truly yours,

C. L. Dodgson

Please have paper ready for 5000 Letters.

---

[1] Dodgson paid seven guineas to have his "Logic Letter" inserted in 4000 copies of the annual edition of *Crockford's Clerical Directory*. On December 9, Frederick Macmillan wrote that the charge "seems to me fairly high," but "of course it would be a first-rate advertisement." In this advertisement, Dodgson makes a strong case for Symbolic Logic as a recreation: in contrast to the "treadmill" of Formal Logic, Symbolic Logic is a "cricket-ground." It is an "'Open Sesame!' to a treasure-house, for students of 12 to 20 years of age and even for children." For more on the Logic Letter and its variants, see *Handbook*, pp. 192–3.

[2] In Frederick Macmillan's absence, Craik replies to this letter two days later: the firm will distribute the books and urge Dodgson to ask for postage in advance. On December 29, Dodgson reports to Craik: "I have sent to Messrs. Clay the MS of the announcement about books to be given away. I am very glad you are able to undertake the distribution. All books, thus given away, should have that fact stamped on the title-page, to secure them from being sold as ordinary copies. This has been already done, if I remember right, with the *Looking-Glass* and *Nursery 'Alice'*: the same stamp will serve for *Sylvie and Bruno*, I should think, if you have it still. Will you let me know what words are on it, and whether it still exists?" On January 1, Frederick Macmillan replies: "I send you an impression of the stamp which was put upon the copies of the *Looking-Glass* and *Nursery 'Alice'* which were given away in January 1894. This will do very well for *Sylvie and Bruno* if the date is altered." For more about the *Circular about Books to Give Away*, see *Handbook*, p. 198.

Christ Church, Oxford
January 28, 1896

Dear Mr. Macmillan,

It is indeed fortunate that it occurred to you to let me see a copy before binding the 500.[1] Your workmen seem to have been trying in how many ways they could disobey the instructions given to them!

I return the two specimen-copies, for reference. Kindly let me have them again, with a *third*, rather more carefully done.

(1) In copy A, I approved of a certain thickness of cover. In B, a thinner one has been used.

(2) In copy A, I *dis*approved of having my name placed, in large type, *between* the two portions of the title, and directed that it should be put *below*, and in *smaller* type. This instruction has been entirely neglected.

(3) After seeing copy A, I directed that the edges should be *sprinkled*. This has not been done.

(4) In copy A, I approved of a certain thickness of paper. In copy B, a paper, one-fifth thicker, has been substituted.[2]

(This last defect is, of course, irremediable with this *first* edition. In the *second*, the right paper must be used.)

Of course I must see another copy before the 500 are bound, even though it will cause delay. I would rather wait a month than offer to the public so unsatisfactory an article as this last specimen.

My confidence in your workmen (or in whoever looks after them) is at a low ebb, and I had better repeat two instructions, lately sent, lest *they* also should be overlooked.

(1)

On December 1, 1895, I requested that a few copies (say 4) of the Circular Letter should be enclosed [in] each of the 200 presentation-copies which you are sending to masters and mistresses: which suggestion you approved of. For this you will have to get about 500 printed. The notice, about books to be given away, should be on the outer page of each.

(2)

On December 22, 1895, I requested that any copies of *Sylvie*, given away in accordance with that notice, should have *plain* covers, like the Hospital *Alice*, and *not* gilt edges.[3]

Very truly yours,

C. L. Dodgson

[1] On the previous day, Frederick Macmillan sent Dodgson "an early" copy (B) of the impending *Symbolic Logic*, "as I should like to be quite sure that you approve of it before the remaining copies are bound up." Copy A is a bound dummy that Dodgson received earlier.

[2] Macmillan explains in his reply of January 30: "It is not the case that the paper is thicker than what was used for the dummy copy. It weighs exactly the same number of pounds to the ream. The volume is certainly thicker than the dummy inasmuch as it contains a greater number of leaves."

[3] In the same letter, Macmillan assures Dodgson that all the points that he raises in his letter will be attended to.

Christ Church, Oxford
January 29, 1896

Dear Mr. Macmillan,

Your letter of January 28 suggests a suspicion that *telegrams*, addressed (as I have been addressing them) to "Publish, London," fail to reach you. You say, in reference to the question of reprinting the 6s. *Alice*-books, "we might discuss this when you come to town next week." Now I sent you a telegram, on January 25, "not coming – send 100 copies care of Parker": and, on January 27, I sent a second telegram, "number required is 140." Did *neither* telegram reach you? I should be glad if you would enquire into this, and let me know the result, in order that, if they were *not* delivered, I may complain to the G.P.O. It is of considerable importance that my telegrams *should* reach you.[1]

As to your suggestion, *not* to reprint the 6s. books,[2] it is surely a sufficient answer to point out that the 6s. *Alice* has sold, in the last $3\frac{1}{2}$ years, at the average rate of 495 a year. But, before entering on the subject, I have a preliminary question to ask. Do you think, remembering the signal "fiasco" which Messrs. Clay made with the last 1000 *Looking-Glass*, that they can be *trusted* to produce a thoroughly artistic result, in case we decided to set up both the books with fresh type, and have new electros taken from the wood-blocks, and to return to the better quality of paper which we discontinued a few years ago? My own *inclination* is, I confess, to employ some other printer: but I shall be largely guided by *your* opinion.[3]

I am preparing corrections for 2nd edition of *Symbolic Logic*, which I *hope* will be wanted at once.

Would you kindly utilise the accompanying 75 leaflets, by shutting them up in any "Lewis Carroll" books that you are selling?[4] If you think it would be worth while to print more of them for the same purpose, please do so.

Very truly yours,

C. L. Dodgson

---

[1] Frederick Macmillan assures Dodgson on the following day that he received both telegrams but had simply "forgotten for the moment" that Dodgson had cancelled his London visit.

[2] The 6s. edition had sold out, and on January 28, Macmillan wrote that as the 2s. 6d. People's Edition was so satisfactory, "it seems to me a question whether it is worth while to have them in any other form." He adds that a fancier book for gift-giving could be provided by binding up some copies "with gilt edges and sides and charging 3s. 6d. instead of 2s. 6d. for them."

[3] In his letter of January 30, Macmillan defends Clay and is "quite sure that under the circumstances they will take the greatest pains." He adds that he does not believe "there is anybody more capable of producing a better result than they."

[4] This must be Dodgson's recent circular letter about books to be given away.

Christ Church, Oxford
February 9, 1896

Dear Mr. Macmillan,

I thank you for your generous refusal to charge a commission on the *Sylvie* books given away.[1] I presume you will not begin to *bind* any, in plain covers, till you have a sufficient number of applications to make it worth while.

If the *Symbolic Logic* comes to a 2nd edition, I should like an alteration made in the cover. The words "PART I. ELEMENTARY" should be rather larger, I think: at present they are too nearly in the same type as "LEWIS CARROLL," and hardly look as if they were a part of the *title*. I should like to see a cover done, with larger types, so as to make those words occupy $3\frac{1}{2}$ inches of width, instead of 3.[2]

I have a question to ask you about the "Serious Poems," which I would like to publish as a thin quarto, with Miss Thomson's pictures. No doubt you were quite right in warning me that it would not pay the expense of printing: but I wish to bring it out even at a loss. My question is, whether you would object to let Mr. Joseph Swain, who has cut the wood-blocks for the pictures, print the book? I will venture to quote what Miss Thomson says on this subject, but I beg you to keep it to yourself, and not to tell Mr. Clay anything of it, as it would wound his feelings needlessly.

She writes, "Would it be possible for Mr. Swain to print the woodcuts instead of the publisher's printers? Being mainly outline, and very delicate, if they are not *very* carefully printed, they will be simply wrecked. These publisher's printers bang the things off in such a reckless, unfeeling fashion. Mr. Swain is really an artist, and would do them beautifully."

Considering that the book will depend largely, if not entirely, on its *pictures* for any success it may have, and remembering Messrs. Clay's reckless conduct in going on with that 60th thousand of *Looking-Glass* when the pictures were such obvious failures, I feel sure that *Swain* had better print it. If (as is very likely) you would yourselves feel a difficulty in employing any printer other than Clay, I hope you would not object to my proceeding as in the case of books I have printed at the University Press and published by you, viz. making my own arrangements with Swain, and simply handing over, to you, the sheets ready for binding. (Swain would willingly undertake the *binding* as well: but I have never seen any reason to be dissatisfied with your binders, and would rather not take the job out of their hands.)[3]

Are you having the Leaflets printed, which I named in my letter of January 29?[4]

Could we have a rather *thinner* paper (but of course not to *show through* at all) for the 2nd edition of the *Logic?* The book looks rather alarmingly thick.[5]

Very truly yours,

C. L. Dodgson

¹ "We cannot agree to accept any payment for the copies of *Sylvie and Bruno* which are given away," Frederick Macmillan wrote on February 5.

² On the day after Dodgson writes this letter, Macmillan replies that all the alterations Dodgson suggested would be made in the second edition and promises to get a sample cover prepared for his approval in the meantime.

³ ". . . we have no objection to employing any printer that you like," Frederick Macmillan writes on February 10, "or to taking the books ready printed if you prefer it. But before putting the thing into Mr. Swain's hands I think it would be advisable for you to assure yourself that he really is a printer. Unless I am very much mistaken he has no printing business proper, and if he undertook the book I think the chances are he would sublet the work to a regular printer. I do not for a moment admit the justice of Miss Thomson's complaints as to the work of what she calls 'publishers' printers' and I will undertake to say that Messrs. Clay can print delicate woodcuts as well if not better than anybody else in this country. The contretemps in connection with the sixtieth thousand of *Through the Looking-Glass* was most unfortunate, but it is not fair to judge of a man's work by an accident of that kind."

⁴ In the same letter, Macmillan assures Dodgson that the leaflets are being printed.

⁵ Macmillan agrees (same letter) that a slightly thinner paper will be used when *Symbolic Logic* is reprinted.

Christ Church, Oxford
February 20, 1896

Dear Mr. Macmillan,

I got your telegram, and hope you got my answer, that the text is now being corrected for the *2nd* edition, so that no more copies can be worked off till all the sheets are again passed for "Press." Have my 100 copies been sent off yet?¹

Your advice about Mr. Swain was wise and opportune. I find he is *not* himself a printer, but would have to sub-let that part of the work, and merely supervise it while being done. So I have given up the idea of getting him to print a book for me.

I have just despatched some more corrections to Messrs. Clay for the 2nd edition of *Symbolic Logic*, and will let you know when they are ready to work off. Please name the *smallest* number, to work off, that will meet the immediate demand: my friends are sure to suggest desirable corrections, and the book will be in transition-state for some time to come. Do you think 250 would be enough to meet the demand for a while?²

Very truly yours,

C. L. Dodgson

¹ *Symbolic Logic, Part I: Elementary* was officially published on February 21, but Macmillan writes on February 20 to say that they would be able to send presentation copies to only one hundred of the two hundred schools that Dodgson has named, to avoid exhausting their stock. One hundred copies went to Dodgson as well, for presentation to friends, and Dodgson records in his *Diaries* (p. 523) on February 21: "Day of publication of *Symbolic Logic, Part I*: 500 were printed, of which 100 are for me to give away, 100 have been presented to schools, etc. (100 more have to be given),

and 50 are to go to America. Orders exhaust the rest of the First Edition, and I am correcting Press for the Second." For more about the book, see *Handbook*, pp. 194–7.
² In his reply of the 21st, Macmillan writes that a printing of 250 would provide only 100 for sale, as the original printing of 500 was oversubscribed by 150. Macmillan's letter of February 28 indicates that another 500 copies were printed.

Christ Church, Oxford
February 24, 1896
Dear Mr. Macmillan,

The second of the enclosed corrections is very important, as, without it, readers will be wasting time and trouble in trying to solve a problem which is, as it stands, insoluble. So will you kindly see how many addresses you have, to which copies have gone, and send halfpenny cards after them with these corrections. You will be the best judge whether it will be best to print them on Official Post Cards, or on blank cards, on which you can put a halfpenny stamp, or on paper, which can then be pasted on the blank cards. The only way, that *won't* do, is to paste paper on Official Cards, which I see is illegal.¹

If you have any copies still unsold, please shut up in each a slip of paper, bearing these corrections.

Very truly yours,

C. L. Dodgson

Please get the cards posted as soon as you conveniently can.
Thanks for the Postal [Order] for 1*s*. 6*d*.²

¹ Frederick Macmillan replies the following day that "the best plan" would be to print the corrections on a slip of paper and mail them in halfpenny envelopes. He also promises to send Dodgson 100 copies of the corrections for his own presentation copies.
² The postal order was to repay Dodgson for the expense incurred when Macmillan sent his copies of *Symbolic Logic* to Christ Church and not to Parker's as Dodgson had directed.

Christ Church, Oxford
March 9, 1896
Dear Mr. Macmillan,

Many thanks for the tickets.

The specimen-cover, which I got from you February 21, was not quite what I want: the letters in line 3 look too large. I telegraphed this, but have not received any further specimen.

I hope to pass for Press all the sheets of the 2nd Edition this week. Will you kindly see that there is paper enough for 500 copies ready. It should be rather thinner than what was used for the 1st Edition. I should like to see a specimen of

what you propose to use, with something printed on it, so that I may feel sure it
will not show through at all.[1]

Also will you kindly secure that the edges shall be *sprinkled*, of the next 500
(darker sprinkling than the specimen you sent me); and that 50 copies shall be
sent, for me, to *Messrs. Parker*, and not to Christ Church.[2]

Very truly yours,

C. L. Dodgson

[1] On March 11, Frederick Macmillan reports that he is sending a book printed on the same paper
that he proposes to use for the second edition of *Symbolic Logic, Part I* to show Dodgson that the type
does not show through.

[2] Dodgson's italics here are reminders of two blunders made with the first edition of *Symbolic Logic,
Part I.* In his letter of February 21, Frederick Macmillan apologized for the binders having
neglected to sprinkle the edges of the book: "it is very annoying and they have no kind of excuse as
their instructions were full and explicit." On the following day, he again apologized for sending
Dodgson's presentation copies of the book to Christ Church when Dodgson had asked that they be
sent to Messrs. Parker, the Oxford stationers and booksellers whom Dodgson had employed since
1874 to pack and send off presentation copies of his books. On February 22, Dodgson recorded in
his Diaries: "Went to Parker's and inscribed 100 copies of *Symbolic Logic*, which are to be sent as
presents."

Christ Church, Oxford
March 22, 1896

Dear Mr. Macmillan,

Thanks for making enquiry about Messrs. Hachette. I shall be much
interested to know the result.[1]

As to the 60 applications for presentation-copies of *Symbolic Logic*, I most
strongly [object] to even a single copy being sent. I have not invited application
for gratis-copies. You can hardly have realised what an extremely awkward
precedent I should create for myself by granting any such application.

But I shall be glad (as I said in my last) to have the list of presentation-copies
increased by (say) 100 more names, if you can find as many as that, which seem
to you eligible. The two criteria should be

(1) that the School is large and important;
(2) that it has *not* applied for a gratis-copy.[2]

The 2nd edition will not be ready, I fear, for some time yet. I begin to think
that Messrs. Clay have undertaken more work than they have hands for, and
that *my* book only gets a few hours, now and then, and perhaps only *one* man, or
boy, can ever be spared to attend to it. I sent corrected sheets on March 2, 6, 8, 9,
and 16, none of which have yet produced any result. I should be *very* glad to get it
done, and have my hands free to get on with Part II and several other books.

Very truly yours,

C. L. Dodgson

1 "I should much like, if it would not be very costly, to get [*Symbolic Logic,*] *Part I* translated into French, and published in Paris," Dodgson wrote to Macmillan on March 18. "It ought to be entirely *French*, printed just like their books, and in a paper cover. Could you ascertain whether any French publisher would undertake [it], and pay us (you and me) a royalty on sale, *I* undertaking cost of supplying them with copies? And could you find a good translator? (I should require him to do a specimen first, for me to submit to friends for criticism.)" On the following day, Macmillan replied: "I think that the best plan will be to find a good French publisher who will undertake to publish it for you on commission. . . . I will make some inquiries and shall be happy to assist you in making arrangements with a publisher, but we could not accept any share of the profits on the French Edition." On the 20th, Dodgson wrote: "Thanks for your letter, and specially for what you say about not accepting any share of the profits, should any such accrue, of a French edition of *Symbolic Logic*. It is by no means the first time that I have had to notice, with gratitude, the handsome way in which my Publishers deal with me." On the following day, Frederick Macmillan reported that he had spoken to Hachette's London agent about the book, but, in the end, although Hachette had published the French *Alice*, they declined *Symbolic Logic* and suggested another publisher whose terms Macmillan considered unfair. On July 6 of this year, Macmillan suggests that Dodgson delay the French edition until the book is in a "fairly final form."

2 Frederick Macmillan wrote on March 21 that they had had about sixty applications for specimen copies of *Symbolic Logic*. Macmillan saw these requests as a favorable sign and reasoned that "a schoolmaster who writes to ask for a specimen copy will at all events consider it seriously if it is sent to him." On the 23rd, Macmillan replies to the present letter that sending specimen copies is a regular practice for school books, and he adds: "Of course if you do not approve of the system we shall not follow it in the case of *Symbolic Logic*, but I think it is worth consideration whether a man who asks for a book is not more likely to adopt it in his class than a man to whom it is sent unasked. Of course we never send to people whom we do not know to be masters in good schools."

Christ Church, Oxford

March 31, 1896

Dear Mr. Macmillan,

I am drawing up a circular letter, which I shall ask you to send, to any master or mistress who applies for a "gratis" copy of the *Symbolic Logic*. One thing I want to tell them is the great *initial* cost that I have incurred, for which I am not attempting to recoup myself by any addition to the *price*, which I have fixed with reference to the *current* cost only; so that nothing but a very large sale can ever make me other than a loser. But I have not the *statistics* needed for this statement. Would you kindly get me the following:

(1) An approximate estimate (I don't care to have the *exact* sum) of the cost incurred *previous* to the issue of the 1st edition, excluding the *current cost* (i.e. the paper, the working off of the 500 copies, binding, and advertising and circular letter);

(2) A similar estimate of the cost already incurred in correcting for 2nd edition;

(3) The price you think might fairly have been charged for the book (more than 200 pages, containing more than 100 different diagrams and a quantity of "table-work").1

I want to make an alteration in my instructions as to *not* giving copies if applied for. In drawing up any additional list of schools to have "gratis" copies, please do not let the fact, of such applications having been made, make any difference *either* way. Let the list be exactly what it would have been if no applications whatever had been made.

You have never told me whether the electros in *America*, of the 6s. editions of the 2 *Alice* books, have been destroyed. I cannot safely proceed to preparing new editions of them, till I know for certain that there is no possibility of the former editions being re-printed.[2]

Thanks for sending me *An Imperative Duty* by "W. D. Howells." There is a curious and very suspicious circumstance, about that book, which I want you to kindly enquire into.

The Lady of the Aroostook, with about 10 other novels, and several plays, are published by Houghton, Mifflin & Co., Boston and New York. The name is given as "W. D. Howells."

An Imperative Duty, with 5 other novels, and several plays, are published by Harper Bros., New York. The name is "William Dean Howells."

The 2 lists of books *have nothing in common*.

I strongly suspect that this second set of books are merely *imitations* of the first, that the name is assumed, and that a very disgraceful fraud is being practised on the public.[3] Believe me

Very truly yours,

C. L. Dodgson

---

[1] Macmillan is away and does not reply until April 9, when he reports that the initial cost of the first edition of *Symbolic Logic* was about £150 and the cost of corrections for the second edition, £12. He does not, however, understand Dodgson's third question and writes: "If by the expression 'might *fairly* have been charged for the book' you mean what price would have enabled the first Edition to pay for its cost, you may say 10s., but I should not like to be understood to say that such a price could *reasonably* have been put upon it."

[2] In his letter of April 9, Macmillan replies that the electrotype plates of the two *Alice* books in America have not been destroyed and for a very good reason. He explains: "As you are aware there is no copyright in these books in the United States and there is no possibility of keeping them out of print by any action of ours. If our New York house let them run out, the books would at once be reprinted by some other American publisher. . . . As soon as you can let us have a new set for America's use, we will see that the old ones are no longer used. In the meantime no American printed copies can be introduced into this country."

[3] In the same letter, Macmillan explains that W. D. Howells and William Dean Howells are one and the same, that the author's earlier works were published by Houghton Mifflin & Co. of Boston, and the later ones by Harper Bros. of New York. Macmillan adds that he has not read any of the latter, but "I know the author has gone in for what is called 'realism' (that generally means dullness) and I think it very likely that his recent books have little in common with his early ones which were charming." *The Lady of The Aroostook* (1879) was written during the years that William Dean Howells (1837–1920) edited the *Atlantic Monthly* in Boston (1866–81). In 1885, Howells moved to New York where Harper Bros. became his publishers and where he published *An Imperative Duty* (1891).

The Chestnuts, Guildford
April 11, 1896

Dear Mr. Macmillan,

I fear I have failed in putting my question clearly enough to be understood. I will try again.

By the expression "might fairly have been charged for the book" I did *not* mean "what price would have enabled it to pay for its cost."

An illustration, with exaggerated statistics, will perhaps make my meaning clear.

Supposing I brought you a number of books ready printed and bound, and said "What would be a fair price to put on these"? You might examine them, and say "Considering the quality of the paper and the binding, the number of pages; the amount of table-work, and the number of the pictures, 10s. would be a fair price." Then if I said "But I had the paper brought from China, and the pictures were done by an eccentric artist who charged £1000, and the book has been reprinted 10 times at enormous cost. To repay the cost I must charge £5 apiece," you would say "Those are details we cannot take account of: the public can only estimate the details they *see*: and the maximum market-price of such a book would be 10s."

Now *that* is the way I want you to answer my present question. Take no account of the *extra* expense caused by an *unusual* amount of re-writing and correcting, but merely look at it as an ordinary outsider would, with nothing but the book itself to go by, and name the maximum price which could be put on it without exceeding the ordinary custom of trade. I want to name the *maximum*, in order that the public may see how unusually low the price of 2s. is.[1]

Very truly yours,

C. L. Dodgson

P.S. Thanks for your answers to my other questions. I would like to write to Mons. Alcan, sending him a Circular Letter, and asking Messrs. Hachette to send on to him the specimen-copy.[2]

[1] Frederick Macmillan replies on April 15 and suggests 3s. as the selling price.
[2] M. Alcan was the French publisher recommended by Hachette when they refused *Symbolic Logic*.

Christ Church, Oxford
May 17, 1896

Dear Mr. Macmillan,

I enclose a copy of the Logic-Circular, marked "Press," for you to forward to Clay with your order for the 20,000. Also please order an extra 100, to be sent to *me*, to give to friends.[1]

Please, this time, do not have them *sewn*. It is quite needless, and must cost a good deal of time and trouble, and additional expense.

Also do not have them cut at top-edge. Simple *folding* will be quite enough, and any one, who wishes to read it through, can easily cut it open for himself.

As to the *Alice* Calendar, which Miss Tress asks leave to publish, will you kindly tell me the grounds on which you think its publication objectionable? My own inclination is to give the required permission: but I do not like to do so, contrary to your advice, as you may have some good reasons, unknown to me, for objecting to its publication.[2] The pictures seem to me well-copied, and coloured with some taste: and I should think that, if its publication had any effect at all on the sale of the book, it would be in its favour rather than against it.

Very truly yours,

C. L. Dodgson

[1] This is again Dodgson's advertisement for *Symbolic Logic*. Dodgson must have asked Macmillan if they would be willing to include the advertisement in some of their other books. On April 27, Frederick Macmillan wrote: "We could if you like have a leaflet such as the enclosed inserted in all the books delivered to us by the binder at the rate of 5*s*. 6*d*. per thousand copies. The leaflet could not be put in when the books leave this place but as we keep a comparatively small stock here, and it is constantly moving, the insertion by the binder comes to very much the same thing. If you determine to have it done please send us as many copies of the leaflet as you wish to circulate in this way." Dodgson's reply is missing, but on May 1, Macmillan wrote again: ". . . roughly speaking, we send out about a million and a half volumes in six months. It would obviously be out of the question to put a copy . . . in every book, but if you will decide how many of the leaflets you would like to distribute in this way we will have them inserted until they are used up. We should use our judgement as to the books in which they should go, or if you prefer it we would take instructions from you on this point." On May 3, Dodgson replied: "May I then understand that you would be willing, for £11.10.0, to shut up, in books sold by you (I would leave it to your discretion to select *which* books to put them in), 20,000 copies of the Letter? If so, I will send you a revised copy (I want to add a sentence about Symbolic Logic being a great *help* in understanding Formal Logic), and you can be getting them worked off." Almost a month after he writes the present letter, on June 13, Dodgson reports to Macmillan that on June 10th "I sent to Clay the 'List of Works,' marked 'Press.' That completes the book [the second edition of *Symbolic Logic, Part I*]. . . ." On June 21, Dodgson writes to Macmillan requesting "50 copies of the 'Examples' part of *Symbolic Logic* done up as a pamphlet, to lend to pupils." This was not the first time that he had parts of his books printed and bound separately for pupils and friends. See, for example, *Handbook*, pp. 80–1, 187.

[2] On May 15, Frederick Macmillan wrote: "We have this morning received the enclosed application for permission to publish an *Alice* Calendar with reproductions of some of the illustrations. I should think you will probably not give the permission which is asked for. I certainly do not think it would be advisable but I send it on to you as a matter of course." In reply to Dodgson's inquiry about his reasons for objecting, Macmillan writes on the following day: "I cannot say that I think the publication of Miss Tress's *Alice* Calendar could do any serious harm, or perhaps even any harm at all to the sale of *Alice*. I simply had an idea that you would not like Sir John Tenniel's pictures to appear in any but your book. However, if you are inclined to grant Miss Tress the necessary permission I cannot say that I have any real ground for advising differently."

Christ Church, Oxford
July 14, 1896
Dear Mr. Macmillan,

I should be very glad to have your opinion on some points connected with the enclosed little book.

It is written by a lady, a cousin of mine, who has written 2 other child-books that seem to me very good. I have had it printed at my own cost (100 copies for private circulation), in a superior style, making it well adapted for giving to little children as prizes or presents.[1]

The question is, would it be possible to publish and sell it so as to repay myself (I don't care about *profits*).

The initial outlay has been 11 guineas (I am *not* including the current cost of the 100 copies).

Five hundred copies would cost me £9.10.0. (i.e. adding in the initial outlay, about 10*d*. each).

One thousand would cost £17 (i.e. nearly 7*d*. each).

I could get the book enlarged to (say) 60 pages, which would add very little to the current cost.

Could *you* see your way to publishing it?[2]

Very truly yours,

C. L. Dodgson

If book were enlarged, I would have more pictures.

---

[1] *The Lost Plum-Cake* by Dodgson's cousin Georgina Wilcox (Mrs. Egerton Allen).
[2] Two days later, Frederick Macmillan replies that he does not think that a very large market exists for a story like *The Lost Plum-Cake* but suggests that if Dodgson would write a few lines of introduction and were willing to have the book published "with a preface by Lewis Carroll," a number of copies, "perhaps a thousand," might be sold. Macmillan writes that he thinks there is not much point to adding more pages or more pictures.

Christ Church, Oxford
July 15, 1896
Dear Mr. Macmillan,

I wish to consult you on the subject of *card-diagrams* for the *Symbolic Logic*.

Our arrangement, with *The Game of Logic*, was to shut up, in each copy, an envelope containing a card, 4 red counters, and 5 grey: and also to offer the envelope, etc., separately, at 3*d*. each.

The first part of the arrangement I do *not* propose to continue with the *Symbolic Logic*. (If we were to begin such a thing, with the 3rd edition, it would make purchasers of the 1st and 2nd editions very discontented!) But I think it might be well, if you do not object to the trouble it would entail, to offer an envelope, etc., *separately*, at 3*d*. each. Please let me know whether or no you would be willing to do this.[1]

Whether you do, or not, at any rate you may destroy all the *existing* cards, with their envelopes: but please, before doing so, empty out the *counters*, and add them to the stock in hand.

I am having a new card printed, $7 \times 3\frac{1}{2}$, for the use of myself and pupils; and, if you approved of the plan of offering them for sale, separately, I would get special envelopes made to hold them, and you could put, into each, 4 red counters and 5 grey.

As to the 190 copies, now on hand, of *The Game of Logic*, will you please put aside 40, which I feel sure will meet *all* future requirements, and the rest may be destroyed.[2]

Very truly yours,

C. L. Dodgson

---

[1] Macmillan's reply is missing, but these card diagrams and counters were produced and sold as Dodgson suggests they should be (see *Handbook*, p. 197).

[2] On June 13, Dodgson wrote to Macmillan: "Now that . . . [*Symbolic Logic, Part I*, 2nd edition] is out, it would not be fair to the public to continue to sell the (very incomplete) earlier book, *The Game of Logic*. So will you kindly withdraw it from Sale."

Christ Church, Oxford
July 24, 1896

Dear Mr. Macmillan,

Many thanks for your letter, received July 17, consenting to publish *A Lost Plum-Cake*. The arrangement you propose will do very well. I will write a little Preface. Also the book will have more text (and perhaps more pictures) which will, I hope, make it more saleable.

On July 22 I passed for Press the whole of the sheets for the 3rd edition of *Symbolic Logic, Part I*, and told Clay to work off 500 copies, and to send me 2 sets: so I suppose he will deliver to you 498 sets. Will you give the necessary orders to the binders? I leave it to your discretion how many to bind.

I see you had on hand, in June 1880, 2 copies of *Determinants*; and I cannot find any further mention of the book in the annual accounts. If they are still on hand, I should like to have them.[1]

Please let me know when the *Logic*s are ready. Don't *send* any, as I am soon leaving here.

Very truly yours,

C. L. Dodgson

Three days later, Frederick Macmillan replies: "With regard to the two copies of *Determinants*, if you will look at the publishing account for the year 1879–80, you will find that these copies were accounted for as sold in that year and were not accounted for as on hand on June 30th, 1880."

2 Bedford Well Road, Eastbourne
August 27, 1896

Dear Mr. Macmillan,

As the 12 copies are gone to Oxford, they may as well stay there, as I have no use here for so many. Please send me *6* more, to the above address.[1] Is there anything like a demand for the 3rd edition? There *ought* to be, I think, as soon as school masters and mistresses have had time to test it.[2] Thanks for the single copy.

I should be glad to have your opinion about reprinting the 6*s. Alice* books. When they were on sale, the annual sale averaged several hundreds of each. My idea would be to print 1000 of each, but keep them in *sheets*, and only bind 100 at a time.

With new type, and new electros of the pictures, and the *better* quality of paper (as originally used) the new copies *ought* to be fully equal, from an artistic point of view, to the original issue. Do you think we may fairly expect this result from Messrs. Clay? I own it is with a rather heavy heart that I contemplate the entrusting so important a task to *them*: but I am much inclined to be guided by *your* opinion.[3]

Very truly yours,

C. L. Dodgson

[1] Dodgson's Eastbourne landlady had moved to new quarters, and Dodgson went with her (see *Letters*, pp. 1080–1, 1096). In a missing letter, Dodgson had apparently asked for twelve copies of *Symbolic Logic*. On August 26, Frederick Macmillan wrote: "The 12 copies of *Symbolic Logic*, 3rd. edition, were sent to Oxford because, as you will remember, the letter in which you asked for them was accidentally dated by you from Christ Church. I am sending you another copy by this post. I presume that you will be able to get the twelve from your rooms in Oxford."

[2] On August 28, Frederick Macmillan writes that the firm has disposed of "about 150 copies" of the third edition of *Symbolic Logic*.

[3] Macmillan replies (same letter) that he does not know of "any printer who would be likely to do them better or even so well as Messrs. Clay."

2 Bedford Well Road, Eastbourne
August 30, 1896

Dear Mr. Macmillan,

I wired to you yesterday to begin on the *Alice* books at once, as you said there was no time to lose. Do you approve of my idea, to print 1000 of each, but only *bind* them 100 at a time?[1]

I should be glad to present 100 copies of the *Symbolic Logic* to Reading Rooms, or similar institutions for working men, in the large towns. Can you suggest any inexpensive way of making the offer known? Would it do to mention it in the

Catalogues you send to the booksellers in large towns? Intelligent working men would, I think, enjoy the study as much as, if not more than, any other class of readers.[2]

Very truly yours,

C. L. Dodgson

[1] On the following day, Frederick Macmillan writes that he approves of Dodgson's suggestion. Under this plan, if sales did not warrant continuing the 6s. edition, the remaining sheets could be bound as the People's Edition.

[2] In the same letter, Macmillan offers to send a list of over 500 of the principal institutions of this kind from which Dodgson could choose 100. Dodgson's reply is missing, but Macmillan's letter of September 3 indicates how they resolve the matter: "We will, as you suggest, send copies of *Symbolic Logic* to 100 of the largest towns on our list, inscribing each copy as 'presented by the Author for the use of the. . . .'"

2 Bedford Well Road, Eastbourne

September 6, 1896

Dear Mr. Macmillan,

I have asked Sir John Tenniel whether the sheets of the 2 *Alice* books may be sent, as fast as they are made up for working off, to *him* instead of to *me*. He writes, "Certainly – I will do what you wish, in regard to supervising the pictures, with much pleasure: of course everything will depend on the *printing*."

It is, of course, needless to say that it would be of no use, at all, to *work off* the 1000 copies of a sheet, and *then* send one to him: what is necessary is that each sheet, containing pictures, should be first "made up" ready to work off, then that one impression should be carefully worked off on the good paper and sent to Sir John Tenniel, and that the rest of the 1000 should *not* be worked off until he has returned the specimen-copy, marked "Press."

May I rely on this system being carried out, with *all* the sheets of *both* books? It is, I consider, absolutely necessary to take all these precautions, under the circumstances.[1]

Very truly yours,

C. L. Dodgson

Sir J. Tenniel,
10 Portsdown Road,
Maida Hill, London.

1 Frederick Macmillan replies on the following day that Dodgson's proposal is totally unworkable as it would involve keeping the printing machines waiting for the approval of each sheet. Macmillan explains that "a printing machine is of course expected to earn a certain amount each day, and if it is kept compulsorily idle as it must necessarily be if your proposal is adopted, it means a serious loss to the printer every time. I do not think we could ask Mr. Clay or any printer to agree

to such an arrangement." On September 9 Macmillan offers an alternative. Clay has suggested that he send careful impressions from the woodcuts for Tenniel's approval. Clay would then take the responsibility for seeing that the impressions in the printed sheets correspond exactly with the prints as passed by Tenniel.

2 Bedford Well Road, Eastbourne
September 10, 1896

Dear Mr. Macmillan,

I am consulting Sir John Tenniel as to your new suggestion, and will write again when I get his reply.

Meanwhile, I should like to know what meaning I am to attach to the sentence "Mr. Clay would then take the responsibility of seeing that the impressions in the printed sheet corresponded exactly with the prints as passed by Sir John."

The phrase "I will take the responsibility" is constantly used *without any meaning at all*. For instance, suppose a man tells me "I will take the responsibility of seeing that the builder calls on you tomorrow." Well, suppose the builder does *not* call, what happens? Simply *nothing*. Of course, if there is *money* involved, the undertaking *does* mean something: for instance, if a man tells me "I will take the responsibility of seeing that the £100 is paid to you tomorrow," if the £100 is *not* paid, I can sue him for the amount, and produce his written promise to pay it.

But, in Mr. Clay's case, suppose, when the books came out, that the pictures did *not* correspond with the prints as passed by Sir John, what then? What would come of his plausible-sounding phrase about "taking the responsibility"? Nothing at all, that I can see.

At present, I have no such confidence in Mr. Clay as to be willing to trust him, in any important matter, without having a written guarantee. You remember, as well as I do, his most discreditable behaviour as to the spoiled 1000 *Looking-Glass*, when he calmly ignored being in *any* degree responsible for the "fiasco," and tacitly assumed the right of sending you sheets unfit for publication, and that it was *your* duty to examine *all* sheets received from him. I see no reason to suppose that he has at all changed his view as to the duty a printer owes to a publisher. So far as I know to the contrary, he would again be ready, in case any of the sheets of the new books happened to fail in the working off, to say nothing about it, but send you the spoiled sheets, in hopes that you would fail to notice them.

"Once bit, twice shy." After the heavy money-loss entailed on me by Mr. Clay's misconduct, I cannot afford to run *any* further risks, in dealing with so untrustworthy a man.[1]

Very truly yours,

C. L. Dodgson

¹ On the following day, Frederick Macmillan replies: "When I said that Mr. Clay would take the responsibility of seeing that the impressions in the printed sheets of the new edition of *Alice* corresponded exactly with the prints passed by Sir John Tenniel, I meant that in case they did not so correspond, he would reprint the sheets at his own risk. Of course in case of any dispute as to whether or not they did so correspond, the matter would have to be referred to an impartial arbitrator, but I really do not think there is any fear of such a question arising."

2 Bedford Well Road, Eastbourne
September 13, 1896

Dear Mr. Macmillan,

Thanks for diagram-cards, and for Press notices of *Symbolic Logic*.¹

As for printing more of *Euclid I, II*, I am ready to be guided by *your* opinion. The book has *very* little chance of sale, there are so many similar ones in the market. And *they* have the advantage of going *further*. I shall *never* have the necessary leisure for doing Books III to VI, which are needed to make the thing complete and give it a fair chance of sale.²

Instead of writing to you, separately, about the re-issue of the 6*s.* editions of the *Alice* books, it will save my time to send, for your perusal, the copy I have thought it desirable to keep of the letter which I have written to Messrs. Clay on the subject.³ Please let me have it back some time.

Very truly yours,

C. L. Dodgson

Can you procure paper, for these 2000 books, which will be *quite* up to the standard of what was used for the original issue?⁴

¹ Although the press notices that Macmillan sent are missing, the critical reception of *Symbolic Logic, Part I* was on the whole favorable. For example, the *Educational Times* (July 1, 1896, p. 316) describes the book as "a *tour de force* of originality, throwing light on its subject from fresh angles." Even the less enthusiastic notice in the *Athenaeum* (October 17, 1896, pp. 520–1) is not damaging: "It is well arranged, its expositions are lucid, it has an excellent stock of examples – many of them worked out, and not a few witty and amusing; and its arguments, even when wrong, are always acute and well worth weighing."

² On September 11, Frederick Macmillan reported that the sixth edition of *Euclid I, II* was "quite exhausted" and, in view of the very slow sales, asked Dodgson's opinion about reprinting. In reply to the present letter, Macmillan writes (the next day): "It is perhaps hardly worth while to reprint *Euclid I, II*."

³ Dodgson's letter to Clay is missing, but Macmillan's reply of the 14th indicates that Dodgson reached some understanding with the printer. Frederick Macmillan writes: "I am quite in hopes that the plan now adopted may work out well."

⁴ In the same letter, Macmillan replies: "As to the paper, I can only say that we have ordered it to be of the best quality that can be made, and the manufacturers intend it to be as nearly as possible like what was used for the early Editions of *Alice*."

2 Bedford Well Road, Eastbourne
September 15, 1896
Dear Mr. Macmillan,

I find the 2*s*. 6*d*. *Alice* books are not at all adapted for reprinting the 6*s*. editions, as I had made many little alterations to suit the new pages, and of course all these have to be altered back again in these 2*s*. 6*d*. copies. I must have recent copies of the 6*s*. editions, to correct. No doubt you can send me one of [the] spoiled 60th thousand of the *Looking-Glass*: but I fear you have no copy of *Alice* that can be sacrificed for this purpose?

Please send *Looking-Glass* at once, and let me know about *Alice*. If *you* have no copy I can use, I will get some copy back, that I have given away lately.[1]

Very truly yours,
C. L. Dodgson

[1] Two days later. Frederick Macmillan writes that Messrs. Clay are sending Dodgson their file copies of the original editions of *Alice* and *Looking-Glass* that he might prepare the new editions. In fact Dodgson borrowed May Barber's copies for the purpose. See Selwyn H. Goodacre, "Lewis Carroll's Alterations for the 1897 . . . *Alice* . . .," *Jabberwocky*, Spring 1982, pp. 67–76.

2 Bedford Well Road, Eastbourne
September 20, 1896
Dear Mr. Macmillan,

I am much obliged by your suggestion, to Messrs. Clay, to send me their file-copies of the 2 books: but I think it would be a pity to spoil them by marking and correcting; so I have got old copies given to me, the spoiling of which does not matter.

What *margins* do you advise that we should allow for the 2 *Alice* books? The first *Alice*s sold in England were taller copies than any sold since, and probably broader also. The most recent of all look rather too much cut down to be really handsome books. I should be glad to have your opinion on this point.[1]

Very truly yours,
C. L. Dodgson

Will you kindly return the enclosed[2] to the "Press Cutting Association," 17 Cockspur Street, and tell them that Mr. Dodgson does not want any such things.

[1] On the following day, Frederick Macmillan recommends paper of which "a fell sheet measures $21\frac{1}{4} \times 32$. This means that when it is folded up each page will be $5\frac{3}{8}$ inches wide and 8 inches high, that is, before the edges are cut." Macmillan adds that even with the edges trimmed, the page would have "a handsome margin."
[2] Missing.

2 Bedford Well Road, Eastbourne
September 30, 1896

Dear Mr. Macmillan,

Thanks for the 2 copies of *Cymbeline*.[1]

Also for your letter, and for the evidence it gives of the thoughtful care you are giving to a matter of so much importance to me.[2]

What you say, about *outer* margin needing to be slightly broader than *inner*, I had never heard *stated* as a rule; but it had occurred to me instinctively that it ought to be so; and, when I wrote those directions, I said to myself "if the pages are printed, on the sheet, $1\frac{1}{2}$ inches apart, so that the inner margin will be, *before binding*, $\frac{3}{4}$ of an inch, a *little* of that will be absorbed in binding (because you never can open a bound book *quite* flat), so that, if the outer margin be made $\frac{3}{4}$ inch, it will *look* a little the broader of the two, as it *ought* to do."

Will you please tell me

(1) how far apart are the pages printed on the unbound sheet?

(2) is any difference made for *outer* and *inner* pages of a sheet? (in a sheet of 16 pages, if pages 1, 16 were, on the sheet, at the *same* distance apart as pages 8, 9, they would, after binding, have rather *less* inner margins).

(3) what alteration do you propose in the instructions to the binder?[3]

Very truly yours,

C. L. D.

---

[1] In 1889 Macmillan & Co. published *Cymbeline* with an introduction and notes by K. Deighton, as part of their English Classics, but we do not know why Dodgson required two copies.

[2] At least two more Dodgson letters on the subject of margins are missing. Frederick Macmillan wrote on September 29: "Your instructions to the binder are explicit and sufficient. There is however one point which I ought to make. You say that you wish to have $\frac{3}{4}$ inch clear margin on each side of the type. It is usual however to have rather more margin on the outside than on the inside, because if this is not done, the type has the appearance of being about to slip off the paper. The difference necessary to give the proper effect is very small but I should like to have your authority to make it."

[3] Macmillan replies on October 1 that "the best thing I can do" is to have a sheet of the new *Alice* printed "on paper of the size we propose to use and then bound up in order that you may determine exactly whether the margins are to your liking." On October 14, Macmillan writes apologizing for the delay in answering Dodgson's questions: "1. This depends on the margins you decide upon. If you will kindly send back the specimen pages, a sheet shall be made up to show the exact spaces between the pages of type in the unbound sheet. 2. When a very thick paper is used a difference in the margins is allowed for in making up the sheet. But no alteration is considered necessary with the paper used for *Looking-Glass* as the thickness of 110 leaves is only $\frac{3}{4}$ of an inch; therefore the varying margin of the outer edge is only $\frac{7}{118}$ of $\frac{3}{4}$ of an inch on each fold. 3. The instruction to the binder will be a printed leaf cut to the exact measurement that you wish. This will be preserved by the binder in his pattern case." On the 14th Dodgson writes indicating that Macmillan has misunderstood two of his three questions and goes on to rephrase them more carefully, but Macmillan's reply to this letter has eluded us.

Christ Church, Oxford
November 13, 1896

Dear Mr. Macmillan,

The enclosed bill[1] ought to go into *your* account.

Thanks for advice (all of which I agree to) to print 500 of the 4th edition of *Logic*, and to have ¾ inch outer margin for the *Alice* books.[2]

I want your advice on the following matter:

Sylvie and Bruno hardly sells at all, to speak of. The public *won't* buy such a book at 7*s.* 6*d.*: but I think it probable that they *would* buy it (as they do the *Alice* books) at 6*s.* So what do you think of announcing that, in future, "6*s.* net" will be the price? Your allowance to me would have to be (I find by Rule of Three) ⅘ of 5*s.* 7½*d.* (i.e. 4*s.* 6*d.*) less 2 percent.[3]

Very truly yours,

C. L. Dodgson

Please secure that 4th edition of *Logic* is printed on *same* quality of paper, and that they don't substitute *thinner* paper.[4]

---

[1] Missing.

[2] On November 9, Dodgson wrote: "I should be glad to know your opinion as to how many copies it would be best to print of the 4th edition of *Symbolic Logic*. . . . as it contains some important alterations, I shall wish it to be put on sale as soon as you can get copies from the binders, and that the then-remaining copies of the 3rd edition should be presented to Reading-Rooms and Institutions." On the following day, Frederick Macmillan wrote: "Unless you are likely to wish to correct *Symbolic Logic* again very soon, I should think it would be safe to print 500 copies as the 4th Edition."

[3] In his reply of November 16, Frederick Macmillan advises Dodgson to abandon this plan. He argues that the reduction of the price would not have the slightest effect on the sale, and he fears that the actual result would be that booksellers (who have a good many copies of the book) would ask for a refund of the difference between the new price and the old.

[4] In the same letter, Macmillan assures Dodgson that the 4th edition would be printed on "exactly the same paper as that used for the 3rd Edition."

Christ Church, Oxford
November 24, 1896

Dear Mr. Macmillan,

I have wired you the date, for the tickets, which I so stupidly omitted, viz. next Saturday afternoon.[1]

As to *The Nursery "Alice"*, I fear I must trouble you to devise some other plan, as I cannot consent to the one you propose. I desire that the booksellers should make a really *handsome* profit on the book: but I consider 300 per cent to be *excessive*.[2]

If you say "but they would not think of asking 4*s.* for it: they would offer it at so-and-so," then, whatever price they would offer it at, I wish to have printed on the title-page, and announced in the "List of Works."

The first question to settle is, what price will the public give for it? I feel no doubt at all that it will "hold its own" among other coloured picture-books, if only it is reduced to their level in *price*: it is *far* better got-up than most of the picture-books, of which the shops are full, and which apparently are in great demand.

The second question is, given that the book is to be offered to the public at so-and-so, what can you offer it at, to the trade, so as to let them make a really handsome profit?

The third question is, what royalty could you allow me, so as to clear, for *yourselves*, a reasonable profit?

My profit may be reduced to a *very* low figure, so long as I don't incur any further *loss*.

Now the following figures are merely suggested for your consideration.

There is such a flood of *shilling*-books on the market, and people will so often overlook all questions of *quality*, that I think quite the best chance for the book is to say "Let it be possible for the booksellers to offer it at 1*s*. net."

Then, for them to be able to do this, I fancy you must offer it to *them* at either 9*d*. or 8*d*., net. I am inclined to propose 8*d*.

Now you are going to charge me 5½*d*. for covering each. Would you be satisfied to give me 7*d*. royalty (less the usual 2 percent), and thus clear a full penny per copy?

I await your reply to these suggestions before saying more.[3]

Very truly yours,

C. L. Dodgson

P.S. If we carry out the proposed arrangement, I propose to tell the public what we are offering it at, and to explain to them that, though the original price of 4*s*. was a fair one, yet, as I find they *won't buy it* at a price so much beyond common picture books, I have decided, in order that the children may *have* the book, to sell the copies in stock at considerably *under* cost-price.

---

[1] On Saturday, November 28, Dodgson attends a matinee performance of G. R. Sims and A. Shirley's *Two Little Vagabonds* at the Princess's Theatre (*Diaries*, p. 530).

[2] On November 16, Dodgson wrote to Macmillan: "I want to have your opinion as to whether, if we lowered the (white) *Nursery 'Alice'* to the ordinary price of picture-books of that size, it would be likely to sell. It had far better be sold, even at a heavy loss on the original outlay, than be wasted. If we did this, of course the 'toned' copies must be priced lower still." On the following day, Frederick Macmillan replied that the only way to move the "enormous stock" of *The Nursery "Alice"* was to offer it at "a very great reduction in price." He suggested terms to the trade of 13 as 12 at 1*s*. a copy, leaving it to the bookseller to get what he could for it.

[3] On November 25, Macmillan replies: ". . . my suggestion was that it should be offered to the trade as 'a remainder.' The bookseller who bought it at a shilling would of course not ask four shillings

for it. They would probably sell it for 1*s*. 6*d*., and the point of the thing would be that they would be able to offer their customers a four shilling book for eighteen pence which would attract the people who like what they call 'a good bargain.' Your proposal is simply to reduce the advertised price of the book from 4*s*. to 1*s*." On December 2, Macmillan adds: ". . . I find that the ordinary price to the trade for such books is one-third off to account, which if *Alice* is made a shilling volume means 8*d*. less 5 percent. The public would in most cases pay 9*d*. If you choose to adopt those terms, we shall be satisfied if you allow us to account to you at 8*d*. less 10 percent for all sold. I send a specimen of a cheaper style of binding which would cost you only 2*d*. a copy and which I think is good enough under the circumstances." Dodgson must have agreed to Macmillan's proposal, but he still insisted that the price be printed on the book. Macmillan concludes arrangements in his letter of December 10: "We will get the title pages of *Nursery 'Alice'* altered at once and will issue the book at a shilling on the terms arranged."

Christ Church, Oxford

December 1, 1896

Dear Mr. Macmillan,

Thanks for the tickets. I want to take *two* ladies; so I enclose them to be changed. Would you kindly send at once, and get me *three* front stalls. If there are not 3 to be had, together, in the front row, then two in the front row and one in the second row, just behind them, would do. If neither plan can be managed, then please get three for Saturday week.[1]

Now I have a *most* important matter to write about. The 2 copies of *Alice* and *Looking-Glass* in one volume, have just arrived: and I am greatly dismayed at finding that *both* of them are *incomplete*, the title-page being omitted in *each* part, so that each frontispiece faces *verses*, instead of a title-page, and looks most unsightly.

You have known me long enough not to be surprised at my regarding this as a *very* serious matter, greatly affecting my reputation as an author. You could scarcely deal a heavier blow at that reputation, whatever it may be, than by selling to the public imperfect copies, as perfect.

You will, I think, agree in all that I am now about to say.

This matter must be looked into *at once*, and *all* the copies, in stock, of this double volume, must be collated: and I shall wish to know how many incomplete copies exist. These *of course* must be withdrawn from sale, and the title-pages inserted.

Then I shall want you to ascertain how the thing has happened, and whether it is a mere accident, or whether a deliberate fraud has been attempted, by supplying you, knowingly, with imperfect copies. On *that* point I say no more till I get your answer.[2]

It can hardly be necessary to add that, if any incomplete copies have been already sold, and are returned to you with complaints, they must be exchanged for [complete] copies.

Nor can it be necessary to add that, whatever expense may be incurred, in completing and rebinding copies, or exchanging incomplete copies, ought *not* to fall on me.

Very truly yours,

C. L. Dodgson

I am returning the bad copies.

---

[1] Dodgson's guests on December 5 were his friend Ethel Hatch and his niece Menella Dodgson: they go (Dodgson for a second time) to *Two Little Vagabonds.* "The play was as enjoyable as ever," Dodgson notes (*Diaries*, p. 531). For more on Ethel Hatch, see *Letters*, esp. p. 185; for Menella Dodgson, see *Letters*, pp. 623, 1106.

[2] "Your letter of yesterday will require a careful answer," Macmillan writes on December 2, "and I must ask you to allow me to take the time necessary to write one. I may say at once that the arrangement of the title page in the double volume was made deliberately in view of the necessity of having the right thousand on the title page of each Edition." On the following day, he continues: ". . . we have been following what we imagine to be the instructions you gave us in January 1891 as per enclosed letter [missing]. . . . We have numbered the thousands of the three books separately and at the present time *Alice's Adventures* is in the 49th thousand, *Through the Looking-Glass* in the 30th thousand and the double volume in its 12th thousand. I really do not see what other plan could have been adopted about the title pages. It would be possible of course to have a separate title for each book in the double volume as well as a double title page, but in that case no thousand must be mentioned on it, and as far as appearance goes I think the present arrangement is much the better. Of course we will do whatever you please in the matter." Dodgson replies on December 5, but that letter is missing; he refers to his decision in that letter, however, on May 6, 1897, on p. 351, below.

Christ Church, Oxford
December 10, 1896

Dear Mr. Macmillan,

I don't keep *copies* of my letters, but only *précis* of them, in a Register: I have referred to the one for February 26, and it entirely confirms what you say: but old age has a feeble memory, and I had quite forgotten it.[1] The arrangement, for opening "Lewis Carroll" letters, was due, I see, to the stream of letters, then coming in, applying for gift-copies of *Sylvie.* If that stream has now ceased, the envelopes need no longer be opened, but letters, addressed to pseudonym, should be *enclosed* to me: those addressed to *real* name will merely need to be re-directed.

The title-page of *Nursery "Alice"* is capitally done – a far better plan than *I* had suggested. You may at once begin the sale at 1*s*. Do you advise any *advertising* of it on the new terms? I have very little faith in that system: and it is very costly.[2]

You do not notice my question of December 7, about numbers of pages in each sheet of the *Alice* books.[3]

Very truly yours,

C. L. Dodgson

¹ Dodgson wrote on December 6 (letter missing) to ask why the publisher was opening letters addressed to "Lewis Carroll" before forwarding them to Christ Church. On December 9, Macmillan replied that they were following Dodgson's own instructions.
² In his reply of December 1, Macmillan advises against spending anything on newspaper advertising for the 1*s*. sale of *The Nursery "Alice"*.
³ Dodgson's letter of December 7 is missing, but Macmillan's reply on the 10th indicates the nature of the question: "I have not the slightest idea why the 6*s*. Editions of the *Alice* books have been printed so as to fold in 8 pages. It has been going on since 1869 as a copy of *Alice* of that date which I saw today proves. I think the new Editions had better be printed so as to fold in 16 pages."

Christ Church, Oxford
April 12, 1897

Dear Mr. Macmillan,

Will you please send (if you have not already done so) a copy of *Symbolic Logic*, 4th edition, to the *Schoolmaster*.¹

Also please let me know how many copies were on hand, of the 3rd edition, when the 4th was ready: and the names of the Institutes, etc., to which you have given, or are giving, them.²

Also please send 2 copies of the shilling *Nursery "Alice"* to Miss M. Wilcox, 38 South Street, Durham.³

Also, please send me, in your next parcel, a copy of 4th edition of *Logic*, in sheets.

Also could you get, from America, without mentioning my name, a copy (I suppose it's out by this time) of that imitation-*Alice* which they wanted *you* to publish?⁴

Very truly yours,

C. L. Dodgson

¹ On March 4, Dodgson wrote Macmillan: "I have now passed for 'Press' the whole of the 4th Edition of *Symbolic Logic*, and have told Messrs. Clay to work off 500 copies." On April 13, Frederick Macmillan reports that a copy of the 4th edition, just published, was sent to the *Schoolmaster*.
² Macmillan writes (same letter) that it is still not possible to ascertain how many 3rd editions remain, as some are in the hands of agents, but he estimates that there will not be more than half a dozen. As soon as these 3rd editions are gathered together, they will be given to "Institutes, etc." as Dodgson directed. On April 24, Macmillan reports that ten copies of the 3rd edition have been given to Free Libraries; he encloses the names, but the enclosure is missing.
³ Frances Menella Wilcox (1869–1932) was the daughter of one of Dodgson's favorite cousins, William Wilcox, and his wife, Fanny. Dodgson was close to the Wilcoxes and had taken a paternal interest in "Nella" and her two brothers after their father died in 1876, when the children were still young.
⁴ In his letter of April 13, Macmillan confirms that he will send a copy of the 4th edition of *Symbolic Logic* in sheets, and he promises to try to obtain a copy of the "American imitation of *Alice*" (for more of which see p. 316, above). On April 14, Dodgson writes: "The copy of the *Logic*, which I want, in order to make corrections for the 5th edition, should be in *folded* sheets, ready for binding, but not bound. I fear I did not describe it rightly, and that the large roll, which has come from you,

contains *un*folded sheets. If this is so, I will send it back. I am keeping it unopened till I hear from you about it."

Christ Church, Oxford
May 6, 1897

Dear Mr. Macmillan,

In the new 5000 of 2*s*. 6*d*. *Alice*, please have the proper "thousand" named on the title-pages, reckoning those that have been used in the double volume, as well as those that have been bound separately. I think they will have to be numbered 66th, 67th, 68th, 69th, and 70th.

When more double volumes are printed, they are to be made up by simply taking single volumes from the stock in hand, and will *not* need a general title-page.

This I said in my letter of December 5, 1896: in which I see by my register that I also said that, when more copies of the 2*s*. 6*d*. books were printed, I should want to alter the title-pages. Please send me a copy of the last issue of the 2*s*. 6*d*. *Alice*, that I may see what alterations are needed.[1]

Very truly yours,

C. L. Dodgson

[1] Frederick Macmillan wrote on May 4 asking permission to reprint the 2*s*. 6*d*. *Alice* as stock stood at only 400–500 copies. His reply to this letter, also dated May 6, confirms that Dodgson's numbering is correct. Macmillan adds: "I am sending you a copy of the current edition of *Alice* that you may see what, if any, alterations are needed in the title-page."

Christ Church, Oxford
May 27, 1897

Dear Mr. Macmillan,

Your people are usually so very careful with my books that I am more inclined to say "What an exceptional thing it is, their having forgotten to correct the 'List of Works' up to date," than to utter a word of blame.

Still, it is a mistake needing prompt correction: so I telegraphed to you about it.

The following mistakes I noticed at first glance.

Alice in Wonderland should be 86th 1000, and the "out of print" notice deleted.

Nursery "Alice" should be 11th, instead of 3rd, 1000 (probably over 11, by this time).

Looking-Glass should be 61st 1000, and the "out of print" notice deleted.

There may be other corrections necessary by this time.

Perhaps it would suffice to insert a slip in *all* copies, bound and unbound, of

"Errata in List of Works," and not to trouble to print fresh copies of the "List" for the unbound ones.[1]

Now I have something to say about the new issue of the 6*s*. *Alice* books. On general grounds, it would not matter to me at *what* time in the year the new issue was put on the market: but, just now, with June close at hand, I think I may reasonably point out to you that this enormous delay, after the books have been passed for Press, is calculated (of course unintentionally) to inflict on me the *maximum* of expense, with the *minimum* of compensation by sale, in the account for June 30, 1897.

I passed the whole of *Alice* for Press, January 12, more than 4 months ago!

I passed *Looking-Glass* for Press, February 22, more than 3 months ago.

Had these books been got out (say) in a month after being passed for Press, there would probably have been a considerable "set-off," by sales, in the June account.

This delay (which is no fault of *mine*) will probably be a serious loss to me, if *all* the outlay goes into this account: so I think I may reasonably ask that some of it should be carried on into the *next* account.[2]

By the way, there is yet *another* unreasonable delay I wish to mention – the design for the cover of *Three Sunsets* which has to be cut in brass. I sent you the drawings, to be re-photographed, on April 30. Does your photographer usually take a whole month to do a negative?[3]

A great wave of inaction seems to have come over your "employés." Is it the approaching Jubilee that has so demoralised them![4]

Very truly yours,

C. L. Dodgson

---

[1] ". . . you must bear in mind that these lists have to be printed at intervals as they are required," George Macmillan writes on the following day, "and cannot be always up to date. We have already arranged to put the thousands of *Alice*, and the *Looking-Glass*, and *Nursery 'Alice'* right in some further copies of the list which are now being printed, and whenever a reprint takes place you may depend upon our making the necessary corrections." He does not take up Dodgson's suggestion for an "Errata" slip.

[2] On January 14 of this year, Frederick Macmillan wrote to say that although both Dodgson and Tenniel had passed the whole of the new edition of *Alice* for the press, "It will not be ready for some little time as Clays have made up their minds to work it with the greatest care and do not intend to be hurried." In his letter of May 28, George Macmillan adds: "Our view has been that perfect printing was of more importance than publication at this time of year." He continues: "We would strongly advise your not publishing . . . until the Jubilee festivities are over. The charge for printing will not be made in this half year's account."

[3] In the May 28 letter, Macmillan reports that the new photograph is on its way.

[4] Jubilee Day, the sixtieth anniversary of Victoria's reign, was celebrated on June 22.

Christ Church, Oxford
May 31, 1897

Dear Mr. Macmillan,

I *intended* to write and ask you to send a copy of the 4th edition of *Symbolic Logic* to "D. Biddle, Esq., Charlton Lodge, Kingston on Thames," but have no record of having done so.[1]

Thanks much for your generous proposal to put the whole charge for printing the re-issues of the *Alice* books into the next account. I suppose that means that they will not be on the market this June? It will do very well, so far as *sale* is concerned, if we can get them out in good time for Xmas.

The photo for the cover of *Three Sunsets* will do quite well now: so it may be cut in brass. When that is done, I should like to see an impression of it, in gold, on the linen we agreed on, so as to be quite sure that the result will look well.

I see that you corrected *Nursery "Alice"*, in the "List of Works," to "Seventh Thousand." This I have re-corrected to "*Eleventh* Thousand" in accordance with the accounts, received from you, of sales.

Very truly yours,

C. L. Dodgson

---

[1] Daniel Biddle (1840–1924), physician, mathematician, statistician, and reformer, practiced medicine in Kingston for over half a century and was for some years Mathematical Editor of the *Educational Times*. He wrote numerous articles and pamphlets on a wide range of subjects (see *Letters*, pp. 589–90).

Christ Church, Oxford
June 9, 1897

Dear Mr. Macmillan,

I am rather dismayed at finding that the current cost of producing 1000 bound copies of the enlarged version of *The Lost Plum-Cake* will be £29.10.0. It will be about 80 pages (i.e. more than double the thickness of the copy you have seen), and will have about 8 pictures. Still, we can hardly price it higher than 1s. net. At that price, what would you be able to allow *me*, on the copies sold? Even putting out of the account the setting up, and correcting, and drawing and cutting the pictures, the current cost is over 7d. a copy. We must not spend much on advertising, evidently.[1]

Yours very truly,

C. L. Dodgson

---

[1] In his reply two days later, Frederick Macmillan writes that if the retail price were 1s. net, "we shall be able to account to you for copies sold at 9d. less 7½ percent."

Christ Church, Oxford
June 19, 1897
Dear Mr. Macmillan,

Will you kindly write a note, for me, to Miss Turnoure, and put it into the enclosed book, and then fasten it up and post it.

Please say that Mr. Carroll is sorry not to be able to comply with her request, which is one that is constantly being made to him. He hopes she will understand that in such a matter he has only two possible courses – to write autographs for all applicants, or to refuse all. He has a strong dislike to all forms of *personal* publicity, and has therefore chosen the latter course.

Did you give the instructions about which I wrote on May 30, to have that design, for the cover of *Three Sunsets*, cut in brass, and a specimen impression of it done, in gold on that green linen that Miss Thomson had approved of for the cover?[1]

Very truly yours,

C. L. Dodgson

---

[1] Five days later, Frederick Macmillan replies: "I have written in accordance with your request to Miss Turnoure. . . ." He adds: "The design for the cover of *Three Sunsets* is being cut in brass in accordance with your instructions. . . ."

2 Bedford Well Road, Eastbourne
August 9, 1897
Dear Mr. Macmillan,

Your binders would have saved themselves much wasted trouble, in doing those seven specimen-covers, if they had remembered that on December 18, 1896, a specimen-board was sent to me, and that I wrote to you next day to say that Miss Thomson *approved* of it. She does not like *any* of these new ones. If the binders retained a piece of the linen sent in December, they had better send me a small piece of it, that I may make sure it is the right kind: if not, the thing can wait till Miss Thomson returns to town in December, when she will look for the former specimen and return it to you.[1]

How many *Symbolic Logic* are now on hand? I have some alterations to make for the 5th edition, but need not trouble Messrs. Clay with them till we are near the time for reprinting.[2]

Very truly yours,

C. L. Dodgson

P.S. Do you want the 7 specimen-covers back again? I think I have already written to ask you to send me another copy of Ball's *Mathematical Recreations*.[3]

¹ Frederick Macmillan replies two days later: "I am sorry that we did not remember that Miss Thomson had approved of a specimen binding in December last. This would not have happened if you had sent it back to us, and in future I shall be obliged if you will make it a rule to return a thing of this kind so it may be marked as approved and filed for reference."

² Macmillan reports (same letter) that over 400 copies of *Symbolic Logic* are on hand "so that it is unlikely that a new edition will be wanted very soon." Dodgson did not live to prepare a 5th edition.

³ Macmillan writes (same letter) that they do not want the rejected specimen covers and that a copy of *Mathematical Recreations* was sent to Dodgson on August 10. This is probably the 3rd edition, published in 1896. It was an enormously popular book that went to ten editions during the lifetime of its author, Walter William Rouse Ball (1850–1925), Director of Mathematical Studies at Cambridge.

2 Bedford Well Road, Eastbourne
August 27, 1897

Dear Mr. Macmillan,

I have a suggestion to make to you, which I hope may prove serviceable to many children.

Numbers of mothers, in the upper classes, take quite *little* children to church with them – children capable, perhaps, of joining intelligently in some of the prayers, and listening to some of the lessons, and joining in some of the hymns, but hopelessly *in*capable of understanding, or taking the least interest in, *sermons* not specially addressed to them. To all such children *sermon-time* is a time of unmitigated *boredom*: and such experiences are distinctly *bad*, and tend to give the child a distaste for religious services (like the little girl, who is said to have written to some friend "I thinks, when I'm growed up, I'll never go to church no more. I thinks I'm getting sermons enough to last me all my life"). What a boon it would be, for all such children, if a book were to be had, that they would really *enjoy* reading to themselves during sermon-time – and if the others had the good sense to *reserve* it for use at those times *only*, and not to waste it by allowing the child to see it at any *other* time! Couldn't you get some of your clerical friends, who have leisure enough for the purpose (I wish *I* could offer to do it, but it is quite impossible to give the necessary *time*), to compile such a book? I would call it "The Sunday Treat." It should contain allegories (such as *Agathos*:¹ there must be many whose copyright has run out), stories suitable for reading in church (hundreds such have been published), and poetry (such as "Little Cristel" in *Lilliput Levée*).² I would suggest publishing a "Part I" at 1*s.*, putting as much matter into it as you can afford. I should expect a *large* sale. You might then try "Part II." It ought to be large, *readable* type: but the *book* not large enough to be tiring to little hands. *Pictures* would no doubt be a welcome addition, but would probably be too costly.³

Have you tried *Symbolic Logic* in America?²⁴

I see, among books published by you, *St. Nicholas Magazine.* Is this the famous American Magazine for children?[5]

Please send me a 2*s.* 6*d. Alice*, a 2*s.* 6*d. Looking Glass*, 2 copies of *Sylvie*, and one of the "Conclusion." Also 2 of *The Nursery "Alice"*s, which you are keeping for me, with *un*altered price.[6]

Very truly yours,

C. L. Dodgson

Also 6 of the new Diagram-Cards, in envelopes with counters.

---

[1] *Agathos and Other Sunday Stories* (1840), by Samuel Wilberforce (1805–73), Bishop of Oxford and Winchester, is a series of ten allegories and stories which, the author explains, he told to his own children on successive Sunday evenings. It became popular, and numerous editions were published in England and the United States; it was also translated into French and German.

[2] *Lilliput Levée* (1864) is a book of poetry for children by Alexander Strahan. "Little Cristel" tells the story of a child who leaves church pondering the preacher's words "Even the youngest, humblest child something may do to please the Lord." Little Cristel then goes about her days doing things for others, with "no thought for herself." When by accident she almost drowns, she is revived by those she helped. At the end of the story she awakens and realizes that she had fallen asleep after church and been dreaming. The poem was reprinted in Macmillan's *Sunday Book of Poetry*.

[3] Frederick Macmillan thanks Dodgson four days later for his suggestion but writes that "it would not be practicable to publish a series of books specially intended to be read by children during Church time." He argues that "there is nothing whatever to prevent children reading such books as their parents approve of already, and I am afraid it would be quite hopeless to ask mothers to *reserve* any books for church reading."

[4] Frederick Macmillan answers this question on September 6: "Very few copies of *Symbolic Logic* have been ordered by our American house. Will you empower me to send out say fifty copies 'on consignment,'" which means that they are not to be paid for unless they are sold? This will give the book a fair chance." Dodgson's reply is missing, but Macmillan's subsequent letter (September 8) indicates what they decide: "We are sending out one hundred copies of *Symbolic Logic* to America and are telling our agents there that they are at liberty to present a certain number of them to the principal American colleges and schools."

[5] In his letter of August 31, Frederick Macmillan confirms that Macmillan were the English agent for "the famous American Magazine for children" and had been for the past two years.

[6] On the following December 7, Dodgson writes: "By all means sell the toned *Nursery 'Alice'* on the same terms as the white ones. You are of course keeping back the 100 white ones, for my own use, whose title-pages were *not* altered," he adds.

2 Bedford Well Road, Eastbourne

October 3, 1897

Dear Mr. Macmillan,

I see I have never answered your question, received on September 18, whether I would like you to present some copies of *Symbolic Logic* to Universities in India, Australia, and New Zealand. By all means do so.[1]

Would you kindly ascertain, from the Editor of *Nature*, whether the announcement of a new rule in Arithmetic would suit its columns?[2] It is a recent discovery of mine, and I should be glad to have it on record as such: it is a pleasure to be the *first* discoverer of such a thing – which I expect will prove to be worth teaching in schools.

If it would not be admissible in *Nature*, is there not some *School* Periodical which would publish it? I have applied to the *Educational Times*, but, as it cannot well be stated as a *Problem*, it does not seem to suit them.

I should use my own name, and would send it as an Article, or as a Letter, as the Editor might prefer.[3]

---

[1] On September 17, Frederick Macmillan reported that sales of *Symbolic Logic* in India were small and suggested that the firm send presentation copies to the Registrars and members of the Boards of Studies at the Indian University as well as to the Professors of Logic in the Universities in Australia and New Zealand.

[2] Norman Lockyer was still *Nature*'s editor. Frederick Macmillan replies on October 6 that the editor would be "very pleased to receive a letter from you with reference to your new rule in arithmetic."

[3] Either Dodgson failed to add a close and signature to this letter or an additional leaf is missing.

2 Bedford Well Road, Eastbourne
October 7, 1897

Dear Mr. Macmillan,

Will you kindly convey the enclosed to the Editor of *Nature*, whose address I do not know.

I find Sir John Tenniel is well pleased with the new *Alice* books, and can only find, "here and there," pictures that are slightly too dark. Please send me 6 more copies of each, to Oxford, after October 18. I will then pick 2 good specimens and insert remarks on any pictures that seem to be capable of improvement, and send them to you, to be put aside as standards to be worked up to in future issues.[1]

Very truly yours,
C. L. Dodgson

---

[1] "Yesterday I got from Macmillan copies of the re-issue of the *Alice* books," Dodgson recorded in his *Diaries* (p. 539) on September 24. "The pictures seem to *me* some under and some over done; but I must get Tenniel's opinion." This is what is usually called the 9th edition of *Alice*, beginning with the 86th thousand. Dodgson wrote a preface for it (dated Christmas 1896). He begins by offering two answers to the riddle "Why is a raven like a writing-desk?" Then he comments on the new edition of *Alice*: "For the eighty-sixth thousand, fresh electrotypes have been taken from the wood-blocks . . . and the whole book has been set up afresh with new type. If the artistic qualities of the re-issue fall short, in any particular, of those possessed by the original issue, it will not be for want of painstaking on the part of the author, publisher, or printer. . . . the *Nursery 'Alice'*, hitherto priced at four shillings, net, is now to be had on the same terms as the ordinary shilling picture-books – although I feel sure that it is, in every quality (except the *text* itself, on which I am not qualified to pronounce), greatly superior to them. Four shillings was a perfectly reasonable price to charge, considering the very heavy initial outlay I had incurred: still, as the Public have practically said 'We will *not* give more than a shilling for a picture-book, however artistically got-

up,' I am content to reckon my outlay on the book as so much dead loss, and, rather than let the little ones, for whom it was written, go without it, I am selling it at a price which is, to me, much the same thing as *giving* it away." For more on the ninth edition, see *Handbook*, p. 36.

2 Bedford Well Road, Eastbourne
October 10, 1897

Dear Mr. Macmillan,

I wonder what has become of the Letter, about a new rule in Arithmetic, which I wrote to the Editor of *Nature*, and which you told me, on October 8, you had forwarded to him? I received from him, also on October 8, a letter in which he asked me if I would write a review of a recent mathematical book, but made no allusion to having received anything from me. If our letters *crossed*, it is a curious coincidence. Since then, I have been expecting, every post, to hear that he has received my letter: but nothing has come. Would you kindly ascertain whether he has received it? And would you also secure that the enclosed reaches him?[1]

Thanks for the interesting, and charmingly illustrated, pamphlet about your new quarters. Now that your business is grown to such a size, can you not find a vacancy in which to try that nephew of mine (aged about 25) about whom I wrote to you a year or two back?[2]

Very truly yours,

C. L. Dodgson

[1] In reply four days later, Frederick Macmillan assures Dodgson that the letter to *Nature* "was delivered on the day it reached me" and is already in type. He adds: "A proof has probably reached you by this time." Dodgson's "Brief Method of Dividing a Given Number by 9 or 11" appeared in *Nature* on October 14 (pp. 565–6). For more on the subject, see *Handbook*, pp. 200–1; *Letters*, pp. 1138–40. We have no indication that Dodgson wrote a review of a mathematical book for *Nature*.

[2] During the 1890s new premises were designed and built for Macmillan & Co. in St. Martin's Street, for the first time constructed entirely to their own specifications. Frederick Macmillan writes (same letter) that the move was "for the purpose of giving more room to our existing staff and we do not expect . . . to increase the number of our employees." The nephew probably was Stuart Dodgson Collingwood, who had taken a B.A. in theology at Christ Church in 1892.

Christ Church, Oxford
November 21, 1897

Dear Mr. Macmillan,

It does not seem to me possible for you to see a copy of *Three Sunsets* printed and bound, *before* fixing the price: since the price has to be named on the title-page.[1] Would it not be enough for you to see the cover (which I presume is now being prepared, as a specimen), and to know that it will be a thin book, of only 68 pages, with 12 pictures? In *my* opinion, 6*s*. would prove to be a prohibitive price: 4*s*. is, I think, the outside that people would give for so small an amount of text. I'll send you a set of printer's proofs, if that will be any help: but of course they would give no idea of the beauty of the *pictures*.[2]

Thanks for the theatre-tickets. Would you kindly send me 3 more – front-stalls – for next Saturday?[3]

Very truly yours,

C. L. Dodgson

[1] Two days earlier, Frederick Macmillan suggested a selling price of 6*s*. for *Three Sunsets*, but added that he did not like to decide until he had an opportunity of seeing a copy printed and bound.

[2] When Macmillan sees the proofs, he replies (November 23) that "for only 68 pages and 12 pictures, it would be inadvisable to ask more than 4*s*." *Three Sunsets* was priced at 4*s*. when it appeared in February 1898.

[3] On the day before Dodgson writes this letter, he had a "delightful day" in London, when he saw J. M. Barrie's *The Little Minister* at the Haymarket (*Diaries*, p. 542), but there is no entry for the following Saturday, for which day he requests tickets here. "*The Little Minister* is a play I should like to see again and again," he records on the 20th; perhaps he intended to see it again on the 27th.

Christ Church, Oxford
November 23, 1897

Dear Mr. Macmillan,

After long consideration of the new issue of the *Alice* books, I have written the enclosed letter to Messrs. Clay, which I request you to read before forwarding. My hopes had been high that the new books would be *faultless*, and I was much disappointed with the result. Some sheets seem to have taken the ink better than others: If you turn over the leaves you will find places in which one of two opposite pages is pale compared with the other. It might be well to see to the *ink* also, and to make sure that, next time the *Alice* books are printed, it is the *blackest* ink procurable. I feel quite sure that more brilliant copies *can* be produced.[1]

By the way, I saw, the other day, a copy of the *Alice* published (and I suppose printed) by the "Macmillan Company" in America. The pictures (and indeed the text also) were wretchedly bad. Can nothing be done to mend matters? I don't like such worthless copies coming out under your auspices.[2]

Very truly yours,

C. L. Dodgson

[1] Dodgson's letter to Clay is missing, of course, but Frederick Macmillan replies on the same day as Dodgson writes this letter: "I do not recognise the faded appearance of which you complain. Of course, the woodcuts would look blacker if the paper on which they were printed was a dead white instead of being of a creamy tone, and it would be possible to have a dead white paper if you care about it, but the creamy paper, if you will remember, was made specially at your request to imitate that used for the first edition."

² Macmillan reports (same letter) that he has not seen the American edition of which Dodgson writes. He suggests that quite possibly the plates are worn and asks Dodgson if he is "inclined" to supply Macmillan & Co. with a duplicate set of plates to use in America.

Christ Church, Oxford
November 24, 1897

Dear Mr. Macmillan,

Thanks. We will have "4*s*." on title-page of *Three Sunsets*. Should it not be "FOUR SHILLINGS NET"?¹

What is the latest date the whole book ought to be passed for Press, to get it out for Christmas? I fear the thing is hopeless now, as one of the pictures has to [be] re-cut. And the New-Year of course has no better chance. However, it doesn't matter much: in any case the book will have a *very* limited sale: I propose to work off only 250 copies. What would you advise as to number?²

Do you want *The Lost Plum-Cake* to have, on its *title-page*, "With an Introduction by Lewis Carroll"? I had *rather* keep myself in the back-ground, unless you think that necessary.³

Very truly yours,

C. L. Dodgson

Thanks for theatre-tickets.

¹ Frederick Macmillan agrees (November 28) that the words should be "FOUR SHILLINGS NET."
² In the same letter, Macmillan writes: "I am afraid that publication before Christmas is quite out of the question" and that it was entirely up to Dodgson how many copies would be printed, although, he adds: "I should have thought that unless there was a chance of selling more than 250 the book is not worth publishing."
³ In the same letter, Macmillan replies that he has no strong feelings about putting "Lewis Carroll" on the title page of *The Lost Plum-Cake*, but adds that he need not tell Dodgson that the book will more likely sell better if the famous name is visible.

Christ Church, Oxford
November 25, 1897

Dear Mr. Macmillan,

I shall be most happy to give to the Macmillan Company in America, for the benefit of their readers, duplicate sets of the new electrotypes for the *Alice* books. The only condition I make is that they shall forthwith destroy the electros they are now using. I *wish* they would use better paper: but that must, I suppose, be left to their discretion.¹

I think it desirable that you should see the enclosed set of prints, of the pictures for *Three Sunsets*, sent by Messrs. Clay, and done from "brought-up" blocks and on the paper they propose to use. You need not return them: I have another set. Please tell me what you think of

(1) the quality of the paper;[2]

(2) the artistic effect of the prints (it might be well to borrow a set of "rubbings," from Messrs. Clay, with which to compare them).

I do *not* want *white* paper for the *Alice* books: but I *think* it would be the best kind for *Three Sunsets*.

Very truly yours,

C. L. Dodgson

When will specimen cover for *Three Sunsets* be done?[3]

---

[1] On the following day, Frederick Macmillan thanks Dodgson for the electrotypes and says that he will do his best "to get them to use paper that you will consider satisfactory."

[2] Macmillan (same letter) approves of the quality of the paper that Dodgson sent him but believes it not nearly thick enough for a book of only 80 pages; he promises to get some other specimens.

[3] Macmillan writes (same letter) that the cover cannot be made until the paper is decided on.

Christ Church, Oxford
November 26, 1897

Dear Mr. Macmillan,

I fear I must be a very bad hand at expressing my meaning, to have given you the impression that I was proposing to omit, from *Lost Plum-Cake*, the "Introduction by Lewis Carroll" which I had agreed to write.

On July 17, 1896, I got your letter saying you were willing to publish it "if with an Introduction by Lewis Carroll." On July 24, 1896, I wrote agreeing to do this. So I thought *that* point was settled: and the Introduction is written and in the printer's hands. I *think*, if you refer to my letter, you will find that it contains no allusions to the "Introduction." The question I *meant* to ask was this:

Do you particularly wish the words "With an Introduction by Lewis Carroll" *to appear on the title-page?*

Unless you particularly wish this, I would rather keep my name in the background, and let it merely appear at the end of the Introduction.

I hope *this* question is clear.[1]

Very truly yours,

C. L. Dodgson

---

[1] "I am afraid it is I who am a bad hand at expressing my meaning," writes Frederick Macmillan on the 29th, "for I certainly did not intend to give you the impression that I proposed that your introduction to *The Lost Plum-Cake* should be omitted. What I meant was that if you thought well of it, the words 'With an Introduction by Lewis Carroll' need not go on the title-page. In other words I quite agree with you about the whole matter." Dodgson's introduction, dated Christmas 1897, is signed "Lewis Carroll," and his name does not appear on the title page. The book was

published in January 1898, and the introduction was the last of his works that he saw come into being. The book has nine illustrations by another artist friend of Dodgson, E. L. Shute, and is subtitled "A Tale for Tiny Boys." For a suggestion that Dodgson also wrote Chapter 11 of *The Lost Plum-Cake*, see Trevor Winkfield, ed., *The Lewis Carroll Circular*, II (1974), 70–4; see also *Handbook*, pp. 201–2; R. B. Shaberman, *A Plum-Cake Lost and Found* (1978).

Christ Church, Oxford
November 30, 1897

Dear Mr. Macmillan,

As to the specimen-cover, for *Three Sunsets*, that I asked for in my letter of September 12, and have frequently mentioned since, you say, in your letter of November 26, "We cannot very well get the cover made [until the paper] has been decided upon." Evidently you suppose that I want a "dummy" copy to be bound. I merely want the binder to take a board, the size it is to be (the page will be $6\frac{1}{2} \times 8$), to cover it, on one side, with the linen chosen by Miss Thomson, and to stamp on it, in gold, her design (which I presume has been by this time cut in brass). Please get that done as soon as you can, that we (Miss Thomson and I) may see what the book will look like.[1]

By the way, I don't like the look of a book with a gold design on the "front" cover (is that the technical name?) and nothing at all on the back-cover. Yet it isn't worth while having a design cut for it. No doubt the binder has, ready cut in brass, ornamental stars, or circles, etc. I should like to see a few specimens. One such ornament, central, would be enough, I think.

As to the *paper* for *Three Sunsets*, Miss Thomson would like it to be, *not* "pure white" as I suggested, but "ivory white, thick, and very smooth." I don't object to "very smooth," but I do *not* like that shiny gloss, reflecting the light, which some papers have, and which makes a book disagreeable to read. I should like to see some specimens of paper.

I give up the idea of publishing *Three Sunsets* this year. It doesn't the least matter when it appears. I don't expect it will sell: and I quite agree with you that an issue of 250 copies will be (commercially speaking) not worth bringing out. It will be published at a loss, no doubt: but I don't mind that.

Very truly yours,

C. L. Dodgson

Miss Thomson does not like the name "Illustrations" for her pictures in *Three Sunsets*. It is no doubt a misnomer. I am altering it to "Fairy-Fancies."[2]

---

[1] On the following day, Frederick Macmillan promises to send the sample design "in a very few days." On December 3, Dodgson writes: "A specimen cover has come: but why was it not made the right size? The *leaf* will be $6\frac{1}{2}$ by 8: so I suppose the cover should be about $6\frac{7}{8} \times 8\frac{3}{4}$: whereas it has been made $6\frac{1}{2} \times 7\frac{3}{4}$! Of course the design looks bad on it, having no margin. I shall not send this to

the artist. Please get one done the right size." Macmillan sends Dodgson another specimen cover on the 9th, "made exactly in accordance with the measurements you gave in your postcard of the 3rd. . . ."
2 The title page of *Three Sunsets* reads "by Lewis Carroll with Twelve Fairy-Fancies by E. Gertrude Thomson" (see *Handbook*, pp. 203–4).

Christ Church, Oxford
December 12, 1897

Dear Mr. Macmillan,

Thanks for the second specimen-cover. It seems large enough: but that is a point of which *you* will be the best judge. The *book* will be 6½ × 8, and I leave it to *you* to say how much, beyond the book, the cover should project. Should it be ⅜ inch? Or would ¼ inch be enough?

Please send me a set of folded sheets of the new *Alice* books. It would be a pity to use *bound* copies for the purpose for which I want them – which is to mark them, page by page, to show *which* pages I think rightly printed, and which *not*.

Very truly yours,
C. L. Dodgson

P.S. I have told Messrs. Clay that I do *not* care to have the paper for *Three Sunsets* very smooth. I quoted that phrase, in my last letter, from Miss Thomson's letter: but I do not now agree with it: she is inexperienced in printing. I have told them that, if they can avoid a *glazed* surface (of which I sent them, as a very marked instance, a leaf of *Nature*), which I particularly object to, I shall not mind its *not* being very smooth. I very much doubt that *very* smooth paper ever taking the ink well enough to show all the fine lines distinctly.[1]

---

[1] On the following day, Frederick Macmillan explains to Dodgson that he "must have got a wrong idea about the effect of a smooth surface on the printing." He continues: "The reason that printers like a smooth surface is that it is much the best for printing fine cuts. A paper with a rough surface is still full of little holes (as you will see if you look through a magnifying glass) and it is impossible, therefore, to put ink on it in such a way that very fine lines will be equally printed all along."

Christ Church, Oxford
December 15, 1897

Dear Mr. Macmillan,

Thanks for your letter. On the question of *smoothness*, for the paper used for *Three Sunsets*, we are practically in agreement. *I* do not object to as *much* smoothness as is needed for the best artistic effect; and *you*, I presume, would not propose *more*. The sooner I can see specimens of paper, the better. It was quite at random that I told Messrs. Clay, in my letter of December 12, that the paper should be at least *3* times as thick as the proofs they had sent. It is a matter on which *you* will be a far better judge.

I have submitted copies of the new *Alice* books to Professor Powell, of Christ Church.[1] He is here considered rather an authority on artistic questions, and he has certainly given a good deal of attention to Art. His opinion is that the general look of the books is *too pale*: and he is quite confident that the ink is not really *black*: he tells me inks differ greatly in blackness. Now Clay, on the other hand, writes that it was the very *best* ink (I presume they mean "the *blackest*") they could procure.[2] Do you know of any independent authority – some one who is an undoubtedly good judge of artistic effect, to whom you could submit copies of the books, without telling him of any opinions already given?[3]

The University Press will be able to get a few copies of *The Lost Plum-Cake* ready.[4]

[1] Frederick York Powell (1850–1904), Student of Christ Church and Regius Professor of Modern History at Oxford. For more on Dodgson and Powell, see *Letters*, p. 509.

[2] "I have this morning seen Mr. Clay and he tells me that it is not the case that the best ink that can be used for printing cuts is necessarily the *blackest* ink," Frederick Macmillan writes on the following day. "Ink has many qualities such as adaptability to paper, freedom from liability to clog, etc. which have to be considered. Clay says that with the same ink he could get a darker impression if he tried, but he reminds us that in the case of the *Alice* blocks he was working to a standard which had been approved of by Sir John Tenniel, and that each sheet as it was put in the machine was carefully compared with the proofs which Sir J. Tenniel had seen and signed."

[3] "I think you had better not do anything more about the *Alice* cuts until you have seen some specimens of paper and ink to be used for *Three Sunsets*," Macmillan writes (same letter). "Clay has promised to send you the specimens printed in three different kinds of ink and he will use whichever of them you like best. If you get a thoroughly satisfactory ink for *Three Sunsets* it can be used for the next Edition of *Alice*."

[4] The letter breaks off here, the concluding sheet missing. Dodgson did not live to see a published copy of *Three Sunsets and Other Poems*. He died at The Chestnuts of pneumonia at half-past two in the afternoon of January 14 and was buried in Guildford.

EXCERPTS FROM *THE BOOKSELLER*

When in 1883 Dodgson required that Macmillan supply his books to booksellers at fixed prices allowing lower than conventional profits for the booksellers, a minor controversy broke out in the press, best reflected in a group of letters and editorials which we reproduce below from *The Bookseller*.

AUGUST 4, 1883

Authors as Dictators.
To the Editor of The Bookseller.

SIR,—A lively era is approaching for retail booksellers. A new regime is inaugurated by Mr. Lewis Carroll. This gentleman is, doubtless, greatly annoyed that the public have been supplied by the trade with his books at discount prices, and he is determined to govern the retailers in future by advertising the published prices of his books, and by refusing to supply the same to them under tenpence in the shilling, with "no odd books." This he no doubt considers a very generous effort on his part to protect the booksellers, who, he believes, are utterly unable, or unwilling, to protect themselves; so he has arranged to sweep into his own pockets all the additional profit on the sales effected; for it may safely be relied upon that, as he dictates his terms to the retailers, so he has dictated his terms to his publishers. Now, let the trade for a moment contemplate its position. Except Ruskin's, Carroll's books at present are the only books published at a cost to the trade of tenpence in the shilling. With all retail booksellers selling Carroll's books, now and in future, it will be necessary to explain to every customer that no discount can be allowed because the author refuses to allow the seller to give it to the purchaser. In eight cases out of ten the statement will be received with suspicion, and more painful incidents will arise between booksellers and their customers in the sale of Carroll's books, and specially with the sale of the new one just announced, than with all the other books to be offered in the coming book season.

Were a workable plan proposed between publishers and booksellers that embraced a large number of books, so that thereby the discount system could be slain, we would at once do our best to help the movement forward, but when an attempt is made to dictate terms to the whole of the booksellers of the United Kingdom by one individual, contrary to all the usages of the trade, and entailing nothing but unpleasantness between buyers and sellers, then the time has evidently come for the trade to say it will not submit to dictation of this kind from any individual, be he who he may; and rather than buy on the terms Mr. Lewis Carroll offers, the trade will do well wholly to refuse to take copies of his books, new or old, so long as he adheres to the terms he has just announced to the trade for their delectation and delight.

                                              A FIRM OF LONDON BOOKSELLERS.
July 24th, 1883.   p. 684

[*Editorial*]

MR. LEWIS CARROLL'S BOOKS.—A complaint is made of the terms on which Mr. Lewis Carroll insists that his books shall be supplied to the trade. Our correspondents are correct in their statement of the case, that tenpence in the shilling and net copies are the terms offered. We take, however, an entirely opposite view of the matter to that expressed in the letter of "A Firm of London Booksellers," and shall watch the experiment with much interest. A few books which cannot be sold under any circumstances whatever at threepence in the shilling discount, is just what is necessary to check the all prevailing evil; and whether it is Mr. Carroll or his publishers who have resolved to risk the trial, the effort deserves support instead of condemnation. Booksellers who advertise to take threepence in the shilling off all new books may for the moment find themselves in an awkward position, but we do not believe the public will hesitate to pay full price for a book they require, provided the price is moderate, and there is no possibility of obtaining it for less. For a popular book, such as Mr. Carroll's forthcoming "Rhyme and Reason" is certain to be, to be sold throughout the trade at full price will be a memorable innovation. Most booksellers who take the trouble to think the matter out will see that, in the long run, the influence of such an example will be beneficial, and casting aside the immediate question of loss or gain by the change, will assist vigorously in promoting what may become a new departure in bookselling, smaller nominal and larger real profits. The mass of correspondence which recently appeared in these columns on the subject of underselling, all tended to confirm the statement that no bookseller can nowadays get full price for new books. His profit is commonly reduced to the difference between scrip, at which he sells to the public, and sale, the odd book and the usual journey order discount. More than one bookseller recommended the reduction of discounts and the abolition of the odd copy as the most promising remedy. This remedy is now offered, and it remains to be seen whether the retail trade will allow the opportunity to pass.

                                                                         p. 683

SEPTEMBER 5, 1883

[*Editorial*]

Mr. Lewis Carroll's Books.—Our correspondents return to the attack upon Mr. Carroll's books, and persist in regarding the revised terms as an attempt to dictate to the trade, chiefly on the ground that the experiment is isolated. If Mr. Carroll is in a position to fix the terms on which his books are to be supplied, so much the better for him, and we entirely fail to see any cause of complaint in his doing so, any more than in a publisher fixing the terms. It is quite conceivable that the altered terms may at first be troublesome to booksellers who have committed themselves unreservedly to threepence in the shilling discount, but to the very large majority of the trade, a sprinkle of popular copyright books at short discounts would be of the greatest possible advantage. It would be injudicious to make short discounts the rule with all books, but it must be obvious that a varying scale would soon upset the universal system of full discounts to the public. We repeat the hope that the trade will take up Carroll's books with spirit, and that they will do their best to support a measure which is entirely to their advantage.

p. 799

Mr. Lewis Carroll and Booksellers.
To the Editor of The Bookseller.

Sir,—The writer of the letter in the August Bookseller signed "A Firm of London Booksellers," is, to my mind, much too severe on Mr. Carroll, and cannot be in earnest when he states his willingness "to assist in slaying the discount system," for the tenor of the letter throughout indicates the reverse of the assertion; especially the culminating point of asking the trade to refuse to take Mr. Carroll's books. The proper spirit of the trade should be to give Mr. Carroll every support in their power, for it is plainly the correct initiative to take to lay the foundation of the new departure, which, sooner or later, must take place. This is hardly an original idea of Mr. Carroll's; for the precise system is carried out with the Christmas numbers of the illustrated papers, which, although not books, are analogous, and would be sold at the cut down prices were they offered to the trade at 13 as 12 for 8s. 6d. instead of the fixed price of 10d. per copy nett, no matter how many are ordered; the public never ask for discount, and not one copy more would be sold if they were offered at 9d. or 10d. Hymn books again are readily sold at published prices and discount is not demanded. The line Mr. Carroll has laid down is deserving of the support of the Bookseller' Union, and I find upon calculation that the profit upon 13 as 12 of any price books sold at a discount of 2*d*. in the 1*s*. at the existing terms allows but a shade more profit than the terms made by Mr. Carroll. For instance, 13 as 12 5*s*. books cost £2 3*s*., and sold at 2*d*. in the 1*s*. discount would realise a profit of 11*s*. 2*d*.; whereas 13 5*s*. books at 4*s*. 2*d*. each would realise 10*s*. 10*d*. profit. But the greatest gain to the bookseller should accrue in orders through the wholesale agents. As a 5*s*. book now costs 3*s*. 10*d*., without allowing any commission for collection, and is sold for 4*s*. 2*d*., giving 4*d*. profit; but on Mr. Carroll's principle we should gain 10*d*. by the transaction; there should be no trouble in arranging extra discounts to wholesale agents, to enable them to charge the stated price, as publisher and author would be gainers as well as the retailers. If Mr. Carroll's plucky resolution is carried into effect, I am convinced that this step, if properly backed up, will successfully stamp out the evil of underselling; in connection with which I may mention the deplorable state the trade is in here at Hastings. A firm of fancy dealers and toymen, laying claim to the distinction of booksellers, are doing the trade with a flaming announcement over their window 3*d*. in the 1*s*. discount off books, and another firm announce 4*d*. in the 1*s*. discount off cloth books, these are the sort of people who do not approve of Mr. Carroll's boldness. Apologising for trespassing.

I am sir,

"A Carrollite."

Hastings, *August*, 1883.   pp. 802–3

Authors as Dictators.
To the Editor of The Bookseller.

Sir,—In your comments on our letter in your August issue, you seem to have lost the point at which we aimed—we did not quarrel *with the terms* as announced by Mr. Carroll, as to pay 5*s*. for a 6*s*. book and to get the 6*s*. is a very great deal better than to get a 6*s*. book for 4*s*. and sell it for 4*s*. 6*d*. Our complaint is, that an isolated individual attempts to rule the whole of the trade in his own fashion, without taking the trade, in any branch of it, as retail booksellers or as publishers, into his counsels; and our point was put very clearly, that the annoyance to which the retail trader would be subjected by this one author would be very injurious to the individual tradesman in many ways.

Let us give you a case in point. At the very time our letter was in your hands, and before it was published, an order was given to us for Carroll's "Alice in Wonderland," at 6*s*., and 4*s*. 6*d*. was paid for it, the 3*d*. in the 1*s*. discount price at which we are perforce driven to supply books. Fully to test the case, we obtained a copy for which our collector paid cash price 5*s*. and for which we had received 4*s*. 6*d*. On sending the book to the customer by messenger a distance of about two miles we sent an invoice for 1*s*. 6*d*., stating the altered condition in which the author had placed us with *his* books. Our customer took the book, refused to pay any additional price— declined to return the book until the cash paid was returned to her, and said "she would go elsewhere for her books." This necessitated a long letter in full explanation, which was not accepted— the money was still refused, and the customer actually brought the book back to return, and would not be satisfied until the very notice issued to the trade by the publishers was shown.

We simply ask the trade, is it worth your while to be subjected to this definite and continuous serious annoyance in all your trade transactions with Mr. Lewis Carroll's books merely to oblige Mr. Lewis Carroll? Let his books be treated like Mr. Ruskin's—if the public want them let them order them, and let them be supplied to order; and not kept in stock. But better still, if the publishers will combine with the respectable and leading retail booksellers to redeem this once important business from the pitiable degradation into which it has been driven, and if it will assist by publishing many books on terms like Carroll's, so that the discount shall be slaughtered, then there will be sound policy in supporting a line of publishing like that to which we now object; but a single author asserting his autocracy over the trade will be of as much avail in curing the evil complained of as if Neptune were to attempt to empty the ocean with his trident.

Yours obediently,

A FIRM OF LONDON BOOKSELLERS.

August 20, 1883.   pp. 802-3

LETTERS OMITTED FROM THE TEXT

Letters that Dodgson wrote to Macmillan on the dates below have been omitted from the body of this work. Where a number in parenthesis follows a date a portion (in some cases the entire text) of the omitted letter appears in a note on the page in parenthesis.

May 2, 1867
November 15, 1867 (58)
December 1, 1867
July 25, 1868
July 28, 1868
December 10, 1868 (74)
February 1, 1870
December 22, 1870
February 2, 1871
December 6, 1875
March 27, 1876 (128–9)
April 14, 1876
January 13, 1877 (135)
March 1, 1877
April 13, 1877
June 25, 1877 (132)
July 18, 1877 (132)
August 7, 1877
November 26, 1877 (134)
February 27, 1878
March 12, 1878
March 19, 1878 (143)
March 21, 1878
March 27, 1878
March 28, 1878 (145)
April 9, 1878
May 7, 1878 (146)
June 10, 1878
June 12, 1878
June 27, 1878
July 2, 1878 (147)
September 10, 1878
October 17, 1878

October 23, 1878 (149)
November 7, 1878
November 10, 1878
January 16, 1879
February 4, 1879 (146)
February 10, 1879
February 14, 1879 (146, 152)
May 18, 1879
May 23, 1879
May 27, 1879
June 16, 1879
June 17, 1879
August 5, 1879
August 14, 1879
October 9, 1879
October 30, 1879
May 23, 1883
June 17, 1883
June 19, 1883
June 21, 1883
June 22, 1883
August 27, 1883
October 23, 1883
October 24, 1883
October 25, 1883
December 3, 1883
November 5, 1885 (194)
September 28, 1886 (208)
October 3, 1886 (208)
October 28, 1886 (212)
November 9, 1886 (212, 213)
November 14, 1886 (213)
December 9, 1886

December 16, 1886
December 22, 1886
February 8, 1887
February 23, 1887
February 27, 1887
March 13, 1887
March 23, 1887 (224)
March 24, 1887
March 28, 1887
March 30, 1887 (225)
April 21, 1887
August 23, 1887
August 29, 1887
September 11, 1887 (236)
September 28, 1887
October 11, 1887 (241)
December 16, 1887 (240)
May 30, 1888 (244)
June 12, 1888
November 8, 1888
December 5, 1888
February 28, 1889
April 29, 1889 (256)
December 15, 1889
January 20, 1890
April 24, 1891 (286)
May 29, 1891
May 31, 1891 (286)
November 24, 1893 (297)
December 2, 1893
December 8, 1893 (300)
December 19, 1893

January 25, 1894 (299)
May 7, 1894
May 18, 1894 (307)
November 1, 1894 (315)
November 12, 1894
January 8, 1895
January 24, 1895
April 17, 1895 (314)
May 8, 1895 (316)
May 20, 1895
June 26, 1895
September 7, 1895 (320)
September 20, 1895
December 29, 1895 (327)
March 18, 1896 (334)
March 20, 1896 (334)
April 20, 1896 (275)
April 22, 1896
May 3, 1896 (337)
June 13, 189 (337)
June 21, 1896 (337)
August 11, 1896
October 14, 1896 (345)
November 9, 1896 (346)
November 16, 1896 (347)
March 4, 1897 (350)
April 14, 1897 (350)
April 28, 1897
July 10, 1897
December 3, 1897 (362)
December 7, 1897 (356)

INDEX

Numbers in bold type represent main biographical notes